The Prose Works of William Wordsworth

edited by W. J. B. Owen and Jane W. Smyser

HEB ☼ Humanities-Ebooks

© The Estate of W. J. B Owen, 2008, 2010, 2013

First published in 1974 by the Clarendon Press, Oxford

Published electronically in 2008 by Humanities-Ebooks, LLP, Tirril Hall, Tirril, Penrith CA10 2JE

This paperback edition published in 2009 and re-issued in 2010 and 2013.

The estate has asserted the right of W. J. B. Owen to be identified as the author of his work.

All rights reserved.

Reading Note:

This paperback is the printed version of an electronic book, which contains features such as hyperlinked symbols and colour text [rendered black in the print version] to assist rapid navigation between the elements of the ebook. Individual purchaser of this title in both the print and electronic versions may claim a refund of half the purchase price of the latter by sending their receipt for the printed copy to Humanities-Ebooks.

ISBN 978-1-84760-077-6 Paperback

Contents

Preface to the Electronic Edition

The establishment of Humanities-Ebooks makes it possible for a new generation of scholars and readers to own this long unobtainable work, in a form that will have some conspicuous benefits, and enable new ways of discovering its virtues.

As befits a monumental piece of scholarship, the editorial apparatus provided by Professor Owen and Professor Smyser has been retained, as indeed has the basic layout of the first edition, with its textual notes at the foot of each page of transcription, and separate editorial commentary on each of the twenty-one texts. The temptation to reduce the number of textual notes, and to eliminate some of the elaborate cross-referencing in the editorial apparatus has been resisted; it soon became apparent that while such changes might aid in the production of a stream-lined reading text, it would also require considerable, and unjustifiable, changes in the introductory matter and would remove from the work a dimension that, while few will be conscious of it, those few will marvel at. The textual notes have, however, been reformatted to make them easier to read and to use. As in the Clarendon edition it is possible to read the 1800 and 1850 versions of the preface to *Lyrical Ballads* as parallel texts (but the presentation is more consistent) and in the ebook the choice is for the reader to make: the pagination of the whole allows for side by side display of the two texts, using the appropriate screen layout.

The benefits of electronic processing will appear mainly in the following respects. First, the entire text is searchable. Second, the presence of editorial commentary is indicated by the symbol in the margin, *or by the line number being in that colour*. Third, the appropriate page of the editors' commentary can be accessed from the text via a hyperlinked button ▶ in the margin. Fourth, the table of contents is itself hyperlinked, and is duplicated in the form of hyperlinked bookmarks at the left of the screen, enabling instant navigation between the 21 separate 'texts' and, in each case, the general introduction, textual introduction, text, appendices (where applicable) and editorial commentary. Fifth, the use of colour, for interlinear emendations, and the separate lineation of columnized textual notes is designed to make these features of the editorial apparatus clearer and easier to construe than in the first edition.

Very minor amendments have been made to the content. A fragmentary essay has been separated from the Commentary to the Preface to *Lyrical Ballads*, as an Addendum to the Commentary of Text 6. Some particularly important passages in Greek and Latin have been translated and some cross-references to Volumes 2 and 3 expanded. *The Fenwick Notes* have not been included, however, despite the reasonable suggestion of some reviewers of the printed edition that they might have been. These are already available from Humanities-Ebooks in a companion edition corrected and revised by Jared Curtis (2007).

In 1989 John O Hayden published a very short article entitled, 'Substantive Errors in the Standard edition of Wordsworth's Prose', *The Library: Transactions of the Bibliographical Society*, sixth series 11:1 (1989) 58–9. The eleven errors listed—based upon examination of the MS or printed source text—included one which bears heavily upon the meaning of the text, the rest being of the order of a changed preposition, an intruded quotation mark, a missed gap in the MS, and so on. These will be corrected in this edition, with due acknowledgement of Professor Hayden's notations interpolated into the commentary.

It is not unlikely, however, that as a result of the scanning process many more errors have been introduced than have been eliminated, despite attempts to replicate the exemplary care Professors Owen and Smyser took with the printed edition. As this is an electronic edition, however, there is a ready-and-easy way to rectify such errors. Suggestions for correction and improvement will be most welcome and will be acted upon as soon as practicable. I am grateful, for varieties of help, to John Beer, Jeff Cowton, Michael John Kooy, Sam Ward, and Averill Buchanan.

Richard Gravil, Tirril, 2008

Postscript, 2013

Some minor scanning errors and one substantive one have been corrected in this 'impression', March 2013. Earlier purchasers of the work are entitled to a free copy of this update. It is now unlikely that Volumes 2 and 3 will be attempted, at least in the labour intensive format employed for this volume. A volume of *Wordsworth's Political Writings* has been produced, with the invaluable commentary converted to footnotes and the textual notes omitted. Similar collections of Wordsworth's critical, topographical and miscellaneous writings may be forthcoming in 2013/14.

Preface to the First Edition

WHEN, at the suggestion of Helen Darbishire, we agreed to collaborate in editing Wordsworth's prose, we decided that each particular work should be assigned to one or the other of us, rather than that both should give full attention to every work. At the outset, however, we found that by coincidence we each had independently edited Wordsworth's three *Essays upon Epitaphs*. We amalgamated this initial work and so stand jointly responsible for the editing of these three essays (*Prose Works*, IX). For the rest, Professor Owen has edited I, III–VIII, XI–XVI, and Professor Smyser, II, X, XVII–XXI. Despite this division of labour and final responsibility, the editing throughout has been closely and happily collaborative.

Our aim has been to publish a complete edition of Wordsworth's prose works with an apparatus of all verbal variants. By definition such an edition includes all extant versions of prose works either published or written with the intent of publication. From a distance the boundaries of the domain are distinctly recognized, but close at hand they are discerned under a trickier light and finally some arbitrary decisions are called for. We have included prose fragments written by Wordsworth in his youth ; when he put them on paper, he may or may not have thought of developing them into publishable prose. On the other hand, we have excluded two extensive sets of prose notes attached to poems: notes published and republished by Wordsworth in numerous volumes of poetry, and notes dictated by him to Isabella Fenwick in 1842–3. With one exception, both sets of notes are now available where they are most useful and most desirable—in *The Poetical Works of William Wordsworth*, edited by E. de Selincourt and Helen Darbishire (Oxford, 1940–9). The one exception is Wordsworth's brief note to 'The Ancient Mariner', first published in the *Lyrical Ballads* of 1800 and frequently reprinted. But despite the availability of Wordsworth's notes, the decision to bar all of them from this edition was a difficult one, and particularly so for his *Memoir of the Rev. Robert Walker* (P.W. iii. 510–22).[1] Because of its length and

1 This reference remains, at present, to the Clarendon Press edition, as with all cross-references to volumes 2 and 3 of *The Prose Works* [RG]..

because of its connection with *An Unpublished Tour*, a prose work now published for the first time, it might be maintained that the *Memoir* should be included in this edition. But we have held fast to our principle of not republishing notes to poems. Had we made an exception of the *Memoir*, we would have been hard pressed to find grounds for excluding other long notes to the poetry. For similar reasons we have not attempted to include in this edition Wordsworth's marginalia.

Another omission is far from intentional. In May 1838, in a letter to Daniel Stuart, formerly the editor of the *Courier*, Wordsworth listed poems and prose contributions which he had published in several journals; among them was 'one article which I was induced to publish in a London newspaper, when Southey and Byron were at war' (*L.Y.*, p. 942). An extensive search has so far failed to uncover for us this lost article. All that we have found is a corroborating allusion in the *Literary Gazette* of 19 January 1822; before reprinting in full Southey's letter of 11 January to the *Courier*, the *Gazette* gives a burlesque account of the 'fight' between Southey and Byron and lists, among a series of episodes, an intervention by the 'Leach-gatherer'. No details of place or date are given. Alert to possibilities of other uncollected prose, we have, nevertheless, not systematically sought for a mysterious essay once mentioned by Hazlitt. In the course of praising Burke's prose style, Hazlitt made an aside: 'I remember Coleridge assuring me … that Wordsworth had written an Essay on Marriage, which, for manly thought and nervous expression, he deemed incomparably superior' (*The Complete Works of William Hazlitt*, ed. P. P. Howe (London, 1931), xii. 228). We have met no other reference to such an essay and rather suspect that, if Hazlitt's recollection is accurate, Coleridge was swelling the corpus of Wordsworth's writing, as he sometimes swelled his own.

The texts of our edition, whether of works published by Wordsworth or of works left unpublished in manuscript, are, with one exception, the last to have been corrected by him. The exception is the Preface to *Lyrical Ballads*, which is here published in two versions on facing pages, the first edition of 1800 and the last edition of 1850.[1] Throughout the whole of our edition, variants, both from manuscripts and earlier editions, are preserved in textual notes and occasionally in longer appendices. The last versions to be corrected by Wordsworth have been adopted as the main texts not only because of the great importance which he attached 'to following strictly the last Copy of the text of an Author' (*L.Y.*, p. 473), but also because of the kinds of revisions that are peculiar to his prose. In the case of unpublished manuscripts, the last corrected version provides

1 In this electronic edition the decision whether to display the pages side by side or alternately is for the reader to make: the viewing toolbar allows for both [RG].

almost invariably the only coherent and clearly intelligible text, for earlier versions are little more than fragmentary rough drafts, with numerous deletions and rewritings. In the case of published works, with the exception just mentioned, Wordsworth did not alter the main arguments of his prose or contradict the original spirit and intent. He merely corrected misprints and factual errors, made stylistic improvements, clarified ambiguous statements, and expanded earlier texts or added new sections. (On the rare occasions when an error was introduced into the final text, we relegate it to the textual apparatus and print instead the most recent correct version.)

In separate introductions we describe in detail not only the various manuscripts but also any departures from our standard procedure in editing them. Here it is only necessary to set forth briefly a few of the principles governing our editorial practice: we preserve the manuscript spellings and abbreviations, with all their inconsistencies; where the manuscript lacks pointing, we silently insert it for the sake of intelligibility, but wherever we alter a mark of punctuation, we record that alteration in a textual note; although we have endeavoured to preserve all deletions, we have not recorded the striking out and the immediate rewriting of identical words and phrases; we have also not recorded transpositions within a sentence of identical words, phrases, and clauses, and only rarely have we recorded the fact that some of the text was inserted, usually by means of a caret, at the very moment of composition. A table of sigla used in the textual notes will be found on p. 11.

Our general introductions are concerned primarily with defining the date, occasion, and background of the particular work, and we have usually refrained from comment on its literary qualities. In our commentaries where we quote or cite the poetry of any major English poet without referring to a specific edition, we are using the edition of his work in the series known as the Oxford Standard Authors. Otherwise, works frequently cited are identified in the list of abbreviations.

For permission to publish manuscripts of Wordsworth's prose and other related manuscripts, we are indebted to the Wordsworth Library in Grasmere, the British Museum, the Victoria and Albert Museum, the Pierpont Morgan Library, the Cornell University Library, Harvard University Library, Northwestern University Library, and Yale University Library. The specific manuscripts of these libraries are all identified and described in subsequent introductions appropriate to them. But it should be added here that the numbering of the manuscripts in the Wordsworth Library at Grasmere, both those which we edit and those to which we briefly refer, is what will some day, no doubt, be called 'Old Style'. New numbers were assigned to all the manuscripts after this edition had gone into page proof, but scholars seeking to examine the manuscripts at Grasmere will find there a table of correspondences for the old and new numbering.

Professor Owen's research has been generously supported by the Humanities Research Council of Canada, the Canada Council, and McMaster University, and Professor Smyser's by a grant from the American Council of Learned Societies and frequent research grants from Connecticut College.

We are also grateful to many scholars and friends who have assisted us in numerous ways and it is pleasant here to express our gratitude to them. Helen Darbishire comes first to mind for she welcomed us to Grasmere and aided us at the very beginning of this undertaking; her wisdom and generosity are unforgettable. The loyal support of Professor Basil Willey, as chairman of the Dove Cottage Trustees, has, over a long period of time, been invaluable; indeed, he and his fellow Trustees have made this edition possible. At Grasmere too we have found in the librarians allies par excellence: first, Miss Phoebe Johnson and later and for a longer time, Miss Nesta Clutterbuck. To them especially, but also to Dr. Stephen Gill, whose librarianship more briefly overlapped our days of research, we are deeply grateful. By their admirable publications Professor Zera S. Fink, the late Professor George H. Healey, Mr. Alan G. Hill, Mrs. Mary Moorman, Professor Mark L. Reed, and Professor Chester L. Shaver have advanced the work of all Wordsworth scholars; in addition they have personally assisted us in prompt and generous ways, which are greatly appreciated. At the Cornell University Library Professor Donald D. Eddy continues the cordial traditions of George Healey and we acknowledge with thanks his many kindnesses. For generous aid of various kinds we are also indebted to Miss Helen K. Aitner, Connecticut College Library; the Revd. T. E. H. Baily, Shap; Dr. Paul F. Betz, Georgetown University; Dr. F. W. Bradbrook, University College of North Wales; Dr. Elizabeth M. Brennan, Westfield College, University of London; Professor A. D. Fitton Brown, University of Leicester; Professor M. L. Clarke, University College of North Wales; Miss Martha A. Connor, Swarthmore College Library; the late Professor John F. Danby, University College of North Wales; Miss Vera Farnell, Grasmere; Mrs. Sylvia Harris, Ambleside; the late Mrs. Beatrix Hogan; Mr. Wilmarth Lewis, Farmington, Connecticut; Mr. J. R. T. Pollard, University College of North Wales; Professor Frederick A. Pottle, Yale University; Professor T. M. Raysor, University of Nebraska; Mr. Kenneth Smith, Tullie House Library; Mr. J. H. Watkins, University College of North Wales; Dr. George J. Willauer, Jr., Connecticut College; Miss Marjorie G. Wynne, Yale University Library.

Finally, to Betty Owen and Hamilton Smyser, our shadow collaborators in countless ways, we give our heartfelt thanks. One particularly generous contribution of

Betty Owen's must, however, be permitted to emerge into full light: she compiled for us a file of all proper names and all place-names that are now entered in our Index. If there are errors there, they are, like errors elsewhere in this work, ours.

W. J. B. OWEN,
McMaster University

JANE WORTHINGTON SMYSER,
Connecticut College

Table of Sigla and Abbreviations

as used in the textual notes

MS.	the first version in the manuscript
MS.^{2}	the second version or first correction
MS.^{3}	the third version or first correction
A^2	the second version or first correction of MS. A.
[ ]	a blank space in the manuscript
[?]	an illegible letter or letters, or an illegible word or words
[? there]	the word may be *there*
[? there *or* their]	the word is either *there* or *their*
[there]	an editorial interpolation
273/4	occurring between lines 273 and 274
corr.	corrected
del.	deleted
ins.	inserted
om.	omitted
subs.	substituted

A sample note:

there 1822: their MS.: here MS.^{2}, 1810–20.

The first occurrence of *there* is in the edition of 1822; the first version of the manuscript reads *their* (we avoid the use of *sic*); the second version of the manuscript and the editions of 1810 to 1820 read *here*.

Abbreviations

Abrams	M. H. Abrams, *The Mirror and the Lamp* (New York, 1953)
Ad. Cintra	Advertisement to *Concerning … the Convention of Cintra*
Addison, *Spectator*	Joseph Addison, *The Spectator,* ed. D. F. Bond (Oxford, 1965)
Address	[Address on the Convention of Cintra]
Ad. L.B.	Advertisement to *Lyrical Ballads* (1798)
Ap. Cintra	Appendix to *Concerning … the Convention of Cintra*
Ap. L.B.	Appendix to *Lyrical Ballads* (1802, etc.)
Autobiog.	*Autobiographical Memoranda*
Barstow	Marjorie L. Barstow, *Wordsworth's Theory of Poetic Diction* (New Haven, Conn., 1917)
Biog. Lit.	S. T. Coleridge, *Biographia Literaria,* ed. J. Shawcross (Oxford, 1907)
Blair	Hugh Blair, *Lectures on Rhetoric and Belles Lettres* (Edinburgh, 1813; first edition, 1783)
Bord.	*The Borderers*
Bowness	Speech at the Laying of the Foundation Stone of the New School in the Village of Bowness, Windermere
[Burke,] *Enquiry*	Edmund Burke, *A Philosophical Enquiry into the Origin of our Ideas of the Sublime and Beautiful,* ed. J. T. Boulton (London, 1958)
[Burke,] *Reflections*	Edmund Burke, *Reflections on the Revolution in France,* in *Works* (Bohn's Standard Library, London, 1886)
Burns	*Letter to a Friend of Robert Burns*
Chiabrera, *Opere*	Gabriello Chiabrera, *Delle Opere di Gabbriello Chiabrera Tomo Secondo* (Venice, 1782)
Cintra	*Concerning ... The Convention of Cintra*
C.L.	*Collected Letters of Samuel Taylor Coleridge,* ed. Earl Leslie Griggs (Oxford, 1956-71)
Clarke	James Clarke, *A Survey of the Lakes of Cumberland, Westmorland, and Lancashire,* second edition (London, 1789)

C.N.B.	*The Notebooks of Samuel Taylor Coleridge,* ed. Kathleen Coburn (New York, 1957–)
Copyright	The Law of Copyright
C.R.	*The Correspondence of Henry Crabb Robinson with the Wordsworth Circle,* ed. Edith J. Morley (Oxford, 1927)
Delille	Jacques Delille, *Discours préliminaire* to his translation of the *Georgics,* in *Oeuvres,* ii (Paris, 1824; first edition, 1770)
Dennis	*Critical Works of John Dennis,* ed. E. N. Hooker (Baltimore, Md., 1939–43)
D.N.B	*Dictionary of National Biography*
[Dryden,] *Essays*	*Essays of John Dryden,* ed. W. P. Ker (Oxford, 1900)
Duff	William Duff, *Essay on Original Genius* (London, 1767)
E. de S.	*Wordsworth's Guide to the Lakes,* ed. Ernest de Selincourt (London, 1906)
E.E.	Essays upon Epitaphs
Elegant Extracts	*Elegant Extracts; or useful and entertaining Pieces of Poetry …,* ed. Vicesimus Knox (London, 1805)
E.S.	Essay, Supplementary to the Preface
Exc.	*The Excursion,* in *P.W.* v.
E.Y.	*The Letters of William and Dorothy Wordsworth: The Early Years, 1787–1806,* ed. Ernest de Selincourt; second edition, revised by Chester L. Shaver (Oxford, 1967)
Fenwick note	I. F. note (see below)
Fink	Z. S. Fink, *The Early Wordsworthian Milieu* (Oxford, 1958)
Fragments	Early Prose Fragments
Freeholders	*Two Addresses to the Freeholders of Westmorland*
Gerard, *Genius*	Alexander Gerard, *Essay on Genius* (London, 1774)
Gerard, *Taste*	Alexander Gerard, *Essay on Taste* (London, 1759)
Gilbert	A. H. Gilbert, *Literary Criticism: Plato to Dryden* (New York, 1940)
Gilpin	William Gilpin, *Observations Relative Chiefly to Picturesque Beauty … Particularly the Mountains, and Lakes of Cumberland, and Westmoreland,* second edition (London, 1788)
Godwin	William Godwin, *Enquiry concerning Political Justice,* ed. F. E. L. Priestley (Toronto, 1946)

Green	William Green, *The Tourist's New Guide, Containing A Description of the Lakes, Mountains, and Scenery in Cumberland, Westmorland, and Lancashire* (Kendal, 1819)
Grosart	*The Prose Works of William Wordsworth,* ed. Alexander B. Grosart (London, 1876)
Guide	*A Guide through the District of the Lakes in the North of England*
G.W.	Gordon Wordsworth's transcript of *Guide* manuscripts in the Wordsworth Library
Hale White	W. Hale White, *Description of the Wordsworth and Coleridge Manuscripts in the Possession of Mr. T. Norton Longman* (London, 1897)
Hartley	Joseph Priestley, *Hartley's Theory of the Human Mind* (London, 1775)
Havens	R. D. Havens, *The Mind of a Poet* (Baltimore, Md., 1941)
H.C.R.	*Henry Crabb Robinson on Books and their Writers,* ed. Edith J. Morley (London, 1938)
Healey	George Harris Healey, *The Cornell Wordsworth Collection* (Ithaca, N.Y., 1957)
Hutchinson, *Excursion*	W[illiam] Hutchinson, *An Excursion to the Lakes in Westmoreland and Cumberland* ... (London, 1776)
Hutchinson, *History*	William Hutchinson, *The History of the County of Cumberland* (Carlisle, 1794)
I.F. note	Notes dictated by Wordsworth to Isabella Fenwick in 1843 and printed in *P.W.*
J.E.G.P.	*Journal of English and Germanic Philology*
[Johnson,] *Lives*	Samuel Johnson, *Lives of the English Poets,* ed. George Birkbeck Hill (Oxford, 1905)
Jordan	John E. Jordan, *De Quincey to Wordsworth* (Berkeley and Los Angeles, CA., 1962)
Journals	*Journals of Dorothy Wordsworth,* ed. Ernest de Selincourt (London, 1941)
Kames	Henry Home, Lord Kames, *Elements of Criticism,* fifth edition (Edinburgh, 1774)
Klopstock	Conversations with Klopstock
Knight, *Prose Works*	*The Prose Works of William Wordsworth,* ed. William Knight (London, 1896)

L.B.	*Lyrical Ballads* (1798, 1800, 1802, 1805)
Llandaff	A Letter to the Bishop of Llandaff …
Lovejoy	A. O. Lovejoy, *Essays in the History of Ideas* (Baltimore, Md., 1948)
L.Y.	*The Letters of William and Dorothy Wordsworth: The Later Years,* ed. Ernest de Selincourt (Oxford, 1939)
Mathetes	Letter of 'Mathetes' (John Wilson) to *The Friend*
M.L.N.	*Modern Language Notes*
M.L.R.	*Modern Language Review*
Moorman, i.	Mary Moorman, *William Wordsworth, a Biography: The Early Years, 1770–1803* (Oxford, 1957)
Moorman, ii.	Mary Moorman, *William Wordsworth, a Biography: The Later Years, 1803–1850* (Oxford, 1965)
Morals	Essay on Morals
M.P.	*Modern Philology*
M.W., Letters	*Letters of Mary Wordsworth,* ed. Mary E. Burton (Oxford, 1958)
M.Y.	*Letters of William and Dorothy Wordsworth: The Middle Years,* ed. Ernest de Selincourt; second edition, revised by Mary Moorman and Alan G. Hill (Oxford, 1969–70)
N.&Q.	*Notes and Queries*
Nat. Ind. and Lib.	*Poems Dedicated to National Independence and Liberty* in *P.W.* iii
Nicolson and Burn	Joseph Nicolson and Richard Burn, *The History and Antiquities of the Counties of Westmorland and Cumberland* (London, 1777)
O.E.D.	*Oxford English Dictionary*
Oman	Charles Oman, *History of the Peninsular War* (Oxford, 1902, etc.)
Owen	*Wordsworth's Preface to 'Lyrical Ballads',* ed. W. J. B. Owen (Copenhagen, 1957)
P. 1815	Preface to the Edition of 1815
[Paine,] *Common Sense*	*Common Sense,* in *The Writings of Thomas Paine,* ed. M. D. Conway (New York, 1906)
[Paine,] *Rights of Man*	*Rights of Man,* in *The Writings of Thomas Paine,* ed. M. D. Conway (New York, 1906)
P. Bord.	Preface to *The Borderers*
Petition	Wordsworth's Petition in *Appendix to the Reports of the Select Committee … on Public Petitions,* Session 1839

P. Exc.	Preface to *The Excursion*
P.L.B.	Preface to *Lyrical Ballads*
PMLA	*Publications of the Modern Language Association of America*
Postscript	Postscript to *Yarrow Revisited and Other Poems*
Prel.	*The Prelude,* ed. Ernest de Selincourt; second edition, revised by Helen Darbishire (Oxford, 1959). The text of 1805 is cited unless otherwise stated.
Priestley, *Oratory*	Joseph Priestley, *A Course of Lectures on Oratory and Criticism* (London, 1775)
P.W.	*Poetical Works of William Wordsworth,* ed. Ernest de Selincourt and Helen Darbishire (Oxford, 1940–9, and revised issues, 1952–9)
Q.R.	*Quarterly Review*
Railway	*Kendal and Windermere Railway*
Recl.	*The Recluse,* in *P.W.* v
Reed	Mark L. Reed, *Wordsworth: the Chronology of the Early Tears* (Cambridge, Mass., 1967)
R.E.L.	*Review of English Literature*
Report	*Report from His Majesty's Commissioners for Inquiring into the Administration and Practical Operation of the Poor Laws* (London, [1834])
R.E.S.	*Review of English Studies*
Reynolds	Sir Joshua Reynolds, *Works* (London, 1798)
R.M.	[Reply to 'Mathetes']
Rousseau	*Du Contrat social,* in *The Political Writings of Jean Jacques Rousseau,* ed. C. E. Vaughan (Cambridge, 1915)
Rydal Mount Catalogue	*Catalogue of the Varied and Valuable Historical, Poetical, Theological, and Miscellaneous Library of the late venerated Poet-laureate, William Wordsworth ...* (Preston, 1859); reprinted in *Transactions of the Wordsworth Society,* No. VI, pp. [195]–257 (Edinburgh, n.d.)
S.C.	S. T. Coleridge, *Shakespearean Criticism,* ed. T. M. Raysor (London, 1960)
Scafell Pike Excursion	Dorothy Wordsworth, Scafell Pike Excursion
S.H., Letters	*The Letters of Sara Hutchinson,* ed. Kathleen Coburn (London, 1954)

Smith	Elsie Smith, *An Estimate of William Wordsworth by his Contemporaries* (Oxford, 1932)
[Southey,] *Life and Correspondence*	C. C. Southey, *Life and Correspondence of Robert Southey* (London, 1849, etc.)
[Southey,] *Selections*	J. W. Warter, *Selections from the Letters of Robert Southey* (London, 1856)
Stewart	Dugald Stewart, *Elements of the Philosophy of the Human Mind* (London, 1792)
Subl. and Beaut.	The Sublime and the Beautiful
S.V.	*Select Views*
Talfourd, *Three Speeches*	T. N. Talfourd, *Three Speeches ... In Favour of a Measure for An Extension of Copyright* (London, 1840)
T.L.S.	*Times Literary Supplement*
Ullswater Excursion	Dorothy Wordsworth, Ullswater Excursion
U.T.	An Unpublished Tour
U.T.Q.	*University of Toronto Quarterly*
[Watson,] *Appendix* or *Sermon*	R[ichard] Watson, *A Sermon Preached Before The Stewards Of The Westminster Dispensary... .With an Appendix (*London, 1785)
Webbs, Part I or II	Sidney and Beatrice Webb, *English Poor Law History* (London, 1927, 1929)
Weever	John Weever, *Ancient Funerall Monuments ....* (London, 1631)
Wells	John Edwin Wells, 'The Story of Wordsworth's *Cintra', Studies in Philology,* xviii (1921), 15–77
West, *Antiquities* (1774)	Thomas West, *The Antiquities of Furness* (London, 1774)
West, *Antiquities* (1805)	Thomas West, *The Antiquities of Furness,* ed. William Close (Ulverston, 1805)
West, *Guide*	Thomas West, *Guide to the Lakes,* ninth edition (Kendal, 1807), unless earlier editions are stated
Wordsworth as Critic	W. J. B. Owen, *Wordsworth as Critic* (Toronto and London, 1969)

1.

Early Prose Fragments

INTRODUCTION: GENERAL

NEARLY all the fragments collected here occur in manuscripts mainly devoted to Wordsworth's early verse. Several are so short that it is difficult to guess at their occasions, but we have thought it useful to print them, especially as two of the Grasmere manuscripts, Verse 3 and Verse 4, will become increasingly difficult to read with increasing age and deterioration. In assigning dates, we have generally followed the suggestions of Mark L. Reed, *Wordsworth: the Chronology of the Early Years, 1770–1799*, but, with the exceptions of Fragments V and X, it is obvious that dating of these pieces is, within the limits of probability suggested by the style and period in which the manuscript concerned is likely to have been used, very largely guesswork. Because of this uncertainty, we have printed them in the order in which they appear in the manuscripts, rather than in a putative chronological order.

Fragment I is clearly connected with a draft description of Wordsworth's imaginative or dream-experiences as a child which is printed in *Prel.*, p. 533:

when in my bed I lay
Alone in darkness, I have seen the gloom
Peopled with shapes arrayed in hues more bright
Than flowers or gems, or than the evening sky;
Processions, multitudes in wake or fair
Assembled, puppet shews with tru[m]pet, fife,
Wild beasts, and standards waving in the [field?].
These mounting ever in a sloping line
Were foll(ow)ed by the tumult of the shew
Or horses [ ]
These vanishing, appeared another scene—
Hounds, and the uproar of the ch[ase?], or steeds
That galloped like the wind through standing corn.
Then headless trunks and faces horrible,
Then came a thron[g] of forms all [ ]
Unutterably, horribly arranged
In parallel lines, in features and in look
All different, yet marvellously akin;
Then files of soldiery with dazzling arms
Still mounting, mounting upwards, each to each
Of all these spectres every band and cl[ass?]
Succeeding with fa[n]tastic difference
And instant, unimaginable change.
[ ] phantoms [ ]

For a discussion of the origins of these images, and further use of them in Wordsworth's mature verse, see W. J. B. Owen, '"A Second-Sight Procession" in Wordsworth's London', *N. & Q.*, N.S. xvi (1969), 49–50. Reed, p. 19, dates the passage 1787.

Fragment II, a piece of Ossianic prose addressed to the 'Spirit of these Mountains', and imposing Gothic imagery on the weather conditions of the Lake District, is probably of similar date, as Reed, pp. 20, 76, suggests. It lacks the autobiographical interest of Fragment I, but Wordsworth's observation of the natural scene can be detected under the verbiage.

Fragment III seems to be the opening of a tale in the sentimental mode represented by Lamb's *Rosamund Gray*. It introduces the figure of the destitute woman who appears in *An Evening Walk*, *Guilt and Sorrow*, *The Borderers*, 'The Thorn', 'Her eyes are wild', 'Beggars', 'The Sailor's Mother' and other poems of the period 1790–1805 or thereabouts. Reed, p. 19, dates the piece 'Possibly ... summer 1787; probably ... c. summer1788, 1789, or later'; cf. Reed, p. 313.

Fragment IV comprises two drafts in prose of an epitaph leading to a version in blank verse (rather than two epitaphs, as Reed describes them, pp. 21, 314). The occasion is unknown. Reed dates the pieces 1788.

Fragment V reflects Wordsworth's experience as a tourist in the Alps in 1790: he mentions 'the valley of Lauterbrunnen' in a letter to his sister of 6 September 1790 (*E.Y.*, p. 35), which is thus a *terminus post quem* for the date of this piece. See Reed, p. 24.

Fragment VI, or the major part of it after the gnomic opening sentence, appears to be another Gothic fragment, of uncertain reference. The content suggests a date about 1788. We have not discovered certainly the passages which Reed (pp. 22, 310) summarizes as 'Descriptions of a warrior moving (apparently) to battle'; if this is it, his date of 'c. summer 1788' seems acceptable.

Fragment VII, lines 1–8, is in the manner of Fragment VI, and is presumably of similar date. We cannot identify this piece in Reed's index of early fragments. The latter part, which may very possibly be distinct from lines 1–8, is a somewhat more restrained description of a winter scene, leading to two lines of related verse.

Fragment VIII is another Gothic fragment with allegorical additions. It appears to be one of the 'Drafts describing someone's madness as the "shipwreck of the soul"' (Reed, pp. 20, 310–11), which Reed dates 1788.

Fragment IX is a prose draft towards the image of the sundial in *An Evening Walk* (1793), 37–42. Reed (pp. 21, 310) dates it early 1788.

Fragment X is a prose description of Dovedale, Derbyshire. The writing, or at least the visit it records, may be fairly certainly dated 8 June 1788 (Moorman, i.105; Reed, p. 86, n. 6; for 'Verse 7' in Reed's note read 'Verse 6').

Fragment XI, comprising five pieces interrelated in subject and literary mode, was first printed by Z. S. Fink in *The Early Wordsworthian Milieu,* pp. 76, 80, 86, 88, 95. The pieces occur in a notebook filled mainly with jottings by Christopher Wordsworth towards a loco-descriptive poem on the Lake District; the fragments printed here occur, apparently at random, at the heads of pages, in the hand of William Wordsworth. Fink (pp. 4–5) connects them with Helen Maria Williams's 'pseudo-ballad *Edwin and Eltruda* (1782), a tale of distress … in which a baron who dwelt by Derwent's side is killed in battle by his daughter's suitor, and Mason's dramatic poem *Elfrida* (1752),… which tells of the bitter enmity between Elfrida's father and her husband and a fatal duel between the latter and King Edgar.' On the basis of these and other literary parallels, Fink dates the fragments 1784–5 (p. 7). Reed, observing similarities between the fragments and others which we have printed from the Gramere notebooks, prefers 1788 (Reed, pp. 311–12). It is unlikely that certainty can be reached. The fact that all the pieces are essentially somewhat inflated similes, in the Ossianic or Gothic manner, but usually draw on Wordsworth's observations of Lakeland or similar scenery, suggest a set of technical exercises in just that field—the application of Lakeland scenery to Gothic narrative, as in several sections of *The Vale of Esthwaite*. It might be reasonable to suppose, therefore, that they are earlier than that poem, so that a date earlier than Reed's, though possibly not quite so early as Fink's, might be conjectured.

INTRODUCTION: TEXTUAL

FRAGMENTS I–X occur in four manuscripts, Verse 3, 4, 5 and 6, in the Wordsworth Library, Grasmere.

Fragments I and II occur in MS. Verse 3, f. 10^{v} and f. 15^{v} respectively. Verse 3 is the remains of a notebook, now containing 19 more or less complete folios, about 11½ in. × 7½ in., and some stubs. The major content of this manuscript is MS. A of *The Vale of Esthwaite*; see *P.W.* i. 368.

Fragments III–VIII occur in MS. Verse 4, as follows: Fragment III, ff. 20^{r}, 21^{r}, 21^{v}, 22^{r} (pp. 40, 42–4 in the present pagination of the manuscript); Fragment IV, ff. 42^{v}–43^{r} (pp. 85–6); Fragment V, f. 49^{r}–49^{v} (pp. 98–9); Fragment VI, f. 64^{v} (p. 129); Fragment VII, f. 65^{r} (p. 130); Fragment VIII, f. 66^{v} (p. 132). Verse 4 is a bound note-book, now containing 70 folios, about 9½ in. × 8 in., plus stubs and endpapers which have been written on. The major content of this manuscript is verse printed by de Selincourt in *P.W.* I, Appendix; see his note to Poem II, *P.W.* I. 366.

Fragment IX occurs in MS. Verse 5, f. 16^{v}. Verse 5 is a home-made notebook of 16 folios, about 7¾ in. × 6¼ in. Its major content is fragments of a translation of the *Georgics* and of *The Vale of Esthwaite*. See Reed, p. 307. Fragment X occurs in MS. Verse 6, f. 1^{r}–1^{v}. Verse 6 is a home-made notebook similar in paper and size to Verse 5, and, like it, contains 16 folios. The major content is verse connected with *The Vale of Esthwaite* and *An Evening Walk*. See Reed, p. 310.

All these fragments are written in Wordsworth's hand, and all except III, which is very formally written until emendation begins, and V and X, which are comparatively neat, are difficult to read.

Fragment XI occurs in a notebook now in the Library of Northwestern University, Evanston, Illinois, described in Z. S. Fink, *The Early Wordsworthian Milieu,* pp. 1–3; it now consists of 10 leaves about 6 in. × 4 in., and 3 loose sheets. The pieces given here occur on pp. 1, 5, 11, 13, and 19 of the notebook. Our text is essentially the same as Fink's: we have made one correction to his (i. 2, 'sides' for 'side'); we have introduced two tentative readings where he preferred to remain doubtful (iii, heading, 'Book 1' for Fink's doubtful 'Book; and v. 3, 'complaisant' where he indicated an illegible inter-lineation); and we have abandoned the line-divisions of the manuscript, where Fink preferred as diplomatic a text as possible.

[In the following texts the symbol ¶ indicates the existence of editorial commentary and the symbol ▶ is hyperlinked to the relevant page of such commentary. RG]

EARLY PROSE FRAGMENTS: THE TEXT

I

NAY since the hours when in my infant bed with closed eyes I saw perpetually rising before me The face of [?] horses as wild as Lions have the forms of [? Men] been [? dear] to me The half formed visions [? of] the long processions of solemn terror been dear [to] me

II

WHAT is it that tells my soul the Sun is setting? For not a straggling ray [? tells] her he is in the Eas[t] or west, tis the brown mist which descends slowly into the valley to [? shed] his burthen of ghosts. See where a son of other worlds is sailing slowly on the lake—no! tis the taper that twinkling in the cottage casts a long wan shadow over the [? lake]. Loud howls the village dog. Spirit of these Mountains I see thee throned on Helvellyn, but thy feet and head are wrapped in mist. Spirit of these mountains if thou can bid the mist break from thy forehead, and nod me thrice farewell. farewell farewell.—[? Soon no] more shall the ghosts leaning from the [? rocks], or looki[ng] from the [? bastions] of the [? screes] listen while thou instructed me in the [? lore] of [? Nature]. Bid the mist break from thy brow [? s] and thrice nod me a farewell

I. 1 infant *Edd.*: in infant MS.
2 horses ... Lions *Edd.*: horses as wild to as Lions MS.[2]: horses wild to me MS.
3 Men] *possibly* them
3 of the] *possibly* or the
4 dear to me *Edd.*: dear me MS.

II. 2 brown. MS.[2]: slow MS.
2 slowly into MS.[2] into MS.
3 his burthen of ghosts MS.[2]: the inhabitants of other worlds MS.
3 other worlds MS.[2]: the other world MS.

III

A Tale.

'God bless you', said a voice to me, in a tone so pathetic that my heart melted at the sound, 'God bless you, and may he that maketh his Sun to rise on the evil and on the good, and sendeth rain on the just and on the unjust—may he give you as much happiness in this world as I trust he will give me in the next.'—

—It was at the very Village, and I was passing by the very churchyard, from which on a Sunday noon about twenty years ago the congregation were issuing when Gray returned from his visit to the vale of Elysium.—My astonishment at being thus unusually accosted did not prevent from observing that the object which addressed me was surrounded by a group of eight or ten Villagers. —The voice proceeded from a woman somewhat above the middle size.

Her dress, if you except a black hat (which bore no other marks than that of being drench'd in rain) tied by a dark green ribband which knotted under chin, was not much more warm or becoming than that of the poor, the lame, and the blind, who have no fire but the light of a Window seen at a distance, and whose candle is the little [ ]. Her eyes were large and blue: and from the wrinkles of her face (which, from their fineness, seemed rather the wrinkles of Sorrow than of Years) it was easy to see they had been acquainted with weeping; yet had not perpetual tears been able to extinguish a certain wild brightness, which, at first view, might have been mistaken for the wildness of great joy. But it was far different—it too plainly indicated she was not in her true and perfect mind.

III. *Between title and line 1* MS. *Inserts in pencil*: [? on looking higher]
4 on the good MS.[2]: the good MS.
4 and on the unjust *Edd.* and the on the unjust MS.
9 prevent from] *So in* ms.
12–13 hat … tied MS.[2]: hat tied MS. *In* MS. hat *seems to be deleted.*
13 under chin] *So in* MS.
14–15 *Above* poor … blind MS. *inserts, but does not work into the sentence*: Such of those numerous wrethces [*sic*].

IV

Epitaph.

Here rest[s] a maid whose form and mind were so lovely, that when
Heav'n [? fearing] age would render the one unworthy of the saw
Age began to prey upon her beauty, heav'n [*illegible deletion*] see so fair a soul in form unworthy of it, took And made her what she was before for immortality was all that need be given [? her]

Epitaph.

Here M— sleeps who lived a patriarchs days, she was so fair in youth that
year[s]
Death mistook her for an angel, and in age so good and pious that he spared
only
her as a saint, Till she died her [? sou] join'd Her former beauty to her present [? soul]

Here M.— sleep[s] who liv'd a patriarch's days
In youth so fair so Heav'nly fair that death
Mistook her for an Angel; and in years
So good and pure he spar'd her as a Saint.

IV. 2a fearing] *possibly* hearing
7 *After* sleeps MS. *deletes* in yo
8 good and pious MS.[2]: good MS.
9 former MS.[2]: youthful MS.
12 so fair MS.[2]: she was MS.

V

THE rivers in Peru are observed to quicken their currents with the first approach of morning; an effect produced by the rays of the sun melting the snow upon the Andes. Similar appearances are striking among the Alps. At the head of the valley of Lauterbrunnen, in order to have a more perfect view of a magnificent waterfall, I crossed over a broad and rapid mountain torrent by the aid of the fragments of rock which strewed its bed. I did not stay above a few minutes; but on my return I found the difficulty of recrossing the stream much encreased; and, being detained among the large stones in its channel, I perceived the water swell every moment, which, with the dizziness of sight produced by the furious dashing of the foam, placed me in a situation of considerable personal danger. Returning down the valley, from a bridge under the arch of which, about two hours before, for the sake of shade, we had retired to eat our dinner, we observed such a quantity of water rolling over our late resting place as would have swept us away before it. It will scarce be necessary to say that these temporary floods will be found on different sides of a valley as the sun changes his position.

VI

IN anger you may sometimes see the bottom of the soul. Sea. Storm. Calm.—

The Spectres are busy in shrouding the vale[? s] with wan white mist, shrieking and wailing and every [? house listens] the solemn knell of the Curfew. And thou shalt be seen at night on tiptoe at the [? smallest sound] [? or] eagerly standing and waving with thy hand, as a sign of Silence. That the long worm may not be startled. ▶

V. *Before text*, MS. *deletes four lines*: The Island. / A Song. / An Idyllium. / It is remarked that

1–2 with ... morning MS.[2]: as the morning advances MS.

8 perceived MS.[2]: observed MS.: found MS.[2]:

13 rolling MS.[2]: rolling down MS.

14 *After* it. MS. *deletes*: These sudden floods are temporary MS.[2]: sudden MS.

15 will be found MS.[2]: are occasioned MS.

15 on MS.[2]: in MS.

VI. 2 wan] *written* wand *in* MS.

3 *Above* house MS. *inserts* [? every]

4 on tiptoe] *Interlined between* night *and* standing (5). *The intention may be* standing on tiptoe

VII

Lightening.

Now death and the Spirit of the lightening sat together in a cave of
black
[? dark clouds] prepare [? d].
Now yoked to the blast they swept along the sky.
[? carried the flames of]
Now like horses of fire they [? trudge] through the cloud with his arm
[? scythed]
extended from a dark car.
And I saw a mighty Spectre standing by the edge of a black Cloud.
A Loud peal of Thunder.—Rocky wood
The boy with open breast hoping to [? catch] the Cot. When the snow
[? shrouded] soft foot
walks like a pale Ghost, [? althou] the wind with hard tread soft foot.—
Comes from the mountain
What [?] the snow with shadowy silent foot
Moves like a pale ghost shrouded oer the [? hill]

VIII

The other powers of the mind ran to wake Reason sleeping on the Deck. He stood up and like Ch still'd the storm.—He stood before him on a sudden like what has been at the altar of a Convent when the moon looks through the window[? s].

ere Zephyrus breath has
waked the rose, Smiling in sleep.—
& in the watry [? wintry] gleam

IX

Human Life is like the [? plate] of a dial, hope brightens the future, Reflection the hour that is past—but the present is always marked with a shadow—

VII. 3 clouds] *possibly* clods

X

Cambridge to Hawkshead June 8

[? Dovedale] Saw noth[ing] [? solidly drawn]
you

SAW nothing particularly striking till I came to Ashburn. Arrived there on Sunday Evening—and rode over to Dovedale. Dovedale is a very narrow valley somewhat better than a mile in length, broken into five or six distinct parts, so that the views it affords are necessarily upon a small scale. The first scene
[? quiet moor]
that strikes you upon descending into the valley, is the River Dove fringed with sedge, and spotted with a variety of small tufts of Grass hurrying between two hills, one of which about six years ago was cloathed with wood; the wood is again getting forwards; the other had a number of cattle grazing upon it. The scene was pleasing—the sun was just sinking behind the hill on the left—which was dark—while his beams cast a faint golden tinge upon the side of the other. The River in that part which was streamy had a glittering splendour which was pleasingly chastized, by the blue tint of intervening pieces of calm water; the fringe of sedge and the number of small islands, with which it is variegated. The view is terminated by a number of rocks scattered upon the side of one of the hills of a form perfectly spiral—

XI

(i)

HIS armour glittered in the [ ] but fear sat on his forehead, as when the sun shoots his beams upon the sides of skiddaw or helvellyn but mists sett[l]e upon his head

X. 5 length] *written* lenghth
7 descending MS.²: enterin[g] MS.
7 River] *written* Riverd
10 the other MS.²: that MS.
10 *After* upon it. MS. *has, in different ink and partly written over,* [? And] hand in hand [?].
12 golden MS.²:[? tinge] MS.
13 part which MS.²:part that MS.
13 had MS.²: glitt MS.

XI. (i) sett[l]e *Edd.*: sette MS.

(ii)

his crest nodded dreadful on his head like an oak shook by the wind upon the top of Teneriff—

when she [?] [?]

As when the moon she rises her orb above the Horizon rests upon the Branches of some tall Oak, which grows upon the summit of the Horizon

(iii)

[? Book 1]

mighty was the [? warrior] dreadful was his countenance yet it was tempered with the placid serenity of deliberate courage, as when a sun beam gilds the top [of] a rugged rock—or when the Sun skirts with gold the top of some dark cloud—They gaze upon each other like two rocks which rise from the sea in dreadful majesty they stand unmoved while the [? waves] dash at their feet, and the Storm howls round their heads.—

(iv)

his consort is sad, the smile of Joy forsakes her face, as when the black shade
of the earth
interposes betwixt the sun and Moon—

(v)

before Winter is expired

their love was mutual

He loved the fair Elfrida, but her Sire denied the completion of their
[? complaisant] reclines upon the lap of the youthfu
happiness, as when the Spring [throws her *del.*] arms around the Youthful Year, the hoory Winter rears his icy arm and dashes her from his embrace. ▶

XI. (ii) 1 oak MS.[2]: oak on the top MS.
XI. (ii) 4 Oak MS.[2]: ash MS.
XI. (iii) 3 top a rugged MS.
XI. (v) 4 hoory] *So in* MS.

COMMENTARY

I

For a parallel passage in a draft towards *The Prelude*, see our introductory note.

2. The word which we have left undeciphered is almost certainly 'fac', i.e. the beginning of a second writing of 'face' which should have been deleted. The following phrase appears to have begun as 'horses wild to me'; then the first 'as' was inserted, 'me' altered roughly to 'as', and 'to' left undeleted.

3. If the correct reading is 'them', the reference is to 'horses' (l.2).

II

Reed (p. 76) observes of this piece that 'The subject suggests a time … about that of W's departure for Cambridge', about 23 October 1787.

3–4. brown … valley] Cf. *Vale of Esthwaite*, 236–7 (*P.W.* i. 275): 'The solemn mists, dark brown or pale, / March slow and solemn down the vale.'

III

2–4. may he … unjust] Matt. 5: 45.

6–8. It was … Elysium] Gray, *Correspondence*, ed. Toynbee and Whibley (Oxford, 1935), p. 1098 (Gray's Journal of his tour of the Lakes, 8 Oct. 1769): 'Past by the little Chappel of Wiborn [Wythburn], out of wch the Sunday-congregation were then issuing.' This passage gives an indication of the approximate date of Wordsworth's piece.

8. Elysium] Gray, *Correspondence*, p. 1079 (Journal of the tour, 2 Oct. 1769): 'pass'd by the side of *Skiddaw* & its cub call'd *Latterrig*, & saw from an eminence at two miles distance the Vale of Elysium [i.e. the Keswick valley] in all its verdure, the sun then playing on the bosom of the lake, & lighting up all the mountains with its lustre.'

16. The blank in the text represents an erasure, of a word which began with *g*-, perhaps 'glowworm'.

21. true and perfect mind] Cf. *P.W.* i. 353, l. 12; *Guilt and Sorrow*, 361, reading of *Lyrical Ballads*, 1798–1800: 'And oft, robb'd of my perfect mind'; *King Lear*, IV. vii. 63: 'I fear I am not in my perfect mind'; generally, Cowper, *The Task*, i. 534–56.

IV

We regard the three pieces printed here as essentially three versions of the one epitaph. The occasion is unknown. Reed (p. 314) refers to *Journals*, i. 103 (28 Jan. 1802), where Dorothy reports that Wordsworth 'had [written an] epitaph, and altered one that he wrote when he was a boy'; but it is obviously impossible to prove, or disprove, any relation between this and our text.

2. The intention of the interlined version seems to have been: 'Heav'n fearing age would render the one unworthy of the [other]' i.e. would render the 'form' unworthy of the 'mind'; but 'other' was either never written or has become lost in the deletion nearby. Above the body of the draft appears these three lines: 'soon as he saw was / rendering one unworthy / of the'. The deleted passage began with 'who' and ended with 'to', and the interlined 'saw' replaces 'to see' of the cancelled version.

11. The verse rhythm indicated that the name of the deceased was disyllabic or virtually disyllabic, e.g. 'Mary' or 'Margaret'.

V

Wordsworth wrote a letter to his sister on 14 September 1790 'at a small village in the road from Grindelwald to Lauterbrunnen', and forecast that 'After viewing Lauterbrunnen we shall have concluded our tour of the more Alpine parts of Swisserland' (*E.Y.*, p. 35). Reed (p. 112) gives reasons for dating the incident described here on that day. His location of the incident in '"the heart" of the valley' is based on a misreading of the manuscript at l. 3 of our text. The date of composition is, of course, not necessarily that of the event. Reed, p. 24, suggests 'by 23 May 1794', on the ground that 'the fragment continues to a stanza' in MS. 1 of *Guilt and Sorrow* (*P.W.*i. 339, st. 51; cf. *P.W.* i. 330–1). It is, however, Wordsworth's information about similar phenomena in Peru which is there used, not the Alpine incident.

1–3. We have not found a certain source of Wordsworth's information about Peru. Mrs. Moorman (i. 146) mentions 'Ovalle's account of Chile, which he could have read in a translation'. Cf. *An Historical Relation of the Kingdom of Chile, By Alonso de Ovalle*, in John Pinkerton, *A General Collection of the Best and Most Interesting Voyages and Travels in All Parts of the World* (London, 1813), xiv, 51 (Chap. VII, 'Of the Fountains, Rivers, and Brooks, of the Cordillera'):

> The brooks and rivers which cross the ways every step are so violent, that there is no head so strong, but it turns to look on their current ... so that it is necessary sometimes to stay two or three days till the sun does not shine; for then these brooks are lower, because there is less snow melted: and for this reason it is always best to pass early in the morning, they having had all the night to run lower.

This work would have been available to Wordsworth in A. and J. Churchill, *A Collection of Voyages and Travels*, published in 1732 and later editions.

VI

Various elements of this piece occur in 'Gothic' passages in *The Vale of Esthwaite*, e.g. *V. E.* 250–3: 'Fix'd at the door she seem'd to stand / And beckoning slowly wav'd her hand. / I rose, above my head a bell / The mansion shook with solemn knell' (cf. 'solemn curfew', *Evening Walk* (1793), 318). A similar figure waves a hand in *V.E.* 336, while the poet is 'On tiptoe' (*V.E.* 325).

4. For *listen* as a transitive verb cf. *Evening Walk* (1793), 435–6: 'All air is ... still, / List'ning th'aërial music of the hill'.

5. on tiptoe at] As we have arranged the text, the sense is 'alerted by'. For another possible arrangement see textual n.

VII

5. carried the flames of] The interlined phrase seems to be an attempted variant of 'trudge', which might have produced some such phrase as 'carried the flames of war / destruction through the cloud', etc.

6. scythed] If this reading is correct, the sense is 'provided with scythes', like the conventional war-chariot of the Britons; see *O.E.D.*, s.v.

9. catch] The obvious word would be 'reach', but this does not seem to be the reading of the manuscript.

VIII

2. still'd the storm] Matt. 8: 23–6; Mark 4: 36–9.

IX

Cf. *An Evening Walk* (1793), 37–42:

Alas! the idle tale of man is found
Depicted in the dial's moral round;
With Hope Reflexion blends her social rays
To gild the total tablet of his days;
Yet still, the sport of some malignant Pow'r.
He knows but from its shade the present hour.

X

Mrs. Moorman (i. 105) and Reed (p. 86) place the visit to Dovedale described here in the summer of 1788, an interlude in Wordsworth's journey from Cambridge to Westmorland at the beginning of his first long vacation; though *Prel*. VI. 209 indicates a visit to 'Dovedale' and the 'Yorkshire Dales' in the summer of 1789.

2. Ashburn] Ashbourne, thirteen miles north-west of Derby, and two or three miles south of Dovedale.

9. about six years ago] Wordsworth is presumably reporting local information, as there is no evidence that he had seen Dovedale in 1782. See Reed, p. 55.

11–12. As the valley runs approximately north and south, and as he was presumably viewing from the south, the scene must have been an approximate duplicate of that Lake District spectacle which Wordsworth mentions in 'Dear native regions', *Vale of Esthwaite*, 508–13, *Prel*. (1850), VIII. 462–75, and elsewhere.

13. streamy] 'Wordsworth's meaning must be "rapid" or "rushing"' (Moorman, i, 105). Another possible sense would be 'broken up into several streams'. Just below we hear of a 'number of small islands' in the river, which presumably divided the main stream. Cf. *Prel*. VII. 561: 'streamy Morven'.

14. chastized] 'chequered' (Moorman, I, 105). A more obvious sense is 'toned down, subdued'.

17. spiral] Mrs Moorman compares *Prel*. (1850), VI. 193: 'Dovedale's spiry rocks'. Cf. *OED*, s.v. *spiry*, a.[2]: 'Curving or coiling in spirals'.

XI. i

2–3. The imagery is that of Fragment II above.

XI. ii

2. The interlined word above 'Horizon' is possibly 'far'.

XI. iii

Heading. The word 'Book' seems fairly certain, the numeral '1' following much less so.

1. warrior] The first four letters are plain in the manuscript; what follows might be 'ed' scribbled over to make 'io'; and there is no certain evidence of a final 'r'. Possibly Wordsworth wrote 'warred' and partially corrected towards 'warrior', which must be the sense intended.

4–5. dark cloud] Cf. Fragment VII, 3, 7.

6. waves] This seems to be the final intention. The first letter looks like 's' but may be an incomplete 'w'; after the 'a' the pen rises as if to make 'l' or 't'; 'ves' follows fairly clearly. Possibly Wordsworth began to write 'salt' and changed his mind as he wrote.

XI. v

3. Although only 'throws her' is deleted, the final intention appears to be given by the interlined reading. The interlined 'complaisant' is very uncertain.

2.

A Letter to the Bishop of Llandaff

INTRODUCTION: GENERAL

DURING his second stay in Paris, in the late autumn and early winter of 1792, Wordsworth sometimes imagined himself taking an active, even a dramatic, role in the Revolution. Although conscious of being 'An insignificant Stranger … and little graced with power / Of eloquence even in my native speech' (*Prel.* X. 131–3), he was eager to do whatever an obscure young Englishman could do who was 'enflam'd with hope' (*Prel.* X. 38) for the new French Republic. In *The Prelude*, as he describes his frame of mind during those final weeks in Paris, one senses genuine regret that his voice, speaking for the Revolution, should go unheard.

In January 1793 Richard Watson, Bishop of Llandaff, unknowingly furnished Wordsworth, who was now living in London, with an occasion for speaking out in defence of republicanism. Announcements of the execution of Louis had appeared in the London papers on 24 January 1793; fuller news of the execution began appearing in the papers the following day. Thoroughly shocked at the course of events in France, Watson hurriedly composed an indignant protest, larded with fervent praise of the British Constitution. Dating his composition 25 January, Watson attached it as an Appendix to a Sermon he had preached some years before;[1] on 30 January the Sermon with its Appendix was advertised in *The Morning Herald* as 'This day … published'; it was similarly advertised in *The Times* a week later (7 February).

Although Watson's Appendix does not strike a modern reader as especially challenging, it is understandable why to Wordsworth Watson would have appeared a formidable and worthy opponent.[2] For many years Watson had spoken for liberal causes: besides numerous publications on Church questions, all in a liberal vein,[3] he

1 For a bibliography of Watson's pamphlet see the first note in our Commentary.

2 For some years Watson's reputation would have been well known to Wordsworth. A native of Heversham, Westmorland, and a fellow of Trinity College, Cambridge, Watson had been Regius Professor of Divinity at Cambridge until 1787. He then retired to Calgarth Park, his estate on Windermere (*Anecdotes of the Life of Richard Watson, Bishop of Landaff; Written by Himself* (London, 1817), pp. 3 and 183–7). Here his extensive tree planting attracted the attention of the young Christopher Wordsworth (*The Early Wordsworthian Milieu*, ed. Zera Fink (Oxford, 1958), pp.11–12, 78, 123–4). For Wordsworth's later acquaintance with Watson see *M.Y.* i. 206, 229; ii. 172, 208, 330; and Moorman ii. 231.

3 e.g. *A Sermon Preached before the University of Cambridge, on October 25, 1776* (Cambridge, 1776), pp. 12–13; *A Letter to His Grace the Archbishop of Canterbury*, 2nd edn. (London, 1783); *A*

had also written in favour of the American Revolution,[1] and even in favour of the French Revolution.[2] Though he had, in his political sermons, deplored all forms of 'Republican Tyranny', his reputation for liberalism was a wide one, and others besides Wordsworth were surprised by what they found in the Appendix. *The Critical Review* (vii [February 1793], 212–15), with its Tory bias, understandably made much of the fact that Watson had come at last to recognize the excellence of the British Constitution. Later that year the reviewer in *The Gentleman's Magazine* (lxiii [July 1793], 633–6) was so impressed with Watson's new arguments that he felt it his 'duty' to give the Appendix 'in its fullest extent'—a duty which he fulfilled by quoting all but the introductory paragraph. But it is a measure of the fearfulness and general anti-Jacobinism of the day that the liberal reviews also found much to praise in the Appendix and voiced only the mildest of reservations.[3] Like Wordsworth (*Llandaff*, 42–8), the reviewer in *The European Magazine* recognized the Watson's arguments would 'probably have more weight with a certain class of men, than if they had come from a more avowed friend of the present Governing Powers', but, unlike Wordsworth, this reviewer went on to praise Watson's 'moderate' sentiments. If the reviews we have cited are typical of the general response to the Appendix, Wordsworth must have felt quite alone as he set out to refute the redoubtable Bishop of Llandaff.

Precisely when the 'Letter' was written is not known. There is no authoritative date on the single surviving manuscript,[4] nor have we found any contemporary reference to the date of composition. But, after a careful study of the topical allusions in the 'Letter' itself, we believe that it was most probably composed in February or March, for *all* the allusions are to events antecedent to the execution of Louis, or the to the 'present convulsions' (54) immediately attendant upon that event.[5] The 'mod-

Charge Delivered to the Clergy of the Archdeaconry of Ely on Thursday, June 12, 1788 (Cambridge, 1788).

1 *The Principles of the Revolution vindicated in a Sermon preached before the University of Cambridge, on Wednesday, May 29, 1776* (Cambridge, 1776); *A Sermon Preached before the Lords Spiritual and Temporal in the Abbey-Church, Westminster* (London, 1784). In his autobiography (*Anecdotes*, p. 59), Watson says that for the former sermon he was 'much abused by ministerial writers, as a man of republican principles'; cf. *Llandaff*, 27–38.

2 *A Charge Delivered to the Clergy of the Diocese of Landaff, June, 1791* (London, 1792).

3 e.g. *European Magazine and London Review*, xxiii (Feb. 1793), 111–13; *Analytical Review*, xv (Mar. 1793), 310–12; *Monthly Review*, x (Apr. 1793), 476–8.

4 On the verso page facing *Llandaff*, 667–8 ('it would ill become an English bishop at the close of the eighteenth century'), some late bewildered reader of the manuscript has written: 'here is the date 1799?'

5 Cf. also *Llandaff*, 654, where Watson, whose *Appendix* is dated 25 Jan., is said to be giving his 'opinions upon the present turbulent crisis'. Charles W. Roberts, who sees a Godwinian influence on

ish lamentation' (49–50) which Watson is rebuked for having joined can hardly have lasted much beyond the formal mourning of the Court, 27 January till 7 February.[1] And had the 'Letter' been written much later than the middle of March, one would expect it to reflect the rapidly changing situation in France. For example, *The Morning Herald*, of 23 March, in reporting the crucial defection of Dumouriez, observed that he had 'now committed exactly the same offence against the French Convention as La Fayette offered to the last National Assembly'; as the details of Dumouriez's treason figured more and more prominently in the London papers, any reference to Lafayette's desertion in August 1792—such as the one in Wordsworth's final paragraph—would become wholly outmoded.

Effectively to counteract Watson's pamphlet, and the favourable reception given it in at least two February journals, Wordsworth needed to be prompt. His own outward circumstances would have permitted him to go to work at once. *Descriptive Sketches* had been published on 29 January;[2] he was unoccupied and in touch with his publisher Joseph Johnson, at whose shop he met other young radicals who would presumably have encouraged a rebuttal of Watson;[3] living at Staple Inn with his brother Richard, he had access to all the London newspapers and journals.[4] But if outward circumstances were favourable to work, the inner turmoil was not. To appreciate

Wordsworth's 'Letter', was the first to argue that *Llandaff* 'could not have been written before June of 1793' ('The Influence of Godwin on Wordsworth's "Letter to the Bishop of Llandaff", *Studies in Philology*, xxix (1932), 591). Pointing to Wordsworth's having referred to the attack on Priestley's house in 1791 as though it were a recent event, Roberts endeavours to persuade us that Wordsworth is inaccurate in his use of such terms as *present crisis*, *lately*, *at the moment*, etc.; but as our note to 234–7 indicates, references to the attack on Priestley were entirely topical during the winter of 1792–3. Roberts's later dating depends chiefly, however, on Wordsworth's reference to parliamentary reform (*Llandaff*, 587–8). According to Roberts, this reference could not have been made until after Grey's motion for reform on 6 May 1793. Again, our note to 587–8 shows that this argument is by no means valid. Unfortunately, Roberts's dating of *Llandaff* has been accepted implicitly by F. M. Todd, *Politics and the Poet* (London, 1957), pp. 58–62, and explicitly by Mark L. Reed, *Wordsworth: the Chronology of the Early Years* (Cambridge, Mass., 1967), p. 142. Mary Moorman (i. 255) and G. W. Meyer (*Wordsworth's Formative Years* [Ann Arbor, 1943], pp. 95, 117) think that the 'spring' of 1793 is the probable date, but neither argues the matter.

1 See n. on 49–50 below.

2 So announced that day in *The Morning Herald*. Cf. Mark L. Reed, op. cit., p. 140.

3 Moorman, i. 218–19; Herschel Baker, *William Hazlitt* (Cambridge, Mass., 1962), pp. 56–7; Andrew Gilchrist, *The Life of William Blake*, ed. W. G. Robertson (New York, 1906), pp. 93–7.

4 For Wordsworth's residence at Staple Inn see Moorman i. 211, and Chester L. Shaver, *Review of English Studies*, N.S. xii (1961), 55–7. If the 'Letter' was, as we think, composed at Staple Inn, then Richard was perhaps remembering it when in May 1794 he wrote to William, urging him to 'be cautious in writing or expressing your political opinions. By the suspension of the Habeas Corpus Acts the Ministers have great powers' (*E.Y.* 121).

the passionate sincerity of Wordsworth's 'Letter to Llandaff', one should read it in conjunction with Book X of *The Prelude*. There brilliantly described is Wordsworth's state of mind following the outbreak of war between England and France. The war had torn 'By violence at one decisive rent / From the best Youth in England, their dear pride, / Their joy, in England' (X. 277–9).

I felt
The ravage of this most unnatural strife
In my own heart; there lay it like a weight
At enmity with all the tenderest springs
Of all my enjoyments. I, who with the breeze
Had play'd, a green leaf on the blessed tree
Of my beloved country; nor had wish'd
For happier fortune than to wither there,
Now from my pleasant station was cut off,
And toss'd about in whirlwinds. (X. 250–9)

Such a mood might nourish passionate bursts of oratory, but it would seem ill-suited to sustained reasoning and historical analysis, especially in a writer uncertain of his powers in prose.[1] And yet, unfinished and occasionally imperfect as the 'Letter' is, Wordsworth's arguments are marshalled into an exposition that is both cogent and powerful.

Some of the sources upon which Wordsworth drew in composing his 'Letter' are indicated in the 'Commentary', but perhaps the most important are not there cited. Basic to the 'Letter' are his own experiences in France, not only in 1791–2, but also in the summer of 1790—the sights he saw, the conversations he had, the speeches he heard, the newspapers he read. In Paris he attended both the National Assembly (having been 'introduced' by a member (*E.Y.*, p. 71)) and the Jacobin Club (*Prel.* IX. 46–9); eagerly he read 'the master Pamphlets of the day (*Prel.* IX. 96), and daily he felt the 'shocks' of public news (*Prel.* IX. 177–82). Carra and Gorsas are the only journalists whom he mentions by name in *The Prelude* (IX. 178), but there were many others he might have mentioned as familiarly. The National Assembly regularly ordered speeches and reports to be printed and circulated through the Departments, and individual deputies were constantly printing their own political views. Of the hundreds of ephemeral writings which he must have seen we can recover very few; in annotating the historical allusions we have, however, been mindful of the dates of his residence in France. Hence, as far as possible, French sources have been used for the historical events of December

1 See *E.Y.*, p. 127 (June 1794): 'I have not been much used to composition of any kind particularly in prose, my style therefore may frequently want fluency and sometimes perhaps perspicuity but these defects will gradually wear off.'

1791 to December 1792, and English sources for those thereafter.

Among the established political writers known to Wordsworth, Rousseau and Paine appear to have exerted the strongest influence upon the 'Letter to Llandaff'.[1] Because the verbal parallels between their writings and Wordsworth's are significantly numerous and often very close, these two writers are frequently referred to in our notes. But in every case an indebtedness is not necessarily implied: the teachings of Paine and Rousseau were 'in the air', and statements of theirs were parroted by hundred of lesser writers and orators, in England as well as France.

Two other possible influences upon Wordsworth's 'Letter' are omitted from our notes. There was in revolutionary France a new and lively interest in English political writers of the seventeenth century; Zera Fink has argued that Wordsworth shared this interest, and that his 'Letter' reflects political theory derived from Milton, Harrington and Algernon Sydney.[2] Because the similarities which Fink points to are similarities of broad theoretical concept rather than of particular phrasing, we have had to omit from our notes references to all but one of these parallels. A second possible influence, omitted from our notes for a different reason, is Godwin's *Political Justice*. The argument for Godwin's influence has been most strongly urged by Charles W. Roberts, and his argument has been recently repeated by F. M. Todd.[3] Apart from the fact that *Political Justice* was not published until after the middle of February 1793,[4] and that Wordsworth would, therefore, have had difficulty in mastering its arguments in time for a reply to Watson's Appendix, there are other reasons which lead us to believe that Godwin exerted no influence upon Wordsworth's 'Letter'.[5] Some of Godwin's most important tenets are in direct contradiction to the very heart of Wordsworth's

1 For Paine's influence, see E. N. Hooker, 'Wordsworth's "Letter to the Bishop of Llandaff"', *Studies in Philology*, xxviii (1931), 522–31.

2 'Wordsworth and the English Republican Tradition', *J.E.G.P.* xlvii (1948), 107–8.

3 Roberts, op. cit.; Todd, op. cit., pp. 60–2. Arthur Beatty (*William Wordsworth, his Doctrine and Art in their Historical Relations*, 2nd edn.(Madison, 1927), p. 31–2) and G. M. Harper (*William Wordsworth*, 3rd edn. (London, 1929), pp. 185–6) also saw a strong influence from Godwin in the Letter.

4 Mark L. Reed (op. cit., p. 141), referring to *The London Chronicle*, gives 16 February as the date of publication. On 16 February *The Morning Herald* repeated an advertisement of *Political Justice* identical with one made on 8 February: 'Next week will be published'. On 21 and 25 February it again carried identical advertisements of *Political Justice*: 'This day is published'. The first advertisement in *The Times* that *Political Justice* was now published appeared on 22 February.

5 Cf. for views similar to ours, R. D. Havens, *The Mind of a Poet* (Baltimore, Md., 1941), 543; F. E. L. Priestley (ed.), *Enquiry Concerning Political Justice* (Toronto, 1946), iii. 102–3; Zera Fink, *J.E.G.P.* xlvii (1948), n. 33, p. 111: Herschel Baker, op. cit., 68–9; Moorman, i. 255 ('whereas the *Letter to the Bishop of Llandaff* shows no trace of Godwin's doctrines, the letter to Matthews of June 1794 certainly does').

'Letter': for example, Godwin repudiates entirely the doctrine of social contract ('it is impossible for any government to derive its authority from an original contract'); he condemns all talk of the 'Rights of Man'; he disavows revolution by violence and all recourse to force; he attacks national assemblies, contemptuously calling decision by vote 'that intolerable insult upon all reason and justice'.[1] Wherever similarities occur between Wordsworth's 'Letter' and Godwin's *Political Justice*, it is possible to find a common source, usually Paine.

There remains one other problem connected with Wordsworth's 'Letter': why was it not published in 1793? Two answers may be suggested. First, although it could have preserved him from the censure of conservative elders within the family, anonymous authorship would not have precluded government inquiry. A Proclamation against seditious writing was made in May 1792, and in December Thomas Paine, although by this time in Paris and a member of the National Convention, was found guilty of sedition for having written *The Rights of Man, Part Second.*[2] Any misgivings inspired in Wordsworth by this condemnation, or by similar actions taken against other writers, may have been seconded by Joseph Johnson. Although he was the publisher of Priestley, Horne Tooke, Godwin, and other radicals, Johnson was not wholly lacking in caution: he had printed *The Rights of Man, Part First*, but 'became frightened after a few copies were out … and the work was transferred to J. S. Jordan'.[3] As Wordsworth's publisher, he may have advised against publication. A second possible answer is that events in France may have checked Wordsworth. If we are correct in assigning February or March as the date of composition, the news of the widespread insurrections in France and of the civil war begun by the Vendean armies—both rumoured in late March and fully reported in the London papers of early April—would have sadly undercut Wordsworth's contention that the revolution expressed the unanimous wish of twenty–five million Frenchmen (*Llandaff*, 150). Signs that Wordsworth may have made the decision not to publish can be found in the manuscript itself: one section is left unfinished (see 357 and our textual n.); sometimes an alternative word or phrase is suggested by an insertion above the line, but no decision is reached (see textual nn. 90, 117, 247, 336, 370); occasional underlinings, presumably made by the author, draw attention to small faults of style, but no emendations are made (e.g. see textual nn. 378, 380, 420, 422). In our description of the manuscript (see below, p. 45) we have explained that the sentence fragment with

1 *An Enquiry Concerning Political Justice* (London, 1793), i. 149, 109–19, 202–3; ii. 571.
2 Phillip Anthony Brown, *The French Revolution in English History* (London, 1918), pp. 84–7.
3 M. D. Conway (ed.), *The Writings of Thomas Paine* (New York, 1906), ii. 260.

which the 'Letter' now ends derives from the loss of one or more folios; but even without that loss, the manuscript, though a fair copy, would require further work from the author before it could go to the printer.

INTRODUCTION: TEXTUAL

THE text of Wordsworth's 'Letter to the Bishop of Llandaff' is derived from the fair copy which is preserved in the Wordsworth Library, Grasmere (MS. Prose 1). We believe that no other manuscript of this work survives. The folios, undoubtedly cut from larger sheets, are of a fairly heavy paper, with horizontal chain lines; the watermark is a crown over the letters GR, and there is also an additional mark of either the letter W or M, but we can find no date watermarked on the paper.

After the single folding, the folios were stacked one upon the other and stitched with a cord at the fold, or spine, to make a notebook of pages measuring 7 in. wide × 9 in. long. The first folio and the last surviving folio are both detached from the stitching.

The title is written on the recto of the first leaf, the verso of which is blank. The text begins on the recto of the second leaf, which we refer to as page [1^{r}], and continues on the recto leaves to the end of the last surviving folio, or pages [48^{r}] and [49^{r}]. (The page numbers now on the top right corner of the recto pages were made by Helen Darbishire, who in her numbering missed page [20^{r}], and then corrected the omission by numbering that page '19*A*'; as a result, page '20' on the manuscript should be '21', and so on, to her page '48', our page [49^{r}].)

The last line, at the very bottom of page [49^{r}], reads: 'Lordship. [Besides the names which I'. At the top of page [49^{v}] a pencilled note by Edward Quillinan reads: 'a leaf of the sequel seems torn out at an interesting stage of the discussion. E.Q.' This note suggests that the last folio was, when Quillinan examined it, stitched to the preceding folios, and that he perhaps saw some evidence which led him to think that 'a leaf' had been 'torn out' at the end. But if Wordsworth's references to 'loose sheet' and 'last page', as given in our textual n. 364–9, are both meant to refer to the same page, then this folio may never have been stitched to the notebook. Grosart, who omits from his edition the last five words of the text ('Besides the names which I'), does quote them in his description of the manuscript, and remarks that 'One folio is lacking' (Grosart, i. xiii). From the present condition of the manuscript we cannot estimate what has been lost from the end, but because the manuscript is a fair copy we suppose that the text had once been brought to a conclusion that is now lost. The large opening bracket pencilled around the word 'Besides' may mark Grosart's intention to omit the following five words from his edition, or, like other brackets earlier on the manuscript (see textual nn. 364–9, 587), may indicate the author's intention to make a transposition or some other emendation.

As a rule, the verso pages are blank, but pages [13v] and [14v] are used to expand the text (see textual n. 161–90); verso pages are twice used for footnotes (*Llandaff*, 56 and 84); and a number of times they are used for brief miscellaneous comments on the text, or for pencilled markings opposite the text on the facing recto.

We are unable to identify the clear, careful hand of the principal scribe. In his description Grosart (i. xiii) said that 'The manuscript is wholly in the handwriting of its author'; to this assertion Gordon Wordsworth, on a slip laid in with MS. Prose 1, replied: 'I cannot accept Dr Grosart's statement … that this manuscript is in the handwriting of Wm Wordsworth.' At one time Helen Darbishire thought that the manuscript was in Wordsworth's hand (see F. M. Todd, *Politics and the Poet* (London, 1957), p. 58, fn. 2), but in two different notes—one to the present editors, 15 December 1960, and the other left in MS. Prose 1—she concluded, 'after a careful scrutiny of the whole MS.', that although 'some words and passages are certainly in Wordsworth's hand', the principal hand is not his, nor one which she could identify. We agree with Miss Darbishire that Wordsworth's hand indubitably writes the footnote to *Llandaff*, 84; the text of *Llandaff*, 87–92 ('of the ministers … violence'); 162–90 ('This passage … republicanism'); 324 ('and for their country?'); 338–41 ('he is well … that they'); 620–6 ('vast is … which I'). These occurrences of Wordsworth's hand cited by Miss Darbishire, as well as a few others which she did not cite, are recorded in our textual apparatus. At the conclusion of her note left with MS. Prose 1, Miss Darbishire writes: 'W. W. is at the elbow of the copyist, dictating or closely overseeing the copy, and changes his mind in process of arriving at final copy'; she then cites as evidence four deletions where the substitutions are made, not by insertions above the line, but immediately on the same line (i. e. textual nn. 97, 278, 292, and 317–8). Other similar examples could be cited.

In addition to variants, our textual notes record various markings made usually on the verso pages facing the text, but sometimes on the rectos, such as the scoring of margins or the placing of a large 'X' opposite a sentence or passage. There is no way of telling when these markings were made, but since they seem to suggest a need for revision, they may have been made soon after the copy was finished. Comments on the text, such as those we record in textual nn. 135, 151–4, 242–3, and 587, may have been made at the same time, although they might have been made later. The comment recorded in textual n. 537 was obviously made much later (see our n. to *Llandaff*, 537).

Although Grosart's textual errors are sometimes so egregious that one wonders whether someone else perhaps made a transcript for him, we have nevertheless adopted his reading on the few occasions where a tear in the manuscript may have occurred after his edition of 1876.

A
Letter
to the
Bishop of Landaff
on the extraordinary avowal of his Political Principles contained in the Appendix to his late Sermon ¶
by a Republican ¶

Title: First his *Grosart*: MS. *torn*

►

LETTER TO THE BISHOP OF LLANDAFF: THE TEXT

My Lord,

Reputation may not improperly be termed the moral life of man. Alluding to our natural existence, Addison, in a sublime allegory well known to your Lordship, has represented us as crossing an immense bridge, from whose surface from a variety of causes we disappear one after another, and are seen no more. Every one, who enters upon public life, has such a bridge to pass, some slip through at the very commencement of their career from thoughtlessness, others pursue their course a little longer till, misled by the phantoms of avarice and ambition, they fall victims to their delusion. Your Lordship was either seen, or supposed to be seen, continuing your way for a long time, unseduced and undismayed; but those, who now look for you, will look in vain, and it is feared you have at last fallen, through one of the numerous trap–doors, into the tide of contempt to be swept down to the ocean of oblivion.

It is not my intention to be illiberal; these latter expressions have been forced from me by indignation. Your Lordship has given a proof that even religious controversy may be conducted without asperity; I hope I shall profit by your example. At the same time with a spirit which you may not approve, for it is a republican spirit, I shall not preclude myself from any truths, however severe, which I may think beneficial to the cause which I have undertaken to defend. You will not then be surprized when I inform you that it is only the name of its author which has induced me to notice an Appendix to a sermon, which you have lately given to the world, with a hope that it may have some effect in calming a perturbation which you say has been *excited* in the minds of the lower orders of the community. While, with a servility which has prejudiced many people against religion itself, the ministers of the church of England have appeared as

Symbols

¶ this symbol in the margin indicates the existence of editorial commentary

▶ click on this symbol to visit the relevant page of that commentary

Textual Notes

10 continuing *Grosart*: continu[*tear*] MS

writers upon public measures only to be the advocates of slavery civil and religious, your Lordship stood almost alone as the defender of truth and political charity. The names of levelling prelate, bishop of the dissenters, which were intended as a dishonour to your character were looked upon by your friends, perhaps by yourself, as an acknowledgement of your possessing an enlarged and philosophic mind; and like the generals in a neighbouring country, if it had been equally becoming your profession, you might have adopted, as an honourable title, a denomination intended as a stigma.

On opening your Appendix, your admirers will naturally expect to find an impartial statement of the grievances which harass this nation, and a sagacious enquiry into the proper modes of redress. They will be disappointed. Sensible how large a portion of mankind receive opinions upon authority, I am apprehensive lest the doctrines which they will find there should derive a weight from your name to which they are by no means intrinsically intitled. I will therefore examine what you have advanced from a hope of being able to do away with any impression left on the minds of such as may be liable to confound with argument a strong prepossession for your Lordship's talents, experiences, and virtues.

Before I take notice of what you appear to have laid down as principles, it may not be improper to advert to some incidental opinions found at the commencement of your political confession of faith. At a period big with the fate of the human race, I am sorry that you attach so much importance to the personal sufferings of the late royal martyr and that an anxiety for the issue of the present convulsions should not have prevented you from joining in the idle cry of modish lamentation which has resounded from the court to the cottage. You wish it to be supposed you are one of those who are unpersuaded of the guilt of Louis XVI. If you had attended to the history of the French revolution as minutely as its importance demands, so far from stopping to bewail his death, you would rather have regretted that the blind fondness of his people had placed a human being in that monstrous situation which rendered him unaccountable before a human

44 take notice of MS.[2]: examine MS.
45 advert to [*in Wordsworth's hand*] MS.[2]: take notice of MS.
54–5 rather ... in that] *A pencilled* X *on the facing verso.*

tribunal. A bishop,* a man of philosophy and humanity as distinguished as your Lordship, declared at the opening of the national convention, and twenty-five millions of men were convinced of the truth of the assertion, that there was not a citizen on the tenth of august who, if he could have dragged before the eyes of Louis the corse of one of his murdered brothers, might not have exclaimed to him, Tyran, voilà ton ouvrage. Think of this and you will not want consolation under any depression your spirits may feel at the contrast exhibited by Louis on the most splendid throne of the universe, and Louis alone in the tower of the Temple or on the scaffold. But there is a class of men who received the news of the late execution with much more heart-felt sorrow than that which you among such a multitude so officiously express. The passion of pity is one of which, above all others, a christian teacher should be cautious of cherishing the abuse: when under the influence of reason, it is regulated by the disproportion of the pain suffered to the guilt incurred. It is from the passion thus directed that the men of whom I have spoken are afflicted by the catastrophe of the fallen monarch. They are sorry that the prejudice and weakness of mankind have made it necessary to force an individual into an unnatural situation, which requires more than human talents and human virtues, and at the same time precludes him from attaining even a moderate knowledge of common life and from feeling a particular share in the interests of mankind. But, above all, these men lament that any combination of circumstances should have rendered it necessary or advisable to veil for a moment the statues of the laws, and that by such emergency the cause of twenty-five millions of people, I may say of the whole human race, should have been so materially injured. Any other sorrow for the death of Louis is irrational and weak. In France royalty is no more; the person of the last anointed is no more also, and I flatter myself I am not alone, even in this *kingdom*, when I wish that it may please the almighty neither by the hands of his

*M. Grégoire

56n. *M. Grégoire *Edd.*: Note *M. Gregoire MS.
64–6 of the late … such a] *A pencilled* X *on the facing verso.*
66–78 The passion … say] *Margins scored and marked with a pencilled* X. *The punctuation in* 67–68 *is editorial.*

priests nor his nobles (I allude to a striking passage of Racine) to raise his posterity to the rank of his ancestors and reillume the torch of extinguished David.*

You say "I fly with terror and abhorrence even from the altar of liberty when I see it stained with the blood of the aged, of the innocent, of the defenceless sex; of the ministers of religion, and of the faithful adherents of a fallen monarch." What! have you so little knowledge of the nature of man as to be ignorant, that a time of revolution is not the season of true Liberty. Alas! the obstinacy & perversion of men is such that she is too often obliged to borrow the very arms of despotism to overthrow him, and in order to reign in peace must establish herself by violence. She deplores such stern necessity, but the safety of the people, her supreme law, is her consolation. This apparent contradiction between the principles of liberty and the march of revolutions, this spirit of jealousy, of severity, of disquietude, of vexation, indispensable from a state of war between the oppressors and oppressed, must of necessity confuse the ideas of morality and contract the benign exertion of the best affections of the human heart. Political virtues are developed at the expence of moral ones; and the sweet emotions of compassion, evidently dangerous where traitors are to be punished, are too often altogether smothered. But is this a sufficient reason to reprobate a convulsion from which is to spring a fairer order of things?

* See *Athalie*, Scene second

Il faut que sur le trône un roi soit élevé
Qui *se souvienne un jour* qu'au rang de ses ancêtres
Dieu l'a fait remonter par la main de ses prêtres,
L'a tiré par leur main de l'oubli du tombeau,
Et de David éteint rallumé le flambeau.

The conclusion of the same speech applies so strongly to the present period that I cannot forbear transcribing it.

Daigne, daigne, mon Dieu, sur Mathan et sur elle
Répandre *cet esprit d'imprudence et d'erreur,*
De la chute des rois funeste avant-coureur.

84n. *See ... *avant-coureur*] *In Wordsworth's hand on the facing verso.*

84n, line 7. conclusion MS.[2]: latter MS.

85 say "I MS.[2]: tell us that you MS. *On the margin, a pencilled* X.

87–92 of the ministers ... violence] *In Wordsworth's hand.*

89 a time ... Liberty] *Margin scored.*

89 the season MS.[2]: that MS.

90 men] a? *is written as a query above* men *but* man *is not substituted for men.*

97 contract [*in Wordsworth's hand*] MS.[3]: contract MS: diminish MS.[2]:

101 reprobate [*in Wordsworth's hand*] MS.[2]: deprecate MS.

It is the province of education to rectify the erroneous notions which a habit of oppression, and even of resistance, may have created, and to soften this ferocity of character proceeding from a necessary suspension of the mild and social virtues; it belongs to her to create a race of men who, truly free, will look upon their fathers as only enfranchised.

I proceed to the sorrow you express for the fate of the French priesthood. The measure by which that body was immediately stripped of part of its possessions, and a more equal distribution enjoined of the rest, does not meet with your Lordship's approbation. You do not question the right of the nation over ecclesiastical wealth; you have voluntarily abandoned a ground which you were conscious was altogether untenable. Having allowed this right, can you question the propriety of exerting it at that particular period? The urgencies of the state were such as required the immediate application of a remedy. Even the clergy were conscious of such necessity; and, aware from the immunities they had long enjoyed that the people would insist upon their bearing some share of the burden, offered of themselves a considerable portion of their superfluities. The assembly were true to justice and refused to compromise the interests of the nation by accepting as a satisfaction the insidious offerings of compulsive charity. They enforced their right: they took from the clergy a considerable portion of their wealth, and applied it to the alleviation of the national misery. Experience shews daily the wise employment of the ample provision which yet remains to them. While you reflect on the vast diminution which some men's fortunes must have undergone, your sorrow for these individuals will be diminished by recollecting the unworthy motives which induced the bulk of them to undertake the office, and the scandalous arts which enabled so many to attain the rank and enormous wealth, which it has seemed necessary to annex to the charge of a christian pastor. You will rather look upon it as a signal act of justice that they should thus unexpectedly be stripped of the rewards of their vices and their crimes. If you should lament the sad reverse by which the hero of the necklace has been divested of about 1,300,000 livres of annual revenue, you

103–4 ferocity MS.[2]: necessary ferocity MS.
105 who, MS.[2]: [? who are] MS.
106 enfranchised] *The* en *is heavily smeared.*
115 clergy MS.[2]: clergy themselves MS.
120–1 considerable portion] *Partly underlined; pencilled above is*: large share ante [cf. 117] *but no deletion is made.*
135–6 the necklace... 1,300,00] *Pencilled on the facing verso is*: Prince de Rohan *but no asterisk is made in the text.*
136 about MS.[2]: nearly MS.

may find some consolation that a part of this prodigious mass of riches is gone to preserve from famine some thousands of curés who were pining in villages unobserved by courts.

I now proceed to principles. Your lordship very properly asserts that "the liberty of man in a state of society consists in his being subject to no law but the law enacted by [the] general will of the society to which he belongs". You approved of the object which the French had in view when in the infancy of the revolution they were attempting to destroy arbitrary power and to erect a temple to liberty on its ruins. It is with suprize then that I find you afterwards presuming to dictate to the world a servile adoption of the British constitution. It is with indignation I perceive you "reprobate" a people for having imagined happiness and liberty more likely to flourish in the open field of a republic than under the shade of monarchy. You are therefore guilty of a most glaring contradiction. Twenty-five millions of Frenchmen have felt they could have no security for their liberties under any modification of monarchical power. They have in consequence unanimously chosen a republic. You cannot but observe that they have only exercised that right in which by your own confession liberty essentially resides.

As to your arguments by which you pretend to justify your anathemas of a republic, if arguments they may be called, they are so concise, that I cannot but transcribe them. "I dislike a republic for this reason, because of all forms of government, scarcely excepting the most despotic, I think a republic the most oppressive to the bulk of the people: they are deceived in it with a shew of liberty; but they live in it, under the most odious of all tyrannies, the tyranny of their equals."

This passage is a singular proof of that fatality by which the advocates of error furnish weapons for their own destruction; while it is merely *assertion* in respect to a justification of your aversion to Republicanism, a strong *argument* may be drawn from it in its favour. Mr Burke, in a philosophical lamentation over the extinction of Chivalry, told us that in those times vice lost half its evil, by losing all its grossness; infatuated moralist! Your Lordship excites compassion as labouring under the same delusion. Slavery is a bitter and a poisonous

142 the Edd.: om. MS.

151–4 They have ... resides] *On the facing verso, this passage is scored and in pencil is written*: N.B. This is very true, on the Bp's premises

161–190 *After* equals." MS. *continues*: Relying upon [cf. 190]. *A caret inserted after* equals." *indicates the place where the expanded text, written in Wordsworth's hand on pp.* [13v], [14v], *should be inserted.*

167 excites MS.[2]: appears the MS.

draught; we have but one consolation under it—that a nation may dash the cup to the ground when she pleases; do not imagine that by taking from its bitterness you weaken its deadly quality; no, by rendering it more palatable you contribute to its power of destruction. We submit without repining to the chastisements of providence, aware that we are creatures, that opposition is vain and remonstrance impossible. But when redress is in our power and resistance is rational, we suffer with the same humility from beings like ourselves, because we are taught from infancy that we were born in a state of inferiority to our oppressors, that they were sent into the world to scourge and we to be scourged. Accordingly we see the bulk of mankind actuated by these fatal prejudices, even more ready to lay themselves under the feet of *the great*, than the great are to trample upon them. Now taking for granted that in republics men live under the tyranny of what you call their equals, the circumstance of this being the most odious of all tyrannies is what a republican would boast of; as soon as tyranny becomes odious, the principal step is made towards its destruction. Reflecting on the degraded state of the mass of mankind, a philosopher will lament that oppression is not odious to them, that the iron, while it eats the soul, is not felt to enter into it. "Tout homme né dans l'esclavage naît pour l'esclavage: rien n'est plus certain: les esclaves perdent tout dans leurs fers, jusqu'au désir d'en sortir; ils aiment leur servitude, comme les compagnons d'Ulysse aimaient leur abrutissement."

I return to the quotation in which you reprobate republicanism. Relying upon the temper of the times, you have surely thought little argument necessary to combat what few will be hardy enough to support: the strongest of auxiliaries, imprisonment and the pillory, have left your arm little to perform. But the happiness of mankind is so closely connected with this subject that I cannot suffer such considerations to deter me from throwing out a few hints which may lead to a conclusion that a republic legitimately constructed contains less of an oppressive principle than any other form of government.

Your Lordship will scarcely question that much of human misery, that the great evils which desolate states, proceed from the governors' having an interest distinct from that of the governed. It should seem a natural deduction

169 draught; *Edd.*: draught, MS.
171 weaken MS.[2]: diminish MS.
184 mass MS.[2]: bulk MS. (Cf. 178.)
185 not felt MS.[2]: scarcely felt MS.
186 l'esclavage: *Edd.* l'esclavage, MS.
190 in which you reprobate republicanism. MS.[2]: which I have just made. MS. *The expanded text* (cf. 162–190) *concludes*: Relying upon the temper of the times &c. *It is not clear whether or not a new paragraph is intended at* 206.
194 so MS.[2]: too MS.

that whatever has a tendency to identify the two must also in the same degree promote the general welfare. As the magnitude of almost all states prevents the possibility of their enjoying a pure democracy, philosophers, from a wish, as far as is in their power, to make the governors and governed one, will turn their thoughts to the system of universal representation, and will annex an equal importance to the suffrage of every individual. Jealous of giving up no more of the authority of the people than is necessary, they will be solicitous of finding out some method by which the office of their delegates may be confined as much as is practicable to the proposing and deliberating upon laws, rather than to enacting them; reserving to the people the power of finally inscribing them in the national code. Unless this is attended to,—as soon as a people has chosen representatives it no longer has a political existence except as it is understood to retain the privilege of annihilating the trust when it shall think proper and of resuming its original power. Sensible that at the moment of election an interest distinct from that of the general body is created, an enlightened legislator will endeavour by every possible method to diminish the operation of such interest. The first and most natural mode that presents itself is that of shortening the regular duration of this trust, in order that the man who has betrayed it may soon be superseded by a more worthy successor. But this is not enough: aware of the possibility of imposition and of the natural tendency of power to corrupt the heart of man, a sensible republican will think it essential that the office of legislator be not intrusted to the same man for a succession of years. He will also be induced to this wise restraint by the grand principle of identification: he will be more sure of the virtue of the legislator by knowing that in the capacity of private citizen tomorrow he must either smart under the oppression or bless the justice of the law which he has enacted today.

Perhaps in the very outset of this inquiry the principle on which I proceed will be questioned and I shall be told that the people are not the proper judges of their own welfare. But, because under every government of modern times till the foundation of the American republic, the bulk of mankind have appeared incapable of discerning their true interests, no conclusion can be drawn against my principle. At this moment have we not daily the strongest proofs of the success with which, in what you call the best of all monarchical governments, the

205 will MS.[2]: will necessarily MS.

213 the trust MS.[2]: those representatives MS. *the trust is inserted in pencil and seems also to be deleted, but no other substitution is made.*

217 mode MS.[2]: method MS.

227 Perhaps MS.[2]: But MS.

popular mind may be debauched? Left to the quiet exercise of their own judgement do you think that the people would have thought it necessary to set fire to the house of the philosophic Priestley and to hunt down his life like that of a traitor or a parricide;—that, deprived almost of the necessities of existence by the burden of their taxes, they would cry out as with one voice for a war from which not a single ray of consolation can visit them to compensate for the additional keenness with which they are about to smart under the scourge of labour, of cold, and of hunger?

Appearing as I do the advocate of republicanism, let me not be misunderstood. I am well aware from the abuse of the executive power in states that there is not a single European nation but what affords a melancholy proof that if at this moment the original authority of the people should be restored, all that could be expected from such restoration would in the beginning be but a change of tyranny. Considering the nature of a republic in reference to the present condition of Europe, your Lordship stops here: but a philosopher will extend his views much farther; having dried up the source from which flows the corruption of the public opinion, he will be sensible that the stream will go on gradually refining itself. I must add also that the coercive power is of necessity so strong in all the old governments that a people could not but at first make an abuse of that liberty which a legitimate republic supposes. The animal just released from its stall will exhaust the overflow of its spirits in a round of wanton vagaries, but it will soon return to itself and enjoy its freedom in moderate and regular delight.

But, to resume the subject of universal representation, I ought to have mentioned before that in the choice of its representatives a people will not immorally hold out wealth as a criterion of integrity, nor lay down as a fundamental rule that to be qualified for the trying duties of legislation a citizen should be possessed of a certain fixed property. Virtues, talents, and acquirements are all that it will look for.

Having destroyed every external object of delusion, let us now see what makes the supposition necessary that the people will mislead themselves. Your

234 debauched? *Edd.* debauched. MS.
237 existence MS.2: life MS.
241 hunger? *Edd.*: hunger. MS.
242–3 Appearing … misunderstood] *On the facing verso, beneath a pencilled* X *is written*: N.B.
247 in reference] *Inserted above* as applicable *but neither phrase is deleted*; *similarly*, condition *is inserted above* state (248) *and neither word is deleted.*
254–5 exhaust … vagaries, but MS.2: commit a thousand vagaries till MS.
260 trying duties MS.2: most important office MS.

Lordship respects "peasants and mechanics when they intrude not themselves into concerns for which their education has not fitted them". Setting aside the idea of a peasant or mechanic being a legislator, what vast education is requisite to enable him to judge amongst his neighbours which is most qualified by his industry and integrity to be intrusted with the care of the interests of himself and of his fellow citizens? But leaving this ground, as governments formed on such a plan proceed in a plain and open manner, their administration would require much less of what is usually called talents and experience, that is of disciplined treachery and hoary machiavelism; and, at the same time, as it would no longer be their interest to keep the mass of the nation in ignorance, a moderate portion of useful knowledge would be universally disseminated. If your lordship has travelled in the democratic cantons of Switzerland you must have seen the herdsmen with the staff in one hand and the book in the other. In the constituent assembly of France was found a peasant whose sagacity was as distinguished as his integrity, whose blunt honesty overawed and baffled the refinements of hypocritical patriots. The people of Paris followed him with acclamations, and the name of Père Gérard will long be mentioned with admiration and respect through the eighty-three departments.

From these hints, if pursued further, might be demonstrated the expediency of the whole people "intruding themselves" on the office of legislation, and the wisdom of putting into force what they may claim as a right. But government is divided into two parts, the legislative and executive. The executive power you would lodge in the hands of an individual. Before we inquire into the propriety of this measure, it will be necessary to state the proper objects of the executive power in governments where the principle of universal representation is admitted. With regard to that portion of this power which is exerted in the application of the laws, it may be observed that much of it would be superseded. As laws, being but the expression of the general will, would be enacted only from an almost universal conviction of their utility, any resistance to such laws, any desire of eluding them, must proceed from a few refractory individuals. As far then as relates to the internal administration of the country, a republic has a manifest advantage over a monarchy, inasmuch as less force is requisite to compel obedience to its laws. From the judicial tribunals of our own country, though we

270–1 such a MS.2: [? this] MS.
278 sagacity MS.2: integrity MS.
283 From...demonstrated] *Altered from* These hints...would demon-
291 As MS.2: The MS.
292 being MS.2: would MS.
292–3 an almost MS.2: a uni MS.
297–8 we labour MS.2: labouring MS.

labour under a variety of partial and oppressive laws, we have an evident proof of the nullity of regal interference; as the king's name is confessedly a mere fiction, and justice is known to be most equitably administered when the judges are least dependent on the crown. I have spoken of laws partial and oppressive; our penal code is so crowded with disproportioned penalties and indiscriminate severity that a conscientious man would sacrifice in many instances his respect for the laws to the common feelings of humanity; and there must be a strange vice in that legislation from which can proceed laws in whose execution a man cannot be instrumental without forfeiting his self–esteem and incurring the contempt of his fellow citizens. But to return from this digression; with regard to the other branches of executive government, which relate rather to original measures than to administering the law, it may be observed, that the power exercised in conducting them is distinguished by almost imperceptible shades from the legislative, and that all such as admit of open discussion, and of the delay attendant on public deliberations, are properly the province of the representative assembly. If this observation be duly attended to, it will appear that this part of executive power will be extremely circumscribed, will be stripped almost entirely of a deliberative capacity, and will be reduced to a mere hand or instrument. As a republican government would leave this power to a select body destitute of the means of corruption, and whom the people, continually controuling, could at all times bring to account, or dismiss, will it not necessarily ensue that a body, so selected and supported, would perform their simple functions with greater efficacy and fidelity, than the complicated concerns of royalty can be expected to meet with in the councils of princes; composed as they usually are of favourites; of men who, from their wealth and interest, have forced themselves into trust; and of statesmen, whose constant object is to exalt themselves by laying pitfalls for their colleagues and for their country?

I shall pursue this subject no further; but, adopting your Lordship's method of argument, instead of continuing to demonstrate the superiority of a repub-

300 most MS.2: the most MS.
304 humanity; MS.2: humanity; and a man who values the esteem of his fellow citizens MS.
313 duly MS.2: properly MS.
317–8 people…at all times MS.2: people could at any ti MS.
319 a MS.2: such a MS.
319–20 simple functions MS.2: functions thus reduced MS.
320 complicated … in the] Inserted by a copyist on the facing verso.
323 object MS.2: objects MS.
324 and for their country?] *Added in Wordsworth's hand.*
325 this MS.2: your MS.
326 continuing MS.2: [? dir.] MS.

lican executive government, I will repeat some of the objections, which have been often made to monarchy, and have never been answered. My first objection to regal government is its instability, proceeding from a variety of causes. Where monarchy is found in its greatest intensity, as in Morocco and Turkey, this observation is illustrated in a very pointed manner; and, indeed, is more or less striking, as governments are more or less despotic. The reason is obvious: as the monarch is the chooser of his ministers, and as his own passions and caprice are, in general, the sole guides of his conduct, these ministers, instead of pursuing directly the one grand object of national welfare, will make it their sole study to vary their measures according to his humours. But a minister *may* be refractory; his successor will naturally run headlong into plans totally the reverse of the former system: for, if he treads in the same path, he is well aware that a similar fate will attend him. This observation will apply to each succession of kings, who, from vanity & a desire of distinction, will, in general, studiously avoid any step, which may lead to a suspicion that they are so spiritless as to imitate their predecessor. That a similar instability is not incident to republics is evident from their very constitution.

As, from the nature of monarchy, particularly of hereditary monarchy, there must always be a vast disproportion, between the duties to be performed, and the powers that are to perform them, and as the measures of government, far from gaining additional vigour, are on the contrary enfeebled by being entrusted to one hand, what arguments can be used for allowing to the will of a single being a weight which, as history shews, will subvert that of the whole body politic? And this brings me to my grand objection to monarchy, which is drawn from the eternal nature of man. The office of king is a trial to which human virtue is not equal. Pure and universal representation, by which alone liberty can be secured cannot, I think, exist together with monarchy. It seems madness to expect a manifestation of the *general* will, at the same time that we

333 his MS.2: his own MS.
335 the one grand MS.3: any gran MS: the gran MS.2.
336 sole] chief? *is inserted as a query above* sole *but no deletion is made* (cf. 334).
336 vary MS.2: adapt MS.
336 But MS.2: But it may happen that MS.
337 run MS.2: pursue MS.
337 plans MS.2: a [?] system MS.
338–42 he is …predecessor] *In Wordsworth's hand, except for the copyist's insertion of* are so spiritless as to [341–2].
342 a similar MS.2: the same MS.
341 step MS.2: [? thin] MS.
343 constitution MS.2: nature MS.
344 As, MS.2: As in hereditary MS. of monarchy MS.2: of hereditary monarchy MS.
346 as MS.2: that MS.
347 gaining MS.2: deriving MS.
354 *general* MS.2: national MS.

allow to a *particular* will that weight, which it must obtain in all governments, that can, with any propriety, be called monarchical. They must war with each other, till one of them is extinguished. It was so in France, and * * * I shall not pursue this topic further, but, as you are a teacher of purity of morals, I cannot but remind you of that atmosphere of corruption, without which it should seem that courts cannot exist.

You seem anxious to explain what ought to be understood by the equality of men in a state of civil society, but your Lordship's success has not answered your trouble. If you had looked in the articles of the rights of man you would have found your efforts superseded. Equality, without which liberty cannot exist, is to be met with in perfection in that state in which no distinctions are admitted but such as have evidently for their object the general good. The end of government cannot be attained without authorising some members of the society to command, and, of course, without imposing on the rest the necessity of obedience. Here then is an inevitable inequality which may be denominated that of power. In order to render this as small as possible, a legislator will be careful not to give greater force to such authority than is essential to its due execution. Government is, at best, but a necessary evil: compelled to place themselves in a state of subordination, men will obviously endeavour to prevent the abuse of that superiority to which they submit: accordingly they will cautiously avoid whatever may lead those in whom it is acknowledged to suppose they hold it as a right. Nothing will more effectually contribute to this than that the person in which authority has been lodged should occasionally descend to the level of private citizen; he will learn from it a wholesome lesson, and the people will be

357 ***] *No insertion or note is given; at the end of this paragraph, a third of the page is left blank.*

361 You seem MS.2: Your lordship seems MS.

361–2 *At the top of the facing verso is written in a small hand*:
Octavius, by 1st wife Octavia major
By 2d wife (Octavia minor
(C. Octavius postea
([? Augustus]

362 society, but *Edd.*: society. but MS.

364–69 Equality … obedience] *Some alteration was apparently intended for this section, although the plan was not worked out in any clear detail and may have been abandoned. A large opening bracket is made around the word* Equality (364) *but no closing bracket follows; a second opening bracket is made at the beginning of the next sentence around the word* The (366) *and again no closing bracket follows. On the facing verso page is written*: But you have deprived yourself of the plea of decorum &c. loose sheet: *beneath this statement and direction is a large* X *and a sweeping scrawl*: See last page. *The clause* But you have … decorum *appears in a complete context* (601) at the top of the page [48r]; *the phrase* But you have &c. *is repeated on page* [47v].

370-1 careful not to give] *Inserted above* scrupulous of giving *but neither seems deleted.*

378 it] *Twice underscored with pencil.*

less liable to confound the person with the power. On this principle, hereditary authority will be proscribed; and on another also,—that on such a system as that of hereditary authority no security can be had for talents adequate to the discharge of the office, and consequently the people can only feel the mortification of having humbled without having protected themselves.

Another distinction will arise amongst mankind, which, though it may be easily modified by government, exists independently of it; I mean the distinction of wealth which always will attend superior talents and industry. It cannot be denied that the security of individual property is one of the strongest and most natural motives to induce men to bow their necks to the yoke of civil government. In order to attain this end of security to property, a legislator will proceed with impartiality. He should not suppose that, when he has ensured to their proprietors the possession of lands and moveables against the depredation of the necessitous, nothing remains to be done. The history of all ages has demonstrated that wealth not only can secure itself but includes even an oppressive principle. Aware of this, and that the extremes of poverty and riches have a necessary tendency to corrupt the human heart, he will banish from his code all laws such as the unnatural monster of primogeniture, such as encourage associations against labour in the form of corporate bodies, and indeed all that monopolising system of legislation whose baleful influence is shewn in the depopulation of the country and in the necessity which reduces the sad relicks to owe their very existence to the ostentatious bounty of their oppressors. If it is true in common life, it is still more true in governments that we should be just before we are generous: but our legislators seem to have forgotten or despised this homely maxim. They have unjustly left unprotected that most important part of property, not less real because it has no material existence, that which ought to enable the labourer to provide food for himself and his family. I appeal to innumerable statutes whose constant and professed object it is to lower the price of labour, to compel the workman to be *content* with arbitrary wages, evidently too small from the necessity of legal enforcement of the acceptance of them. Even from the astonishing amount of the sums raised for the support of one description of the poor may be concluded the extent and greatness of that oppression, whose effects have rendered it possible for the few to afford

380 on such] *Twice underscored with pencil.*
392 nothing MS.2: that nothing MS.
400 bounty MS.2: charity MS.
402 legislators seem MS.2: legislature seems MS.
407 with MS.2: with his MS.
408 legal MS.2: the legal MS.
411 afford MS.2: [? se] MS.

so much, and have shewn us that such a multitude of our brothers exist in even helpless indigence. Your lordship tells us that the science of civil government has received all the perfection of which it is capable. For my part, I am more enthusiastic: the sorrow I feel from the contemplation of this melancholy picture is not unconsoled by a comfortable hope that the class of wretches called mendicants will not much longer shock the feelings of humanity; that the miseries entailed upon the marriage those who are not rich will no longer tempt the bulk of mankind to fly to that promiscuous intercourse to which they are impelled by the instincts of nature, and the dreadful satisfaction of escaping the prospect of infants, sad fruit of such intercourse, whom they are unable to support. If these flattering prospects be ever realised, it must be owing to some wise and salutary regulations counteracting that inequality among mankind which proceeds from the present *forced* disproportion of their possessions.

I am not an advocate for the agrarian law, nor for sumptuary regulations, but I contend that the people amongst whom the law of primogeniture exists, and among whose corporate bodies are encouraged and immense salaries annexed to useless and indeed hereditary offices, is oppressed by an inequality in the distribution of wealth which does not necessarily attend men in a state of civil society.

Thus far we have considered inequalities inseparable from civil society. But other arbitrary distinctions exist among mankind, either from choice or usurpation. I allude to titles, to stars, ribbands, and garters and other badges of fictitious superiority. Your lordship will not question the grand principle on which this enquiry set out; I look upon it, then, as my duty to try the propriety of these distinctions by that criterion, & think it will be no difficult task to prove that these separations among mankind are absurd, impolitic, and immoral. Considering hereditary nobility as a reward for services rendered to the state, and it is to my charity that you owe the permission of taking upon the question on this ground, what services can a man render to the state adequate to such a compensation that the making of laws, upon which the happiness of millions is to depend, shall be lodged in him and his posterity, however depraved may be their principles, however contemptible their understandings? But here I may be

416 by MS.2: with MS. 464 tempt MS.2: imp M.S.: compel MS.2.
420. prospect] *Twice underscored with pencil.*
422 prospects] *Twice underscored with pencil.*
424 possessions] *Followed by an* X.
427 annexed MS.2: are annexed MS.
434 superiority. MS.2: superiority. I imagine MS.
436 it will be *Edd.*: it will be MS.
438–41 and it … compensation] *On the facing verso, a pencilled* X.

accused of sophistry; I ought to subtract every idea of power from such distinction though from the weakness of mankind it is impossible to disconnect them: what services then can a man render to society to compensate for the outrage done to the dignity of our nature when we bind ourselves to address him and his posterity with humiliating circumlocutions, calling him most noble, most honourable, most high, most august, serene, excellent, eminent and so forth: when it is more than probable that such unnatural flattery will but generate vices which ought to consign him to neglect and solitude, or make him the perpetual object of the finger of scorn. And does not experience justify the observation that, where titles, a thing very rare, have been conferred as the rewards of merit, those to whom they have descended, far from being thereby animated to imitate their ancestor, have presumed upon that lustre which they supposed thrown round them, and prodigally relying on such resources lavished what alone was their own, their personal reputation.

It would be happy if this delusion were confined to themselves; but alas! the world is weak enough to grant the indulgence which they assume. Vice which is forgiven in one character will soon cease to meet with sternness of rebuke when found in others. Even at first she will intreat pardon with confidence, assured that ere long she will be charitably supposed to stand in no need of it.

But let me ask you seriously, from the mode in which these distinctions are originally conferred, is it not almost necessary that, far from being the rewards of services rendered to the state, they should usually be the recompense of an industrious sacrifice of the general welfare to the particular aggrandizement of that power by which they are bestowed? Let us even alter their source, and consider them as proceeding from the nation itself, and deprived of their hereditary quality: even here I should proscribe them and for this most evident reason; that a man's past services are no sufficient security for his future character: he who today merits the civic wreath may tomorrow deserve the Tarpeian rock. Besides where respect is not perverted, where the world is not taught to reverence men without regarding their conduct, the esteem of mankind will have a very different value, and, when a proper independence is secured, will be regarded as a sufficient recompense for services however important, and will be a much surer

452 scorn MS.2: infamy MS.
456 such MS.2: such a MS.
458 It would be] *On the facing verso a pencilled* X.
473 without regarding MS.2: independent of MS.
475 surer MS.2: stronger MS.

guarantee of the continuance of such virtues as may deserve it.

I have another strong objection to nobility which is that it has a necessary tendency to dishonour labour, a prejudice which extends far beyond its own circle; that it binds down whole ranks of men to idleness while it gives the enjoyment of a reward which exceeds the hopes of the most active exertions of human industry. The languid tedium of this noble repose must be dissipated; and gaming with the tricking manoeuvres of the horse-race, afford occupation to hours, which it would be happy for mankind had they been totally unemployed. Reflecting on the corruption of the public manners, does your lordship shudder at the prostitution which miserably deluges our streets? You may find the cause in our aristocratical prejudices. Are you disgusted with the hypocrisy and sycophancy of our intercourse in private life? You may find the cause in the necessity of dissimulation which we have established by regulations which oblige us to address as our superiours, indeed as our masters, men whom we cannot but internally despise. Do you lament that such large portions of mankind should stoop to occupations unworthy the dignity of their nature? You may find in the pride and luxury thought necessary to nobility how such servile arts are encouraged. Besides where the most honourable of the land do not blush to accept such offices as groom of the bedchamber, master of the hounds, lords in waiting, captain of the honourable band of gentlemen pensioners, is it astonishing that the bulk of the people should not ask of an occupation, what is it? but what might be gained by it? If the long equestrian train of equipage should make your lordship sigh for the poor who are pining in hunger, you will find that little is thought of snatching the bread from their mouths to eke out the "*necessary* splendor" of nobility.

I have not time to pursue this object farther, but am so strongly impressed with the baleful influence of aristocracy and nobility upon human happiness and virtue that if, as I am persuaded, monarchy cannot exist without such supporters, I think that reason sufficient for the preference I have given to the republican system.

It is with reluctance that I quit the subjects I have just touched upon; but the nature of this address does not permit me to continue the discussion. I proceed to what more immediately relates to this kingdom, at the present crisis. You ask

478 dishonour labour] *On the facing verso a pencilled* X.
481 dissipated MS.2: diverted and MS.
483 would be MS.2: had been for MS.
489–90 us...despise] *On the facing verso a pencilled* X.
494 groom MS.2: grooms MS.

with triumphant confidence, to what other law are the people of England subject than to the general will of the society to which they belong? Is your lordship to be told that acquiescence is not choice, and that obedience is not freedom? If there is a single man in Great Britain, who has no suffrage in the election of a representative, the will of the society of which he is a member is not generally expressed; he is a helot in that society. You answer the question, so confidently put, in this singular manner. "The King, we are all justly persuaded, has not the inclination; and we all know that, if he had the inclination, he has not the power, to substitute his will in the place of law. The house of lords has no such power. The house of commons has no such power." This passage, so artfully and unconstitutionally framed to agree with the delusions of the moment, cannot deceive a thinking reader. The expression of your full persuasion of the upright intentions of the king can only be the language of flattery. You are not to be told that it is constitutionally a maxim not to attribute to the person of the king the measures and misconduct of government. Had you chosen to speak, as you ought to have done, openly and explicitly, you must have expressed your just persuasion and implicit confidence in the integrity, moderation, and wisdom of his majesty's ministers. Have you forgot the avowed ministerial maxims of Sir Robert Walpole? are you ignorant of the overwhelming corruption of the present day?

You seem unconscious of the absurdity of separating what is inseperable even in imagination. Would it have been any consolation to the miserable Romans under the second triumvate to have been asked insultingly, is it Octavius, is it Anthony, or is it Lepidus that has caused this bitterness of affliction? and when the answer could not be returned with certainty, to have been reproached that their sufferings were imaginary? The fact is that the king *and* lords *and* commons, by what is termed the omnipotence of parliament, have constitutionally the right of enacting whatever laws they please, in defiance of the petitions or remonstrances of the nation; they have the power of doubling our enormous debt of 240 millions, and *may* pursue measures, which could never be supposed the emanation of the general will, without concluding the people stripped of reason, of sentiment, and even of the first instinct, which prompts them to preserve their own existence.

512 election MS.2: choice MS.
514 he is...society] On the facing verso a pencilled X.
520 a MS.2: the MS.
534 imaginary? Edd.: imaginary. MS.
537 nation MS.2: people MS.
538 240] Twice underscored with pencil and on the facing verso is written: ? was it not more, even then? it is now above 800?

I congratulate your lordship upon your enthusiastic fondness for the judicial proceedings of this country. I am happy to find you have passed through life not having your fleeces torn from your back in the thorny labyrinth of litigation. But you have not lived always in colleges, and must have passed by some victims whom it cannot be supposed, without a reflection on your heart, that you have forgotten. Here I am reminded of what I have said on the subject of representation; to be qualified for the office of legislation you should have felt like the bulk of mankind; their sorrows should be familiar to you, of which if you are ignorant how can you redress them? As a member of the assembly which, from a confidence in its experience, sagacity, and wisdom, the constitution has invested with the supreme appellant jurisdiction to determine the most doubtful points of an intricate jurisprudence, your lordship cannot, I presume, be ignorant of the consuming expenses of our never-ending process, the verbosity of unintelligible statutes, and the perpetual contrariety in our judicial decisions.

"The greatest freedom that can be enjoyed by man in a state of civil society; the greatest security that can be given him with respect to the protection of his character, property, personal liberty, limb and life is afforded to every individual by our present constitution."

"Let it never be forgotten by ourselves and let us impress the observation upon the hearts of our children that we are in possession of both (liberty and equality), of as much of both, as can be consistent with the end for which civil society was introduced among mankind."

Many of my readers will hardly believe me when I inform them that these passages are copied verbatim from your appendix. Mr Burke roused the indignation of all ranks of men, when by a refinement in cruelty superiour to that which in the East yokes the living to the dead he strove to persuade us that we and our posterity to the end of time were riveted to a constitution by the indissoluble compact of a dead parchment, and were bound to cherish a corse at the bosom, when reason might call aloud that it should be entombed. Your lordship aims at the same detestable object by means more criminal because more dangerous and insidious. Attempting to lull the people of England into a belief that any enquiries directed towards the nature of liberty and equality can in no other

544-6 in the … cannot] *On the facing verso an* X.
550 them? *Edd.*: them. MS.
553–5 *After* ignorant *of approximately 1¼ in. were cut from the bottom of the page; on the facing verso the rest of the sentence was written once, heavily deleted, and rewritten.*
555 unintelligible statutes MS.2: our statue MS.
568 riveted *Edd.*: rivetted MS.
569 at the MS.2: in our MS.

way lead to their happiness than by convincing them that they have already arrived at perfection in the science of government, what is your object but to exclude them for ever from the most fruitful field of human knowledge? Besides, it is another cause to execrate this doctrine that the consequence of such fatal delusion would be that they must entirely draw off their attention not only from the government but from their governors; that the stream of public vigilance, far from chearing and enriching the prospect of society, would by its stagnation consign it to barrenness and by its putrefaction infect it with death. You have aimed an arrow at liberty and philosophy, the eyes of the human race:—why, like the inveterate enemy of Philip, in putting your name to the shaft, did you not declare openly its destination?

As a teacher of religion your lordship cannot be ignorant of a class of breaches of duty which may be denominated faults of omission. You profess to give your opinions upon the present turbulent crisis, expressing a wish that they might have some effect in tranquillizing the minds of the people. From your silence respecting the general call for a parliamentary reform, supported by your assertion that we at present enjoy as great a portion of liberty and equality as is consistent with civil society, what can be supposed but that you are a determined enemy to the redress of what the people of England call and feel to be grievances?

From your omitting to speak upon the war, and your general disapprobation of French measures and French principles expressed particularly at this moment, we are necessarily led also to conclude that you have no wish to dispel an infatuation which is now giving up to the sword so large a portion of the poor and consigning the rest to the more slow and more painful consumption of want. I could excuse your silence on this point as it would ill become an English

577 execrate MS.2: curse MS.

584 destination? *Edd.* destination, MS.

588 people. From MS.2: people. Whence comes it then that the two grand causes of this working of the popular mind are passed over in silence? Your lordship's conduct may bring to mind [*altered from* remind] the story of a company of strolling comedians who gave out the play of Hamlet as the performance of the evening, the audience were not a little surprised to be told, on the drawing up of the curtain that from circumstances of particular convenience it was hoped they would dispense with the omission of the character of—Hamlet. But to be serious, for the subject is serious in the extreme; from MS. *Square brackets enclose the deleted passage, although the lines of deletion do not strike out the whole passage; on the facing verso is written*: [omit] This is poor X. *The bracketed* [omit] *seems to be pencilled in another hand—Edward Quillinan's*?

593 grievances? MS.2: grievances? Why then did you not speak openly MS.

596 dispel MS.2: prevent MS.

bishop at the close of the eighteenth century to make the pulpit the vehicle of exhortations which would have disgraced the incendiary of the crusades, the hermit Peter. But you have deprived yourself of the plea of decorum by giving no opinion on the reform of the legislature: as undoubtedly, you have some secret reason for the reservation of your sentiments on this latter head, I cannot but apply the same reason to the former. Upon what principle is your conduct to be explained? In some parts of England it is quaintly said, when a drunken man is seen reeling towards his home, that he has business on both sides of the road. Observing your lordship's tortuous path, the spectators will be far from insinuating that you have partaken on Mr Burke's intoxicating bowl; they will content themselves, shaking their heads as you stagger along, with remarking that you have business on both sides of the road.

The friends of liberty congratulate themselves upon the odium under which they are at present labouring; as the causes which have produced it have obliged so many of her false adherents to disclaim with officious earnestness any desire to promote her interest; nor are they disheartened by the diminution which their body is supposed already to have sustained. Conscious that an enemy lurking in our ranks is ten times more formidable than when drawn out against us, that the unblushing aristocracy of a Maury or a Cazalès is far less dangerous than the insidious mask of patriotism assumed by a La Fayette or a Mirabeau, we thank you for your desertion. Political convulsions have been said particularly to call forth concealed abilities; but it has been seldom observed how vast is their consumption of them. Reflecting upon the fate of the greatest portion of the members of the constituent and legislative assemblies, we must necessarily be struck with a prodigious annihilation of human talents.—Aware that this necessity is attached to a struggle for Liberty, we are the less sorry that we can expect no advantage from the mental endowments of your Lordship. Besides the names which I

602 ff. But you have] *Written in pencil on page* [47v] *is*: But you *Beneath that in ink is written*: But you have &c. (*Cf. textual n.*, 364–9)
614 desire MS.2: inten MS.
618 unblushing MS.2: avowed MS.
618 aristocracy Grosart. [tear]ocracy MS.
621–2 vast … of them MS.2: great their necessary effect in MS.
624 a MS.2: the MS.2
624 that MS.2: [? in] MS.
626 from Grosart: [tear]om MS.
626 Besides … I] *Enclosed with an opening bracket in pencil. After* I *text breaks off, see* Textual Introduction.

COMMENTARY

Title: Appendix to his late Sermon] A / SERMON / PREACHED BEFORE THE / *STEWARDS* / OF THE / WESTMINSTER DISPENSARY / AT THEIR ANNIVERSARY MEETING, / IN / CHARLOTTE-STREET CHAPEL., APRIL 1785. / WITH AN APPENDIX. / *BY R. WATSON, D. D.* / LORD BISHOP OF LLANDAFF. / LONDON: / PRINTED FOR T. CADELL IN THE STRAND; AND T. EVANS IN / PATERNOSTER-ROW. / 1793 / Our references to the two parts of this work will hereafter be abbreviated *Sermon* or *Appendix*, respectively. Two copies of this edition are in the British Museum, and two in the Yale University Library. A second edition (London, 1793) was reviewed in *The Gentleman's Magazine*, lxiii (July 1793), 633–6 (see above, p. 39, and n. on 22–3). Single copies of 'The Third Edition; are in the Boston Athenaeum and in the New York Public Library; both copies show signs of careless printing. Although it is announced on the title-page, and although the beginning of the catchword [APPEN-] appears at the foot of the final page, the *Appendix* is completely missing from the Athenaeum copy. The copy in the New York Public Library does print the *Appendix* (the text is the same as that of the first edition), but the pages are numbered in a curious fashion: the *Sermon* ends on p, 20; the *Appendix* begins on p [21]; the second page of the *Appendix* is properly numbered 22, but the following page is strangely numbered 7, and thereafter the numbers run 8, 9, 10, and so on to 22, where the *Appendix* ends. Grosart, who reprinted somewhat carelessly the *Appendix* (Grosart, i. 24–30), also gives the title-page of a separate edition of the *Appendix* (Loughborough, 1793); see Grosart, i. xi. Perhaps the copy at the New York Public Library was made up from sheets left over from this separate edition.

Title: by a Republican] In calling himself a Republican, Wordsworth indicates immediately his sympathy with the Republic of France (cf. *Prel.* X. 24–31) and his opposition to the British Constitution. In the English press of 1792–3 the word *Republican* was anathematized by almost daily notices from the 'Association for preserving Liberty and Property against Republicans and Levellers'. In February 1793 Joseph Priestley was quoted as saying: 'A dread of every thing tending to *Republicanism* is manifestly increased of late years.... The very term is become one of the most opprobrious in the English language' (*Gentleman's Magazine*, lxiii, 136). A year later (May 1794) Wordsworth wrote to Mathews: 'You know perhaps already that I am of that odious class of men called democrats, and of that class I shall for ever continue' (*E.Y.*, p. 119); the substitution of *democrat* for *Republican* is congruous with the Godwinian position so clearly maintained in the letters to Matthews in 1794. For Godwin's use of the word *democrat* see *Political Justice* (London, 1793), ii. 489–94.

3. Addison, in a sublime allegory] '*The first Vision of* Mizrah' (*The Spectator*, ed. D. F. Bond (Oxford, 1965), No. 159, ii. 121–6). At Cambridge Wordsworth had 'translated the Vision of Mizra, and two or three other papers of the Spectator, into Italian' (*Autobiog*. 106–7). Cf. also *Miscellaneous Sonnets*, VIII (*P.W.* iii. 5).

12–13. through one of … oblivion] Addison's allegory continues to supply the metaphorical figures: 'As I looked more attentively, I saw several of the Passengers dropping thro' the Bridge, into the great Tide that flowed underneath it; and upon further Examination, perceived there were innumerable Trap-doors that lay concealed in the Bridge, which the Passengers no sooner trod upon, but they fell through them into the Tide and immediately disappeared' (*The Spectator*, ii. 123). The 'tide of contempt' and 'the ocean of oblivion' are Wordsworth's own terms; Addison had identified the water as 'Part of the great Tide of Eternity', or 'that Portion of Eternity which is called Time'.

15–16. Your Lordship … asperity] Before 1793 Watson's most notable religious controversy was one with Edward Gibbon. Attempting to refute Gibbon's fifteenth chapter, Watson published *An Apology for Christianity, in a Series of Letters, Addressed to Edward Gibbon* (Cambridge, 1776). This volume went through many editions; in *A Vindication of Some Passages in the Fifteenth and Sixteenth Chapters of the History of the Decline and Fall of the Roman Empire* (London, 1779) Gibbon praised the 'liberal and philosophic cast' of Watson's thought and the 'politeness and moderation' of his expression (p. 93).

22–3. with a hope … community] *Appendix*, p. [17]: 'If it [the *Sermon*] shall have any effect in calming the perturbation which has been lately excited, and which still subsists in the minds of the lower classes of the community, I shall not be ashamed of having given to the world a composition in every other light uninteresting.' This sentence is from the opening paragraph of the *Appendix*, the one paragraph not quoted in the review of Watson in *The Gentleman's Magazine*, lxiii (July 1793), 633.

25–27. the ministers … and religious] Evidence supporting this charge may be found in W. T. Laprade, *England and the French Revolution* (Baltimore, Md., 1909), pp. 70–1 and 84. For reviews and summaries of typical sermons see, for example, *Gentleman's Magazine*, lxiii (Feb. 1793), 155–7; ibid. lxiii (Mar. 1793), 249; *European Magazine*, xxiii (Feb. 1783), 129 and 136.

28. bishop of the dissenters] Cf. Parliamentary Proceedings of 9 May 1792, reported in *The Gentleman's Magazine*, lxii (Nov. 1792), 1014: 'The Right Reverend Prelate … being perhaps what his brother of Landaff is, a *Dissenting* Bishop'; *Analytical Review*, xv (Mar. 1793), 311: 'The bishop of Landaff has long been misrepresented as a dissenter and a republican.' Watson had urged toleration towards Dissenters in *A Sermon Preached before the University of Cambridge* (Cambridge, 1776), pp. 12–13, and in *A Charge Delivered to the Clergy of the Diocese of Landaff* (London, 1792), pp. 11–20.

31. like the generals ... country] In France a general was sometimes addressed as *Citoyen général* and was regularly spoken of as *le général*. According to *Larousse du XX*[e] *siècle* (s.v. *général*) at the time of the Revolution the titles *généraux de brigade* and *généraux de division* replaced respectively the earlier titles *les maréchaux de camp* and *les lieutenants généraux*.

48. the late royal martyr] Louis XVI was executed on 21 January 1793. The phrase 'late royal martyr' quickly became a cliché, but conscious irony was probably Wordsworth's intent.

49–50. joining in ... cottage] Although strongly put, Watson's expression of grief for Louis was confined to a single sentence: 'My heart sinks within me when I see it [the altar of Liberty] streaming with the blood of the monarch himself' (*Appendix*, p. 19). Examples of 'modish lamentation' which took place in London are the observance of an elaborate mourning in the Court (see instructions from the Lord Chamberlain's Office, printed in *The Times* and *The Morning Herald*, 28 Jan. 1793); obsequies held in the Spanish Chapel, 28 January (see *The Times*, 28 Jan., and *The Gentleman's Magazine*, lxiii (Mar. 1793), 252); and the flocking of citizens to a model of the Temple erected in Haymarket (see *The Morning Herald*, 30 Jan. 1793 and n. on 63–4 below).

50–2. You wish ... Louis XVI] Wordsworth exaggerates Watson's view on the guilt of Louis; cf. *Appendix*, p. 20:

> The monarch, you will tell me, was guilty of perfidy and perjury.—I know not, that he was guilty of either; but admitting that he has been guilty of both—who, alas! of the sons of men, is so confident in the strength of his own virtue ... as to be certain, that under similar temptations he would not have been guilty of similar offences? Surely it would have been no dimunition of the sternness of new republican virtue ... if it had pardoned the perfidy which its own oppression had occasioned—if it had remitted the punishment of the perjury of the king, to the tribunal of Him by whom *kings reign and princes decree justice*.

55. monstrous situation] Cf. 72 and nn. 72–5.

56–7. Grégoire in the National Convention, 15 November 1792 (*Archives parlementaires*, Première Série, liii, 426): 'J'évoque ici tous les martyrs de la liberté, victimés depuis trois ans. Est-il un parent, un ami de nos frères immolés sur la frontière our dans la journée du 10 août, qui n'ait eu le droit de traîner le cadavre aux pieds de Louis XVI, en lui disant ... Voilà ton ouvrage ... et cet homme ne serait pas jugeable!' Grégoire had been elected Bishop of Blois in February 1791 (*Réimpression de L'Ancien Moniteur*, vii. 396), and according to G. M. Harper (*William Wordsworth*, 3rd edn.(London, 1929), pp. 117–18), he attended meetings of the Society of the Friends of the Constitution in Blois, meetings which Wordsworth may also have attended. Cf. Mark L. Reed, *Wordsworth* (Cambridge, Mass., 1967), p. 130.

63–4. the tower of the Temple] The Temple, an ancient monastery of the Knights Templar, had a residential wing, but its tower was a grim medieval keep. After the rising of 10 August the deputies would have imprisoned Louis in the Luxembourg palace, but the Paris commune insisted upon the tower of the Temple (J. M. Thompson, *The French Revolution* (Oxford, 1955), pp. 290–1). Visiting Paris in 1820, Wordsworth struck a different note: 'The exterior of Paris is much changed since I last visited it in 1792. I miss many antient Buildings, particularly the Temple, where the poor king and his family were so long confined' (*M.Y.* ii. 642). See also *Prel.* X 42–4.

66–7. Wordsworth's meaning is somewhat obscure. Probably, he means that a Christian teacher should be careful lest he abuse the passion of pity; when pity is properly influenced by reason, its degree is measured by ('is regulated by') the disproportion of the pain suffered by a Louis on the scaffold to the guilt which he had incurred on the throne. Some of the difficulty of this passage may be owing to Wordsworth's attempting to counteract Watson's appeal to pity: speaking of the 'sanguinary, savage, more than brutal' methods adopted by the French, Watson said that these methods 'not merely fill the heart of every individual with commiseration for the unfortunate sufferers; but they exhibit to the eye of contemplation, an humiliating picture of human nature, *when its passions are not regulated by religion*, or controlled by law' (*Appendix*, p. 19—the italics are ours).

72–5. to force ... of mankind] Cf. *Common Sense*, in *The Writings of Thomas Paine*, ed. M. D. Conway (New York, 1906), i. 73 and 82:

> There is something exceedingly ridiculous in the composition of Monarchy; it first excludes a man from the means of information, yet empowers him to act in cases where the highest judgement is required. The state of a king shuts him from the World, yet the business of a king requires him to know it thoroughly.... the world they [hereditary monarchs] act in differs so materially from the world at large, that they have but little opportunity of knowing its true interests.

77. to veil ... the laws] Cf. Burke, *Reflections on the Revolution in France*, in *Works* (Bohn's Standard Library, London, 1886), ii. 405–6: if the nobility in France had indeed been such 'objects of horror' as the revolutionists had maintained they were, then he would admit that 'too critical an inquiry might not be advisable into the means of freeing the world from such a nuisance. The statues of Equity and Mercy might be veiled for a moment.' In its formal report on the questions relative to the judgement of Louis (7 Nov. 1792), the *Comité de législation* quoted a similar expression from Montesquieu: '"j'avoue ... que l'usage des peuples les plus libres qui aient jamais été sur la terre me fair croire qu'il y a des cas où il faut mettre pour un moment un voile sur la liberté, comme l'on cache les statues des dieux"' (*Réimpression de L'Ancien Moniteur*, xiv. 420).

78–9. the cause ... human race] Cf. *Prel.* IX. 530–3: *Rights of Man*, in *The Writings of Thomas Paine*, ed. M. D. Conway (New York, 1906), ii. 272: 'The cause of the French people is that of all Europe, or rather the whole world.'

84, fn. *Athalie*, I. ii, in *Œuvres complètes*, ed. R. Picard (Paris, 1951), p. 903. The italics are Wordsworth's. In 1820 Wordsworth 'did not wish to see it [*Athalie*] acted, as it would never come up to the high imagination he had formed in reading it, of the prophetic inspiration of the priests' (*Tom Moore's Diary*, cited by M. L. Peacock, *The Critical Opinions of William Wordsworth* (Baltimore, Md., 1950), p. 329).

85–9. *Appendix*, p. 19: verbatim, except for minor variations in punctuation.

88–102. Wordsworth's recognition of the need for violence in effecting a major revolution parallels James Mackintosh, *Vindiciæ Gallicæ* (London, 1792 [lot 52 in Rydal Mount Catalogue]), pp. 162–4, and innumerable speeches in the National Convention. Cf. also *Prel.* X 746 ff. By June 1794 Wordsworth had, however, arrived at a diametrically opposite view: 'I recoil from the bare idea of a revolution.... I am a determined enemy to every species of violence.... I deplore the miserable situation of the French' (*E.Y.*, p. 124).

90, textual n. The suggested emendation of 'man' for 'men' would provide an antecedent for 'him' in 91, but since it is clearly the despot who is to be overthrown, Wordsworth's meaning could be clarified only by the substitution of 'the despot' for 'despotism' (98). Even so, the thought would remain somewhat obscure. Probably Wordsworth means that those men whom Watson had characterized as 'the faithful adherents of a fallen monarch' (87) are actually men debased by 'obstinancy & perversion' (90). Their faults would thus be comparable to the faults of those who out of 'blind fondness' (54) or 'prejudice and weakness' (71) had established monarchy in the first place.

93. the safety of the people, her supreme law] A commonplace in French oratory: e.g. Osselin in the National Convention, 31 October 1792: 'Le salut public est la suprême, la dernière loi' (*Réimpression de L'Ancien Moniteur*, xiv. 363).

100–1. But is this ... things] Cf. Wordsworth's paean on the Revolution in *Descriptive Sketches* (1793), 780–3 (*P.W.* i. 88):

> Yet, yet rejoice, tho' Pride's perverted ire
> Rouze Hell's own aid, and wrap thy hills in fire.

> Lo! From th'innocuous flames, a lovely birth!
> With it's own Virtues springs another earth.

107–39. Wordsworth exaggerates Watson's views on the confiscation of Church property, for actually his mild censure was confined to a single sentence (*Appendix*, p. 18): 'I thought that the state ought not in justice to have seized any part of the property of the church, till it had reverted, as it were, to the community, by the death of its immediate possessors.' Earlier, in *A Charge Delivered to the Clergy of the Diocese of Landaff, June 1791* (London, 1792), pp. 8–10, Watson had discussed at some length the Church reforms in France, and praised wholeheartedly the suppression of the monasteries and the more equitable distribution of ecclesiastical wealth. For Wordsworth's apparent ignorance of Watson's other writings see also n. on 169–73.

114–21. On 30 October 1798 in the National Assembly, Boisgelin, Archbishop of Aix, offered in behalf of the Church an advance of 400,000,000 livres to help the State pay its indebtedness. Three days later the motion of Mirabeau that all ecclesiastical property should be at the disposal of the nation was passed by a vote of 568 to 346 (*Réimpression de L'Ancien Moniteur*, ii. 116, and A. Mathiez, *The French Revolution*, trans. C. A. Phillips (New York, 1929), pp. 97–8). For Burke's views on Boisgelin's 'extravagant' offer, see *Reflections*, ii. 391–2.

135 ff. the hero of the necklace] Cardinal-Bishop Prince de Rohan was one of the principal figures in the scandal of the Diamond Necklace (1785–6), a complicated and still unsolved case of Court intrigue and fraud, involving Rohan's relationship with Marie Antionette. A famous literary account of this episode is Thomas Carlysle's 'The Diamond Necklace', reprinted in his *Critical and Miscellaneous Essays*. The fullest modern account is Frances Mossiker, *The Queen's Necklace* (New York, 1961). For a brief summary see 'Diamond Necklace', *Encyclopædia Britannica*, 11th edn. Rohan's preferments are said to have brought him an income of 2,500,000 livres (s.v. 'Rohan', ibid.).

140–2. *Appendix*, pp. 20–1. For slight variations between Wordsworth's quotation and Watson's statement, see n. on 567–9.

142–5. *Appendix*, pp. [17]–18:

> the object which the French seemed to have in view at the commencement of their revolution, had my hearty approbation. The object was to free themselves and their prosperity from arbitrary power. I hope there is not a man in Great Britain so little sensible of the blessings of that free Constitution under which he has the happiness to live; so entirely dead to the interests of general humanity, as not to wish that a Constitution similar to our own might be established, not only in France, but in every despotic state in Europe; not only in Europe, but in every quarter of the globe.

147. "reprobate"] *Appendix*, pp. 18–19: 'The French have abandoned the constitution they had at first established, and have changed it for another. No one can reprobate with more truth than I do both the means, and the end of this change.—The end has been the establishment of a republic.' Watson's word *reprobate* seems to be scornfully echoed by Wordsworth, not only here, but also in 101 and 190.

150–2. Cf. Paine, *Rights of Man*, ii. 278: 'That which a whole nation chooses to do it has a right to do.' Wordsworth's statement that 'Twenty-five millions of Frenchmen ... have ... unanimously chosen a republic' is hyperbole. In 1791 he himself had observed in Orleans the disfavour with which men of 'wealth and circumstance' regarded the Revolution (*E.Y.*, p. 70), and later in Blois he recognized the existence of great numbers of counter-revolutionists (*E.Y.*, p. 78). Furthermore, only five million Frenchmen were enfranchised, and of these only one million voted in the election of 1792. Although none of the deputies elected was a royalist, only the Paris deputies had been instructed to move for a republic. In the second session of the Convention (21 Sept.) the abolition of royalty was decreed, and on the following day it was decreed that all public acts should thereafter bear the date *l'an premier de la République française*. Thus the Republic was not even formally proclaimed, but instead its existence was merely recognized indirectly. (On the franchise and the establishment of the Republic see *Archives parlementaires*, Première Série, lii, 80; J. M. Thompson, *The French Revolution* (Oxford, 1955), pp. 310–15; A. Aulard, *The French Revolution*, trans. B. Miall (New York, 1910), ii. 150–3).

157–61. *Appendix*, p. 19: 'Now, a republic is a form of government, which, of all others, I most dislike—and I dislike it for this reason; because' etc., as quoted by Wordsworth, except the 'shew' rather than 'a shew' (172). Watson was here repeating sentiments which he had voiced some ten years earlier in *A Letter to His Grace the Archbishop of Canterbury*, 2nd edn. (London, 1783), p. 15: 'The principles of those who have spoken against the influence of the Crown, have been either much misunderstood, or much misrepresented; they have been accused ... of wishing to introduce the most tyrannous (in my apprehension) of all Governments, a Republick, in the form of a limited Monarchy.' Even in 1791, when he was writing favourably of the French Revolution, he similarly qualified his approval: 'I cannot but rejoice in the Emancipation of the French Nation from the Tyranny of Regal Despotism: but detesting the Despotism both of popular and aristocratic Demagogues, still more than that of Individual Monarchs, my rejoicing is held back, lest that Emancipation should be more apparent than real' (*A Charge Delivered to the Clergy of the Diocese of Landaff, June 1791* (London, 1792), p. 6). Here, as well as in 107–39, it would appear that Wordsworth was more familiar with Watson's reputation than with his actual writing.

165–7. M[r] Burke ... moralist] *Reflections*, ii. 348: 'But the age of chivalry is gone.... It is gone, that sensibility of principle, that chastity of honour, which felt a stain like a wound, which inspired courage whilst it mitigated ferocity, which ennobled whatever it touched, and under which vice itself lost half its evil, by losing all its grossness.' The famous passage, inspired by the misfortunes of Marie Antionette, was also contemptuously treated by Paine, *Rights of Man*, ii. 287. For Wordsworth's later tributes to the 'Genius of Burke' see *Prel.* (1850), VII. 512–43, and *Freeholders*, 199–201.

185–6. the iron ... into it] Ps. 105: 18, Book of Common Prayer: 'Whose feet they hurt in the stocks: the iron entered into his soul.'

186–9. *Du Contrat social*, ii. 26n. in *The Political Writings of Jean Jacques Rousseau*, ed. C. E. Vaughan (Cambridge, 1915).

194. imprisonment and the pillory] For accounts of the repressive measures taken by the Government in 1792 and the spring of 1793 see Phillip Anthony Brown, *The French Revolution in English History* (London, 1918), pp. 82–99; notices of trials and convictions for seditious words appear in *The Morning Herald*, 10 and 11 January 1793, and 23 March 1793.

202–6. As the magnitude ... individual] That a 'pure democracy' is an impossibility in a large State was a view held both by Rousseau (ii. 72) and by Paine (*Rights of Man*, ii. 422–3). In proposing representation as the best form for the government of a large State, Wordsworth is closer to Paine: 'the original simple democracy...is incapable of extension, not from its principle, but from the inconvenience of its form...Retaining, then, democracy as the ground...the representative system naturally presents itself; remedying at once the defects of the simple democracy as to form' (*Rights of Man*, ii. 423). Rousseau (ii. 98) had opposed representation as being destructive of liberty: 'Quoi qu'il en soit, à l'instant qu'un people se donne des Représentants, il n'est plus libre.' On the 'suffrage of every individual' see n. on 511–3.

208–11. the office ... code] Here it seems that Wordsworth would deny legislative power to the elected representatives, and would substitute legislation by referendum, as recommended by Rousseau (ii. 96): 'La souveraineté ne peut être représentee.... Elle consiste essentiellement dans la volonté générale, et la volonté ne se représente point.... Les Députés du people ne sont donc, ni ne peuvent être, ses représentants; ils ne sont que ses commissaires; ils ne peuvent rien conclure définitivement. Toute loi que le people en personne n'a pas ratifiée est nulle; ce n'est point une loi.' And yet in 307–13 Wordsworth maintains that the legislation of 'original measures' should fall to the 'representative assembly'. This apparent contradiction may stem from Article 6 of *Droits de L' Homme et du Citoyen*, which loosely permits the adoption of either method: 'La loi est l'expression de la volonté générale. Tous les citoyens ont droit de concourir personnellement, our par leurs représentants, à sa formation.' Similar vacillation is to be found in French action and debate at the opening of the Convention (see A. Aulard, *The French Revolution* (New York, 1910), ii. 160–1). In a speech delivered on the first day of the Convention (21 Sept.) Lasource distinguished between 'les lois constitutionelles et générales' and 'les lois particulières': the former, he said, should be ratified by the people, but the latter need not be. This distinction, however, was not carefully observed in the subsequent action, for although the first decree passed that day declared that 'il ne peut y avoir de constitution que lorsqu'elle est acceptée par le peuple', the Convention immediately thereafter passed three other major decrees—including the abolition of royalty——none of which entailed a referendum. (See *Réimpression de L'Ancien Moniteur*, xiv, 7–8.)

213–4. the privilege ... power] Cf. Paine, *Rights of Man*, ii. 432: government 'is altogether a trust, in right of those by whom that trust is delegated, and by whom it is always resumable'; and Rousseau, ii. 100–1.

214–26. Sensible that ... today] Cf. Paine, *Common Sense*, i. 71:

> and that the *elected* might never form to themselves an interest separate from the *electors*, prudence will point out the propriety of having elections often: because as the *elected* might by that means return and mix again with the general body of the *electors* in a few months, their fidelity to the public will be secured by the prudent reflection of not making a rod for themselves. And as this frequent interchange will establish a common interest with every part of the community, they will mutually and naturally support each other, and on this, (not on the unmeaning name of king,) depends the *strength of government, and the happiness of the governed*. [The italics are Paine's.]

220–1. tendency of power ... man] Cf. [John Almon], *Anecdotes of the Life of The Right Hon. William Pitt, Earl of Chatham* (Dublin, 1792), ii. 21: Pitt is speaking in the House of Lords, 9 January 1770, 'Unlimited power is apt to corrupt the minds of those who possess it.'

223. principle of identification] i.e. 'of interests' (215–19).

234–7. Left to ... parricide] The house of Joseph Priestley was burned on 14 July 1791, during the Birmingham riots. References to these riots are so numerous in journals and newspapers throughout 1792–3 that Wordsworth's allusion is perfectly topical; and his implication that the rioters had been surreptitiously incited to this action was a charge voiced in the House of Commons in May 1792, and referred to throughout the winter of 1792–3. (See, for example, Sheridan in the House of

Commons, 4 Mar., as reported in *The Times*, 5 Mar. 1793, p. 2, col. 3; *Gentleman's Magazine*, lxii (Dec. 1792), 1109–11; *European Magazine*, xxii (Dec. 1792), 470, and xxiii (Mar. 1793), 209–10; Robespierre on 5 Nov. 1792—see *Réimpression de L'Ancien Moniteur*, xiv. 390).

237–41. deprived almost ... hunger] Cf. 664–6. In the House of Lords, 1 February 1793, Stanhope in speaking against a war with France similarly emphasized the hardships war would bring to the poor: 'the necessaries of life are taxed so high, as to preclude the poor almost from the means of existence' (*Morning Herald*, 2 Feb. 1793).

249–51. having dried ... itself] The image is of two streams, one of public opinion, and the other, a kind of tributary, which, until its source is dried up, will continue to inject corruption into the first.

251–6. I must ... delight] Cf. *Prel.* X. 430–40.

257–62. Cf. Article 6, *Droits de L'Homme et du Citoyen*: 'Tous les citoyens ... sont également admissibles à toutes dignités, places et emplois publics, selon leur capacité et sans autre distinction que celles de leurs vertus et de leurs talents.'

264–6. *Appendix*, pp. 26–7:

> I think it [the British Constitution] far too excellent to be amended by peasants and mechanics. I do not mean to speak of peasants and mechanics with any degree of disrespect ... peasants and mechanics are as useful to the state as any other order of men; but their utility consists in their discharging well the duties of their respective stations; it ceases when they affect to become legislators; when they intrude themselves into concerns, for which their education has not fitted them.

Burke was probably as much Wordsworth's target as Watson, for in his *Reflections* (ii. 314–19) Burke attacked at length the quality of men elected to the National Assembly; he deplored their lack of practical experience in statecraft; he contemned the 'country clowns, who have seats in that assembly, some of whom are said not to be able to read and write' (ii. 316); and he found among the representatives of the clergy 'a very large proportion of mere country curates ... men who never had seen the state so much as in a picture; men who knew nothing of the world beyond the bounds of an obscure village' (ii. 319).

275–7. If your Lordship ... the other] Cf. the portrait of the Swiss herdsman in *Descriptive Sketches* (1793), 532–5 (*P.W.* i. 74).

> The slave of none, of beasts alone the lord,
> He marches with his flute, his book, and sword,
> Well taught by that to feel his rights, prepar'd
> With this "the blessings he enjoys to guard."

277–82. Michel Gérard (1737–1815), deputy from Rennes to the Estates-General. Wearing always the garb of a Breton peasant, Gérard was singled out for popular acclaim in the Procession of 4 May 1789. Affectionately called 'le père Gérard' by the Assembly, he voted with the *bourgeois* leader, Le Chapelier, and is not, therefore, a wholly appropriate figure for Wordsworth to select as a model republican. Perhaps Wordsworth derived his impression of Gérard not from reports of Assembly proceedings, but either from paintings of him done by David (see R. Valentiner, *Jacques Louis David and the French Revolution* (New York, 1929) and D. L. Dowd, *Pageant-Master of the Republic* (University of Nebraska Studies, 1948)), or from the fictional portrait of him by Collot d' Herbois in his immensely popular book, *Almanach du père Gérard pour 1792* (Paris, 1792). For information on Gérard see *La Grande Encyclopédie* and *Nouvelle Biographie générale*.

285–6. But government ... executive] Like Paine, Wordsworth apparently regards the judicial branch of government as being subsumed under the executive. Cf. *Rights of Man*, ii. 443.

290–3. With regard ... utility] Cf. Rousseau, ii. 103: 'Un État ainsi [simplement] gouverné a besoin de très peu de lois; et, à mesure qu'il devient nécessaire d'en promulger de nouvelles, cette nécessité se voit universellement.'

291–2. laws being ... the general will] Article 6, *Droits de L'Homme et du Citoyen*: 'La loi est l'expression de la volonté générale.'

294. a few refractory individuals] *les prêtres réfractaires* was a stock phrase in France for the clergy who refused to take the oath to the Civil Constitution; s.v. *réfractaire* in *Petit Larousse illustré*.

304. common feelings of humanity] Cf. *E.E.* I. 315–6.

307–13. See n. on 208–11.

318. could at all times bring to account] Cf. Article 15, *Droit de L'Homme et du Citoyen*: 'La société a le droit de demander compte à tout agent public de son administration.' Cf. also 213–4 and n.

319–20. simple functions ... complicated concerns] The antithesis here (and in 270–3) recalls the antithetical governments of the Lilliputians and the Houyhnhyms in Swift's *Gulliver's Travels*. Complexity in government was advocated by Burke (*Reflections*, ii. 334); simplicity in government, by Rousseau (ii. 102–3).

328. never] Owen and Smyser have 'not'. John O Hayden corrects from DCMS.8.

328–43. My first objection ... constitution] C.f. Rousseau, ii. 80:

> Une suite de ce défaut de cohérence est l'inconstance du Government royal, qui se réglant tantôt sur un plan et tantôt sur un autre, selon le caractère du prince qui règne ou des gens qui règnent pour lui, ne peut avoir longtemps un object

fixe ni une conduite conséquente: variation qui rend toujours l'État flottant de maxime en maxime, de projet en projet ... de la maxime commune à tous les ministres, et presque à tous les rois, étant de prendre en toute chose le contre-pied de leur prédécesseur.

And Paine, *Rights of Man*, ii. 416: a monarchy 'has no fixed character. To-day it is one thing; to-morrow it is something else. It changes with the temper of every succeeding individual, and is subject to all the varieties of each. It is government through the medium of passions and accidents.'

350–2. my grand objection ... not equal] Cf. 81–5 and n. Zera Fink (*J.E.G.P.* xlvii (1948), 115–16) cites Algernon Sydney, *Discourses concerning Government*, ii. xix, as Wordsworth's source.

351–5. *general* will ... *particular* will] The terms are Rousseau's.

359–60. that atmosphere of ... exist] A commonplace in anti-monarchial writers, but cf. *Prel.* IX. 349–61 and Paine, *Common Sense*, i. 78.

361–3. You seem anxious ... trouble] *Appendix*, p. 22: 'The equality of man in a state of civil society, does not consist in an equality of wisdom, honesty, ingenuity, industry,—nor in an equality of property resulting from a due exertion of these talents; but in being equally subject to, equally protected by the same laws.'

363–6. If you had ... good] Although one here expects a simple translation of Article 1 of *Droits de L'Homme et du Citoyen* ('Les homes naissent et demeurent libres et égaux en droits. Les distinctions socials ne peuvent être fondées que sur l'utilité commune'), Wordsworth seems also to be drawing on Rousseau, ii. 61: 'Si l'on recherché en quoi consiste précisément le plus grand bien de tous ... on trouvera qu'il se réduit à deux objets principaux: la *liberté* et l'*égalité* ... l'égalité, parce que la liberté ne peut subsister sans elle.'

372. Government ... necessary evil] Paine, *Common Sense*,i. 69: 'Government, even in its best state, is but a necessary evil.'

376–9. Nothing ... with the power] Cf. 233–47 and n.

384–430. Cf. Rousseau, ii. 61, fn. 4: 'Voulez-vous donc donner à l'État de la consistence? rapprochez les degrés extrêmes autant qu'il est possible; ne souffrez ni des gens opulents ni des gueux. Ces deux états, naturellement inséparables, sont également funestes au bien commun.'

394–424. Cf. *Postscript*, 19–361 (Ch. XVII below).

396. unnatural monster of primogeniture] Cf. Paine, *Rights of Man*, ii. 322: 'To restore, therefore, parents to their children, and children to their parents ... and to exterminate the monster aristocracy, root and branch—the French Constitution has destroyed the law of PRIMOGENITURESHIP.' Paine makes a further attack on primogeniture as being 'unnatural and unjust' (ii. 500).

403–30. They have unjustly ... society] Cf. Paine, *Rights of Man*, ii. 501: 'Several laws are in existence for regulating and limiting work-men's wages.... Personal labour is all they have.' The 'innumerable statutes' to which Wordsworth refers are the wage assessment clauses of the Act of 1563, whereby Justices of Peace established wage rates for all kinds of labour within a country; classic economists, such as J. E. Thorold Rogers (*Six Centuries of Work and Wages* (London, 1884), ii. 389–9, 437–8), agree with Wordsworth that these assessments were unfair to labour; but modern economic histories show that in the eighteenth century assessments were comparatively rare, that where they existed the actual wages were generally higher than the assessment, and that in the period 1790–3 wages rose steadily. (See E. Lipson, *The Economic History of England* (London, 1931). Iii. 270; E. W. Gilboy, *Wages in Eighteenth Century England* (Cambridge, Mass., 1934), pp. 110–12, 175; Gayer, Rostow, Schwartz, *The Growth and Fluctuation of the British Economy, 1790–1850* (Oxford, 1953), i. 25.)

In the course of this vigorous attack on England's economic condition it is surprising that Wordsworth does not refer to Watson's *Sermon*, for in the *Sermon* Watson tries to reconcile the poor to their condition. One example of his effort should suffice: 'Every man amongst us is equally capable of acquiring property ... through the faults or the misfortunes of his progenitors he may have been born in a low situation, but it must be through his own if he continues in it' (p. 4). Ironically, Wordsworth's own views on England's economy had but recently been almost as complacent as Watson's. As late May 1792 he had written to Mathews: 'You have the happiness of being born in a free country, where every road is open, where talents and industry are more liberally rewarded than amongst any other nation of the Universe' (*E.Y.*, p. 77).

413–4. Your lordship ... capable] Watson's approval of the British Constitution implies such a view as that which Wordsworth here ascribes to him; e.g. *Appendix*, p. 29: 'look round the globe, and see if you can discover a single nation on all its surface, so powerful, so rich, so beneficent, so free and happy as our own? May Heaven avert from the minds of my countrymen the slightest wish to abolish their constitution!' But in the heat of debate Wordsworth ignores Watson's fuller statement (pp. 26–7): 'That the constitution of this country is so perfect as neither to require, or admit of any improvement, is a proposition to which I never did, or ever can assent.... No danger need be apprehended from a candid examination of our own constitution, or from a display of the advantages of any other: it will bear to be contrasted with the best; but all men are not qualified to make the comparison.'

424. infants ... unable to support] It will be recalled that Wordsworth's daughter

Caroline was born to Annette Vallon on 15 December 1792 (Moorman, i. 187), and that he had returned 'Reluctantly to England… / Compell'd by nothing less than absolute want / Of funds for my support' (*Prel.* X. 190–2).

425. agrarian law … sumptuary regulations] The terminology is, of course, classical, but the statement is topical because of Girondist opposition to threats of egalitarianism made during August and September 1792. (See A. Aulard, *The French Revolution* (New York, 1910), ii. 132–5; A. Mathiez, *The French Revolution* (New York, 1927), pp. 918–213.) On 25 March 1793 *The Morning Herald* reported that the preceding week the National Convention had pronounced 'The punishment of death … against whoever should propose *Agrarian* Laws, or any others, subversive of the property of commerce and industry'.

434. the grand principle] i.e. the 'happiness' of a people or the 'general welfare'. Cf. 210, 219. 490, 518–19.

437–57. Considering hereditary … reputation] Cf. Swift, *Gulliver's Travels*, III, viii; Paine, *Common Sense*, i. 79: hereditary nobility is 'an insult and imposition on posterity. For all men being originally equals, no one by birth could have a right to set up his own family in perpetual preference to all others for ever, and tho' himself might deserve some decent degree of honours of his contemporaries, yet his descendants might be far too unworthy to inherit them.'

451–2. make him … scorn] The alteration (see textual n.) moves towards a reminiscence of *Othello*, IV. ii. 52–4.

470–1. he who … Tarpeian rock] The Tarpeian rock on the Capitoline, from which condemned criminals were hurled, was a popular metaphor in French oratory. When Mirabeau's intrigues were exposed (5 Dec. 1792), it was proposed in the Convention that public honours henceforth be deferred until ten years after a man's death, and it was recalled that Mirabeau himself had said 'qu'il n'y avait pas loin du Capitole au mont Tarpeïan' (*Réimpression de L'Ancien Moniteur*, xiv, 666).

493–7. Besides where … gained by it] Cf. Paine, *Rights of Man*, ii. 368 and 472.

498. the poor … hunger] Cf. *Guilt and Sorrow*, 368–9 (*P.W.* i. 114).

500. "*necessary* splendor"] The phrase is not Watson's, although the concept is: 'I cannot wish to see the splendor of the crown reduced to nothing, lest its proper weight in the scale of the constitution should be thereby destroyed' (*Appendix*, p. 25).

508–10. You ask … belong] *Appendix*, pp. 20–1: 'the liberty of a man in a state of society, consists in his being subject to no law, but to the law enacted by the general will of the society to which he belongs.—And to what other law is any man in Great

Britain subject?'

511–4. If there is ... society] 'will annex an equal importance to the suffrage of every individual' (205–6). In England, manhood suffrage, annual elections, and reform in parliamentary representation were the aims of a number of radical societies during the early seventeen-eighties (see Phillip A. Brown, *The French Revolution in English History* (London, 1918), pp. 13–26). Again in 1791, under the impact of the French Revolution, English radical groups, notably the London Corresponding Society, with its affiliated societies in other parts of the country, began working for the same ends (ibid., pp. 55–74). In France, Grégoire and Robespierre had spoken for universal suffrage in the debates on the franchise at the close of 1789; but the franchise voted by the Assembly, and the one which governed the elections of 1790–1, bore a tax-payment qualification which disqualified nearly two million adult Frenchmen. Manhood suffrage was established only after the insurrection of 10 August 1792. (See Aulard, *The French Revolution*, i. 179–89, 203–11, 239–47, ii. 77–8; J. M. Thomson, *The French Revolution* (Oxford, 1955), pp. 122–6, 296; R. R. Palmer, *The Age of the Democratic Revolution* (Princeton, N. J., 1959), i. 501, 522–6.)

515–18. *Appendix*, p. 21. Except for variations in punctuation and the omission of 'the' before 'law' in 518, the quotation is verbatim.

526. the avowed ... Walpole] Notably, 'Every man has his price.' (For early ascriptions of this maxim to Walpole see *N. & Q.* vii (1907), 367, 470–2, 492.)

538. debt of 240 millions] Cf. textual n. 600. The following relevant figures for the National Debt are from *Parliamentary Papers, 1868–9*, reprinted in *English Historical Documents, 1783–1832*, ed. A. Aspinall and E. A. Smith (London, 1959), p. 578:

1792—£239,663,421
1793—£247,874,434
1813—£788,093,781
1814—£813,140,176

542–55. Cf. *Appendix*, pp. 21–2: 'The courts of British justice are impartial and incorrupt; they respect not the persons of men; the poor man's lamb is, in their estimation, as sacred as the monarch's crown; with inflexible integrity they adjudge to every man his own. Your property under their protection is secure.' Wordsworth's own experience with the litigation of the Lonsdale debt undoubtedly invigorates his condemnation of the English courts. (See Moorman, i. 167–9.)

545. you have not ... colleges] Graduated from Trinity College, Cambridge, in 1759, Watson was elected a Fellow in the following year. In 1764 he was elected

Professor of Chemistry, and in 1771 Regius Professor of Divinity. (See *Anecdotes of the Life of Richard Watson, Bishop of Landaff; Written by Himself* (London, 1817), pp. 7–38.)

546–7. Here I am ... representation] See 202 ff, 257 ff.

556–9. *Appendix*, p. 22, verbatim.

560–63. *Appendix*, pp. 23–4: 'Other nations may deluge their land with blood in struggling for liberty and equality; but let it never be forgotten by ourselves, and let us impress the observation upon the hearts of our children, that we are in possession of both; of as much of both, as can be consistent with the end for which civil society was introduced amongst mankind.'

565–9. Mr Burke ... parchment] Burke, writing on the Act of Settlement, *Reflections*, ii. 297: 'The law, by which this royal family is specifically destined to the succession, is the act of the 12th and 13th of King William. The term of this act bind "us and our *heirs*, and our *posterity*, to them, their *heirs*, and their *posterity*," being Protestants, to the end of time, in the same words as the Declaration of Right had bound us to the heirs of King William and Queen Mary.' Wordsworth's 'dead parchment' (633–4) recalls Paine's reiterated attacks on this passage in Burke (*Rights of Man*, ii. 276–84), and particularly Paine's contempt for the 'musty records and mouldy parchments' (*Rights of Man*, ii, 282, 284) upon which Burke had based his arguments.

567. in the East ... dead] This example of cruelty, as far as we can discover, is an invention not of the East, but of the Etruscan tyrant Mezentius, in the Aeneid, viii, 485: 'mortua quin etiam iungebat corpora vivis.' Cf. Wordsworth's *Imitation of Juvenal—Satire VIII*, 5–6 (*P.W.* i. 302): 'Even he who yoked the living to the dead, / Rivall'd by you, hides the diminish'd head.'

572–6. But see n. on 413–4.

583–4. like the inveterate enemy ... destination] The 'inveterate enemy' is, presumably, Demosthenes. If the metaphor of the arrow is Wordsworth's (and we recognize no allusion to Demosthenes' marking the shaft of his arrow and declaring Philip to be its destination), the comparison turns upon Demosthenes' plainly calling his speeches *Phillipics*, whereas Watson, although putting his name to his attack on liberty, was unwilling to acknowledge that it *was* an attack on liberty.

586–7. You profess ... the people] See n. on 22–3.

588. the general call ... reform] For the reform movement in 1792–3 see W. T. Laprade, *England and the French Revolution* (Baltimore, Md., 1909), pp. 55–60, 135–43, and Phillip A. Brown, *The French Revolution in English History* (London, 1918), pp. 53–68. Throughout the winter of 1792–3 reform was a leading topic in periodicals, books and Parliamentary debates. (See, for example, the numerous books and pamphlets on reform published July 1792–June 1793, listed in *The Analytical Review*, xiv (Dec., 1792), 533–4, and xvi (Aug. 1793), 533–6; reports on Parliamentary Proceedings in *The Gentleman's Magazine*, lxii (Oct. 1792), 913, and lxii (Jan. 1793), 46 in *The Morning Herald*, 29 Mar. 1793, and in *The European Magazine*, xiii (Mar. 1793), 217–18; editorials urging reform in *The Morning Chronicle*, 5 and 6 Dec. 1792; 'Report of the Society of the Friends of the People on the state of representation, 9 Feb. 1793', in *English Historical Documents*, ed. A. Aspinall and E. A. Smith (London, 1959), pp. 216–21. On 28 January 1793 *The Times* advertised, as published that day by J. Johnson, *The Necessity of a Speedy and Effectual Reform in Parliament* by George Phillips.) Thus Wordsworth was justified in rebuking Watson's silence on the reform question, even though Grey's famous motion on reform was not made until 6 May 1793.

594–9. From your omitting ... want] Despite the fact that Watson dated his *Appendix* 25 January, or one week before the French declaration of war, Wordsworth could rightly expect some comment by Watson on war with France. Since the King's Proclamation of 1 December, drawing out the Militia Forces, war with France was the dominant topic in both Houses of Parliament, and so too in all London newspapers and journals. Nor did the declaration of war preclude Wordsworth's raising the issue, for debate on the war continued in both Houses for some time afterwards: Stanhope and Fox moved condemnations of the Ministers 'for having drawn us into a war by refusing to negotiate' (*Morning Herald*, 13 Feb. 1793), and on 21 February Grey made a similar motion (*European Magazine*, xxiii (Mar. 1793), 214–17). For Watson's 'disapprobation of French measures' see n. on 147.

602. the hermit Peter] A priest of Amiens who instigated the crusade of the *pauperes*, 1096, and in legend was made the author of the First Crusade.

618. Maury ... Cazalès] Jean-Siffrein Maury, 1746–1817: deputy of the clergy of Péronne to the Estates General: a leader of the extreme right, and an outspoken defender of clerical property; emigrated to Rome in 1791. Jacques-Antoine-Marie de Cazalès, 1768–1805: deputy for the nobility of Rivière-Verdun to the Estates General; fought to keep the three orders separate and independent; defended the clergy's refusal to take the oath; resigned as deputy after the arrest of Louis at Varennes and withdrew to Germany; returned to France in February 1792, but emigrated after 10 August. In England he was well received by important statesmen, especially by Burke, 'qui avait pour lui la plus haute admiration'. (S.v.v. 'Maury' and 'Cazalès', *Biographie universelle*.) Whereas in France the two names were linked in opprobrium (e.g. *Réimpression de L'Ancien Moniteur*, xiv, 138). Burke had linked the names Maury and Cazalés in an encomium (*Letter to a Member of the National Assembly*, in *Works* (Bohn's Standard Library, London, 1886), ii. 546).

618. mask of patriotism] The phrase *le masque du patriotisme* appears in Louvet's speech against Robespierre (*Réimpression de L'Ancien Moniteur*, xiv, 88, 214, 407), a speech described in The Prelude (X. 83–103); others in the Convention also used the phrase (e.g. see *Réimpression de L'Ancien Moniteur*, xiv, 88, 214, 207).

618. La Fayette ... Mirabeau] Once a national hero, Lafayette rapidly fell into universal distrust through his support of a constitutional monarchy. Following the invasion of the Tuileries (20 June 1792), he left his command in the north, and before the Assembly demanded punishment of the perpetrators, but instead the Assembly indicted him for leaving his post. His acquittal on 8 August in part precipitated the rising of 10 August; on 19 August, after failing to hold the loyalty of his troops, he crossed the border into Belgium. (See J. M. Thompson, *The French Revolution* (Oxford, 1955), p. 275, 285.) Mirabeau, still a popular hero at the time of his death (2 Apr. 1791), was given a state funeral and buried in the Pantheon (ibid., pp. 197–8); but when his intrigues with the Court were publicly uncovered during the debates on the King's trial, it was proposed that his ashes be removed from the Pantheon and the Convention decreed (5 Dec.) that his statue be veiled. (See *Réimpression de L'Ancien Moniteur*, xiv. 666–7.)

619–20. Political convulsions ... abilities] Cf. James Mackintosh, *Vindiciæ Gallicæ* (London, 1792), p. 130; and Paine, *Rights of Man*, ii. 420: 'It appears to general observation, that revolutions create genius and talents; but those events do no more than bring them forward. There is existing in man, a mass of sense lying in a dormant state.'

622–5. Reflecting upon ... talents] This statement is somewhat baffling, for Wordsworth could hardly have regretted the disappearance of the nobility and non-juring clergy from the National Assembly. J. M. Thompson (*The French Revolution* (Oxford, 1955)) has pointed out that in the Convention 'one out of every three deputies had already sat either in the Constituent Assembly of '89 or in the Legislative Assembly of '91' (p. 318), and that the members of the Convention differed very little in their talents and experience from the members of the earlier Assemblies (p. 312). But to Wordsworth in Paris at the end of 1792 things may have seemed very different: denunciations and decrees of accusation were almost daily fare in the Convention; Louvet, in the speech referred to in our n. on 618, said that in September 'l'autorité nationale, représentée par l'Assemblée legislative, était indignement méconnue, avilie, foulée aux pieds'; in combating a motion that would in the future prohibit all public office to the present deputies, Barrère said (27 Oct.), 'Jugez du peu de danger de la rééligibilité par l'exemple de l'Assemblée constituante: sur 1200 hommes, passés à travers la filière de l'opinion publique, 80 ou 90 seulement sont revenues à la Convention nationale' (*Réimpression de L'Ancien Moniteur*, xiv. 320); on 10 November Cambon, recalling the situation of 10 August, said, 'Le côté droit était atteré; il ne restait que deux cents ou deux cent-six députés, ceux qui avaient conservé la confiance publique en votant contre Lafayette, qui pussent parler encore' (ibid. xiv. 449).

3.

Preface to *The Borderers*

INTRODUCTION: GENERAL

WORDSWORTH himself traced the origin of *The Borderers* and its Preface to his observation of men and motives in revolutionary France:

> The study of human nature suggests this awful truth, that, as in the trials to which life subjects us, sin and crime are apt to start from their very opposite qualities, so are there no limits to the hardening of the heart, and the perversion of the understanding to which they may carry their slaves. During my long residence in France, while the revolution was rapidly advancing to its extreme of wickedness, I had frequent opportunities of being an eye-witness of this process, and it was while that knowledge was fresh upon my memory, that the Tragedy of 'The Borderers' was composed.
>
> ... while I was composing this Play I wrote a short essay illustrative of that constitution and those tendencies of human nature which make the apparently *motiveless* actions of bad men intelligible to careful observers. This was partly done with reference to the character of Oswald, and his persevering endeavour to lead the man he disliked into so heinous a crime; but still more to preserve in my distinct remembrance what I had observed of transition in character, and the reflections I had been led to make during the time I was a witness of the changes through which the French Revolution passed [*P.W.* i. 342–3].

Wordsworth was an effective observer of French affairs at first-hand from November 1791 until December 1792. During this period he was close to the following political events, which he records in the early lines of *The Prelude*, Book X: the fall of the King (9–10 August 1792; *Prel.* X. 8–9); the invasion of France by the allies and its repulse (August–October 1792; *Prel.* X. 9–20); the September massacres (2–4 September 1792; *Prel.* X. 64–6); the denunciation and triumph of Robespierre (29 October, 5 November 1792; *Prel.* X. 83–128). Of these, only the last two suggest the kind of event Wordsworth had in mind when he linked *The Borderers* to French affairs; and indeed *The Prelude* is not especially illuminating on the sort of mind which Wordsworth saw in France and which he might have thought he was portraying in Oswald. A few passages in Book X are perhaps relevant:

> The indecision on their part whose aim
> Seem'd best, and the straightforward path of those
> Who in attack or in defence alike
> Were strong through their impiety ... (113–16)

> [faith], theirs who throned
> The human understanding paramount
> And made of that their God ... (318–20)

In the depth
Of those enormities, even thinking minds
Forgot at seasons whence they had their being,
Forgot that such a sound was ever heard
As Liberty upon earth; yet all beneath
Her innocent authority was wrought,
Nor could have been, without her blessed name. (346–52)

Of these, the first two suggest the nature of Oswald as Preface and play present him; the third suggests the behaviour (in another context) of Marmaduke, or the starting of 'sin and crime … from their very opposite qualities'. This may also be the intention of certain items in the list, X. 316–22, even including, possibly, those described in 318–20, cited above.

The tone of *The Prelude* when it discusses these matters suggests in Wordsworth in late 1792 a frame of mind at first hopeful (X. 31–9), but later uneasy. Shortly he was answering Bishop Watson in *Llandaff*, which says little to our present purpose, except to note that in a nation newly released from tyranny excesses are likely but will eventually subside (cf. *Prel.* X. 34–7).

The possibility that Wordsworth visited France in October 1793 and, as he reported to Carlyle, actually witnessed the execution of Gorsas should be taken into account.[1] Prior to this date he had, so far as we know, never actually seen the brutality of the Jacobins in action. It is conceivable, though it certainly cannot be proved, that, if Wordsworth really saw this execution, the spectacle might have roused in him sufficient revulsion to account for the change in his attitude to France which is evident in a series of letters to William Mathews beginning in early 1794. The first of these (17 February 1794; *E.Y.*, p. 113) uses the jargon of progressive politics in some questions about Portugal; the second (23 May 1794; *E.Y.*, p. 119) identifies Wordsworth as 'of that odious class of men called democrats'; and the third (8 June 1794; *E.Y.*, pp. 123–4) proceeds, in the manner of *Llandaff*, to 'disapprove of monarchical and aristocratical governments … Hereditary distinctions, and privileged orders of every species', and the like. Yet 'The destruction of those institutions which I condemn appears to me to be hastening on too rapidly. I recoil from the bare idea of a revolution'. A programme of education may assist a reform without violence. 'I am a determined enemy to every species of violence … I deplore the miserable situation of the French … [we should express] our detestation of the execrable measures pursued in France [but also] hold up to the approbation of the world such of their regulations and

1 See Reed, *Chronology of the Early Years*, p. 147.

decrees as are dictated by the spirit of Philosophy' (*E.Y.*, pp. 124–9).[1] In spite of the 'execrable measures pursued in France', Wordsworth in November still opposes the war and the government (*E.Y.*, p. 135), and in December 'rejoices' at the acquittal of Horne Tooke and others (*E.Y.*, p. 137). Between late 1795 and early 1797 his adaptation of Juvenal's eighth Satire (*E.Y.*, pp. 156 ff.) indicates that at the time of writing *The Borderers* (*E.Y.*, p. 177) his political sympathies were still with the Left, even though they had shifted from France.

It is our opinion that the documents we have cited do not fully substantiate Wordsworth's claim to have deduced the character of Oswald from his observation of Frenchmen and French affairs. There is ample evidence, to be sure, in French history for the statement that 'sin and crime are apt to start from their very opposite qualities', i.e. for the transformation of liberal thinkers into political tyrants whose tyranny seeks to be justified in the name of freedom; and hence there is empirical evidence for the kind of action which led Oswald into the career he describes in Bord. 1688 ff., and which will similarly lead Marmaduke into the crime of exposing Herbert in the belief that he is encouraging or permitting the operation of some divine or natural justice. The belief that a violent means is justified by an end of national importance can be seen time and again in the procedures of Robespierre and others. Two books by revolutionaries which came into Wordsworth's hands about the time he was writing the play make such a point (on Wordsworth's knowledge of these books see *E.Y.*, 166):

> In relating a few facts of the political lives of our friends [the Girondins] ... I have imputed to them some faults: but let it be remembered ... that they are too great to be flattered. Besides, all their faults were the faults of virtue: they originated from the purity of their manners, from the extreme goodness of their hearts. They were too virtuous to credit crimes, till the very day they fell victims to them.[2]
>
> It is not easy to command our passions in the time of a revolution: there is indeed no instance of one accomplished without their assistance. Great obstacles are to be overcome; and this cannot be effected without an ardour, and a devotion to the causes, bordering upon enthusiasm, or tending to produce it. Hence it is that we grasp with avidity at every thing that seems to serve our purpose, and lose the faculty of perceiving what may prove injurious.[3]

But neither these works nor Wordsworth's utterances on the Revolution outside our

1 Godwin had written against violent revolution in *Political Justice*, Book IV, Ch. Ii (ed. F. E. L. Priestley (Toronto, 1946), i. 263 ff.; cf. for the version of 1793). Wordsworth would have had time to read Godwin by the date of this letter.

2 Jean-Baptiste Louvet, *Narrative of the Dangers to which I have been Exposed* ... (London, 1795), pp. v–vi.

3 *An Appeal to Impartial Posterity, by Madame Roland* ... (London, 1796), i., 60–1. .

text and the immediately related notes seem to us to provide empirical authority for Oswald, the man who, having acted like some French revolutionaries in the mistaken belief that by violence he serves justice, supposes that, by the victory he secures over the remorse which follows upon the discovery of his error, he has made the decisive step towards an intellectual freedom otherwise unobtainable, and then proceeds to obtain satisfaction by vicariously repeating the crime. We find in French history the revolutionary who (rationally, perhaps) removes the reactionary, or supposedly reactionary, enemies of the progressive State at which the revolutionary aims. What we do not find is the revolutionary who supposes, as Oswald does or says he does, that the act of removal, is in itself a criterion whereby the right-mindedness of colleagues is to be judged.[1] The act of removal is judged by the criterion of expediency, not as an initiation into a condition of intellectual advancement or freedom, seen as the right intellectual milieu for a new political entity. No doubt many atrocities in France derived from power guided by 'the immediate law, / From the clear light of circumstances, flashed / Upon an independent Intellect' (*Bord.* 1494–6); but their aim, in their authors' judgements, seems usually to have been to promote the interests of the State by obliterating its enemies. It is also true, no doubt, that many such atrocities arose when their authors supposed themselves guided by such a law as Oswald postulates, when in fact they were guided, perhaps unconsciously, by jealousy, personal fear, or other baser motives. But in neither instance does the act of terror seem to have been undertaken with the aim of educating the intellects of right-minded survivors.

Critics of the play have constantly discussed the character of Oswald and devised various explanations of it, related or unrelated to Wordsworth's account of its origins in his observations in France. Since Émile Legouis's notable exposition, in his *Early Life of William Wordsworth*,[2] the influence of William Godwin on the poet and one the character of Oswald has been canvassed or denied. Oswald has been seen as a warning against Godwin's thinking,[3] as a failed Godwinian,[4] or as no Godwinian at all,[5] or merely a reflection of the over-rational thinking found in many theorists of politics and morals in the eighteenth century.[6] In view of Wordsworth's known inter-

1 Such criteria are not, of course, incredible in themselves..

2 Trans. J. W. Matthews, 2nd edn. (London, 1921), pp. 253–78, especially pp. 269 ff.

3 By Legouis, and by Ernest de Selincourt, 'Wordsworth's Preface to "The Borderers",' in *Oxford Lectures on Poetry* (Oxford, 1934), pp. 157–79.

4 By H.W. Garrod, *Wordworth* (Oxford, 1923), p. 92.

5 By G. W. Meyer, *Wordsworth's Formative Years* (Ann Arbor, Mich., 1943), pp. 153 ff.

6 R. D. Havens, *The Mind of a Poet* (Baltimore, Md., 1941), p. 543; Alan Grob, 'Wordsworth and Godwin: a Reassessment', *Studies in Romanticism*, vi (1967), 98–119.

est in *Political Justice*,[1] his personal contacts with Godwin in 1795,[2] and his direct and critical reference to him in the fragmentary 'Essay on Morals' of 1798, we see no reason, until convincing parallels with other writers are discovered, against believing that the various 'Godwinian' utterances of Oswald in the play[3] arise from Wordsworth's contact with and rejection of Godwin and his book.

Oswald has also been seen as a 'Gothic' villain of the type developed in the 'frantic novels, sickly and stupid German tragedies', of which Wordsworth complained in the Preface to *Lyrical Ballads*,[4] and which will be more clearly defined in the Satanic, Faustean (or Promethean, according to point of view) figure which dominates some of the larger works of Byron and Shelley. As Legouis, again, made clear in one telling quotation from Mrs. Radcliffe, the Godwinian and Satanic types are by no means mutually exclusive.[5]

In the process of exposition, critical emphases are sometimes disconcertingly reversed. According to Lascelles Abercrombie, Oswald's real interest is in manipulating Marmaduke's mind, while his confessed jealousy and hatred are only superficial motives towards his seduction of Marmaduke. Thorslev, on the contrary, thinks that Oswald's Satanic desire to spread intellectual freedom, which he achieves, or thinks he achieves, in the seduction of Marmaduke, is a rationalization and concealment of his real motives, 'envy and wounded pride'.[6]

In our view, neither Wordsworth's own claim that he found models in revolutionary France nor the invocation of literary types by some modern critics wholly explains the character of Oswald, though the suggestions are obviously not irrelevant. We tend to agree with critics such as Legouis and de Selincourt that the character springs rather from the impact of rational ways of thought (including Godwin's) on Wordsworth's mind as he sought to understand the collapse of his revolutionary ideals; and we would agree especially with the able analysis of Roger Sharrock,[7] when

1 *E.Y.*, pp. 124, 170.

2 Moorman, i. 262 ff.

3 e.g. *Bord.* 1484–98, 1560–7, 1834–7, 1855–7.

4 P. L. Thorslev, Jr., 'Wordsworth's *Borderers* and the Romantic Villain-Hero', *Studies in Romanticism*, v (1966), 84–103.

5 Legouis, *Early Life*, pp. 271–2.

6 Lascelles Abercrombie, *The Art of Wordsworth* (London, 1952), p. 71; Thorslev, p. 100.

7 '*The Borderers*: Wordsworth on the Moral Frontier', *Durham University Journal*, lv (1964), 170–83; the phrases quoted are on pp. 175–6. With Sharrock's account of the play as emerging from 'a state of disillusion with the liberal experience … the suspension of all accepted codes, the rejection of traditional custom and habit, the fresh start *ex nihilo*' (p. 171), cf. the subtle account in Geoffrey H. Hartman, *Wordsworth's Poetry, 1787–1814* (New Haven, Conn., and London, 1964, 1964), pp. 125 ff. 369. See also Robert Osborn, 'Meaningful Obscurity: The Antecedents and Character of Rivers', in

he finds in Oswald and Marmaduke 'the two aspects of [Wordsworth's] divided mind' and shows that Oswald is 'a stage he [Wordsworth] himself could have taken'.

Bicentenary Wordsworth Studies in Memory of John Alban Finch, ed. J. Wordsworth (Ithaca, N. Y. and London, 1970), pp. 393–424.

INTRODUCTION: TEXTUAL

THE text of Wordsworth's Preface to *The Borderers* is derived from two manuscripts preserved in the Wordsworth Library, Grasmere. What appears to be the earlier (Grasmere MS. Verse 13; MS. A in our notes) consists of eight and a half pages, 9 in. × 7¼ in.; the first three pages down to 'sophism' are written in an unknown hand, the remainder in the hand of Dorothy Wordsworth, except the motto from Pope (184–7), which according to the Library Catalogue is in Wordsworth's hand. The later version (Grasmere MS. Verse 15; MS. B in our notes) is contained in a vellum-bound notebook, 7½in. × 6 in., which contains also MS. B of *The Borderers* and MS. U of *The Prelude* (see *P.W.* i. 344; *Prel.*, p. Xxviii). The hand is Mary Wordsworth's, except for the heading 'A Tragedy' and the motto from Pope (168–71), which are perhaps in the hand of Dorothy Wordsworth. MS. A cannot be dated with any precision; the paper is watermarked 1795, and the writing is presumably not earlier than late 1796 or early 1797 (*P.W.* i. 343–4); MS. B belongs to 1799 or 1800 (ibid.).

Our text is based primarily on MS. B, mainly on the ground that it seems to be later than MS. A, and that its characteristic readings[1] are likely to represent Wordsworth's second thoughts. On the other hand, it is sometimes inferior to MS. A, for it contains copyist's errors[2] which can be corrected from MS. A. MS. A, however, can hardly serve as copy-text; for it is itself a copy,[3] and does not, therefore carry holograph authority; and its first three pages contain many curious and almost illiterate spellings ('tumuluous', 'desirts', 'talants'; 'exausts'; 'intrested', 'reccollection', 'folled', 'exibition', 'sufficiant', 'Aristo' and (possibly) 'Candenio', 'scociety', 'dispises').[4] We have therefore followed MS. B, except where it is obviously or very probably in error.

---

1 See, for example, 119, 167, 172, textual notes.

2 See 21–2, 168, textual notes; probably 31, textual n. and Commentary; and perhaps 66, textual n. and Commentary.

3 At 110 the duplication of 'habit' is probably an error; at 112 'more' is dittographed; and at 115–6 the group 'where the mind ... in that action' is dittographed and deleted at a second writing.

4 These suggest an inaccurate speller following dictation rather than copying. Perhaps Wordsworth began to dictate, gave up when he saw the result, and then wrote a draft which Dorothy copied as a continuation of the work of the unknown amanuensis. Professor Mark L. Reed tells us that he believes the hand to be John Wordsworth's and the manuscript to have been written in 1800.

[PREFACE TO *THE BORDERERS*]

LET us suppose a young man of great intellectual powers, yet without any solid principles of genuine benevolence. His master passions are pride and the love of distinction—He has deeply imbibed a spirit of enterprise in a tumultuous age. He goes into the world and is betrayed into a great crime.—That influence on which all his happiness is built immediately deserts him. His talents are robbed of their weight—his exertions are unavailing, and he quits the world in disgust, with strong misanthropic feelings. In his retirement, he is impelled to examine the reasonableness of established opinions, & the force of his mind exhausts itself in constant efforts to separate the elements of virtue and vice. It is his pleasure & his consolation to hunt out whatever is bad in actions usually esteemed virtuous, & to detect the good in actions which the universal sense of mankind teaches us to reprobate. While the general exertion of his intellect seduces him from the remembrance of his crime, the particular conclusions to which he is led have a tendency to reconcile him to himself. His feelings are interested in making him a moral sceptic, &, as his scepticism increases, he is raised in his own esteem. After this process has been continued some time, his natural energy and restlessness impel him again into the world. In this state, pressed by the recollection of his guilt, he seeks relief from two sources, action and meditation. Of actions, those are most attractive which best exhibit his own powers, partly from the original pride of his character, and still more because the loss of authority and influence which followed upon his crime was the first circumstance which impressed him with the magnitude of that crime, & brought along with it those tormenting sensations by which he is assailed. The recovery of his original importance & the exhibition of his own powers are therefore in his mind almost identified with the extinction of those painful feeling which attend the recollection of his guilt. Perhaps there is no cause which has greater weight in preventing the return of bad men to virtue than that good actions being for the most part in their nature silent & regularly progressive, they do not present those sudden results which can afford a sufficient stimulus

The title is editorial.
12 exertion A^2B: exertions A.
21–2 was the first ... crime A: *om.* crime B.
27 than *Edd.*: then AB.

to a troubled mind. In processes of vice the effects are more frequently immediate, palpable, and extensive. Power is much more easily manifested in destroying than in creating. A child, Rousseau has observed, will tear in pieces fifty toys before he will think of making one. From these causes, assisted by disgust and misanthropic feeling, the character we are now contemplating will have a strong tendency to vice. His energies are most impressively manifested in works of devastation. He is the Orlando of Ariosto, the Cardenio of Cervantes, who lays waste the groves that should shelter him. He has rebelled against the world & the laws of the world, & he regards them as tyrannical masters; convinced that he is right in some of his conclusions, he nourishes a contempt for mankind the more dangerous because he has been led to it by reflexion. Being in the habit of considering the world as a body which is in some sort at war with him, he has a feeling borrowed from that habit which gives an additional zest to his hatred of those members of society whom he hates & to his contempt of those whom he despises. Add to this, that a mind fond of nourishing sentiments of contempt will be prone to the admission of those feelings which are considered under any uncommon bond of relation (as must be the case with a man who has quarrelled with the world), the feelings will mutually strengthen each other. In this morbid state of mind he cannot exist without occupation, he requires constant provocatives, all his pleasures are prospective, he is perpetually chasing a phantom, he commits new crimes to drive away the memory of the past. But the lenitives of his pain are twofold; meditation as well as action. Accordingly, his reason is almost exclusively employed in justifying his past enormities & in enabling him to commit new ones. He is perpetually imposing upon himself, he has a sophism for every crime. The *mild* effusions of thought, the milk of human reason, are unknown to him. His imagination is powerful, being strengthened by the habit of picturing possible forms of society where his crimes would be no longer crimes, and he would enjoy that estimation to which, from his intellectual attainments, he deems himself entitled. The nicer shades of manners he disregards, but whenever, upon looking back upon past ages, or in surveying the practices of different countries in the age in which he lives, he find such contrarieties as seem to affect the principles of *morals*, he exults over

31 manifested A: magnifested B (*an attempt to correct* magnified).

35–6 manifested A: manifest B.

45 which B: *om.* A.

49 provocatives AB: provocations [or provocation] A^2.

50 chasing A: ch[*tear*]ing B.

51 twofold: *Edd.*: twofold, A: twofold B.

59 upon looking B: in looking A.

his discovery, and applies it to his heart as the dearest of his consolations. Such a mind cannot but discover some truths, but he is unable to profit by them, and in his hands they become instruments of evil.

He presses truth and falshood into the same service. He looks at society through an optical glass of a peculiar tint; something of the forms of objects he takes from objects, but their colour is exclusively what he gives them; it is one, and it is his own. Having indulged a habit, dangerous in a man who has fallen, of dallying with moral calculations, he becomes an empiric, and a daring & unfeeling empiric. He disguises from himself his own malignity by assuming the character of a spectator in morals, and one who has the hardihood to realize his speculations.

It will easily be perceived that to such a mind those enterprizes which are the most extraordinary will in time appear the most inviting. His appetite from being exhausted becomes unnatural. Accordingly, he will struggle so [ ] to characterize & to exalt actions, little and contemptible in themselves, by a forced greatness of *manner*, and will chequer & degrade enterprizes great in their atrocity by grotesque littleness of manner, and fantastic obliquities. He is like a worn out voluptuary—he finds his temptation in strangeness, he is unable to suppress a low hankering after the *double entendre* in vice; yet his thirst after the extraordinary buoys him up, and, supported by a habit of constant reflexion, he frequently breaks out into what has the appearance of greatness; and, in sudden emergencies, when he is called upon by surprize & thrown out of the part of his regular habits, or when dormant associations are awakened tracing the revolutions through which his character has passed, in painting his former self he really *is* great.

Benefits conferred on a man like this will be the seeds of a worse feeling than ingratitude. They will give birth to positive hatred. Let him be deprived of power, though by means which he despises, & he will never forgive. It will scarcely be denied that such a mind, by very slight external motives, may be led to the commission of the greatest enormities. Let its malignant feelings be fixed on a particular object, & the rest follows of itself.

Having shaken off the obligations of religion & morality in a dark and tempestuous age, it is probable that such a character will be infected with a tinge

65 service. A: service B.

75 *A blank space after* so *in both manuscripts.*

77 *manner,* A: *manner* B.

80 *entendre*] altered to *entente* in pencil in A.

84 regular A^{2}B: general A.

of superstition. The period in which he lives teems with great events, which he feels he cannot controul. That influence which his pride makes him unwilling to allow to his fellow-men he has no reluctance to ascribe to invisible agents: his pride impels him to superstition and shapes out the nature of his belief: his creed is his own: it is made & not adopted.

A character like this, or some of its features at least, I have attempted to delineate in the following drama. I have introduced him deliberately prosecuting the destruction of an amiable young man by the most atrocious means, & with a pertinacity, as it should seem, not to be accounted for but on the supposition of the most malignant injuries. No such injuries, however, appear to have been sustained. What are, then, his motives? First, it must be observed that to make the non-existence of a common motive itself a motive to action is a practice which we are never so prone to attribute exclusively to madmen as when we forget ourselves. Our love of the marvellous is not confined to external things. There is no object on which it settles with more delight than on our own minds. This habit is in the very essence of the habit which we are delineating.

But there are particles of that poisonous mineral of which Iago speaks gnawing his inwards, his malevolent feelings are excited, & he hates the more deeply because he feels he ought not to hate.

We all know that the dissatisfaction accompanying the first impulses towards a criminal action, where the mind is familiar with guilt, acts as a stimulus to proceed in that action. Uneasiness must be driven away by fresh uneasiness, obstinacy, waywardness, & wilful blindness are alternatives resorted to, till there is an universal insurrection of every depraved feeling of the heart.

Besides, in a course of criminal conduct every fresh step that we make appears a justification of the one that preceded it, it seems to bring back again the moment of liberty and choice; it banishes the idea of repentance, and seems to remorse at defiance. Every time we plan a fresh accumulation of our guilt, we have restored to us something like that original state of mind, that perturbed pleasure, which first made the crime attractive.

If, after these general remarks, I am asked what are Rivers's motives to the atrocity detailed in the drama? I answer: they are founded chiefly in the very constitution of his character; in his pride which borders even upon madness, in

105 are, then, *Edd.*: are then B: then are A.
119–20 appears B, *written over deln.*: seems A.
120 that B: which A.
122 of B: to A.
125 I am asked] *inserted in pencil into a blank* A: blank b.
126 drama? B: drama A.
126 founded B: found A.

his restless disposition, in his disturbed mind, in his superstition, in irresistible propensities to embody in practical experiments his worst & most extravagant speculations, in his thoughts & in his feelings, in his general habits & his particular impulses, in his perverted reason justifying his perverted instincts. The general moral intended to be impressed by the delineation of such a character is obvious: it is the shew the dangerous use which may be made of reason when a man has committed a great crime.

There is a kind of superstition which makes us shudder when we find moral sentiments to which we attach a sacred importance applied to vicious purposes. In real life this is done every day, and we do not feel the disgust. The difference is here. In works of imagination we see the motive and the end. In real life we rarely see either the one or the other; and, when the distress comes, it prevents us from attending to the cause. This superstition of which I have spoken is not without its use; yet it appears to be one great source of our vices; it is our constant engine in seducing each other. We are lulled asleep by its agency, and betrayed before we know that an attempt is made to betray us.

I have endeavoured to shake this prejudice, persuaded that in so doing I was well employed. It has been a further object with me to shew that, from abuses interwoven with the texture of society, a bad man may be furnished with sophisms in support of his crimes which it would be difficult to answer.

One word more upon the subject of motives. In private life what is more common than, when we hear of law–suits prosecuted to the utter ruin of the parties, and the most deadly feuds in families, to find them attributed to trifling and apparently inadequate sources? But when our malignant passions operate, the original causes which called them forth are soon supplanted, yet when we account for the effect we forget the immediate impulse, and the whole is attributed to the force from which the first motion was received. The vessel keeps sailing on, and we attribute her progress in the voyage to the ropes which first towed her out of harbour.

To this must be added that we are too apt to apply our own moral sentiments

133 obvious: *Edd.*: obvious, AB.
136 vicious A^{2}B: virtuous A.
151 sources? *Edd.*: sources. AB.

as a measure of the conduct of others. We insensibly suppose that a criminal action assumes the same form to the agent as to ourselves. We forget that his feelings and his reason are equally busy in contracting its dimensions and pleading for its necessity.

A Tragedy

On human actions reason though you can,
It may be reason, but it is not man;
His principle of action once explore,
That instant 'tis his principle no more.
Pope.

167 A tragedy B: *om.* A.
168 On A *recte*: Of B.
172 Pope. B: *om.* A.

COMMENTARY

2. benevolence] Godwin's usual criterion for moral worth: *Enquiry Concerning Political Justice*, ed. F. E. L. Priestley (Toronto, 1946), i. 149: 'virtue [is] any action or actions of an intelligent being, proceeding from kind and benevolent intentions, and having a tendency to contribute to general happiness'; i. 433: 'Benevolent intention is essential to virtue.'

4. betrayed into a great crime] See *Bord.* 1689 ff. Oswald explains how he was duped by a ship's company into marooning the ship's captain, and thus ensuring his death, in the mistaken belief that the captain had plotted 'Against my honour' (1691); so that what appeared an act of justice turned out to be a virtual murder.

4. influence] Oswald's influence over others; cf. 21: 'the loss of authority and influence which followed upon his crime'; *Bord,* 1761–3: 'my power at once / Shrunk from me; plans and schemes, and lofty hopes – / All vanished.'

6–7. he quits the world in disgust] See *Bord.* 1766–8: 'I hid my head within a Convent, there / Lay passive as a dormouse in mid winter. / That was no life for me.'

7–19. In his retirement ... action & meditation] See Oswald's account, *Bord.* 1771–94; note the reading of MS. B (1782–7, textual n.): 'Thirsting for some exploits of power and terror.'

8. examine the reasonableness of established opinions] Cf. *Bord.* 1815–16: 'I turned to contemplate / The World's opinions and her usages.'

12–13. While ... crime] Cf. *Bord.* 1560–2: 'Remorse— / It cannot live with thought; think on, think on, / And it will die.' Oswald indulges in purely rational speculations to escape from his emotions, like Coleridge: 'not to think of what I needs must feel, / But ... by abstruse research to steal / From my own nature all the natural man' ('Dejection', 87–90).

17. his natural energy ... into the world] Cf. *Bord.* 1780–1: 'I saw that every possible shape of action / Might lead to good—I saw it and burst forth'; 1787–90: 'I had within me evermore / A salient spring of energy; I mounted / From action up to action with a mind / That never rested.'

19. meditation] See 57 ff.

21–2, textual n. The copyist of MS. B copied down to 'crime' (24) and resumed after 'crime' (25).

27–31. good actions … extensive] Cf. *E. E.* II. 55–61: 'it is the nature of Vice to force itself upon notice, both in the act and by its consequences.... on the contrary, the virtues … are retired.'

31–2. Power … creating] Cf. *Bord.* 1432–4: 'Power is life to him / And breath and being; where he cannot govern, / He will destroy.'

32–3. A child … one] The nearest parallel we have found in Rousseau is in *Émile*, in *Œuvres complètes de J. J.Rousseau* (Paris, 1882), ii. 36:

> Avant l'âge de raison, nous faisons le bien et le mal sans le connoître; et il n'y a point de moralité dans nos actions … Un enfant veut déranger tout ce qu'il voit; il casse, il brise tout ce qu'il peut atteindre; il empoigne un oiseau comme il empoignerait une pierre, et l'etouffe sans savoir ce qu'il fait … L'activité défaillante se concentre dans le cœur du viellard; dans celui de l'enfant elle est surabondante et s'étend au dehors; il se sent, pour ainsi dire, assez de vie pour animer tout ce qui l'environne. Qu'il fasse ou qu'il défasse, il n'importe; il suffit qu'il change l'état des choses, et tout changement est une action. Que s'il semble avoir plus de penchant à détruire, ce n'est point par méchanceté, c'est que l' action qui forme est toujours lente, et que celle qui détruire, ce n'est point par méchanceté, c'est que l'action qui forme est toujours lente, et que celle qui détruit, étant plus rapide, convient mieux à sa vivacité.

35. manifested] MS. B ('manifest') makes sense, but the reading of MS. A is probably correct: cf. 32 above. The ending *–ed* in MS. A is now very close to the right-hand margin of a verso page, and was probably at one time obscured by stitching (now removed from the manuscript); it may therefore have escaped the copyist's notice.

36. Orlando … shelter him] *Orlando Furioso*, xxiii. 131–5. In *Don Quixote*, Book III, Chs. ix–x, Cardenio is seen, and described as being, in a savage state, and in Ch. xiii he himself relates his lapse into savage madness. He does not, however, appear to 'lay waste the groves that should shelter him'. Wordsworth is perhaps confused, since in this context (Ch. xi) Don Quixote himself proposes to emulate the violence of Orlando's madness.

37. He has rebelled … laws of the world] Cf. *Bord.* 596–7: 'these disputed tracts, that own / No law but what each man makes for himself.'

41–2. Being … war with him] Cf. *Bord.* 1827–30: 'I felt that merit has no surer test / Than obloquy; that, if we wish to serve / The world … / We must become obnoxious to its hate.'

44–5. Add … contempt] Cf. *Bord.* 18–19: 'he [Oswald] despised alike Mohammedan and Christian'; 553–4: 'The insult bred / More of contempt than hatred [in Oswald].'

45–6. which are considered under any uncommon bond of relation] A difficult phrase; if the text is right, the sense is perhaps: 'which are not usually considered in such mutual connection as that in which he considers them'. Cf. the discussion of unwarranted antithesis in Popean epitaphs, *E.E.* II. 447 ff.

47–8. the feelings ... other] Cf. *Prel.* XI. 326–7: 'feeling comes in aid / Of feeling.'

50, textual n. The reading of MS. A is more like 'chusing' than 'chasing'. MS. B has been rubbed or scraped to a hole at this point, possibly in an attempt to correct 'chusing' (or 'choosing') when it was realized that this reading hardly gives sense.

52–4. his reason ... crime] Cf. *Morals*, 46–52: 'when we have been unworthily employed...we are all activity & keenness; then it is that we repair to systems of morality for arguments in defence of ourselves;& sure enough are we to find them.... lifeless words, & abstract propositions, will not be destitute of power to lay asleep the spirit of self-accusation & exclude the uneasiness of repentance.' For the last phrase in the present passage, cf. 146–7: 'sophisms in support of his crimes which it would be difficult to answer'.

55. the milk of human reason] *Macbeth*, I. V. 18: 'the milk of human kindness'. Cf. *Bord.* 620–8, textual n.: 'compassion's milk' (reading of MS. B).

56–7. possible forms ... no longer crimes] Cf. *Bord.* 1818–19: 'a region of futurity / Whose natural element was freedom', 1855–6: 'Let us be fellow-labourers, then, to enlarge / Man's intellectual empire.'

59, textual n. MS. B 'upon looking' may be an anticipation of 'upon past ages'; MS. A 'in looking ... or in surveying' is perhaps more natural idiom.

73–4. those enterprizes ... inviting] Cf. *Bord.* 1436: 'There is no crime from which this man would shrink.'

75, textual n. The blank space after 'so' in both MSS. seems to have been left for the insertion of an adverb; but in fact the sentence would be expected to take the form: 'so to characterize ... that...'. As it stands, it would be incomplete without 'so'.

84–6. when dormant ... *is* great] Oswald is engaged in 'painting his former self' in *Bord.* 1684–1844; and though the revelation is perhaps the most fascinating part of the play, it is not clear in what sense he is 'really ... great' in this passage.

87–8. Benefits ... hatred] Cf. *Bord.* 27–31: 'You know that you have saved his life ... / And that he hates you! ... gratitude's a heavy burden / To a proud Soul'; 918–21: 'this Stripling / Must needs step in, and save my life. The look / With which he gave the boon—I see it now! / The same that tempted me to loathe the gift.' Gratitude is excluded from virtue by Godwin, *Political Justice*, ed. cit., i. 128–9:

> Every voluntary benefit ... entitles the bestower to some kindness and retribution. Why? Because a voluntary benefit is an evidence of benevolent intention, that is, in a certain degree, of virtue ... But the merit of this disposition is equal, whether the benefit were conferred upon me or upon another ... Gratitude therefore, if by gratitude we understand a sentiment of preference which I entertain towards another, upon the ground of my having been the subject of his benefits, is no part either of justice or virtue.

Godwin does not, however, claim that gratitude is a burden on the mind of the man benefited.

88–9. Let him ... forgive] Oswald is insulted because the Borderers chose Marmaduke for their chief, instead of himself (*Bord.* 551–5).

94–8. a tinge of superstition ... his pride impels him to superstition] Cf. *Bord.* 1440–1: 'his pride has built / Some uncouth superstition of its own'; and the following anecdote, *Bord.* 1442–7.

96–7. That influence ... agents] Cf. *Bord.* 1452–5: 'Such Minds as find amid their fellow-men / No heart that loves them, none that they can love, / Will turn perforce and seek for sympathy / In dim relation to imagined Beings.'

99. his creed ... adopted] Cf. n. on 41–2.

105–8. What are ... ourselves] Cf. *Bord.* 1427–32: 'But for the motive? Natures such as his / Spin motives out of their own bowels ... there needs no other motive / Than that most strange incontinence in crime / Which haunts this Oswald.' Did a recollection of this passage suggest Coleridge's remark on Iago's 'motive-hunting of motiveless malignity' (*S.C.* i. 44)?

108–9. Our love ... minds] Cf. *Bord.* 1168–70: 'the mind of man, upturned, / Is in all natures a strange spectacle; / In some a hideous one [Is a strange spectacle! MS. B].'

110. habit ... habit] Though this is clearly the reading of both MSS., the sense is unconvincing, and possibly the second 'habit' has been written for some word now irrecoverable, such as 'man' or 'character'; cf. 100: 'A character like this...I have attempted to delineate', 126–7: 'Rivers's [Oswald's] motives...are founded chiefly in the very constitution of his character'. In the following paragraph, the pronouns 'his' and 'he', clearly referring to Oswald (except in the phrase 'his [Iago's] inwards'), seem to require a personal antecedent, not the abstract 'habit', and there is no such antecedent nearby in the present text.

111–2, that poisonous ... inwards] *Othello*, II. i. 308–9: 'the thought ... / Doth like a poisonous mineral gnaw my inwards'. Cf. *Bord.* 1566–7: 'the thing had never been / Whose very shadow gnaws us to the vitals.'

119–24. Cf. *Bord.* 1431–2, cited above, n. to 105–8.

125, textual n. I am asked] In his printing of *P. Bord.* In *Oxford Lectures on Poetry* (Oxford, 1934), pp. 157–79 (there reprinted from *Nineteenth Century*, Nov. 1926), de Selincourt notes (p. 169) that he 'supplied these words to fill a blank space in the manuscript'. At this date, or at any rate in 1926, de Selincourt knew only our MS. B of *P. Bord.* (*Lectures*, pp. 164–5). It seems likely, therefore, that the pencilled insertion in MS. A derives directly or indirectly from de Selincourt rather than from a Wordsworthian source; but as some such phrase is required by the sense, we have accepted it in our text. The proper name 'Rivers' belongs to the state of the play represented by MS. B of *Bord.*, of which MS.B of *P. Bord.* is a part. There is not sufficient evidence to determine when the alteration in our MS. A was made, but it may have been in 1842 or even later (*P.W.* i. 343–4).

127. his pride which borders even upon madness ... his restless disposition] Cf. *Bord.* 1448 ff.: 'A most subtle doctor / Were that man, who could draw the line that parts / Pride ... from Madness, / ... Restless Minds... / Will ... seek for sympathy / In dim relation to imagined Beings'; 1788–90: 'I mounted / From action up to action with a mind / That never rested.'

129. practical experiments] Cf. *Bord.* 1782–7, textual n. (reading of MS. B): 'my brain ... teemed with projects / Which seemed to have no limit'. Coleridge called Iago 'a preconceiving *experimenter*' (*S.C.* i. 40).

135–43. A possible explanation of this difficult paragraph, and of the use of 'superstition', is given in Moorman, i. 305. Another follows:

> In real life, moral sentiments are constantly applied to vicious purposes, but usually we do not feel any disgust because the total situation is not clear to us, i.e. we usually do not see the viciousness of the purpose, and therefore we do not see the incongruity between the sentiment and the purpose which would, if seen, occasion the disgust. In art, the total situation is clear, and so, therefore, is the incongruity. In real life, moreover, the distress arising from a vicious action, if we happen to be the victims of it, helps to prevent us from seeing the total situation. We shudder, however, when we do see, or think we see, the incongruity (in real life or in art); and our shuddering is, as it were, that of a superstitious man in the presence of what he regards as the supernatural.
>
> This superstition can be morally useful because, when the shudder occurs, we recognize it as a sign or warning that moral sentiments are being perverted to vicious purposes. If, however, the shudder can be roused in us when the situation does not in fact warrant it, it may serve as an 'engine in seducing each other', because the man subject to it supposes that he sees the whole situation clearly, whereas his view of it is false or partial, and he is therefore an easy target for 'betrayal'. It is thus an unreliable moral guide, and Wordsworth wishes to expose its unreliability.

Superstition in this version means 'superstitious cast of mind' (as in 95, 98 above), rather than 'superstitious belief', which is represented rather by Wordsworth;s 'prejudice' (144). Situations of the kind envisaged are those of *Othello* and *The Borderers*: Iago induces Othello to see an incongruity between Desdemona's protestations of innocence and generous behaviour on behalf of Cassio, and her supposed sexual infidelity; Oswald induces Marmaduke to see an incongruity between Herbert's language of tender fatherhood and his supposed aim of virtually selling his daughter into prostition (cf. *Bord.* 249: 'Her [Idonea's] virtues are his [Herbert's] instruments'). In each case, the 'shudder' of the betrayed hero leads him to bring about the destruction of the innocent victim.—We are indebted to Julian Patrick for suggestions towards this note.

145. abuses] The evil reputation of Lord Clifford (*Bord.* 279–80, 540–2, 568–9, etc.)? The false witness of the beggar-woman, or, rather, her poverty which leaves her open to bribery (*Bord.* 364 ff., etc.)?

148–51. In private ... sources?] On Wordsworth's experience with lawsuits see Moorman, i. 167–9. He would hardly have attributed the efforts of his own family against Lord Lonsdale to 'trifling and apparently inadequate sources'. Cf. *Llandaff*, 541–54 and n.

165–6. pleading for its necessity] Cf. *Paradise Lost*, IV. 393–4: 'neccessitie / The Tyrants plea'; *Prel.* X. 310–1 (of the reaction in France to the British declaration of war in 1793): 'Tyrants, strong before, / In devilish pleas were ten times stronger now.'

168–71. On human ... no more] Pope, 'Epistle to Cobham', 35–8 [25–8]. No authoritative text appears to read 'Of' (184), which is no doubt a copyist's error in MS. B.

4.

Conversations with Klopstock

INTRODUCTION

THE conversations of Wordsworth and Coleridge with Klopstock during their stay in Hamburg are recorded in Wordsworth's hand in a small notebook (MS. Journal 5) preserved in the Wordsworth Library, Grasmere. The main content of the book is Dorothy Wordsworth's Journal for 14 February–2 May 1802, but it must have been in use in 1798, since it contains part of her Journal of the Wordsworth's visit to Germany; it also contains the drafts for *The Prelude*, Book I, known as MS. JJ, and the prose fragment which we have called 'Essay on Morals'. The text of the Conversations has reached its present state by corrections and alterations made usually *currente calamo*; these are mostly of small significance, having to do with the layout rather than the substance of sentences, and our record of them is therefore selective. Apart from full stops and the dash which sometimes does duty therefor, the manuscript is inadequately punctuated, and we have added a minimum of pointing for the sake of intelligibility.

The notes record three meetings with Klopstock (1–43, 54–144, 145 ff.), though they do not make it clear at the proper point whether the visit to Remnant's bookshop (44 ff.) was an interlude in the first visit or a prelude to the second. Coleridge (*C.L.* i. 441–3) records the first visit as taking place on 21 September 1798, and his account of that visit gives nothing which Wordsworth records later than 43 except a reference to 'Nelson's Victory' (cf. 49). Wordsworth must therefore have made a second visit to Klopstock's house, without Coleridge, and on the same day (145) he dined with Klopstock's brother and had 'a third interview with the poet'. The dinner took place on 26 September (*Journals*, i. 24; cf. *C.L.* i, 443–5). Wordsworth, we surmise, wrote down his notes between this date and 20 November, when Coleridge presumably drew on them for his account of the dinner (*C.L.* i. 443–5).

In *The Friend*, No. 18 (21 December 1809), and in *Biog. Lit.* ii. 169–79, Coleridge drew on Wordsworth's notes for the make-weight essays called *Satyrane's Letters*. The latter part of the passage which concerns us (*Biog. Lit.* ii. 175–9) is quoted almost verbatim from the notes printed here (42 ff.); the earlier part (especially *Biog. Lit.* ii 169–71) is a conflation of Coleridge's letter to Poole of 20 November 1798 (*C.L.* i. 441–3) with Wordsworth's notes, rather than a mere revision of this letter, as is implied by Shawcross (*Biog. Lit.* ii, 295) and Griggs (*C.L.* iii. 261, n. 3): note, for instance, 'commonplace' (3), 'beyond which ... roads' (5), 'detachment ... entertainment' (13–15), 'By the bye ... dirt' (32–34), all passages which occur in Wordsworth's notes but not in Coleridge's letter to Poole. Coleridge's 'I looked ... German poetry' (*Biog.Lit.* ii. 171; *C.L.* i. 442) may have been suggested by *Journals*, i, 25: 'I could not ... sensible emotion'; but the borrowing, if any, may be in the conflated text there are variants between Wordsworth's manuscript and Coleridge's printed version; but as we have no reason to think that any Wordsworthian authority attaches to these variants we have not usually recorded them.

[CONVERSATIONS WITH KLOPSTOCK]

MR KLOPSTOCK took us to see his brother the poet, who lives about a qr of a mile out of the town. In chusing his residence, the poet does not seem to have been influenced by poetic ideas. His house is one amongst a range of commonplace houses with four or five rows of trees of a few years growth before the windows, beyond which is a green, and a dead flat intersected with several roads; but no object whatsoever to interest the eye. We were ushered into a plain, decent room, ornamented with a few drawings or plates (I believe from the Messiah), and the figures of two of the muses. We had not been here two minutes before the poet himself made his appearance. I was somewhat disappointed in his countenance, in which I was not able to discover the marks either of sublimity or enthusiasm. We began a conversation in french upon the events which had just taken place in Ireland. He spoke with great liveliness and spirit upon the surrender of the detachment of french troops under General Humbert; and their proceedings with regard to the committee which they have appointed and the rest of their organizing system seemed to have given him great entertainment.

—He said they had in the german language no history of german poetry. He did not appear to have regularly studied the poetry of his country before his own times—He spoke in terms of approbation of [ ] He preferred the blank verse of Glover (each verse separately considered) to that of Milton—but agreed with me that the true harmony of blank verse consisted in the periods and not in a succession of musical lines. He showed us a new edition of his works in quarto which is printing at Leipsig; and read us some passages from his odes in which he has adopted the latin measures. I must candidly [? avow] that my ear was unable to discover the alcaic movement in the specimens which he read us—He said he had read a translation of Milton when he was fourteen years old. He spoke with great animation on the powers of the german language, particularly on the score of compression—He observed that his first ode was 50 years elder than the last. He is now in his 74th year. His teeth are almost entirely gone, and ▶

3 range MS.²: row MS.
12 upon MS.²: upon the subject of MS.
16 He said MS.²: I enquired if MS.
16 no MS.²: any MS.
17 poetry MS.²: poetry. He answered in the negative MS.

his legs are much swelled. Yet he expresses himself with the liveliness of a girl of seventeen—this is striking to an Englishman, and rendered him an interesting object; and such I found him, notwithstanding his enormous powdered and frizzled periwig. By the bye, old men ought never to wear powder—the contrast between a large snow white wig and the colour of an old man's skin is disgusting; and wrinkles in such a neighbourhood appear only channels for dirt.

C spoke of a work which he wished to execute, namely, a history of german poetry; and added that he hoped to have the pleasure of translating some of his odes as specimens. He begged that if he did so he would likewise give some fragments of the Messiah to *revenge* him of the man who had made so execrable, so detestable a translation of that work. He spoke with much feeling on this subject. He mentioned Ebert's translation of Leonidas and Young's Night Thoughts as the best translation from the English which they had. By the bye, Ebert was his particular friend. He wished to see the Calvary of Cumberland, and asked what [? we *or* ? was] thought of it in England.—

Went to Remnant, the English bookseller, where I procured the analytical review in which is contained the review of Cumberland's Calvary. I remembered to have read there some specimens of a blank verse translation of the Messiah. I had mentioned this to Klopstock, and he had a great desire to have a sight of them. I walked over to his house and put the book into his hand[? s]. We talked of admiral Nelson's rumoured victory; he was all [? faith]. I had my doubts. He began the Messiah when he was seventeen; he devoted three entire years to the plan without composing a single word. He was greatly at a loss in what manner to execute his work. There were no successful specimens of versification in the german language before his time. The first three cantos he wrote in a species of measured or numerous prose. This, though done with much labour and some success, was far from satisfying him. He had composed hexameters both latin and greek as a school exercise, and there had been also in the german language attempts in that style of versification. These were only of very moderate merit.—One day he was struck with the idea of trying what could be done in this way. He kept his room a whole day, even went without his dinner, and found that in the evening he had written 23 hexameters, versifying a part of what he had before written in prose. From that time, pleased with his efforts, he composed no more in prose. Today he informed me that he had finished his

32 periwig MS.[2]: periwig which he wore MS.
32 powder— MS.[2]: powder— With a powdered wig MS.
32 contrast MS.[2]: contrast is so striking MS.
52 There were MS.[2]: [?He had] MS.

plan before he read Milton. He was enchanted to see an author who before him had trod the same path. This is a contradiction of what he said before. He did not wish to speak of his poem to any one till it was finished: but some of his friends who had seen what he had finished tormented him till he consented to publish a few books in a journal—He was then, I believe, very young, about 25. The rest were printed at different periods, [? four *or* ? five] books at a time. The reception given to the first specimen[? s] was highly flattering. He was near thirty years in finishing the whole poem, but of these thirty years not more than two were employed in the composition. He only composed in favourable moments. Besides, he had other occupations.—He values himself upon the plans of his odes, and accuses the modern lyrical writers of gross deficiency in this respect. I laid the same accusation against Horace; he would not hear of it. But we waived the discussion.

He called Rousseau's ode to Fortune a moral dissertation in stanzas. I spoke of Dryden's Cecilia, but he did not seem familiar with our writers. He wished to know the distinctions between our dramatic & epic blank verse.—He recommended to me to read his drama on the story of Arviragus before I read either his Messiah or his odes. He flattered himself that some time or other these would be known in England. He had not heard of Cowper. He thought that Voss in his translation of the iliad had done violence to the idiom of the germans & had sacrificed it to the greek, not remembering sufficiently that each language has its particular spirit and genius. He said Lessing was the first of their dramatic authors. I complained of Nathan [ ] as tedious—He said there was not enough of action in it, but that Lessing was the most chaste of their writers. He spoke favourably of Goethe, but said that his sorrows of Werter was his best work, better than any of his dramas. He preferred the first written to the rest of Goethe's dramas. Schiller's robbers he found so extravagant that he could not read it. I spoke of the scene of the setting sun. He did not know it. He said Schiller could not live. He thought Don Carlos might be the best of his dramas, but said that the plot was inextricable—It was evident he knew little of Schiller's work [? s], indeed he said he could not read them. Bürger, he said, was a true poet an[d] would live; that Schiller, on the contrary, must soon be forgotten, that he gave himself up to the imitation of Shakespear, who often was extravagant, but that Schiller was ten thousand times more so. He spoke very slightingly of Kotzebue as an immoral author in the first place, and next as deficient in power;

64 is MS.[2]: [? In some degree] MS.

at Vienna, said he, they are transported with him, but we do not reckon the people of Vienna either wisest or the wittiest people of Germany. He said Wieland was a charming author, and a sovereign Master of his own language; that in this respect Goethe could not be compared to him, nor, indeed, anybody else. He said that his fault was to be fertile to exuberance. I told him the Oberon had just been translated into English. He asked if I was not delighted with the poem. I answered that I thought the story began to flag about 7th or eighth book; and observed that it was unworthy of a man of genius to make the interest of a long poem turn entirely upon animal gratification. He seemed at first disposed to excuse this by saying that there are different subjects for poetry, and that poets are not willing to be restricted in their choice. I answered that I thought the passion of love as well suited to the purpose[? s] of poetry as any other passion, but that it was a cheap way of pleasing to fix the attention of the reader through a long poem on the mere sexual enjoyment. Well, but, said [*or* ? says] he, you see that such poems please every body. I answered that it was the province of a great poet to raise people up to his own level, not to descend to theirs. He agreed, and confessed that on no account whatsoever would he have written a work like the Oberon. He spoke in raptures of Wieland's style, and pointed out the passage where Retzia is delivered of her child as exquisitely beautiful. I said that I did not perceive any very striking passages in the poem, but that I made allowance for the imperfections of a translation. Of the thefts of Wieland he said they were so exquisitely managed that the greatest writers might be proud to steal as he did. He considered the books and fables of the old [? roman *or* ? romance] writers in the light of the antient mythology as a sort of common property from which a man was free to take whatever he could make good use of.—An Englishman had presented him with the odes of Collins; he had read them with pleasure—He seemed to know little or nothing of Gray except his churchyard. He complained of the fool in Lear. I observed that he seemed to give a terrible wildness to the distress. That might be, but still he complained. Upon the whole he did not seem to be at all familiar with our writers—He asked whether it was not allowed that Pope had written rhyme poetry with more skill than any of our writers. I said I preferred Dryden, because his couplets had greater variety in their movement. He thought my reason a good one, but asked whether the

99 either wisest] *so in* MS.
102 I told him MS.[2]: He asked if MS.
104 about 7th] *so in* MS.
107 there *Edd*,: their MS.
109 any MS.[2]: what MS.
119–20 as he did MS.[2]: like him MS.
122 was free to MS.[2]: might MS.

rhymes of Pope were not more exact. This question I understood as applying to the final terminations; and I observed to him that I believed it was the case, but that I thought it easy to excuse some inaccuracy if the final sounds in the general sweep of the verse was superior. I told him that we were not so exact with regard to the final endings of lines as the french. He did not seem to know that we made no distinction between masculine & feminine rimes; at least he put inquiries to me upon this subject. He seemed to think that no language could ever be so far formed as that it might no be enriched by idioms borrowed from another tongue. I said I thought this a very dangerous practice—and, like him, that I thought Milton had often injured both his prose and his verse by taking this liberty too frequently. I recommended to him the prose works of Dryden as models of pure and native English.—I was treading on tender ground, as I have reason to suppose that he has himself liberally indulged in the practice I took upon me to condemn.—

The same day we dined at Mr Klopstock's, when I had the pleasure of a third interview with the poet. We talked principally about indifferent things. I asked him what he thought of Kant. He said that his reputation was much on the decline in Germany. That for his own part he was not suprised to find it so, as the works of Kant were to him utterly incomprehensible.—He said he had often been pestered by the Kanteans; that he was rarely in the practice of arguing with them; that his custom was to produce the book, open it, and point to a passage and beg they would explain it. This they ordinarily attempted to do by substituting their own ideas. I do not want, said he, an explanation of your ideas, but of the passage which is before us. In this way I generally bring the dispute to an immediate conclusion. He spoke of Wolfe as the first metaphysician they [? had *or* ? have] had in Germany. Wolfe had followers but they could hardly be called a sect; and luckily, till the appearance of Kant about ten years ago, Germany had not been pestered by any sect of philosophers whatsoever; but that each man had separately pursued his enquiries uncontrolled by the dogmas of a master. Kant had appeared ambitious to be the founder of a sect; that he had succeeded; but that the germans were now coming to their senses again. That Nicolai & Engel had, in different ways, contributed to disenchant the Nation, but, above all, the incomprehensibility of the philosopher & his philosophy. He seemed pleased to hear that, as yet, Kant's doctrines had not met with many admirers

131 Pope MS.[2]: Dryden MS.

143 practice MS.[2]: practice that MS.

in England; did not doubt but that we had too much wisdom to be duped by a writer who set at defiance the common sense and the common understandings of men.—We talked of tragedy; he seemed to rate too highly the power of exciting tears. I said that nothing was more easy than to deluge an audience. That it was done every day by the meanest writers.

(Ariosto—

165 did not doubt but that MS.[2]: [? and hoped that] MS.
165 too much wisdom *Edd.*: wisdom MS.[2]: had too much [?sen] MS.
166 writer MS.[2]: [? philos] MS.
167 to rate *Edd.*: to be rate MS.

COMMENTARY

1. the poet] Friedrich Gottlieb Klopstock (1724–1803). His brother, 'Mr. Klopstock', was 'a sort of Merchant in the agency line ... the Proprietor of one of the Hamburgh Newspapers', introduced to Coleridge by his partner, 'Mr Chatterley' (*C.L.* i. 436–7).

7. Messiah] *Der Messias*, Klopstock's major work, an epic in twenty cantos, was published (as is indicated below, 67–71), in instalments from 1748 to 1773.

11–3. events ... Humbert] On 22 August 1798 General Joseph Amable Humbert (1767–1823) and about 1,000 French troops landed at Killala, County Mayo, with the intention of supporting an Irish rebellion. They took Castlebar on 27 August, and, after manœuvres and skirmishes, in which they received no effective support from the Irish, they surrendered to overwhelming forces under Cornwallis at Ballinamuck on 8 September. It is not clear whether the 'committee' next mentioned (16) is connected with some episode in this campaign which we have not found recorded, or whether the reference is to the general conduct of the war by the French.

19. Glover] Richard Glover (1712–85), author of *Leonidas* (1737), an epic in blank verse; cf. 40.

21. a new edition] *Werke*, 12 vols., 1798–1817.

25. a translation of Milton] That of Johann Jakob Bodmer (1698–1783), published in 1732.

35–6. a history of german poetry] Shortly after this interview, Wordsworth was asking Coleridge, 'Have you been able to get any information concerning the earlier poets of Germany?' and offering possible sources of information (*E.Y.*, p. 235). The 'history' appears soon to have been transformed into 'a Life of Lessing–& interweaved with it a true state of German Literature, in it's rise & present state (*C.L.* i. 455; 4 Jan. 1799); cf. also *C.L.* i. 518 (21 May 1799): 'a history of the Belles Lettres in Germany before the time of Lessing.' After this, references to the Life of Lessing are comparatively frequent, but the projected history seems to disappear until 1816 (*C.L.* iv. 664).

38–9. the man who ... translation] Klopstock's *Der Messias* was translated into English prose by Mary and Joseph Collyer (*The Messiah. Attempted from the German of Mr. Klopstock. To which is prefixed his Introduction on Divine Poetry*, 2 vols., 1763).

40. Ebert's translation] Johann Arnold Ebert (1723–95) translated Glover's *Leonidas* (1766) and Young's *Night Thoughts* (1751–2, and later revised editions). The catalogue of the Wordsworth Library, Grasmere, lists Wordsworth's copy of Ebert's *Epistelen, und vermischte Gedichte*, Zweiter Theil, ed. J. J. Eschenburg, which is said to have been 'given by Klopstock, 1798'.

42–6. Calvary ... Messiah] *Analytical Review*, xiii (June 1792), 121–38, reviews '*Calvary: or, The Death of Christ. A Poem, in eight Books.* By Richard Cumberland ... 1792.' Lengthy excerpts from the poem are given on pp. 124–6, 127, 128–9. On p. 130 the review compares Milton and Klopstock, and speaks of the 'execrable prose translation, which can scarcely be said to convey the skeleton of [Klopstock's] plan'. The review concludes (pp. 130–8) with specimens of a translation, presumably by the reviewer ('R.R.'), in Miltonic blank verse, corresponding to *Der Messias* (1748), II. 427–736 and IV. 110–71 (in *Werke*, ed. Hamel, Deutsche National-Litteratur, Berlin and Stuttgart, n. d, i. 91–111, 180–3).

49. Nelson's rumoured victory] The Battle of the Nile, 1 August 1798.

67–8. a few books ... at a time.] Cantos 1–3 of *Der Messias* were published in *Bremer Beiträge* for 1748; they were reprinted, with Cantos 4–5, as Vol. I of the work, in 1751. Cantos 1–10 appeared in a two-volume edition published in Copenhagen in 1755. Cantos 11–15 appeared in 1768, Cantos 16–20 in 1773. Edition of Klopstock's *Works* appeared in 1781 and 1798 (mentioned above, 25). If Wordsworth reported Klopstock correctly, the reading 'five' must be accepted, and Coleridge's 'four' (*Biog. Lit.* ii. 176) is wrong. Apart from the initial *f*-, the word is almost illegible in the manuscript.

76. Rousseau's ode to Fortune] Jean-Baptiste Rousseau (1671–1741), 'Ode à la Fortune', in *Les Œuvres de M*[r] *Rousseau* (Paris, 1716), i. 96–103.

77. Dryden's Cecilia] *A Song for St. Cecilia's Day November 22, 1687.*

79. Drama ... Arviragus] The manuscript has clearly 'Arviragus', but Wordsworth should have written 'Arminius'; he may have misheard Klopstock, or, by homoeotopy, substituted the more familiar Shakespearean name for Klopstock's word beginning with the same letter-group. The play referred to must be Klopstock's *Hermanns Schlacht* (1769).

81–2. Voss ... iliad] Johann Heinrich Voss (1751–1826); his translation of the *Iliad* appeared in 1793. Cf. *E.S.* 300.

84–6. Lessing ... action in it] Gotthold Ephraim Lessing (1729–81), *Nathan de Weise* (1779), based on the not very lively plot of Boccaccio, *Decameron*, i. 3. A translation by R. E. Raspe in prose was published in 1781; William Taylor's, which

Wordsworth might have seen, was privately printed in 1791 and published in 1805. The blank in the manuscript was probably left for the completing of the title.

87–9. Goethe ... dramas] Johann Wolfgang Goethe (1749–1832); *Die Leiden des jungen Werthers*, 1774, translated by Richard Graves, *The Sorrows of Werter. A German Story. Founded on Fact*, 2 vols., 1779. By 'the first written' Klopstock probably intended *Götz von Berlichingen* (1773), Goethe's first important drama. There was no English translation until 1799, when two (by Rose Laurence and Walter Scott) appeared; this would account for Wordsworth's seeming ignorance of the title.

87–92. Schiller's robbers ... inextricable] Johann Christoph Friedrich Schiller (1759–1805); *Die Räuber*, 1781, translated by Alexander F. Tytler, *The Robbers, a Tragedy translated from the German of Frederick Schiller*, 1792. The 'scene of the setting sun' is presumably Act III, Sc. ii, where Karl Moor, moved by a beautiful sunset, laments his lost innocence. *Don Carlos* (1787) appeared in two English translations, by Symonds and by G. H. Noehden and J. Stoddart, in 1798.

93. Bürger] Gottfried August Bürger (1747–94); best known in England at this time for his *Lenore*, of which at least five translations appeared in 1796 (by J. T. Stanley, W. R. Spencer, J. H. Pye, W. Taylor, and Walter Scott). Cf. *E.S.* 524–50.

96–7. Kotzebue] August Friedrich Ferdinand Kotzebue (1761–1819); for a lengthy list of his plays translated into English in the nineties, see Allardyce Nicoll, *History of Late Eighteenth Century Drama, 1750–1800* (Cambridge, 1927), pp. 64–5.

99. Wieland] Christoph Martin Wieland (1733–1813); *Oberon*, 1780, translated by William Sotheby, 1798.

115. the passage] Canto VIII, ll. 4969–5064.

128. rhyme poetry] Coleridge (*Biog. Lit.* ii. 178) emends to 'rhymed poetry'; but cf. *E.Y.*, p. 236: 'Rhyme poems'.

146. Klopstock's view of Kant's reputation is severely criticized by Coleridge (*Biog. Lit.* ii. 174–5). Kant's 'appearance ... about ten years ago' (179) perhaps coincided in Klopstock's mind with the publication of the *Kritik der praktischen Vernunft* (1788); Kant had been publishing since the fifties and had been Professor at Königsberg since 1770.

155. Wolfe] Presumably Christian Wolff (1679–1754), follower of Leibniz and Professor of Mathematics at Halle from 1706, a tenure interrupted by a period of banishment in Saxony for his rationalistic opinions.

161–2. Nicolai & Engel] Christoph Friedrich Nicolai (1733–1811), an opponent of Kant in his *Geschichte eines dicken Mannes* (1794) and his *Leben und Meinungen*

Sempronius Gondiberts, eines deutschen Philosophen (1798). Johann Jakob Engel (1741–1802); we have not traced his hostility to Kant.

168. I said … writers.] An anticipation of the attack on 'sickly and stupid German Tragedies', *P.L.B.* 167, and, by implication, of the discussion of what 'may be [more easily] endured in metrical composition … than in prose', *P.L.B.* 548–9.

170. Ariosto] The name appears thus in the manuscript, but whether it is to be connected with what precedes by contrast, or similarity, or at all, is not clear.

5.

Essay on Morals

INTRODUCTION: GENERAL

WORDSWORTH's fragmentary 'Essay on Morals' is written in a notebook (MS. Journal 5) preserved in the Wordsworth Library, Grasmere, which contains, *inter alia*, the 'Conversations with Klopstock' and MS. JJ of *The Prelude*. Its place in the notebook, after *Klopstock* and before the drafts for *The Prelude*, suggests that it was written in Germany in the last quarter of 1798, as proposed by Reed, *Chronology of the Early Years*, p. 34, and by Geoffrey Little, 'An Incomplete Wordsworth Essay upon Moral Habits', *R.E.L.* ii (1961), 9–20 (Little, p. 10, suggests 'probably in October or early November'). How far the Essay proceeded after the available text breaks off is uncertain. The breaking off arises from the removal of five leaves from the notebook, and of these only the first is, like the Essay, written in ink on the stub; the remaining four are written in pencil. This may suggest, but is far from proving, that Wordsworth did not continue the Essay much beyond the point where it now breaks off.

The occasion of the fragment is equally uncertain. Its connection with Wordsworth's distaste in the nineties for over-rationalized systems of thinking, such as Godwin's, is explicit in the early lines, and implicit in the clear parallel, near the end, with the discussion of the rationalization of guilt-feelings in the Preface to *The Borderers* (see nn. to 4, 41–3). It appears to anticipate the theorizing on literature as an instrument for moral improvement, or at least for improvement of moral insight, which Wordsworth shortly was to sketch in the Preface to *Lyrical Ballads* and in various drafts towards *The Prelude (see nn. on 8, 14–25, 32–3), a*nd which he was to discuss more fully in the 'Essays upon Epitaphs'. It is thus an obvious reflection of Wordsworth's thinking in 1798, after the completion of the *Lyrical Ballads*, which was to be dicussed with hindsight in the Prefaces of 1800 and 1802, and a parallel in miniature to the argument of *The Prelude*, Books X–XII, which traces the rejection of over-rational ways of thinking, leading eventually to the project of 'making Verse / Deal boldly with substantial things' (*Prel*. XII 233–4).

INTRODUCTION: TEXTUAL

OUR text of the 'Essay on Morals' is based on MS. Journal 5 in the Wordsworth Library, Grasmere. The hand is Wordsworth's own, and transcription is often difficult and occasionally uncertain. The text in Little's paper mentioned in our Introduction (the only other complete transcription of the fragment) agrees with ours in all significant details except at 21 and 43, where we read 'examined' and 'sure' against Little's 'experienced' and 'rare [? rash]'.

[ESSAY ON MORALS]

I THINK publications in which we formally & systematically lay down rules for the actions of Men cannot be too long delayed. I shall scarcely express myself too strongly when I say that I consider such books as Mr Godwyn's, Mr. Paley's, & those of the whole tribe of authors of that class as impotent [? in *or* ? to] all their intended good purposes; to which I wish I could add that they were equally impotent to all bad one[s]. This sentence will, I am afraid, be unintelligible. You will at least have a glimpse of my meaning when I observe that our attention ought principally to be fixed upon that part of our conduct & actions which is the result of our habits. In a [? strict] sense all our actions are the result of our habits—but I mean here to exclude those accidental & indefinite actions, which do not regularly & in common flow from this or that particular habit. As, for example: a tale of distress is related in *a mixed company*, relief for the sufferers proposed. The vain man, the proud man, the avaricious man &c., all contribute, but from very different feelings. Now in all the cases except in that of the affectionate & benevolent man, I would call the act of giving more or less accidental—I return to our habits—Now, I know no book or system of moral philosophy written with sufficient power to melt into our affection[? s], to incorporate itself with the blood & vital juices of our minds, & thence to have any influence worth our notice in forming those habits of which I am speaking. Perhaps by the plan which these authors pursue this effect is rendered unattainable. Can it be imagined by any man who has deeply examined his own heart that an old habit will be foregone, or a new one formed, by a series of propositions, which, presenting no image to the [? mind] can convey no feeling which has any connection with the supposed archetype or fountain of the proposition existing in human life? These moralists attempt to strip the mind of all its old clothing when their object ought to be to furnish it with new. All this is the consequence of an undue value set upon that faculty which we call reason. The whole secret of this juggler's trick[? s] lies (not in fitting words to things (which would be a noble employment) but) in fitting things to words—I have said that

14 from] from from MS.
14 feelings MS.^{2}: motives MS.
25 life? *Edd.*: life. MS.
29 noble] *perhaps underscored in* MS.

these bald & naked reasonings are impotent over our habits, they cannot form them; from the same cause they are equally powerless in regulating our judgments concerning the value of men & things. They contain no picture of human life; they *describe* nothing. They in no respect enable us to be practically useful by informing us how men placed in such or such situations will necessarily act, & thence enabling us to apply ourselves to the means of turning them into a more beneficial course, if necessary, or of giving them new ardour & new knowledge when they are proceeding as they ought.

We do not *argue* in defence of our *good* actions, we feel internally their beneficial effect; we are satisfied with this delicious sensation; &, even when we are called upon to justify our conduct, we perform the task with languor & indifference. Not so when we have been unworthily employed; then it is that we are all activity & keenness; then it is that we repair to systems of morality for arguments in defence of ourselves; & sure enough are we to find them. In this state of our mind[? s] lifeless words, & abstract propositions, will not be destitute of power to lay asleep the spirit of self-accusation & exclude the uneasiness of repentance. Thus confirmed & comforted, we are prepared immediately to transgress [? anew], &, following up this process, we shall find that I have erred when I said that

COMMENTARY

3–4. Mr Godwyn's, Mr. Paley's] William Godwin (1756–1836); Wordsworth refers here primarily to his *Enquiry Concerning Political Justice* (1793). On Wordsworth's meetings with Godwin in the nineties see Moorman, i. 262–5, 297. William Paley (1743–1805), author of several ethical and theological works; Wordsworth presumably refers to his *Principles of Moral and Political Philosophy* (1785). We cite Godwin from the edition of F. E. L. Priestley (Toronto, 1946); Paley from *Works* (Edinburgh, 1828).

Wordsworth's interest in Godwin and his thinking is well known; it is difficult to guess why he should have singled out Paley for particular mention. The *Principles*, a book which might be called, according to point of view, a rather wooden and unimaginative account of morals and politics from a more or less Christian stance, which nevertheless contrives to be fairly utilitarian, or a work 'notable for its lucidity' (V. H. H. Green in *Chambers's Encyclopœdia*, x (1959), 374), might be expected to have interested Wordsworth far less than Godwin's thorough-going rationalism.

8. that part ... habits] Godwin (i. 64 ff.) is strongly opposed to reliance upon habit for moral guidance, urging that all action should be preceded by a rational decision based on current circumstances:

> Every action ... so far as it is perfectly voluntary, flows solely from the decision of the judgment ... In proportion as our experience enlarges, the subjects of voluntary action becomes more numerous. In this state of the human being, he soon comes to perceive a considerable similarity between situation and situation. In consequence he feels inclined to abridge the process of deliberation, and to act today conformably to the determination of yesterday. Thus the understanding fixes for itself resting places, is no longer a novice, and is not at the trouble continually to go back and revise the original reasons which determined it to a course of action. Thus the man acquires habits, from which it is very difficult to wean him, and which he obeys without being able to assign either to himself or others, any explicit reason for his proceeding. This is the history of prepossession and prejudice... In the mean time it is obvious to remark, that the perfection of the human character consists in approaching as nearly as possible to the perfectly voluntary state. We ought to be upon all occasions prepared to render a reason of our actions... We should be cautious of thinking it a sufficient reason for an action, that we are accustomed to perform it, and that we once thought it right.

Paley (p. 10) agrees with Godwin that

> Mankind act more from habit than reflection. It is on few only and great occasions that men deliberate at all; on fewer still, that they institute any thing like a regular inquiry into the moral rectitude or depravity of what they are about to do; or wait for the result of it. We are for the most part determined at once; and by an impulse, which is the effect and energy of pre-established habits.

But he proceeds, in agreement with Wordsworth:

> And this constitution seems well adapted to the exigencies of human life, and to the imbecility of our moral principle. In the current occasions and rapid opportunities of life, there is oftentimes little leisure for reflection; and were there more, a man, who has to reason about his duty, when the temptation to transgress it is upon him, is almost sure to reason himself into an error. If we are in so great a degree passive under our habits; Where, it is asked, is the exercise of virtue, the guilt of vice, or any use of moral and religious knowledge? I answer, in the *forming and contracting* of these habits.

For Wordsworth on the formation of habits of moral evaluation in connection with the production of poetry see *P.L.B.* 113–31; Owen, pp. 40–4.

12–16. As … accidental] A similar example appears at least twice in Paley, the first occurrence shortly after the passage cited in 8, n.:

> A beggar, with the appearance of extreme distress, asks our charity. If we come to argue the matter, whether the distress be real, whether it be not brought upon himself, [etc., etc.], it may appear very doubtful, whether we ought or ought not to give any thing. But when we reflect, that the misery before our eyes excites our pity, whether we will or not; (etc., etc.], a wise man … will give way to his compassion … A man of confirmed good habits, will act in the same manner without any consideration at all [p. 10]. A beggar solicits your charity, by a story of the most pitiable distress; you promise to relieve him, if he will call again:—In the interval you discover his story to be made up of lies;—this discovery, no doubt, releases you from your promise [p. 29].

Various kinds of charity, including the relief of beggars ('the lowest exertion of benevolence') are discussed in Book III, Part II, Ch. V (pp. 50–3). On the moral value for various individuals of habitual charity see 'The Old Cumberland Beggar', 87–161 (*P.W.* iv. 237–9).

13–14. The vain … feelings] Presumably the vain man contributes so that his public image may be enhanced, the proud man so that his public image may be maintained, and the avaricious man so that his private image may be concealed. It is not clear that the first two act contrary to habit.

14–25. Now … human life?] In *P.L.B.* Wordsworth will propose literature as a modifier of moral judgements: 'If my conclusions are admitted … , our judgements concerning the works of the greatest Poets both ancient and modern will be far different from what they are at present…our moral feelings influencing and influenced by these judgements will … be corrected and purified' (285 ff). If the poet's intellectual discipline has been correct, 'such habits of mind will be produced, that, by obeying blindly and mechanically the impulses of those habits, we shall describe objects, and utter sentiments, of such a nature, and in such connection with each other, that the understanding of the Reader must necessarily be in some degree enlightened, and his affections strengthened and purified' (126–31). A little later, Wordsworth suggests that *Lyrical Ballads* might have a slight effect in counteracting the 'degrading thirst after outrageous stimulation; in the literature and life of his own day, especially if the book acts in conjunction with 'certain inherent and indestructible qualities of the human mind, and ... certain powers in the great and permanent objects that act upon it ... equally inherent and indestructible'. The 'qualities' might include an innate moral sense, such as is postulated in 'The Old Cumberland Beggar', 77: 'a spirit and pulse of good', and *E.E.* III. 12: 'the moral principle which can never be extinguished in the mind', and such as is denied by Godwin (e.g. i. 30–1, 195) and Paley (p. 5)—a sense matured under the influence if natural objects, 'Foster'd alike by beauty and by fear' (*Prel.* I. 306).

18. blood & vital juices] For the figure, cf. *P.L.B.* 276–6: poetry 'can boast of no celestial ichor that distinguishes her vital juices from those of prose'/

27. an undue value ... reason] This is Godwin's argument *passim*. See especially i. 170 ff.: 'To a rational being there can be but one rule of conduct, justice, and one mode of ascertaining that rule, the exercise of his understanding... Understanding, particularly as it is concerned with moral subjects, is the percipient of truth. In reality, by as many instances as I act contrary to the unbiassed dictate of my own judgement, by so much I abdicate the most valuable part of the character of man.'

32–3. They contain ... *describe* nothing] Presumably Wordsworth is still thinking of literature as a better moral teacher than Godwin or Paley. The next sentence suggests the concept of Aristotelean general truth which Wordsworth will introduce into *P.L.B.* ii 1802 (343); it is hardly true, however, that the rational moralists fail, or do not attempt, to inform 'us how men placed in such or such situations will necessarily act'; for a minor example see Paley on charity, cited above, 12–16, n.

41–3. Not so ... find them] Cf. *P. Bord.* 52–4: 'his reason is almost exclusively employed in justifying his past enormities & in enabling him to commit new ones [cf. Essay 46–7: 'we are prepared immediately to transgress anew']...he has a sophism for every crime.'

6.

Advertisement, Preface and Appendix to *Lyrical Ballads*

INTRODUCTION: GENERAL

OF the three critical documents concerned with *Lyrical Ballads*, the earliest, shortest, and simplest is the Advertisement which prefaces the edition of 1798. It exists in one version only. We have found no precise evidence for dating it, but it was presumably written after the first published mention of *Lyrical Ballads*, 30 April 1798 (*E.Y.* 216), and certainly before 13 September 1798, when the book was 'printed, but not published' (*E.Y.*, 227; on the following day Wordsworth sailed for Germany). Most of the ideas of the Advertisement, as our Commentary indicates, are repeated, with or without modification, in the Preface of 1800.

The more famous, or notorious, Preface appears in its simplest form in *Lyrical Ballads*, 1800. For reasons made clear elsewhere,[1] we regard the Preface of 1800 as a work differing in various important respects from subsequent versions, and we have, therefore, printed it separately. References to it are made by line-numbers enclosed in square brackets. The Preface reappeared, in expanded form, in *Lyrical Ballads*, 1802 and 1805, and in all later collected editions of Wordsworth's poems issued by him. Modifications of substance appear in 1836 and subsequent editions, where the text of 1802 is somewhat shortened and the pronoun of the first person, especially in the form 'I', is fairly rigorously excluded.

The Appendix on 'what is usually called POETIC DICTION' appeared first in *Lyrical Ballads*, 1802, and was reprinted, modified from time to time, in all subsequent editions containing the Preface.

The Preface was being written in September 1800; Dorothy Wordsworth 'corrected the last sheet' (of manuscript)[2] on 1 October (*Journals*, i. 61–2). Certain modifications to the text of 1800 which took place during the printing of *Lyrical Ballads*, 1800, are recorded in our textual notes. At this time Wordsworth was also meditating an 'essay for the second volume of "L.B."' (*Journals*, i. 63), but by December 1800 he had abandoned the project (*E.Y.*, pp. 307–8, 309). The substance of this essay may

1 See W. J. B. Owen, *Wordsworth's Preface to* Lyrical Ballads (Copenhagen, 1957), Introduction, or W. J. B. Owen, *Wordsworth as Critic* (Toronto, 1969), pp. 3–114, where this and related problems are discussed at length.

2 The 'last sheet' of the Yale manuscript contains the latter part of Wordsworth's note to 'The Thorn' (*P.W.* ii. 531). his supercilious note on The Ancient Mariner, the note of 1800 on 'Tintern Abbey' (*P.W.* ii 517), and various instructions to the printer.

have been incorporated in the additions made to the Preface in 1802, or in the Appendix; but as neither passage is overloaded with 'many quotations to illustrate the argument', and as no certain trace of the work can be found (cf. *P. L. B. 695* ff., n.), speculation on its content is largely idle.

By the end of June 1801, *Lyrical Ballads* was 'sold to within 130 copies', and Wordsworth was to 'prepare another' edition (*E.Y.*, p. 337). The edition of 1802 was in print by April of that year, as Longman's Impression Book shows,[1] so that Wordsworth probably revised the Preface and wrote the Appendix between June 1801 and April 1802. At least some of the revision was probably undertaken between late January and April 1802, since Wordsworth, in the added passages concerning the similarities and differences between the Poet and the Scientist (*P.L.B.* 382 ff), seems to be aware of the arguments of Humphry Davy in his *Introductory Discrouse* to a series of lectures on chemistry at the Royal Institution, delivered 21 January 1802 (see n. on 390). This is consistent with our tentative suggestion that Wordsworth may have gained some knowledge of Lessing's *Laokoon* about February 1802 (see n. on 322–7).

The Preface to *Lyrical Ballads* is Wordsworth's best-known critical work, and his most original essay in aesthetics, in the sense that it often appears to be the result of his introspective examination of his own poetic processes. It is less original than has sometimes been thought, however, in that many of its aesthetic, psychological, and sociological presuppositions are quite commonplace, especially in the numerous writings on aesthetics in English which appeared during the eighteenth century, based often on the associationist psychology of Locke and Hartley or on the primitvistic theories of culture and literature which are characteristic of Scottish 'Common-sense' philosophers. It is only rarely possible to point to specific sources,[2] but our Commentary makes clear Wordsworth's general debt to the eighteenth century.

A more specific debt was claimed by Coleridge in two letters written in July 1802:

> It is most certain, that the P[reface arose from] the heads of our mutual Conversations &c—& the f[irst pass]ages were indeed partly taken from notes of mine[3] ... altho' Wordsworth's Preface is half a child of my own Brain/& so arose out of Conversations, so frequent, that with few exceptions we could scarcely

1 See *The Library*, 5th Ser. xii (1957), 94.

2 Attempts to find such general sources, such as that of A. A. Mendilow, 'Robert Heron and Wordsworth's Critical Essays', *M. L. R.* lii (1957), 329–38, merely add to the list of commonplaces without producing parallels sufficiently close to define a source.

3 Does the 'first passages' mean 'the first sentences of the Preface', or 'the first parts of the Preface to be written down'?

> either of us perhaps positively say, which first started any particular Thought—I am speaking of the Preface as it stood in the second Volume[1]—yet I am far from going all lengths with Wordsworth. (*C.L.* ii, 811, 830)

Wordsworth, indeed, admits that Coleridge urged him to the composition of the Preface (see n. on 26–31), but he does not, so far as we have discovered, acknowledge any profound debt to Coleridge for its matter. Of the alleged debt the only trace now remaining appears to be *C.N.B.* i. 787 (see n. on 584–611); and here, as our note suggests, it is difficult to see who is the debtor. It is also difficult to believe, in view of the criticisms made in the two letters just cited, and the latter discussions in *Biographia Literaria*, Chs. XV ff., that Coleridge was as sympathetic to the Preface as the letters suggest. True, the letters criticize mainly the additions of 1802; but in *Biographia Literaria* Coleridge quotes the text of 1800 and later versions with equal disapproval.[2]

Closer parallels, and one probable specific source, can be found for the Appendix; for the basic assumptions implicit in the early part of this document are commonplaces of the primitivistic theories of poetry which abound in the eighteenth century. See, for convenient general discussion, Lois Whitney, 'English Primitivistic Theories of Epic Origins', *M. P.* xxi (1924), 337–78, and Abrams, pp. 78–84. A typical exposition can be found in Blair, iii. 92–3:

> Poetry, however, in its ancient original condition, was perhaps more vigorous than it is in its modern state. It included then, the whole burst of the human mind; the whole exertion of its imaginative faculties. It spoke then the language of passion, and no other; for to passion it owed its birth. Prompted and inspired by objects which to him seemed great, by events which interested his country or his friends, the early bard arose and sung. He sung indeed in wild and disorderly strains; but they were the native effusions of his heart; they were the ardent conceptions of admiration or resentment, of sorrow or friendship, which he poured forth. It is no wonder, therefore, that in the rude and artless strains of the first poetry of all nations, we should often find somewhat that captivates and transports the mind. In after ages, when poetry became a regular art, studied for reputation and for gain, authors began to affect what they did not feel. Composing coolly in their closets, they endeavoured to imitate passion, rather than to express it; they tried to force their imagination into raptures, or to supply the defect of native warmth, by those artificial ornaments which might give composition a splendid appearance.

Wordsworth's account of these matters probably owes something to William

1 As Grigg indicates, Coleridge no doubt means 'edition' (that of 1800) rather than 'Volume'.

2 The following passages in *Biog. Lit.* are probably or certainly cited from the text of *P. L. B.* (1800) (others are either indifferent or certainly from later texts); ii. 35, ll. 21–3; ii. 38, ll 13–21; ii. 41, ll. 9–11 ('*I propose... of men*'); ii, 63, ll. 6, 7–13 (there is no authority for 'voluntary', l. 8, in any Wordsworthian text).

Enfield's paper, 'Is Verse Essential to Poetry?', *Monthly Magazine*, ii (1796; see especially *P.L.B.* 202–57, and n.). Thus with Appendix 51, textual n.: 'with the spirit of a fraternity, they arrogated [an artificial language] to themselves as their own', cf. *Monthly Magazine*, p. 453: 'it may not be thought presumptuous to enquire, whether that spirit of monopoly, which has proved so injurious to ecclesiastical and civil society, has not found its way into the republic of letters … an arrogant assumption … has been made in favour of poets. That ambitious race [cf. 10–11: "Men ambitious of the fame of Poets"] … have … conjured up a wall of separation between themselves and other writers.' With 8–10: 'The earliest poets … and figurative', cf. *Monthly Magazine*, p. 454: 'In the rude state of nature, before the art of versification was known, men felt strong passions, and expressed them strongly. Their language would be bold and figurative' (noted by Barstow, p. 121). With 38–9: 'To this language… superadded', cf. ibid.:

> These first expressions of passion and sentiment would be poetry, but they would not assume the regular form of verse. So artificial a production must have been the result of innumerable efforts, and could not attain any high degree of perfection but in a period of great refinement. "No one can doubt," says Quintilian, "that poetry, at first, flowed, without art; and that it was reduced to feet after the ear had discovered, by frequent observation, the regular intervals of melodious sounds."

Our Commentary on Advertisement, Preface, and Appendix to *Lyrical Ballads* is necessarily indebted to that in the separate edition by W. J. B. Owen, cited above.

[Reading Note: In this electronic edition, line numbers to 1800 are in red, those to 1850 in blue. If read in single page view the two texts alternate: to see the text in parallel, readers should select double page view in the lower right-hand corner of the screen.]

INTRODUCTION: TEXTUAL

OUR text of *Ad. L.B.* is from *Lyrical Ballads, With a Few Other Poems* (London, 1798; Healey, item 4), with one editorial insertion.

Our text of *P.L.B.* (1800) is from *Lyrical Ballads, With Other Poems. In Two Volumes* (London, 1800; Healey, item 6). An incomplete manuscript of this text, in fact the printer's copy, in the hand of Dorothy Wordsworth, is preserved in the library of Yale University; it extends from the beginning of the Preface to 'the most interesting parts' ([220] of our text), and from 'of his abandoning ([490–1]) to the end. This version is cited in our textual notes as 1800a. Copies of *Lyrical Ballads*, 1800, with original leaf *a3* (see Healey, p. 6, and plate facing p. 80) are cited as 1800b; and copies with cancel-leaf *a3* are cited as 1800c. A reading common to 1800b–c (or to 1800a–c) is cited as 1800.

Our main text of *P.L.B.*, to which our textual apparatus and Commentary primarily refer, is from *Poetical Works* (London, 1850; Healey, item 151); our apparatus gives the variants in *Lyrical Ballads*, 1802 and 1805 (Healey, items 12, 17) and in Wordsworth's collected editions of 1815, 1820, 1827, 1832, 1836–7 and reprints, 1845 and reprints (Healey, items 30, 64, 76, 83, 101, 135).

Our text of *Ap. L.B.* is also from *Poetical Works* (London, 1850); and variants are given from *Lyrical Ballads*, 1802, 1805, and the collected editions cited above. Manuscript readings of this work, cited as 1802a, are transcribed from W. Hale White, *Description of the Wordsworth & Coleridge Manuscripts in the Possession of Mr. T. Norton Longman* (London, 1897), pp. 47–50; the present whereabouts of the manuscript concerned we have been unable to discover.

ADVERTISEMENT

IT is the honourable characteristic of Poetry that its materials are to be found in every subject which can interest the human mind. The evidence of this fact is to be sought, not in the writings of Critics, but in those of Poets themselves.

The majority of the following poems are to be considered as experiments. They were written chiefly with a view to ascertain how far the language of conversation in the middle and lower classes of society is adapted to the purposes of poetic pleasure. Readers accustomed to the gaudiness and inane phraseology of many modern writers, if they persist in reading this book to its conclusion, will perhaps frequently have to struggle with feelings of strangeness and aukwardness: they will look round for poetry, and will be induced to enquire by what species of courtesy these attempts can be permitted to assume that title. It is desirable that such readers, for their own sakes, should not suffer the solitary word Poetry, a word of very disputed meaning, to stand in the way of their gratification; but that, while they are perusing this book, they should ask themselves if it contains a natural delineation of human passions, human characters, and human incidents; and if the answer be favorable to the author's wishes, that they should consent to be pleased in spite of that most dreadful enemy to our pleasures, our own pre-established codes of decision.

Readers of superior judgment may disapprove of the style in which many of these pieces are executed: it must be expected that many lines and phrases will not exactly suit their taste. It will perhaps appear to them, that wishing to avoid the prevalent fault of the day, the author has sometimes descended too low, and that many of his expressions are too familiar, and not of sufficient dignity. It is apprehended, that the more conversant the reader is with our elder writers, and with those in modern times who have been the most successful in painting manners and passions, the fewer complaints of this kind will he have to make.

An accurate taste in poetry, and in all the other arts, Sir Joshua Reynolds has observed, is an acquired talent, which can only be produced by severe thought, and a long continued intercourse with the best models of composition. This is mentioned not with so ridiculous a purpose as to prevent the most inexperi-

20 executed: it *Edd.*: executed it 1798.

enced reader from judging for himself; but merely to temper the rashness of decision, and to suggest that if poetry be a subject on which much time has not been bestowed, the judgment may be erroneous, and that in many cases it necessarily will be so.

The tale of Goody Blake and Harry Gill is founded on a well- authenticated fact which happened in Warwickshire. Of the other poems in the collection, it may be proper to say that they are either absolute inventions of the author, or facts which took place within his personal observation or that of his friends. The poem of the Thorn, as the reader will soon discover, is not supposed to be spoken in the author's own person: the character of the loquacious narrator will sufficiently shew itself in the course of the story. The Rime of the Ancyent Marinere was professedly written in imitation of the *style*, as well as of the spirit, of the elder poets; but with a few exceptions, the Author believes that the language adopted in it has been equally intelligible for these three last centuries. The lines entitled Expostulation and Reply, and those which follow, arose out of conversation with a friend who was somewhat unreasonably attached to modern books of moral philosophy.

PREFACE [1800]

THE first volume of these Poems has already been submitted to general perusal. It was published, as an experiment, which, I hoped, might be of some use to ascertain, how far, by fitting to metrical arrangement a selection of the real language of men in a state of vivid sensation, that sort of pleasure and that quantity of pleasure may be imparted, which a Poet may rationally endeavour to impart.

I had formed no very inaccurate estimate of the probable effect of those Poems: I flattered myself that they who should be pleased with them would read them with more than common pleasure: and, on the other hand, I was well aware that by those who should dislike them, they would be read with more than common dislike. The result has differed from my expectation in this only, that I have pleased a greater number, than I ventured to hope I should please.

For the sake of variety and from a consciousness of my own weakness I was induced to request the assistance of a Friend, who furnished me with the

[1] THE ... submitted] The first Volume of these Poems, under the title of Lyrical Ballads has already been presented *Wordsworth to Biggs and Cottle, 6/7 October 1800* (*E.Y.*, p. 304).

[14–16] I was ... LOVE.] I have again requested the assistance of a Friend who contributed largely to the first volume*, and who has now furnished me with the [long and beautiful *del.* 1800a] Poem of Christabel, without which I should not yet have ventured to present a second volume to the public.

*The Poems [furnished *del.* 1800a] supplied by my Friend, are the ANTIENT MARINER, the FOSTER-MOTHER'S TALE, the NIGHTINGALE, the DUNGEON, and the Poem entitled, LOVE 1800a–b.

Wordsworth to Biggs and Cottle, 6/7 October 1800 (*E.Y.*, pp. 304–5), *cancels the paragraph* 'down to the words "do almost entirely coincide"' ([22–3]), *and orders the following to be substituted*:

It is proper to inform the Reader that the Poems entitled the ancient Mariner, the Foster Mother's Tale, the Nightingale, the Dungeon, and Love, are written by a friend, who has also furnished me with a few of those Poems in the second volume, which are classed under the title of "Poems on the Naming of Places."

On 18 December 1800 (*E.Y.*, p. 307), *Wordsworth orders another version, agreeing verbally with the cancel of 1800c. The cancel exists in two states but without verbal variation; see Healey, plate facing p. 80.*

APPENDIX, PREFACES,

ETC. ETC.

MUCH the greatest part of the foregoing Poems has been so long before the Public that no prefatory matter, explanatory of any portion of them, or of the arrangement which has been adopted, appears to be required; and had it not been for the observations contained in those Prefaces upon the principles of Poetry in general they would not have been reprinted even as an Appendix in this Edition.

PREFACE

TO THE SECOND EDITION OF SEVERAL OF THE FOREGOING POEMS, PUBLISHED, WITH AN ADDITIONAL VOLUME, UNDER THE TITLE OF "LYRICAL BALLADS."

[*Note.*—In succeeding Editions, when the Collection was much enlarged and diversified, this Preface was transferred to the end of the Volumes as having little of a special application to their contents.]

THE first volume of these Poems has already been submitted to general perusal. It was published, as an experiment, which, I hoped, might be of some use to ascertain, how far, by fitting to metrical arrangement a selection of the real language of men in a state of vivid sensation, that sort of pleasure and that quantity of pleasure may be imparted, which a Poet may rationally endeavour to impart.

I had formed no very inaccurate estimate of the probable effect of those Poems: I flattered myself that they who should be pleased with them would read them with more than common pleasure: and, on the other hand, I was well aware, that by those who should dislike them, they would be read with

Heading and 1–6 APPENDIX ... Edition. 1845: *om.* 1802–36.
6–9 PREFACE ... BALLADS." 1815: PREFACE. 1802–5.
10–12 [*Note.* ... contents.] 1845: *om.* 1802–36.
20 flattered 1800a²: had flattered 1800a.

Poems of the Ancient Mariner, the Foster-Mother's Tale, the Nightingale, the Dungeon, and the Poem entitled Love. I should not, however, have requested this assistance, had I not believed that the poems of my Friend would in great measure have the same tendency as my own, and that, though there would be found a difference, there would be found no discordance in the colours of our style; as our opinions on the subject of poetry do almost entirely coincide.

Several of my Friends are anxious for the success of these Poems, from a belief, that, if the views with which they were composed were indeed realized, a class of Poetry would be produced, well adapted to interest mankind permanently, and not unimportant in the multiplicity, and in the quality of its moral relations: and on this account they have advised me to prefix a systematic defence of the theory, upon which the poems were written. But I was unwilling to undertake the task, because I knew that on this occasion the Reader would look coldly upon my arguments, since I might be suspected of having been principally influenced by the selfish and foolish hope of *reasoning* him into an approbation of these particular Poems: and I was still more unwilling to undertake the task, because, adequately to display my opinions, and fully to enforce my arguments, would require a space wholly disproportionate to the nature of a preface. For, to treat the subject with the clearness and coherence of which I believe it susceptible, it would be necessary to give a full account of the present state of the public taste in this country, and to determine how far this taste is healthy or depraved; which again could not be determined, without pointing out, in what manner language and the human mind act and react on each other, and without retracing the revolutions, not of literature alone but likewise of society itself. I have therefore altogether declined to enter regularly upon this defence; yet I am sensible, that there would be some impropriety in abruptly obtruding upon the Public, without a few words of introduction, Poems so materially different from those upon which general approbation is at present bestowed.

It is supposed, that by the act of writing in verse an Author makes a formal engagement that he will gratify certain known habits of association; that he not

[27] knew 1800a: know 1800a.

more than common dislike. The result has differed from my expectation in this only, that a greater number have been pleased than I ventured to hope I should please.

* * * * * *

Several of my Friends are anxious for the success of these Poems, from a belief, that, if the views with which they were composed were indeed realized, a class of Poetry would be produced, well adapted to interest mankind permanently, and not unimportant in the quality, and in the multiplicity of its moral relations: and on this account they have advised me to prefix a systematic defence of the theory upon which the Poems were written. But I was unwilling to undertake the task, knowing that on this occasion the Reader would look coldly upon my arguments, since I might be suspected of having been principally influenced by the selfish and foolish hope of *reasoning* him into an approbation of these particular Poems: and I was still more unwilling to undertake the task, because, adequately to display the opinions, and fully to enforce the arguments, would require a space wholly disproportionate to a preface. For, to treat the subject with the clearness and coherence of which it is susceptible, it would be necessary to give a full account of the present state of the public taste in this country, and to determine how far this taste is healthy or depraved; which, again, could not be determined, without pointing out in what manner language and the human mind act and re-act on each other, and without retracing the revolutions, not of literature alone, but likewise of society itself. I have therefore altogether declined to enter regularly upon this defence; yet I am sensible, that there would be something like impropriety in abruptly obtruding upon the Public, without a few words of introduction, Poems so materially different from those upon which general approbation is at present bestowed.

It is supposed, that by the act of writing in verse an Author makes a formal engagement that he will gratify certain known habits of association; that he not

24 that ... than 1836: 1802–32 *as* [12–13].
25 *After* please. 1802–5 *insert*: For the sake ... coincide, *as* [13–20] *but omitting* the DUNGEON.
29 quality 1800a[a]: quantity 1800a.
29 in ... of 1836: 1802–32 *as* [24–5].
32 knowing 1836: 1802–32 *as* [27].
33-4 influenced 1800a[2]: [? interested] 1800a.
36 the ... the 1836: 1802–32 *as* [31–2].
37 to a 1836: 1802–32 *as* [32].
38 it is 1836: 1802–32 *as* [33].
45 something like 1845: 1802–36 *as* [40].
45 obtruding 1800a[2]: intruding 1800a.
49 that he will 1802–15, 1827–50: to 1820.
49 that he 1802–15, 1827–50: and he 1820.

only thus apprizes the Reader that certain classes of ideas and expressions will be found in his book, but that others will be carefully excluded. This exponent or symbol held forth by metrical language must in different æras of literature have excited very different expectations: for example in the age of Catullus, Terence, and Lucretius, and that of Statius or Claudian; and in our own country, in the age of Shakespeare and Beaumont and Fletcher, and that of Donne and Cowley, or Dryden, or Pope. I will not take upon me to determine the exact import of the promise which by the act of writing in verse an Author in the present day makes to his Reader: but I am certain it will appear to many persons that I have not fulfilled the terms of an engagement thus voluntarily contracted. I hope therefore the Reader will not censure me, if I attempt to state what I have proposed to myself to perform; and also, (as far as the limits of a preface will permit) to explain some of the chief reasons which have determined me in the choice of my purpose: that at least he may be spared any unpleasant feeling of disappointment, and that I myself may be protected from the most dishonourable accusation which can be brought against an Author, namely, that of an indolence which prevents him from endeavouring to ascertain what is his duty, or, when his duty is ascertained prevents him from performing it.

The principal object then which I proposed to myself in these Poems was to make the incidents of common life interesting by tracing in them, truly though not ostentatiously, the primary laws of our nature: chiefly as far as regards the

48] Catullus, *Edd.*: Catullus 1800.

[49] Lucretius 1800a: Lucretia 1800b–c (*corrected in Errata*).

only thus apprises the Reader that certain classes of ideas and expressions will be found in his book, but that others will be carefully excluded. This exponent or symbol held forth by metrical language must in different eras of literature have excited very different expectations: for example, in the age of Catullus, Terence, and Lucretius, and that of Statius or Claudian; and in our own country, in the age of Shakespeare and Beaumont and Fletcher, and that of Donne and Cowley, or Dryden, or Pope. I will not take upon me to determine the exact import of the promise which, by the act of writing in verse, an Author, in the present day makes to his reader: but it will undoubtedly appear to many persons that I have not fulfilled the terms of an engagement thus voluntarily contracted. They who have been accustomed to the gaudiness and inane phraseology of many modern writers, if they persist in reading this book to its conclusion, will, no doubt, frequently have to struggle with feelings of strangeness and awkwardness: they will look round for poetry, and will be induced to inquire by what species of courtesy these attempts can be permitted to assume that title. I hope therefore the reader will not censure me for attempting to state what I have proposed to myself to perform; and also (as far as the limits of a preface will permit) to explain some of the chief reasons which have determined me in the choice of my purpose: that at least he may be spared any unpleasant feeling of disappointment, and that I myself may be protected from one of the most dishonourable accusations which can be brought against an Author, namely, that of an indolence which prevents him from endeavouring to ascertain what is his duty, or, when his duty is ascertained, prevents him from performing it.

The principal object, then, proposed in these Poems was to choose incidents and situations from common life, and to relate or describe them, throughout, as far as was possible in a selection of language really used by men, and, at the same time, to throw over them a certain colouring of imagination, whereby ordinary things should be presented to the mind in an unusual aspect; and, further, and above all, to make these incidents and situations interesting by tracing in them, truly though not ostentatiously, the primary laws of our nature: chiefly, ▶

54–5 that … that 1802–15, 1827–50: in that … in that 1820.
58 it … appear 1836: 1802–32 *as* [53]
65 for attempting 1836: 1802–32 *as* [55].
69–70 one … accusations 1836: 1802–32 *as* [60].
73 proposed 1836: 1802–32 *as* [63].
77 aspect 1836: way 1802–32.

manner in which we associate ideas in a state of excitement. Low and rustic life was generally chosen because in that situation the essential passions of the heart find a better soil in which they can attain their maturity, are less under restraint, and speak a plainer and more emphatic language; because in that situation our elementary feelings exist in a state of greater simplicity and consequently may be more accurately contemplated and more forcibly communicated; because the manners of rural life germinate from those elementary feelings; and from the necessary character of rural occupations are more easily comprehended; and are more durable; and lastly, because in that situation the passions of men are incorporated with the beautiful and permanent forms of nature. The language too of these men is adopted (purified indeed from what appear to be its real defects, from all lasting and rational causes of dislike or disgust) because such men hourly communicate with the best objects from which the best part of language is originally derived; and because, from their rank in society and the sameness and narrow circle of their intercourse, being less under the influence of social vanity they convey their feelings and notions in simple and unelaborated expressions. Accordingly such a language arising out of repeated experience and regular feelings is a more permanent and a far more philosophical language than that which is frequently substituted for it by Poets, who think that they are conferring honour upon themselves and their art in proportion as they separate themselves from the sympathies of men, and indulge in arbitrary and capricious habits of expression, in order to furnish food for fickle tastes and fickle appetites of their own creation.*

I cannot be insensible of the present outcry against the triviality and meanness both of thought and language, which some of my contemporaries have occasionally introduced into their metrical compositions; and I acknowledge that this defect where it exists, is more dishonourable to the Writer's own character than false refinement or arbitrary innovation, though I should contend at

* It is worth while here to observe that the affecting parts of Chaucer are almost always expressed in language pure and universally intelligible even to this day.

[69] situation 1800a: state 1800a. [

as far as regards the manner in which we associate ideas in a state of excitement. Humble and rustic life was generally chosen, because, in that condition, the essential passions of the heart find a better soil in which they can attain their maturity, are less under restraint, and speak a plainer and more emphatic language; because in that condition of life our elementary feelings coexist in a state of greater simplicity, and, consequently, may be more accurately contemplated, and more forcibly communicated; because the manners of rural life germinate from those elementary feelings, and, from the necessary character of rural occupations, are more easily comprehended, and are more durable; and, lastly, because in that condition the passions of men are incorporated with the beautiful and permanent forms of nature. The language, too, of these men has been adopted (purified indeed from what appear to be its real defects, from all lasting and rational causes of dislike or disgust) because such men hourly communicate with the best objects from which the best part of language is originally derived; and because, from their rank in society and the sameness and narrow circle of their intercourse, being less under the influence of social vanity, they convey their feelings and notions in simple and unelaborated expressions. Accordingly, such a language, arising out of repeated experience and regular feelings, is a more permanent, and a far more philosophical language, than that which is frequently substituted for it by Poets, who think that they are conferring honour upon themselves and their art, in proportion as they separate themselves from the sympathies of men, and indulge in arbitrary and capricious habits of expression, in order to furnish food for fickle tastes, and fickle appetites, of their own creation.*

I cannot, however, be insensible to the present outcry against the triviality and meanness, both of thought and language, which some of my contemporaries have occasionally introduced into their metrical compositions; and I acknowledge that this defect, where it exists, is more dishonourable to the Writer's own character than false refinement or arbitrary innovation, though I should

* It is worth while here to observe that the affecting parts of Chaucer are almost always expressed in language pure and universally intelligible even to this day.

81 Humble 1832: 1802–27 *as* [66].
90–1 has been 1836: 1802–32 *as* [76].
91 appear 1802–5, 1832–50: appears 1815–27.
103 *fn.* to observe 1802–27, 1836–50: to be observe *[sic]* 1832.
103 *fn* always 1800a^2: [? uniformly] 1800a.
104 I ... to 1836: I cannot, however, be insensible of 1802–32.
107 more 1800a^2, 1800a: [? somewhat] more 1800a^2.

the same time that it is far less pernicious in the sum of its consequences. From such verses the Poems in these volumes will be found distinguished at least by one mark of difference, that each of them has a worthy *purpose.* Not that I mean to say, that I always began to write with a distinct purpose formally conceived; but I believe that my habits of meditation have so formed my feelings, as that my descriptions of such objects as strongly excite those feelings, will be found to carry along with them a *purpose.* If in this opinion I am mistaken I can have little right to the name of a Poet. For all good poetry is the spontaneous overflow of powerful feelings; but though this be true, Poems to which any value can be attached, were never produced on any variety of subjects but by a man who being possessed of more than usual organic sensibility had also thought long and deeply. For our continued influxes of feeling are modified and directed by our thoughts, which are indeed the representatives of all our past feelings; and as by contemplating the relation of these general representatives to each other, we discover what is really important to men, so by the repetition and continuance of this act feelings connected with important subjects will be nourished, till at length, if we be originally possessed of much organic sensibility, such habits of mind will be produced that by obeying blindly and mechanically the impulses of those habits we shall describe objects and utter sentiments of such a nature and in such connection with each other, that the understanding of the being to whom we address ourselves, if he be in a healthful state of association, must necessarily be in some degree enlightened, his taste exalted, and his affections ameliorated.

I have said that each of these poems has a purpose. I have also informed my Reader what this purpose will be found principally to be: namely to illustrate the manner in which our feelings and ideas are associated in a state of excitement. But speaking in less general language, it is to follow the fluxes and refluxes of the mind when agitated by the great and simple affections of our nature. This object I have endeavoured in these short essays to attain by various means; by tracing the maternal passion through many of its more subtle windings, as in ¶ the poems of the IDIOT BOY and the MAD MOTHER; by accompanying the last ▶ struggles of a human being at the approach of death, cleaving in solitude to life and society, as in the Poem of the FORSAKEN INDIAN; by shewing, as in the Stanzas entitled WE ARE SEVEN, the perplexity and obscurity which in childhood attend our notion of death, or rather our utter inability to admit that notion; or

120] But 1800a[2]: And 1800a.

contend at the same time, that it is far less pernicious in the sum of its consequences. From such verses the Poems in these volumes will be found distinguished at least by one mark of difference, that each of them has a worthy *purpose*. Not that I always began to write with a distinct purpose formerly conceived; but habits of meditation have, I trust, so prompted and regulated my feelings, that my descriptions of such objects as strongly excite those feelings, will be found to carry along with them a *purpose*. If this opinion be erroneous, I can have little right to the name of a Poet. For all good poetry is the spontaneous overflow of powerful feelings: and though this be true, Poems to which any value can be attached were never produced on any variety of subjects but by a man who, being possessed of more than usual organic sensibility, had also thought long and deeply. For our continued influxes of feeling are modified and directed by our thoughts, which are indeed the representatives of all our past feelings; and, as by contemplating the relation of these general representatives to each other, we discover what is really important to men, so, by the repetition and continuance of this act, our feelings will be connected with important subjects, till at length, if we be originally possessed of much sensibility, such habits of mind will be produced, that, by obeying blindly and mechanically the impulses of those habits, we shall describe objects, and utter sentiments, of such a nature, and in such connexion with each other, that the understanding of the Reader must necessarily be in some degree enlightened, and his affections strengthened and purified.

It has been said that each of these poems has a purpose. Another

113 Not that I 1836: 1802–15 *as* [96]: I do not mean to say, that I 1820: Not that I mean to say, I 1827–32.
114–5 habits ... that 1836: 1802–20 *as* [98]: my habits of meditation have so formed my feelings, as that 1827–32.
116 If ... erroneous 1836: 1802–32 *as* [100].
118 and 1815: 1802–5 *as* [102].
122 representatives 1800a^2: representations 1800a.
130 Reader 1836: 1802–32 *as* [113–4].
130–1 enlightened ... purified 1836: enlightened, and his affections ameliorated 1802–32.
132–36 It... feeling 1845: 1802–36 *as* [117–46], *except:* [117] I have said 1802–32: It has been said 1836; [117–8] I have also informed my Reader 1802–52: The Reader has also been informed 1836; [120] But speaking in less general language 1800: But, speaking in language somewhat more appropriate 1802–36; [124] Mad Mother 1802–32: one beginning, "Her eyes are wild," &c. 1836; [136] the Old 1800: the Two April Mornings, The Fountain, The Old 1802–56; [140] proper that I should 1802–32: proper to 1836.

by displaying the strength of fraternal, or to speak more philosophically, of moral attachment when early association with the great and beautiful objects of nature, as in The Brothers; or, as in the Incident of Simon Lee, by placing my Reader in the way of receiving from ordinary moral sensations another and more salutary impression than we are accustomed to receive from them. It has also been part of my general purpose to attempt to sketch characters under the influence of less impassioned feelings, as in the Old Man Travelling, The Two Thieves, &c. characters of which the elements are simple, belonging rather to nature than to manners, such as exist now and will probably always exist, and which from their constitution may be distinctly and profitably contemplated. I will not abuse the indulgence of my Reader by dwelling longer upon this subject; but it is proper that I should mention one other circumstance which distinguishes these Poems from the popular Poetry of the day; it is this, that the feeling therein developed gives importance to the action and situation and not the action and situation to the feeling. My meaning will be rendered perfectly intelligible by referring my Reader to the Poems entitled Poor Susan and the Childless Father, particularly to the last Stanza of the latter Poem.

I will not suffer a sense of false modesty to prevent me from asserting, that I point my Reader's attention to this mark of distinction far less for the sake of these particular Poems than from the general importance of the subject. The subject is indeed important! For the human mind is capable of excitement without the application of gross and violent stimulants; and he must have a very faint perception of its beauty and dignity who does not know this, and who does not further know that one being is elevated above another in proportion as he possesses this capability. It has therefore appeared to me that to endeavour to produce or enlarge this capability is one of the best services in which, at any period, a Writer can be engaged; but this service, excellent at all times, is especially so at the present day. For a multitude of causes unknown to former times are now acting with a combined force to blunt the discriminating powers

[132] another 1800a[2]: a different 1800a.
accustomed 1800[2]: [? ordinarily] accustomed 1800a.

circumstance must be mentioned which distinguishes these Poems from the popular Poetry of the day; it is this, that the feeling therein developed gives importance to the action and situation, and not the action and situation to the feeling.

A sense of false modesty shall not prevent me from asserting, that the Reader's attention is pointed to this mark of distinction, far less for the sake of these particular Poems than from the general importance of the subject. The subject is indeed important! For the human mind is capable of being excited without the application of gross and violent stimulants; and he must have a very faint ▶ perception of its beauty and dignity who does not know this, and who does not further know, that one being is elevated above another, in proportion as he possesses this capability. It has therefore appeared to me, that to endeavour to produce or enlarge this capability is one of the best services in which, at any period, a Writer can be engaged; but this service, excellent at all times, is especially so at the present day. For a multitude of causes, unknown to former times, are now acting with a combined force to blunt the discriminating powers of the

137–8 A ... pointed 1836: 1802–32 *as* [148].

of the mind, and unfitting it for all voluntary exertion to reduce it to a state of almost savage torpor. The most effective of these causes are the great national events which are daily taking place, and the encreasing accumulation of men in cities, where the uniformity of their occupations produces a craving for extraordinary incident which the rapid communication of intelligence hourly gratifies. To this tendency of life and manners the literature and theatrical exhibitions of the country have conformed themselves. The invaluable works of our elder writers, I had almost said the works of Shakespear and Milton, are driven into neglect by frantic novels, sickly and stupid German Tragedies, and deluges of idle and extravagant stories in verse.—When I think upon this degrading thirst after outrageous stimulation I am almost ashamed to have spoken of the feeble effort with which I have endeavoured to counteract it; and reflecting upon the magnitude of the general evil, I should be oppressed with no dishonourable melancholy, had I not a deep impression of certain inherent and indestructible qualities of the human mind, and likewise of certain powers in the great and permanent objects that act upon it which are equally inherent and indestructible; and did I not further add to this impression a belief that the time is approaching when the evil will be systematically opposed by men of greater powers and with far more distinguished success.

Having dwelt thus long on the subjects and aim of these Poems, I shall request the Reader's permission to apprize him of a few circumstances relating to their *style,* in order, among other reasons, that I may not be censured for not having performed what I never attempted. Except in a very few instances the Reader will find no personifications of abstract ideas in these volumes, not that I mean to censure such personifications: they may be well fitted for certain sorts of composition, but in these Poems I propose to myself to imitate, and, as far as is possible, to adopt the very language of men, and I do not find that such personifications make any regular or natural part of that language. I wish to keep my Reader in the company of flesh and blood, persuaded that by so

[185] as is possible 1800a: as possible 800b–c.

mind, and, unfitting it for all voluntary exertion, to reduce it to a state of almost savage torpor. The most effective of these causes are the great national events which are daily taking place, and the increasing accumulation of men in cities, where the uniformity of their occupations produces a craving for extraordinary incident, which the rapid communication of intelligence hourly gratifies. To this tendency of life and manners the literature and theatrical exhibitions of the country have conformed themselves. The invaluable works of our elder writers, I had almost said the works of Shakspeare and Milton, are driven into neglect by frantic novels, sickly and stupid German Tragedies, and deluges of idle and extravagant stories in verse.—When I think upon this degrading thirst after outrageous stimulation, I am almost ashamed to have spoken of the feeble endeavour made in these volumes to counteract it; and, reflecting upon the magnitude of the general evil, I should be oppressed with no dishonourable melancholy, had I not a deep impression of certain inherent and indestructible qualities of the human mind, and likewise of certain powers in the great and permanent objects that act upon it, which are equally inherent and indestructible; and were there not added to this impression a belief, that the time is approaching when the evil will be systematically opposed, by men of greater powers, and with far more distinguished success.

Having dwelt thus long on the subjects and aim of these Poems, I shall request the Reader's permission to apprise him of a few circumstances relating to their *style,* in order, among other reasons, that he may not censure me for not having performed what I never attempted. The Reader will find that personifications of abstract ideas rarely occur in these volumes; and are utterly rejected, as an ordinary device to elevate the style, and raise it above prose. My purpose was to imitate, and, as far as is possible, to adopt the very language of men; and assuredly such personifications do not make any natural or regular part of that language. They are, indeed, a figure of speech occasionally prompted by passion, and I have made use of them as such; but have endeavoured utterly to reject them as a mechanical device of style, or as a family language which Writers in metre seem to lay claim to by prescription. I have wished to keep the Reader in the company of flesh and blood, persuaded that by so doing I shall

159–60 endeavour ... volumes 1836: 1802–32 *as* [170].
164–5 were ... added 1836: 1802–32 *as* [175].
170 he ... me 1836: 1802–32 *as* [180].
172 and are 1836: and, I hope, are 1802–32.
173–4 My purpose was 1836: I have proposed to myself 1802–32.
177 but have 1836: but I have 1802–32.
179 the Reader 1836: 1802–32 *as* [187].

doing I shall interest him. Not but that I believe that others who pursue a different track may interest him likewise: I do not interfere with their claim, I only wish to prefer a different claim of my own. There will also be found in these volumes little of what is usually called poetic diction; I have taken as much pains to avoid it as others ordinarily take to produce it; this I have done for the reason already alleged, to bring my language near to the language of men; and further, because the pleasure which I have proposed to myself to impart is of a kind very different from that which is supposed by many persons to be the proper object of poetry. I do not know how without being culpably particular I can give my Reader a more exact notion of the style in which I wished these poems to be written than by informing him that I have at all times endeavoured to look steadily at my subject; consequently I hope it will be found that there is in these Poems little falsehood of description, and that my ideas are expressed in language fitted to their respective importance. Something I must have gained by this practice, as it is friendly to one property of all good poetry, namely, good sense; but it has necessarily cut me off from a large portion of phrases and figures of speech which from father to son have long been regarded as the common inheritance of Poets. I have also thought it expedient to restrict myself still further, having abstained from the use of many expressions, in themselves proper and beautiful, but which have been foolishly repeated by bad Poets till such feelings of disgust are connected with them as it is scarcely possible by any art of association to overpower.

If in a Poem there should be found a series of lines, or even a single line, in which the language, though naturally arranged and according to the strict laws of metre, does not differ from that of prose, there is a numerous class of critics who, when they stumble upon these prosaisms as they call them, imagine that they have made a notable discovery, and exult over the Poet as over a man ignorant of his own profession. Now these men would establish a canon of criticism which the Reader will conclude he must utterly reject if he wishes to be pleased with these volumes. And it would be a most easy task to prove to him that not

[192] ordinarily $1800a^2$: usually 1800a.

interest him. Others who pursue a different track will interest him likewise; I do not interfere with their claim, but wish to prefer a claim of my own. There will also be found in these volumes little of what is usually called poetic diction; as much pains has been taken to avoid it as is ordinarily taken to produce it; this has been done for the reason already alleged, to bring my language near to the language of men; and further, because the pleasure which I have proposed to myself to impart, is of a kind very different from that which is supposed by many persons to be the proper object of poetry. Without being culpably particular, I do not know how to give my Reader a more exact notion of the style in which it was my wish and intention to write, than by informing him that I have at all times endeavoured to look steadily at my subject; consequently, there is I hope in these Poems little falsehood of description, and my ideas are expressed in language fitted to their respective importance. Something must have been gained by this practice, as it is friendly to one property of all good poetry, namely, good sense: but it has necessarily cut me off from a large portion of phrases and figures of speech which from father to son have long been regarded as the common inheritance of Poets. I have also thought it expedient to restrict myself still further, having abstained from the use of many expressions, in themselves proper and beautiful, but which have been foolishly repeated by bad Poets, till such feelings of disgust are connected with them as it is scarcely possible by any art of association to overpower.

If in a poem there should be found a series of lines, or even a single line, in which the language, though naturally arranged, and according to the strict laws of metre, does not differ from that of prose, there is a numerous class of critics, who, when they stumble upon these prosaisms, as they call them, imagine that they have made a notable discovery, and exult over the Poet as over a man ignorant of his own profession. Now these men would establish a canon of criticism which the Reader will conclude he must utterly reject, if he wishes to be pleased with these volumes. and it would be a most easy task to prove to him, that not only the language of a large portion of every

181 Others 1836: I am, however, well aware that others 1802–32.
181 will 1836: 1802–32 *as* [189].
182 but 1836: 1802–32 *as* [189].
182 a claim 1832: 1802–27 *as* [190].
183–4 as ... taken 1836: 1802–32 *as* [191].
184 has been 1836: 1802–32*as* [192].
188–9 Without... to 1836: 1802–32 *as* [196].
191 there is I hope 1836: I hope that there is 1802–32.
192 and 1836: 1802–32 *as* [200].
193 must have been 1836: 1802–32*as* [201].
209 a most easy 1800a^{2}: the eas 1800a.

only the language of a large portion of every good poem, even of the most elevated character, must necessarily, except with reference to the metre, in no respect differ from that of good prose, but likewise that some of the most interesting parts of the best poems will be found to be strictly the language of prose when prose is well written. The truth of this assertion might be demonstrated by innumerable passages from almost all the poetical writings, even of Milton himself. I have not space for much quotation; but, to illustrate the subject in a general manner, I will here adduce a short composition of Gray, who was at the head of those who by their reasonings have attempted to widen the space of separation betwixt Prose and Metrical composition, and was more than any other man curiously elaborate in the structure of his own poetic diction.

> In vain to me the smiling mornings shine,
> And reddening Phœbus lifts his golden fire:
> The birds in vain their amorous descant join,
> Or chearful fields resume their green attire:
> These ears alas! for other notes repine;
> *A different object do these eyes require;*
> *My lonely anguish melts no heart but mine;*
> *And in my breast the imperfect joys expire;*
> Yet Morning smiles the busy race to cheer,
> And new-born pleasure brings to happier men;
> The fields to all their wonted tribute bear;
> To warm their little loves the birds complain.
> *I fruitless mourn to him that cannot hear*
> *And weep the more because I weep in vain.*

It will easily be perceived that the only part of this Sonnet which is of any value is the lines printed in Italics: it is equally obvious that except in the rhyme, and in the use of the single word "fruitless" for fruitlessly, which is so far a defect, the language of these lines does in no respect differ from that of prose.

Is there then, it will be asked, no essential difference between the language of prose and metrical composition? I answer that there neither is nor can be any essential difference. We are fond of tracing the resemblance between Poetry and Painting, and, accordingly, we call them Sisters: but where shall we find good poem, even of the most elevated character, must necessarily, except with reference to the metre, in no respect differ from that of good prose, but likewise that some of the most interesting parts of the best poems will be found to be strictly the language of prose when prose is well written. The truth of this assertion might be demonstrated by innumerable passages from almost all the poetical writings, even of Milton himself. To illustrate the subject in a general manner, I will here adduce a short composition of Gray, who was at the head of those who, by their reasonings, have attempted to widen the space of separation betwixt Prose and Metrical composition, and was more than any other man curiously elaborate in the structure of his own poetic diction.

> 'In vain to me the smiling mornings shine,
> And reddening Phœbus lifts his golden fire:
> The birds in vain their amorous descant join,
> Or chearful fields resume their green attire:
> These ears alas! for other notes repine;
> *A different object do these eyes require;*
> *My lonely anguish melts no heart but mine;*
> *And in my breast the imperfect joys expire;*
> Yet Morning smiles the busy race to cheer,
> And new-born pleasure brings to happier men;
> The fields to all their wonted tribute bear;
> To warm their little loves the birds complain.
> *I fruitless mourn to him that cannot hear,*
> *And weep the more because I weep in vain.'*

It will easily be perceived, that the only part of this Sonnet which is of any value is the lines printed in Italics; it is equally obvious, that, except in the rhyme, and in the use of the single word 'fruitless' for fruitlessly, which is so far a defect, the language of these lines does in no respect differ from that of prose.

By the foregoing quotation it has been shown that the language of Prose may yet be well adapted to Poetry; and it was previously asserted, that a large portion of the language of every good poem can in no respect differ from that

216 To illustrate 1836: 1802–32 *as* [224].
241 it has been 1836: I have 1802–32.
242 it was 1836: I have 1802–32.

bonds of connection sufficiently strict to typify the affinity betwixt metrical and prose composition? They both speak by and to the same organs; the bodies in which both of them are clothed may be said to be of the same substance, their affections are kindred and almost identical, not necessarily differing even in degree; *Poetry sheds no tears "such as Angels weep," but natural and human tears; she can boast of no celestial Ichor that distinguishes her vital juices from those of prose; the same human blood circulates through the veins of them both.

If it be affirmed that rhyme and metrical arrangement of themselves constitute a distinction which overturns what I have been saying on the strict affinity of metrical language with that of prose, and paves the way for other distinctions which the mind voluntarily admits, I answer that

[the 1800 text continues on page 170]

* I here use the word "Poetry" (though against my own judgement) as opposed to the word Prose, and synonymous with metrical composition. But much confusion has been introduced into criticism by this contradistinction of Poetry and Prose, instead of the more philosophical one of Poetry and Science. The only strict antithesis to Prose is Metre.

of good Prose. We will go further. It may be safely affirmed, that there neither is, nor can be, any *essential* difference between the language of prose and metrical composition. We are fond of tracing the resemblance between Poetry and Painting, and, accordingly, we call them Sisters: but where shall we find bonds of connexion sufficiently strict to typify the affinity betwixt metrical and prose composition? They both speak by and to the same organs; the bodies in which both of them are clothed may be said to be of the same substance, their affections are kindred, and almost identical, not necessarily differing even in degree; Poetry* sheds no tears 'such as Angels weep,' but natural and human tears; she can boast of no celestial ichor that distinguishes her vital juices from those of prose; the same human blood circulates through the veins of them both.

If it be affirmed that rhyme and metrical arrangement of themselves constitute a distinction which overturns what has just been said on the strict affinity of metrical language with that of prose, and paves the way for other artificial distinctions which the mind voluntarily admits, I answer that the language of such Poetry as is here recommended is, as far as is possible, a selection of the language really spoken by men; that this selection, wherever it is made with true taste and feeling, will of itself form a distinction far greater than would at first be imagined, and will entirely separate the composition from the vulgarity and meanness of ordinary life; and, if metre be superadded thereto, I believe that a dissimilitude will be produced altogether sufficient for the gratification of a rational mind. What other distinction would we have? Whence is it to come? And where is it to exist? Not, surely, where the Poet speaks through the mouths of his characters: it cannot be necessary here, either for elevation of style, or any of its supposed ornaments: for, if the Poet's subject be judiciously chosen, it will naturally, and upon fit occasion, lead him to passions the language of which, if selected truly and judiciously, must necessarily be dignified and

* I here use the word 'Poetry' (though against my own judgement) as opposed to the word Prose, and synonymous with metrical composition. But much confusion has been introduced into criticism by this contradistinction of Poetry and Prose, instead of the more philosophical one of Poetry and Matter of Fact, or Science. The only strict antithesis to Prose is Metre; nor is this, in truth, a *strict* antithesis, because lines and passages of metre so naturally occur in writing prose, that it would be scarcely possible to avoid them, even were it desirable.

244 We 1836: I 1802–32.
244 It may 1836: I do not doubt that it may 1802–32.
245 *essential* 1836: essential 1802–32.
256 has ... said 1836: 1802–32 *as* [259].
259 is here recommended 1836: I am recommending 1802–32.
259 as is possible 1802–15, 1827–50: as possible 1820.

[the 1800 text continues on page 170]

variegated, and alive with metaphors and figures. I forbear to speak of an incongruity which would shock the intelligent Reader, should the Poet interweave any foreign splendour of his own with that which the passion naturally suggests: it is sufficient to say that such addition is unnecessary. And, surely, it is more probable that those passages, which with propriety abound with metaphors and figures, will have their due effect, if, upon other occasions where the passions are of a milder character, the style also be subdued and temperate.

But, as the pleasure which I hope to give by the Poems now presented to the Reader must depend entirely on just notions upon this subject, and, as it is in itself of high importance to our taste and moral feelings, I cannot content myself with these detached remarks. And if, in what I am about to say, it shall appear to some that my labour is unnecessary, and that I am like a man fighting a battle without enemies, such persons may be reminded, that, whatever be the language outwardly holden by men, a practical faith in the opinions which I am wishing to establish is almost unknown. If my conclusions are admitted, and carried as far as they must be carried if admitted at all, our judgements concerning the works of the greatest Poets both ancient and modern will be far different from what they are at present, both when we praise, and when we censure: and our moral feelings influencing and influenced by these judgements will, I believe, be corrected and purified.

Taking up the subject, then, upon general grounds, let me ask, what is meant by the word Poet? What is a Poet? To whom does he address himself? And what language is to be expected from him?—He is a man speaking to men: a man, it is true, endowed with more lively sensibility, more enthusiasm and tenderness, who has a greater knowledge of human nature, and a more comprehensive soul, than are supposed to be common among mankind; a man pleased with his own passions and volitions, and who rejoices more than other men in the spirit of life that is in him; delighting to contemplate similar volitions and passions as manifested in the goings-on of the Universe, and habitually impelled to create them where he does not find them. To these qualities he has added a disposition to be affected more than other men by absent things as if they were present; an ability of conjuring up in himself passions, which are indeed far from being the same as those produced by real events, yet (especially in those parts of the general

278 now presented 1836: I now present 1802–32.
280 high 1836: the highest 1802–32.
283 such ... reminded 1836: I would remind such persons 1802–32.
283 be 1836: may be 1802–32.
291 let me ask 1836: I ask 1802–32.
294 endowed 1836: endued 1802–32.

[the 1800 text continues on page 170]

sympathy which are pleasing and delightful) do more nearly resemble the passions produced by real events, than anything which, from the motions of their own minds merely, other men are accustomed to feel in themselves:— whence, and from practice, he has acquired a greater readiness and power in expressing what he thinks and feels, and especially those thoughts and feelings which, by his own choice, or from the structure of his own mind, arise in him without immediate external excitement.

But whatever portion of this faculty we may suppose even the greatest Poet to possess, there cannot be a doubt that the language which it will suggest to him, must often, in liveliness and truth, fall short of that which is uttered by men in real life, under the actual pressure of those passions, certain shadows of which the Poet thus produces, or feels to be produced, in himself.

However exalted a notion we would wish to cherish of the character of a Poet, it is obvious, that while he describes and imitates passions, his employment is in some degree mechanical, compared with the freedom and power of real and substantial action and suffering. So that it will be the wish of the Poet to bring his feelings near to those of the persons whose feelings he describes, nay, for short spaces of time, perhaps, to let himself slip into an entire delusion, and even confound and identify his own feelings with theirs; modifying only the language which is thus suggested to him by a consideration that he describes for a particular purpose, that of giving pleasure. Here, then, he will apply the principle of selection which has been already insisted upon. He will depend upon this for removing what would otherwise be painful or disgusting in the passion; he will feel that there is no necessity to trick out or to elevate nature: and, the more industriously he applies this principle, the deeper will be his faith that no words, which *his* fancy or imagination can suggest, will be to be compared with those which are the emanations of reality and truth.

But it may be said by those who do not object to the general spirit of these remarks, that, as it is impossible for the Poet to produce upon all occasions language as exquisitely fitted for the passion as that which the real passion itself suggests, it is proper that he should consider himself as in the situation of

312 that 1836: but that 1802–32.
313 must often 1845: must 1802–36.
313 short 1845: far short 1802–36.
317–8 employment ... mechanical 1845: situation is altogether slavish and mechanical 1802–32: situation is slavish and mechanical 1836.
325–6 principle ... this 1836: principle on which I have so much insisted, namely, that of selection; on this he will depend 1802–32.
329 *his* 1815: his 1802–5.

[the 1800 text continues on page 170]

a translator, who does not scruple to substitute excellencies of another kind for those which are unattainable by him; and endeavours occasionally to surpass his original, in order to make some amends for the general inferiority to which he feels that he must submit. But this would be to encourage idleness and unmanly despair. Further, it is the language of men who speak of what they do not understand; who talk of Poetry as of a matter of amusement and idle pleasure; who will converse with us as gravely about a *taste* for Poetry, as they express it, as if it were a thing as indifferent as a taste for rope-dancing, or Frontiniac or Sherry. Aristotle, I have been told, has said, that Poetry is the most philosophic of all writing: it is so: its object is truth, not individual and local, but general, and operative; not standing upon external testimony, but carried alive into the heart by passion; truth which is its own testimony, which gives competence and confidence to the tribunal to which it appeals, and receives them from the same tribunal. Poetry is the image of man and nature. The obstacles which stand in the way of the fidelity of the Biographer and Historian, and of their consequent utility, are incalculably greater than those which are to be encountered by the Poet who comprehends the dignity of his art. The Poet writes under one restriction only, namely, the necessity of giving immediate pleasure to a human Being possessed of that information which may be expected from him, not as a lawyer, a physician, a mariner, an astronomer, or a natural philosopher, but as a Man. Except this one restriction, there is no object standing between the Poet and the image of things; between this, and the Biographer and Historian, there are a thousand.

Nor let this necessity of producing immediate pleasure be considered as a degradation of the Poet's art. It is far otherwise. It is an acknowledgement of the beauty of the universe, an acknowledgement the more sincere, because not formal, but indirect; it is a task light and easy to him who looks at the world in the spirit of love: further, it is a homage paid to the native and naked dignity of man, to the grand elementary principle of pleasure, by which he knows, and feels, and lives, and moves. We have no sympathy but what is propagated by

335 does ... substitute 1836: deems himself justified when he substitutes 1802–32.
335 excellencies 1827: excellences 1802–20.
342 Frontiniac 1802–15, 1827–50: for Frontiniac 1820.
343 has 1836: hath 1802–32.
346–7 competence and confidence 1836: strength and divinity 1802–32.
351 comprehends 1836: has an adequate notion of 1802–32.
352 namely, the necessity 1836: namely, that of the necessity 1802–32.
360 because not 1836: because it is not 1802–32.

[the 1800 text continues on page 170]

pleasure: I would not be misunderstood; but wherever we sympathize with pain, it will be found that the sympathy is produced and carried on by subtle combinations with pleasure. We have no knowledge, that is, no general principles drawn from the contemplation of particular facts, but what has been built up by pleasure, and exists in us by pleasure alone. The Man of science, the Chemist and Mathematician, whatever difficulties and disgusts they may have had to struggle with, know and feel this. However painful may be the objects with which the Anatomist's knowledge is connected, he feels that his knowledge is pleasure; and where he has no pleasure he has no knowledge. What then does the Poet? He considers man and the objects that surround him as acting and re-acting upon each other, so as to produce an infinite complexity of pain and pleasure; he considers man in his own nature and in his ordinary life as contemplating this with a certain quantity of immediate knowledge, with certain convictions, intuitions, and deductions, which from habit acquire the quality of intuitions; he considers him as looking upon this complex scene of ideas and sensations, and finding everywhere objects that immediately excite in him sympathies which, from the necessities of his nature, are accompanied by an overbalance of enjoyment.

To this knowledge which all men carry about with them, and to these sympathies in which, without any other discipline than that of our daily life, we are fitted to take delight, the Poet principally directs his attention. He considers man and nature as essentially adapted to each other, and the mind of man as naturally the mirror of the fairest and most interesting properties of nature. And thus the Poet, prompted by this feeling of pleasure, which accompanies him through the whole course of his studies, converses with general nature, with affections akin to those, which, through labour and length of time, the Man of science has raised up in himself, by conversing with those particular parts of nature which are the objects of his studies. The knowledge both of the Poet and the Man of science is pleasure; but the knowledge of the one cleaves to us as a necessary part of our existence, our natural and unalienable inheritance; the other is a personal and individual acquisition, slow to come to us, and by no habitual and direct sympathy connecting us with our fellow-beings. The Man of science seeks truth as a remote

369, 390 science ... science 1836: Science ... Science 1802–32.

378 from ... quality 1836: by habit become of the nature 1802–32.

387 properties 1836: qualities 1802–32.

392–422 science ... science ... science ... science ... science ... science 1836: Science ... Science ... Science ... Science ... Science ... Science 1802–32.

[the 1800 text continues on page 170]

and unknown benefactor; he cherishes and loves it in his solitude: the Poet, singing a song in which all human beings join with him, rejoices in the presence of truth as our visible friend and hourly companion. Poetry is the breath and finer spirit of all knowledge; it is the impassioned expression which is in the countenance of all Science. Emphatically may it be said of the Poet, as Shakspeare hath said of man, 'that he looks before and after.' He is the rock of defence for human nature; an upholder and preserver, carrying everywhere with him relationship and love. In spite of difference of soil and climate, of language and manners, of laws and customs: in spite of things silently gone out of mind, and things violently destroyed; the Poet binds together by passion and knowledge the vast empire of human society, as it is spread over the whole earth, and over all time. The objects of the Poet's thoughts are everywhere; though the eyes and senses of man are, it is true, his favourite guides, yet he will follow wheresoever he can find an atmosphere of sensation in which to move his wings. Poetry is the first and last of all knowledge—it is as immortal as the heart of man. If the labours of Men of science should ever create any material revolution, direct or indirect, in our condition, and in the impressions which we habitually receive, the Poet will sleep then no more than at present; he will be ready to follow the steps of the Man of science, not only in those general indirect effects, but he will be at his side, carrying sensation into the midst of the objects of the science itself. The remotest discoveries of the Chemist, the Botanist, or Mineralogist, will be as proper objects of the Poet's art as any upon which it can be employed, if the time should ever come when these things shall be familiar to us, and the relations under which they are contemplated by the followers of these respective sciences shall be manifestly and palpably material to us as enjoying and suffering beings. If the time should ever come when what is now called science, thus familiarised to men, shall be ready to put on, as it were, a form of flesh and blood, the Poet will lend his divine spirit to aid the transfiguration, and will welcome the Being thus produced, as a dear and genuine inmate of the household of man.—It is not, then, to be supposed that any one, who holds that sublime notion of Poetry which I have attempted to convey, will break in upon the sanctity and truth of his pictures by transitory and accidental ornaments, and endeavour to excite admiration of himself by arts, the necessity of which must manifestly depend upon the assumed meanness of his subject.

What has been thus far said applies to Poetry in general; but especially to

402 for 1836: of 1802–32.
414 he 1836: but he 1802–32.
420 sciences 1832: Sciences 1802–27.
450 has been 1836: I have 1802–32.

[the 1800 text continues on page 170]

those parts of composition where the Poet speaks through the mouths of his characters; and upon this point it appears to authorize the conclusion that there are few persons of good sense, who would not allow that the dramatic parts of composition are defective, in proportion as they deviate from the real language of nature, and are coloured by a diction of the Poet's own, either peculiar to him as an individual Poet or belonging simply to Poets in general; to a body of men who, from the circumstance of their compositions being in metre, it is expected will employ a particular language.

It is not, then, in the dramatic parts of composition that we look for this distinction of language; but still it may be proper and necessary where the Poet speaks to us in his own person and character. To this I answer by referring the Reader to the description before given of a Poet. Among the qualities there enumerated as principally conducing to form a Poet, is implied nothing differing in kind from other men, but only in degree. The sum of what was said is, that the Poet is chiefly distinguished from other men by a greater promptness to think and feel without immediate external excitement, and a greater power in expressing such thoughts and feelings as are produced in him in that manner. But these passions and thoughts and feelings are the general passions and thoughts and feelings of men. And with what are they connected? Undoubtedly with our moral sentiments and animal sensations, and with the causes which excite these; with the operations of the elements, and the appearances of the visible universe; with storm and sunshine, with the revolutions of the seasons, with cold and heat, with loss of friends and kindred, with injuries and resentments, gratitude and hope, with fear and sorrow. These, and the like, are the sensations and objects which the Poet describes, as they are the sensations of other men, and the objects which interest them. The Poet thinks and feels in the spirit of human passions. How, then, can his language differ in any material degree from that of all other men who feel vividly and see clearly? It might be *proved* that it is impossible. But supposing that this were not the case, the Poet might then be allowed to use a peculiar language when expressing his feelings for his own gratification, or that of men like himself. But Poets do not write for Poets alone, but for men. Unless therefore we are advocates for that admiration

452 authorise ... that 1836: have such weight that I will conclude, 1802–32.
461–2 the Reader 1836: my Reader 1802–32.
462 description before 1836: description which I have before 1802–32.
462 there 1836: which I have 1802–32.
464 was 1836: I have there 1802–32.
477 human passions 1836: the passions of men 1802–32.

the distinction of rhyme and metre is regular and uniform, and not, like that which is produced by what is usually called poetic diction, arbitrary and subject to infinite caprices upon which no calculation whatever can be made. In the one case the Reader is utterly at the mercy of the Poet respecting what imagery or diction he may choose to connect with the passion; whereas in the other the metre obeys certain laws, to which the Poet and Reader both willingly submit because they are certain, and because no interference is made by them with the passion but such as the concurring testimony of ages has shewn to heighten and improve the pleasure which co-exists with it.

It will now be proper to answer an obvious question, namely, why, professing these opinions have I written in verse? To this in the first place I reply, because, however I may have restricted myself, there is still left open to me what confessedly constitutes the most valuable object of all writing whether in prose or verse, the great and universal passions of men, the most general and interesting of their occupations, and the entire world of nature, from which I am at liberty to supply myself with endless combinations of forms and imagery. Now, granting for a moment that whatever is interesting in these objects may be as vividly described in prose, why am I to be condemned if to such description I have endeavoured to superadd the charm which by the consent of all nations is acknowledged to exist in metrical language? To this it will be answered, that a very small part of the pleasure given by Poetry depends upon the metre, and that it is injudicious to write in metre unless it be accompanied with the other which subsists upon ignorance, and that pleasure which arises from hearing what we do not understand, the Poet must descend from this supposed height; and, in order to excite rational sympathy, he must express himself as other men express themselves. To this it may be added, that while he is only selecting from the real language of men, or, which amounts to the same thing, composing accurately in the spirit of such selection, he is treading upon safe ground, and we know what we are to expect from him. Our feelings are the same with respect to metre; for, as it may be proper to remind the Reader, the distinction of metre is regular and uniform, and not, like that which is produced by what is usually called Poetic Diction, arbitrary, and subject to infinite caprices upon which no calculation whatever can be made. In the one case, the Reader is utterly at the mercy of the Poet, respecting what imagery or diction he may choose to connect with the passion; whereas, in the other, the metre obeys certain laws, to which the Poet and Reader both willingly submit because they are certain, and because no interference is made by them with the passion, but such as the concurring testimony of ages has shown to heighten and improve the pleasure which co-exists with it.

It will now be proper to answer an obvious question, namely, Why, professing these opinions, have I written in verse? To this, in addition to such answer as is included in what has been already said, I reply, in the first place, Because, however I may have restricted myself, there is still left open to me what confessedly constitutes the most valuable object of all writing, whether in prose or verse; the great and universal passions of men, the most general and interesting of their occupations, and the entire world of nature before me—to supply endless combinations of forms and imagery. Now, supposing for a moment that whatever is interesting in these objects may be as vividly described in prose, why should I be condemned for attempting to superadd to such description the charm which, by the consent of all nations, is acknowledged to exist in metrical language? To this, by such as are yet unconvinced, it may be answered that a very small part of the pleasure given by Poetry depends upon the metre, and that it is injudicious to write in metre, unless it be accompanied with the other artificial distinctions of style with which metre is usually accompanied, and

483 subsists 1836: depends 1802–32.
502 has been 1836: I have 1802–32.
506 nature ... supply 1836: 1802–32 *as* [271–8].
509 should I 1836: 1802–32 *as* [280].
509 for ... description 1836: 1802–32 *as* [280].
511 To ... may 1836: To this, by such as are unconvinced by what I have already said, it may 1802–32.

artificial distinctions of style with which metre is usually accompanied, and that by such deviation more will be lost from the shock which will be thereby given to the Reader's associations than will be counterbalanced by any pleasure which he can derive from the general power of numbers. In answer to those who thus contend for the necessity of accompanying metre with certain appropriate colours of style in order to the accomplishment of its appropriate end, and who also, in my opinion, greatly under-rate the power of metre in itself, it might perhaps be almost sufficient to observe that poems are extant, written upon more humble subjects, and in a more naked and simple style than what I have aimed at, which poems have continued to give pleasure from generation to generation. Now, if nakedness and simplicity be a defect, the fact here mentioned affords a strong presumption that poems somewhat less naked and simple are capable of affording pleasure at the present day; and all that I am now attempting is to justify myself for having written under the impression of this belief.

But I might point out various causes why, when the style is manly, and the subject of some importance, words metrically arranged will long continue to impart such a pleasure to mankind as he who is sensible of the extent of that pleasure will be desirous to impart. The end of Poetry is to produce excitement in coexistence with an overbalance of pleasure. Now, by the supposition, excitement is an unusual and irregular state of the mind; ideas and feelings do not in that state succeed each other in accustomed order. But if the words by which this excitement is produced are in themselves powerful, or the images and feelings have an undue proportion of pain connected with them, there is some danger that the excitement may be carried beyond its proper bounds. Now the co-presence of something regular, something to which the mind has been accustomed when in an unexcited or less excited state, cannot but have great efficacy in tempering and restraining the passion by an intertexture of ordinary feeling. This may be that, by such deviation, more will be lost from the shock which will thereby be given to the Reader's associations than will be counterbalanced by any pleasure which he can derive from the general power of numbers. In answer to those who still contend for the necessity of accompanying metre with certain appropriate colours of style in order to the accomplishment of its appropriate end, and who also, in my opinion, greatly underrate the power of metre in itself, it might, perhaps, as far as relates to these Volumes, have been almost sufficient to observe, that poems are extant, written upon more humble subjects, and in a still more naked and simple style, which have continued to give pleasure from generation to generation. Now, if nakedness and simplicity be a defect, the fact here mentioned affords a strong presumption that poems somewhat less naked and simple are capable of affording pleasure at the present day; and, what I wish *chiefly* to attempt, at present, was to justify myself for having written under the impression of this belief.

But various causes might be pointed out why, when the style is manly, and the subject of some importance, words metrically arranged will long continue to impart such a pleasure to mankind as he who proves the extent of that pleasure will be desirous to impart. The end of Poetry is to produce excitement in co-existence with an overbalance of pleasure; but, by the supposition, excitement is an unusual and irregular state of the mind; ideas and feelings do not, in that state, succeed each other in accustomed order. If the words, however, by which this excitement is produced be in themselves powerful, or the images and feelings have an undue proportion of pain connected with them, there is some danger that the excitement may be carried beyond its proper bounds. Now the co-presence of something regular, something to which the mind has been accustomed in various moods and in a less excited state, cannot but have great efficacy in tempering and restraining the passion by an intertexture of ordinary feeling, and of feeling not strictly and necessarily connected with the passion. This is unquestionably true; and hence, though the opinion will at first appear paradoxical, from the tendency of metre to divest language, in a certain degree, of its reality, and thus to throw a sort of half-consciousness of unsubstantial existence over the whole composition, there can be little doubt but that more

515 thereby be 1827: 1802–20 *as* [286].
521 Volumes 1836: Poems 1802–32.
523 still ... which 1836: more naked and simple style than I have aimed at, which poems 1802–32.
529 But ... out 1836: 1802–32 *as* [300].
531 proves 1836: 1802–32 *as* [302].
533 pleasure; but 1836: 1802–32 *as* [304].
535 If ... however, 1836: 1802–32 *as* [306].
536 be 1836: 1802–32 *as* [307].

illustrated by appealing to the Reader's own experience of the reluctance with which he comes to the re-perusal of the distressful parts of Clarissa Harlowe, or the Gamester. While Shakespeare's writings, in the most pathetic scenes, never act upon us as pathetic beyond the bounds of pleasure—an effect which is in a great degree to be ascribed to small, but continual and regular impulses of pleasurable surprise from the metrical arrangement.—On the other hand (what it must be allowed will much more frequently happen) if the Poet's words should be incommensurate with the passion, and inadequate to raise the Reader to a height of desirable excitement, then, (unless the Poet's choice of his metre has been grossly injudicious) in the feelings of pleasure which the Reader has been accustomed to connect with metre in general, and in the feeling, whether chearful or melancholy, which he has been accustomed to connect with that particular movement of metre, there will be found something which will greatly contribute to impart passion to the words, and to effect the complex end which the Poet proposes to himself.

If I had undertaken a systematic defence of the theory upon which these poems are written, it would have been my duty to develope the various causes upon which the pleasure received from metrical language depends. Among the chief of these causes is to be reckoned a principle which must be well known to those who have made any of the Arts the object of accurate reflection; I mean the pleasure which the mind derives from the perception of similitude in dissimilitude. This principle is the great spring of the activity of our minds and their chief feeder. From this principle the direction of the sexual appetite, and all the passions connected with it take their origin: It is the life of our ordinary conversation; and upon the accuracy with which similitude in dissimilitude, and dissimilitude in similitude are perceived, depend our taste and our moral feelings. It would not have been a useless employment to apply this principle pathetic situations and sentiments, that is, those which have a greater proportion of pain connected with them, may be endured in metrical composition, especially in rhyme, than in prose. The metre of the old ballads is very artless; yet they contain many passages which would illustrate this opinion; and, I hope, if the following Poems be attentively perused, similar instances will be found in them. This opinion may be further illustrated by appealing to the Reader's own experience of the reluctance with which he comes to the re-perusal of the distressful parts of Clarissa Harlowe, or the Gamester; while Shakspeare's writings, in the most pathetic scenes, never act upon us, as pathetic, beyond the bounds of pleasure—an effect which, in a much greater degree than might at first be imagined, is to be ascribed to small, but continual and regular impulses of pleasurable surprise from the metrical arrangement.—On the other hand (what it must be allowed will much more frequently happen) if the Poet's words should be incommensurate with the passion, and inadequate to raise the Reader to a height of desirable excitement, then, (unless the Poet's choice of his metre has been grossly injudicious) in the feelings of pleasure which the Reader has been accustomed to connect with metre in general, and in the feeling, whether cheerful or melancholy, which he has been accustomed to connect with that particular movement of metre, there will be found something which will greatly contribute to impart passion to the words, and to effect the complex end which the Poet proposes to himself.

If I had undertaken a SYSTEMATIC defence of the theory here maintained, it would have been my duty to develope the various causes upon which the pleasure received from metrical language depends. Among the chief of these causes is to be reckoned a principle which must be well known to those who have made any of the Arts the object of accurate reflection; namely, the pleasure which the mind derives from the perception of similitude in dissimilitude. This principle is the great spring of the activity of our minds, and their chief feeder. From this principle the direction of the sexual appetite, and all the passions connected with it, take their origin: it is the life of our ordinary conversation; and upon the accuracy with which similitude in dissimilitude, and dissimilitude in similitude are perceived, depend our taste and our moral feelings. It would not be a useless employment to apply this principle to the consideration of metre, and to show that metre is hence enabled to afford much pleasure, and to point

568 here maintained 1836: 1802–32 *as* [328–9].
572 namely, 1836: 1802–32 *as* [332].
579–80 be ... apply ... show ... point 1836: 1802–32 *as* [339–41].

to the consideration of metre, and to have shown that metre is hence enabled to afford much pleasure, and to have pointed out in what manner that pleasure is produced. But my limits will not permit me to enter upon this subject, and I must content myself with a general summary.

I have said that Poetry is the spontaneous overflow of powerful feelings: it takes its origin from emotion recollected in tranquillity: the emotion is contemplated till by a species of reaction the tranquillity gradually disappears, and an emotion, similar to that which was before the subject of contemplation, is gradually produced, and does itself actually exist in the mind. In this mood successful composition generally begins, and in a mood similar to this it is carried on; but the emotion, of whatever kind and in whatever degree, from various causes is qualified by various pleasures, so that in describing any passions whatsoever, which are voluntarily described, the mind will upon the whole be in a state of enjoyment. Now if Nature be thus cautious in preserving in a state of enjoyment a being thus employed, the Poet ought to profit by the lesson thus held forth to him, and ought especially to take care, that whatever passions he communicates to his Reader, those passions, if his Reader's mind be sound and vigorous, should always be accompanied with an overbalance of pleasure. Now the music of harmonious metrical language, the sense of difficulty overcome, and the blind association of pleasure which has been previously received from works of rhyme or metre of the same or similar construction, all these imperceptibly make up a complex feeling of delight, which is of the most important use in tempering the painful feeling which will always be found intermingled with powerful descriptions of the deeper passions. This effect is always produced in pathetic and impassioned poetry; while in lighter compositions the ease and gracefulness with which the Poet manages his numbers are themselves confessedly a principal source of the gratification of the Reader. I might perhaps include all which it is *necessary* to say upon this subject by affirming what few persons will deny, that of two descriptions, either of passions, manners, or characters, each of them equally well executed, the one in prose and the other in verse, the verse will be read a hundred times where the prose is read once. We see that Pope by the power of verse alone, has contrived to render the plainest out in what manner that pleasure is produced. But my limits will not permit me to enter upon this subject, and I must content myself with a general summary.

I have said that poetry is the spontaneous overflow of powerful feelings: it takes its origin from emotion recollected in tranquillity: the emotion is contemplated till, by a species of re-action, the tranquillity gradually disappears, and an emotion, kindred to that which was before the subject of contemplation, is gradually produced, and does itself actually exist in the mind. In this mood successful composition generally begins, and in a mood similar to this it is carried on; but the emotion, of whatever kind, and in whatever degree, from various causes, is qualified by various pleasures, so that in describing any passions whatsoever, which are voluntarily described, the mind will, upon the whole, be in a state of enjoyment. If Nature be thus cautious to preserve in a state of enjoyment a being so employed, the Poet ought to profit by the lesson held forth to him, and ought especially to take care, that, whatever passions he communicates to his Reader, those passions, if his Reader's mind be sound and vigorous, should always be accompanied with an overbalance of pleasure. Now the music of harmonious metrical language, the sense of difficulty overcome, and the blind association of pleasure which has been previously received from works of rhyme or metre of the same or similar construction, an indistinct perception perpetually renewed of language closely resembling that of real life, and yet, in the circumstance of metre, differing from it so widely—all these imperceptibly make up a complex feeling of delight, which is of the most important use in tempering the painful feeling always found intermingled with powerful descriptions of the deeper passions. This effect is always produced in pathetic and impassioned poetry; while, in lighter compositions, the ease and gracefulness with which the Poet manages his numbers are themselves confessedly a principal source of the gratification of the Reader. All that it is *necessary* to say, however, upon this subject, may be effected by affirming, what few persons will deny, that, of two descriptions, either of passions, manners, or characters, each of them equally well executed, the one in prose and the other in verse, the verse will be read a hundred times where the prose is read once.

592 If 1836: 1802–32 *as* [353].
592 to preserve 1836: 1802–32 *as* [353].
593 so 1836: 1802–32 *as* [354].
593 lesson held 1836: 1802–32 *as* [354–5].
603 always 1845: 1802–36 *as* [362].
607–8 All ... effected 1836: 1802–32 *as* [366–7].
611 *After* once. 1802–36 *insert:* We see that Pope ... usual in Ballads, *as* [370–9], *except:* [375] I wished 1802–32: My wish was 1836.

common sense interesting, and even frequently to invest it with the appearance of passion. In consequence of these convictions I related in metre the Tale of GOODY BLAKE AND HARRY GILL, which is one of the rudest of this collection. I wished to draw attention to the truth that that power of the human imagination is sufficient to produce such changes even in our physical nature as might almost appear miraculous. The truth is an important one; the fact (for it is a *fact*) is a valuable illustration of it. And I have the satisfaction of knowing that it has been communicated to many hundreds of people who would never have heard of it, had it not been narrated as a Ballad, and in a more impressive metre than is usual in Ballads.

Having thus adverted to a few of the reasons why I have written in verse, and why I have chosen subjects from common life, and endeavoured to bring my language near to the real language of men, if I have been too minute in pleading my own cause, I have at the same time been treating a subject of general interest; and it is for this reason that I request the Reader's permission to add a few words with reference solely to these particular poems, and to some defects which will probably be found in them. I am sensible that my associations must have sometimes been particular instead of general, and that, consequently, giving to things a false importance, sometimes from diseased impulses I may have written upon unworthy subjects; but I am less apprehensive on this account, than that my language may frequently have suffered from those arbitrary connections of feelings and ideas with particular words, from which no man can altogether protect himself. Hence I have no doubt that in some instances feelings even of the ludicrous may be given to my Readers by expressions which appeared to me tender and pathetic. Such faulty expressions, were I convinced they were faulty at present, and that they must necessarily continue to be so, I would willingly take all reasonable pains to correct. But it is dangerous to make these alterations on the simple authority of a few individuals, or even of certain classes of men; for where the understanding of an Author is not convinced, or his feelings altered, this cannot be done without great injury to himself: for his own feelings are his stay and support; and if he sets them aside in one instance, he may be induced to repeat this act till his mind loses all confidence in itself and becomes utterly debilitated. To this it may be added, that the Reader ought never to forget that he is himself exposed to the same errors as the Poet and,

Having thus explained a few of my reasons for writing in verse, and why I have chosen subjects from common life, and endeavoured to bring my language near to the real language of men, if I have been too minute in pleading my own cause, I have at the same time been treating a subject of general interest; and for this reason a few words shall be added with reference solely to these particular poems, and to some defects which will probably be found in them. I am sensible that my associations must have sometimes been particular instead of general, and that, consequently, giving to things a false importance, I may have sometimes written upon unworthy subjects; but I am less apprehensive on this account, than that my language may frequently have suffered from those arbitrary connexions of feelings and ideas with particular words and phrases, from which no man can altogether protect himself. Hence I have no doubt, that, in some instances, feelings, even of the ludicrous, may be given to my Readers by expressions which appeared to me tender and pathetic. Such faulty expressions, were I convinced they were faulty at present, and that they must necessarily continue to be so, I would willingly take all reasonable pains to correct. But it is dangerous to make these alterations on the simple authority of a few individuals, or even of certain classes of men; for where the understanding of an Author is not convinced, or his feelings altered, this cannot be done without great injury to himself: for his own feelings are his stay and support; and, if he set them aside in one instance, he may be induced to repeat this act till his mind shall lose all confidence in itself, and become utterly debilitated. to this it may be added, that the critic ought never to forget that he is himself exposed to the same errors as the Poet, and, perhaps, in a much greater degree: for there can be no presumption in saying of most readers, that it is not probable they will be so

612 my … writing 1836: 1802–32 *as* [382].
616 for … added 1836: 1802–32 *as* [386–7].
619–20 I may have sometimes 1836: 1802–32 *as* [390].
632 set 1836: 1802–32 *as* [402].
633 shall lose 1836: 1802–32 *as* [403].
633 become 1836 *[also* 1832, *wrongly*]: 1802–27 *as* [404].
634 critic 1836: 1802–32 *as* [404].
636 of … they 1836: 1802–32 *as* [404 ff].

perhaps in a much greater degree: for there can be no presumption in saying that it is not probable he will be so well acquainted with the various stages of meaning through which words have passed, or with the fickleness or stability of the relations of particular ideas to each other; and above all, since he is so much less interested in the subject, he may decide lightly and carelessly.

Long as I have detained my Reader, I hope he will permit me to caution him against a mode of false criticism which has been applied to Poetry in which the language closely resembles that of life and nature. Such verses have been triumphed over in parodies of which Dr. Johnson's Stanza is a fair specimen.

"I put my hat upon my head
And walk'd into the Strand,
And there I met another man
Whose hat was in his hand."

Immediately under these lines I will place one of the most justly admired stanzas of the "*Babes* in the Wood."

"These pretty Babes with hand in hand
Went wandering up and down;
But never more they saw the Man
Approaching from the town."

In both of these stanzas the words, and the order of the words, in no respect differ from the most unimpassioned conversation. There are words in both, for example, "the Strand," and "the Town," connected with none but the most familiar ideas; yet the one stanza we admit as admirable, and the other as a fair example of the superlatively contemptible. Whence arises this difference? Not from the metre, not from the language, not from the order of the words; but the *matter* expressed in Dr. Johnson's stanza is contemptible. The proper method of treating trivial and simple verses to which Dr. Johnson's stanza would be a fair parallelism is not to say this is a bad kind of poetry, or this is not poetry; but this wants sense; it is neither interesting in itself, nor can *lead* to anything interesting; the images neither originate in that sane state of feeling which arises out of thought, nor can excite thought or feeling in the Reader. This is the only sensible manner of dealing with such verses: Why trouble yourself about the species till you have previously decided upon the genus? Why take pains to prove that an Ape is not a Newton when it is self-evident that he is not a man.

I have one request to make of my Reader, which is, that in judging these well acquainted with the various stages of meaning through which words have passed, or with the fickleness or stability of the relations of particular ideas to each other; and, above all, since they are so much less interested in the subject, they may decide lightly and carelessly.

Long as the Reader has been detained, I hope he will permit me to caution him against a mode of false criticism which has been applied to Poetry, in which the language closely resembles that of life and nature. Such verses have been triumphed over in parodies, of which Dr. Johnson's stanza is a fair specimen:—

'I put my hat upon my head
And walked into the Strand,
And there I met another man
Whose hat was in his hand.'

Immediately under these lines let us place one of the most justly admired stanzas of the "*Babes in the Wood.*"

'These pretty Babes with hand in hand
Went wandering up and down;
But never more they saw the Man
Approaching from the Town.'

In both these stanzas the words, and the order of the words, in no respect differ from the most unimpassioned conversation. There are words in both, for example, 'the Strand,' and 'the town,' connected with none but the most familiar ideas; yet the one stanza we admit as admirable, and the other as a fair example of the superlatively contemptible. Whence arises this difference? Not from the metre, not from the language, not from the order of the words; but the *matter* expressed in Dr. Johnson's stanza is contemptible. The proper method of treating trivial and simple verses, to which Dr. Johnson's stanza would be a fair parallelism, is not to say, this is a bad kind of poetry, or, this is not poetry; but, this wants sense; it is neither interesting in itself nor can *lead* to anything interesting; the images neither originate in that sane state of feeling which arises out of thought, nor can excite thought or feeling in the Reader. This is the only sensible manner of dealing with such verses. Why trouble yourself about the species till you have previously decided upon the genus? Why take pains to prove that an ape is not a Newton, when it is self-evident that he is not a man?

One request I must make of my reader, which is, that in judging these Poems he would decide by his own feelings genuinely, and not by reflection upon what

641 Long … detained 1836: 1802–32 *as* [411]. 670 One … must 1836: 1802–32 *as* [460].
649 let us 1836: 1802–32 *as* [419].

Poems he would decide by his own feelings genuinely, and not by reflection upon what will probably be the judgment of others. How common is it to hear a person say, "I myself do not object to this style of composition or this or that expression, but to such and such classes of people it will appear mean or ludicrous." This mode of criticism so destructive of all sound unadulterated judgement is almost universal: I have therefore to request that the Reader would abide independently by his own feelings, and that if he finds himself affected he would not suffer such conjectures to interfere with his pleasure.

If an Author by any single composition has impressed us with respect for his talents, it is useful to consider this as affording a presumption, that, on other occasions where we have been displeased, he nevertheless, may not have written ill or absurdly; and, further, to give him so much credit for this one composition as may induce us to review what has displeased us with more care than we should otherwise have bestowed upon it. This is not only an act of justice, but in our decisions upon poetry especially, may conduce in a high degree to the improvement of our own taste: for an *accurate* taste in Poetry and in all the other arts, as Sir Joshua Reynolds has observed, is an *acquired* talent, which can only be produced by thought and a long continued intercourse with the best models of composition. This is mentioned not with so ridiculous a purpose as to prevent the most inexperienced Reader from judging for himself, (I have already said that I wished him to judge for himself;) but merely to temper the rashness of decision, and to suggest that if Poetry be a subject on which much time has not been bestowed, the judgement may be erroneous; and that in many cases it necessarily will be so.

I know that nothing would have so effectually contributed to further the end which I have in view as to have shewn of what kind the pleasure is, and how the pleasure is produced which is confessedly produced by metrical composition essentially different from what I have here endeavoured to recommend; for the Reader will say that he has been pleased by such composition and what can I do more for him? The power of any art is limited and he will suspect that if I propose to furnish him with new friends it is only upon condition of his abandoning his old friends. Besides, as I have said, the Reader is himself conscious of the pleasure which he has received from such composition, composition to will probably be the judgment of others. How common is it to hear a person say, I myself do not object to this style of composition, or this or that expression, but, to such and such classes of people it will appear mean or ludicrous! This mode of criticism, so destructive of all sound unadulterated judgement, is almost universal: let the Reader then abide, independently, by his own feelings, and, if he finds himself affected, let him not suffer such conjectures to interfere with his pleasure.

If an Author, by any single composition, has impressed us with respect for his talents, it is useful to consider this as affording a presumption, that on other occasions where we have been displeased, he, nevertheless, may not have written ill or absurdly; and further, to give him so much credit for this one composition as may induce us to review what has displeased us, with more care than we should otherwise have bestowed upon it. This is not only an act of justice, but, in our decisions upon poetry especially, may conduce, in a high degree, to the improvement of our own taste; for an *accurate* taste in poetry, and in all the other arts, as Sir Joshua Reynolds has observed, is an *acquired* talent, which can only be produced by thought and a long-continued intercourse with the best models of composition. This is mentioned, not with so ridiculous a purpose as to prevent the most inexperienced Reader from judging for himself, (I have already said that I wish him to judge for himself), but merely to temper the rashness of decision, and to suggest, that, if Poetry be a subject on which much time has not been bestowed, the judgement may be erroneous; and that, in many cases, it necessarily will be so.

Nothing would, I know, have so effectually contributed to further the end which I have in view, as to have shown of what kind the pleasure is, and how that pleasure is produced, which is confessedly produced by metrical composition essentially different from that which I have here endeavoured to recommend: for the Reader will say that he has been pleased by such composition; and what more can be done for him? The power of any art is limited; and he will suspect, that, if it be proposed to furnish him with new friends, that can be only upon condition of his abandoning his old friends. Besides, as I have said, the Reader is himself conscious of the pleasure which he has received from such composition, composition to which he has peculiarly attached the endear-

676 let ... then 1836: 1802–32 *as* [466].
677 and, ... him 1836: 1802–32 *as* [467].
695 Nothing ... know, 1836: 1802–32 *as* [485].
700 more ... done 1836: 1802–32 *as* [489–90].
701 it be proposed 1836: 1802–32 *as* [490–1].
701 that can be 1836: 1802–32 *as* [491].
703 himself 1800a^2: of himself 1800a.

which he has peculiarly attached the endearing name of Poetry; and all men feel an habitual gratitude, and something of an honorable bigotry for the objects which have long continued to please them: we not only wish to be pleased, but to be pleased in that particular way in which we have been accustomed to be pleased. There is a host of arguments in these feelings; and I should be the less able to combat them successfully, as I am willing to allow, that in order entirely to enjoy the Poetry which I am recommending, it would be necessary to give up much of what is ordinarily enjoyed. But would my limits have permitted me to point out how this pleasure is produced, I might have removed many obstacles, and assisted my Reader in perceiving that the powers of language are not so limited as he may suppose; and that it is possible that poetry may give other enjoyments, of a purer, more lasting, and more exquisite nature. But this part of my subject I have been obliged altogether to omit: as it has been less my present aim to prove that the interest excited by some other kinds of poetry is less vivid, and less worthy of the nobler powers of the mind, than to offer reasons for presuming, that, if the object which I have proposed to myself were adequately attained, a species of poetry would be produced, which is genuine poetry; in its nature well adapted to interest mankind permanently, and likewise important in the multiplicity and quality of its moral relations.

From what has been said, and from a perusal of the Poems, the Reader will be able clearly to perceive the object which I have proposed to myself: he will determine how far I have attained this object; and what is a much more important question, whether it be worth attaining; and upon the decision of these two questions will rest my claim to the approbation of the public.

ing name of Poetry; and all men feel an habitual gratitude, and something of an honourable bigotry, for the objects which have long continued to please them: we not only wish to be pleased, but to be pleased in that particular way in which we have been accustomed to be pleased. There is in these feelings enough to resist a host of arguments; and I should be the less able to combat them successfully, as I am willing to allow, that, in order entirely to enjoy the Poetry which I am recommending, it would be necessary to give up much of what is ordinarily enjoyed. But, would my limits have permitted me to point out how this pleasure is produced, many obstacles might have been removed, and the Reader assisted in perceiving that the powers of language are not so limited as he may suppose; and that it is possible for poetry to give other enjoyments, of a purer, more lasting, and more exquisite nature. This part of the subject has not been altogether neglected, but it has not been so much my present aim to prove, that the interest excited by some other kinds of poetry is less vivid, and less worthy of the nobler powers of the mind, as to offer reasons for presuming, that if my purpose were fulfilled, a species of poetry would be produced, which is genuine poetry; in its nature well adapted to interest mankind permanently, and likewise important in the multiplicity and quality of its moral relations.

From what has been said, and from a perusal of the Poems, the Reader will be able clearly to perceive the object which I had in view: he will determine how far it has been attained; and, what is a much more important question, whether it be worth attaining: and upon the decision of these two questions will rest my claim to the approbation of the Public.

708–9 in these … arguments 1845: 1802–32 *as* [498]: in these feelings enough to outweigh a host of arguments 1836.
713 many … removed 1836: 1802–32 *as* [502].
713 the Reader assisted 1836: 1802–32 *as* [503].
715 for poetry to 1820: 1802–15 *as* [504].
716–7 This … neglected, 1836: This party of my subject I have not altogether neglected; 1802–32.
717 but … much 1836: but it has been less 1802–32.
719 as 1836: 1802–32 *as* [508].
719–20 my … fulfilled 1836: 1802–32 *as* [509–10].
724 had in view 1836: 1802–32 *as* [514].
725 it … attained 1836: 1802–32 *as* [515].

APPENDIX

See page [171]—'by what is usually called Poetic Diction.'

Perhaps, as I have no right to expect that attentive perusal, without which, confined, as I have been, to the narrow limits of a preface, my meaning cannot be thoroughly understood, I am anxious to give an exact notion of the sense in which the phrase poetic diction has been used; and for this purpose, a few words shall here be added, concerning the origin and characteristics of the phraseology, which I have condemned under that name.

The earliest poets of all nations generally wrote from passion excited by real events; they wrote naturally, and as men: feeling powerfully as they did, their language was daring, and figurative. In succeeding times, Poets, and Men ambitious of the fame of Poets, perceiving the influence of such language, and desirous of producing the same effect without being animated by the same passion, set themselves to a mechanical adoption of these figures of speech, and made use of them, sometimes with propriety, but much more frequently applied them to feelings and thoughts with which they had no natural connection whatsoever. A language was thus insensibly produced, differing materially from the real language of men in *any situation.* The Reader or Hearer of this distorted language found himself in a perturbed and unusual state of mind: when affected by the genuine language of passion he had been in a perturbed and unusual state of mind also: in both cases he was willing that his common judgement and understanding should be laid asleep, and he had no instinctive and infallible perception of the true to make him reject the false; the one served as a passport for the other. The emotion was in both cases delightful, and no wonder if he

1 See page 1827: See Preface, page 1802–20.

2–4 Perhaps ... am 1836: As perhaps I have no right to expect from a Reader of an introduction to a volume of Poems that attentive perusal without which it is impossible, imperfectly as I have been compelled to express my meaning, that what I have said [what is said 1827–32] in the Preface should throughout be fully understood, I am the more 1802–32

5 the phrase ... used 1836: I use the phrase *poetic diction* 1802–32.

5–6 a few ... added 1836: I will here add a few words 1802–32.

6 and characteristics 1836: *om.* 1802–32.

12 being ... same 1836: having the same animating 1802–32.

13 these 1815: those 1802–5.

15 thoughts 1836: ideas 1802–32.

23 emotion was 1836: agitation and confusion of mind were 1802–32.

confounded the one with the other, and believed them both to be produced by the same, or similar causes. Besides, the Poet spake to him in the character of a man to be looked up to, a man of genius and authority. Thus, and from a variety of other causes, this distorted language was received with admiration; and Poets, it is probable, who had before contented themselves for the most part with misapplying only expressions which at first had been dictated by real passion, carried the abuse still further, and introduced phrases composed apparently in the spirit of the original figurative language of passion, yet altogether of their own invention, and characterised by various degrees of wanton deviation from good sense and nature.

It is indeed true, that the language of the earliest Poets was felt to differ materially from ordinary language, because it was the language of extraordinary occasions; but it was really spoken by men, language which the Poet himself had uttered when he had been affected by the events which he described, or which he had heard uttered by those around him. To this language it is probable that metre of some sort or other was early superadded. This separated the genuine language of Poetry still further from common life, so that whoever read or heard the poems of these earliest Poets felt himself moved in a way in which he had not been accustomed to be moved in real life, and by causes manifestly different from those which acted upon him in real life. This was the great temptation to all the corruptions which have followed: under the protection of this feeling succeeding Poets constructed a phraseology which had one thing, it is true, in common with the genuine language of poetry, namely, that it was not heard in ordinary conversation; that it was unusual. But the first Poets, as I have said, spake a language which, though unusual, was still the language of men. This circumstance, however, was disregarded by their successors; they found that they could please by easier means: they became proud of modes of expression which they themselves had invented, and which were uttered only by themselves. In process of time metre became a symbol or promise of this unusual language, and whoever took upon him to write in metre, according as he possessed more or less of true poetic genius, introduced less or more of this

32 characterised 1836: distinguished 1802–32.
50–1 modes of expression 1836: a language 1802–32.
51 were 1836: was 1802–32.
52 themselves. 1836: themselves; and, with the spirit of a fraternity, they arrogated it to themselves as their own. 1802–32.
52 or 1802–7, 1836–50: of [*sic*] 1832.

adulterated phraseology into his compositions, and the true and the false were inseparably interwoven until, the taste of men becoming gradually perverted, this language was received as a natural language: and at length, by the influence of books upon men, did to a certain degree really become so. Abuses of this kind were imported from one nation to another, and with the progress of refinement this diction became daily more and more corrupt, thrusting out of sight the plain humanities of nature by a motley masquerade of tricks, quaintnesses, hieroglyphics, and enigmas.

It would not be uninteresting to point out the causes of the pleasure given by this extravagant and absurd diction. It depends upon a great variety of causes, but upon none, perhaps, more than its influence in impressing a notion of the peculiarity and exaltation of the Poet's character, and in flattering the Reader's self-love by bringing him nearer to a sympathy with that character; an effect which is accomplished by unsettling ordinary habits of thinking, and thus assisting the Reader to approach to that perturbed and dizzy state of mind in which if he does not find himself, he imagines that he is *balked* of a peculiar enjoyment which poetry can and ought to bestow.

The sonnet quoted from Gray, in the Preface, except the lines printed in Italics, consists of little else but this diction, though not of the worst kind; and indeed, if one may be permitted to say so, it is far too common in the best writers both ancient and modern. Perhaps in no way, by positive example could more easily be given a notion of what I mean by the phrase *poetic diction* than by referring to a comparison between the metrical paraphrases which we have of passages in the Old and New Testament, and those passages as they exist in our common Translation. See Pope's "Messiah" throughout; Prior's 'Did sweeter sounds adorn my flowing tongue,' &c. &c. 'Though I speak with the tongues of men and of angels,' &c. &c., 1st Corinthians, chap. xiii. By way of immediate example take the following of Dr. Johnson:

54–5 were … until, 1845: became so inseparably interwoven that 1802–36. becoming 1845: was 1802–36.

55 perverted, this 1845: perverted; and this 1802–36.

62 not be uninteresting 1836: be highly interest 1802–32.

63 diction. It 1836: language; but this is not the place; it 1802–32.

71 quoted 1836: which I have quoted 1802–32.

73 one 1836: I 1802–32.

74–5 in… given 1836: I can in no way, by positive example, more easily give my Reader 1802–32.

76 referring 1836: referring him 1802–32.

77 paraphrases 1802–5 *recte*: paraphrase 1815–50.

80 1st…xiii 1836: See 1st Corinthians Chapter 13th [*or* xiiith] 1802–32.

'Turn on the prudent Ant thy heedless eyes,
Observe her labours, Sluggard, and be wise;
No stern command, no monitory voice,
Prescribes her duties, or directs her choice;
Yet, timely provident, she hastes away
To snatch the blessings of a plenteous day;
When fruitful Summer loads the teeming plain,
She crops the harvest, and she stores the grain.
How long shall sloth usurp thy useless hours,
Unnerve thy vigour, and enchain thy powers?
While artful shades thy downy couch enclose,
And soft solicitation courts repose,
Amidst the drowsy charms of dull delight,
Year chases year with unremitted flight,
Till Want now following, fraudulent and slow,
Shall spring to seize thee, like an ambush'd foe.'

From this hubbub of words pass to the original. 'Go to the Ant, thou Sluggard, consider her ways, and be wise: which having no guide, overseer, or ruler, provideth her meat in the summer, and gathereth her food in the harvest. How long wilt thou sleep, O Sluggard? when wilt thou arise out of thy sleep? Yet a little sleep, a little slumber, a little folding of the hands to sleep. So shall thy poverty come as one that travelleth, and thy want as an armed man.' Proverbs, chap. vi.

One more quotation, and I have done. It is from Cowper's Verses supposed to be written by Alexander Selkirk:—

105 vi 1827: 6th [*or* vith] 1802–20. *After* vi. 1802a (*Hale White, pp. 47–8*) *inserts and cancels*: In order further to point out some of the ordinary and less disgusting shapes which Misdiction puts on at the present day, I will transcribe a poem published a few years ago, which, though of great merit, is crowded with these defects. [printed opposite]

The Reader has only to translate this sonnet into such language as any person of good sense and lively sensibility, one, I mean who does not talk out of books—would use upon such occasion in real life, and he will at once perceive in what manner the passages printed in italics are defective.

Could then the Babes from yon *unshelter'd* cot
Implore thy *passing charity* in vain?
Too thoughtless Youth! what though *thy happier lot*
Insult their life of poverty and pain.
What though their Maker doom'd them thus forlorn
To brook the mockery of the *taunting throng*
Beneath the *Oppressor's iron scourge* to mourn
To *mourn, but not to murmur* at *his wrong*!
Yet when their *last late* evening shall decline
Their evening chearful though their day distrest,
A Hope perhaps more *heavenly bright* than thine,
A Grace by thee unsought, and unpossest,
A Faith more fix'd, a rapture more divine
Shall gild their passage to eternal rest.—RUSSEL.

'Religion! what treasure untold
Resides in that heavenly word!
More precious than silver and gold,
Or all that this earth can afford.
But the sound of the church-going bell
These valleys and rocks never heard,
Ne'er sighed at the sound of a knell,
Or smiled when a sabbath appeared.

Ye winds, that have made me your sport
Convey to this desolate shore
Some cordial endearing report
Of a land I must visit no more.
My Friends, do they now and then send
A wish or a thought after me?
O tell me I yet have a friend,
Though a friend I am never to see.'

This passage is quoted as an instance of three different styles of composition. The first four lines are poorly expressed; some Critics would call the language prosaic; the fact is, it would be bad prose, so bad, that it is scarcely worse in metre. The epithet 'church-going' applied to a bell, and that by so chaste a writer as Cowper, is an instance of the strange abuses which Poets have introduced into their language, till they and their Readers take them as matters of course, if they do not single them out expressly as objects of admiration. The two lines 'Ne'er sighed at the sound,' &c., are, in my opinion, an instance of the language of passion wrested from its proper use, and, from the mere circumstance of the composition being in metre, applied upon an occasion that does not justify such violent expressions; and I should condemn the passage, though perhaps few Readers will agree with me, as vicious poetic diction. The last stanza is throughout admirably expressed: it would be equally good whether in prose or verse, except that the Reader has an exquisite pleasure in seeing such natural language so naturally connected with metre. The beauty of this stanza tempts me to conclude with a principle which ought never to be lost sight of, and which

124 This ... quoted 1836: I have quoted this passage 1802–32.

139–45 to conclude ... judicious 1836: here to add a sentiment which ought to be the pervading spirit of a system, detached parts of which have been imperfectly explained in the Preface, namely, that in proportion as ideas and feelings are valuable, whether the composition be in prose or in verse, they require and exact one and the same language 1802–20: to conclude with a principle which ought never to be lost sight of,—namely, that in works of imagination and sentiment, in proportion as ideas and feelings are valuable, whether the composition be in prose or in verse, they require and exact one and the same language. Metre is but adventitious to composition, and the phraseology for which has been my chief guide in all I have said,—namely, that in works *of imagination and sentiment,* for of these only have I been treating, in proportion as ideas and feelings are valuable, whether the composition be in prose or in verse, they require and exact one and the same language. Metre is but adventitious to composition, and the phraseology for which that passport is necessary, even where it may be graceful at all, will be little valued by the judicious.

that passport is necessary, even where it is graceful at all, will be little valued by the judicious 1827–32.

143 *After* language. 1802a (*Hale White, pp. 49–50*) *inserts and cancels*: The Reader, I hope, will believe that it is with great reluctance I have presumed, in this note, to censure so freely the writings of other Poets, and that I should not have done this, could I otherwise have made my meaning intelligible. The passages which I have condemned I have condemned upon principle, and I have given my reasons, else I should have been inexcusable. Without an appeal to laws and principles there can be no criticism. What passes under that name is, for the most part, little more than a string of random and extempore judgements, a mode of writing more cheap than any other, and utterly worthless. When I contrast these summary decisions with the pains and anxiety of original composition, especially in verse, I am frequently reminded of a passage of Drayton on this subject which, no doubt, he wrote with deep feeling:

Detracting what laboriously we do
Only by that which he but idly saith.

COMMENTARY: ADVERTISEMENT

1–2. It is ... mind.] Stated at much greater length in *P.L.B.* 351–55, 383-5, and especially 468–77.

5–7. Modified in wording, and to some extent in general sense, in *P.L.B.* 14–18, 73–5, 90–103.

7–11. Repeated in *P.L.B.* 60–64.

11–18. Restated in *P.L.B.* 670–78.

24. elder writers] It is difficult to see who these are, unless writers of ballads are intended: cf. 48–50, where *The Ancient Mariner* is said to imitate 'the *style* ... of the elder poets'. On the other hand, Shakespeare and Milton are associated with 'our elder writers', *P.L.B.*, 165–6.

25. those in modern times] Probably Burns and Cowper: cf. *E.Y.*, pp. 255–6: 'Now I find no manners in Burger; in Burns you have manners everywhere ... Burns also is energetic solemn and sublime in sentiment, and profound in feeling'; 'At the Grave of Burns, 1803', 31–6 (*P.W.*, iii, 66, and see *P. W.* iii. 441–2); Russell Noyes, 'Wordsworth and Burns', *PMLA* lix (1944), 813 ff. especially pp. 830–1; Thomasina Dennis to Davies Giddy, 23 June 1798, cited in R. S. Woolf, 'Coleridge and Thomasina Dennis', *U.T.Q.* xxxii (1962), 39: 'I was surprized to hear [Coleridge] says that Burns and Cowper were the only modern writers that deserve the Name of poet', and Woof's comments. For the meaning of *manners* see *P.L.B.* 86, [137], and nn.

27–34. Repeated almost verbatim in *P.L.B.* 686–94; see n. ad loc.

35–6. Cf. *P.L.B.* [373–9]. For the 'authentication' of the story, see *P.W.* iv. 439–40.

39–41. Cf. the expanded explanation of 1800–5, *P.W.* ii. 512–13.

43–5. Cf. *P.L.B.* 103, fn. Why 1498 should here be taken as Wordsworth's point of reference is not clear: did he mean to refer to Chaucer, as in *P.L.B.*, and miscalculate by a century? According to Hazlitt, *Works*, ed. Howe, xvii (London, 1933), 120, Coleridge made the upper limit 'the days of Henry II'. Arthur Beatty, *William Wordsworth: his Doctrine and Art* (2nd edn., Madison, Wis., 1927), p. 56, suggests that 'this is a slip for "Henry VII"', which would agree with 'these three last centuries' here. Possibly Wordsworth intended to refer to the language as it appears after the developments of the fifteenth century, in the works of such poets as Skelton, Wyatt and Surrey.

46. a friend] Said to be Hazlitt; see *P.W.* iv. 411.

COMMENTARY: PREFACE

6–7. PREFACE TO THE SECOND EDITION] The basis of the standard text is rather the Preface to the third edition of *L.B.* (1802); see textual apparatus *passim.*

14–15. *L.B.* (1800), vol. i, in the main reprints the poems of 1798, omitting 'The Convict', adding Coleridge's 'Love', and dividing 'Lines written near Richmond' into two poems.

16. language] 'idiom', 'style', 'mode of expression' in general, rather than 'vocabulary' as often interpreted. See especially *E.Y.*, p. 365: 'The Leech-Gatherer' 'is throughout written in the language of men—"I suffered much by a sickness had by me long ago" is a phrase which anybody might use, as well as "a sickness which I had long ago"', where 'the language of men' is to Wordsworth authority for one syntactical method (passive voice) as opposed to another (active voice), not for a particular vocabulary. See also n. on 238 below.

16–17. 'A selection from the language which men actually use when they are feeling intensely.' For another definition see 91–2, and n.

19–25. For an account of the criticism of *L.B.* (1798) see Smith, pp. 29–42.

[**14–16**], textual n. The complexity of the apparatus here arises mainly from the decision not to include 'Christabel' in *L.B.* (1800), taken 6 October 1800 (*Journals*, i. 64; *E.Y.*, pp. 304–5). What poems of Coleridge's might have been included 'under the title of "Poems on the Naming of Places"' cannot now be discovered; conceivably, parts of 'The Brook', projected in 1797 (*Biog. Lit.* i. 129). See also Hale White, pp. 18–20; *C.L.* i. 631, 637, 643.

26–31. The 'friends' would seem to be Coleridge. See *L.Y.*, pp. 910, 1248–9: 'Though prevailed upon by Mr. Coleridge to write the first Preface to my Poems'; 'The Prefaces...were written solely to gratify Coleridge'; note to Barron Field's memoir of Wordsworth, B.M. Add. MS. 41325, fol. 111^{v}: 'I never cared a straw about the theory—& the Preface was written at the request of Coleridge out of sheer good nature—I recollect the very spot, a deserted Quarry in the Vale of Grasmere where he pressed the thing upon me, & but for that it would never have been thought of.'

40–3. See 147–53, and *E.S. passim.*

60–4. Repeated from *Ad. L.B.* 6–11.

73–81. Cf. *Biog. Lit.* ii. 5–6, and Shawcross's n. to line 25, ibid., pp. 264–5.

81–97. Cf. *Exc.* I. 341 ff:

> much did he see of men,
> Their manners, their enjoyments, and pursuits,
> Their passions and their feelings; chiefly those
> Essential and eternal in the heart,
> That 'mid the simpler forms of rural life,
> Exist more simple in their elements,
> And speak a plainer language.

This passage was written by 1798 (*P.W.* v. 378). Cf. also *Exc.* V. 116–19: 'he prized / The ancient rural character, composed / Of simple manners, feelings unsupprest / And undisguised, and strong and serious thought'; *Recl.* I. i. 401–26. The language of eighteenth-century primitivistic critics is similar, e.g. Duff, pp. 269–70:

> The simple manners which prevail among most nations in the infancy of society, are peculiarly favourable to [the] exertions [of Poetic Genius]. In this primitive state of nature, the manners, sentiments, and passions are ... perfectly ORIGINAL. They are the dictates of nature, unmixed and undisguised: they are therefore more easily comprehended [cf. *P.L.B.* 73] AND DESCRIBED ... Their tastes, dispositions, and manners are thrown into the same mould, and generally formed upon one and the same model;

James Beattie, *Dissertations Moral and Critical* (London, 1783), pp. 191–2: 'accurate representations of human manners, especially in that state of primitive simplicity, in which they give a full display of the character [are pleasing]'.

86. manners] 'The modes of life, customary rules of behavior, conditions of society, prevailing in a people' (*O.E.D.*, sense 4. c). Cf. *E.Y.*, p. 255: 'I do not so ardently desire character in poems like Burger's, as manners, not transitory manners reflecting the wearisome unintelligible obliquities of city-life, but manners connected with the permanent objects of nature and partaking of the simplicity of those objects.'

89. incorporated] Seems to mean 'associated, closely connected'; cf. [129–30]: 'the strength of fraternal ... attachment when early associated with the great and beautiful objects that act upon ['the human mind']; *E.Y.*, p. 255: 'manners connected with the permanent objects of nature'.

90. nature] The sense of this word differs from context to context in this Preface and throughout Wordsworth's writings. Here it means 'external nature, natural surroundings'; cf. *E.Y.*, p. 255, where Etna is one of the 'permanent objects of nature'.

91–2. On the defects of rustic language see *Recl.* I. i. 341–6:

> That Shepherd's voice, it may have reached mine ear
> Debased and under profanation, made
> The ready Organ of articulate sounds

From ribaldry, impiety, or wrath
Issuing when shame hath ceased to check the brawls
Of some abused Festivity

(in MSS. A and B: 'An organ for the sounds articulate / Of ribaldry and blasphemy, and wrath / When drunkenness hath kindled senseless frays'); a passage perhaps written a few months before the Preface (*P.W.* v. 475). See also *Biog. Lit.* ii, 38: 'a rustic's language, purified from all provincialism and grossness'; Grosart, iii. 426: Wordsworth 'said his principle had been to give the oral part as nearly as he could in the very words of the speakers, where he narrated a real story, dropping, of course, all vulgarisms or provincialisms, and borrowing sometimes a Bible turn of expression: those former were mere accidents, not essential to the truth in representing how the human heart and passions worked'. The process described here does not seem to be identical with that of 'selection' emphasized especially in the texts of 1802 and later: for 'purification' is applied to the language of rustics, whatever the rustic may be expressing, whereas 'selection' is applied to the language of passion, whoever expresses it (see 258–65, 324–8).

98. philosophical language] Hartley, p. 149, defines it thus: 'If we suppose mankind possessed of such a language, as that they could at pleasure denote all their conceptions adequately, *i.e.* without any deficiency, superfluity, or equivocation; if, moreover, this language depended upon a few principles assumed, not arbitrarily, but because they were the shortest and best possible, and grew on from the same principles indefinitely, so as to correspond to every advancement in the knowledge of things, this language might be termed a philosophical one.' So Priestley, *Lectures on Language* (Warrington, 1762), p. 8: 'one of the last and greatest atchievements of human genius, viz. a philosophical and universal language, which shall be the most natural and perfect expression of human ideas and sentiments'. So 'to speak more philosophically' ([129–30]) means 'to speak more precisely'; cf. the equivalent phrase 'speaking with more precision', *E.Y.*, p. 627; 'more philosophical' (252, fn.) means 'more accurate, more precise'.

99–103. Cf. *E.E.* II. 403–17.

101–3. Cf. *Ap. L.B.* 8–62.

103. fn. According to Hale White, p. 19, this note appears in 1800a in Coleridge's hand. This is not obvious from a photograph of the MS.; the hand is, we believe, Dorothy Wordsworth's, written small so as to confine the note to the page concerned. Coleridge wrote a marginal instruction (next to 'creation'): 'See Bottom of page for Note to be printed, like the other notes at the Bottom of the page.'

104–6. We cannot identify the poets or their critics with certainty. Some of Southey's ballads and *English Eclogues* of the period might qualify for this description. Possibly Wordsworth is making a surreptitious hit at Southey in revenge for his review of *L.B.*, 1798. In similar vein, he told Robinson in 1812 that 'S[outhey] ... never inquires ... on what idea his poem is to be wrought, what feeling or passion is to be excited ... he does not give anything which impresses the mind strongly and is recollected in solitude' (*H.C.R.*, p. 87).

115. descriptions ... feelings] Cf. *Monthly Magazine*, ii (1796), 455: 'if it be the province of the poet, to observe, with a discriminating eye, the objects which are adapted to excite emotions, and to represent them with such distinctness and force as to make a vivid impression upon the reader's fancy ... '.

120. organic] Probably *O.E.D.*, sense 5: 'Belonging to or inherent in the organization or constitution (bodily or mental) of a living being; constitutional; fundamental', rather than sense 3: 'Of or pertaining to the bodily organs.'

121–31. Various passages in, or, related to, *The Prelude* seem relevant. Cf. *Prel.* III. 149–50: 'steady moods of thoughtfulness, matur'd / To inspiration'; and, for the notion of habitual (139–41) valuing ('important', 137, 138) of experience (probably on a moral basis), cf. the fragments from MS. W. cited in *Prel.*, pp. 535, 621: 'enjoyments ... / Instructing [the mind] to value, and to know / What it possess'd though slighted and unused'; the poet 'whose habits must have needs / Been such as shall have fitted him ... / For moral greatness' also *Exc.* IV. 1230–49, and especially an early draft of this in MS. B of 'The Ruined Cottage' (1798; *P.W.* v. 401):

> And further, by contemplating these forms
> In the *relations* which they bear to man
> We shall *discover* what a power is theirs
> To stimulate our minds, and multiply
> The spiritual presences of absent things.
> Then weariness shall cease. We shall acquire
> The [ ] *habit* by which sense is made
> Subservient still to *moral* purposes ...
> Nor shall we meet an *object* but may read
> Some sweet and tender lesson to our minds
> Of human suffering or of human joy. [Our italics.]

There are general resemblances between the passage under consideration and the later remarks on 'emotion recollected in tranquility' (585 ff.), on the one hand, and, on the other, certain tenets of John Dennis, especially Dennis, i. 217:

> Poetical Enthusiasm, is a Passion guided by Judgement, whose Cause is not comprehended by us ... let us inquire, what the Cause of Poetical Enthusiasm is, that has been hitherto not comprehended by us. That Enthusiasm moves, is plain to Sense; why then it mov'd the Writer: But if it mov'd the Writer, it mov'd

> him while he was thinking. Now what can move a Man while he is thinking, but the Thoughts that are in his Mind? In short, Enthusiasm, as well as ordinary Passions, must proceed from the Thoughts ... but the Reason why we know not the Causes of Enthusiastick, as well as of ordinary Passions, is, because we are not so us'd to them, and because they proceed from Thoughts, that latently, and unobserv'd by us, carry Passion along with them. Here it would be no hard matter to prove, that most of our Thoughts, are naturally attended with some sort, and some degree of Passion. And 'tis the Expression of this Passion, which gives us so much Pleasure, both in Conversation, and in Human Authors ... If any one asks, What sort of Passions these are, that thus, unknown to us, flow from these Thoughts? to him I answer, That the same sort of Passions flow from the Thoughts, that would do from the Things of which those Thoughts are Ideas.

Cf. also n. to 'The Thorn' (1800; *P.W.* ii. 513): 'Poetry is passion', with Dennis, i, 199, 211, 215: 'Passion is the principal Thing in Poetry ... Passion making the Greatness and Beauty of Poetry ... That Passion is the chief Thing in Poetry.' In 1842 De Quincey claimed that he 'once collected [Dennis's] ridiculous pamphlets to oblige Wordsworth, who (together with S.T.C.) had an absurd "craze" about him' (cited in Dennis, ii, p. lxxiii). For Wordsworth's later and more obvious use of Dennis see *P. 1815*, 311 and n.; *E.S.* 138–9, 755–8, 781–804, and nn.

128. sentiments] 'Every thought prompted by passion is termed a *sentiment*' (Kames, i. 451).

129–30. understanding ... affections] Hartley's definitions (Hartley, p. iii) seem relevant: 'The understanding is that faculty, by which we contemplate mere sensations and ideas, pursue truth, and assent to, or dissent from, propositions. The affections have the pleasures and pains for their objects; as the understanding has the mere sensations and ideas. By the affections we are excited to pursue happiness, and all its mean, fly from misery, and all its apparent causes.' The understanding is the 'judging power', *E.E.*, Appendix I. 27.

[123–4]. In 'The Idiot Boy' and 'The Mad Mother' the 'maternal passion' is seen in 'its more subtle windings', since in the one case it is exercised on an abnormal object, in the other by an abnormal subject.

[137]. nature] *O.E.D.*, sense 2. B: 'The general inherent character or disposition of mankind'. Cf. the last line of 'The Two Thieves', and the following phrases in the context here.

[137] manners] See n. on 86 above. The sense cited there may be intended, or Wordsworth may mean something like 'individual character'; cf. *O.E.D.*, sense 4. e. *Nature* and *manners* are contrasted, and *nature* carries a wider sense than *manners*.

[145]. **Poor Susan ... Childless Father**] The situation of a country girl living in London is not inherently important; the emotions which the song of a thrush excites

(by association) 'give importance to the action and situation'. Similarly, the situation of a hunt is not important in itself; it is important in that it recalls to a childless father his loss and loneliness. Cf. *Prel.* XII. 286–9: 'the array / Of outward circumstance and visible form / Is to the pleasure of the human mind / What passion makes it'.

140–4. Cf. *Prel.* XIII. 90–102: 'higher minds ... build up greatest things / From least suggestions ... / They need not extraordinary calls / To rouze them'.

150. savage torpor] Itinerant pedlars are 'Apt instruments to soften and refine / Rude minds, and savage torpor to dispel' (*Exc.* VIII. 66–7, reading of MS.).

150–3. The most ... gratifies] Cf. *Cintra* 3974–80: 'Manufactures and Commerce have [in Spain] in far less degree than elsewhere—by unnaturally clustering the people together—enfeebled their bodies, inflamed their passions by intemperance, vitiated from childhood their moral affections, and destroyed their imaginations. Madrid is no enormous city, like Paris; over-grown, and disproportionate; sickening and bowing down, by its corrupt humours, the frame of the body politic.'

150. national events] No doubt the fortunes of the French war.

151. accumulation of men in cities] On this subject, see, for instance, Witt Bowden, *Industrial Society in England towards the End of the Eighteenth Century* (New York, 1925), pp. 95 ff. Manchester is said to have doubled its population in the period 1760–90 (op. cit., pp. 106–7).

153. rapid communication of intelligence] The mail-coach and the telegraph were recent inventions at the time.

157. frantic novels] Presumably the 'Gothic' novels of Horace Walpole and others. Wordsworth was concerned with the conventional materials of the form in some of his juvenilia: see *P.W.* i. Appendix, Nos. VII, VIII, X, XV, XXVIII; Ernest de Selincourt, 'The Early Wordsworth', in *Wordsworthian and Other Studies* (Oxford, 1947), pp. 1–33; Z. S. Fink, *The Early Wordsworthian Milieu* (Oxford, 1958), pp. 20–1.

157. German Tragedies] See Allardyce Nicoll, *History of Late Eighteenth Century Drama, 1750–1800* (Cambridge, 1927), pp. 61–9. 'While the German influences on our drama can be traced back to the early eighties of the century, the enthusiasm for the drama of Kotzebue and his companions did not reach a height till the years 1798–1800' (op. cit., p. 66).

158. stories in verse] Many were published in the magazines of the day; see Robert Mayo, 'The Contemporaneity of the *Lyrical Ballads*', *PMLA*, lxix (1954), 486–522.

161. with no dishonourable melancholy] Wordsworth means 'with a not dishonourable melancholy'.

171–6, [181–6]. In the text of 'The Female Vagrant', 1800, some of the personifications of the text of 1798 remain: see, for instance, *P.W.* i. 111 ff., textual notes to 297/8, 351/2. The removal of some of these in 1802 permits Wordsworth to use the stronger language of the main text.

Personification as a means of distinguishing poetry from prose was perhaps rejected as a counterblast to the theory of Erasmus Darwin in the first prose Interlude to his *Loves of the Plants* (3rd edn., London, 1791, pp. 48–9), the object of which is to discover 'the essential difference between Poetry and Prose' (cf. *P.L.B.* [248–9], 244–6). The difference is 'that Poetry admits of but few words expressive of very abstracted ideas, whereas Prose abounds in them.' Moreover, 'as our ideas derived from visible objects are more distinct than those derived from the objects of our other senses, the words expressive of those ideas belonging to vision make up the principal part of poetic language. That is, the Poet writes principally to the eye, the Prose-writer uses more abstracted terms.' This aim may be achieved by using 'Personifications and Allegories', because 'These are … arts of bringing objects before the eye; or of expressing sentiments in the language of vision.' Wordsworth referred in 1842 to 'the mischievous influence of Darwin's dazzling manner … upon my taste and natural tendencies' (*P.W.* iii. 442).

176–7. Cf. Blair, i. 384, 386, on 'the third and highest degree' of personification, 'when inanimate objects are introduced, not only as feeling and acting, but as speaking to us, or hearing and listening when we address ourselves to them': 'it is the style of strong passion only; and, therefore, never to be attempted, unless when the mind is considerably heated and agitated …. The first rule is, never to attempt [this sort of personification], unless when prompted by strong passion.'

177–9. Cf. *Ap. L.B.* 49–55, and textual n. to *Ap. L.B.* 50.

198–200. Cf. *Ap. L.B.* 10 ff.

202–57. Cf. Dennis, i. 24: '*Beaum*[*ont*]. Why, will you allow nothing to be said in Verse that may not be said in Prose too? *Freem*[*an*]. Yes, an Expression may be too florid, or too bold for Prose, and yet be very becoming of Verse. But every Expression that is false English in Prose, is barbarous and absurd in Verse too.' Wordsworth may have known this passage, but more probably the terms of this theory are derived from [William Enfield,] 'Is Verse Essential to Poetry?', *Monthly Magazine*, ii (1796), 455:

> The character of poetry, which may seem most to require that it be limited to verse, is its appropriate diction. It will be admitted, that metaphorical language, being more impressive than general terms, is best suited to poetry. That excited state of mind, which poetry supposes, naturally prompts a figurative style. But the language of fancy, sentiment, and passion is not peculiar to verse. Whatever is the natural and proper expression of any conception or feeling in metre or

> rhyme, is its natural or proper expression in prose. All beyond this is a departure from the true principles of taste. If the artificial diction of modern poetry would be improper, on similar occasions, in prose, it is equally improper in verse. In support of this opinion, the appeal may be made, not only to the general sense of propriety, but to those perfect models of fine writing, the Greek poets. The language of these great masters is always is so consonant to nature, that, thrown out of rhythm, it would become the proper expression of the same sentiment in prose. If modern poetry will seldom bear to be brought to the same taste [*? misprint for* test], it is because the taste of the moderns has been refined to a degree of fastidiousness, which leads them to prefer the meretricious ornaments of art, to the genuine simplicity of nature.

The drift of this article is to show that 'metaphorical' and 'figurative' prose may reasonably be called *poetry*, rather than to demonstrate Wordsworth's thesis. But he almost certainly knew the article: see 252, fn., and n.; 507–11 and n.; introductory n. to *Ap. L.B.*; Moorman, i. 309.

218. by their reasonings] Wordsworth probably remembers Gray's dictum that 'the language of the age is never the language of poetry'; see *Correspondence*, ed. Toynbee and Whibley (Oxford, 1935), pp. 192–3.

222–35. Gray, 'Sonnet on the Death of Richard West'.

238. The use … fruitlessly] The point made is that Gray's Latinate idiom, subject: adjective: verb, does not agree with the normal English prose-idiom subject: verb: adverb. In *Guilt and Sorrow*, 376, Wordsworth substituted 'Dismally tolled' for 'How dismal tolled' in texts later than 1800 (see also *E.Y.*, p. 329). See n. on 16.

247. call them Sisters] Cf. *E.S.* 827. A commonplace in eighteenth-century aesthetics; see, for instance, Gerard, *Taste*, p. 84; Mason, *Art of Painting*, in Reynolds, *Works* (London, 1798), iii. 27; Reynolds, *Works*, i. 71.

252, fn. Cf. *Monthly Magazine*, ii (1796), 456: 'the terms *poetry* and *prose* are incorrectly opposed to each other. *Verse* is, properly, the contrary of *prose*; and because poetry speaks the language of fancy, passion, and sentiment, and philosophy speaks the language of reason, these two terms should be considered as contraries, and writing should be divided, not into poetry and prose, but into *poetry* and *philosophy*' (noted by Barstow, p. 122). The distinction between 'Poetry' and 'Matter of Fact' (not in 1800) is perhaps an echo of Aristotle's distinction between poetry and history: cf. 343–57 (a passage also added after 1800). For the distinction between poetry and science, see 383–425; *E.S.* 22–7. For the last part of the footnote cf. Dryden, Epistle Dedicatory of *The Rival Ladies*, in *Essays*, i. 6: 'Shakespeare (who … had undoubtedly a larger soul of poesy than ever any of our nation) was the first who … invented that kind of writing which we call blank verse … into which the English tongue so naturally slides, that, in writing prose, it is hardly to be avoided'; and so

Dennis, ii. 4–5. See also n. on 295 below.

252. 'such as Angels weep'] *Paradise Lost*, I. 620.

265. Whence is it to come?] 'What other factor distinguishing the language of poetry from that really spoken by men could be added?'

265. where] 'In what parts of the composition' or 'in what sorts of composition'.

268 ff. That figurative language is the 'natural' expression of passion is a commonplace of eighteenth-century critical theory. Cf. 176–7; Dennis, i. 135: 'The Sentiments ought to be bold and figurative; and the more violent the Passions are, the bolder may the Language be'; i. 215: 'a Discourse that is every where extremely pathetick, and, consequently, every where bold and figurative, is certainly Poetry without Numbers'; i. 359: 'figurative Language is but a Consequence of the Enthusiasm, that being the natural Language of the Passions'; Francis Hutcheson, *Inquiry into the Original of our Ideas of Beauty and Virtue* (2nd edn., London, 1726), p. 258: 'The various Figures of Speech, are the several Manners which a lively Genius, warm'd with Passions suitable to the Occasion, naturally runs into ... and they only move the *Hearers*, by giving a lively Representation of the Passions of the *Speaker*; which are communicated to the *Hearers*'; Kames, i. 497–8: 'figures are not equally the language of every passion: pleasant emotions, which elevate or swell the mind, vent themselves in strong epithets and figurative expression; but humbling and dispiriting passions affect to speak plain ... Figurative expression, being the work of an enlivened imagination, cannot be the language of anguish or distress'; Priestley, *Oratory*, p. 188: Metaphors 'are ... very properly put into the mouth of a person under any emotion of mind; and the stronger are his emotions, the bolder figures he naturally uses'; Blair, i. 319: 'Figures ... may be described to be that language, which is prompted either by the imagination, or by the passions.' Only passion (and imagination, according to Blair) can justify the use of figures': cf. 176 ff.; *App. L.B.* 8 ff.; Blair i. 322: 'it is ... the sentiment or passion, which lies under the figured expression that gives it any merit'; ii. 2: Figures 'are beautiful, then only, when they are prompted by fancy, or by passion. They must arise of their own accord'; *Monthly Magazine*, ii (1796), 455: 'That excited state of mind, which poetry supposes, naturally prompts a figurative style'; Coleridge to Sotheby, 13 July 1802 (*C.L.* ii. 812): 'every phrase, every metaphor, every personification, should have it's justifying cause in some *passion* either of the Poet's mind, or of the Characters described by the poet.'

274–7. The sentence is grammatically incomplete: it should proceed to the effect: 'than if the whole composition is characterized by metaphors and figures'. Alternatively delete *more* in 274. The general sense is that the 'metaphors and figures' justified by 'passion' will gain in effect by contrast with 'subdued and temperate' passages, which should not, therefore, be inflated by 'artificial distinctions' for which there is no justification in 'passion'.

280. moral feelings] Wordsworth connects these with aesthetic judgements in some way which he does not explain; cf. 29–30, 289–90, 578, 721–2; and especially *E.E.*, Appendix I, 1–28. In 1808 Wordsworth

> spoke at length on the connection of poetry with moral principles as well as with a knowledge of the principles of human nature. He said he could not respect the mother who could read without emotion his poem, *Once in a lonely hamlet I sojourned*. He said he wrote his *Beggars* to exhibit the power of physical beauty and health and vigour in childhood even in a state of moral depravity. He wished popularity for his *Two voices are there, one is of the Sea* as a test of elevation and moral purity [*H.C.R.*, pp. 10–11; cf. *C.R.*, p. 53].

From such passages it appears that Wordsworth has some notion of a 'moral sense', akin to the aesthetic sense ('taste'), and similar to that postulated by such moralists as Shaftesbury and Hutcheson; and regarded (though not as innate) by Hartley (pp. ii, 202–3) as the highest of, and 'generated' by a combination of the lower varieties of, the 'intellectual affections'. Hartley recognizes the affinity of his 'moral sense' with that proposed by others 'as an instinct' (p. 332); he notes also the connection of its 'pleasures and pains' with those of the imagination (p. 330), which include poetry (pp. 262 ff.) and other arts. So Gerard, *Taste*, p. 74: 'The moral sense is not only itself a taste of a superior order … but it also spreads its influence over all the most considerable works of art and genius'; Reynolds, *Discourse VII*, in *Works* (London, 1798), i. 224–5: 'the good and virtuous man alone can acquire this true or just relish even of works of art … The same disposition, the same desire to find something steady, substantial and durable on which the mind can lean … and rest with safety, actuates us [in both art and life]'; *C.L.* ii. 1054 (1 Feb. 1804): 'the intimate Connection of Taste & Morals'.

295. comprehensive] Perhaps 'that grasps or understands (a thing) fully' (*O.E.D.*, sense 2. a): more probably, 'embracing many things, broad in mental grasp, sympathies, or the like' (sense 2. b). Probably remembered from Dryden on Shakespeare: 'the man who … had the … .most comprehensive soul', *Essays of Dramatic Poetry* in *Essays*, i, 79; and cf. n. on 252, fn., above,

299. to create them] Presumably by attributing them to inanimate objects: the boy Wordsworth found retributive purpose in the mountain which 'strode after him' (*Prel.* I. 372–427): 'the breeze [is] gifted with that love of the sound which the Poet feels' in 'O Nightingale' (*P. 1815*, 225–6).

300–1. Cf. Quintilian, *Inst. Orat.* VI. ii. 29: 'visiones … per quas imagines rerum absentium ita repraesentantur animo, ut eas cernere oculis ac praesentes habere videamur'. Wordsworth owned two copies of Quintilian (Rydal Mount Catalogue, lots 389, 413).

304, sympathy] 'Common feelings' rather than 'mutual feeling'; *general sympathy* seems to mean 'the conglomerate of feelings common to all individuals'. Cf. 'undistinguishable sympathies' ('When, to the attractions', 107; *P.W.* ii. 122): John Wordsworth and his brother feel the same feelings towards Grasmere; 'traditionary sympathies / Of a most rustic ignorance' (*Exc.* IV. 614–15), which seems to mean 'the traditional feelings [of superstition] common to ignorant rustics'; *The Borderers*, 2276: 'links of sympathy', i.e. the remorse which both Marmaduke and Oswald will feel. In *E.E.* I. 315 ff., general sympathy is used more or less as a synonym for 'the common or universal feeling of humanity', and is contrasted with 'particular thoughts, actions, images,—circumstances of age, occupation, manner of life' etc. Cf. also *E.E.* ii. 574–8, III. 4–7, 132–4, 335–6.

312–5, 317–9, 332–4. The notion that strong feeling prompts an adequate or eloquent utterance is found in Quintilian, X, vii. 15: 'Pectus est enim, quod disertos facit, et vis mentis. Ideoque imperitis quoque, si modo sint aliquot adfectu concitati, verba non desunt.' This passage is cited by Wordsworth in his letter to Fox of 14 Jan. 1801 (*E.Y.*, p. 315), and is used as a motto on the half-title of *L.B.*, edns. of 1802 and 1805. The passage immediately preceding in Quintilian refers back to VI. ii. 29; see n. on 328–30. So Blair, ii. 165:

> the high eloquence which I have last mentioned, is always the offspring of passion. By passion, I mean that state of the mind in which it is agitated and fired, by some object it has in view ... Passion, when in such a degree as to rouse and kindle the mind, without throwing it out of the possession of itself, is universally found to exalt all the human powers ... Almost every man, in passion, is eloquent. Then, he is at no loss for words and arguments. He transmits to others, by a sort of contagious sympathy, the warm sentiments which he feels.

313. liveliness and truth] Cf. *Prel.* XII, 260 ff.: 'Men [rustics] may be found ... / Expressing liveliest thoughts in lively words / As native passion dictates'; and XII. 181/2, deleted reading of MS. Y: 'There [on country walks] I heard, / [And in the tongue of truest eloquence] / From mouths of lowly men and of obscure / A tale of honour.'

319–22. Cf. Aristotle, *Poetics*, 1455ᵃ30–2: πιθανώτατοι γὰρ ἀπὸ τῆς αὐτῆς φύσεως οἱ ἐν τοῖς πάθεσίν εἰσιν καὶ χειμαίνει ὁ χειμαζόμενος καὶ χαλεπαίνει ὁ ὀργιζόμενος ἀληθινώτατα [Greek transcriptions here and later kindly checked by Hazel Dunn and translated by John Beer, for this ebook edition: 'since a natural affinity makes those in the grip of emotions the most convincing, and the truest distress or anger is conveyed by one who actually feels these things']; Horace, *Ars Poetica*, 102–3: 'si vis me flere, dolendum est / Primum ipsi tibi' [If you wish to draw tears from me, you must first feel pain yourself]; Quintilian, VI. ii. 26 ff., especially 27: 'Quare in iis, quae esse verisimilia volemus, simus ipsi similes eorum qui vere patiuntur adfectibus' ['Consequently, where we wish to give an impression of reality, let us assimilate ourselves to the emotions of those who really suffer']; cf. notes on 300–1, 312–5. So Dennis, i. 291: 'For a Comick Poet is obliged to put off himself, and transform himself into his several Characters; to enter into the Foibles of his several persons, and all the Recesses and secret turns of their minds, and to make their Passions, their Interests, and their Concern his own'; James Beattie, *Essays on Poetry and Music* (3rd edn., London, 1779), p. 53: 'if [the poet] would have his heroes and heroines speak the language of love or sorrow, devotion or courage [etc.], his heart must be susceptible of those emotions, and in some degree feel them, as long at least as he employs himself in framing words for them'; Blair, ii. 365: 'In order to be probable in narration, it is material to enter into the characters of the persons of whom we speak'; so ii. 386, citing the passage from Quintilian cited above; iii. 308–9: 'To paint passion … requires the author to have the power of entering deeply into the characters which he draws; of becoming for a moment the very person whom he exhibits, and of assuming all his feelings … there is no possibility of speaking properly the language of any passion, without feeling it'; Gerard, *Genius*, p. 357:

> the passions and affections of the soul … can be expressed only by the person whose sensibility of heart enables him to conceive the passion with vivacity, to catch it as if by infection … it is the fancy, excited by the lively conception of the passion, running into the same thoughts which the passion, if really working, would suggest, and placing the artist in the situation in which he would then be, that puts it in his power to imagine, and consequently to represent, its causes and its objects in a way proper for infusing it into others.

The notion of imaginative identification with others, and hence of the author with his characters, is common in the late eighteenth century. See Walter Jackson Bate, *From Classic to Romantic* (Cambridge, Mass., 1946), pp. 129–59. Wordsworth makes use of the idea in 'Inscription for a Seat' (*P.W.* i. 300), 7–12. Cf. also *The Borderers*, 1553–9 and 1862–5.

In the state described, the poet's utterance is, as it were, automatic; see Duff, pp. 152–4: the epic poet

> will admirably succeed in the invention of PATHETIC as well as SUBLIME sentiments; if an Author can be said to invent sentiments which rise to the imagination, in a manner by simple volition, without any labour, and almost without any effort. Such a person being endued with a vivacity and vigour of Imagination, as well as an exquisite sensibility of every emotion, whether pleasant or painful, which can

> affect the human heart, has nothing else to do, in order to move the passions of others, but to represent his own feelings in a strong and lively manner; and to exhibit the object, event or action ... in that particular attitude or view, which has most powerfully interested his own affections, for that will most certainly interest ours: we shall feel the same concern, and share in the same distress .... The sentiments of an Author of this kind are the natural dictates of the heart, not fictitious or copied, but original.

So Priestley, *Oratory*, p. 172: 'A person who represents another as under the influence of any passion, should almost forget that he is only describing, and should feel himself: otherwise his mind will be in so different a situation from that of the person he is describing, that it will be absolutely impossible that the same thoughts should occur to him.'

Some eighteenth-century critics make a distinction between the description and the imitation (or representation) of passions, characters, and the like, e.g. Gerard, *Genius*, pp. 169, 172–3:

> a fault very common in dramatic poetry: persons are made to express their passions, not as if they were really actuated by them, but as if they were spectators of them in others; the poet gives not a natural *representation* of the passion, but a laboured *description* of it ... an indifferent poet ... feels not the passion, he has not force of genius or sensibility of heart sufficient for conceiving how it would affect a person who felt it, or for entering into the sentiments which it would produce in him ... in order to conceive sentiments natural to him, the poet ought to have confined himself to the consideration of the object from this one point of view, as strictly connected with a passion and suggested by it; he ought to indulge only such a train of thought, as it would lead to in these circumstances, or such a train as the passion with which it is presently connected, would introduce into the mind of a person under the power of that passion.

So Lord Monboddo, *Of the Origin and Progress of Language* (Edinburgh, 1776), iii. 125–6; Blair, iii. 309; Kames, i. 451; Priestley, *Oratory*, p. 103. Wordsworth's phrase 'describes and imitates' may echo this distinction.

322–7. Cf. *Burns*, 194–8; *E.E.* I. 335–40. Wordsworth's views show some affinity with those of Lessing (*Laokoon*, Ch. ii) on the plastic arts:

> the aim of knowledge is truth; truth is necessary to the soul, and it becomes tyranny to do it the smallest violence in the gratification of this essential need. The aim of art, on the contrary, is pleasure ... There are passions, and degrees of passion, which are expressed by the ugliest possible contortions of countenance, and throw the whole body into such a forced position that all the beautiful lines which cover its surface are lost. From all such emotions the ancient master either abstained entirely, or reduced them to that lower degree in which they are capable of a certain measure of beauty. [Thus Timanthus in his painting of the sacrifice of Iphigeneia concealed the face of Agamemnon (though he was quite capable of portraying it distorted with grief), and in the Laokoon the sculptor has softened the father's shriek to a sigh.] It is certain that this softening down of

> extreme bodily pain to a lower degree of feeling is perceptible in several productions of ancient art [trans. E. C. Beasley, in *Selected Prose Works*, Bohn edn., London, 1913, pp. 13–18].

Lessing proceeds to argue, contrary to Wordsworth's view, that the poet does not need the process of 'softening', unless in drama in which stage performance is envisaged.

We find no direct evidence that Wordsworth read *Laokoon*. But the Preface was presumably revised between June 1801 and April 1802 (see Introd.); we therefore note that in February 1802 Dorothy Wordsworth was reading German, including 'Lessing's Fables' and another work which she calls 'Lessing's Essay' (*Journals*, i. 107, 117). In 1798 Wordsworth 'complained of Nathan ... as tedious' (*Klopstock*, 85), and Lessing was evidently under discussion with Coleridge in 1799 (*E.Y.*, p. 255).

322–3. Wordsworth means 'modifying the language ... only by a consideration' etc.

328. nature] Probably 'natural utterance'; cf. 482: 'the real language of nature'; *Ap. L.B.* 30–3: 'phrases ... characterised by various degrees of wanton deviation from good sense and nature'; *Ap. L.B.* 60–1: '[poetic] diction ... thrusting out of sight the plain humanities of nature'; *E.E.* II. 413–15: a misguided mourner 'thought that the further he wandered from nature in his language the more would he honour his departed Consort'; Lovejoy, p. 72, sense 15: 'Self-expression without self-consciousness; freedom from premeditation or deliberate and reflective design, artlessness.'

335–8. translator ... submit] Probably from Delille, *Discours*, p. xlix:

> Il n'y a pas dans Virgile un seul endroit imitatif, pour lequel je n'aie fait les mêmes efforts: mais comme il n'est pas possible que j'aie toujours réussi, je m'en suis dédommagé, autant que je l'ai pu, en mettant de l'harmonie imitative dans plusieurs vers, où Virgile n'en a point mis; car il faut être quelquefois supérieur à son original, précisément parcequ'on lui est très inférieur; [pp. l–li:] Quiconque se charge de traduire, contracte une dette; il faut, pour l'acquitter, qu'il paie, non avec la même monnoie, mais la même somme: quand il ne peut rendre une image, qu'il y supplée par une pensée; si'l ne peut peindre à l'oreille, qu'il peigne à l'espirit [etc.]; en sorte qu'il établisse par-tout une juste compensation.

By 1822 Wordsworth had come round to Delille's view: 'Having been displeased in modern translations with the additions of incongruous matter, I began to translate [the *Aeneid*] with a resolve to keep clear of that fault, by adding nothing; but I became convinced that a spirited translation can scarcely be accomplished in the English language without admitting a principle of compensation' (*P.W.* iv. 470).

343. philosophic] Probably 'precise, authentic, adequate to the subject matter' (cf. n. on 109); not Aristotle's sense. Aristotle does not say what Wordsworth here attributes to him, but that poetry is more philosophical than history. *Poetics*, $1451^{b}5$–7: διὸ καὶ φιλοσοφώτερον καὶ σπονδαιότερον ποίησις ἱστορίας ἐστίν· 'η μὲν γὰρ ποίησις μᾶλλον τὰ καθόλου, ἡ δ' ἱστορία τὰ καθ' ἕκαστον λέγει ['Consequently, poetry is more philosophical and more elevated than history, since poetry relates more of the universal, while history relates particulars']. Coleridge, presumably the source of Wordsworth's information, makes Aristotle say what Wordsworth here attributes to him: *Biog. Lit.* ii. 101, σπουδαιότατον καὶ φιλοσοφώτατον γένος ['the noblest and most philosophical mode'] is written for φιλοσοφώτερον καὶ σπουδαιότερον. It is improbable that Wordsworth had any first-hand knowledge of the *Poetics* at this date. The distinction between poet and historian in *Prel.* XI. 91–2 sounds like a more accurate echo of Aristotle.

344–5. its object ... operative] Wordsworth is 'sensible that my associations must have sometimes been particular instead of general' (618–9), and that therefore the subjects concerned are unsuitable for poetry. For *operative*, cf. Davenant's 'truth narrative and past is the idol of historians, (who worship a dead thing), and truth operative, and by effects continually alive, is the mistress of poets', cited in *Biog. Lit.* ii. 102.

348. obstacles] The difficulties of biographical and historical research, which the poet does not have to face, since he deals with men, not with particular men. Cf. *Burns*, 71–3: it is improbable for 'a biographer to relate the truth, the *whole* truth, and nothing *but* the truth'.

351 ff. Truth 'Uplifts her fair proportions at the call / Of pleasure her best minister' (*P.W.* v. 342). Cf. *Burns*, 295–6, 394–5: 'the intrinsic efficacy of his poetry—to please, and to instruct ... imparting solid instruction through the medium of unalloyed pleasure'.

359–60. Since the poet deals with 'the universe', and since his poems are designed to produce pleasure in the reader, it follows that 'the universe; as the poet reveals it must be characterized by 'beauty'. This sounds Coleridgean: see *Biog. Lit.* ii, 223–4: poetry is 'the excitement of emotion for the purpose of immediate pleasure [cf. *P.L.B.* 387–8], through the medium of beauty'; also *Biog. Lit.* ii, 10, and other references in Shawcross's index, s. v. *Pleasure*.

362–3. Cf. *Exc.* VI. 666: 'The native grandeur of the human soul'. Wordsworth seems to mean that the reader receives pleasure, and justly, from perceiving the dignity of man as portrayed by the poet; and that 'the necessity of producing immediate pleasure' is consonant with 'the grand elementary principle of pleasure'.

363. ff. Cf. *Prel.* XII, 244–7. Pleasure as a universal motive is discussed by Dennis, i. 148–9: ' 'Tis universally acknowledg'd by Mankind, that Happiness consists in Pleasure, which is evident from this, that whatever a Man does, ... Pleasure is, at least, the chief and the final Motive to it, if it is not the immediate one ... . Man, in every Thing that he does, proposes pleasure to himself'; i. 337: 'we are mov'd by Pleasure which is Happiness, to do every thing we do.'

364–7. Cf. James Beattie, *Essays on Poetry and Music* (London, 1779), p. 117: 'there is something very peculiar in the nature of pity. The pain, however exquisite, that accompanies this amiable affection, is such, that a man of a generous mind would not disqualify himself for it, even if he could: nor is the "luxury of woe", that we read of in poetry, a mere figure of speech, but a real sensation ... The exercise of pity, even towards imaginary sufferings, cannot fail to give pleasure, if attended ... with the approbation of reason and conscience.'

367–9. Cf. *Exc.* IV. 346: 'For knowledge is delight' (written in 1800; see *P.W.* v. 370, 478).

371–3. Possibly suggested by Burke, *Enquiry* p. 108: 'How different is the satisfaction of an anatomist, who discovers the use of the muscles and of the skin ... from the affection which possesses an ordinary man at the sight of a delicate smooth skin, and all the other parts of beauty which require no investigation to be perceived? In the former case, whilst we look up to the Maker with admiration and praise, the object which causes it may be odious and distasteful.'

378–9. which ... intuitions] Qualifies only *deductions*; there is no comma after *deductions* in edns. 1802–5.

385–7. Cf. *P. Exc.* 120–6: 'my voice proclaims / How exquisitely the individual Mind / ... to the external World / Is fitted:—and how exquisitely, too ... / The external World is fitted to the Mind'; *Prel.* VIII. 756–8: 'all objects, being / Themselves capacious, also found in me / Capaciousness and amplitude of mind'; *Prel.*, p. 576: the future poet 'feels that, be his mind however great / In aspiration, the universe in which / He lives is equal to his mind, that each / Is worthy of the other; if the one / Be insatiate, the other is inexhaustible'; and with *P.L.B.* 385–6, cf. *Prel.*, p. 576:

Whatever dignity there be [ ]
Within himself, from which he gathers hope,
There doth he feel its counterpart the same
In kind before him outwardly express'd,
With difference that makes the likeness clear,
Sublimities, grave beauty, excellence,
Not taken upon trust, but self-displayed
Before his proper senses;

Misc. Son. I. x, especially MS. version cited in *P.W.* iii. 6–7.

389. general nature] The object of the 'knowledge which all men carry about with them' (383).

390. the Man of science] The distinction made here and below between the poet and the scientist no doubt represents Wordsworth's reaction to the claims of Humphry Davy on behalf of science, and in particular to Davy's introductory lecture given at the Royal Institution on 21 January 1802. See Roger Sharrock, 'The Chemist and the Poet: Sir Humphry Davy and the Preface to *Lyrical Ballads*', *Notes and Records of the Royal Society of London*, xvii (1962), 57–76; and for another instance of guarded approval of scientific achievement see *Cintra*, 4238, textual n.

400–1. impassioned ... Science] As an 'impassioned expression' gives meaning and unity to the separate features of the face, so poetry gives meaning and unity to 'all Science'. But Wordsworth appears to be saying above and below that science (= 'physical science') is not, or is not yet, suitable material for poetry. The figure is thus obscure.

402. 'that he ... after'] *Hamlet*, IV. iv, 37: 'Looking before and after'.

403. carrying ... relationship] Seems to mean 'bringing relationship to objects where it is not usually perceived', i.e. imaginatively imposing relationship. Cf. 296–300 above, and *Prel.* II. 403–5: 'observation of affinities / In objects where no brotherhood exists / To common [passive 1850] minds'; and II. 408–9: 'the great social principle of life, / Coercing all things into sympathy'.

409–10. atmosphere of sensation] Another obscure figure. If *atmosphere* is used equivocally to mean both 'mere appearance, semblance' and 'the medium of flight', the drift may be: 'though the poet will usually draw on such materials as are available to him through sense–experience yet he will also draw on meterial to which sense experience is in even the smallest degree relevant'. Cf. 415–6: 'carrying sensation into the midst of the objects of the science itself'.

411–25. Wordsworth looks forward to a time when scientific knowledge will become part of general truth, part of our 'natural and unalienable inheritance' (394), not, as when he writes, 'a personal and individual acquisition ... by no habitual and direct sympathy connecting us with our fellow–beings' (394–6). Cf. 'Steamboats, Viaducts, and Railways' (*P.W.* iv. 47).

425–8. Cf. *E.E.* II. 272–6.

453–8. Cf. *Ap. L.B.* 8–62, especially 49–55, and textual n. to 49–50.

477. in the spirit of human passions] 'In terms of human feelings', such as those just listed.

482–7. Similarly, 'an epitaph is not a proud writing shut up for the studious: it is exposed to all—to the wise and most ignorant' (*E.E.* I. 399–401).

495. certain] 'fixed', as the relative clause following shows.

507. imagery] 'Sensible objects really existing, and felt to exist, are *imagery*; and they may form the materials of a descriptive poem, where objects are delineated as they are' (Grosart, iii. 464). 'Images' are included in 'external things', *Prel.* I. 166; cf. I. 429–31: 'Thou Soul ... / That giv'st to forms and images a breath / And everlasting motion'; and *Prel.*, p. 636: 'The visible imagery of all the world'.

509–11. Cf. *Monthly Magazine*, ii (1796), 533: 'what is undoubtedly a very pleasing and impressive part of poetical composition, and has been a favourite of all nations, savage and civilized—the art of versification'; James Beattie, *Essays on Poetry and Music* (London, 1779), pp. 275–6: 'That the rhythm and measures of verse are naturally agreeable ... is evident from this, that children and illiterate people ... are exceedingly delighted with them.'

532 ff. The terminology is Hartleian; cf. 358–82, and see Owen, pp. 32–3, 84–5. Cf. also *Monthly Magazine*, ii. (1796), 455: 'That excited state of mind, which poetry supposes.' For the notion of the tempering of painful passion, cf. 592–6; *Prel.* XII. 245–7: 'Sorrow that is not sorrow, but delight, / And miserable love that is not pain / To hear of.'

535–8. Hartley, pp. 49–50: 'admitting the powers of ... association, compound or mental pains will arise from simple bodily ones by means of words, symbols, and associated circumstances ... the mere words denoting bodily pains, though not formed into propositions and threatening, affect children ... the very words, *burn*, *wound*, &c. seem even in adults ... to excite ... a perception of the disagreeable kind.' Wordsworth appears to follow some such account as this.

538 ff. Cf. *Biog. Lit.* ii. 49.

538–49. Cf. Johnson, *Rambler*, No. 88: 'that harmony [of metre] ... that shackles attention, and governs passions'; Priestley, *Oratory*, pp. 264–6:

> the strong sensations, excited by scenes of terror and compassion [in tragedy], are so much diminished by a conviction of their being only imaginary, as to fall within the limits of pleasure: since pleasure hath been defined to consist of sensations moderately vigorous, and pain of sensations exceeding that degree. [Metre is a means towards this conviction, since] several circumstances, which every moment demonstrate the scene to be no reality, have a good effect. Otherwise *prose* would be universally more agreeable than *verse*, because no person ever speaks seriously in verse;

C.L. ii. 814 (19 July 1802): 'wild Ducks *shaping* their rapid flight in forms always regular (a still better image of Verse)'.

554. the Gamester] A prose drama of family life by Edward Moore, published in 1753 and in many subsequent editions.

558. surprise] At the recognition that the pathos is, after all, under control, of which the metre is a symbol? Or at variation from the expected metrical norm? Cf. *C.N.B.* ii,

2516 (Mar. 1805): 'two kinds of pleasure are procured, in the two master-movements & impulses of man, the gratification of the Love of Variety with the grat. of the Love of Uniformity—and that by a recurrence, delightful as a painless and yet exciting act of memory, tiny breezelets of surprise, each one destroying the ripplets which the former had made, yet all together keeping the surface of the mind in a bright dimple-smile!'

558–67. Cf. Dennis, i. 364–5:

> great Passions naturally threw [the ancient Greeks] upon Harmony and figurative Language, as they must of necessity do any Poet, as long as he continues Master of them ... never any one, while he was wrapt in Enthusiasm, or with ordinary Passion, wanted either Words or Harmony; and therefore Poetry is more harmonious than Prose, because it is more pathetick ... And in Poetry, they who write with a great deal of Passion, are generally very harmonious ... At the same time 'tis a little odd to consider, that Passion, which disturbs the Soul, should occasion it to produce Harmony, which seems to imply that Order and Composure of it. Whether this proceeds from the secret Effort that the Soul makes to compose it self, or whatever the Cause is, the Effect is certain. But as Passion, which is the disorder of the Soul, produces Harmony, which is agreement; so Harmony, which is Concord, augments and propagates Passion, which is Discord ... Numbers are proper to move Passion, and for that reason are inseparable from Poetry, which has no other Design. [i. 376:] Harmony may be said to be both the Father and the Child of Passion: 'tis produced by it, and begets it; and the more pathetick any Discourse is, the more harmonious it must of Necessity be.

Harmony to Dennis means, or includes, metrical form: four elements of it are 'Number, Measure, Cadence, and Rime' (i. 376). Cf. also Wordsworth's note to 'The Thorn' (*P.W.* ii. 512): he wished that 'words, which in [certain] minds are impregnated with passion, should likewise convey passion to Readers who are not accustomed to sympathize with men feeling in that manner or using such language. It seemed to me that this might be done by calling in the assistance of Lyrical and rapid Metre.'

573. perception of similitude in dissimilitude] A commonplace of eighteenth-century aesthetics: Hutcheson, *Inquiry into ... Beauty and Virtue* (2nd edn., London, 1726), p. 17: 'The Figures which excite in us the Ideas of Beauty, seem to be those in which there is *Uniformity amidst Variety*'; Kames, i. 278–9: 'Resemblance among objects of the same kind, and dissimilitude among objects of different kinds, are too obvious and familiar to gratify our curiosity in any degree: its gratification lies in discovering differences among things where resemblance prevails, and resemblances where difference prevails.' Nearer to Wordsworth's statement, and anticipating Coleridge's distinction between imitation and copy, is Adam Smith, *Of the Nature of that Imitation which takes place in ... the Imitative Arts*, in *Works* (London, 1811), v. 243 ff. Smith urges that aesthetic pleasure arises from the sense of difficulty overcome in the production of the artifact, which, again, is based on the recognition of a disparity between the object imitated and the imitative medium. Thus painting attempts to imitate three dimensions in two; marble imitates the human body, etc. A completely realistic imitation (a Coleridgean 'copy') is aesthetically undesirable: Smith cites 'the works of Mrs. Wright', i.e. waxworks, a stock example of bad art in several critics (Reynolds, *Discourse XI*, in *Works* (London, 1798), ii. 46–7; Priestley, *Oratory*, pp. 264–5; *S.C.* ii, 80; *Biog. Lit.* ii. 256). Similarly James Beattie, *Essays on Poetry and Music* (London, 1779), p. 87: 'that which is properly termed *Imitation* has always in it something which is not in the original. If the prototype and transcript be exactly alike ... we may call the latter a representative, a copy, a draught, or a picture, of the former; but we never call it an imitation'; and so Gerard, *Taste*, p. 56; Priestley, *Oratory*, pp. 261–74; Reynolds, *Discourses III, XIII*, in *Works*, i. 52–3, ii. 122–3, 135–6.

575–6. The force of this application of the principle escapes us, unless it refers merely to the perception that the male and female bodies are at once alike and unlike.

584–611. The opening lines of *Prel.* XII, are perhaps parallel: 'From nature doth emotion come, and moods / Of calmness equally are nature's gift ... Genius ... exists by interchange / Of peace and excitation', etc. Cf. also *P.W.* v. 343–4, Fragment IV. vi. Both these passages stress that the 'emotion', 'impression of delight', or 'sentiment' originates in 'nature', which seems to mean 'natural objects'. There is no suggestion of this in *P.L.B.*, for Wordsworth is here concerned with 'the general passions and thoughts and feelings of men' (468–9). Nor does *P.L.B.* confine itself to 'The original impression of *delight*' (*P.W.* v 344). Cf. also 'The Waggoner', IV, 209–15 (*P.W.* v. 344). The notion of an inevitable time-lag between emotion felt and the consequent composition of a poem is not unknown in eighteenth-century aesthetics: see especially Diderot, *Paradoxe sur le comédien*, in *Œuvres*, ed. Billy Bibliothèque de la Pléiade, xxv (Paris. 1951), 1055:

> Est-ce au moment où vous venez de perdre votre ami ou votre maîtresse que vous composerez un poème sur sa mort? Non. Malheur à celui qui jouit alors de son talent! C'est lorsque la grande doleur est passée: quand l'extrême sensibilité est amortie, lorsqu'on est loin de la catastrophe, que l'âme est calme, qu'on se rapelle son bonheur éclipsé, qu'on est capable d' apprécier la perte qu'on a faite, que la mémoire se réunit à l'imagination, l'une pour retracer, l'autre pour exagérer la douceur d'un temps passé; qu'on se possède et qu'on parle bien. On dit qu'on pleure, mais on ne pleure pas lorsqu'on poursuit une épithète énergique qui se refuse; on dit qu'on pleure, mais on ne pleure pas lorsqu'on s'occupe à rendre son vers harmonieux: ou si les larmes coulent, la plume tombe des mains, on se livre à son sentiment et l'on cesse de composer.

Schiller, 'Über Bürgers Gedichte', in *Sämtliche Werke*, ed. Petersen (Stuttgart and Berlin, n.d.), xvi. 239:

> Ein Dichter nehme sich ja in Acht, mitten im Schmerz den Schmerz zu besingen. So, wie der Dichter selbst bloß leidender Teil ist, muß seine Empfindung unausbleiblich von ihrer idealischen Allgemeinheit zu einer unvollkommenen Individualität herabsinken. Aus der sanften und fernenden Erinnerung mag er dichten, und dann desto besser für ihn, je mehr er an sich erfahren hat, was er besingt; aber ja niemals inter der gegenwärtigen Herrschaft des Affekts, den er uns schön versinnlichen soll.

It has been claimed that Wordsworth knew this latter passage, or its drift, from Coleridge: see L. A. Willoughby, 'Wordsworth and Germany', in *German Studies presented to H. G. Fiedler* (Oxford, 1938), pp. 443–5. An obscure passage in *C.N.B.* i. 787 seems to have some relation to Wordsworth's theory here: 'recalling of passion in tranquillity [cf. *P.L.B.* 628] ... Metre district and artificial—till at length poetry forgot its essence in those forms which were only hieroglyphic of it' (cf. *Ap. L.B.* 38–9, 52 ff, 143). Since this passage can neither be read nor dated precisely, it is impossible to decide who is quoting whom.

597. difficulty] Of disciplining, the 'language of prose' into metrical form. Cf. Delille, *Discours*, p. xl: 'Un autre charme de la poésie, ... c'est la difficulté vaincue. Une des choses qui nous frappent le plus dans ... un poëme ... c'est que des vers, malgré la gêne de la mesure, aient la même liberté que le langage ordinaire'; Priestley, *Oratory*, p. 267: 'Why is the pleasure we receive from *verse* ... superior to the pleasure we should receive from the same things said in *prose* ... ? It is more *difficult* to compose in verse than in prose [and more difficult to write in rhyme than in blank verse].'

609. *manners* is again distinguished from *characters*; cf. notes on 86, [137].

645–54. Wordsworth's source for Johnson's stanza seems to have been (directly or indirectly) *The London Magazine*, Apr. 1785; for this is apparently the only printed source up to 1800 which preserves this, Johnson's own, version. See *Poems*, ed. Nichol Smith and McAdam (Oxford, 1941), pp. 157–8. Mr. F. W. Bateson informs us that, in an exhaustive inspection of texts of *The Babes in the Wood* available in the British Museum, he found only one which combines Wordsworth's text and title: a pamphlet date 1800 [?], shelf-mark 11623 m.4 (22). Percy's version, which Wordsworth might have been expected to follow, is entitled *The Children in the Wood*; for the third line quoted it has 'But never more could see the man' (*Reliques of Ancient English Poetry*, 4th edn., London, 1794, iii, 175).

668–9. Pope, *Essay on Man*, II. 31–4: 'Superiour beings, when of late they saw / A mortal Man unfold all Nature's law, / Admir'd such wisdom in an earthly shape. / And shew'd a NEWTON as we shew an Ape.'

686–94. Repeated from *Ad. L.B.* Reynolds makes remarks to this effect in various places: see, for instance, *Works* (London, 1798), i. 11 (*Discourse I*), i. 25–6, 29

(*Discourse II*), i. 222–3 (*Discourse VII*), and especially ii. 95 (*Discourse XII*): 'The habit of contemplating and brooding over the ideas of great geniuses, till you find yourself warmed by the contact, is the true method of forming an artist-like mind … Besides the general advantage of forming the taste by such an intercourse, there is another …'; *Works*, iii. 136 (Notes on Mason's translation of du Fresnoy's *Art of Painting*): 'Taste … may be acquired by a continued contemplation of the works of [great] Painters.' The closest parallel we have found is in Reynolds's 'loose papers', reported by Malone in his Biographical Introduction to the *Works*, i, pp. xvii–xviii:

> Having since that period frequently revolved this subject in my mind, I am now clearly of opinion, that a relish for the higher excellencies of art is an acquired taste, which no man ever possessed without long cultivation, and great labour and attention … A just poetical taste, and the acquisition of a nice discriminative musical ear, are equally the work of time.

The difficulty in the way of assuming that this is Wordsworth's source is that in 1804 he refers to Malone's edition and 'the life' in terms which indicate that he read it in that year for the first time (*E.Y.*, pp. 490–1).

695 ff. See *Ap. L.B.* 17–72. In 1808 Wordsworth 'said he thought of writing an essay, "Why bad poetry pleases." He never wrote it—a loss to our literature' (*H.C.R.*, p. 10). SEE ALSO the ADDENDUM on the next three pages: pp 215–7.

716–7. This part … neglected] See [504–5]. The alteration was no doubt made in view of the long insertion (258–489) in the text of 1802.

719–22. Repeated from 27–30.

ADDENDUM TO THE COMMENTARY
(Wordsworth's Fragment on 'transpositions')

695 ff. See *Ap. L.B.* 17–72. In 1808 Wordsworth 'said he thought of writing an essay, "Why bad poetry pleases." He never wrote it—a loss to our literature' (*H.C.R.*, p. 10). In a damaged and interleaved copy of Coleridge's *Poems*, 1796, now preserved at Grasmere (MSS. Verse 42 and 43), on the interleaf between pp. 174 and 175, there appears the following fragment in Wordsworth's hand:

> Frequently [? done] in any class of Composition which has taken deep hold of the affections of the People. By imitating such transpositions a Poet may sometimes revive the pleasurable feelings attached to the recollection of these poems in the mind of his Reader, & by so doing may produce a pleasure which will more than counterbalance any displeasure which such transposition w[d.] otherwise occasion. But this liberty must be used with great caution. Not wantonly & capriciously but under the control of certain fixed laws—What I have said upon metre to which this subject is nearly akin may be applied here.
>
> From this review imperfect as it is the Reader will be able to collect how small must be the stock of words & phrases, how few the peculiarities of language to which the Poet, even when he speaks in his own person can have any relational claim.

Textual Notes on the above Fragment

1 any class of Composition MS.[2]: Composition MS.
3 revive MS.[4]: excite a [? revolt] MS.: call forth MS.[2]: excite MS.[3].
4 produce MS.[2]: give MS.
5 displeasure MS.[2]: dislike [? or] aversion MS.
6 occasion MS.[2] Excite MS.
7 the control of certain MS.[2]: certain MS.
10 collect MS.[2]: perceive MS.
10–11 how small MS.[2]: what MS.
12 when he speaks MS.[2]: speaking MS. [–ing *undeleted*].

Commentary on the above Fragment

Connection with *P.L.B.* (1850) 510 ff is indicated by close verbal parallels, as follows:

1–2. which has taken … People] Cf. *P.L.B.* 510, the appeal to 'the consent of all nations' in order to prove the 'charm' of metrical language; and *P.L.B.* 523–4, on ballads (?) which 'have continued to give pleasure from generation to generation'.

4–6. by so doing … occasion] Cf. *P.L.B.* 515–7: 'by such deviation [from conventional diction], more will be lost from the shock which will thereby be given to the Reader's associations than will be counterbalanced by any pleasure which he can derive from the general power of numbers'; and 529 ff., the discussion of pain and pleasure in poetry.

5. With the original reading, 'dislike or aversion' cf. *P.L.B.* 102: 'dislike or disgust'.

7. wantonly & capriciously] Cf. *P.L.B.* 99–102: 'Poets … indulge in arbitrary and capricious habits of expression'; 492–3: 'Poetic Diction, arbitrary, and subject to infinite caprices upon which no calculation whatever can be made.'

7–8. under the control … laws] Cf. *P.L.B.* 495–6: 'the distinction of [rhyme and 1800] metre is regular and uniform … the metre obeys certain laws, to which the Poet and Reader both willingly submit because they are certain.'

11–13. how few … relational claim] Cf. *P.L.B.* 487–9: 'It is not, then, in the dramatic parts of composition that we look for this distinction of language; but still it may be proper and necessary where the Poet speaks to us in his own person and character'; and for the latter phrases cf. *P.L.B.* 178–9: 'a family language which Writers in metre seem to lay claim to by prescription'.

The major part of the fragment seems to discuss the possible use by the poet of conventional 'transpositions', presumably deviations from 'normal' idiom or, more especially, normal word-order (that of 'the language of prose'?), such as might be found, for instance, in traditional ballads. Wordsworth says that such deviation usually causes 'displeasure' to the reader, but that, if it is introduced 'under the control of certain fixed laws', it may be poetically useful by reviving 'pleasurable feelings' associated with traditional poetry.

The final paragraph of the fragment appears to conclude a wider argument showing that the range of traditional 'poetic' clichés which the poet can justifiably use is almost negligibly small; the major part is a concession in this argument which does not affect its general drift.

It is possible that the fragment is (1) a draft towards the Preface of 1800 which

Wordsworth eventually cut; his apology for this concealed cut is then given in the phrase of 1800, [504–5]: 'But this part of my subject [the appeal of conventional poetry] I have been obliged altogether to omit'; or (2) a draft towards the essay proposed for *L.B.* (1800), vol. ii (*Journals*, i. 63; *E.Y.*, pp. 307–8) which was never published and presumably never written in full; or (3) a draft towards the revised Preface of 1802. We think the last of these suggestions indicative, at any rate, of the latest possible date of the fragment, because *P.L.B.* 459–61 (cf. 479–81), first appearing in 1802, seems to show Wordsworth retorting to his own argument of the fragment in the phraseology of the fragment, and finally rejecting even the minor concession towards conventional diction which the fragment proposed.

COMMENTARY: APPENDIX

8–10. On the source of this doctrine in eighteenth-century primitivistic theories of poetry, see Introd.

37–9. See Introd. The passage from Quintilian translated in *Monthly Magazine* is *Inst. Orat.* IX. iv. 114: 'Quasi vero numeri non fuerint in compositione deprehensi: sicut poema nemo dubitaverit imperito quodam initio fusum, et aurium mensura, et similiter decurrentium spatiorum observatione esse generatum, mox in eo repertos pedes (text of G. L. Spalding, Leipzig, 1808; the sources are corrupt). It will be seen that the author has misinterpreted the passage, and that it provides no authority for his suggestions that metre is a late addition to poetry: all that Quintilian says is that the material for a theory of prosody was available in poetry before the theory was evolved. Cf. Ibid. 115: 'Ante enim carmen est quam observation carminis.' If *The Monthly Magazine* is Wordsworth's source, he has followed the misinterpretation.

39–40. Cf. *P.L.B.* 255–65.

49–50. The virtual equivalence of 'modes of expression' and 'a language' (see textual n.) indicates that *language* does not mean 'vocabulary'. See n. on *P.L.B.* 16. So below, 64, 'language' is replaced by 'diction' = 'the manner in which anything is expressed in words' (*O.E.D.*, sense 4).

52–57. Cf. *P.L.B.* 43–72, 255–6, 456–8.

67–71. an effect ... bestow] Cf. *P.L.B.* 532–5: 'The end of Poetry is to produce excitement [which is] an unusual and irregular state of the mind; ideas and feelings do not, in that state, succeed each other in accustomed order'. Thus poetic diction appears to achieve 'the end of Poetry'.

75–104. This source of exemplification, though common enough in eighteenth-century criticism, was perhaps suggested by *Monthly Magazine*, p. 455: 'If ... it were required, that examples should be adduced of writings in prose, which possess all the properties of genuine poetry, except its metrical numbers, it would be easy ... to point out many passages sublimely poetical in the prose parts of the Hebrew scriptures.'

79–80, 83 ff. Prior, 'Charity. A Paraphrase on the Thirteenth Chapter of the First Epistle to the Corinthians', in *Poems on Several Occasions*, ed. Waller (Cambridge, 1905), pp. 204–6; Johnson, 'The Ant', in *Poems*, ed. Nichol Smith and McAdam (Oxford, 1941), pp. 151–2. Wordsworth appears to follow the text of Johnson's *Works*, 1787.

105, textual n. 'This is Sonnet X in "Sonnets and Miscellaneous Poems, by the late Thomas Russell, Fellow of New College"' (Hale White, p. 48). Hale White observes that Wordsworth borrowed the last four lines in the sonnet 'Iona' (*P.W.* iv. 42–3).

127. church-going] *O.E.D.*, s.v. *church-going*, vbl. sb., cites only Cowper's line in illustration of this usage. Note Wordsworth's attempted improvement, 'The church-inviting bells' delightful chime', *P.W.* i 106, textual n.

143, textual n. Drayton] *Moses his Birth and Miracles*, II. 165–8, in *Works*, ed. Hebel, iii (Oxford, 1932), 383: 'We that calumnious Critick may eschew, / That blasteth all things with his poys'ned breath, / Detracting what laboriously we doe, / Onely with that which he but idely saith.'

7.

The Convention of Cintra

INTRODUCTION: GENERAL

In August 1807 Napoleon attempted to bring Portugal within the Continental System by demanding that by 1 September the Prince-Regent should declare war on Great Britain and seize British subjects and property in Portugal. After some temporizing by the Prince-Regent, unsatisfactory to France, the French and Spanish ambassadors left Lisbon on 30 September; and in October a French army under Junot entered Spain on its way to Portugal. It reached Salamanca on 12 November; thereafter it hastened its march by way of Alcantara, the Tagus valley, and Abrantes; and, with considerable difficulty and loss of men and armament, though without significant Portuguese opposition, began to arrive in Lisbon on 30 November. The day before, the Prince-Regent, who had meanwhile complied with most of Napoleon's demands without being able thereby to conciliate him, had set sail with his court for Rio de Janeiro. Junot settled down in Lisbon to rule and tyrannize over the Portuguese; there was no organized opposition for some months.

Meanwhile disturbances in the Spanish Court, arising from the incompetence of King Charles IV and the hostility of his son Ferdinand, Prince of the Asturias, towards the Court favourite Manuel Godoy, provided a favourable opportunity for French interference. On 27 October 1807 Ferdinand was arrested on a charge of treason; on the day of his arrest there was signed by France and Spain the secret Treaty of Fontainebleau, which proposed a division of Portuguese territory between France and Spain, and which permitted the entry of French troops into Spain to ensure this division.[1] By 22 November a force of 25,000 under Dupont had crossed the Spanish border from Bayonne, and on 8 January 1808 another force of 30,000 under Moncey entered Spain. These forces occupied strong positions in northern Spain without attempting to enter Portugal, where, indeed, they were not required. Between mid-February and mid-March 1808 French forces, casting aside the pretence that they were in passage for Portugal, seized four Spanish border fortresses (Pampeluna, Barcelona, San Sebastian, and Figueras), and advanced towards Madrid; their command was taken over by Murat. The Spanish Court, already removed to Aranjuez, prepared to move to Seville. Riots aimed at Godoy at Aranjuez on 17 March prevented this; they

1 The text was printed in *Courier,* 10 Oct. 1808.

were quietened when Ferdinand was produced and Godoy's dismissal promised, and on 19 March Charles abdicated in favour of Ferdinand.

Instead of opposing the French, Ferdinand entered Madrid on 24 March, one day after Murat's arrival, and proposed co-operation and marital alliance with Napoleon. Murat ignored him, and entered into communication with Charles and the Queen; and Charles prepared a protest against his abdication, claiming that it had been forced upon him. Early in April, Ferdinand was lured north to meet a proposed visit by Napoleon; he arrived at Bayonne on 20 April, ostensibly to confirm his throne in the eyes of Napoleon, but actually to receive the news that a French king would assume the rule of Spain. After ten days of argument and protest, Napoleon confronted Ferdinand with Charles and the renunciation of his abdication. Further debates ensued between Ferdinand and his parents as to who should rule; but by 6 May news arrived of the riots of 2 May in Madrid against Murat; whereupon Napoleon's tone became threatening, and Ferdinand resigned his throne in favour of his father. Charles had already signed a treaty resigning his throne to Napoleon; and Ferdinand being compelled to sign away his expectations on 10 May, the way was clear for the appointment of Joseph Bonaparte as King of Spain.

By the end of April the early events of this series were known to the people of Madrid; on 1 May Murat proposed to send relatives of Ferdinand after him to Bayonne; and on 2 May riots broke out in protest against their removal. These were savagely put down by Murat's troops. A deputation of Spaniards nominated by Napoleon went to Bayonne in late May to beg from him that Joseph Bonaparte might be appointed to rule Spain.[1]

News of the Madrid riots and of their suppression called forth a general revolt in Spain, beginning in Asturias on 24 May, then in Galicia (where there was appreciable Spanish military strength) on 30 May. Asturian envoys to Britain secured promises of British aid in early June.

The French authorities, in the early stages of the struggle, appear to have underestimated the size of the Spanish revolt, and proposed to deal with it by means of comparatively small and isolated forces. Bessières was to watch the northern lines of communication, detaching a force against Saragossa. Dupont moved south from Madrid on Cordova and Seville, and Moncey south-east to Valencia. Dupont took and sacked Cordova on 7 June, but shortly found his communications to Madrid cut by revolt in his rear, and a Spanish army under Castanos advancing on his front. He withdrew on 16 June to Andujar, where he remained for a month.

1 Cf. *Cintra*, 642 ff.

Meanwhile Moncey pressed on towards Valencia, avoiding Spanish forces which might have ambushed his small army at suitable points; and on 26 June he began a siege. He was repulsed with considerable losses in two assaults, and, like Dupont, had had his communications cut. He withdrew without meeting further opposition, and reached Madrid on 15 July.

The French had greater success in the north-west, where detachments of Bessières's force under Lasalle and Merle defeated Cuesta on 12 June at Cabezon; a month later, on 13–14 July, Bessières won a crushing victory over Cuesta and Blake at Medina de Rio Seco. This success cleared the French lines from Bayonne to Madrid, and Joseph Bonaparte entered the capital on 20 July. In the north-east, however, Saragossa under Joseph Palafox withstood its first siege by Lefebvre-Desnouettes, and subsequently by Verdier, in June, July, and August.

Joseph Bonaparte had hardly entered Madrid when he moved out again (1 August); for news shortly arrived of the defeat and surrender of Dupont's army at Baylen (13–19 July). The resulting convention between Dupont and Castanos removed some 17,000 French troops from the war.

The Spanish revolt cut the communications of Junot's force in Portugal, and encouraged Portuguese resistance. In early June a Spanish division under Belesta, which had been garrisoning northern Portugal on behalf of Junot, moved into Spain, taking with it General Quesnel, the French governor of Oporto, and other prisoners. Junot prevented a similar defection of the Spanish troops at Lisbon under Caraffa, by disarming them (9 June) and imprisoning them in hulks covered by the Lisbon artillery. Oporto rose in revolt on 18 June, and there were minor risings in the south. Junot concentrated his troops in and near Lisbon by early July, and during that month sent out small forces on local expeditions. But on 1 August the British expeditionary force under Wellesley was landing on the Portuguese coast at Mondego Bay.

Wellesley began to advance on Lisbon on 9 August; he was hampered by lack of horses and vehicles, and by the unco-operative attitude of the Portuguese forces under General Freire. He was opposed on 17 August at Roliça by a small French force under Delaborde, who retreated skilfully before superior strength. Wellesley took up positions at Vimiero, covering the landing of two reinforcing brigades at Maceira. Here, on 21 August, he was attacked by Junot, who suffered a severe defeat. Pursuit was prevented by the arrival of Wellesley's successor, Sir Harry Burrard, on 22 August. Sir Hew Dalrymple, who almost immediately superseded Burrard, landed and confirmed the policy of caution, at any rate until the support of Sir John Moore's division should have been obtained. But on the same day Kellermann, who had commanded Junot's reserve in the battle, appeared in the British camp to appeal for a convention, which was negotiated between 23 and 30 August. The text of this document, which was to occupy Wordsworth's attention for some time to come, is given in his Appendix.

II

News of the Convention of Cintra was published in British newspapers on 16 September 1808. By 27 September 1808 Wordsworth was complaining to Richard Sharp: 'We are all here cut to the heart by the conduct of Sir Hew and his Brother Knight in Portugal' (*M.Y.* i. 267, cf. i. 269). A Board of Inquiry began to sit on the subject of the Armistice and Convention on 14 November 1808. During October and November Wordsworth and others made efforts to follow, and to better, the example of the City of London by holding a public meeting which might approve an address to the King on the subject of the Convention. The following documents[1] indicate the course of these efforts, and their eventual failure, which led to Wordsworth's voicing of his discontent in *Cintra:*

(l) Southey to Humphrey Senhouse, 19 October 1808 *(Life and Correspondence,* iii. 175–7; our text mainly from Raymond D. Havens, 'A Project of Wordsworth's', *R.E.S.* v (1929), 320–2):

> I have had a visit this morning from Wordsworth & Spedding upon the subject of this accursed convention in Portugal. They & some of their friends are very desirous of bringing before the country in some regular form the main iniquity of the business ... these sentiments [on Dalrymple's conduct] would appear with most effect if they were embodied in a County Address, of which the ostensible purport might be to thank his Majesty for having instituted an Enquiry, and to request that he would be pleased to appoint a day of national humiliation for this grievous national disgrace. This would not be liable to the reproof with which he thought proper to receive the city address, because it prejudges nothing.... Spedding & Calvert know many persons who will come forward at such a meeting. Coleridge or Wordsworth will be ready to speak, & will draw up resolutions to be previously approved, & brought forward by some proper person. We will prepare the way by writing in the county papers.

1 The following authorities, as well as others in more general use, are referred to in the ensuing discussion and in our Commentary: C. C. Southey, *Life and Correspondence of Robert Southey* (London, 1849, etc.; cited as *'Life and Correspondence')* ; J. W. Warter, *Selections from the Letters of Robert Southey* (London, 1856; cited as *'Selections')*; John E. Jordan, *De Quincey to Wordsworth* (Berkeley, Calif., 1962; cited as 'Jordan'); J. E. Wells, 'The Story of Wordsworth's *Cintra*', *S.P.* xviii (1921), 15–77 (cited as 'Wells'). Where we have been able to discover them, we have used the manuscripts of Southey's letters rather than the printed texts cited above; and as our transcripts of De Quincey's correspondence were made before the appearance of Professor Jordan's book, we have used these rather than his.

(2) Southey to Tom Southey, 30 October 1808 (B.M. Add. MS. 30927, fol. 143; cf. *Selections,* ii. 116–17):

> There is a talk [sic] of an address from this county,—but Lord Lonsdale will do all he can to prevent a meeting, or oppose any thing that may be done at once. ... If anything is done in Cumberland here it will originate with Wordsworth, he & I & Coleridge will set the business in its true light in the county newspapers,—& frame the resolutions, to be brought forward by some weighty persons,—& Wordsworth will speak at the meeting, he being a freeholder. We are all to meet Curwen ... at Calverts on Friday next:—& then I suppose the plan of operations will be settled. It was wished not to make this a party matter, & therefore Lord Lonsdale was applied to thro H. Senhouse,—but it seems he "views the Convention in a very different light!" God help poor England!

(3) Southey to Walter Scott, 6 November 1808 *(Life and Correspondence,* iii. 180):

> Wordsworth ... left me to-day ... he is about to write a pamphlet upon this precious convention, which he will place in a more philosophical point of view than any body has yet done.

(4) Southey to Tom Southey, 22 November 1808 (B.M. Add. MS. 30927, fol. 146):

> Our projected county meeting came to nothing. Lord Lonsdale set his face against it, & upon consultation with Curwen, we were convinced that it was hopeless to muster force against his merry men, who would have bellowed as loudly against us at the meeting, as they would have done against the cursed Convention before they were under orders of mum. So Wordsworth went home to ease his heart by writing a pamphlett, which you may be sure will be a right good one, & contain more true philosophy & true patriotism than has for many a long year appeared in such a form. How he gets on with it I have not heard.

(5) Southey to W. S. Landor, 26 November 1808 (MS. F.48.D.32, Forster Collection, Victoria and Albert Museum, fol. 6; cf. *Life and Correspondence,* iii. 197):

> We used our endeavours here to obtain a County Meeting & send in a petition which should have taken up the damned Convention upon its true grounds of honour & moral feeling, keeping all pettier considerations out of sight. But Lord Lonsdale had received Mum as the word of command from those who move his strings, & he moves the puppets of two Counties! Wordsworth who left me when we found the business hopeless, went home to ease his heart in a pamphlett, which I daily expect to hear he has completed.

In brief, Wordsworth and his friends made efforts to arrange a public meeting, for which Wordsworth appears to have drafted the speech mentioned by Southey in documents (l) and (2) above (see our Appendix I); but these efforts were frustrated by what seem to have been covert threats by Lord Lonsdale to break up the meeting with organized rowdyism. In consequence, Wordsworth, as he says in the Advertisement to *Cintra,* began to write the pamphlet in November 1808, probably in the first half of the month.

III

Southey's expectation that Wordsworth's pamphlet would be completed by late November 1808 was excessively optimistic, and the lengthy and complex progress of the work towards publication falls into three more or less distinct phases during the next six months: (A) publication by instalments in Daniel Stuart's daily newspaper *The Courier;* (B) publication in book form under the supervision of Stuart; and (C) publication in book form under the supervision of De Quincey.

Phase A.

The following documents trace the early stages of the book's development:

(6) Wordsworth to Wrangham, 3 December 1808 *(M.Y.* i. 278): Wordsworth is

> very deep in this subject [Spain], and about to publish upon it; first, I believe in a newspaper for the sake of immediate and wide circulation; and next, the same matter in a separate pamphlet.

(7) Dorothy Wordsworth to Jane Marshall, 4 December 1808 *(M.Y.* i. 280):

> my brother is deeply engaged in writing a pamphlet upon the Convention of Cintra ...

(8) Coleridge to Poole, 4 December 1808 *(C.L.* iii. 131):

> ... the Cintra Convention—on which Wordsworth has nearly finished a most eloquent & well-reasoned Pamphlet.

(9) (*a*) Coleridge to Daniel Stuart, *c.* 6 December 1808 (*C.L.* iii. 134):

> Wordsworth has nearly finished a series of most masterly Essays on the affairs of Portugal & Spain—and by my advice he will first send them to you, that if they suit the Courier, they may be inserted;

(and so (*b*) Coleridge to Humphry Davy, 7 December 1808 (*C.L.* iii. 136)).

(10) Coleridge to T. G. Street, 7 December 1808 *(C.L.* iii. 137):

> Wordsworth has nearly finished a series of most masterly Essays on [the Convention]—and I shall send the two first to Mr Stuart by the next post—and the others, as soon as ever I hear from him or you.

(11) Dorothy Wordsworth to Catherine Clarkson, 8 December 1808 (*M.Y.* i. 282–3):

> William and Mary ... in William's study, where she is writing for him (he dictating). He is engaged in ... a pamphlet of considerable length. ... I believe it will first appear in the *Courier* in different sections.

(12) Coleridge to Stuart, *c.* 14 December 1808 (*C.L.* iii. 142):

> Wordsworth's first Essay, I hope, the two first, will be sent to you by this or the following Post.

(13) Stuart to Coleridge, 16 December 1808 (ms. in Wordsworth Library, Grasmere):

> The Essays on Spain & Portugal from M[r] Wordsworth have not arrived; but we shall be very glad indeed to receive them, & to pay for them too, if you think that will be agreeable. But at any rate let us have them.

(14) Stuart to Coleridge, P.S. of 24 December to letter of 17 December 1808 (manuscript in Wordsworth Library, Grasmere):

> I have just received M[r] Wordsworth's Packet & shall take it to Brompton to read.

(15) *The Courier,* 27 December 1808, prints *Cintra,* 1–187; see *Ad. Cintra,* 6–7, and n.

(16) Coleridge to Stuart, 28 December 1808 (*C.L.* iii. 151):

> I am afraid that Wordsworth's fifth cannot go off, as was intended, in this Frank—it is finished all but the corrections—but [Wordsworth has been ill]. Consequently, such are our Posts, it cannot go off from Kendal till Saturday Morning [31 December 1808].

(17) Coleridge to Stuart, 3 January 1809 (*C.L.* iii. 160):

> William received your Letter this Morning at 11 o/clock—we have been hard at work ever since ... the Essay has probably benefited by the accident—at all events, it has been increased in size—We are very sorry, you should have had so much ... anxiety about the loss of the papers.

(18) Coleridge to Basil Montagu, 7 January 1809 (*C.L.* iii. 161):

> In the Courier one Essay of [Wordsworth's] has appeared, signed G.—the second was lost in London, and so was re-written & sent again.

(19) Coleridge to Stuart, 9 January 1809 (*C.L.* iii. 164):

> You will long ere this (on Friday Morning [6 January], I calculate) have received Wordsworth's second Essay re-written by me, and in some parts re-composed.

(20) *The Courier,* 13 January 1809, prints *Cintra,* 188–503; see *Ad. Cintra,* 6–7, and n.

From documents (12)–(20) it appears that the first instalment of *Cintra* was sent to Stuart in the third week of December 1808 for publication in *The Courier;* whether this copy coincided with the instalment actually printed in *The Courier* of 27 December, or exceeded it, cannot be determined. Further copy must have been sent before 28 December, when Coleridge promises that the 'fifth' part will leave Kendal by 31 December. Of this further copy, all or some was lost in the post (cf. *Ad. Cintra,* 11–13), and, in response to a letter from Stuart received 2 or 3 January 1809, Wordsworth and Coleridge rewrote what was necessary.[1] This material was published, or forms part of what was published, in *The Courier,* 13 January 1809.

1 See Coleridge, *EOT,* 3, 98.n. for Coleridge's claim to have in some sense 're-composed' or at least amplified several hundred lines from draft. The passage in question is lines 375–536. I am indebted to Michael John Kooy for drawing this to my attention and to Jeff Cowton for providing a scan of EOT 3: 98–103 containing Coleridge's supposed 'recomposition' [RG].

Phase B.

There were no further instalments in *The Courier.* The reason is given by Wordsworth: 'the pressure of public business rendering it then [mid-January 1809] improbable that room could be found, in the columns of the paper, regularly to insert matter extending to such a length—this plan of publication was given up' *(Ad. Cintra,* 13–15; see n. ad loc.). This decision was perhaps taken by about 20 January, in view of (21) Coleridge to Stuart, 23 January 1809 (*C.L.* iii. 169): 'In answer to that part of your Letter (which I have just now received) respecting Wordsworth's Copy . . .'; almost certainly by 26 January, when Stuart writes to Coleridge (22), giving specimen printing charges, in connection with *The Friend,* and states that 'For such as Wordsworths Pamphlet [I was asked] 2 G[s] [a sheet] for 500 [copies]' (manuscript in Wordsworth Library, Grasmere); and certainly by 3 February, in view of (23) Coleridge to Poole, 3 February 1809 (*C.L.* iii. 174):

> An accident in London delayed the publication ten days—the whole therefore is now publishing as a Pamphlet, & I believe, with a more comprehensive Title.

This procedure had, of course, been envisaged from the first conception of the work (documents (3)–(8) above), and early in January, or even late in December, Stuart had been negotiating, or offering to negotiate, for a publisher on Wordsworth's behalf (*C.L.* iii. 160; 3 January 1809). He was shortly engaged in supervising the printing; this is probably indicated by document (21) above, and is clear from (24) Coleridge to Stuart, 4 June 1809 (*C.L.* iii. 210):

> I was forced to be so troublesome just at the very time when your Kindness had prompted you to take upon yourself the equal or greater Task of superintending the interests of W. Wordsworth's Pamphlet;

and from (25) *M.Y.* i. 288 (postmarked 9 February 1809, written 'Sunday', i.e. 5 February), which indicates that Wordsworth was sending copy to Stuart.

In spite of Stuart's supervision, Wordsworth continued to read proofs of the book at this time; for (26) De Quincey on 25 March 1809 (Jordan, p. 119) mentions '[sheet] M, which was the last proof that Mr. Wordsworth saw'. Moreover, it is obvious that the main reason for De Quincey's taking over the supervision was so that proofs could be read in London rather than in Grasmere; so Wordsworth told Stuart (27) on 25 May (*M.Y.* i. 344):

> My inducement for placing it in Mr De Quincey's hands was to save time and expense (our situation being so inconvenient for the post) and also to save you trouble;

and so (28) *M.Y.* i. 351 (? 28 May 1809).

Phase C.

When the decision to entrust the supervision to De Quincey was taken is not clear. It is perhaps indicated by Coleridge to Stuart, 8 February 1809 (*C.L.* iii. 177), where Coleridge gives Stuart a description of De Quincey, as if Stuart was expecting to meet De Quincey shortly. Stuart replies (to Coleridge, 14 February 1809; manuscript in Wordsworth Library, Grasmere): 'I recollect M[r.] De Quincey perfectly & envy him the pleasure he will feel in pursuing his proposed Plan.' At any rate, De Quincey left Grasmere about 20 February 1809 and arrived in London on 25 February (Jordan, pp. 91–5). The progress of *Cintra* under his supervision can be traced in some detail, though not with absolute completeness, from his correspondence with the Wordsworths; the Wordsworthian half of this correspondence is by no means complete.

At the time of De Quincey's arrival in London Wordsworth himself had seen proof of the book up to and including sheet M (document (26) above). Again, De Quincey writes on 28 March 1809 that 'up to page 96 [the last page of sheet M] inclusively, none of the errors are imputable to me' (Jordan, p. 124). Thus De Quincey's handling of the printing begins, generally speaking, with sheet N of the text of 1809 (in our text, 'people knew', 2162). However, the printer had manuscript material later than sheet M which passed through De Quincey's hands only in proof; for on 1 April he writes that the phrase 'at least from the animating efforts of the Peninsula' (*Cintra,* 2425–6; in 1809, p. 108, sheet O) occurs 'in a part of the M.S. sent up to London before I arrived' (Jordan, p. 136). Moreover, on 14 March he reports that he has emended 'refined' to 'defined' (*Cintra,* 2511; cf. *M.Y.* i. 298) in proof (Jordan, p. 110); and, as his habit was, obviously, to check Wordsworth's copy before handing it to the printer, this passage also must belong to copy sent before his arrival.

On 5 March he acknowledges receipt, on 4 March, of '2 packets (containing 4 M.S. sheets)' (Jordan, p. 97), and, according to the same letter, these four sheets contained *Cintra,* 2925–30: 'The former source … stock of knowledge', and 3083–4: 'for reasons … given'. Thus when De Quincey reached London, the printer had already received copy, either directly from Wordsworth or through Stuart, which extends at least up to *Cintra,* 2511, and at most up to *Cintra*, 2925.

On 11 March De Quincey reports the receipt, on 7 March, of '1 single letter', which may have contained text, or at least emendations. On 9 March he received '2 [single letters] containing the winding-up of the pamphlet'; and on 10 March he received *M.Y.,* Letters 140 and 141; Letter 141 must be dated 6 March (Jordan, pp.

104–5).[1] On 11 March he received 'the supplementary intercalation, beginng—"*In Madrid, in Ferrol, in Corunna*" ' (*Cintra,* 3539; Jordan, pp. 106–7). This last is evidently the additional matter promised on 7 March *(M.Y.* i. 294), which was to extend to 'about a Folio sheet', and which was to be inserted after 'career in the fulness of [her joy]' (*Cintra,* 4313). But it was later moved to an earlier position; for on 25 March De Quincey writes: 'I *believe* that I have made out, in Mr Wordsworth's note (contained in your last letter) where the addition—"In Madrid—Ferrol" &c. is to come in' (Jordan, p. 120). At this date, 'your last letter' (unpreserved) means a letter of 'Friday afternoon', 17 March, received by De Quincey on 21 March (Jordan, p. 114, cf. p. 119). On 28 March (Jordan, p. 125), De Quincey says that he has inserted 'In Madrid', etc., 'Directly after *"and hope has inwardly accompanied me to the end"* ' (*Cintra,* 3537), 'all along to the *end* of the addition. Then, in a new parag. I resume *"Whilst I was writing the earlier part of this tract"* up to *"feed and uphold" the bright consum. flower* [*Cintra,* 4289] —where the press will stop.' The final text of *Cintra* contains no such 'new parag.', but the significance of the passage concerned will appear shortly.

In the letter just quoted (Jordan, p. 124), De Quincey tells Dorothy Wordsworth that he has not '*yet* (viz. Tuesday, after the delivery of the letters) received anything from you since this day last week [21 March], when I had your letter.—However, I dare say, something will come tomorrow or Thursday; and (if there does) not the least delay will have been occasioned at the press by this long pause on your part', because the printers have, for various reasons, been fully occupied. Again, on 29 March, he writes that Stuart thinks that 'the remainder of the copy should be sent up' (Jordan, p. 131). These passages, and the promise of 28 March to stop the press, indicate that in late March De Quincey and Stuart were expecting further copy from Wordsworth; and on 30 March De Quincey received four letters sent off from Grasmere on 26 March (Jordan, p. 132).

Of these four letters, one was *M.Y.* Letter 143, to be dated about 26 March. Some or all of the remaining three were copy, or copy was sent off at approximately the same time *(M.Y.* i. 295: 'the last sheets of the Pamphlet'). This copy was matter to be *inserted,* since De Quincey had received 'the winding-up' on 9 March; it concerns

1 Mrs. Moorman follows de Selincourt's dating of Letter 141 (26 Mar.), on the grounds that 'D. W.'s postscript makes it clear that she wrote on Monday, 27 Mar.' *(M.Y.* i. 294). Dorothy's postscript appears to us to prove nothing except that it was written on a Monday. De Quincey's letter of 11 March, however, acknowledges receipt of a letter 'dated Monday morng before your walk to Rydale'; Dorothy's postscript is dated 'Monday Morning', and says that 'Wm and I proceed to the post at Rydale where we hope to find a letter from you.'

'the hopes of the Spaniards and principles of the contest' *(M.Y.* i. 296), and 'the great body' of it begins at *Cintra,* 3539, or, more precisely, at 3537: 'But I began' (*M.Y.* i. 299). The limits of these additions we shall now attempt to define.

In a series of letters, beginning 26 March, Wordsworth makes various corrections to, or comments on, the text of *Cintra,* in such a way as to suggest that he is correcting, or commenting on, matter recently written. We shall therefore assume that all or most of these corrections refer to copy sent to De Quincey on 26 March. Except for corrections concerned with (*a*) *Cintra,* 3537 ff., (*b*) passages which Wordsworth suspected to be libellous, and (*c*) a passage in the Advertisement, the passages concerned are as follows, in the order in which Wordsworth corrects them: *Cintra,* 3905–08 and Appendix E, 4019–21 and Appendix F (*M.Y.* i. 299–300); 2998-9, 3718, 3796 (*M.Y.,* i. 300–1); 3770–76, 4061–2, 4080, 4085 (*M.Y.* i. 304).

Again, on 1 April, when he acknowledges receipt of the four letters sent on 26 March, De Quincey comments on two passages in the manuscript which is 'sent to the printer' (Jordan, p. 134). These passages were presumably part of the copy which he has just received; they are *Cintra,* 4077–8 and 3805–7.

It will be seen that, with one exception (*Cintra,* 2998–9), all these passages fall within a well-consolidated continuum of writing extending from *Cintra,* 3718 to 4085, or, from beginning to end of paragraphs, from *Cintra,* 3700 to 4087.

The limits just arrived at, however, are minimal, in that the addition of 26 March may begin earlier than *Cintra,* 3700, and may end later than 4087. That it does begin earlier is indicated by *M.Y.* i. 299, which says that 'The great body of additions sent, since the conclusion was sent [i.e. after the matter received by De Quincey on 9 March], will begin' at *Cintra,* 3537. The passage beginning here, or rather at 3539, is, as we have seen, the 'supplementary intercalation' received by De Quincey on 11 March and promised by Wordsworth on 7 March (*M.Y.* i. 294); it was to be 'about a Folio sheet', it was originally to be inserted after 'fulness of her joy' (*Cintra,* 4313), but, as we have also seen, it was moved to its present position in accordance with instructions issued by Wordsworth about 17 March).

A folio sheet, regularly written, corresponds to about 150 lines of our text, so that the matter concerned extends from *Cintra,* 3539 to about 3632, or, to end of paragraph, 3666; and the addition of 26 March begins at *Cintra,* 3667.

This point, thus hypothetically arrived at, in fact corresponds with the beginning of the text in a sheet of manuscript preserved in the Wordsworth Library, Grasmere, and more fully described elsewhere in this Introduction. We suggest that this manuscript is the first sheet of the copy (or, rather, a draft of it) sent from Grasmere on 26 March, received by De Quincey on 30 March, and acknowledged by him on 1 April (Jordan, p. 132). Since it is cued to follow 3666, and since 3666 at this date occupied approximately its present position (Jordan, p. 125; Wordsworth's instructions of ?17 March), the general disposition of the added matter must have been clear in Wordsworth's mind at this date. This is indeed indicated by *M.Y.* i. 299, 305, where Wordsworth repeats instructions requiring a general removal of inserted material from somewhere 'near the conclusion' to an earlier position; but we make the point, since it is to be suspected that in mid-March Wordsworth proposed to make a major insertion after 4289 'where the press will stop' (Jordan, p. 125, referring to Wordsworth's instructions of ?17 March). Such a proposal would account, generally, for De Quincey's and Stuart's expectation of the copy of 26 March before it arrived (Jordan, p. 131), and also for Wordsworth's dismissal, in late March, of a large insertion 'near the conclusion' of the work *(M.Y.* i. 299). In fact, there is now no evidence of an insertion or a stopping of the press at 4289; for the paragraph which now follows after this point belongs, in some form or other, to the early 'winding-up' of the work, since its last phrase is mentioned on 7 March *(M.Y. i.* 294). In sum: we suggest that on 21 March De Quincey received, with Dorothy's letter of 17 March, 'M[r] Wordsworth's note' which gave new directions for inserting 'In Madrid, in Ferrol,' etc., in its present position, 3539, rather than after 4313 as is suggested by *M.Y.* i. 294; that the note forecast a bulky insertion to be placed after 4289 (Jordan, p. 125); but that when the insertion actually arrived on 30 March it was cued to follow 3666.

Where the addition of 26 March ends is more difficult to determine. On 6 March, immediately after sending the 'winding-up' of the work, Wordsworth sent to De Quincey corrections of *Cintra,* 4200–06 and 4274–5 *(M.Y. i.* 294–5, to be dated 5 or 6 March). Therefore the original text of *Cintra* contained 4205 ff., and the additions of 26 March must precede, or be interpolated into, 4205–4376. The bulk of the matter which precedes 4205 extends, as we saw above, probably to 4087 at least; so that between 44088 and 4205 we must seek a point of junction between the original matter and that of 26 March.

The paragraphs 4088–126 appear to belong to the addition, since they mention the second siege of Saragossa as completed. The fall of Saragossa, which occurred on 20 February 1809, was first heard of by De Quincey on 10 March (Jordan, p. 112). These passages, therefore, must have been written, or substantially revised, by Wordsworth after 10 March (probably after 13 or 14 March).

The paragraph 4125–73, concerned mainly with quotations from Sir Philip Warwick and Charles Vaughan, does not seem to offer any evidence, unless a date can be established for Wordsworth's reading of the second edition of Vaughan's pamphlet (see Commentary, n. on 4161).

The paragraph beginning at 4174 seems to show signs of patching in its early sentences. The phrase 'in the earlier part of this tract' (4175) appears to be a remnant of a 'new parag. ... "Whilst I was writing the earlier part of this tract" ' at which the text was, in De Quincey's understanding on 28 March, to 'resume' after 'the *end* of the addition' (Jordan, p. 125). The present paragraph refers to 'details given, in the earlier part of this tract, concerning the course which ... might with advantage be pursued in Spain', i.e. to the argument either for a very large military effort, or for helping Spain 'rather in *Things* than in Men' (3214–381), a passage which closely precedes the point (3405) at which Wordsworth, obviously writing in late February or early March, describes himself as 'drawing towards a conclusion' (see Commentary, nn. on 3214 ff., 3405–08). Further, these early sentences of the paragraph beginning at 4174 echo phrases in the same earlier region of the work, shortly preceding the point (3537) at which we know that 'the great body of additions' begins (*M.Y.* i. 299): note 3502: 'the same disinterested generous passions', and 4180: 'the grand and disinterested passions'; 3501: 'a blessing', and 4195: 'this of blessedness'. These references and echoes suggest that in the early sentences of 4174 ff. Wordsworth is endeavouring to knit together two portions of his original argument (one ending at 3536/9, the other beginning at some point closely preceding 4205) which have become separated by the insertion of 'the great body of additions' made after 5 March. The precise point at which this patching ends and Wordsworth's original text recommences is impossible to define without manuscript evidence. But we may guess that it lies between about 4187 or 4189 (where the last of the summarizing, retrospective perfect tenses occurs) and 4200, where the sentence emended by Wordsworth on 6 March begins. Thus, if for 'the action of these powers' (4190) we were to write 'hope', then the sentence beginning 'If, however, there should be men' (4188), or that beginning 'Oppression, its own blind' (4194) would follow satisfactorily after '. . . justified my hope' (3539). We suggest tentatively that the major interpolation in *Cintra,* comprising both the 'intercalation' of early March and the additions of late March, begins at 3536/9 and ends at about 4188 or 4194.

At least one other paragraph, lying outside these limits, must be an interpolation or revision, since it too refers to the fall of Saragossa. This is 4314–36, which follows the phrase 'fulness of her joy', in a position which was once to be occupied by the 'intercalation' of early March, beginning 'In Madrid, in Ferrol'. We suggest that the present paragraph 4314–36 is part of the addition of 26 March; cf. *M.Y.* i. 298, on 'what is now sent' concerning Saragossa. This suggestion is consistent with Jordan, pp. 155–6 (10 May 1809), which reports that

> the final part beginning at—"feed and uphold the bright consummate flower" [*Cintra,* 4289]—having been sent on a sheet containing a letter to me—and having besides a Latin quotation [? *Cintra,* 4358–67] in it which was not written quite distinctly enough to prevent the printer f^m^ making blunders—and being, in a manner, matted into the preface (which, from the alterations and insertions since sent, it was necessary should be written out fair)—for all these reasons I thought it better to write all this over again . . .

De Quincey's transcript of the passage concerned, beginning at 'feed and uphold' (*Cintra,* 4289) and proceeding to 'fulness of her joy' (4313), is preserved in the Cornell MS. of his Postscript, pp. 56–7. After 'joy.' this transcript proceeds: 'But we may turn &c. [from these thoughts; for the present juncture is most auspicious. &c. *del.*] see page marked III.' We may infer from De Quincey's breaking off at this point that the paragraph beginning 'But we may turn' (4314–36) was on a sheet ('marked III') other than that which De Quincey thought it necessary to transcribe, and that the sheet 'marked III' was, unlike De Quincey's exemplar both before and after this paragraph, legible enough for the printer. It is therefore likely to have been an insertion. It is unlikely that the insertion extended beyond 4336, since the following paragraph, 4337–77, is probably that referred to by Wordsworth, in terms suggesting that it was part of the original version, as 'the Paragraph before' the concluding quotation, containing a 'simile not ... sufficiently upon a level with ordinary imaginations' to stand at the end of the book (*M.Y.* i. 299).[1]

1 On 11 March 1809 De Quincey had regretted 'that the work ends with a *quotation'* (Jordan, p. 107); Wordsworth here replies to this comment. There are various passages in this and another letter which, as Wells (p. 36) pointed out, indicate Wordsworth's confusion as to the paragraphing of the final pages of *Cintra.* He proceeds immediately: 'Does what you will now find added require an alteration in the first words of the last Paragraph?' Later in the same letter (*M.Y.* i. 302), he writes: 'N.B.—If Austria should not appear to join in the war, the two last paragraphs will require a slight alteration, an *"if"* or something that you can easily give.' And on 29 March he writes (*M.Y.* i. 309): 'The concluding paragraph need not be altered on account of Palafox's reported Death.' In the first of these passages Wordsworth must refer, if our assumptions are correct, to the first words of the paragraph 4337–49, which is the third from the end of *Cintra.* In the second passage, he appears to refer to the paragraph 4314–36, which mentions Austria twice, as 'the two last paragraphs'; or, if we take the reference to Hungary (4307) as relevant, he refers to the two paragraphs 4292–336 as 'the two last paragraphs'. In the third passage he again refers to the paragraph 4314–36 as 'The concluding paragraph'. If all this is not mere confusion, we may attempt to clarify Wordsworth's remarks thus: in the first passage cited (*M.Y.* i. 299), 'the last Paragraph' should be interpreted as 'the last [mentioned] Paragraph', that containing the 'simile': Wordsworth is asking whether the insertion of 4314–36 requires alteration of the words immediately following (for instance, the word 'surviving', 4337, might have been inserted by De Quincey to take account of' Palafox's reported Death'). In the second and third passages (*M.Y.* i. 302,

The original text of *Cintra,* therefore, the latter parts of which were received by De Quincey in six or seven sheets of manuscript by 9 March 1809, seems to have been approximately 1–3536, 4188–313, and 4337–77. The extent of these six or seven sheets cannot be defined with precision, since we are not in fact certain whether they numbered six or seven, nor of the exact extent of a single sheet of manuscript. We know of them that they included (*a*) *Cintra*, 2975–80 and 3083–4 (Jordan, p. 97; 5 March 1809; included in the four sheets received on that date); (*b*) a passage about 'the incompetence of ordinary Statesmen to deal with indefinite things', probably *Cintra,* 2985 ff. (Jordan, p. 107; 11 March 1809); (*c*) a quotation at the end of the work, either 4358–67, or 4370–7, or both (ibid.); (*d*) *Cintra,* 3230, 3473, 3176, 3393–5, passages commented on by De Quincey on 14 March 1809 (Jordan, pp. 110–11).

The six or seven sheets therefore begin at earliest at 2511, at latest at 2925. Their maximum extent is thus 2511–3536, 4188–313, and 4337–77, a total of about 1191 lines; and their minimum extent is 2925–3536, 4188–313, and 4337–77, about 691+143+46 = 776 lines of our text. The maximum extent postulates manuscript at the rate of 198 (six sheets) or 170 (seven sheets) lines of our text per sheet; the minimum postulates manuscript at 129 or 110 lines per sheet.

Any of these rates is theoretically possible. The manuscript of *Cintra* seems to have been written in the first instance by Mary Wordsworth from Wordsworth's dictation (*M.Y.* i. 283); whether this arrangement persisted throughout the composition is uncertain. The printer's copy, however, was not, or not usually, the work of the original amanuensis, since various passages indicate that Wordsworth retained the original manuscript, and that a fair copy was sent to De Quincey (*M.Y.* i. 299: 'I cannot find the passage in my MS. … I cannot find the MS.'; i. 315: 'We have hunted out the MS. from which your copy was taken and it is exactly as you say'). The scribes of the printer's copy were in fact mainly Sara Hutchinson and Dorothy Wordsworth (Jordan, p. 196). A 'single sheet' in the terminology used for describing letters at this date is what we should call a double foolscap sheet, i.e. four pages approximately 13 in. x 8 in. The manuscript of *Cintra,* 3667–785, preserved at Grasmere, is such a sheet; it is written (probably) in the hand of Sara Hutchinson, and shows that a regularly written page in a largish, fairly formal hand corresponds to about 37 lines of our text (about 148 lines of our text to a four–page sheet).[1] A sheet containing an address

309) Wordsworth is thinking of the paragraph 4314–36 as the last of the matter sent on 26 March.

1 I have not attempted to recalculate the figures in this paragraph, that is, relating to the number of lines in our [Clarendon] text accounted for by a page of manuscript. References to line numbers in the

panel (about four inches deep) might be 11 or 12 lines shorter (136 or 137 lines of our text). A cramped page may contain noticeably more: the last page of the sheet at Grasmere, even though it contains an address panel, contains the equivalent of about 46 lines of our text, and, if the address panel had been used for text, might have contained 56 or 58 lines of our text; so that a 'single sheet' so written might contain as much as 232 lines of our text. (That the Grasmere sheet effectively contains only 134 lines of our text is explained by the large deletions eventually made in it.) The first sheet of the Yale manuscript of *P.L.B.,* wholly in the hand of Dorothy Wordsworth and containing an address panel, contains about 255 lines of our text. The manuscript of *R.M.,* in the hand of Mary Wordsworth, contains 48–50 lines of our text per page, i.e. 192–200 lines per four-page sheet. Thus the printer's copy for *Cintra* might contain as much as about 250 lines of our text per sheet or as little as about 150, or less in a sheet which was not full or which was much emended or cancelled. Six (or seven) sheets at 250 lines per sheet will more than fill the gap postulated above (1371 lines at most); we therefore give two specimen calculations, assuming manuscript at the rate of 200 and 150 lines of our [Clarendon] text per sheet:

(*a*) 200 [Clarendon] lines per sheet. The two sheets of the 'winding-up' are the last 400 lines of the original text as defined above, i.e. 3348–3536 (188 lines), 4188–313 (125 lines), and 4337–77 (41 lines). The other sheets (800 or 1000 lines) are 2633–3347 or 2486–3347; the latter figure comes within thirty lines of the postulated earliest possible point at which the passage can begin (2511).

(*b*) 150 [Clarendon] lines per sheet. The two sheets of the 'winding-up' are the last 300 lines of the original text, i.e. 3438–3536 (98 lines), 4188–313 (125 lines), and 4337–77 (41 lines). The remaining four or five sheets (600 or 750 lines) are 2907–3437 or 2795–3437.

It is clear from these calculations that the extent of a 'single sheet' of manuscript cannot be defined with sufficient precision to give a clear indication of the point at which the six or seven sheets concerned begin; moreover, all calculations are based on the assumptions that the scribe or scribes maintained a constant rate per sheet, and that all sheets were filled with the text of *Cintra.* Neither of these assumptions is true: the first because of the variation in rate revealed by the Grasmere manuscript, the second because we know that the sheet containing 4289 ff. contained also a letter to De Quincey, and all or some of *Ad. Cintra* (Jordan, p. 155). However, the calculations will serve to show that six (and, *a fortiori,* seven) sheets of manuscript, written at credible rates, will amply fill the gap which has to be accounted for. They are,

---

Cintra text have, however, all been changed to the line numbers in the e-text. [RG]

moreover, consistent with the following points which have not so far appeared in our arguments:

(1) On 25 March (Jordan, p. 119) De Quincey states that the printer is ready to print off 'at least' sheets N, O, P, Q. These correspond to *Cintra,* 2162 ('people knew')—2895 ('Power of'). Copy for this, according to our calculations, was in the printer's hands well before 25 March.

(2) On 1 April (Jordan, p. 133) De Quincey says that sheet P has been printed by that date (it was later cancelled because Wordsworth rejected De Quincey's note on Saragossa), and that Q, R, S, T, U have been composed. Sheets Q–U now correspond to *Cintra,* 2895–3649, i.e. to matter received by De Quincey by 11 March. This matter, moreover, was at the time swollen by De Quincey's note on Saragossa, so that sheet U must, on 1 April, have ended rather earlier than 3649 of the present text.

(3) The reference to Lord Henry Petty's motion in the Commons of 22 February (*Cintra,* 3402 ff.) as a recent event is placed either in the 'winding-up' itself (calculation *a* above), or very near the end of the sheets received by De Quincey by 4 or 7 March, within sight of the 'winding-up' (calculation *b* above). In either case, it belongs to writing of late February or early March, when Wordsworth was, as he says, 'drawing towards a conclusion' (3405).

(4) Wordsworth's second reference to Lord Peterborough (*Cintra,* 4034–8) draws on a book which he mentions on 26 March as having been procured, presumably recently; this reference, therefore, belongs to the additions of 26 March, where our calculations place it.

The difficulties and delays in publication did not by any means end with De Quincey's receipt and correction of Wordsworth's manuscript. His letters are full of complaints about the inefficiency of Baldwin's compositors. As early as 7 March he mentions that the compositor 'was [on 6 March] (according to established practice) celebrating the orgies of St Monday' (Jordan, p. 101). On 11 March he records that composing is going on 'rather slowly;—chiefly on account of Mrs. Clarke; whose Memoirs &c. are now pleaded at every press in London as an apology for neglecting all other business' (Jordan, p. 107).[1] On 21 March he records remodelling Appendix A 'since the appearance of an official Report of the Board of Inquiry's proceedings' (Jordan, p. 116) . On 25 March he writes that, because of 'proneness to modify any word, though misspelt, into the word which one is anticipating—added to the daily instances of extreme carelessness of the compositor', he is now insisting on seeing

1 Sara Hutchinson to Mary Monkhouse, 19 Apr. 1809, in *S. H., Letters,* pp. 20–1, is based on this information.

three proofs (Jordan, p. 119). In punctuation, 'the stupid compositor [has] attended to my alterations, or not, *ad libitum'* (Jordan, p. 123; 28 March 1809). Moreover,

> (partly in consequence of neither Mr Stewart's nor the pressmen's having discovered a line of the *interlineary corrections* until I came to Town) there was a good deal of time spent in getting the press to rights—which, added to the different Monthly publications ... and to Mrs Clarke's memoirs, so delayed the printing for the 1st fortnight—that I shall not receive a 1st proof of the *last part of the M.S. which can be printed before the whole arrives* until to-morrow morning [29 March] [Jordan, p. 124].

On 30 March, as we have seen, De Quincey received additional copy to be inserted into the text, and instructions which involved cancelling sheet P. Nevertheless, he writes on 1 April that he has 'explained to the printer that no further delay will arise on the part of the author; ... the utmost expedition shall be used to get the work out (if possible) by Monday after Easter:[1] I will take care that they shall not wait for me' (Jordan, p. 136). On 5 April he reports receipt on 3 April of '*both* the letters relating to the note on Sir J. Moore [*M.Y.* Letter 145 and another]; which shall be done as well as I can do it' (Jordan, pp. 137–8); the Cornell manuscript of De Quincey's Postscript shows the extent of his labour, some passages existing in as many as six versions. He complains in the same letter that, because of Easter holidays, 'the pamphlet has languished since Saturday [1 April]: however to-day, if the men can be made to attend, the overseer promises that it shall begin to advance again by forced marches ... if I give [the printers] half an hour's respite, they are ready to make that an excuse for going off to some other work ... the pamphlet [may be] out (as I am promised) by Monday next [10 April]' (Jordan, p. 139). On 15 April, however,

> The pamphlet ... is not yet finished: what is the cause of the delay, I cannot learn ... there remains at least a whole sheet of which I have not yet seen a proof; and the whole of the Appendix (about 3 half-sheets).[2] ... I fear therefore that it is in vain to hope that the pamphlet can be ready for publication before Wednesday night next [19 April] ... Mr Baldwin ... assured me that his "best endeavours" &c. should be used to get it done as soon as possible: but this it is impossible to believe from the pace at which they have advanced since.—Easter Week, however, accounts for some part of the delay; as most of the workmen made a jubilee week of it—seldom staying but a few hours of the day—and many of them none at all [Jordan, pp. 143–4].
>
> [On 25 April,] it is not yet finished ... last week, out of the six days, the man attended *two;* and must then undoubtedly have been drunk from the absurd blunders and omissions which he made;—and they will not (they say, *cannot*) put any other compositor to the work ... [Stuart] has either guessed—or been told at

1 Probably Monday, 10 April, rather than the day commonly called Easter Monday, 3 April.

2 Sheets Bb, Cc, Dd.

> the press—that it is the multitude of my corrections which causes [the delay; but the real point is that] if I have troubled them with numerous corrections—it is because they have troubled me with numerous blunders [Jordan, pp. 144–6].[1]

On 29 April, 'though the pamphlet is not finished, it will go on without stopping; as they promised on Thursday [27 April] to put a new workman to it ... on Wednesday [3 May], I should hope, it will be published' (Jordan, pp. 147–8). On 9 May De Quincey records receipt of '3 letters from Grasmere' (*M.Y.* Letters 154, 156, 158), the second of which initiates further disorder arising from Wordsworth's fears that he has written libel, especially at *Cintra,* 2170 ff.; De Quincey, Stuart, and Baldwin have attended to the cancellation of leaf N1 (Jordan, pp. 151–3). De Quincey has in proof 'only the 1st half sheet of the Appendix'; but two compositors are now working, and he has 'hopes that the last proof (i.e. the Title-page and Advertisement) should be in my hands on Wednesday [10 May] and that the pamphlet should be in Longman's hands for publication on Thursday [11 May]' (Jordan, p. 152). His letter of 10 May gives a long report of delays concerned with the last pages of 'the *body* of the pamphlet' and the Appendix: he has been accused, evidently by the printers through Stuart,[2] of holding back copy; but in fact the only copy he has held back is matter for which the compositors were not ready (Jordan, pp. 155–8). On 12 May he reports that the pamphlet is almost finished (Jordan, p. 161); on 13 May he receives 'Mr Wordsworth's letter of Wednesday night' *(M.Y.* Letter 159), which delays progress further with more Wordsworthian fears about libel. He extracts possible libels for Stuart's opinion; Stuart inspects them on Monday, 15 May, and thinks 'not one of these libellous;—but ... thought one which I had not suspected ... a libel' (*Cintra,* 3384). He disagrees with

1 On 26 April Stuart writes to Coleridge: 'I ... was much vexed to hear Mr Baldwins account of [*Cintra*]. He says that in the whole course of his Business, he never knew so much chopping & changing, so much cancelling & correction, that he supposes he has got the whole but in forming that supposition he has several times already been deceived, & that he cannot say when it will be done, till it is done. He plainly told me that the multitude of alterations, corrections & cancels would greatly [? inflame] the expence of printing. ... I of myself changed the long notes into an appendix as I know notes inflame the expence, & I ordered only 500 to be printed distinctly stating to Wordsworth that there would soon be an opportunity to making a second Edition in which he might set all to rights. ... About 3 or 4 weeks ago I informed Mr De Quincey to the same effect & even remonstrated against notes & many great alterations; urging the necessity of publishing immediately after the Easter Holidays & making him promise to write to Wordsworth. Now the whole of my prudence is upset. The Expence of printing will be great, the Edition small, the Season nearly expired. ... I wish Mr Wordsworth had trusted to himself to send the Pamphlet to Press. We got on much faster when it was in his own hands. I am quite satisfied of Mr de Quinceys amiable character & kind intentions;—but these are nothing on such an occasion' [Grasmere manuscript].

2 See the letter cited in the last note. Stuart was asked by Wordsworth on 26 April *(M.Y.* i. 321) to 'procure the immediate finishing of the work'.

Stuart and is confirmed in his opinion by Baldwin, thereby arousing Wordsworth's displeasure (Jordan, pp. 162–6; *M.Y.* i. 342, 344). On 16 May 'there remains now only the last half-sheet and the advertisement—to be *corrected'* (Jordan, p. 166) by the compositor. On Wednesday (17 May) he makes his final proof-corrections; dates the Advertisement 20 May, alters the date in his Postscript on Moore 'from April 20th to May 18th that I might lie with consistency'; and only the printing of corrected sheets remains (Jordan, pp. 167–8). He sends off four advance copies to Wordsworth on 17 May (Jordan, p. 168; cf. *M.Y.* i. 341); the printing is finished on 18 May, in spite of instructions from Stuart not to print till he gives permission (cf. *M.Y.* i. 349–50); but the sheets will take till Monday (22 May) to dry. However, Orme of Longman's 'promised me that, if 50 for immediate distribution could be sent up, they should be stitched and circulated in 2 hours: accordingly by 6 that evening (Thursday last [18 May]), 50 were sent up to [*tear*] by the fire' (Jordan, p. 171). Yet on 24 May, to De Quincey's mystification, the book remains unpublished (Jordan, p. 173). On 27 May he reports that he 'was at Longman's last night; and I had at length the pleasure of finding that the pamphlet was in a course of delivery; Mr Orme has promised to send up the remaining 10 copies for you this morning'[1] (Jordan, p. 181). The book was advertised in *The Courier* of 27 May; the advertisement, appropriately, as it were, to the general progress of the book, misprints 'CENTRA' and 'WONDSWORTH'.

Here the record of *Cintra* from De Quincey's side ends, except for a discussion about misprints on 31 May 1809 (Jordan, pp. 192–6), and a report to Dorothy Wordsworth, 7 July 1809, that by 30 June 170 copies of the book had been sold (Jordan, p. 238). As to Wordsworth, he found the delays in publication tiresome. He learned 'from Coleridge, that the Printers accuse Mr. de Quincey and myself of being the cause of the delay of the publication, by the chopping and changing that has taken place. As for myself, the charge gives me no concern; whatever harm has been occasioned by the delay cannot now be remedied' (*M.Y. i.* 328; 3 May 1809). He returns to this charge in another letter to Stuart of 25 May: 'I have no doubt that Mr De Quincey was the *occasion,* though I am at the same time assured that he neither was, nor could be, the necessary *cause* of the delay. The MSS was transmitted to him, now nearly two months ago, nor has a single syllable of the *body of the work* been altered, either by him or me, since that time—it is now printed exactly as I sent it at that time' (*M.Y.* i. 344). This statement is not, of course, true, for many alterations of word and phrase were made by De Quincey and Wordsworth, as their correspondence makes clear;

1 Wordsworth had asked for fourteen copies for himself on 6 March *(M.Y.* i. 295); he had already had four, sent on 17 May.

but it is also clear that De Quincey made nearly all of them in copy, before it reached the printer, and the only major alterations affecting the printing were the removal of De Quincey's note on Saragossa and the cancellation of leaf N1 because of Wordsworth's fear of libel. It is obvious that 'Mr De Quincey must have insisted upon his punctuation being attended to', but Wordsworth's inference that 'the Printer must have been put out of humour by this and therefore refused to go on with the work' (*M.Y.* i. 344, cf. i. 351) does not necessarily follow. De Quincey was over-meticulous in his anxiety to serve Wordsworth, as Coleridge saw (*C.L.* iii. 205–6), and as a glance at De Quincey's prolix explanations in his letters will show; but, except for his insistence on three proofs in the latter stages of the printing, most of his fussiness seems to have been exercised before the manuscript reached the printer. And there seem to have been gaps in the compositor's work which are hardly explicable except on the grounds that he or his employer preferred to spend his time on other work, such as Mrs. Clarke's memoirs or 'Monthly publications (of which this printer prints a great many)' or '*bills* &c.' (Jordan, pp. 124, 143). And whatever the printer or Coleridge (*C.L.* iii. 213) thought of De Quincey's system of punctuation, Wordsworth thought it 'admirable' (*M.Y.* i. 348). De Quincey, again, could hardly be blamed for the errors of collation of which Wordsworth complained on 4 June (*M.Y.* i. 353–4).

At some time, perhaps up to the point when he sent the 'winding-up' to De Quincey on 5 March, Wordsworth must have been at least considering a sequel to *Cintra.* On 11 March De Quincey speaks of the work 'as being only a *first* part' (Jordan, p. 107). Some trace of this intention seems to remain in the present text at 4263 ff., and as late as 5 April De Quincey questioned whether this passage ought to stand. He evidently received no instructions to cancel it; but on 26 March Wordsworth had already stated that 'The Title-Page need not state "first part". I do not wish to engage myself so far, having now said so much' (*M.Y.* i. 302). This passage suggests that the ground of the proposed sequel, or comparable ground, was covered by the additions of 26 March; other suggestions are made in our note on *Cintra,* 4263. In a letter to Stuart of 2 May, Coleridge, regretting De Quincey's 'unwise anxiety to let nothing escape', commented that had Wordsworth 'brought it out, such as it was, he might now have been adding all, he wished, to a second Edition' (*C.L.* iii. 206). Wordsworth himself had hopes of a second edition (*M.Y.* i. 354, 358), which he did not propose to revise except by correcting errors. A few weeks later Dorothy Wordsworth sadly records that 'nobody buys' *Cintra* (*M.Y.* i. 370); and the dry records of Longman's accounts show that, two years after publication, the 178 copies of the book which remained were sold as waste paper.[1]

Certain bibliographical peculiarities in the book emerged from the long and complicated printing. In some copies leaf N1 remained un-cancelled, as Wordsworth complained to Stuart on 4 June; he was the more mystified because the uncorrected copies he saw 'contain … the errata which were printed on another part of the same half sheet' (*M.Y.* i. 354; cf. Jordan, p. 152).[2]

A variant title-page was reported by T. J. Wise in his *Bibliography* ... of *William Wordsworth* (London, 1916), pp. 74–6: it reads, in Wise's copy of *Cintra* (B.M. Ashley 4628): 'CONCERNING/ THE / CONVENTION OF CINTRA, / *IN RELATION TO* / THE PRINCIPLES BY WHICH THE INDEPENDENCE OF / NATIONS MUST BE PRESERVED OR RECOVERED. / [rule] / LONDON: / PRINTED FOR LONGMAN, HURST, REES, AND ORME, / PATERNOSTER ROW. / [rule] / 1809.' Two other copies of the book are known to preserve this version; in each case the usual title-page is present also (Healey, item 22). The usual arrangement of the book is described by Healey as follows: 'The old title-page was A1 of a quarto gathering. It was replaced not by a single leaf but by a two-leaf fold; the second leaf carried a new addition to the book, the "Advertisement". Furthermore, an errata leaf was printed and inserted in the middle of this new fold. Cancellandum A1 was replaced, therefore, by three leaves.' The reason for the existence of two title-pages is not fully explicable. Two preliminary versions, nearly identical, are given in *M.Y.* i. 278, 283 (early December 1808), and two further versions appear at the head of the two instalments in *The Courier* (see Commentary, n. on *Ad. Cintra,* 6–8). These versions and the earlier title-page all give prominence to the matter beginning at *'those Principles'* in the later and commoner title-page; so that Wordsworth's revision is concerned with widening the scope of the title to include 'the relation of Great Britain, Spain, and Portugal, to each other, and to the common enemy'. This version is first announced in a letter to Stuart of 26 March (*M.Y.* i. 295–6, cf. *M.Y.* i. 310, 312);[3] and Wells (p. 42) may have been correct in inferring that Wordsworth made the change in order to take account of the additions made to *Cintra* in late March.

1 See W. J. B. Owen, 'Costs, Sales, and Profits of Longman's Editions of Wordsworth', *The Library,* 5th Ser. xii (1967), 93–107.

2 'The cancel [N1] has luckily been so contrived by a fortunate spare leaf which they calculate on having at the end … that only one leaf of that half-sheet will be lost.' This seems to be the basis of Wordsworth's statement. T. J. Wise *(Bibliography,* p. 79) claimed that the paper of the errata leaf is 'slightly thinner than that employed for the body of the work, and for the two cancel-leaves', but Wells (p. 74) doubted this.

3 This letter to Wrangham, dated April 1809 by de Selincourt, must belong to the last week of March, where Mrs. Moorman places it: note 'I sent off the last sheets only a day or two since', and cf. *M.Y.* i. 295.

Yet as early as 3 February Coleridge had mentioned 'a more comprehensive Title' than that used in *The Courier* (*C.L.* iii. 174); and it would seem that the change must have been made before the copy for the additions of late March was received by De Quincey, for on 29 March, in urging early completion of the book, De Quincey says that 'The change in the title would indeed alone have secured it a better chance for immediate circulation' (Jordan, pp. 131–2). The last letter he had had from the Wordsworths at this date seems to have been from Dorothy, 17 March, receipt of which he acknowledges on 21 March. This letter of Dorothy's is not preserved, but may have contained the revised title designed to cover the additions which Wordsworth was in mid-March in process of writing.[1] The early title-page seems to exist because it was set at the beginning of the printing of the book. For originally it occupied A1^r; the text of *Cintra* begins on A2^r, not, as might have been expected, on A1^r, with title-page and preliminaries on unsigned sheets.

On 5 April De Quincey is inquiring whether to add after the author's name on the title-page 'Author of "the Lyrical Ballads" and of other "Poems" ' (Jordan, p. 139); on 9 April he is told that this 'must by no means be done' *(M.Y.* i. 320), perhaps, as we have suggested elsewhere, because Wordsworth was still smarting at the reception of the *Poems* of 1807, and thought that such a reminder to the public would be injudicious. On 9 May 'the Title-page and Advertisement' is 'the last proof to be corrected; on 13 May 'printing the New title-page and the advertisement' remains to be done, and so again on 17 May, though De Quincey has on this day 'gone—for the last time—over last half-sheet—title-page—advertisement—table of Errata'.

The dubious readings of all copies of 1809 that we have seen at *Cintra,* 131, are mentioned in Commentary, n. ad loc. Another curious typographical feature of the book is the presence in the edition of 1809 of abnormally long dashes at certain points in the latter half [not replicated in the Clarendon edition or here]: It is possible that the dashes at 2674 after Madrid; and 2685 after slavery were used to fill space which fell vacant with the removal of De Quincey's note on Saragossa, which must once have stood on sheet P in their neighbourhood; no such explanation presents itself for

1 It may have been sent even earlier, if not as early as Coleridge's reference of 3 February. Some, perhaps the major part, of *Ad. Cintra* was sent with the last parts of the manuscript which De Quincey received by 9 March. De Quincey had to transcribe these parts for the sake of legibility (see above). Since the printing of the Advertisement was involved with the printing of the new title-page, the final version of the title-page may have been sent at the same time, i.e. by 9 March. If this is so, the revision of the title does not depend on the additions sent on 26 March. Sheet A, containing the original title-page, must have been read by Wordsworth well before this date, since he had read as far as sheet M when De Quincey reached London.

the other instances.

We have preserved in our text the variant spellings 'Portugueze/ Portuguese' from 1809. The first of these is confined to parts of the book proof-read by Wordsworth, the second to parts proof-read by De Quincey; and we assume that the difference arises from the difference in proof-readers.

Our Commentary on this, Wordsworth's largest work in prose, is necessarily less close than elsewhere. We have, however, tried to identify Wordsworth's literary sources, to clarify his references to current affairs, and to give the sources of his information on current affairs where we have been able to discover them. It is clear that Wordsworth relied almost entirely on daily newspapers for his information about the Peninsula, and wherever possible we have looked for his sources in *The Courier,* which he obviously read regularly: see the references in *M.Y.,* Index, i. 532–3; and De Quincey, *Reminiscences of the English Lake Poets,* ed. Jordan (Everyman's Library, London, 1961), p. 122, fn. Where *The Courier* lacks information, or where its files in the British Museum and the Library of Guildhall are deficient, we have used *The Times.* From these journals we have given, as well as references for Wordsworth's citing of documents, a certain amount of editorial comment on current affairs which parallels Wordsworth's. In citing such comment we have not meant to suggest so much that Wordsworth necessarily borrowed it (though he may have done so), as that many of his feelings on Peninsular affairs were shared by contemporary Opposition journalists.

For general historical information on the war in our Introduction and Commentary we have relied primarily on Charles Oman, *History of the Peninsular War* (Oxford, 1902, etc.), and occasionally on W. F. P. Napier, *History of the War in the Peninsula* (London, 1828, etc.).

INTRODUCTION: TEXTUAL

Our text of *Cintra* is derived primarily from the printed text of 1809, the genesis of which has been described above; see also Healey, item 22. Corrections to the text of 1809 are provided by its own list of *Errata* (so referred to in our apparatus), and by a list of errata appended to Wordsworth's letter to to De Quincey, 24 May 1809, printed in *M.Y.* i. 342–3. A similar list of errata is appended to Wordsworth to Daniel Stuart, p.m. 31 May 1809 (*M.Y.* i. 350–1); this list omits the corrections given in *M.Y.* i. 342–3, for *Cintra,* 3359, 3477, and 3854, confuses the correction given there for 2780 by requiring 'to' (the reading of 1809) to be read for 'of' (which does not occur in 1809 at all), and, in giving the correction for 4103, reads 'honour' instead of 'triumph'.

Variants from the text of *Cintra,* 1–503, as printed in *The Courier,* 27 December 1808 and 13 January 1809 (see *Ad. Cintra,* 6–8, and n.), are referred to in our apparatus as *Courier.*

Our apparatus records also the significant variants from 1809 of two fragmentary manuscript drafts of *Cintra.* The first of these, in Wordsworth's hand, appears deleted at the head of Wordsworth to Daniel Stuart, p.m. 9 February 1809, dated 'Sunday Evening', presumably 5 February 1809 (*M.Y.* i. 288; B.M. Add. MS. 34046, fol. 207). This draft, cited as BM in our apparatus, corresponds to *Cintra,* 2239–65; the reason for its revision in early February 1809 is suggested in our note ad loc.

The second manuscript draft is a single sheet, i.e. four foolscap pages, 12.9 in. x 7.8 in., preserved in the Wordsworth Library, Grasmere. It has been folded as a letter and is addressed to De Quincey at Great Titchfield Street, London. It has been sealed and opened, but not, apparently, postmarked. The first page opens with the following, in Wordsworth's hand:

> My dear Friend I am very sorry that I must [?draw] upon your patience for two days more—I [was *del.*] had a miserable head-ache yesterday and was occupied with visitors a great part of the day before
>
> I don't remember the last words but they were about avoided

In the left-hand margin, also in Wordsworth's hand:

> you filled up the [lacu *del.*] gap with the proper word

The last sentence of the note places the text of the manuscript where it now stands, after *Cintra,* 3666: 'much to be avoided', etc.; the marginal remark replies to De Quincey's request for something to fill 'a *lacuna,* as the critics say' (Jordan, p. 97; 5 March 1809). The text, written in the hand of Sara Hutchinson (probably) or Mary Wordsworth, begins at 'There is yet' and ends at 'position' (*Cintra,* 3667–3785). This manuscript is cited as G in our apparatus.

Jordan (p. 66) thinks that this sheet was sent early in the period of De Quincey's supervision of the printing; but he gives no evidence for this view, and there are reasons against it, and, indeed, reasons for thinking that the sheet now preserved at Grasmere was never sent to De Quincey. We think it probable that the matter on the sheet is part of Wordsworth's addition to *Cintra* finally sent to De Quincey on 26 March and received by him on 30 March, but that, though the sheet preserved at Grasmere was prepared for posting to the extent of being sealed, it was subsequently opened by the Wordsworths and copied, with revisions, in more legible form. Indeed, if this is not so, it is hard to account for the preservation of one particular sheet out of the many which made up the copy for 1809.

As to the date: the marginal note quoted above, by its use of the word 'lacu[na]', evidently refers to De Quincey's letter of 5–7 March (Jordan, p. 97), which could not have been received by the Wordsworths before 10 or 11 March; by which date Wordsworth had sent, and De Quincey had received, not only the original 'winding-up' of *Cintra* but also 'the supplementary intercalation', *Cintra,* 3539 ff. (Jordan, pp. 104–7). As there is no evidence that De Quincey received further copy until 30 March (Jordan, p. 132), it seems clear that the Grasmere manuscript must be later than 10–11 March, and therefore part of, or a draft of part of, the copy sent on 26 March.

As to the nature of the manuscript: the absence of postmark is consistent with our views, but can also be accounted for by supposing that the sheet was enclosed in a packet (cf. Jordan, p. 97: '2 packets'); and that this sheet was one of several written about the same date is clear from the fact that it breaks off in the middle of a sentence, and also from a direction to 'see the end of last sheet' (3727, textual n., ad fin.) which is repeated in Sara Hutchinson's hand on the address panel: 'You will find the interlined passage, which may be difficult to read plainly written at the end of the *last* Sheet. God bless you!' There are other characteristics of the sheet, however, which suggest that it did not reach De Quincey. It shows no signs of having been handled by a printer; its punctuation is inadequate (as may be seen from 3727, textual n.), whereas De Quincey's letters of 5 March and 25 April (Jordan, pp. 97, 145–6) indicate that he punctuated the copy before passing it to the printer; and certain variants from the text of 1809 suggest the revision of the author at first-hand rather than by letter. Thus, whereas the comparatively lengthy passage 3769–76 is inserted by Wordsworth in a letter sent immediately after the additions of 26 March (*M.Y.* i. 304), the substitution of a single word for another (see, e.g., textual notes to 3684, 3691, 3726, 3743, 3757) does not seem a revision of a kind commonly made by Wordsworth in his letters; at least two examples (3726 and 3757) are so insignificant that it is hard to imagine Wordsworth taking the trouble to write about them, though they are revisions (if indeed they are not slips) such as could easily emerge in the recopying of a manuscript. Further, at 3758 the word 'anticipations' is clearly deleted from the manuscript; its appearance in the printed text suggests restoration by the author reconsidering his manuscript rather than in a written instruction. The absence from Wordsworth's letters of all revisions to the text contained in the manuscript, except the addition 3769–76, is consistent with these views, though not evidence for them, since letters may have been lost; at least one, of possibly relevant date, has been (Jordan, p. 137). Again, the manuscript is legible in parts only with difficulty, and would have been recopied with advantage; and Wordsworth's own scribbled efforts to write the sentence 3753–5 on the address panel have made the address itself almost illegible. Lastly, since the passage recorded in 3727, textual n., is in fact eventually deleted entirely, we should expect that, if the manuscript had been sent to De Quincey, Sara Hutchinson's note concerning this passage would have been deleted accordingly from the address panel.

CONCERNING

THE RELATIONS

OF

GREAT BRITAIN, SPAIN, AND PORTUGAL,

TO EACH OTHER, AND TO THE COMMON ENEMY,

AT THIS CRISIS;

AND SPECIFICALLY AS AFFECTED BY

THE

CONVENTION OF CINTRA:

The whole brought to the test of those Principles, by which alone the Independence and Freedom of Nations can be Preserved or Recovered.

Qui didicit patriae quid debeat;——
Quod sit conscripti, quod judicis officium; quae
Partes in bellum missi ducis.

BY WILLIAM WORDSWORTH.

London:

PRINTED FOR LONGMAN, HURST, REES, AND ORME,
PATERNOSTER-ROW.

1809.

[MOTTO]

Bitter and earnest writing must not hastily be condemned; for men cannot contend coldly, and without affection, about things which they hold dear and precious. A politic man may write from his brain, without touch and sense of his heart; as in a speculation that appertaineth not unto him;—but a feeling Christian will express, in his words, a character of hate or love,

Lord Bacon.

ADVERTISEMENT

The following pages originated in the opposition which was made by his Majesty's ministers to the expression, in public meetings and otherwise, of the opinions and feelings of the people concerning the Convention of Cintra. For the sake of immediate and general circulation, I determined (when I had made a considerable progress in the manuscript) to print it in different portions in one of the daily newspapers. Accordingly two portions of it (extending to page [266]) *were printed, in the months of December and January, in the Courier,—as being one of the most impartial and extensively circulated journals of the time. The reader is requested to bear in mind this previous publication: otherwise he will be at a loss to account for the arrangement of the matter in one instance in the earlier part of the work. An accidental loss of several sheets of the manuscript delayed the continuance of the publication in that manner, till the close of the Christmas holidays; and—the pressure of public business rendering it then improbable that room could be found, in the columns of the paper, regularly to insert matter extending to such a length—this plan of publication was given up.*

MOTTO:
hate *M.Y.* i. 342: zeal 1809.

It may be proper to state that, in the extracts which have been made from the Spanish Proclamations, I have been obliged to content myself with the translations which appeared in the public journals; having only in one instance had access to the original. This is, in some cases, to be regretted—where the language falls below the dignity of the matter: but in general it is not so; and the feeling has suggested correspondent expressions to the translators; hastily as, no doubt, they must have performed their work.

I must entreat the reader to bear in mind that I began to write upon this subject in November last; and have continued without bringing my work earlier to a conclusion, partly from accident, and partly from a wish to possess additional documents and facts. Passing occurrences have made changes in the situation of certain objects spoken of; but I have not thought it necessary to accommodate what I had previously written to these changes: the whole stands without alteration; except where additions have been made, or errors corrected.

As I have spoken without reserve of things (and of persons as far as it was necessary to illustrate things, but no further); and as this has been uniformly done according to the light of my conscience; I have deemed it right to prefix my name to these pages, in order that this last testimony of a sincere mind might not be wanting.

May 20*th,* 1809.

CONCERNING THE CONVENTION OF CINTRA

The Convention, recently concluded by the Generals at the head of the British army in Portugal, is one of the most important events of our time. It would be deemed so in France, if the Ruler of that country could dare to make it public with those merely of its known bearings and dependences with which the English people are acquainted; it has been deemed so in Spain and Portugal as far as the people of those countries have been permitted to gain, or have gained, a knowledge of it; and what this nation has felt and still feels upon the subject is sufficiently manifest. Wherever the tidings were communicated, they carried agitation along with them—a conflict of sensations in which, though sorrow was predominant, yet, through force of scorn, impatience, hope, and indignation, and through the universal participation in passions so complex, and the sense of power which this necessarily included—the whole partook of the energy and activity of congratulation and joy. Not a street, not a public room, not a fire-side in the island which was not disturbed as by a local or private trouble; men of all estates, conditions, and tempers were affected apparently in equal degrees. Yet was the event by none received as an open and measurable affliction: it had indeed features bold and intelligible to every one; but there was an under-expression which was strange, dark, and mysterious—and, accordingly as different notions prevailed, or the object was looked at in different points of view, we were astonished like men who are overwhelmed without forewarning—fearful like men who feel themselves to be helpless, and indignant and angry like men who are betrayed. In a word, it would not be too much to say that the tidings of this event did not spread with the commotion of a storm which sweeps visibly over our heads, but like an earthquake which rocks the ground under our feet.

4 dependences ... acquainted 1809: dependences which the English people are acquainted with *Courier*.

11 and through the ... included 1809: and the universal participation in passion ... which it necessarily included *Courier*.

20 astonished 1809: astounded *Courier*.

How was it possible that it could be otherwise? For that army had been sent upon a service which appealed so strongly to all that was human in the heart of this nation—that there was scarcely a gallant father of a family who had not his moments of regret that he was not a soldier by profession, which might have made it his duty to accompany it; every high-minded youth grieved that his first impulses, which would have sent him upon the same errand, were not to be yielded to, and that after-thought did not sanction and confirm the instantaneous dictates or the reiterated persuasions of an heroic spirit. The army took its departure with prayers and blessings which were as widely spread as they were fervent and intense. For it was not doubted that, on this occasion, every person of which it was composed, from the General to the private soldier, would carry both into his conflicts with the enemy in the field, and into his relations of peaceful intercourse with the inhabitants, not only the virtues which might be expected from him as a soldier, but the antipathies and sympathies, the loves and hatreds of a citizen—of a human being—acting, in a manner hitherto unprecedented under the obligation of his human and social nature. If the conduct of the rapacious and merciless adversary rendered it neither easy nor wise—made it, I might say, impossible to give way to that unqualified admiration of courage and skill, made it impossible in relation to him to be exalted by those triumphs of the courteous affections, and to be purified by those refinements of civility which do, more than any thing, reconcile a man of thoughtful mind and humane dispositions to the horrors of ordinary war; it was felt that for such loss the benign and accomplished soldier would upon this mission be abundantly recompensed by the enthusiasm of fraternal love with which his Ally, the oppressed people whom he was going to aid in rescuing themselves, would receive him; and that this, and the virtues which he would witness in them, would furnish his heart with never-failing and far nobler objects of complacency and admiration. The discipline of the army was well known; and as a machine, or a vital organized body, the Nation was assured that it could not but be formidable; but thus to the standing excellence of

33 or 1809: of *Courier.*
36 private 1809: meanest *Courier.*
38 virtues *Errata:* virtue *Courier,* 1809.
43–5 to give way … exalted 1809: to give way in connection with him to that unqualified admiration of courage and skill, to be exalted *Courier.*
45–6 to be purified 1809: purified *Courier.*
46 do, … reconcile 1809: do more than anything to reconcile *Courier.*
47 humane 1809: benign *Courier.*
48–9 for such … mission 1809: upon this mission the soldier would *Courier.*
49 fraternal 1809: paternal *Courier.*

mechanic or organic power seemed to be superadded, at this time, and for this service, the force of *inspiration:* could any thing therefore be looked for, but a glorious result? The army proved its prowess in the field; and what has been the result is attested, and long will be attested, by the downcast looks—the silence—the passionate exclamations—the sighs and shame of every man who is worthy to breathe the air or to look upon the green-fields of Liberty in this blessed and highly-favoured Island which we inhabit.

If I were speaking of things however weighty, that were long past and dwindled in the memory, I should scarcely venture to use this language; but the feelings are of yesterday—they are of to-day; the flower, a melancholy flower it is! is still in blow, nor will, I trust, its leaves be shed through months that are to come: for I repeat that the heart of the nation is in this struggle. This just and necessary war, as we have been accustomed to hear it styled from the beginning of the contest in the year 1793, had, some time before the Treaty of Amiens, viz. after the subjugation of Switzerland, and not till then, begun to be regarded by the body of the people, as indeed both just and necessary; and this justice and necessity were by none more clearly perceived, or more feelingly bewailed, than by those who had most eagerly opposed the war in its commencement, and who continued most bitterly to regret that this nation had ever borne a part in it. Their conduct was herein consistent: they proved that they kept their eyes steadily fixed upon principles; for, though there was a shifting or transfer of hostility in their minds as far as regarded persons, they only combated the same enemy opposed to them under a different shape; and that enemy was the spirit of selfish tyranny and lawless ambition. This spirit, the class of persons of whom I have been speaking, (and I would now be understood, as associating them with an immense majority of the people of Great Britain, whose affections, notwithstanding all the delusions which had been practised upon them, were, in the former part of the contest, for a long time on the side of their nominal enemies,) this spirit, when it became undeniably embodied in the French government, they wished, in spite of all dangers, should be opposed by war; because peace was not to be procured without submission, which could not but be followed by a communion, of which the word of greeting would be, on the one part, insult,—and, on the other, degradation. The people now wished for war, as their rulers had done before, because open

60 exclamations 1809: exclamation *Courier.*

81 associating them with 1809: including with them *Courier.*

war between nations is a defined and effectual partition, and the sword, in the hands of the good and the virtuous, is the most intelligible symbol of abhorrence. It was in order to be preserved from spirit-breaking submissions—from the guilt of seeming to approve that which they had not the power to prevent, and out of a consciousness of the danger that such guilt would otherwise actually steal upon them, and that thus, by evil communications and participations, would be weakened and finally destroyed, those moral sensibilities and energies, by virtue of which alone, their liberties, and even their lives, could be preserved,—that the people of Great Britain determined to encounter all perils which could follow in the train of open resistance.—There were some, and those deservedly of high character in the country, who exerted their utmost influence to counteract this resolution; nor did they give to it so gentle a name as want of prudence, but they boldly termed it blindness and obstinacy. Let them be judged with charity! But there are promptings of wisdom from the penetralia of human nature, which a people can hear, though the wisest of their practical Statesmen be deaf towards them. This authentic voice, the people of England had heard and obeyed: and, in opposition to French tyranny growing daily more insatiate and implacable, they ranged themselves zealously under their Government; though they neither forgot nor forgave its transgressions, in having first involved them in a war with a people then struggling for its own liberties under a twofold affliction—confounded by inbred faction, and beleaguered by a cruel and imperious external foe. But these remembrances did not vent themselves in reproaches, nor hinder us from being reconciled to our Rulers, when a change or rather a revolution in circumstances had imposed new duties: and, in defiance of local and personal clamour, it may be safely said, that the nation united heart and hand with the Government in its resolve to meet the worst, rather than stoop its head to receive that which, it was felt, would not be the garland but the yoke of peace. Yet it was an afflicting alternative; and it is not to be denied, that the effort, if it had the determination, wanted the cheerfulness of duty. Our condition savoured too much of a grinding constraint—too much of the vassalage of necessity;—it had too much of fear, and therefore of selfishness, not to be contemplated in the main with rueful emotion. We desponded though we did not despair. In fact a deliberate and preparatory fortitude—a sedate and stern melancholy, which had no sunshine

94–5 actually *Errata:* aetually 1809.
97 their lives 1809: lives *Courier.*
111 beleaguered *Edd.:* beleagured *Courier,* 1809.
111 external 1809: eternal *Courier.*

and was exhilarated only by the lightnings of indignation—this was the highest and best state of moral feeling to which the most noble-minded among us could attain.

But, from the moment of the rising of the people of the Pyrenean peninsula, there was a mighty change; we were instantaneously animated; and, from that moment, the contest assumed the dignity, which it is not in the power of any thing but hope to bestow, and, if I may dare to transfer language, prompted by a revelation of a state of being that admits not of decay or change, to the concerns and interests of our transitory planet, from that moment 'this corruptible put on incorruption, and this mortal put on immortality.' This sudden elevation was on no account more welcome—was by nothing more endeared, than by the returning sense which accompanied it of inward liberty and choice, which gratified our moral yearnings, inasmuch as it would give henceforward to our actions as a people, an origination and direction unquestionably moral—as it was free—as it was manifestly in sympathy with the species—as it admitted therefore of fluctuations of generous feeling—of approbation and of complacency. We were intellectualized also in proportion; we looked backward upon the records of the human race with pride, and, instead of being afraid, we delighted to look forward into futurity. It was imagined that this new-born spirit of resistance, rising from the most sacred feelings of the human heart, would diffuse itself through many countries; and not merely for the distant future, but for the present, hopes were entertained as bold as they were disinterested and generous.

Never, indeed, was the fellowship of our sentient nature more intimately felt—never was the irresistible power of justice more gloriously displayed than when the British and Spanish Nations, with an impulse like that of two ancient heroes throwing down their weapons and reconciled in the field, cast off at once their aversions and enmities, and mutually embraced each other—to solemnize this conversion of love, not by the festivities of peace, but by combating side by side through danger and under affliction in the devotedness of perfect brotherhood. This was a conjunction which excited hope as fervent as it was rational. On the one side was a nation which brought with it sanction and authority, inasmuch as it had tried and approved the blessings for which the other had risen to contend: the one was a people which, by the help of the

127 *Errata indicates a new paragraph at this point; Courier and* 1809 *run on from* 141.

131 of a state *Courier recte:* ofa state *or* oft state 1809. *See note.*

surrounding ocean and its own virtues, had preserved to itself through ages its liberty, pure and inviolated by a foreign invader; the other a high-minded nation, which a tyrant, presuming on its decrepitude, had, through the real decrepitude of its Government, perfidiously enslaved. What could be more delightful than to think of an intercourse beginning in this manner? On the part of the Spaniards their love towards us was enthusiasm and adoration; the faults of our national character were hidden from them by a veil of splendour; they saw nothing around us but glory and light; and, on our side, we estimated *their* character with partial and indulgent fondness;—thinking on their past greatness, not as the undermined foundation of a magnificent building, but as the root of a majestic tree recovered from a long disease, and beginning again to flourish with promise of wider branches and a deeper shade than it had boasted in the fulness of its strength. If in the sensations with which the Spaniards prostrated themselves before the religion of their country we did not keep pace with them—if even their loyalty was such as, from our mixed constitution of government and from other causes, we could not thoroughly sympathize with,—and if, lastly, their devotion to the person of their Sovereign appeared to us to have too much of the alloy of delusion,—in all these things we judged them gently: and, taught by the reverses of the French revolution, we looked upon these dispositions as more human—more social—and therefore as wiser, and of better omen, than if they had stood forth the zealots of abstract principles, drawn out of the laboratory of unfeeling philosophists. Finally, in this reverence for the past and present, we found an earnest that they were prepared to contend to the death for as much liberty as their habits and their knowledge enabled them to receive. To assist them and their neighbours the Portuguese in the attainment of this end, we sent to them in love and in friendship a powerful army to aid—to invigorate—and to chastise:—they landed; and the first proof they afforded of their being worthy to be sent on such a service—the first pledge of amity given by them was the victory of Vimiera; the second pledge (and this was from the hand of their Generals,) was the Convention of Cintra.

The reader will by this time have perceived, what thoughts were uppermost in my mind, when I began with asserting, that this Convention is among the most important events of our times:—an assertion, which was made deliberately, and after due allowance for that infirmity which inclines us to magnify things present and passing, at the expence of those which are past. It is my aim

185 on 1809: upon *Courier.* 189 among 1809: aiming *Courier.*

to prove, wherein the real importance of this event lies: and, as a necessary preparative for forming a right judgment upon it, I have already given a representation of the sentiments, with which the people of Great Britain and those of Spain looked upon each other. I have indeed spoken rather of the Spaniards than of the Portuguese; but what has been said, will be understood as applying in the main to the whole Peninsula. The wrongs of the two nations have been equal, and their cause is the same: they must stand or fall together. What their wrongs have been, in what degree they considered themselves united, and what their hopes and resolutions were, we have learned from public Papers issued by themselves and by their enemies. These were read by the people of this Country, at the time when they were severally published, with due impression.—Pity, that those impressions could not have been as faithfully retained as they were at first received deeply! Doubtless, there is not a man in these Islands, who is not convinced that the cause of Spain is the most righteous cause in which, since the opposition of the Greek Republics to the Persian Invader at Thermopylae and Marathon, sword ever was drawn! But this is not enough. We are actors in the struggle; and, in order that we may have steady PRINCIPLES to controul and direct us, (without which we may do much harm, and can do no good,) we ought to make it a duty to revive in the memory those words and facts, which first carried the conviction to our hearts: that, as far as it is possible, we may see as we then saw, and feel as we then felt. Let me therefore entreat the Reader seriously to peruse once more such parts of those Declarations as I shall extract from them. I feel indeed with sorrow, that events are hurrying us forward, as down the Rapid of an American river, and that there is too much danger *before,* to permit the mind easily to turn back upon the course which is past. It is indeed difficult.—But I need not say, that to yield to the difficulty, would be degrading to rational beings. Besides, if from the retrospect, we can either gain strength by which we can overcome, or learn prudence by which we may avoid, such submission is not only degrading, but pernicious. I address these words to those who have feeling, but whose judgment is overpowered by their feelings:—such as have not, and who are mere slaves of curiosity, calling perpetually for something new, and being able to create nothing new for themselves out of old materials, may be left to wander about under

200 have 1809: had *Courier.*
207 Republics 1809: Republic *Courier.*
218 not say *Errata, Courier:* not to say 1809.
221 avoid, such submission is 1809: avoid such submission, is *Courier.*
225 out of 1809: from *Courier.*

the yoke of their own unprofitable appetite.—Yet not so! Even these I would include in my request: and conjure them, as they are men, not to be impatient, while I place before their eyes, a composition made out of fragments of those Declarations from various parts of the Peninsula, which, disposed as it were in a tesselated pavement, shall set forth a story which may be easily understood; which will move and teach, and be consolatory to him who looks upon it. I say, consolatory: and let not the Reader shrink from the word. I am well aware of the burthen which is to be supported, of the discountenance from recent calamity under which every thing, which speaks of hope for the Spanish people, and through *them* for mankind, will be received. But this, far from deterring, ought to be an encouragement; it makes the duty more imperious. Nevertheless, whatever confidence any individual of meditative mind may have in these representations of the principles and feelings of the people of Spain, both as to their sanctity and truth, and as to their competence in ordinary circumstances to make these acknowledged, it would be unjust to recall them to the public mind, stricken as it is by present disaster, without attempting to mitigate the bewildering terror which accompanies these events, and which is caused as much by their nearness to the eye, as by any thing in their own nature. I shall, however, at present confine myself to suggest a few considerations, some of which will be developed hereafter, when I resume the subject.

It appears then, that the Spanish armies have sustained great defeats, and have been compelled to abandon their positions, and that these reverses have been effected by an army greatly superior to the Spanish forces in number, and far excelling them in the art and practice of war. This is the sum of those tidings, which it was natural we should receive with sorrow, but which too many have received with dismay and despair, though surely no events could be more in the course of rational expectation. And what is the amount of the evil?—It is manifest that, though a great army may easily defeat or disperse another *army,* less or greater, yet it is not in a like degree formidable to a determined *people,* nor efficient in a like degree to subdue them, or to keep them in subjugation—much less if this people, like those of Spain in the present instance, be numerous, and, like them, inhabit a territory extensive and strong by nature. For a great army, and even several great armies, cannot accomplish this by marching about the country, unbroken, but each must split itself into

238–9 both … truth, 1809: *om. Courier.*
244 suggest 1809: point out *Courier.*
253 It 1809: Now, it *Courier.*
284 success 1809: final success *Courier.*

many portions, and the several detachments become weak accordingly, not merely as they are small in size, but because the soldiery, acting thus, necessarily relinquish much of that part of their superiority, which lies in what may be called the enginery of war; and far more, because they lose, in proportion as they are broken, the power of profiting by the military skill of the Commanders, or by their own military habits. The experienced soldier is thus brought down nearer to the plain ground of the inexperienced, man to the level of man: and it is then, that the truly brave man rises, the man of good hopes and purposes; and superiority in moral brings with it superiority in physical power. Hence, if the Spanish armies have been defeated, or even dispersed, it not only argues a want of magnanimity, but of sense, to conclude that the cause *therefore* is lost. Supposing that the spirit of the people is not crushed, the war is now brought back to that plan of conducting it, which was recommended by the Junta of Seville in that inestimable paper entitled "PRECAUTIONS," which plan ought never to have been departed from, except by compulsion, or with a moral certainty of success; and which the Spaniards will now be constrained to re-adopt, with the advantage, that the lesson, which has been received, will preclude the possibility of their ever committing the same error. In this paper it is said, "let the first object be to avoid all general actions, and to convince ourselves of the very great hazards without any advantage or the hope of it, to which they would expose us." The paper then gives directions, how the war ought to be conducted as a war of partizans, and shews the peculiar fitness of the country for it. Yet, though relying solely on this unambitious mode of warfare, the framers of the paper, which is in every part of it distinguished by wisdom, speak with confident thoughts of success. To this mode of warfare, then, after experience of calamity from not having trusted in it; to this, and to the people in whom the contest originated, and who are its proper depository, that contest is now referred.

Secondly, if the spirits of the Spaniards be not broken by defeat, which is impossible, if the sentiments that have been publicly expressed be fairly characteristic of the nation, and do not belong only to particular spots or to a few individuals of superior mind,—a doubt, which the internal evidence of these publications, sanctioned by the resistance already made, and corroborated by the universal consent with which certain qualities have been attributed to the Spaniards in all ages, encourages us to repel;—then are there mighty resources

292 sanctioned by 1809: in addition to *Courier*. 295 not yet 1809: not *Courier*.

in the country which have not yet been called forth. For all has hitherto been done by the spontaneous efforts of the people, acting under little or no compulsion of the Government, but with its advice and exhortation. It is an error to suppose, that, in proportion as a people are strong, and act largely for themselves, the Government must therefore be weak. This is not a necessary consequence even in the heat of Revolution, but only when the people are lawless from want of a steady and noble object among themselves for their love, or in the presence of a foreign enemy for their hatred. In the early part of the French Revolution, indeed as long as it was evident that the end was the common safety, the National Assembly had the power to turn the people into any course, to constrain them to any task, while their voluntary efforts, as far as these could be exercised, were not abated in consequence. That which the National Assembly did for France, the Spanish Sovereign's authority acting through those whom the people themselves have deputed to represent him, would, in their present enthusiasm of loyalty, and condition of their general feelings, render practicable and easy for Spain. The Spaniards, it is true, with a thoughtfulness most hopeful for the cause which they have undertaken, have been loth to depart from established laws, forms, and practices. This dignified feeling of self-restraint they would do well to cherish so far as never to depart from it without some reluctance;—but, when old and familiar means are not equal to the exigency, new ones must, without timidity, be resorted to, though by many they may be found harsh and ungracious. Nothing but good would result from such conduct. The well-disposed would rely more confidently upon a Government which thus proved that it had confidence in itself. Men, less zealous, and of less comprehensive minds, would soon be reconciled to measures from which at first they had revolted; the remiss and selfish might be made servants of their country, through the influence of the same passions which had prepared them to become slaves of the Invader; or, should this not be possible, they would appear in their true character, and the main danger to be feared from them would be prevented. The course which ought to be pursued is plain. Either the cause has lost the people's love, or it has not. If it has, let the struggle be abandoned. If it has not, let the Government, in whatever shape it may exist, and however great may be the calamities under which it may labour, act

297 with 1809: from *Courier.*
298 a people 1809: the people *Courier.*
299 themselves, the 1809: themselves, that the *Courier.*
309 condition 1809: the condition *Courier.*
315 ones 1809: one *Courier.*
316 harsh 1809: hard *Courier.*

up to the full stretch of its rights, nor doubt that the people will support it to the full extent of their power. If, therefore, the Chiefs of the Spanish Nation be men of wise and strong minds, they will bring both the forces, those of the Government and of the people, into their utmost action; tempering them in such a manner that neither shall impair or obstruct the other, but rather that they shall strengthen and direct each other for all salutary purposes.

Thirdly, it was never dreamt by any thinking man, that the Spaniards were to succeed by their army; if by their *army* be meant any thing but the people. The whole people is their army, and their true army is the people, and nothing else. Five hundred men, who in the early part of the struggle had been taken prisoners,—I think it was at the battle of Rio Seco—were returned by the French General under the title of Galician Peasants, a title, which the Spanish General, Blake, rejected and maintained in his answer that they were genuine soldiers, meaning regular troops. The conduct of the Frenchman was politic, and that of the Spaniard would have been more in the spirit of his cause and of his own noble character, if, waiving on this occasion the plea of any subordinate and formal commission which these men might have, he had rested their claim to the title of Soldiers on its true ground, and affirmed that this was no other than the rights of the cause which they maintained, by which rights every Spaniard was a soldier who could appear in arms, and was authorized to take that place, in which it was probable, to those under whom he acted, and on many occasions to himself, that he could most annoy the enemy. But these patriots of Galicia were not clothed alike, nor perhaps armed alike, nor had the outward appearance of those bodies, which are called regular troops; and the Frenchman availed himself of this pretext, to apply to them that insolent language, which might, I think, have been more nobly repelled on a more comprehensive principle. For thus are men of the gravest minds imposed upon by the presumptuous; and through these influences it comes, that the strength of a tyrant is in opinion—not merely in the opinion of those who support him, but alas! even of those who willingly resist, and who would resist effectually, if it were not that their own understandings betray them, being already half enslaved by shews and forms. The whole Spanish nation ought to be encouraged to deem themselves an army, embodied under the authority of their country and of human nature. A military spirit should be there, and a military action,

334 or 356 to 478 See Commentary: Coleridge claims to have composed or 'recomposed' this long paragraph (or possibly from the dash in line 356) from WW's draft.

not confined like an ordinary river in one channel, but spreading like the Nile over the whole face of the land. Is this possible? I believe it is: if there be minds among them worthy to lead, and if those leading minds cherish a *civic* spirit by all warrantable aids and appliances, and, above all other means, by combining a reverential memory of their elder ancestors with distinct hopes of solid advantage, from the privileges of freedom, for themselves and their posterity—to which the history and the past state of Spain furnish such enviable facilities; and if they provide for the sustenance of this spirit, by organizing it in its primary sources, not timidly jealous of a people, whose toils and sacrifices have approved them worthy of all love and confidence, and whose failing of excess, if such there exist, is assuredly on the side of loyalty to their Sovereign, and predilection for all established institutions. We affirm, then, that a universal military spirit may be produced; and not only this, but that a much more rare and more admirable phenomenon may be realized—the civic and military spirit united in one people, and in enduring harmony with each other. The people of Spain, with arms in their hands, are already in an elevated mood, to which they have been raised by the indignant passions, and the keen sense of insupportable wrong and insult from the enemy, and its infamous instruments. But they must be taught, not to trust too exclusively to the violent passions, which have already done much of their peculiar task and service. They must seek additional aid from affections, which less imperiously exclude all individual interests, while at the same time they consecrate them to the public good.—But the enemy is in the heart of their land! We have not forgotten this. We would encourage their military zeal, and all qualities especially military, by all rewards of honourable ambition, and by rank and dignity conferred on the truly worthy, whatever may be their birth or condition, the elevating influence of which would extend from the individual possessor to the class from which he may have sprung. For the necessity of thus raising and upholding the military spirit, we plead: but yet the *professional* excellencies of the soldier must be contemplated according to their due place and relation. Nothing is done, or worse than nothing, unless something higher be taught, *as* higher, something more fundamental, *as* more fundamental. In the moral virtues and qualities of passion which belong to a people, must the ultimate salvation of a people be sought for. Moral qualities of a high order, and vehement passions,

365 by all warrantable aids and appliances *Errata:* by all aids and appliances in their power *Courier:* warrantable, by all aids and appliances 1809.

and virtuous as vehement, the Spaniards have already displayed; nor is it to be anticipated, that the conduct of their enemies will suffer the heat and glow to remit and languish. These may be trusted to themselves, and to the provocations of the merciless Invader. They must now be taught, that their strength *chiefly* lies in moral qualities, more silent in their operation, more permanent in their nature; in the virtues of perseverance, constancy, fortitude, and watchfulness, in a long memory and a quick feeling, to rise upon a favourable summons, a texture of life which, though cut through (as hath been feigned of the bodies of the Angels) unites again—these are the virtues and qualities on which the Spanish People must be taught *mainly* to depend. These it is not in the power of their Chiefs to create; but they may preserve and procure to them opportunities of unfolding themselves, by guarding the Nation against an intemperate reliance on other qualities and other modes of exertion, to which it could never have resorted in the degree in which it appears to have resorted to them without having been in contradiction to itself, paying at the same time an indirect homage to its enemy. Yet, in hazarding this conditional censure, we are still inclined to believe, that, in spite of our deductions on the score of exaggeration, we have still given too easy credit to the accounts furnished by the enemy, of the rashness with which the Spaniards engaged in pitched battles, and of their dismay after defeat. For the Spaniards have repeatedly proclaimed, and they have inwardly felt, that their strength was from their cause—of course, that it was moral. Why then should they abandon this, and endeavour to prevail by means in which their opponents are confessedly so much superior? Moral strength is their's; but physical power for the purposes of immediate or rapid destruction is on the side of their enemies. This is to them no disgrace, but, as soon as they understand themselves, they will see that they are disgraced by mistrusting their appropriate stay, and throwing themselves upon a power which for them must be weak. Nor will it then appear to them a sufficient excuse, that they were seduced into this by the splendid qualities of courage and enthusiasm, which, being the frequent companions, and, in given circumstances, the necessary agents of virtue, are too often themselves hailed as virtues by their own title. But courage and enthusiasm have equally characterised the best and the worst beings, a Satan, equally with an ABDIEL—a BONAPARTE equally with a LEONIDAS. They are indeed indispensible to the Spanish soldiery, in order that, man to man, they may not be inferior to their enemies

419 power 1809: powers *Courier*.

in the field of battle. But inferior they are and long must be in warlike skill and coolness; inferior in assembled numbers, and in blind mobility to the preconceived purposes of their leader. If therefore the Spaniards are not superior in some superior quality, their fall may be predicted with the certainty of a mathematical calculation. Nay, it is right to acknowledge, however depressing to false hope the thought may be, that from a people prone and disposed to war, as the French are, through the very absence of those excellencies which give a contra-distinguishing dignity to the Spanish character; that, from an army of men presumptuous by nature, to whose presumption the experience of constant success has given the confidence and stubborn strength of reason, and who balance against the devotion of patriotism the superstition so naturally attached by the sensual and disordinate to the strange fortunes and continual felicity of their Emperor; that, from the armies of such a people a more manageable enthusiasm, a courage less under the influence of accidents, may be expected in the confusion of immediate conflict, than from forces like the Spaniards, united indeed by devotion to a common cause, but not equally united by an equal confidence in each other, resulting from long fellowship and brotherhood in all conceivable incidents of war and battle. Therefore, I do not hesitate to affirm, that even the occasional flight of the Spanish levies, from sudden panic under untried circumstances, would not be so injurious to the Spanish cause; no, nor so dishonourable to the Spanish character, nor so ominous of ultimate failure, as a paramount reliance on superior valour, instead of a principled reposal on superior constancy and immutable resolve. Rather let them have fled once and again, than direct their prime admiration to the blaze and explosion of animal courage, in slight of the vital and sustaining warmth of fortitude; in slight of that moral contempt of death and privation, which does not need the stir and shout of battle to call it forth or support it, which can smile in patience over the stiff and cold wound, as well as rush forward regardless, because half senseless of the fresh and bleeding one. Why did we give our hearts to the present cause of Spain with a fervour and elevation unknown to us in the commencement of the late Austrian or Prussian resistance to France? Because we attributed to the former an heroic temperament which would render their transfer to such domination an evil to human nature itself, and an affrightening perplexity in the dispensations of Providence. But if in oblivion of the prophetic wisdom

447–8 brotherhood … I 1809. brotherhood.—In all conceivable incidents of war and battle therefore I *Courier.*

of their own first leaders in the cause, they are surprised beyond the power of rallying, utterly cast down and manacled by fearful thoughts from the first thunder-storm of defeat in the field, wherein do they differ from the Prussians and Austrians? Wherein are they a PEOPLE, and not a mere army or set of armies? If this be indeed so, what have we to mourn over but our own honourable impetuosity, in hoping where no just ground of hope existed? A nation, without the virtues necessary for the attainment of independence, have failed to attain it. This is all. For little has that man understood the majesty of true national freedom, who believes that a population, like that of Spain, in a country like that of Spain, may want the qualities needful to fight out their independence, and yet possess the excellencies which render men susceptible of true liberty. The Dutch, the Americans, did possess the former; but it is, I fear, more than doubtful whether the one ever did, or the other ever will, evince the nobler morality indispensible to the latter.

It was not my intention that the subject should at present have been pursued so far. But I have been carried forward by a strong wish to be of use in raising and steadying the minds of my countrymen, an end to which every thing that I shall say hereafter (provided it be true) will contribute. For all knowledge of human nature leads ultimately to repose; and I shall write to little purpose if I do not assist some portion of my readers to form an estimate of the grounds of hope and fear in the present effort of liberty against oppression, in the present or any future struggle which justice will have to maintain against might. In fact, this is my main object, "the sea-mark of my utmost sail:" in order that, understanding the sources of strength and seats of weakness, both in the tyrant and in those who would save or rescue themselves from his grasp, we may act as becomes men who would guard their own liberties, and would draw a good use from the desire which they feel, and the efforts which they are making, to benefit the less favoured part of the family of mankind. With these as my ultimate objects, I have undertaken to examine the Convention of Cintra; and, as an indispensible preparative for forming a right judgment of this event, I have already faithfully exhibited the feelings of the people of Great Britain and of Spain towards each other, and have shewn by what sacred bonds they were united. With the same view, I shall next proceed to shew by what barrier of aversion, scarcely less sacred, the people of the *Peninsula* were divided from

468 Austrians 1809: Austrian *Courier.*
468 set 1809: sets *Courier.*
475 which 1809: that *Courier.*
481 that 1809: which *Courier.*

their enemies,—their feelings towards them, and their hopes for themselves; trusting, that I have already mitigated the deadening influences of recent calamity, and that the representation I shall frame, in the manner which has been promised, will speak in its true colours and life to the eye and heart of the spectator.

The government of Asturias, which was the first to rise against their oppressors, thus expresses itself in the opening of its Address to the People of that Province. "Loyal Asturians! beloved Countrymen! your wishes are already fulfilled. The Principality, discharging those duties which are most sacred to men, has already declared war against France. You may perhaps dread this vigorous resolution. But what other measure could or ought we to adopt? Shall there be found one single man among us, who prefers the vile and ignominious death of slaves, to the glory of dying on the field of honour, with arms in his hand, defending our unfortunate monarch, our homes, our children, and our wives? If, in the very moment when those bands of banditti were receiving the kindest offices and favours from the inhabitants of our Capital, they murdered in cold blood upwards of two thousand people, for no other reason than their having defended their insulted brethren, what could we expect from them, had we submitted to their dominion? Their perfidious conduct towards our king and his whole family, whom they deceived and decoyed into France under the promise of an eternal armistice, in order to chain them all, has no precedent in history. Their conduct towards the whole nation is more iniquitous, than we had the right to expect from a horde of Hottentots. They have profaned our temples; they have insulted our religion; they have assailed our wives; in fine, they have broken all their promises, and there exists no right which they have not violated. To arms, Asturians! to arms!" The Supreme Junta of Government, sitting at Seville, introduces its declaration of war in words to the same effect. "France, under the government of the emperor Napoleon the First, has violated towards Spain the most sacred compacts—has arrested her monarchs—obliged them to a forced and manifestly void abdication and renunciation; has behaved with the same violence towards the Spanish Nobles whom he keeps in his power—has declared that he will elect a king of Spain, the most horrible attempt that is recorded in history—has sent his troops into Spain, seized her fortresses and her Capital, and scattered his troops throughout the country—has committed against Spain all sorts of assassinations, robberies, and unheard-of cruelties; and this he has done with the most enormous ingratitude to the services which the Spanish nation has rendered France, to the friendship it has shewn her, thus treating it with the most dreadful perfidy, fraud, and treachery, such as was never committed against any nation or monarch by the most barbarous or ambitious king or people. He has in fine declared, that he will trample down our monarchy, our fundamental laws, and bring about the ruin of our holy catholic religion.—The only remedy therefore to such grievous ills, which are so manifest to all Europe, is in war, which we declare against him." The injuries, done to the Portuguese Nation and Government, previous to its declaration of war against the Emperor of the French, are stated at length in the manifesto of the Court of Portugal, dated Rio Janeiro, May 1st, 1808; and to that the reader may be referred: but upon this subject I will beg leave to lay before him, the following extract from the Address of the Supreme Junta of Seville to the Portuguese nation, dated May 30th, 1808. "PORTUGUESE,—Your lot is, perhaps, the hardest ever endured by any people on the earth. Your princes were compelled to fly from you, and the events in Spain have furnished an irrefragable proof of the absolute necessity of that measure.—You were ordered not to defend yourselves, and you did not defend yourselves. Junot offered to make you happy, and your happiness has consisted in being treated with greater cruelty than the most ferocious conquerors inflict on the people whom they have subdued by force of arms and after the most obstinate resistance. You have been despoiled of your princes, your laws, your usages, your customs, your property, your liberty, even your lives, and your holy religion, which your enemies never have respected, however they may, according to their custom, have promised to protect it, and however they may affect and pretend to have any sense of it themselves. Your nobility has been annihilated,—its property confiscated in punishment of its fidelity and loyalty. You have been basely dragged to foreign countries, and compelled to prostrate yourselves at the feet of the man who is the author of all your calamities, and who, by the most horrible perfidy, has usurped your government, and rules you with a sceptre of iron. Even now your troops have left your borders, and are travelling in chains to die in the defence of him who has oppressed you; by which means his deep malignity may accomplish his purpose,—by destroying those who should constitute your strength, and by rendering their lives subservient to his triumphs, and to the savage glory to which he aspires.—Spain beheld your slavery, and the horrible evils which followed it, with mingled sensations of grief and despair. You are her brother, and she panted to fly to your assistance. But certain Chiefs, and a Government either weak or corrupt, kept her in chains, and were preparing the means by which the ruin of our king, our laws, our independence, our liberty, our lives, and even the holy religion in which we are united, might accompany your's,—by which a barbarous people might consummate their own triumph, and accomplish the slavery of every nation in Europe:—our loyalty, our honour, our justice, could not submit to such flagrant atrocity! We have broken our chains,—let us then to action." But the story of Portuguese sufferings shall be told by Junot himself; who, in his proclamation to the people of Portugal (dated Palace of Lisbon, June 26,) thus speaks to them: "You have earnestly entreated of him a king, who, aided by the omnipotence of that great monarch, might raise up again your unfortunate Country, and replace her in the rank which belongs to her. Doubtless at this moment your new monarch is on the point of visiting you.—He expects to find faithful Subjects—shall he find only rebels? I expected to have delivered over to him a peaceable kingdom and flourishing cities—shall I be obliged to shew him only ruins and heaps of ashes and dead bodies?—Merit pardon by prompt submission, and a prompt obedience to my orders; if not, think of the punishment which awaits you.—Every city, town, or village, which shall take up arms against my forces, and whose inhabitants shall rise upon the French troops, shall be delivered up to pillage and totally destroyed, and the inhabitants shall be put to the sword—every individual taken in arms shall be instantly shot." That these were not empty threats, we learn from the bulletins published by authority of the same Junot, which at once shew his cruelty, and that of the persons whom he employed, and the noble resistance of the Portuguese. "We entered Beia," says one of those dismal chronicles, "in the midst of great carnage. The rebels left dead on the field of battle; all those taken with arms in their hands were put to the sword, and all the houses from which we had been fired upon were burned." Again in another, "The spirit of insanity, which had led astray the inhabitants of Beia and rendered necessary the terrible chastisement which they have received, has likewise been exercised in the north of Portugal." Describing another engagement, it is said, "the lines endeavoured to make a stand, but they were forced; the massacre was terrible—more than a thousand dead bodies remained on the field of battle, and General Loison, pursuing the remainder of these wretches, entered Guerda with fixed bayonets." On approaching Alpedrinha, they found the *rebels* posted in a kind of redoubt— "it was forced, the town of Alpedrinha taken, and delivered to the flames:" the whole of this tragedy is thus summed up— "In the engagements fought in these different marches, we lost twenty men killed, and 30 or 40 wounded. The insurgents have left at least 13000 dead in the field, the melancholy consequence of a frenzy which nothing can justify, which forces us to multiply victims, whom we lament and regret, but whom a terrible necessity obliges us to sacrifice." "It is thus," continues the writer, "that deluded men, ungrateful children as well as culpable citizens, exchange all their claims to the benevolence and protection of Government for misfortune and wretchedness; ruin their families; carry into their habitations desolation, conflagrations, and death; change flourishing cities into heaps of ashes—into vast tombs; and bring on their whole country calamities which they deserve, and from which (feeble victims!) they cannot escape. In fine, it is thus that, covering themselves with opprobrium and ridicule at the same time that they complete their destruction, they have no other resource but the pity of those they have wished to assassinate—a pity which they never have implored in vain, when acknowledging their crime, they have solicited pardon from Frenchmen, who, incapable of departing from their noble character, are ever as generous as they are brave.—By order of Monseigneur le duc d'Abrantes, Commander in chief."—Compare this with the Address of Massaredo to the Biscayans, in which there is the like avowal that the Spaniards are to be treated as Rebels. He tells them, that he is commanded by his master, Joseph Bonaparte, to assure them—"that, in case they disapprove of the insurrection in the City of Bilboa, his majesty will consign to oblivion the mistake and error of the Insurgents, and that he will punish only the heads and beginners of the insurrection, with regard to whom *the law must take its course.*"

To be the victim of such bloody-mindedness is a doleful lot for a Nation; and the anguish must have been rendered still more poignant by the scoffs and insults, and by that heinous contempt of the most awful truths, with which the Perpetrator of those cruelties has proclaimed them.—Merciless ferocity is an evil familiar to our thoughts; but these combinations of malevolence historians have not yet been called upon to record; and writers of fiction, if they have ever ventured to create passions resembling them, have confined, out of reverence for the acknowledged constitution of human nature, those passions to reprobate Spirits. Such tyranny is, in the strictest sense, intolerable; not because it aims at the extinction of life, but of every thing which

624 brave.—*Edd.:* brave."—1809

gives life its value—of virtue, of reason, of repose in God, or in truth. With what heart may we suppose that a genuine Spaniard would read the following impious address from the Deputation, as they were falsely called, of his apostate countrymen at Bayonne, seduced or compelled to assemble under the eye of the Tyrant, and speaking as he dictated? "Dear Spaniards, Beloved Countrymen!—Your habitations, your cities, your power, and your property, are as dear to us as ourselves; and we wish to keep all of you in our eye, that we may be able to establish your security.—We, as well as yourselves, are bound in allegiance to the old dynasty—to her, to whom an end has been put by that God-like Providence which rules all thrones and sceptres. We have seen the greatest states fall under the guidance of this rule, and our land alone has hitherto escaped the same fate. An unavoidable destiny has now overtaken our country, and brought us under the protection of the invincible Emperor of France.—We know that you will regard our present situation with the utmost consideration; and we have accordingly, in this conviction, been uniformly conciliating the friendship to which we are tied by so many obligations. With what admiration must we see the benevolence and humanity of his imperial and royal Majesty outstep our wishes—qualities which are even more to be admired than his great power! He has desired nothing else, than that we should be indebted to him for our welfare. Whenever he gives us a sovereign to reign over us in the person of his magnanimous brother Joseph, he will consummate our prosperity.—As he has been pleased to change our old system of laws, it becomes us to obey, and to live in tranquillity: as he has also promised to reorganize our financial system, we may hope that then our naval and military power will become terrible to our enemies, &c."—That the Castilians were horror-stricken by the above blasphemies, which are the habitual language of the French Senate and Ministers to their Emperor, is apparent from an address dated Valladolid,—"He (Bonaparte) carries his audacity the length of holding out to us offers of happiness and peace, while he is laying waste our country, pulling down our churches, and slaughtering our brethren. His pride, cherished by a band of villains who are constantly anxious to offer incense on his shrine, and tolerated by numberless victims who pine in his chains, has caused him to conceive the fantastical idea of proclaiming himself Lord and Ruler of the whole world. There is no atrocity which he does not commit to attain that end * * * * * *. Shall these outrages, these iniquities, remain unpunished while Spaniards—and Castilian Spaniards—yet exist?"

Many passages might be adduced to prove that the carnage and devastation spread over their land have not afflicted this noble people so deeply as this more searching warfare against the conscience and the reason. They groan less over the blood which has been shed, than over the arrogant assumptions of beneficence made by him from whose order that blood has flowed. Still to be talking of bestowing and conferring, and to be happy in the sight of nothing but what he thinks he has bestowed or conferred, this, in a man to whom the weakness of his fellows has given great power, is a madness of pride more hideous than cruelty itself. We have heard of Attila and Tamerlane who called themselves the scourges of God, and rejoiced in personating the terrors of Providence; but such monsters do less outrage to the reason than he who arrogates to himself the gentle and gracious attributes of the Deity: for the one acts professedly from the temperance of reason, the other avowedly in the gusts of passion. Through the terrors of the Supreme Ruler of things, as set forth by works of destruction and ruin, we see but darkly; we may reverence the chastisement, may fear it with awe, but it is not natural to incline towards it in love: moreover, devastation passes away—a perishing power among things that perish: whereas to found, and to build, to create and to institute, to bless through blessing, this has to do with objects where we trust we can see clearly,—it reminds us of what we love,—it aims at permanence,—and the sorrow is, (as in the present instance the people of Spain feel) that it may last; that, if the giddy and intoxicated Being who proclaims that he does these things with the eye and through the might of Providence be not overthrown, it will last; that it needs must last:—and therefore would they hate and abhor him and his pride, even if he were not cruel; if he were merely an image of mortal presumption thrust in between them and the piety which is natural to the heart of man; between them and that religious worship which, as authoritatively as his reason forbids idolatry, that same reason commands. Accordingly, labouring under these violations done to their moral nature, they describe themselves, in the anguish of their souls, treated as a people at once dastardly and *insensible.* In the same spirit they make it even matter of complaint, as comparatively a far greater evil, that they have not fallen by the brute violence of open war, but by deceit and perfidy, by a subtle undermining, or contemptuous overthrow of those principles of good faith, through prevalence of which, in some degree, or under some modification or other, families, communities, a people, or any frame of human society, even destroying armies themselves can exist.

But enough of their wrongs; let us now see what were their consolations, their resolves, and their hopes. First, they neither murmur nor repine; but with genuine religion and philosophy they recognize in these dreadful visitations the ways of a benign Providence, and find in them cause for thankfulness. The Council of Castile exhort the people of Madrid "to cast off their lethargy, and purify their manners, and to acknowledge the calamities which the kingdom and that great capital had endured as a punishment necessary to their correction." General Morla in his address to the citizens of Cadiz thus speaks to them:— "The commotion, more or less violent, which has taken place in the whole peninsula of Spain, has been of eminent service to rouse us from the state of lethargy in which we indulged, and to make us acquainted with our rights, our glory, and the inviolable duty which we owe to our holy religion and our monarch. We wanted some electric stroke to rouse us from our paralytic state of inactivity; we stood in need of a hurricane to clear the atmosphere of the insalubrious vapours with which it was loaded."—The unanimity with which the whole people were affected they rightly deem an indication of wisdom, an authority, and a sanction,—and they refer it to its highest source. "The defence of our country and our king," (says a manifesto of the Junta of Seville) "that of our laws, our religion, and of all the rights of man, trodden down and violated in a manner which is without example, by the Emperor of the French, Napoleon I. and by his troops in Spain, compelled the whole nation to take up arms, and choose itself a form of government; and, in the difficulties and dangers into which the French had plunged it, all, or nearly all the provinces, as it were by the inspiration of heaven, and in a manner little short of miraculous, created Supreme Juntas, delivered themselves up to their guidance, and placed in their hands the rights and the ultimate fate of Spain. The effects have hitherto most happily corresponded with the designs of those who formed them."

With this general confidence, that the highest good may be brought out of the worst calamities, they have combined a solace, which is vouchsafed only to such nations as can recal to memory the illustrious deeds of their ancestors. The names of Pelayo and The Cid are the watch-words of the address to the people of Leon; and they are told that to these two deliverers of their country, and to the sentiments of enthusiasm which they excited in every breast, Spain owes the glory and happiness which she has *so long* enjoyed. The Biscayans are called to cast their eyes upon the ages which are past, and they will see their ancestors at one time repulsing the Carthaginians, at another destroying the hordes of Rome; at one period was granted to them the distinction of serving in the van of the army; at another the privilege of citizens. "Imitate," says the address, "the glorious example of your worthy progenitors." The Asturians, the Gallicians, and the city of Cordova, are exhorted in the same manner. And surely to a people thus united in their minds with the heroism of years which have been long departed, and living under such obligation of gratitude to their ancestors, it is not difficult, nay it is natural, to take upon themselves the highest obligations of duty to their posterity; to enjoy in the holiness of imagination the happiness of unborn ages to which they shall have eminently contributed; and that each man, fortified by these thoughts, should welcome despair for himself, because it is the assured mother of hope for his country.— "Life or Death," says a proclamation affixed in the most public places of Seville, "is in this crisis indifferent;—ye who shall return shall receive the reward of gratitude in the embraces of your country, which shall proclaim you her deliverers;—ye whom heaven destines to seal with your blood the independence of your nation, the honour of your women, and the purity of the religion which ye profess, do not dread the anguish of the last moments; remember in these moments that there are in our hearts inexhaustible tears of tenderness to shed over your graves, and fervent prayers, to which the Almighty Father of mercies will lend an ear, to grant you a glory superior to that which they who survive you shall enjoy." And in fact it ought never to be forgotten, that the Spaniards have not wilfully blinded themselves, but have steadily fixed their eyes not only upon danger and upon death, but upon a deplorable issue of the contest. They have contemplated their subjugation as a thing possible. The next extract, from the paper entitled Precautions, (and the same language is holden by many others) will show in what manner alone they reconcile themselves to it. "Therefore, it is necessary to sacrifice our lives and property in defence of the king, and of the country; and, though our lot (which we hope will never come to pass) should destine us to become slaves, let us become so fighting and dying like gallant men, not giving ourselves up basely to the yoke like sheep, as the late infamous government would have done, and fixing upon Spain and her slavery eternal ignominy and disgrace."

But let us now hear them, as becomes men with such feelings, express more cheering and bolder hopes rising from a confidence in the supremacy of justice,—hopes which, however the Tyrant from the iron fortresses of his policy may scoff at them and at those who entertained them, will render their memory dear to all good men, when his name will be pronounced with universal abhorrence.

"All Europe," says the Junta of Seville, "will applaud our efforts and hasten to our assistance: Italy, Germany, and the whole North, which suffer under the despotism of the French nation, will eagerly avail themselves of the favourable opportunity, held out to them by Spain, to shake off the yoke and recover their liberty, their laws, their monarchs, and all they have been robbed of by that nation. France herself will hasten to erase the stain of infamy, which must cover the tools and instruments of deeds so treacherous and heinous. She will not shed her blood in so vile a cause. She has already suffered too much under the idle pretext of peace and happiness, which never came, and can never be attained, but under the empire of reason, peace, religion, and laws, and in a state where the rights of other nations are respected and preserved." To this may be added a hope, the fulfilment of which belongs more to themselves, and lies more within their own power, namely, a hope that they shall be able in their progress towards liberty, to inflict condign punishment on their cruel and perfidious enemies. The Junta of Seville, in an Address to the People of Madrid, express themselves thus: "People of Madrid! Seville has learned, with consternation and surprize, your dreadful catastrophe of the second of May; the weakness of a government which did nothing in our favour,—which ordered arms to be directed against you; and your heroic sacrifices. Blessed be ye, and your memory shall shine immortal in the annals of our nation!—She has seen with horror that the author of all your misfortunes and of our's has published a proclamation, in which he distorted every fact, and pretended that you gave the first provocation, while it was he who provoked you. The government was weak enough to sanction and order that proclamation to be circulated; and saw, with perfect composure, numbers of you put to death for a pretended violation of laws which did not exist. The French were told in that proclamation, that French blood profusely shed was crying out for vengeance! And the Spanish blood, does not *it* cry out for vengeance? That Spanish blood, shed by an army which hesitated not to attack a disarmed and defenceless people, living under their laws and their king, and against whom cruelties were committed, which shake the human frame with horror. We, all Spain, exclaim—the Spanish blood shed in Madrid cries aloud for revenge! Comfort yourselves, we are your brethren: we will fight like you, until we perish in defending our king and country. Assist us with your good wishes, and your continual prayers offered up to the Most High, whom we adore, and who cannot forsake us, because he never forsakes a just cause." Again, in the conclusion of their address to the People of Portugal, quoted before, "The universal cry of Spain is, we will die in defence of our country, but we will take care that those infamous enemies shall die with us. Come then, ye generous Portugueze, and unite with us. You have among yourselves the objects of your vengeance—obey not the authors of your misfortunes—attack them—they are but a handful of miserable panic-struck men, humiliated and conquered already by the perfidy and cruelties which they have committed, and which have covered them with disgrace in the eyes of Europe and the world! Rise then in a body, but avoid staining your honourable hands with crimes, for your design is to resist them and to destroy them—our united efforts will do for this perfidious nation; and Portugal, Spain, nay, all Europe, shall breathe or die free like men."—Such are their hopes; and again see, upon this subject, the paper entitled "*Precautions*;" a contrast this to the impious mockery of Providence, exhibited by the Tyrant in some passages heretofore quoted! "Care shall be taken to explain to the nation, and to convince them that, when free, as we trust to be, from this civil war, to which the French have forced us, and when placed in a state of tranquillity, our Lord and King, Ferdinand VII, being restored to the throne of Spain, under him and by him, *the Cortes will be assembled, abuses reformed,* and such laws shall be enacted, as the circumstances of the time and experience may dictate for the public good and happiness. Things which we Spaniards know how to do, which we have done as well as other nations, without any necessity that the vile French should come to instruct us, and, according to their custom, under the mask of friendship, should deprive us of our liberty, our laws, &c. &c."

One extract more and I shall conclude. It is from a proclamation dated Oviedo, July 17th. "Yes—Spain with the energies of Liberty has to contend with France debilitated by slavery. If she remain firm and constant, Spain will triumph. A whole people is more powerful than disciplined armies. Those, who unite to maintain the independence of their country, must triumph over tyranny. Spain will inevitably conquer, in a cause the most just that has ever raised the deadly weapon of war; for she fights, not for the concerns of a day, but for the security and happiness of ages; not for an insulated privilege, but for the rights of human nature; not for temporal blessings, but for eternal happiness; not for the benefit of one nation, but for all mankind, and even for France herself."

I will now beg of my reader to pause a moment, and to review in his own mind the whole of what has been laid before him. He has seen of what kind, and how great have been the injuries endured by these two nations; what they have suffered, and what they have to fear; he has seen that they have felt with that unanimity which nothing but the light of truth spread over the inmost concerns of human nature can create; with that simultaneousness which has led Philosophers upon like occasions to assert, that the voice of the people is the voice of God. He has seen that they have submitted as far as human nature could bear; and that at last these millions of suffering people have risen almost like one man, with one hope; for whether they look to triumph or defeat, to victory or death, they are full of hope—despair comes not near them—they will die, they say—each individual knows the danger, and, strong in the magnitude of it, grasps eagerly at the thought that he himself is to perish; and more eagerly, and with higher confidence, does he lay to his heart the faith that the nation will survive and be victorious;—or, at the worst, let the contest terminate how it may as to superiority of outward strength, that the fortitude and the martyrdom, the justice and the blessing, are their's and cannot be relinquished. And not only are they moved by these exalted sentiments of universal morality, and of direct and universal concern to mankind, which have impelled them to resist evil and to endeavour to punish the evil-doer, but also they descend (for even this, great as in itself it is, may be here considered as a descent) to express a rational hope of reforming domestic abuses, and of re-constructing, out of the materials of their ancient institutions, customs, and laws, a better frame of civil government, the same in the great outlines of its architecture, but exhibiting the knowledge, and genius, and the needs of the present race, harmoniously blended with those of their forefathers. Woe, then, to the unworthy who intrude with their help to maintain this most sacred cause! It calls aloud for the aid of intellect, knowledge, and love, and rejects every other. It is in vain to send forth armies if these do not inspire and direct them. The stream is as pure as it is mighty, fed by ten thousand springs in the bounty of untainted nature; any augmentation from the kennels and sewers of guilt and baseness may clog, but cannot strengthen it.—It is not from any thought that I am communicating new information, that I have dwelt thus long upon this subject, but to recall to the reader his own knowledge, and to re-infuse into that knowledge a breath and life of appropriate feeling; because the bare sense of wisdom is nothing without its powers, and it is only in these feelings that the powers of wisdom exist.

If then we do not forget that the Spanish and Portugueze Nations stand upon the loftiest ground of principle and passion, and do not suffer on our part those sympathies to languish which a few months since were so strong, and do not negligently or timidly descend from those heights of magnanimity to which as a nation we were raised, when they first represented to us their wrongs and entreated our assistance, and we devoted ourselves sincerely and earnestly to their service, making with them a common cause under a common hope; if we are true in all this to them and to ourselves, we shall not be at a loss to conceive what actions are entitled to our commendation as being in the spirit of a friendship so nobly begun, and tending assuredly to promote the common welfare; and what are abject, treacherous, and pernicious, and therefore to be condemned and abhorred. Is then, I may now ask, the Convention of Cintra an act of this latter kind? Have the Generals, who signed and ratified that agreement, thereby proved themselves unworthy associates in such a cause? And has the Ministry, by whose appointment these men were enabled to act in this manner, and which sanctioned the Convention by permitting them to carry it into execution, thereby taken to itself a weight of guilt, in which the Nation must feel that it participates, until the transaction shall be solemnly reprobated by the Government, and the remote and immediate authors of it brought to merited punishment? An answer to each of these questions will be implied in the proof which will be given that the condemnation, which the People did with one voice pronounce upon this Convention when it first became known, was just; that the nature of the offence of those who signed it was such, and established by evidence of such a kind, making so imperious an exception to the ordinary course of action, that there was no need to wait here for the decision of a Court of Judicature, but that the People were compelled by a necessity involved in the very constitution of man as a moral Being to pass sentence upon them. And this I shall prove by trying this act of their's by principles of justice which are of universal obligation, and by a reference to those moral sentiments which rise out of that retrospect of things which has been given.

I shall now proceed to facts. The dispatches of Sir Arthur Wellesley, containing an account of his having defeated the enemy in two several engagements, spread joy through the nation. The latter action appeared to have been decisive, and the result may be thus briefly reported, in a never to be forgotten sentence of Sir Arthur's second letter. "In this action," says he, "in which the whole of the French force in Portugal was employed, under the command of the DUC D'ABRANTES in person, in which the enemy was certainly superior in cavalry and artillery, and in which not more than half of the British army was actually engaged, he sustained a signal defeat, and has lost thirteen pieces of cannon, &c. &c." In the official communication, made to the public of these dispatches, it was added, that "a General officer had arrived at the British head-quarters to treat for terms." This was joyful intelligence! First, an immediate, effectual, and honourable deliverance of Portugal was confidently expected: secondly, the humiliation and captivity of a large French army, and just punishment, from the hands of the Portugueze government, of the most atrocious offenders in that army and among those who, having held civil offices under it, (especially if Portugueze) had, in contempt of all law, civil and military, notoriously abused the power which they had treasonably accepted: thirdly, in this presumed surrender of the army, a diminution of the enemy's military force was looked to, which, after the losses he had already sustained in Spain, would most sensibly weaken it: and lastly, and far above this, there was an anticipation of a shock to his power, where that power is strongest, in the imaginations of men, which are sure to fall under the bondage of long- continued success. The judicious part of the nation fixed their attention chiefly on these results, and they had good cause to rejoice. They also received with pleasure this additional proof (which indeed with the unthinking many, as after the victory of Maida, weighed too much,) of the superiority in courage and discipline of the British soldiery over the French, and of the certainty of success whenever our army was led on by men of even respectable military talents against any equal or not too greatly disproportionate number of the enemy. But the pleasure was damped in the minds of reflecting persons by several causes. It occasioned regret and perplexity, that they had not heard more of the Portugueze. They knew what that People had suffered, and how they had risen;—remembered the language of the proclamation addressed to them, dated August the 4th, and signed CHARLES COTTON and ARTHUR WELLESLEY, in which they (the Portugueze) were told, that "The British Army had been sent in consequence of ardent supplications from all parts of Portugal; that the glorious struggle, in which they are engaged, is for all that is dear to man; that the noble struggle against the tyranny and usurpation of France will be *jointly* maintained by Portugal, Spain, and England." Why then, it was asked, do we not hear more of those who are at least coequals with us, if not principals, in this contest? They appeared to have had little share in either engagement; (*See*

Appendix A.) and, while the French were abundantly praised, no word of commendation was found for *them.* Had they deserved to be thus neglected? The body of the People by a general rising had proved their zeal and courage, their animosity towards their enemies, their hatred of them. It was therefore apprehended, from this silence respecting the Portugueze, that their Chiefs might either be distracted by factions, or blinded by selfish interests, or that they mistrusted their Allies. Situated as Portugal then was, it would argue gross ignorance of human nature to have expected that unanimity should prevail among all the several authorities or leading persons, as to the *means* to be employed: it was enough, that they looked with one feeling to the *end,* namely, an honourable deliverance of their country and security for its Independence in conjunction with the liberation and independence of Spain. It was therefore absolutely necessary to make allowance for some division in conduct from difference of opinion. Instead of acquiescing in the first feelings of disappointment, our Commanders ought to have used the best means to win the confidence of the Portugueze Chiefs, and to induce them to regard the British as dispassionate arbiters; they ought to have endeavoured to excite a genuine patriotic spirit where it appeared wanting, and to assist in creating for it an organ by which it might act. Were these things done? or, if such evils existed among the Portugueze, was *any* remedy or alleviation attempted? Sir Arthur Wellesley has told us, before the Board of Inquiry, that he made applications to the Portugueze General, FRERE, for assistance, which were acceded to by General FRERE upon such conditions only as made Sir Arthur deem it more advisable to refuse than accept his co-operation: and it is alleged that, in his general expectations of assistance, he was greatly disappointed. We are not disposed to deny, that such cause for complaint *might* exist; but that it *did,* and upon no provocation on our part, requires confirmation by other testimony. And surely, the Portugueze have a right to be heard in answer to this accusation, before they are condemned. For they have supplied no fact from their own hands, which tends to prove that they were languid in the cause, or that they had unreasonable jealousies of the British Army or Nation, or dispositions towards them which were other than friendly. Now there is a fact, furnished by Sir Arthur Wellesley himself, which may seem to render it in the highest degree probable that, previously to any recorded or palpable act of disregard or disrespect to the situation and feelings of the Portugueze, the general tenour of his bearing towards them might have been such that they could not look favourably upon him; that he was not a man framed to conciliate them, to compose their differences, or to awaken or strengthen their zeal. I allude to the passage in his letter above quoted, where, having occasion to speak of the French General, he has found no name by which to designate him but that of Duc d'Abrantes—words necessarily implying, that Bonaparte, who had taken upon himself to confer upon General Junot this Portugueze title with Portugueze domains to support it, was lawful Sovereign of that Country, and that consequently the Portugueze Nation were rebels, and the British Army, and he himself at the head of it, aiders and abettors of that rebellion. It would be absurd to suppose, that Sir Arthur Wellesley, at the time when he used these words, was aware of the meaning really involved in them: let them be deemed an oversight. But the capability of such an oversight affords too strong suspicion of a deadness to the moral interests of the cause in which he was engaged, and of such a want of sympathy with the just feelings of his injured Ally as could exist only in a mind narrowed by exclusive and overweening attention to the *military* character, led astray by vanity, or hardened by general habits of contemptuousness. These words, "Duke of Abrantes *in person,*" were indeed words of bad omen: and thinking men trembled for the consequences. They saw plainly, that, in the opinion of the exalted Spaniards—of those assuredly who framed, and of all who had felt, that affecting Proclamation addressed by the Junta of Seville to the Portugueze people, he must appear utterly unworthy of the station in which he had been placed. He had been sent as a deliverer—as an assertor and avenger of the rights of human nature. But these words would carry with them every where the conviction, that Portugal and Spain, yea, all which was good in England, or iniquitous in France or in Frenchmen, was forgotten, and his head full only of himself, miserably conceiting that he swelled the importance of his conquered antagonist by sounding titles and phrases, come from what quarter they might; and that, in proportion as this was done, he magnified himself and his atchievements. It was plain, then, that here was a man, who, having not any fellow-feeling with the people whom he had been commissioned to aid, could not know where their strength lay, and therefore could not turn it to account, nor by his example call it forth or cherish it; but that, if his future conduct should be in the same spirit, he must be a blighting wind wherever his influence was carried: for he had neither felt the wrongs of his allies nor been induced by common worldly prudence to affect to feel them, or at least to disguise his insensibility; and therefore what could follow, but, in despite of victory and outward demonstrations of joy, inward disgust and depression? These reflections interrupted the satisfaction of many; but more from fear of future consequences than for the immediate enterprize, for here success seemed inevitable; and a happy and glorious termination was confidently expected, yet not without that intermixture of apprehension, which was at once an acknowledgment of the general condition of humanity, and a proof of the deep interest attached to the impending event.

Sir Arthur Wellesley's dispatches had appeared in the Gazette on the 2d of September, and on the 16th of the same month suspence was put an end to by the publication of Sir Hew Dalrymple's letter, accompanied with the Armistice and Convention. The night before, by order of ministers, an attempt had been made at rejoicing, and the Park and Tower guns had been fired in sign of good news.—Heaven grant that the ears of that great city may be preserved from such another outrage! As soon as the truth was known, never was there such a burst of rage and indignation—such an overwhelming of stupefaction and sorrow. But I will not, I cannot dwell upon it—it is enough to say, that Sir Hew Dalrymple and Sir Arthur Wellesley must be bold men if they can think of what must have been reported to them without awe and trembling; the heart of their country was turned against them, and they were execrated in bitterness.

For they had changed all things into their contraries, hope into despair; triumph into defeat; confidence into treachery, which left no place to stand upon; justice into the keenest injury.—Whom had they delivered but the Tyrant in captivity? Whose hands had they bound but those of their Allies, who were able of themselves to have executed their own purposes? Whom had they punished but the innocent sufferer? Whom rewarded but the guiltiest of Oppressors? They had reversed every thing:—favour and honour for their enemies—insult for their friends—and robbery (they had both protected the person of the robber and secured to him his booty) and opprobrium for themselves;—to those over whom they had been masters, who had crouched to them by an open act of submission, they had made themselves servants, turning the British Lion into a beast of burthen, to carry a vanquished enemy, with his load of iniquities, when and whither it had pleased him.

Such issue would have been a heavy calamity at any time; but now, when we ought to have risen above ourselves, and if possible to have been foremost in the strife of honour and magnanimity; now, when a new-born power had been arrayed against the Tyrant, the only one which ever offered a glimpse of hope to a sane mind, the power of popular resistance rising out of universal reason, and from the heart of human nature,—and by a peculiar providence disembarrassed from the imbecility, the cowardice, and the intrigues of a worn-out government—that at this time we, the most favoured nation upon earth, should have acted as if it had been our aim to level to the ground by one blow this long-wished-for spirit, whose birth we had so joyfully hailed, and by which even our own glory, our safety, our existence, were to be maintained; this was verily a surpassing affliction to every man who had a feeling of life beyond his meanest concerns!

As soon as men had recovered from the shock, and could bear to look somewhat steadily at these documents, it was found that the gross body of the transaction, considered as a military transaction, was this; that the Russian fleet, of nine sail of the line, which had been so long watched, and could not have escaped, was to be delivered up to us; the ships to be detained till six months after the end of the war, and the sailors sent home by us, and to be by us protected in their voyage through the Swedish fleet, and to be at liberty to fight immediately against our ally, the king of Sweden. Secondly, that a French army of more than twenty thousand men, already beaten, and no longer able to appear in the field, cut off from all possibility of receiving reinforcements or supplies, and in the midst of a hostile country loathing and abhorring it, was to be transported with its arms, ammunition, and plunder, at the expence of Great Britain, in British vessels, and landed within a few days march of the Spanish frontier,—there to be at liberty to commence hostilities immediately!

Omitting every characteristic which distinguishes the present contest from others, and looking at this issue merely as an affair between two armies, what stupidity of mind to provoke the accusation of not merely shrinking from future toils and dangers, but of basely shifting the burthen to the shoulders of an ally, already overpressed!—What infatuation, to convey the imprisoned foe to the very spot, whither, if he had had wings, he would have flown! This last was an absurdity as glaring as if, the French having landed on our own island, we had taken them from Yorkshire to be set on shore in Sussex; but ten thousand times worse! from a place where without our interference they had been virtually blockaded, where they were cut off, hopeless, useless, and disgraced, to become an efficient part of a mighty host, carrying the strength of their numbers, and alas! the strength of their glory, (not to mention the sight of their plunder) to animate that host; while the British army, more numerous in the proportion of three to two, with all the population and resources of the peninsula to aid it, within ten days sail of it's own country, and the sea covered with friendly shipping at it's back, was to make a long march to encounter this same enemy, (the British forfeiting instead of gaining by the treaty as to superiority of numbers, for that this would be the case was clearly foreseen) to encounter, in a new condition of strength and pride, those whom, by its deliberate act, it had exalted,—having taken from itself, meanwhile, all which it had conferred, and bearing into the presence of its noble ally an infection of despondency and disgrace. The motive assigned for all this, was the great importance of gaining time; fear of an open beach and of equinoctial gales for the shipping; fear that reinforcements could not be landed; fear of famine;—fear of every thing but dishonour! (*See Appendix, B*.)

The nation had expected that the French would surrender immediately at discretion; and, supposing that Sir Arthur Wellesley had told them the whole truth, they had a right to form this expectation. It has since appeared, from the evidence given before the Board of Inquiry, that Sir Arthur Wellesley earnestly exhorted his successor in command (Sir Harry Burrard) to pursue the defeated enemy at the battle of Vimiera; and that, if this had been done, the affair, in Sir Arthur Wellesley's opinion, would have had a much more satisfactory termination. But, waiving any considerations of this advice, or of the fault which might be committed in not following it; and taking up the matter from the time when Sir Hew Dalrymple entered upon the command, and when the two adverse armies were in that condition, relatively to each other, that none of the Generals has pleaded any difference of opinion as to their ability to advance against the enemy, I will ask what confirmation has appeared before the Board of Inquiry, of the reasonableness of the causes, assigned by Sir Hew Dalrymple in his letter, for deeming a Convention adviseable. A want of cavalry, (for which they who occasioned it are heavily censurable,) has indeed been proved; and certain failures of duty in the Commissariat department with respect to horses, &c; but these deficiencies, though furnishing reasons against advancing upon the enemy in the open field, had ceased to be of moment, when the business was to expel him from the forts to which he might have the power of retreating. It is proved, that, though there are difficulties in landing upon that coast, (and what military or marine operation can be carried on without difficulty?) there was not the slightest reason to apprehend that the army, which was then abundantly supplied, would suffer hereafter from want of provisions;

proved also that heavy ordnance, for the purpose of attacking the forts, was ready on ship-board, to be landed when and where it might be needed. Therefore, so far from being exculpated by the facts which have been laid before the Board of Inquiry, Sir Hew Dalrymple and the other Generals, who deemed *any* Convention necessary or expedient upon the grounds stated in his letter, are more deeply criminated. But grant, (for the sake of looking at a different part of the subject,) grant a case infinitely stronger than Sir Hew Dalrymple has even hinted at;—why was not the taste of some of those evils, in apprehension so terrible, actually tried? It would not have been the first time that Britons had faced hunger and tempests, had endured the worst of such enmity, and upon a call, under an obligation, how faint and feeble, compared with that which the brave men of that army must have felt upon the present occasion! In the proclamation quoted before, addressed to the Portugueze, and signed Charles Cotton and Arthur Wellesley, they were told, that the objects, for which they contended, "could only be attained by distinguished examples of fortitude and constancy." Where were the fortitude and constancy of the teachers? When Sir Hew Dalrymple had been so busy in taking the measure of his own weakness, and feeding his own fears, how came it to escape him, that General Junot must also have had *his* weaknesses and *his* fears? Was it nothing to have been defeated in the open field, where he himself had been the assailant? Was it nothing that so proud a man, the servant of so proud a man, had stooped to send a General Officer to treat concerning the evacuation of the country? Was the hatred and abhorrence of the Portugueze and Spanish Nations nothing? the people of a large metropolis under his eye—detesting him, and stung almost to madness, nothing? The composition of his own army made up of men of different nations and languages, and forced into the service,—was there no cause of mistrust in this? And, finally, among the many unsound places which, had his mind been as active in this sort of inquiry as Sir Hew Dalrymple's was, he must have found in his constitution, could a bad cause have been missed—a worse cause than ever confounded the mind of a soldier when boldly pressed upon, or gave courage and animation to a righteous assailant? But alas! in Sir Hew Dalrymple and his brethren, we had Generals who had a power of sight only for the strength of their enemies and their own weakness.

Let me not be misunderstood. While I am thus forced to repeat things, which were uttered or thought of these men in reference to their military conduct, as heads of that army, it is needless to add, that their personal courage is in no wise implicated in the charge brought against them. But, in the name of my countrymen, I do repeat these accusations, and tax them with an utter want of *intellectual* courage—of that higher quality, which is never found without one or other of the three accompaniments, talents, genius, or principle;—talents matured by experience, without which it cannot exist at all; or the rapid insight of peculiar genius, by which the fitness of an act may be instantly determined, and which will supply higher motives than mere talents can furnish for encountering difficulty and danger, and will suggest better resources for diminishing or overcoming them. Thus, through the power of genius, this quality of intellectual courage may exist in an eminent degree, though the moral character be greatly perverted; as in those personages, who are so conspicuous in history, conquerors and usurpers, the Alexanders, the Caesars, and Cromwells; and in that other class still more perverted, remorseless and energetic minds, the Catilines and Borgias, whom poets have denominated "bold, bad men." But, though a course of depravity will neither preclude nor destroy this quality, nay, in certain circumstances will give it a peculiar promptness and hardihood of decision, it is not on this account the less true, that, to *consummate* this species of courage, and to render it equal to all occasions, (especially when a man is not acting for himself, but has an additional claim on his resolution from the circumstance of responsibility to a superior) *Principle* is indispensibly requisite. I mean that fixed and habitual principle, which implies the absence of all selfish anticipations, whether of hope or fear, and the inward disavowal of any tribunal higher and more dreaded than the mind's own judgment upon its own act. The existence of such principle cannot but elevate the most commanding genius, add rapidity to the quickest glance, a wider range to the most ample comprehension; but, without this principle, the man of ordinary powers must, in the trying hour, be found utterly wanting. Neither, without it, can the man of excelling powers be trustworthy, or have at all times a calm and confident repose in himself. But he, in whom talents, genius, and principle are united, will have a firm mind, in whatever embarrassment he may be placed; will look steadily at the most undefined shapes of difficulty and danger, of possible mistake or mischance; nor will they appear to him more formidable than they really are. For his attention is not distracted—he has but one business, and that is with the object before him. Neither in general conduct nor in particular emergencies, are his plans subservient to considerations of rewards, estate, or title: these are

1188 than *Edd.*: that 1809.

not to have precedence in his thoughts, to govern his actions, but to follow in the train of his duty. Such men, in ancient times, were Phocion, Epaminondas, and Philopoemen; and such a man was Sir Philip Sidney, of whom it has been said, that he first taught this country *the majesty of honest dealing.* With these may be named, the honour of our own age, Washington, the deliverer of the American Continent; with these, though in many things unlike, Lord Nelson, whom we have lately lost. Lord Peterborough, who fought in Spain a hundred years ago, had the same excellence; with a sense of exalted honour, and a tinge of romantic enthusiasm, well suited to the country which was the scene of his exploits. Would that we had a man, like Peterborough or Nelson, at the head of our army in Spain at this moment! I utter this wish with more earnestness, because it is rumoured, that some of those, who have already called forth such severe reprehension from their countrymen, are to resume a command, which must entrust to them a portion of those sacred hopes in which, not only we, and the people of Spain and Portugal, but the whole human race are so deeply interested. (See Appendix C.)

I maintain then that, merely from want of this intellectual courage, of courage as generals or chiefs, (for I will not speak at present of the want of other qualities equally needful upon this service,) grievous errors were committed by Sir Hew Dalrymple and his colleagues in estimating the relative state of the two armies. A precious moment, it is most probable, had been lost after the battle of Vimiera; yet still the inferiority of the enemy had been proved; they themselves had admitted it—not merely by withdrawing from the field, but by proposing terms:—monstrous terms! and how ought they to have been received? Repelled undoubtedly with scorn, as an insult. If our Generals had been men capable of taking the measure of their real strength, either as existing in their own army, or in those principles of liberty and justice which they were commissioned to defend, they must of necessity have acted in this manner;—if they had been men of common sagacity for business, they must have acted in this manner;—nay, if they had been upon a level with an ordinary bargain-maker in a fair or a market, they could not have acted otherwise.—Strange that they should so far forget the nature of their calling! They were soldiers, and their business was to fight. Sir Arthur Wellesley had fought, and gallantly; it was not becoming his high situation, or that of his successors, to treat, that is, to beat down, to chaffer, or on their part to propose: it does not become any general at the head of a victorious army so to do.* They were to *accept,*—and, if the terms offered were flagrantly presumptuous, our commanders ought to have rejected them with dignified scorn, and to have referred the proposer to the sword for a lesson of decorum and humility. This is the general rule of all high-minded men upon such occasions; and meaner minds copy them, doing in prudence what they do from principle. But it has been urged, before the Board of Inquiry, that the conduct of the French armies upon like occasions, and their known character, rendered it probable that a determined resistance would in the present instance be maintained. We need not fear to say that this conclusion, from reasons which have been adverted to, was erroneous. But, in the mind of him who had admitted it upon whatever ground, whether false or true, surely the first thought which followed, ought to have been, not that we should bend to the enemy, but that, if they were resolute in defence, we should learn from that example to be courageous in attack. The tender feelings, however, are pleaded against this determination; and it is said, that one of the motives for the cessation of hostilities was to prevent the further effusion of human blood.—When, or how? The enemy was delivered over to us; it was not to be hoped that, cut off from all assistance as they were, these, or an equal number of men, could ever be reduced to such straits as would ensure their destruction as an enemy, with so small a sacrifice of life on their part, or on ours. What then was to be gained by this tenderness? The shedding of a few drops of blood is not to be risked in Portugal to-day, and streams of blood must shortly flow from the same veins in the fields of Spain! And, even if this had not been the assured consequence, let not the consideration, though it be one which no humane man can ever lose sight of, have more than its due weight. For national independence and liberty, and *that* honour by which these and other blessings are to be preserved, honour—which is no other than the most elevated and pure conception of justice which can be formed, these are more precious than life: else why have we already lost so many brave men in this struggle?—Why not submit at once, and let the Tyrant mount upon his throne of universal dominion, while the world lies prostrate at his feet in indifference and apathy, which he will proclaim to it is peace and happiness? But peace and happiness can exist only by knowledge and virtue; slavery has no enduring

* Those rare cases are of course excepted, in which the superiority on the one side is not only fairly to be presumed but positive—and so prominently obtrusive, that to *propose* terms is to *inflict* terms.

connection with tranquillity or security—she cannot frame a league with any thing which is desirable—she has no charter even for her own ignoble ease and darling sloth. Yet to this abject condition, mankind, betrayed by an ill-judging tenderness, would surely be led; and in the face of an inevitable contradiction! For neither in this state of things would the shedding of blood be prevented, nor would warfare cease. The only difference would be, that, instead of wars like those which prevail at this moment, presenting a spectacle of such character that, upon one side at least, a superior Being might look down with favour and blessing, there would follow endless commotions and quarrels without the presence of justice any where,—in which the alternations of success would not excite a wish or regret; in which a prayer could not be uttered for a decision either this way or that;—wars from no impulse in either of the combatants, but rival instigations of demoniacal passion. If, therefore, by the faculty of reason we can prophecy concerning the shapes which the future may put on,—if we are under any bond of duty to succeeding generations, there is high cause to guard against a specious sensibility, which may encourage the hoarding up of life for its own sake, seducing us from those considerations by which we might learn when it ought to be resigned. Moreover, disregarding future ages, and confining ourselves to the present state of mankind, it may be safely affirmed that he, who is the most watchful of the honour of his country, most determined to preserve her fair name at all hazards, will be found, in any view of things which looks beyond the passing hour, the best steward of the *lives* of his countrymen. For, by proving that she is of a firm temper, that she will only submit or yield to a point of her own fixing, and that all beyond is immutable resolution, he will save her from being wantonly attacked; and, if attacked, will awe the aggressor into a speedier abandonment of an unjust and hopeless attempt. Thus will he preserve not only that which gives life its value, but life itself; and not for his own country merely, but for that of his enemies, to whom he will have offered an example of magnanimity, which will ensure to them like benefits; an example, the re-action of which will be felt by his own countrymen, and will prevent them from becoming assailants unjustly or rashly. Nations will thus be taught to respect each other, and mutually to abstain from injuries. And hence, by a benign ordinance of our nature, genuine honour is the hand-maid of humanity; the attendant and sustainer—both of the sterner qualities which constitute the appropriate excellence of the male character, and of the gentle and tender virtues which belong more especially to motherliness and womanhood. These general laws, by which mankind is purified and exalted, and by which Nations are preserved, suggest likewise the best rules for the preservation of individual armies, and for the accomplishment of all equitable service upon which they can be sent.

Not therefore rashly and unfeelingly, but from the dictates of thoughtful humanity, did I say that it was the business of our Generals to fight, and to persevere in fighting; and that they did not bear this duty sufficiently in mind; this, almost the sole duty which professional soldiers, till our time, (happily for mankind) used to think of. But the victories of the French have been attended every where by the subversion of Governments; and their generals have accordingly united *political* with military functions; and with what success this has been done by them, the present state of Europe affords melancholy proof. But have they, on this account, ever neglected to calculate upon the advantages which might fairly be anticipated from future warfare? Or, in a treaty of to-day, have they ever forgotten a victory of yesterday? Eager to grasp at the double honour of captain and negociator, have they ever sacrificed the one to the other; or, in the blind effort, lost both? Above all, in their readiness to flourish with the pen, have they ever overlooked the sword, the symbol of their power, and the appropriate instrument of their success and glory? I notice this assumption of a double character on the part of the French, not to lament over it and its consequences, but to render somewhat more intelligible the conduct of our own Generals; and to explain how far men, whom we have no reason to believe other than brave, have, through the influence of such example, lost sight of their primary duties, apeing instead of imitating, and following only to be misled.

It is indeed deplorable, that our Generals, from this infirmity, or from any other cause, did not assume that lofty deportment which the character and relative strength of the two armies authorized them, and the nature of the service upon which they were sent, enjoined them to assume;—that they were in such haste to treat—that, with such an enemy (let me say at once,) and in such circumstances, they should have treated at all. Is it possible that they could ever have asked themselves who that enemy was, how he came into that country, and what he had done there? From the manifesto of the Portugueze government, issued at Rio Janeiro, and from other official papers, they might have learned, what was notorious to all Europe, that this body of men commissioned by Bonaparte, in the time of profound peace, without a declaration of war, had invaded Portugal under the command of Junot, who had perfidiously entered the country, as the General of a friendly and allied Power, assuring the people, as he advanced, that he came to protect their Sovereign against an invasion of the English; and that, when in this manner he had entered a peaceable kingdom, which offered no resistance, and had expelled its lawful Sovereign, he wrung from it unheard-of contributions, ravaged it, cursed it with domestic pillage and open sacrilege; and that, when this unoffending people, unable to endure any longer, rose up against the tyrant, he had given their towns and villages to the flames, and put the whole country, thus resisting, under military execution.—Setting aside all natural sympathy with the Portugueze and Spanish nations, and all prudential considerations of regard or respect for *their feelings* towards these men, and for *their expectations* concerning the manner in which they ought to be dealt with, it is plain that the French had forfeited by their crimes all right to those privileges, or to those modes of intercourse, which one army may demand from another according to the laws of war. They were not soldiers in any thing but the power of soldiers, and the outward frame of an army. During their occupation of Portugal, the laws and customs of war had never been referred to by them, but as a plea for some enormity, to the aggravated oppression of that unhappy country! Pillage, sacrilege, and murder—sweeping murder and individual assassination, had been proved against them by voices from every quarter. They had outlawed themselves by their offences from membership in the community of war, and from every species of community acknowledged by reason. But even, should any one be so insensible as to question this, he will not at all events deny, that the French ought to have been dealt with as having put on a double character. For surely they never considered themselves merely as an army. They had dissolved the established authorities of Portugal, and had usurped the civil power of the government; and it was in this compound capacity, under this two-fold monstrous shape, that they had exercised, over the religion and property of the country, the most grievous oppressions. What then remained to protect them but their power?—Right they had none,—and power! it is a mortifying consideration, but I will ask if Bonaparte, (nor do I mean in the question to imply any thing to his honour,) had been in the place of Sir Hew Dalrymple, what would he have thought of their power?—Yet before this shadow the solid substance of *justice* melted away.

And this leads me from the contemplation of their errors in the estimate and application of means, to the contemplation of their heavier errors and worse blindness in regard to ends. The British Generals acted as if they had no purpose but that the enemy should be removed from the country in which they were, upon *any* terms. Now the evacuation of Portugal was not the prime object, but the manner in which that event was to be brought about; this ought to have been deemed first both in order and importance;—the French were to be subdued, their ferocious warfare and heinous policy to be confounded; and in this way, and no other, was the deliverance of that country to be accomplished. It was not for the soil, or for the cities and forts, that Portugal was valued, but for the human feeling which was there; for the rights of human nature which might be there conspicuously asserted; for a triumph over injustice and oppression there to be atchieved, which could neither be concealed nor disguised, and which should penetrate the darkest corner of the dark Continent of Europe by its splendour. We combated for victory in the empire of reason, for strongholds in the imagination. Lisbon and Portugal, as city and soil, were chiefly prized by us as a *language;* but our Generals mistook the counters of the game for the stake played for. The nation required that the French should surrender at discretion;—grant that the victory of Vimiera had excited some unreasonable impatience—we were not so overweening as to demand that the enemy should surrender within a given time, but that they should surrender. Every thing, short of this, was felt to be below the duties of the occasion; not only no service, but a grievous injury. Only as far as there was a prospect of forcing the enemy to an unconditional submission, did the British nation deem that they had a right to interfere;—if that prospect failed, they expected that their army would know that it became it to retire, and take care of itself. But our Generals have told us, that the Convention would not have been admitted, if they had not judged it right to effect, even upon these terms, the evacuation of Portugal—as ministerial to their future services in Spain. If this had been a common war between two established governments measuring with each other their regular resources, there might have been some appearance of force in this plea. But who does not cry out at once, that the affections and opinions, that is, the souls of the people of Spain and Portugal, must be the inspiration and the power, if this labour is to be brought to a happy end? Therefore it was worse than folly to think of supporting Spain by physical strength, at the expence of moral. Besides, she was strong in men; she never earnestly solicited troops from us; some of the Provinces had even refused them when offered,—and all had been lukewarm in the acceptance of them. The Spaniards could not *ultimately* be benefited but by allies acting under the same impulses of honour, rouzed by a sense of their wrongs, and sharing their loves and hatreds—above all, their *passion* for justice. They had themselves given an example, at Baylen, proclaiming to all the world what ought to be aimed at by those who would uphold their cause, and be associated in arms with them. And was the law of justice, which Spaniards, Spanish peasantry, I might almost say, would not relax in favour of Dupont, to be relaxed by a British army in favour of Junot? Had the French commander at Lisbon, or his army, proved themselves less perfidious, less cruel, or less rapacious than the other? Nay, did not the pride and crimes of Junot call for humiliation and punishment far more importunately, inasmuch as his power to do harm, and therefore his will, keeping pace with it, had been greater? Yet, in the noble letter of the Governor of Cadiz to Dupont, he expressly tells him, that his conduct, and that of his army, had been such, that they owed their lives only to that honour which forbad the Spanish army to become executioners. The Portugueze also, as appears from various letters produced before the Board of Inquiry, have shewn to our Generals, as boldly as their respect for the British nation would permit them to do, what *they* expected. A Portugueze General, who was also a member of the regency appointed by the Prince Regent, says, in a protest addressed to Sir Hew Dalrymple, that he had been able to drive the French out of the provinces of Algarve and Alentejo; and therefore he could not be convinced, that such a Convention was necessary. What was this but implying that it was dishonourable, and that it would frustrate the efforts which his country was making, and destroy the hopes which it had built upon its own power? Another letter from a magistrate inveighs against the Convention, as leaving the crimes of the French in Portugal unpunished; as giving no indemnification for all the murders, robberies, and atrocities, which had been committed by them. But I feel that I shall be wanting in respect to my countrymen, if I pursue this argument further. I blush that it should be necessary to speak upon the subject at all. And these are men and things, which we have been reproved for condemning, because evidence was wanting both as to fact and person! If there ever was a case, which could not, in any rational sense of the word, be prejudged, this is one. As to the fact—it appears, and sheds from its own body, like the sun in heaven, the light by which it is seen; as to the person—each has written down with his own hand, *I am the man.* Condemnation of actions and men like these is not, in the minds of a people, (thanks to the divine Being and to human nature!) a matter of choice; it is like a physical necessity, as the hand must be burned which is thrust into the furnace—the body chilled which stands naked in the freezing north-wind. I am entitled to make this assertion here, when the *moral* depravity of the Convention, of which I shall have to speak hereafter, has not even been touched upon. Nor let it be blamed in any man, though his station be in private life, that upon this occasion he speaks publickly, and gives a decisive opinion concerning that part of this public event, and those measures, which are more especially military. All have a right to speak, and to make their voices heard, as far as they have power. For these are times, in which the conduct of military men concerns us, perhaps, more intimately than that of any other class; when the business of arms comes unhappily too near to the fire side; when the character and duties of a soldier ought to be understood by every one who values his liberty, and bears in mind how soon he may have to fight for it. Men will and ought to speak upon things in which they are so deeply interested; how else are right notions to spread, or is error to be destroyed? These are times also in which, if we may judge from the proceedings and result of the Court of Inquiry, the heads of the army, more than at any other period, stand in need of being taught wisdom by the voice of the people. It is their own interest, both as men and as soldiers, that the people should speak fervently and fearlessly of their actions:—from no other quarter can they be so powerfully reminded of the duties which they owe to themselves, to their country, and to human nature. Let any one read the evidence given before that Court, and he will there see, how much the intellectual and moral constitution of many of our military officers, has suffered by a profession, which, if not counteracted by admonitions willingly listened to, and by habits of meditation, does, more than any other, denaturalize—and therefore degrade the human being;—he will note with sorrow, how faint are their sympathies with the best feelings, and how dim their apprehension of some of the most awful truths, relating to the happiness and dignity of man in society. But on this I do not mean to insist at present; it is too weighty a subject to be treated incidentally: and my purpose is—not to invalidate the authority of military men, *positively* considered, upon a military question, but *comparatively;*—to maintain that there are military transactions upon which the people have a right to be heard, and upon which their authority is entitled to far more respect than any man or number of men can lay claim to, who speak merely with the ordinary professional views of soldiership;—that there are such military transactions;—and that *this* is one of them.

The condemnation, which the people of these islands pronounced upon the Convention of Cintra considered as to its main *military* results, that is, as a treaty by which it was established that the Russian fleet should be surrendered on the terms specified; and by which, not only the obligation of forcing the French army to an unconditional surrender was abandoned, but its restoration in freedom and triumph to its own country was secured;—the condemnation, pronounced by the people upon a treaty, by virtue of which these things were to be done, I have recorded—accounted for—and thereby justified.—I will now proceed to another division of the subject, on which I feel a still more earnest wish to speak; because, though in itself of the highest importance, it has been comparatively neglected;—I mean the political injustice and moral depravity which are stamped upon the front of this agreement, and pervade every regulation which it contains. I shall shew that our Generals (and with them our Ministers, as far as they might have either given directions to this effect, or have countenanced what has been done)—when it was their paramount duty to maintain at all hazards the noblest principles in unsuspected integrity; because, upon the summons of these, and in defence of them, their Allies had risen, and by these alone could stand—not only did not perform this duty, but descended as far below the level of ordinary principles as they ought to have mounted above it;—imitating not the majesty of the oak with which it lifts its branches towards the heavens, but the vigour with which, in the language of the poet, it strikes its roots downwards towards hell:—

Radice in Tartara tendit.

The Armistice is the basis of the Convention; and in the first article we find it agreed, "That there shall be a suspension of hostilities between the forces of his Britannic Majesty, and those of his Imperial and Royal Majesty, Napoleon I." I will ask if it be the practice of military officers, in instruments of this kind, to acknowledge, in the person of the head of the government with which they are at war, titles which their own government—for which they are acting—has not acknowledged. If this be the practice, which I will not stop to determine, it is grossly improper; and ought to be abolished. Our Generals, however, had entered Portugal as allies of a Government by which this title had been acknowledged; and they might have pleaded this circumstance in mitigation of their offence; but surely not in an instrument, where we not only look in vain for the name of the Portugueze Sovereign, or of the Government which he appointed, or of any heads or representatives of the Portugueze armies or people as a party in the contract,—but where it is stipulated (in the 4th article) that the British General shall engage to include the Portugueze armies in this Convention. What an outrage!—We enter the Portugueze territory as allies; and, without their consent—or even consulting them, we proceed to form the basis of an agreement, relating—not to the safety or interests of our own army—but to Portugueze territory, Portugueze persons, liberties, and rights,—and engage, out of our own will and power, to include the Portugueze army, they or their Government willing or not, within the obligation of this agreement. I place these things in contrast, viz. the acknowledgement of Bonaparte as emperor and king, and the utter neglect of the Portugueze Sovereign and Portugueze authorities, to shew in what spirit and temper these agreements were entered upon. I will not here insist upon what was our duty, on this occasion, to the Portugueze—as dictated by those sublime precepts of justice which it has been proved that they and the Spaniards had risen to defend,—and without feeling the force and sanctity of which, they neither could have risen, nor can oppose to their enemy resistance which has any hope in it; but I will ask, of any man who is not dead to the common feelings of his social nature—and besotted in understanding, if this be not a cruel mockery, and which must have been felt, unless it were repelled with hatred and scorn, as a heart-breaking insult. Moreover, this conduct acknowledges, by implication, that principle which by his actions the enemy has for a long time covertly maintained, and now openly and insolently avows in his words—that power is the measure of right;—and it is in a steady adherence to this abominable doctrine that his strength mainly lies. I do maintain then that, as far as the conduct of our Generals in framing these instruments tends to reconcile men to this course of action, and to sanction this principle, they are virtually his Allies: their weapons may be against him, but he will laugh at their weapons,—for he knows, though they themselves do not, that their souls are for him. Look at the preamble to the Armistice! In what is omitted and what is inserted, the French Ruler could not have fashioned it more for his own purpose if he had traced it with his own hand. We have then trampled upon a fundamental principle of justice, and countenanced a prime maxim of iniquity; thus adding, in an unexampled degree, the foolishness of impolicy to the heinousness of guilt. A conduct thus grossly unjust and impolitic, without having the hatred which it inspires neutralised by the contempt, is made contemptible by utterly wanting that colour of right which authority and power, put forth in defence of our Allies—in asserting their just claims and avenging their injuries, might have given. But we, instead of triumphantly displaying our power towards our enemies, have ostentatiously exercised it upon our friends; reversing here, as every where, the practice of sense and reason;—conciliatory even to abject submission where we ought to have been haughty and commanding,—and repulsive and tyrannical where we ought to have been gracious and kind. Even a common law of good breeding would have served us here, had we known how to apply it. We ought to have endeavoured to raise the Portugueze in their own estimation by concealing our power in comparison with theirs; dealing with them in the spirit of those mild and humane delusions, which spread such a genial grace over the intercourse, and add so much to the influence of love in the concerns of private life. It is a common saying, presume that a man is dishonest, and that is the readiest way to make him so: in like manner it may be said, presume that a nation is weak, and that is the surest course to bring it to weakness,—if it be not rouzed to prove its strength by applying it to the humiliation of your pride. The Portugueze had been weak; and, in connection with their allies the Spaniards, they were prepared to become strong. It was, therefore, doubly incumbent upon us to foster and encourage them—to look favourably upon their efforts—generously to give them credit upon their promises—to hope with them and for them; and, thus anticipating and foreseeing, we should, by a natural operation of love, have contributed to create the merits which were anticipated and foreseen. I apply these rules, taken from the intercourse between individuals, to the conduct of large bodies of men, or of nations towards each other, because these are nothing but aggregates of individuals; and because the maxims of all just law, and the measures of all sane practice, are only an enlarged or modified application of those dispositions of love and those principles of reason, by which the welfare of individuals, in their connection with each other, is promoted. There was also here a still more urgent call for these courteous and humane principles as guides of conduct; because, in exact proportion to the physical weakness of Governments, and to the distraction and confusion which cannot but prevail, when a people is struggling for independence and liberty, are the well-intentioned and the wise among them remitted for their support to those benign elementary feelings of society, for the preservation and cherishing of which, among other important objects, government was from the beginning ordained.

Therefore, by the strongest obligations, we were bound to be studious of a delicate and respectful bearing towards those ill-fated nations, our allies: and consequently, if the government of the Portugueze, though weak in power, possessed their affections, and was strong in right, it was incumbent upon us to turn our first thoughts to that government—to look for it if it were hidden—to call it forth,—and, by our power combined with that of the people, to assert its rights. Or, if the government were dissolved and had no existence, it was our duty, in such an emergency, to have resorted to the nation, expressing its will through the most respectable and conspicuous authority, through that which seemed to have the best right to stand forth as its representative. In whatever circumstances Portugal had been placed, the paramount right of the Portugueze nation, or government, to appear not merely as a party but a principal, ought to have been established as a primary position, without the admission of which, all proposals to treat would be peremptorily rejected. But the Portugueze *had* a government; they had a lawful prince in Brazil; and a regency, appointed by him, at home; and generals, at the head of considerable bodies of troops, appointed also by the regency or the prince. Well then might one of those generals enter a formal protest against the treaty, on account of its being "totally void of that deference due to the prince regent, or the government that represents him; as being hostile to the sovereign authority and independence of that government; and as being against the honour, safety, and independence of the nation." I have already reminded the reader, of the benign and happy influences which might have attended upon a different conduct; how much good we might have added to that already in existence; how far we might have assisted in strengthening, among our allies, those powers, and in developing those virtues, which were producing themselves by a natural process, and to which these breathings of insult must have been a deadly check and interruption. Nor would the evil be merely negative; for the interference of professed friends, acting in this manner, must have superinduced dispositions and passions, which were alien to the condition of the Portugueze;—scattered weeds which could not have been found upon the soil, if our ignorant hands had not sown them. Of this I will not now speak, for I have already detained the reader too long at the threshold;—but I have put the master-key into his possession; and every chamber which he opens will be found loathsome as the one which he last quitted. Let us then proceed.

By the first article of the Convention it is covenanted, that all the places and forts in the kingdom of Portugal, occupied by the French troops, shall be delivered to the British army. Articles IV. and XII. are to the same effect—determining the surrender of Portugueze fortified places, stores, and ships, to the English forces; but not a word of their being to be holden in trust for the prince regent, or his government, to whom they belonged! The same neglect or contempt of justice and decency is shewn here, as in the preamble to these instruments. It was further shewn afterwards, by the act of hoisting the British flag instead of the Portugueze upon these forts, when they were first taken possession of by the British forces. It is no excuse to say that this was not intended. Such inattentions are among the most grievous faults which can be committed; and are *impossible,* when the affections and understandings of men are of that quality, and in that state, which are required for a service in which there is any thing noble or virtuous. Again, suppose that it was the purpose of the generals, who signed and ratified a Convention containing the articles in question, that the forts and ships, &c. should be delivered immediately to the Portugueze government,—would the delivering up of them wipe away the affront? Would it not rather appear, after the omission to recognize the right, that we had ostentatiously taken upon us to bestow—as a boon—that which they felt to be their own?

Passing by, as already deliberated and decided upon, those conditions, (Articles II. and III.) by which it is stipulated, that the French army shall not be considered as prisoners of war, shall be conveyed with arms, &c. to some port between Rochefort and L'Orient, and be at liberty to serve, I come to that memorable condition, (Article V.) "that the French army shall carry with it all its equipments, that is to say, its military chests and carriages, attached to the field commissariat and field hospitals, or shall be allowed to dispose of such part, as the Commander in Chief may judge it unnecessary to embark. In like manner all individuals of the army shall be at liberty to dispose of *their private property* of *every* description, with full security hereafter for the purchasers." This is expressed still more pointedly in the Armistice,—though the meaning, implied in the two articles, is precisely the same. For, in the fifth article of the Armistice, it is agreed provisionally, "that all those, of whom the French army consists, shall be conveyed to France with arms and baggage, *and* all their private property of every description, no part of which shall be wrested from them." In the Convention it is only expressed, that they shall be at liberty to depart, (Article II.) with arms and baggage, and (Article V.) to dispose of their private property of every description. But, if they had a right to dispose of it, *this* would include a right to carry it away—which was undoubtedly understood by the French general. And in the Armistice it is expressly said, that their private property of every description shall be conveyed to France along with their persons. What then are we to understand by the words, *their private property of every description?* Equipments of the army in general, and baggage of individuals, had been stipulated for before: now we all know that the lawful professional gains and earnings of a soldier must be small; that he is not in the habit of carrying about him, during actual warfare, any accumulation of these or other property; and that the ordinary private property, which he can be supposed to have a *just* title to, is included under the name of his *baggage;*—therefore this was something more; and what it was—is apparent. No part of their property, says the Armistice, shall be *wrested from them.* Who does not see in these words the consciousness of guilt, an indirect self-betraying admission that they had in their hands treasures which might be lawfully taken from them, and an anxiety to prevent that act of justice by a positive stipulation? Who does not see, on what sort of property the Frenchman had his eye; that it was not property by right, but their *possessions*—their plunder—every thing, by what means soever acquired, that the French army, or any individual in it, was possessed of? But it has been urged, that the monstrousness of such a supposition precludes this interpretation, renders it impossible that it could either be intended by the one party, or so understood by the other. What right they who signed, and he who ratified this Convention, have to shelter themselves under this plea—will appear from the 16th and 17th articles. In these it is stipulated, "that all subjects of France, or of Powers in alliance with France, domiciliated in Portugal, or accidentally in the country, shall have their property of every kind—moveable and immoveable—guaranteed to them, with liberty of retaining or disposing of it, and passing the produce into France:" the same is stipulated, (Article XVII.) for such natives of Portugal as have sided with the French, or occupied situations under *the French Government.* Here then is a direct avowal, still more monstrous, that every Frenchman, or native of a country in alliance with France, however obnoxious his crimes may have made him, and every traitorous Portugueze, shall have his property guaranteed to him (both previously to and after the reinstatement of the Portugueze government) by the British army! Now let us ask, what sense the word property must have had fastened to it in *these* cases. Must it not necessarily have included all the rewards which the Frenchman had received for his iniquity, and the traitorous Portugueze for his treason? (for no man would bear a part in such oppressions, or would be a traitor for nothing; and, moreover, all the rewards, which the French could bestow, must have been taken from the Portugueze, extorted from the honest and loyal, to be given to the wicked and disloyal.) These rewards of iniquity must necessarily have been included; for, on our side, no attempt is made at a distinction; and, on the side of the French, the word *immoveable* is manifestly intended to preclude such a distinction, where alone it could have been effectual. Property, then, here means—possessions thus infamously acquired; and, in the instance of the Portugueze, the fundamental notion of the word is subverted; for a traitor can have no property, till the government of his own country has remitted the punishment due to his crimes. And these wages of guilt, which the master by such exactions was enabled to pay, and which the servant thus earned, are to be guaranteed to him by a British *army!* Where does there exist a power on earth that could confer this right? If the Portugueze government itself had acted in this manner, it would have been guilty of wilful suicide; and the nation, if it had acted so, of high treason against itself. Let it not, then, be said, that the monstrousness of covenanting to convey, along with the persons of the French, their plunder, secures the article from the interpretation which the people of Great Britain gave, and which, I have now proved, they were bound to give to it.—But, conceding for a moment, that it was not intended that the words should bear this sense, and that, neither in a fair grammatical construction, nor as illustrated by other passages or by the general tenour of the document, they actually did bear it, had not unquestionable voices proclaimed the cruelty and rapacity—the acts of sacrilege, assassination, and robbery, by which these treasures had been amassed? Was not the perfidy of the French army, and its contempt of moral obligation, both as a body and as to the individuals which composed it, infamous through Europe?—Therefore, the concession would signify nothing: for our Generals, by allowing an army of this character to depart with its equipments, waggons, military chest, and baggage, had provided abundant means to enable it to carry off whatsoever it desired, and thus to elude and frustrate any stipulations which might have been made for compelling it to restore that which had been so iniquitously seized. And here are we brought back to the fountain-head of all this baseness; to that apathy and deadness to the principle of justice, through influence of which, this army, outlawed by its crimes, was suffered to depart from the land, over which it had so long tyrannized—other than as a band of disarmed prisoners.—I maintain, therefore, that permission to carry off the booty was distinctly expressed; and, if it had not been so, that the principle of justice could not here be preserved; as a violation of it must necessarily have followed from other conditions of the treaty. Sir Hew Dalrymple himself, before the Court of Inquiry, has told us, in two letters (to Generals Beresford and Friere,) that "such part of the plunder as was in money, it would be difficult, if not impossible, to identify;" and, consequently, the French could not be prevented from carrying it away with them. From the same letters we learn, that "the French were intending to carry off a considerable part of their plunder, by calling it public money, and saying that it belonged to the military chest; and that their evasions of the article were most shameful, and evinced a want of probity and honour, which was most disgraceful to them." If the French had given no other proofs of their want of such virtues, than those furnished by this occasion, neither the Portugueze, nor Spanish, nor British nations would condemn them, nor hate them as they now do; nor would this article of the Convention have excited such indignation. For the French, by so acting, could not deem themselves breaking an engagement; no doubt they looked upon themselves as injured,—that the failure in good faith was on the part of the British; and that it was in the lawlessness of power, and by a mere quibble, that this construction was afterwards put upon the article in question.

Widely different from the conduct of the British was that of the Spaniards in a like case:—with high feeling did they, abating not a jot or a tittle, enforce the principle of justice. "How," says the governor of Cadiz to General Dupont in the same noble letter before alluded to, "how," says he, after enumerating the afflictions which his army, and the tyrant who had sent it, had unjustly brought upon the Spanish nation, (for of these, in *their* dealings with the French, they never for a moment lost sight,) "how," asks he, "could you expect, that your army should carry off from Spain the fruit of its rapacity, cruelty, and impiety? how could you conceive this possible, or that we should be so stupid or senseless?" And this conduct is as wise in reason as it is true to nature. The Spanish people could have had no confidence in their government, if it had not acted thus. These are the sympathies which prove that a government is paternal,—that it makes one family with the people: besides, it is only by such adherence to justice, that, in times of like commotion, popular excesses can either be mitigated or prevented. If we would be efficient allies of Spain, nay, if we would not run the risk of doing infinite harm, these sentiments must not only be ours as a nation, but they must pervade the hearts of our ministers and our generals—our agents and our ambassadors. If it be not so, they, who are sent abroad, must either be conscious how unworthy they are, and with what unworthy commissions they appear, or not: if they do feel this, then they must hang their heads, and blush for their country and themselves; if they do not, the Spaniards must blush for them and revolt from them; or, what would be ten thousand times more deplorable, they must purchase a reconcilement and a communion by a sacrifice of all that is excellent in themselves. Spain must either break down her lofty spirit, her animation and fiery courage, to run side by side in the same trammels with Great Britain; or she must start off from her intended yoke-fellow with contempt and aversion. This is the alternative, and there is no avoiding it.

I have yet to speak of the influence of such concessions upon the French Ruler and his army. With what Satanic pride must he have contemplated the devotion of his servants and adherents to *their* law, the steadiness and zeal of their perverse loyalty, and the faithfulness with which they stand by him and each other! How must his heart have distended with false glory, while he contrasted these qualities of his subjects with the insensibility and slackness of his British enemies! This notice has, however, no especial propriety in this place; for, as far as concerns Bonaparte, his pride and depraved confidence may be equally fed by almost all the conditions of this instrument. But, as to his army, it is plain that the permission, (whether it be considered as by an express article formally granted, or only involved in the general conditions of the treaty,) to bear away in triumph the harvest of its crimes, must not only have emboldened and exalted it with arrogance, and whetted its rapacity; but that hereby every soldier, of which this army was composed, must, upon his arrival in his own country, have been a seed which would give back plenteously in its kind. The French are at present a needy people, without commerce or manufactures,—unsettled in their minds and debased in their morals by revolutionary practices and habits of warfare; and the youth of the country are rendered desperate by oppression, which, leaving no choice in their occupation, discharges them from all responsibility to their own consciences. How powerful then must have been the action of such incitements upon a people so circumstanced! The actual sight, and, far more, the imaginary sight and handling of these treasures, magnified by the romantic tales which must have been spread about them, would carry into every town and village an antidote for the terrors of conscription; and would rouze men, like the dreams imported from the new world when the first discoverers and adventurers returned, with their ingots and their gold dust—their stories and their promises, to inflame and madden the avarice of the old. "What an effect," says the Governor of Cadiz, "must it have upon the people," (he means the Spanish people,) "to know that a single soldier was carrying away 2580 livres tournois!" What an effect, (he might have said also,) must it have upon the French!—I direct the reader's attention to this, because it seems to have been overlooked; and because some of the public journals, speaking of the Convention, (and, no doubt, uttering the sentiments of several of their readers,)—say "that they are disgusted with the transaction, not because the French have been permitted to carry off a few diamonds, or some ingots of silver; but because we confessed, by consenting to the treaty, that an army of 35,000 British troops, aided by the Portugueze nation, was not able to compel 20,000 French to surrender at discretion." This is indeed the root of the evil, as hath been shewn; and it is the curse of this treaty, that the several parts of it are of such enormity as singly to occupy the attention and to destroy comparison and coexistence. But the people of Great Britain are disgusted both with the one and the other. They bewail the violation of the principle: if the value of the things carried off had been in itself trifling, their grief and their indignation would have been scarcely less. But it is manifest, from what has been said, that it was not trifling; and that therefore, (upon that account as well as upon others,) this permission was no less impolitic than it was unjust and dishonourable.

In illustrating these articles of the Armistice and Convention, by which the French were both expressly permitted and indirectly enabled to carry off their booty, we have already seen, that a concession was made which is still more enormous; viz. that all subjects of France, or of powers in alliance with France, domiciliated in Portugal or resident there, and all natives of Portugal who have accepted situations under *the French government,* &c., shall have their *property* of every kind guaranteed to them by the British army. By articles 16th and 17th, their *persons* are placed under the like protection. "The French" (Article XVI.) "shall be at liberty either to accompany the French army, or to remain in Portugal;" "And the Portugueze" (Article XVII.) "shall not be rendered accountable for their political conduct during the period of the occupation of the country by the French army: they all are placed under the protection of the

British commanders, and shall sustain no injury in their property or persons."

I have animadverted, heretofore, upon the unprofessional eagerness of our Generals to appear in the character of negotiators when the sword would have done them more service than the pen. But, if they had confined themselves to mere military regulations, they might indeed with justice have been grievously censured as injudicious commanders, whose notion of the honour of armies was of a low pitch, and who had no conception of the peculiar nature of the service in which they were engaged: but the censure must have stopped here. Whereas, by these provisions, they have shewn that they had never reflected upon the nature of military authority as contradistinguished from civil. French example had so far dazzled and blinded them, that the French army is suffered to denominate itself *"the French government;"* and, from the whole tenour of these instruments, (from the preamble, and these articles especially,) it should seem that our Generals fancied themselves and their army to be *the British government.* For these regulations, emanating from a mere military authority, are purely civil; but of such a kind, that no power on earth could confer a right to establish them. And this trampling upon the most sacred rights—this sacrifice of the consciousness of a self-preserving principle, without which neither societies nor governments can exist, is not made by our generals in relation to subjects of their own sovereign, but to an independent nation, our ally, into whose territories we could not have entered but from its confidence in our friendship and good faith. Surely the persons, who (under the countenance of too high authority) have talked so loudly of prejudging this question, entirely overlooked or utterly forgot this part of it. What have these monstrous provisions to do with the relative strength of the two armies, or with any point admitting a doubt? What need here of a court of judicature to settle who were the persons (their names are subscribed by their own hands), and to determine the quality of the thing? Actions and agents like these, exhibited in this connection with each other, must of necessity be condemned the moment they are known: and to assert the contrary, is to maintain that man is a being without understanding, and that morality is an empty dream. And, if this condemnation must after this manner follow, to utter it is less a duty than a further inevitable consequence from the constitution of human nature. They, who hold that the formal sanction of a court of judicature is in this case required before a people has a right to pass sentence, know not to what degree they are enemies to that people and to mankind; to what degree selfishness, whether arising from their peculiar situation or from other causes, has in them prevailed over those faculties which are our common inheritance, and cut them off from fellowship with the species. Most deplorable would be the result, if it were possible that the injunctions of these men could be obeyed, or their remonstrances acknowledged to be just. For, (not to mention that, if it were not for such prompt decisions of the public voice, misdemeanours of men high in office would rarely be accounted for at all,) we must bear in mind, at this crisis, that the adversary of all good is hourly and daily extending his ravages; and, according to such notions of fitness, our indignation, our sorrow, our shame, our sense of right and wrong, and all those moral affections, and powers of the understanding, by which alone he can be effectually opposed, are to enter upon a long vacation; their motion is to be suspended—a thing impossible; if it could, it would be destroyed.

Let us now see what language the Portugueze speak upon that part of the treaty which has incited me to give vent to these feelings, and to assert these truths. "I protest," says General Friere, "against Article XVII., one of the two now under examination, because it attempts to tie down the government of this kingdom not to bring to justice and condign punishment those persons, who have been notoriously and scandalously disloyal to their prince and the country by joining and serving the French party, and, even if the English army should be allowed to screen them from the punishment they have deserved, still it should not prevent their expulsion—whereby this country would no longer have to fear being again betrayed by the same men." Yet, while the partizans of the French are thus guarded, not a word is said to protect the loyal Portugueze, whose fidelity to their country and their prince must have rendered them obnoxious to the French army; and who in Lisbon and the environs, were left at its mercy from the day when the Convention was signed, till the departure of the French. Couple also with this the first additional article, by which it is agreed, "that the individuals in the civil employment of the army," (including all the agitators, spies, informers, all the jackals of the ravenous lion,) "made prisoners either by the British troops or the Portugueze in any part of Portugal, will be restored (*as is customary*) without exchange." That is, no stipulations being made for reciprocal conditions! In fact, through the whole course of this strange interference of a military power with the administration of civil justice in the country of an ally, there is only one article (the 15th) which bears the least shew of attention to Portugueze interests. By this it is stipulated, "That, from the date of the ratification of the Convention, all arrears of contributions, requisitions, or claims whatever of the French Government against subjects of Portugal, or any other individuals residing in this country, founded on the occupation of Portugal by the French troops in the month of December 1807, which may not have been paid up, are cancelled: and all sequestrations, laid upon their property moveable or immoveable, are removed; and the free disposal of the same is restored to the proper owners." Which amounts to this. The French are called upon formally to relinquish, in favour of the Portugueze, that to which they never had any right; to abandon false claims, which they either had a power to enforce, or they had not: if they departed immediately and had *not* power, the article was nugatory; if they remained a day longer and *had* power, there was no security that they would abide by it. Accordingly, loud complaints were made that, after the date of the Convention, all kinds of ravages were committed by the French upon Lisbon and its neighbourhood: and what did it matter whether these were upon the plea of old debts and requisitions; or new debts were created more greedily than ever—from the consciousness that the time for collecting them was so short? This article, then, the only one which is even in shew favourable to the Portugueze, is, in substance, nothing: inasmuch as, in what it is silent upon, (viz. that the People of Lisbon and its neighbourhood shall not be vexed and oppressed by the French, during their stay, with new claims and robberies,) it is grossly cruel or negligent; and, in that for which it actually stipulates, wholly delusive. It is in fact insulting; for the very admission of a formal renunciation of these claims does to a certain degree acknowledge their justice. The only decent manner of introducing matter to this effect would have been by placing it as a bye clause of a provision that secured the Portugueze from further molestations, and merely alluding to it as a thing understood of course. Yet, from the place which this specious article occupies, (preceding immediately the 16th and 17th which we have been last considering,) it is clear that it must have been intended by the French General as honey is smeared upon the edge of the cup—to make the poison, contained in those two, more palateable.

Thus much for the Portugueze, and their particular interests. In one instance, a concern of the Spanish Nation comes directly under notice; and that nation also is treated without delicacy or feeling. For by the 18th article it is agreed, "that the Spaniards, (4000 in number) who had been disarmed, and were confined on ship-board in the port of Lisbon by the French, should be liberated."

And upon what consideration? Not upon their *right* to be free, as having been treacherously and cruelly dealt with by men who were part of a power that was labouring to subjugate their country, and in this attempt had committed inhuman crimes against it;—not even exchanged as soldiers against soldiers:—but the condition of their emancipation is, that the British General engages "to obtain of the Spaniards to restore such French subjects, either military or civil, as have been detained in Spain, without having been taken in battle or in consequence of military operations, but on account of the *occurrences* of the 29th of last May and the days immediately following." "*Occurrences!*" I know not what are exactly the features of the face for which this word serves as a veil: I have no register at hand to inform me what these events precisely were: but there can be no doubt that it was a time of triumph for liberty and humanity; and that the persons, for whom these noble-minded Spaniards were to be exchanged, were no other than a horde from among the most abject of the French Nation; probably those wretches, who, having never faced either the dangers or the fatigues of war, had been most busy in secret preparations or were most conspicuous in open acts of massacre, when the streets of Madrid, a few weeks before, had been drenched with the blood of two thousand of her bravest citizens. Yet the liberation of these Spaniards, upon these terms, is recorded (in the report of the Court of Enquiry) "as one of the advantages which, in the contemplation of the Generals, would result from the Convention!"

Finally, "If there shall be any doubt (Article XIV.) as to the meaning of any article, it shall be explained favourably to the French Army; and Hostages (Article XX.) of the rank of Field Officers, on the part of the British Army and Navy, shall be furnished for the guarantee of the present Convention."

I have now gone through the painful task of examining the most material conditions of the CONVENTION OF CINTRA:—the whole number of the articles is twenty-two, with three additional ones—a long ladder into a deep abyss of infamy!—

Need it be said that neglects—injuries—and insults—like these which we have been contemplating, come from what quarter they may, let them be exhibited towards whom they will, must produce not merely mistrust and jealousy, but alienation and hatred. The passions and feelings may be quieted or diverted for a short time; but, though out of sight or seemingly asleep, they must exist; and the life which they have received cannot, but by a long course

1997 twenty–two *Errata:* twenty–three 1809.

of justice and kindness, be overcome and destroyed. But why talk of a long course of justice and kindness, when the immediate result must have been so deplorable? Relying upon our humanity, our fellow-feeling, and our justice, upon these instant and urgent claims, sanctioned by the more mild one of ancient alliance, the Portugueze People by voices from every part of their land entreated our succour; the arrival of a British Army upon their coasts was joyfully hailed; and the people of the country zealously assisted in landing the troops; without which help, as a British General has informed us, that landing could not have been effected. And it is in this manner that they are repaid! Scarcely have we set foot upon their country before we sting them into self-reproaches, and act in every thing as if it were our wish to make them ashamed of their generous confidence as of a foolish simplicity—proclaiming to them that they have escaped from one thraldom only to fall into another. If the French had any traitorous partizans in Portugal, (and we have seen that such there were; and that nothing was left undone on our part, which could be done, to keep them there, and to strengthen them) what answer could have been given to one of these, if (with this treaty in his hand) he had said, "The French have dealt hardly with us, I allow; but we have gained nothing: the change is not for the better, but for the worse: for the appetite of their tyranny was palled; but this, being new to its food, is keen and vigorous. If you have only a choice between two masters, (such an advocate might have argued) chuse always the stronger: for he, after his evil passions have had their first harvest, confident in his strength, will not torment you wantonly in order to prove it. Besides, the property which he has in you he can maintain; and there will be no risk of your being torn in pieces—the unsettled prey of two rival claimants. You will thus have the advantage of a fixed and assured object of your hatred: and your fear, being stripped of doubt, will lose its motion and its edge: both passions will relax and grow mild; and, though they may not turn into reconcilement and love, though you may not be independent nor be free, yet you will at least exist in tranquillity,—and possess, if not the activity of hope, the security of despair." No effectual answer, I say, could have been given to a man pleading thus in such circumstances. So much for the choice of evils. But, for the hope of good!—what is to become of the efforts and high resolutions of the Portugueze and Spanish Nations, manifested by their own hand in the manner which we have seen? They may live indeed and prosper; but not by us, but in despite of us.

Whatever may be the character of the Portugueze Nation; be it true or not, that they had a becoming sense of the injuries which they had received from the French Invader, and were rouzed to throw off oppression by a universal effort, and to form a living barrier against it;—certain it is that, betrayed and trampled upon as they had been, they held unprecedented claims upon humanity to secure them from further outrages.—Moreover, our conduct towards them was grossly inconsistent. For we entered their country upon the supposition that they had such sensibility and virtue; we announced to them publickly and solemnly our belief in this: and indeed to have landed a force in the peninsula upon any other inducement would have been the excess of folly and madness. But the Portugueze *are* a brave people—a people of great courage and worth! Conclusions, drawn from intercourse with certain classes of the depraved inhabitants of Lisbon only, and which are true only with respect to them, have been hastily extended to the whole nation, which has thus unjustly suffered both in our esteem and in that of all Europe. In common with their neighbours the Spaniards, they *were* making a universal, zealous, and fearless effort; and, whatever may be the final issue, the very act of having risen under the pressure and in the face of the most tremendous military power which the earth has ever seen—is itself evidence in their favour, the strongest and most comprehensive which can be given; a transcendent glory! which, let it be remembered, no subsequent failures in duty on their part can forfeit. This they must have felt—that they had furnished an illustrious example; and that nothing can abolish their claim upon the good wishes and upon the gratitude of mankind, which is—and will be through all ages their due. At such a time, then, injuries and insults from any quarter would have been deplorable; but, proceeding from us, the evil must have been aggravated beyond calculation. For we have, throughout Europe, the character of a sage and meditative people. Our history has been read by the degraded Nations of the Continent with admiration, and some portions of it with awe; with a recognition of superiority and distance, which was honourable to us—salutary for those to whose hearts, in their depressed state, it could find entrance—and promising for the future condition of the human race. We have been looked up to as a people who have acted nobly; whom their constitution of government has enabled to speak and write freely, and who therefore have thought comprehensively; as a people among whom philosophers and poets, by their surpassing genius—their wisdom—and knowledge of human nature, have circulated—and made familiar—divinely-tempered sentiments and the purest notions concerning the duties and true dignity of individual and social man in all situations and under all trials. By so readily acceding to the prayers with which the Spaniards and Portugueze entreated our assistance, we had proved to them that we were not wanting in fellow-feeling. Therefore might we be admitted to be judges between them and their enemies—unexceptionable judges—more competent even than a dispassionate posterity, which, from the very want comparatively of interest and passion, might be in its examination remiss and negligent, and therefore in its decision erroneous. We, their contemporaries, were drawn towards them as suffering beings; but still their sufferings were not ours, nor could be; and we seemed to stand at that due point of distance from which right and wrong might be fairly looked at and seen in their just proportions. Every thing conspired to prepossess the Spaniards and Portugueze in our favour, and to give the judgment of the British Nation authority in their eyes. Strange, then, would be their first sensations, when, upon further trial, instead of a growing sympathy, they met with demonstrations of a state of sentiment and opinion abhorrent from their own. A shock must have followed upon this discovery, a shock to their confidence—not perhaps at first in us, but in themselves: for, like all men under the agitation of extreme passion, no doubt they had before experienced occasional misgivings that they were subject to error and distraction from afflictions pressing too violently upon them. These flying apprehensions would now take a fixed place; and that moment would be most painful. If they continued to respect our opinion, so far must they have mistrusted themselves: fatal mistrust at such a crisis! Their passion of just vengeance, their indignation, their aspiring hopes, every thing that elevated and cheared, must have departed from them. But this bad influence, the *excess* of the outrage would mitigate or prevent; and we may be assured that they rather recoiled from allies who had thus by their actions discountenanced and condemned efforts, which the most solemn testimony of conscience had avouched to them were just;—that they recoiled from us with that loathing and contempt which unexpected, determined, and absolute hostility, upon points of dearest interest will for ever create.

Again: independence and liberty were the blessings for which the people of the Peninsula were contending—immediate independence, which was not to be gained but by modes of exertion from which liberty must ensue. Now, liberty—healthy, matured, time-honoured liberty—this is the growth and peculiar boast of Britain; and nature herself, by encircling with the ocean the country which we inhabit, has proclaimed that this mighty nation is for ever to be her own ruler, and that the land is set apart for the home of immortal independence. Judging then from these first fruits of British Friendship, what bewildering and depressing and hollow thoughts must the Spaniards and Portugueze have entertained concerning the real value of these blessings, if the people who have possessed them longest, and who ought to understand them best, could send forth an army capable of enacting the oppression and baseness of the Convention of Cintra; if the government of that people could sanction this treaty; and if, lastly, this distinguished and favoured people themselves could suffer it to be held forth to the eyes of men as expressing the sense of their hearts—as an image of their understandings.

But it did not speak their sense—it was not endured—it was not submitted to in their hearts. Bitter was the sorrow of the people of Great Britain when the tidings first came to their ears, when they first fixed their eyes upon this covenant—overwhelming was their astonishment, tormenting their shame; their indignation was tumultuous; and the burthen of the past would have been insupportable, if it had not involved in its very nature a sustaining hope for the future. Among many alleviations, there was one, which, (not wisely, but overcome by circumstances) all were willing to admit;—that the event was so strange and uncouth, exhibiting such discordant characteristics of innocent fatuity and enormous guilt, that it could not without violence be thought of as indicative of a general constitution of things, either in the country or the government; but that it was a kind of *lusus naturae* in the moral world—a solitary straggler out of the circumference of nature's law—a monster which could not propagate, and had no birthright in futurity. Accordingly, the first expectation was that the government would deem itself under the necessity of disannulling the Convention; a necessity which, though in itself a great evil, appeared small in the eyes of judicious men, compared with the consequences of admitting that such a contract could be binding. For they, who had signed and ratified it, had not only glaringly exceeded all power which could be supposed to be vested in them as holding a military office; but, in the exercise of political functions, they had framed ordinances which neither the government, nor the nation, nor any power on earth, could confer upon them a right to frame: therefore the contract was self-destroyed from the beginning. It is a

2145 self–destroyed *M.Y.* i. 342: self–destroying 1809.

wretched oversight, or a wilful abuse of terms still more wretched, to speak of the good faith of a nation as being pledged to an act which was not a shattering of the edifice of justice, but a subversion of its foundations. One man cannot sign away the faculty of reason in another; much less can one or two individuals do this for a whole people. Therefore the contract was void, both from its injustice and its absurdity; and the party, with whom it was made, must have known it to be so. It could not then but be expected by many that the government would reject it. Moreover, extraordinary outrages against reason and virtue demand that extraordinary sacrifices of atonement should be made upon their altars; and some were encouraged to think that a government might upon this impulse rise above itself, and turn an exceeding disgrace into true glory, by a public profession of shame and repentance for having appointed such unworthy instruments; that, this being acknowledged, it would clear itself from all imputation of having any further connection with what had been done, and would provide that the nation should as speedily as possible, be purified from all suspicion of looking upon it with other feelings than those of abhorrence. The people knew what had been their own wishes when the army was sent in aid of their allies; and they clung to the faith, that their wishes and the aims of the Government must have been in unison; and that the guilt would soon be judicially fastened upon those who stood forth as principals, and who (it was hoped) would be found to have fulfilled only their own will and pleasure,—to have had no explicit commission or implied encouragement for what they had done,—no accessaries in their crime. The punishment of these persons was anticipated, not to satisfy any cravings of vindictive justice (for these, if they could have existed in such a case, had been thoroughly appeased already: for what punishment could be greater than to have brought upon themselves the sentence passed upon them by the voice of their countrymen?); but for this reason—that a judicial condemnation of the men, who were openly the proximate cause, and who were forgetfully considered as the single and sole originating source, would make our detestation of the effect more signally manifest.

These thoughts, if not welcomed without scruple and relied upon without fear, were at least encouraged; till it was recollected that the persons at the head of government had ordered that the event should be communicated to the inhabitants of the metropolis with signs of national rejoicing. No wonder if,

2172 sentence ... voice 1809 *cancel* N1: unremoveable contempt and hatred 1809 *cancellandum* N1.

when these rejoicings were called to mind, it was impossible to entertain the faith which would have been most consolatory. The evil appeared no longer as the forlorn monster which I have described. It put on another shape, and was endued with a more formidable life—with power to generate and transmit after its kind. A new and alarming import was added to the event by this open testimony of gladness and approbation; which intimated—which declared—that the spirit, which swayed the individuals who were the ostensible and immediate authors of the Convention, was not confined to them; but that it was widely prevalent: else it could not have been found in the very council-seat; there, where if wisdom and virtue have not some influence, what is to become of the nation in these times of peril? rather say, into what an abyss is it already fallen!

His Majesty's ministers, by this mode of communicating the tidings, indiscreet as it was unfeeling, had committed themselves. Yet still they might have recovered from the lapse, have awakened after a little time. And accordingly, notwithstanding an annunciation so ominous, it was matter of surprise and sorrow to many, that the ministry appeared to deem the Convention binding, and that its terms were to be fulfilled. There had indeed been only a choice of evils: but, of the two, the worse—ten thousand times the worse—was fixed upon. The ministers, having thus officially applauded the treaty,—and, by suffering it to be carried into execution, made themselves a party to the transaction,—drew upon themselves those suspicions which will ever pursue the steps of public men who abandon the direct road which leads to the welfare of their country. It was suspected that they had taken this part against the dictates of conscience, and from selfishness and cowardice; that, from the first, they reasoned thus within themselves:—"If the act be indeed so criminal as there is cause to believe that the public will pronounce it to be; and if it shall continue to be regarded as such; great odium must sooner or later fall upon those who have appointed the agents: And this odium, which will be from the first considerable, in spite of the astonishment and indignation of which the framers of the Convention may be the immediate object, will, when the astonishment has relaxed, and the angry passions have died away, settle (for many causes) more heavily upon those who, by placing such men in the command, are the original source of the guilt and the dishonour. How then is this most effectually to be prevented? By endeavouring to prevent or to destroy, as far as may be, the odium attached to the act itself." For which purpose it was suspected that the rejoicings had been ordered; and that afterwards (when the people had declared themselves so loudly),—partly upon the plea of the good faith of the nation being pledged, and partly from a false estimate of the comparative force of the two obligations,—the Convention, in the same selfish spirit, was carried into effect; and that the ministry took upon itself a final responsibility, with a vain hope that, by so doing and incorporating its own credit with the transaction, it might bear down the censures of the people, and overrule their judgment to the superinducing of a belief, that the treaty was not so unjust and inexpedient: and thus would be included—in one sweeping exculpation—the misdeeds of the servant and the master.

But,—whether these suspicions were reasonable or not, whatever motives produced a determination that the Convention should be acted upon,—there can be no doubt of the manner in which the ministry wished that the people should appreciate it; when the same persons, who had ordered that it should at first be received with rejoicing, availed themselves of his Majesty's high authority to give a harsh reproof to the City of London for having prayed "that an enquiry might be instituted into this dishonourable and unprecedented transaction." In their petition they styled it also "an afflicting event—humiliating and degrading to the country, and injurious to his Majesty's Allies." And for this, to the astonishment and grief of all sound minds, the petitioners were severely reprimanded; and told, among other admonitions, "that it was inconsistent with the principles of British jurisprudence to pronounce judgement without previous investigation."

Upon this charge, as re-echoed in its general import by persons who have been over-awed or deceived, and by others who have been wilful deceivers, I have already incidentally animadverted; and repelled it, I trust, with becoming indignation. I shall now meet the charge for the last time formally and directly; on account of considerations applicable to all times; and because the whole course of domestic proceedings relating to the Convention of Cintra, combined with menaces which have been recently thrown out in the lower House of Par-

2242 charge ... by 1809: charge in its general import as reechoed by BM.
2239–40 persons ... deceivers, 1809: a part of the Public BM.
2241 incidentally BM, *Errata:* incidently 1809. animadverted; 1809: animadverted with sober reason BM.
2241 it 1809: it also BM.
2242 indignation 1809: indignation at the outrage committed by it against the understanding and moral feelings of mankind BM.
2242 meet ... charge 1809: both for its relation to this particular question, and for the general importance of the subject, meet it BM.
2243–53 on account ... purposes 1809: *om.* BM.

liament, renders it too probable that a league has been framed for the purpose of laying further restraints upon freedom of speech and of the press; and that the reprimand to the City of London was devised by ministers as a preparatory overt act of this scheme; to the great abuse of the Sovereign's Authority, and in contempt of the rights of the nation. In meeting this charge, I shall shew to what desperate issues men are brought, and in what woeful labyrinths they are entangled, when, under the pretext of defending instituted law, they violate the laws of reason and nature for their own unhallowed purposes.

If the persons, who signed this petition, acted inconsistently with the principles of British jurisprudence; the offence must have been committed by giving an answer, before adequate and lawful evidence had entitled them so to do, to one or other of these questions:—"What is the act? and who is the agent?"—or to both conjointly. Now the petition gives no opinion upon the agent; it pronounces only upon the act, and that some one must be guilty; but *who*—it does not take upon itself to say. It condemns the act; and calls for punishment upon the authors, whosoever they may be found to be; and does no more. After the analysis which has been made of the Convention, I may ask if there be any thing in this which deserves reproof; and reproof from an authority which ought to be most enlightened and most dispassionate,—as it is, next to the legislative, the most solemn authority in the land.

It is known to every one that the privilege of complaint and petition, in cases where the nation feels itself aggrieved, *itself* being the judge, (and who else ought to be, or can be?)—a privilege, the exercise of which implies condemnation of something complained of, followed by a prayer for its removal or correction—not only is established by the most grave and authentic charters of Englishmen, who have been taught by their wisest statesmen and legislators to be jealous over its preservation, and to call it into practice upon every

2254–57 acted … questions 1809, BM[3]: had violated the principles of British jurisprudence by prejudging the case that is deciding upon it without adequate and lawful evidence, it must have been [?] one or other of these [?] BM: had violated … it must have been by giving an answer before they were entitled so to do by adequate and [lawful evidence] to one or other of these questions BM[2].

2258–59 pronounces only 1809: only pronounces BM.

2261–63 After … any thing 1809: Is there any thing BM: After the [? line or ? hint] which we have taken of [? this transaction] is there any thing BM[2]: After the examination [analysis BM[4]] which we have made of the convention I may ask if there be any thing BM[3].

2263 which BM[2], 1809: that BM. reproof 1809: that reproof BM.

2264 most enlightened and most dispassionate 1809: the most enlightened and [*tear*] most dispassionate BM.

2265 legislative, the most 1809: Legislati[? ve] [?assembly] [*tear*] most BM.

reasonable occasion; but also that this privilege is an indispensable condition of all civil liberty. Nay, of such paramount interest is it to mankind, existing under any frame of Government whatsoever; that, either by law or custom, it has universally prevailed under all governments—from the Grecian and Swiss Democracies to the Despotisms of Imperial Rome, of Turkey, and of France under her present ruler. It must then be a high principle which could exact obeisance from governments at the two extremes of polity, and from all modes of government inclusively; from the best and from the worst; from magistrates acting under obedience to the stedfast law which expresses the general will; and from depraved and licentious tyrants, whose habit it is—to express, and to act upon, their own individual will. Tyrants have seemed to feel that, if this principle were acknowledged, the subject ought to be reconciled to any thing; that, by permitting the free exercise of this right alone, an adequate price was paid down for all abuses; that a standing pardon was included in it for the past, and a daily renewed indulgence for every future enormity. It is then melancholy to think that the time is come when an attempt has been made to tear, out of the venerable crown of the Sovereign of Great Britain, a gem which is in the very front of the turban of the Emperor of Morocco.—(*See Appendix D.*)

To enter upon this argument is indeed both astounding and humiliating: for the adversary in the present case is bound to contend that we cannot pronounce upon evil or good, either in the actions of our own or in past times, unless the decision of a Court of Judicature has empowered us so to do. Why then have historians written? and why do we yield to the impulses of our nature, hating or loving—approving or condemning according to the appearances which their records present to our eyes? But the doctrine is as nefarious as it is absurd. For those public events in which men are most interested, namely, the crimes of rulers and of persons in high authority, for the most part are such as either have never been brought before tribunals at all, or before unjust ones: for, though offenders may be in hostility with each other, yet the kingdom of guilt is not wholly divided against itself; its subjects are united by a general interest to elude or overcome that law which would bring them to condign punishment. Therefore to make a verdict of a Court of Judicature a necessary condition for enabling men to determine the quality of an act, when the "head and front"—the life and soul of the offence may have been, that it eludes or rises above the reach of all judicature, is a contradiction which would be too gross to merit notice, were it not that men willingly suffer their understandings to stagnate. And hence this rotten bog, rotten and unstable as the crude consistence of Milton's Chaos, "smitten" (for I will continue to use the language of the poet) "by the petrific mace—and bound with Gorgonian rigour by the look"—of despotism, is transmuted; and becomes a high-way of adamant for the sorrowful steps of generation after generation.

Again: in cases where judicial inquiries can be and are instituted, and are equitably conducted, this suspension of judgment, with respect to act or agent, is only supposed necessarily to exist in the court itself; not in the witnesses, the plaintiffs or accusers, or in the minds even of the people who may be present. If the contrary supposition were realized, how could the arraigned person ever have been brought into court? What would become of the indignation, the hope, the sorrow, or the sense of justice, by which the prosecutors, or the people of the country who pursued or apprehended the presumed criminal, or they who appear in evidence against him, are actuated? If then this suspension of judgment, by a law of human nature and a requisite of society, is not supposed *necessarily* to exist—except in the minds of the court; if this be undeniable in cases where the eye and ear-witnesses are few;—how much more so in a case like the present; where all, that constitutes the essence of the act, is avowed by the agents themselves, and lies bare to the notice of the whole world?—Now it was in the character of complainants and denunciators, that the petitioners of the City of London appeared before his Majesty's throne; and they have been reproached by his Majesty's ministers under the cover of a sophism, which, if our anxiety to interpret favourably words sanctioned by the First Magistrate—makes us unwilling to think it a deliberate artifice meant for the delusion of the people, must however (on the most charitable comment) be pronounced an evidence of no little heedlessness and self-delusion on the part of those who framed it.

To sum up the matter—the right of petition (which, we have shewn as a general proposition, supposes a right to condemn, and is in itself an act of qualified condemnation) may in too many instances take the ground of absolute condemnation, both with respect to the crime and the criminal. It was confined, in this case, to the crime; but, if the City of London had proceeded farther, they would have been justifiable; because the delinquents had set their hands to their own delinquency. The petitioners, then, are not only clear of all blame; but are entitled to high praise: and we have seen whither the doctrines lead, upon which they were condemned.—And now, mark the discord which will ever be found in the actions of men, where there is no inward harmony of reason or virtue to regulate the outward conduct.

Those ministers, who advised their Sovereign to reprove the City of London for uttering prematurely, upon a measure, an opinion in which they were supported by the unanimous voice of the nation, had themselves before publickly prejudged the question by ordering that the tidings should be communicated with rejoicings. One of their body has since attempted to wipe away this stigma by representing that these orders were given out of a just tenderness for the reputation of the generals, who would otherwise have appeared to be condemned without trial. But did these rejoicings leave the matter indifferent? Was not the *positive* fact of thus expressing an opinion (above all in a case like this, in which surely no man could ever dream that there were any features of splendour) far stronger language of approbation, than the *negative* fact could be of disapprobation? For these same ministers who had called upon the people of Great Britain to rejoice over the Armistice and Convention, and who reproved and discountenanced and suppressed to the utmost of their power every attempt at petitioning for redress of the injury caused by those treaties, have now made publick a document from which it appears that, "when the instruments were first laid before his Majesty, the king felt himself compelled *at once*" (i.e. previously to all investigation) "to express his disapprobation of those articles, in which stipulations were made directly affecting the interests or feelings of the Spanish and Portugueze nations."

And was it possible that a Sovereign of a free country could be otherwise affected? It is indeed to be regretted that his Majesty's censure was not, upon this occasion, radical—and pronounced in a sterner tone; that a council was not in existence sufficiently intelligent and virtuous to advise the king to give full expression to the sentiments of his own mind; which, we may reasonably conclude, were in sympathy with those of a brave and loyal people. Never surely was there a public event more fitted to reduce men, in all ranks of society, under the supremacy of their common nature; to impress upon them one belief; to infuse into them one spirit. For it was not done in a remote corner by persons of obscure rank; but in the eyes of Europe and of all mankind; by the leading authorities, military and civil, of a mighty empire. It did not relate to a petty immunity, or a local and insulated privilege—but to the highest feelings of honour to which a nation may either be calmly and gradually raised by a long course of independence, liberty, and glory; or to the level of which it may be lifted up at once, from a fallen state, by a sudden and extreme pressure of violence and tyranny. It not only related to these high feelings of honour; but to the fundamental principles of justice, by which life and property, that is the means of living, are secured.

A people, whose government had been dissolved by foreign tyranny, and which had been left to work out its salvation by its own virtues, prayed for our help. And whence were we to learn how that help could be most effectually given, how they were even to be preserved from receiving injuries instead of benefits at our hands,—whence were we to learn this but from their language and from our own hearts? They had spoken of unrelenting and inhuman wrongs; of patience wearied out; of the agonizing yoke cast off; of the blessed service of freedom chosen; of heroic aspirations; of constancy, and fortitude, and perseverance; of resolution even to the death; of gladness in the embrace of death; of weeping over the graves of the slain, by those who had not been so happy as to die; of resignation under the worst final doom; of glory, and triumph, and punishment. This was the language which we heard—this was the devout hymn that was chaunted; and the responses, with which our country bore a part in the solemn service, were from her soul and from the depths of her soul.

O sorrow! O misery for England, the land of liberty and courage and peace; the land trustworthy and long approved; the home of lofty example and benign precept; the central orb to which, as to a fountain, the nations of the earth "ought to repair, and in their golden urns draw light;"—O sorrow and shame for our country; for the grass which is upon her fields, and the dust which is in her graves;—for her good men who now look upon the day;—and her long train of deliverers and defenders, her Alfred, her Sidneys, and her Milton; whose voice yet speaketh for our reproach; and whose actions survive in memory to confound us, or to redeem!

For what hath been done? look at it: we have looked at it: we have handled it: we have pondered it steadily: we have tried it by the principles of absolute and eternal justice; by the sentiments of high-minded honour, both with reference to their general nature, and to their especial exaltation under present circumstances; by the rules of expedience; by the maxims of prudence, civil and military: we have weighed it in the balance of all these, and found it wanting; in that, which is most excellent, most wanting.

Our country placed herself by the side of Spain, and her fellow nation; she sent an honourable portion of her sons to aid a suffering people to subjugate or destroy an army—but I degrade the word—a banded multitude of perfidious oppressors, of robbers and assassins, who had outlawed themselves from society in the wantonness of power; who were abominable for their own crimes, and on account of the crimes of him whom they served—to subjugate or destroy these; not exacting that it should be done within a limited time; admitting even that they might effect their purpose or not; she could have borne either issue, she was prepared for either; but she was not prepared for such a deliverance as hath been accomplished; not a deliverance of Portugal from French oppression, but of the oppressor from the anger and power (at least from the animating efforts) of the Peninsula: she was not prepared to stand between her allies, and their worthiest hopes: that, when chastisement could not be inflicted, honour—as much as bad men could receive—should be conferred: that them, whom her own hands had humbled, the same hands and no other should exalt: that finally the sovereign of this horde of devastators, himself the destroyer of the hopes of good men, should have to say, through the mouth of his minister, and for the hearing of all Europe, that his army of Portugal had "DICTATED THE TERMS OF ITS GLORIOUS RETREAT."

I have to defend my countrymen: and, if their feelings deserve reverence, if there be any stirrings of wisdom in the motions of their souls, my task is accomplished. For here were no factions to blind; no dissolution of established authorities to confound; no ferments to distemper; no narrow selfish interests to delude. The object was at a distance; and it rebounded upon us, as with force collected from a mighty distance; we were calm till the very moment of transition; and all the people were moved—and felt as with one heart, and spake as with one voice. Every human being in these islands was unsettled; the most slavish broke loose as from fetters; and there was not an individual—it need not be said of heroic virtue, but of ingenuous life and sound discretion—who, if his father, his son, or his brother, or if the flower of his house had been in that army, would not rather that they had perished, and the whole body of their countrymen, their companions in arms, had perished to a man, than that a treaty should have been submitted to upon such conditions. This was the feeling of the people; an awful feeling: and it is from these oracles that rulers are to learn wisdom.

For, when the people speaks loudly, it is from being strongly possessed either by the Godhead or the Demon; and he, who cannot discover the true spirit from the false, hath no ear for profitable communion. But in all that regarded the destinies of Spain, and her own as connected with them, the voice of Britain had the unquestionable sound of inspiration. If the gentle passions of pity, love, and gratitude, be porches of the temple; if the sentiments of admiration and rivalry be pillars upon which the structure is sustained; if, lastly, hatred, and anger, and vengeance, be steps which, by a mystery of nature, lead to the House of Sanctity;—then was it manifest to what power the edifice was consecrated; and that the voice within was of Holiness and Truth.

Spain had risen not merely to be delivered and saved;—deliverance and safety were but intermediate objects;—regeneration and liberty were the end, and the means by which this end was to be attained; had their own high value; were determined and precious; and could no more admit of being departed from, than the end of being forgotten.—She had risen—not merely to be free; but, in the act and process of acquiring that freedom, to recompense herself, as it were in a moment, for all which she had suffered through ages; to levy, upon the false fame of a cruel Tyrant, large contributions of true glory; to lift herself, by the conflict, as high in honour—as the disgrace was deep to which her own weakness and vices, and the violence and perfidy of her enemies, had subjected her.

Let us suppose that our own land had been so outraged; could we have been content that the enemy should be wafted from our shores as lightly as he came,—much less that he should depart illustrated in his own eyes and glorified, singing songs of savage triumph and wicked gaiety?—No.—Should we not have felt that a high trespass—a grievous offence had been committed; and that to demand satisfaction was our first and indispensable duty? Would we not have rendered their bodies back upon our guardian ocean which had borne them hither; or have insisted that their haughty weapons should submissively kiss the soil which they had polluted? We should have been resolute in a defence that would strike awe and terror: this for our dignity:—moreover, if safety and deliverance are to be so fondly prized for their own sakes, what security otherwise could they have? Would it not be certain that the work, which had been so ill done to-day, we should be called upon to execute still more imperfectly and ingloriously to-morrow; that we should be summoned to an attempt that would be vain?

In like manner were the wise and heroic Spaniards moved. If an Angel from heaven had come with power to take the enemy from their grasp (I do not fear to say this, in spite of the dominion which is now re-extended over so large a portion of their land), they would have been sad; they would have looked round them; their souls would have turned inward; and they would have stood like men defrauded and betrayed.

For not presumptuously had they taken upon themselves the work of chastisement. They did not wander madly about the world—like the Tamerlanes, or the Chengiz Khans, or the present barbarian Ravager of Europe—under a mock title of Delegates of the Almighty, acting upon self-assumed authority. Their commission had been thrust upon them. They had been trampled upon, tormented, wronged—bitterly, wantonly wronged—if ever a people on the earth was wronged. And this it was which legitimately incorporated their law with the supreme conscience, and gave to them the deep faith which they have expressed—that their power was favoured and assisted by the Almighty.—These words are not uttered without a due sense of their awful import: but the Spirit of evil is strong: and the subject requires the highest mode of thinking and feeling of which human nature is capable.—Nor in this can they be deceived; for, whatever be the immediate issue for themselves, the final issue for their Country and Mankind must be good;—they are instruments of benefit and glory for the human race; and the Deity therefore is with them.

From these impulses, then, our brethren of the Peninsula had risen; they could have risen from no other. By these energies, and by such others as (under judicious encouragement) would naturally grow out of and unite with these, the multitudes, who have risen, stand; and, if they desert them, must fall.—Riddance, mere riddance—safety, mere safety—are objects far too defined, too inert and passive in their own nature, to have ability either to rouze or to sustain. They win not the mind by any attraction of grandeur or sublime delight, either in effort or in endurance: for the mind gains consciousness of its strength to undergo only by exercise among materials which admit the impression of its power,—which grow under it, which bend under it,—which resist,—which change under its influence,—which alter either through its might or in its presence, by it or before it. These, during times of tranquillity, are the objects with which, in the studious walks of sequestered life, Genius most loves to hold intercourse; by which it is reared and supported;—these are the qualities in action and in object, in image, in thought, and in feeling, from communion with which proceeds originally all that is creative in art and science, and all that is magnanimous in virtue.—Despair thinks of *safety,* and hath no purpose; fear thinks of safety; despondency looks the same way:—but these passions are far too selfish, and therefore too blind, to reach the thing at which they aim; even when there is in them sufficient dignity to have an aim.—All courage is a projection from ourselves; however short-lived, it is a motion of hope. But these thoughts bind too closely to something inward,—to the present and to the past,—that is, to the self which is or has been. Whereas the vigour of the human soul is from without and from futurity,—in breaking down limit, and losing and forgetting herself in the sensation and image of Country and of the human race; and, when she returns and is most restricted and confined, her dignity consists in the contemplation of a better and more exalted being, which, though proceeding from herself, she loves and is devoted to as to another.

In following the stream of these thoughts, I have not wandered from my course: I have drawn out to open day the truth from its recesses in the minds of my countrymen.—Something more perhaps may have been done: a shape hath perhaps been given to that which was before a stirring spirit. I have shewn in what manner it was their wish that the struggle with the adversary of all that is good should be maintained—by pure passions and high actions. They forbid that their noble aim should be frustrated by measuring against each other things which are incommensurate—mechanic against moral power—body against soul. They will not suffer, without expressing their sorrow, that purblind calculation should wither the purest hopes in the face of all-seeing justice. These are times of strong appeal—of deep-searching visitation; when the best abstractions of the prudential understanding give way, and are included and absorbed in a supreme comprehensiveness of intellect and passion; which is the perfection and the very being of humanity.

How base! how puny! how inefficient for all good purposes are the tools and implements of policy, compared with these mighty engines of Nature! There is no middle course: two masters cannot be served:—Justice must either be enthroned above might, and the moral law take place of the edicts of selfish passion; or the heart of the people, which alone can sustain the efforts of the people, will languish: their desires will not spread beyond the plough and the loom, the field and the fireside: the sword will appear to them an emblem of no promise; an instrument of no hope; an object of indifference, of disgust, or fear. Was there ever—since the earliest actions of men which have been transmitted by affectionate tradition or recorded by faithful history, or sung to the impassioned harp of poetry—was there ever a people who presented themselves to the reason and the imagination, as under more holy influences than the dwellers upon the Southern Peninsula; as rouzed more instantaneously from a deadly sleep to a more hopeful wakefulness; as a mass fluctuating with one motion under the breath of a mightier wind; as breaking themselves up, and settling into several bodies, in more harmonious order; as reunited and embattled under a standard which was reared to the sun with more authentic assurance of final victory?—The superstition (I do not dread the word), which prevailed in these nations, may have checked many of my countrymen who would otherwise have exultingly accompanied me in the challenge which, under the shape of a question, I have been confidently uttering; as I know that this stain (so the same persons termed it) did, from the beginning, discourage their hopes for the cause. Short-sighted despondency! Whatever mixture of superstition there might be in the religious faith or devotional practices of the Spaniards; this must have necessarily been transmuted by that triumphant power, wherever that power was felt, which grows out of intense moral suffering—from the moment in which it coalesces with fervent hope. The chains of bigotry, which enthralled the mind, must have been turned into armour to defend and weapons to annoy. Wherever the heaving and effort of freedom was spread, purification must have followed it. And the types and ancient instruments of error, where emancipated men shewed their foreheads to the day, must have become a language and a ceremony of imagination; expressing, consecrating, and invigorating, the most pure deductions of Reason and the holiest feelings of universal Nature.

When the Boy of Saragossa (as we have been told), too immature in growth and unconfirmed in strength to be admitted by his Fellow-citizens into their ranks, too tender of age for them to bear the sight of him in arms—when this Boy, forgetful or unmindful of the restrictions which had been put upon him, rushed into the field where his Countrymen were engaged in battle, and, fighting with the sinew and courage of an unripe Hero, won a standard from the enemy, and bore his acquisition to the Church, and laid it with his own hands upon the Altar of the Virgin;—surely there was not less to be hoped for his Country from this act, than if the banner, taken from his grasp, had, without any such intermediation, been hung up in the place of worship—a direct offering to the incorporeal and supreme Being. Surely there is here an object which the most meditative and most elevated minds may contemplate with absolute delight; a well-adapted outlet for the dearest sentiments; an organ by which they may act; a function by which they may be sustained.—Who does not recognise in this presentation a visible affinity with deliverance, with patriotism, with hatred of oppression, and with human means put forth to the height for accomplishing, under divine countenance, the worthiest ends?

Such is the burst and growth of power and virtue which may rise out of excessive national afflictions from tyranny and oppression;—such is the hallowing influence, and thus mighty is the sway, of the spirit of moral justice in the heart of the individual and over the wide world of humanity. Even the very faith in present miraculous interposition, which is so dire a weakness and cause of weakness in tranquil times when the listless Being turns to it as a cheap and ready substitute upon every occasion, where the man sleeps, and the Saint, or the image of the Saint, is to perform his work, and to give effect to his wishes;—even this infirm faith, in a state of incitement from extreme passion sanctioned by a paramount sense of moral justice; having for its object a power which is no longer sole nor principal, but secondary and ministerial; a power added to a power; a breeze which springs up unthought-of to assist the strenuous oarsman;—even this faith is subjugated in order to be exalted; and—instead of operating as a temptation to relax or to be remiss, as an encouragement to indolence or cowardice; instead of being a false stay, a necessary and definite dependence which may fail—it passes into a habit of obscure and infinite confidence of the mind in its own energies, in the cause from its own sanctity, and in the ever-present invisible aid or momentary conspicuous approbation of the supreme Disposer of things.

Let the fire, which is never wholly to be extinguished, break out afresh; let but the human creature be rouzed; whether he have lain heedless and torpid in religious or civil slavery—have languished under a thraldom, domestic or foreign, or under both these alternately—or have drifted about a helpless member of a clan of disjointed and feeble barbarians; let him rise and act;—and his domineering imagination, by which from childhood he has been betrayed, and the debasing affections, which it has imposed upon him, will from that moment participate the dignity of the newly ennobled being whom they will now acknowledge for their master; and will further him in his progress, whatever be the object at which he aims. Still more inevitable and momentous are the results, when the individual knows that the fire, which is reanimated in him, is not less lively in the breasts of his associates; and sees the signs and testimonies of his own power, incorporated with those of a growing multitude and not to be distinguished from them, accompany him wherever he moves.—Hence those marvellous atchievements which were performed by the first enthusiastic followers of Mohammed; and by other conquerors, who with their armies have swept large portions of the earth like a transitory wind, or have founded new religions or empires.—But, if the object contended for be worthy and truly great (as, in the instance of the Spaniards, we have seen that it is); if cruelties have been committed upon an ancient and venerable people, which "shake the human frame with horror;" if not alone the life which is sustained by the bread of the mouth, but that—without which there is no life—the life in the soul, has been directly and mortally warred against; if reason has had abominations to endure in her inmost sanctuary;—then does intense passion, consecrated by a sudden revelation of justice, give birth to those higher and better wonders which I have described; and exhibit true miracles to the eyes of men, and the noblest which can be seen. It may be added that,—as this union brings back to the right road the faculty of imagination, where it is prone to err, and has gone farthest astray; as it corrects those qualities which (being in their essence indifferent), and cleanses those affections which (not being inherent in the constitution of man, nor necessarily determined to their object) are more immediately dependent upon the imagination, and which may have received from it a thorough taint of dishonour;—so the domestic loves and sanctities which are in their nature less liable to be stained,—so these, wherever they have flowed with a pure and placid stream, do instantly, under the same influence, put forth their strength as in a flood; and, without being sullied or polluted, pursue—exultingly and with song—a course which leads the contemplative reason to the ocean of eternal love.

I feel that I have been speaking in a strain which it is difficult to harmonize with the petty irritations, the doubts and fears, and the familiar (and therefore frequently undignified) exterior of present and passing events. But the theme is justice: and my voice is raised for mankind; for us who are alive, and for all posterity:—justice and passion; clear-sighted aspiring justice, and passion sacred as vehement. These, like twin-born Deities delighting in each other's presence, have wrought marvels in the inward mind through the whole region of the Pyrenëan Peninsula. I have shewn by what process these united powers sublimated the objects of outward sense in such rites—practices—and ordinances of Religion—as deviate from simplicity and wholesome piety; how they converted them to instruments of nobler use; and raised them to a conformity with things truly divine. The same reasoning might have been carried into the customs of civil life and their accompanying imagery, wherever these also were inconsistent with the dignity of man; and like effects of exaltation and purification have been shewn.

But a more urgent service calls me to point to further works of these united powers, more obvious and obtrusive—works and appearances, such as were hailed by the citizen of Seville when returning from Madrid;— "where" (to use the words of his own public declaration) "he had left his countrymen groaning in the chains which perfidy had thrown round them, and doomed at every step to the insult of being eyed with the disdain of the conqueror to the conquered; from Madrid threatened, harassed, and vexed; where mistrust reigned in every heart, and the smallest noise made the citizens tremble in the bosom of their families; where the enemy, from time to time, ran to arms to sustain the impression of terror by which the inhabitants had been stricken through the recent massacre; from Madrid a prison, where the gaolers took pleasure in terrifying the prisoners by alarms to keep them quiet; from Madrid thus tortured and troubled by a relentless Tyrant, to fit it for the slow and interminable evils of Slavery";—when he returned, and was able to compare the oppressed and degraded state of the inhabitants of that metropolis with the noble attitude of defence in which Andalusia stood. "A month ago," says he, "the Spaniards had lost their country;—Seville has restored it to life more glorious than ever; and those fields, which for so many years have seen no steel but that of the plough-share, are going amid the splendour of arms to prove the new cradle of their adored country."—"I could not," he adds, "refrain from tears of joy on viewing the city in which I first drew breath—and to see it in a situation so glorious!"

We might have trusted, but for late disgraces, that there is not a man in these islands whose heart would not, at such a spectacle, have beat in sympathy with that of this fervent Patriot—whose voice would not be in true accord with his in the prayer (which, if he has not already perished for the service of his dear country, he is perhaps uttering at this moment) that Andalusia and the city of Seville may preserve the noble attitude in which they then stood, and are yet standing; or, if they be doomed to fall, that their dying efforts may not be unworthy of their first promises; that the evening—the closing hour of their freedom may display a brightness not less splendid, though more aweful, than the dawn; so that the names of Seville and Andalusia may be consecrated among men, and be words of life to endless generations.

Saragossa!—She also has given bond, by her past actions, that she cannot forget her duty and will not shrink from it.* Valencia is under the seal of the same obligation. The multitudes of men who were arrayed in the fields of Baylen, and upon the mountains of the North; the peasants of Asturias, and the students of Salamanca; and many a solitary and untold-of hand, which, quitting for a moment the plough or the spade, has discharged a more pressing debt to the country by levelling with the dust at least one insolent and murderous Invader;—these have attested the efficacy of the passions which we have been contemplating—that the will of good men is not a vain impulse, heroic desires a delusive prop;—have proved that the condition of human affairs is not so forlorn and desperate, but that there are golden opportunities when the dictates of justice may be unrelentingly enforced, and the beauty of the inner mind substantiated in the outward act;—for a visible standard to look back upon; for a point of realized excellence at which to aspire; a monument to record;—for a charter to fasten down; and, as far as it is possible, to preserve.

Yes! there was an annunciation which the good received with gladness; a bright appearance which emboldened the wise to say—We trust that Regeneration is at hand; these are works of recovered innocence and wisdom:

> Magnus ab integro seclorum nascitur ordo;
> *Jam* redit et Virgo, redeunt Saturnia regna;
> *Jam* nova progenies coelo demittitur alto.

The spirits of the generous, of the brave, of the meditative, of the youthful and undefiled—who, upon the strongest wing of human nature, have accompanied me in this journey into a fair region—must descend: and, sorrowful to think! it is at the name and remembrance of Britain that we are to stoop from the balmy air of this pure element. Our country did not create, but there was created for her, one of those golden opportunities over which we have been rejoicing: an invitation was offered—a summons sent to her ear, as if from heaven, to go forth also and exhibit on her part, in entire coincidence and perfect harmony, the beneficent action with the benevolent will; to advance in the career of renovation upon which the Spaniards had so gloriously entered; and to solemnize yet another marriage between victory and justice. How she acquitted herself of this duty, we have already seen and lamented: yet on this—and on this duty only—ought the mind of that army and of the govern-

* Written in February.

ment to have been fixed. Every thing was smoothed before their feet;—Providence, it might almost be said, held forth to the men of authority in this country a gracious temptation to deceive them into the path of the new virtues which were stirring;—the enemy was delivered over to them; and they were unable to close their infantine fingers upon the gift.—The helplessness of infancy was their's—oh! could I but add, the innocence of infancy!

Reflect upon what was the temper and condition of the Southern Peninsula of Europe—the noble temper of the people of this mighty island sovereigns of the all-embracing ocean; think also of the condition of so vast a region in the Western continent and its islands; and we shall have cause to fear that ages may pass away before a conjunction of things, so marvellously adapted to ensure prosperity to virtue, shall present itself again. It could scarcely be spoken of as being to the wishes of men,—it was so far beyond their hopes.—The government which had been exercised under the name of the old Monarchy of Spain—this government, imbecile even to dotage, whose very selfishness was destitute of vigour, had been removed; taken laboriously and foolishly by the plotting Corsican to his own bosom; in order that the world might see, more triumphantly set forth than since the beginning of things had ever been seen before, to what degree a man of bad principles is despicable—though of great power—working blindly against his own purposes. It was a high satisfaction to behold demonstrated, in this manner, to what a narrow domain of knowledge the intellect of a Tyrant must be confined; that if the gate by which wisdom enters has never been opened, that of policy will surely find moments when it will shut itself against its pretended master imperiously and obstinately. To the eyes of the very peasant in the field, this sublime truth was laid open—not only that a Tyrant's domain of knowledge is narrow, but melancholy as narrow; inasmuch as—from all that is lovely, dignified, or exhilarating in the prospect of human nature—he is inexorably cut off; and therefore he is inwardly helpless and forlorn.

Was not their hope in this—twofold hope; from the weakness of him who had thus counteracted himself; and a hope, still more cheering, from the strength of those who had been disburthened of a cleaving curse by an ordinance of Providence—employing their most wilful and determined enemy to perform for them the best service which man could perform? The work of liberation was virtually accomplished—we might almost say, established. The interests of the people were taken from a government whose sole aim it had been to prop up the last remains of its own decrepitude by betraying those whom it was its duty to protect;—withdrawn from such hands, to be committed to those of the people; at a time when the double affliction which Spain had endured, and the return of affliction with which she was threatened, made it impossible that the emancipated nation could abuse its new-born strength to any substantial injury of itself.—Infinitely less favourable to all good ends was the condition of the French people when, a few years past, a revolution made them, for a season, their own masters,—rid them from the incumbrance of superannuated institutions—the galling pressure of so many unjust laws—and the tyranny of bad customs. The Spaniards became their own masters: and the blessing lay in this, that they became so at once: there had not been time for them to court their power: their fancies had not been fed to wantonness by ever-changing temptations: obstinacy in them could not have leagued itself with trivial opinions: petty hatreds had not accumulated to masses of strength conflicting perniciously with each other: vanity with them had not found leisure to flourish—nor presumption: they did not assume their authority,—it was given them,—it was thrust upon them. The perfidy and tyranny of Napoleon "*compelled*," says the Junta of Seville in words before quoted, "the whole Nation to take up arms and *to choose itself a form of government;* and, in the difficulties and dangers into which the French had plunged it, all—or nearly all—the provinces, as it were *by the inspiration of Heaven* and *in a manner little short of miraculous,* created Supreme Juntas—delivered themselves up to their guidance—and placed in their hands the rights and the ultimate fate of Spain."—Governments, thus newly issued from the people, could not but act from the spirit of the people—be organs of their life. And, though misery (by which I mean pain of mind not without some consciousness of guilt) naturally disorders the understanding and perverts the moral sense,—calamity (that is suffering, individual or national, when it has been inflicted by one to whom no injury has been done or provocation given) ever brings wisdom along with it; and, whatever outward agitation it may cause, does inwardly rectify the will.

But more was required; not merely judicious desires; not alone an eye from which the scales had dropped off—which could see widely and clearly; but a mighty hand was wanting. The government had been formed; and it could not but recollect that the condition of Spain did not exact from her children, as *a first* requisite, virtues like those due and familiar impulses of spring-time by

2780 of *M.Y.* i. 342: to 1809. 2787 could *M.Y.* i. 350: would 1809.

which things are revived and carried forward in accustomed health according to established order—not power so much for a renewal as for a birth—labour by throes and violence;—a chaos was to be conquered—a work of creation begun and consummated;—and afterwards the seasons were to advance, and continue their gracious revolutions. The powers, which were needful for the people to enter upon and assist in this work, had been given; we have seen that they had been bountifully conferred. The nation had been thrown into—rather, lifted up to—that state when conscience, for the body of the people, is not merely an infallible monitor (which may be heard and disregarded); but, by combining—with the attributes of insight to perceive, and of inevitable presence to admonish and enjoin—the attribute of passion to enforce, it was truly an all-powerful deity in the soul.

Oh! let but any man, who has a care for the progressive happiness of the species, peruse merely that epitome of Spanish wisdom and benevolence and "amplitude of mind for highest deeds" which, in the former part of this investigation, I have laid before the reader: let him listen to the reports—which they, who really have had means of knowledge, and who are worthy to speak upon the subject, will give to him—of the things done or endured in every corner of Spain; and he will see what emancipation had there been effected in the mind;—how far the perceptions—the impulses—and the actions also—had outstripped the habit and the character, and consequently were in a process of permanently elevating both; and how much farther (alas! by infinite degrees) the principles and practice of a people, with great objects before them to concentrate their love and their hatred, transcend the principles and practice of governments; not excepting those which, in their constitution and ordinary conduct, furnish the least matter for complaint.

Then it was—when the people of Spain were thus rouzed; after this manner released from the natal burthen of that government which had bowed them to the ground; in the free use of their understandings, and in the play and "noble rage" of their passions; while yet the new authorities, which they had generated, were truly living members of their body, and (as I have said) organs of their life; when that numerous people were in a stage of their journey which could not be accomplished without the spirit which was then prevalent in them, and which (as might be feared) would too soon abate of itself;—then it was that we—not we, but the heads of the British army and nation—when, if they could not breathe a favouring breath, they ought at least to have stood at an awful distance—stepped in with their forms, their impediments, their rotten customs and precedents, their narrow desires, their busy and purblind fears; and called out to these aspiring travellers to halt—"For ye are in a dream;" confounded them (for it was the voice of a seeming friend that spoke); and spell-bound them, as far as was possible, by an instrument framed "in the eclipse" and sealed "with curses dark."—In a word, we had the power to act up to the most sacred letter of justice—and this at a time when the mandates of justice were of an affecting obligation such as had never before been witnessed; and we plunged into the lowest depths of injustice:—We had power to give a brotherly aid to our allies in supporting the mighty world which their shoulders had undertaken to uphold; and, while they were expecting from us this aid, we undermined—without forewarning them—the ground upon which they stood. The evil is incalculable; and the stain will cleave to the British name as long as the story of this island shall endure.

Did we not (if, from this comprehensive feeling of sorrow, I may for a moment descend to particulars)—did we not send forth a general, one whom, since his return, Court, and Parliament, and Army, have been at strife with each other which shall most caress and applaud—a general, who, in defending the armistice which he himself had signed, said in open court that he deemed that the French army was *entitled* to such terms. The people of Spain had, through the Supreme Junta of Seville, thus spoken of this same army: "Ye have, among yourselves, the objects of your vengeance;—attack them;—they are but a handful of miserable panic-struck men, humiliated and conquered already by their perfidy and cruelties;—resist and destroy them: our united efforts will extirpate this perfidious nation." The same Spaniards had said (speaking officially of the state of the whole Peninsula, and no doubt with their eye especially upon this army in Portugal)—"Our enemies have taken up exactly those positions in which they may most easily be destroyed."—Where then did the British General find this right and title of the French army in Portugal? "Because," says he in military language, "it was not broken."—Of the Man, and of the understanding and heart of the man—of the Citizen, who could think and feel after this manner in such circumstances, it is needless to speak; but to the General I will say, This is most pitiable pedantry. If the instinctive wisdom of your ally could not be understood, you might at least have remembered the resolute policy of your enemy. The French army was not broken? Break it then—wither it—pursue it with unrelenting warfare—hunt it out of its holds;—if impetuosity be not justifiable, have recourse to patience—to watchfulness—to obstinacy: at all events, never for a moment forget who the foe is—and that he is in your power. This is the example which the French Ruler and his Generals have given you at Ulm—at Lubeck—in Switzerland—over the whole plain of Prussia—every where;—and this for the worst deeds of darkness; while your's was the noblest service of light.

This remonstrance has been forced from me by indignation:—let me explain in what sense I propose, with calmer thought, that the example of our enemy should be imitated.—The laws and customs of war, and the maxims of policy, have all had their foundation in reason and humanity; and their object has been the attainment or security of some real or supposed—some positive or relative—good. They are established among men as ready guides for the understanding, and authorities to which the passions are taught to pay deference. But the relations of things to each other are perpetually changing; and in course of time many of these leaders and masters, by losing part of their power to do service and sometimes the whole, forfeit in proportion their right to obedience. Accordingly they are disregarded in some instances, and sink insensibly into neglect with the general improvement of society. But they often survive when they have become an oppression and a hindrance which cannot be cast off decisively, but by an impulse—rising either from the absolute knowledge of good and great men,—or from the partial insight which is given to superior minds, though of a vitiated moral constitution,—or lastly from that blind energy and those habits of daring which are often found in men who, checked by no restraint of morality, suffer their evil passions to gain extraordinary strength in extraordinary circumstances. By any of these forces may the tyranny be broken through. We have seen, in the conduct of our Countrymen, to what degree it tempts to weak actions,—and furnishes excuse for them, admitted by those who sit as judges. I wish then that we could so far imitate our enemies as, like them, to shake off these bonds; but not, like them, from the worst—but from the worthiest impulse. If this were done, we should have learned how much of their practice would harmonize with justice; have learned to distinguish between those rules which ought to be wholly abandoned, and those which deserve to be retained; and should have known when, and to what point, they ought to be trusted.—But how is this to be? Power of mind is wanting, where there is power of place. Even we cannot, as a beginning of a new journey, force or win our way into the current of success, the flattering motion of which would awaken intellectual courage—the only substitute which is able to perform any arduous part of the secondary work of "heroic wisdom;"—I mean, execute happily any of its prudential regulations. In the person of our enemy and his chieftains we have living example how wicked men of ordinary talents are emboldened by success. There is a kindliness, as they feel, in the nature of advancement; and prosperity is their Genius. But let us know and remember that this prosperity, with all the terrible features which it has gradually assumed, is a child of noble parents—Liberty and Philanthropic Love. Perverted as the creature is which it has grown up to (rather, into which it has passed),—from no inferior stock could it have issued. It is the Fallen Spirit, triumphant in misdeeds, which was formerly a blessed Angel.

If then (to return to ourselves) there be such strong obstacles in the way of our drawing benefit either from the maxims of policy or the principles of justice: what hope remains that the British nation should repair, by its future conduct, the injury which has been done?—We cannot advance a step towards a rational answer to this question—without previously adverting to the original sources of our miscarriages; which are these:—First; a want, in the minds of the members of government and public functionaries, of knowledge indispensible for this service; and, secondly, a want of power, in the same persons acting in their corporate capacities, to give effect to the knowledge which individually they possess.—Of the latter source of weakness,—this inability as caused by decay in the machine of government, and by illegitimate forces which are checking and controuling its constitutional motions,—I have not spoken, nor shall I now speak: for I have judged it best to suspend my task for a while: and this subject, being in its nature delicate, ought not to be lightly or transiently touched. Besides, no *immediate* effect can be expected from the soundest and most unexceptionable doctrines which might be laid down for the correcting of this evil.—The former source of weakness,—namely, the want of appropriate and indispensible knowledge,—has, in the past investigation, been reached, and shall be further laid open; not without a hope of some result of *immediate* good by a direct application to the mind; and in full confidence that the best and surest way to render operative that knowledge which is already possessed—is to increase the stock of knowledge.

Here let me avow that I undertook this present labour as a serious duty; rather, that it was forced (and has been unremittingly pressed) upon me by a perception of justice united with strength of feeling;—in a word, by that power of conscience, calm or impassioned, to which throughout I have done reverence as the animating spirit of the cause. My work was begun and prosecuted under this controul:—and with the accompanying satisfaction that no charge of presumption could, by a thinking mind, be brought against me: though I had taken upon myself to offer instruction to men who, if they possess not talents and acquirements, have not title to the high stations which they hold; who also, by holding those stations, are understood to obtain certain benefit of experience and of knowledge not otherwise to be gained; and who have a further claim to deference—founded upon reputation, even when it is spurious (as much of the reputation of men high in power must necessarily be; their errors being veiled and palliated by the authority attached to their office; while that same authority gives more than due weight and effect to their wiser opinions). Yet, notwithstanding all this, I did not fear the censure of having unbecomingly obtruded counsels or remonstrances. For there can be no presumption, upon a call so affecting as the present, in an attempt to assert the sanctity and to display the efficacy of principles and passions which are the natural birthright of man; to some share of which all are born; but an inheritance which may be alienated or consumed; and by none more readily and assuredly than by those who are most eager for the praise of policy, of prudence, of sagacity, and of all those qualities which are the darling virtues of the worldly-wise. Moreover; the evidence to which I have made appeal, in order to establish the truth, is not locked up in cabinets; but is accessible to all; as it exists in the bosoms of men—in the appearances and intercourse of daily life—in the details of passing events—and in general history. And more especially is its right import within the reach of Him who—taking no part in public measures, and having no concern in the changes of things but as they affect what is most precious in his country and humanity—will doubtless be more alive to those genuine sensations which are the materials of sound judgment. Nor is it to be overlooked that such a man may have more leisure (and probably will have a stronger inclination) to communicate with the records of past ages.

Deeming myself justified then in what has been said,—I will continue to lay open (and, in some degree, to account for) those privations in the materials of judgment, and those delusions of opinion, and infirmities of mind, to which practical Statesmen, and particularly such as are high in office, are more than other men subject;—as containing an answer to that question, so interesting at this juncture,—How far is it in our power to make amends for the harm done?

After the view of things which has been taken,—we may confidently affirm that nothing, but a knowledge of human nature directing the operations of our government, can give it a right to an intimate association with a cause which is that of human nature. I say, an I intimate association founded on the right of thorough knowledge;—to contradistinguish this best mode of exertion from another which might found *its* right upon a vast and commanding military power put forth with manifestation of sincere intentions to benefit our allies—from a conviction merely of policy that their liberty, independence, and honour, are our genuine gain;—to distinguish the pure brotherly connection from this other (in its appearance at least more magisterial) which such a power, guided by such intention uniformly displayed, might authorize. But of the former connection (which supposes the main military effort to be made, even at present, by the people of the Peninsula on whom the moral interest more closely presses), and of the knowledge which it demands, I have hitherto spoken—and have further to speak.

It is plain *à priori* that the minds of Statesmen and Courtiers are unfavourable to the growth of this knowledge. For they are in a situation exclusive and artificial; which has the further disadvantage, that it does not separate men from men by collateral partitions which leave, along with difference, a sense of equality—that they, who are divided, are yet upon the same level; but by a degree of superiority which can scarcely fail to be accompanied with more or less of pride. This situation therefore must be eminently unfavourable for the reception and establishment of that knowledge which is founded not upon things but upon sensations;—sensations which are general, and under general influences (and this it is which makes them what they are, and gives them their importance);—not upon things which may be *brought;* but upon sensations which must be *met.* Passing by the kindred and usually accompanying influence of birth in a certain rank—and, where education has been pre-defined from childhood for the express purpose of future political power, the tendency of such education to warp (and therefore weaken) the intellect;—we may join at once, with the privation which I have been noticing, a delusion equally common. It is this: that practical Statesmen assume too much credit to themselves for their ability to see into the motives and manage the selfish passions of their immediate agents and dependants; and for the skill with which they baffle or resist the aims of their opponents. A promptness in looking through the most superficial part of the characters of those men—who, by the very circumstance of their contending ambitiously for the rewards and honours of government, are separated from the mass of the society to which they belong—is mistaken for a knowledge of human kind. Hence, where higher knowledge is a prime requisite, they not only are unfurnished; but, being unconscious that they are so, they look down contemptuously upon those who endeavour to supply (in some degree) their want.—The instincts of natural and social man; the deeper emotions; the simpler feelings; the spacious range of the disinterested imagination; the pride in country for country's sake, when to serve has not been a formal profession—and the mind is therefore left in a state of dignity only to be surpassed by having served nobly and generously; the instantaneous accomplishment in which they start up who, upon a searching call, stir for the land which they love—not from personal motives, but for a reward which is undefined and cannot be missed; the solemn fraternity which a great nation composes—gathered together, in a stormy season, under the shade of ancestral feeling; the delicacy of moral honour which pervades the minds of a people, when despair has been suddenly thrown off and expectations are lofty; the apprehensiveness to a touch unkindly or irreverent, where sympathy is at once exacted as a tribute and welcomed as a gift; the power of injustice and inordinate calamity to transmute, to invigorate, and to govern—to sweep away the barriers of opinion—to reduce under submission passions purely evil—to exalt the nature of indifferent qualities, and to render them fit companions for the absolute virtues with which they are summoned to associate—to consecrate passions which, if not bad in themselves, are of such temper that, in the calm of ordinary life, they are rightly deemed so—to correct and embody these passions—and, without weakening them (nay, with tenfold addition to their strength), to make them worthy of taking their place as the advanced guard of hope, when a sublime movement of deliverance is to be originated;—these arrangements and resources of nature, these ways and means of society, have so little connection with those others upon which a ruling minister of a long-established government is accustomed to depend; these—elements as it were of a universe, functions of a living body—are so opposite, in their mode of action, to the formal machine which it has been his pride to manage;—that he has but a faint perception of their immediate efficacy; knows not the facility with which they assimilate with other powers; nor the property by which such of them—as, from necessity of nature, must change or pass away—will, under wise and fearless management, surely generate lawful successors to fill their place when their appropriate work is performed. Nay, of the majority of men, who are usually found in high stations under old governments, it may without injustice be said; that, when they look about them in times (alas! too rare) which present the glorious product of such agency to their eyes, they have not a right to say—with a dejected man in the midst of the woods, the rivers, the mountains, the sunshine, and shadows of some transcendant landscape—

> "I see, not feel, how beautiful they are:"

These spectators neither see nor feel. And it is from the blindness and insensibility of these, and the train whom they draw along with them, that the throes of nations have been so ill recompensed by the births which have followed; and that revolutions, after passing from crime to crime and from sorrow to sorrow, have often ended in throwing back such heavy reproaches of delusiveness upon their first promises.

I am satisfied that no enlightened Patriot will impute to me a wish to disparage the characters of men high in authority, or to detract from the estimation which is fairly due to them. My purpose is to guard against unreasonable expectations. That specific knowledge,—the paramount importance of which, in the present condition of Europe, I am insisting upon,—they, who usually fill places of high trust in old governments, neither do—nor, for the most part, can—possess: nor is it necessary, for the administration of affairs in ordinary circumstances, that they should.—The progress of their own country, and of the other nations of the world, in civilization, in true refinement, in science, in religion, in morals, and in all the real wealth of humanity, might indeed be quicker, and might correspond more happily with the wishes of the benevolent,—if Governors better understood the rudiments of nature as studied in the walks of common life; if they were men who had themselves felt every strong emotion "inspired by nature and by fortune taught;" and could calculate upon the force of the grander passions. Yet, at the same time, there is temptation in this. To know may seduce; and to have been agitated may compel. Arduous cares are attractive for their own sakes. Great talents are naturally driven towards hazard and difficulty; as it is there that they are most sure to find their exercise, and their evidence, and joy in anticipated triumph—the liveliest of all sensations. Moreover; magnificent desires, when least under the bias of personal feeling, dispose the mind—more than itself is conscious of—to regard commotion with complacency, and to watch the aggravations of distress with welcoming; from an immoderate confidence that, when the appointed day shall come, it will be in the power of intellect to relieve. There is danger in being a zealot in any cause—not excepting that of humanity. Nor is it to be forgotten that the incapacity and ignorance of the regular agents of long-established governments do not prevent some progress in the dearest concerns of men; and that society may owe to these very deficiencies, and to the tame and unenterprizing course which they necessitate, much security and tranquil enjoyment.

Nor, on the other hand, (for reasons which may be added to those already given) is it so desirable as might at first sight be imagined, much less is it desirable as an absolute good, that men of comprehensive sensibility and tutored genius—either for the interests of mankind or for their own—should, in ordinary times, have vested in them political power. The Empire, which they hold, is more independent: its constituent parts are sustained by a stricter connection: the dominion is purer and of higher origin; as mind is more excellent than body—the search of truth an employment more inherently dignified than the application of force—the determinations of nature more venerable than the accidents of human institution. Chance and disorder, vexation and disappointment, malignity and perverseness within or without the mind, are a sad exchange for the steady and genial processes of reason. Moreover; worldly distinctions and offices of command do not lie in the path—nor are they any part of the appropriate retinue—of Philosophy and Virtue. Nothing, but a strong spirit of love, can counteract the consciousness of pre-eminence which ever attends pre-eminent intellectual power with correspondent attainments: and this spirit of love is best encouraged by humility and simplicity in mind, manners, and conduct of life; virtues, to which wisdom leads. But,—though these be virtues in a Man, a Citizen, or a Sage,—they cannot be recommended to the especial culture of the Political or Military Functionary; and still less of the Civil Magistrate. Him, in the exercise of his functions, it will often become to carry himself highly and with state; in order that evil may be suppressed, and authority respected by those who have not understanding. The power also of office, whether the duties be discharged well or ill, will ensure a never-failing supply of flattery and praise: and of these—a man (becoming at once double-dealer and dupe) may, without impeachment of his modesty, receive as much as his weakness inclines him to; under the shew that the homage is not offered up to himself, but to that portion of the public dignity which is lodged in his person. But, whatever may be the cause, the fact is certain—that there is an unconquerable tendency in all power, save that of knowledge acting by and through knowledge, to injure the mind of him who exercises that power; so much so, that best natures cannot escape the evil of such alliance. Nor is it less certain that things of soundest quality, issuing through a medium to which they have only an arbitrary relation, are vitiated: and it is inevitable that there should be a reäscent of unkindly influence to the heart of him from whom the gift, thus unfairly dealt with, proceeded.—In illustration of these remarks, as connected with the management of States, we need only refer to the Empire of China—where superior endowments of mind and acquisitions of learning are the sole acknowledged title to offices of great trust; and yet in no country is the government more bigotted or intolerant, or society less progressive.

To prevent misconception; and to silence (at least to throw discredit upon) the clamours of ignorance;—I have thought proper thus, in some sort, to strike a balance between the claims of men of routine—and men of original and accomplished minds—to the management of State affairs in ordinary circumstances. But ours is not an age of this character: and,—after having seen such a long series of misconduct, so many unjustifiable attempts made and sometimes carried into effect, good endeavours frustrated, disinterested wishes thwarted, and benevolent hopes disappointed,—it is reasonable that we should endeavour to ascertain to what cause these evils are to be ascribed. I have directed the attention of the Reader to one primary cause: and can he doubt of its existence, and of the operation which I have attributed to it?

In the course of the last thirty years we have seen two wars waged against Liberty—the American war, and the war against the French People in the early stages of their Revolution. In the latter instance the Emigrants and the Continental Powers and the British did, in all their expectations and in every movement of their efforts, manifest a common ignorance—originating in the same source. And, for what more especially belongs to ourselves at this time, we may affirm—that the same presumptuous irreverence of the principles of justice, and blank insensibility to the affections of human nature, which determined the conduct of our government in those two wars *against* liberty, have continued to accompany its exertions in the present struggle *for* liberty,—and have rendered them fruitless. The British government deems (no doubt), on its own part, that its intentions are good. It must not deceive itself: nor must we deceive ourselves. Intentions—thoroughly good—could not mingle with the unblessed actions which we have witnessed. A disinterested and pure intention is a light that guides as well as cheers, and renders desperate lapses impossible.

Our duty is—our aim ought to be—to employ the true means of liberty and virtue for the ends of liberty and virtue. In such policy, thoroughly understood, there is fitness and concord and rational subordination; it deserves a higher name—organization, health, and grandeur. Contrast, in a single instance, the two processes; and the qualifications which they require. The ministers of that period found it an easy task to hire a band of Hessians, and to send it across the Atlantic, that they might assist *in bringing the Americans* (according to the phrase then prevalent) *to reason.* The force, with which these troops would attack, was gross—tangible,—and might be calculated; but the spirit of resistance, which their presence would create, was subtle—ethereal—mighty—and incalculable. Accordingly, from the moment when these foreigners landed—men who had no interest, no business, in the quarrel, but what the wages of their master bound him to, and he imposed upon his miserable slaves;—nay, from the first rumour of their destination, the success of the British was (as hath since been affirmed by judicious Americans) impossible.

The British government of the present day have been seduced, as we have seen, by the same common-place facilities on the one side; and have been equally blind on the other. A physical auxiliar force of thirty-five thousand men is to be added to the army of Spain: but the moral energy, which thereby *might* be taken away from the principal, is overlooked or slighted; the material being too fine for their calculation. What does it avail to graft a bough upon a tree; if this be done so ignorantly and rashly that the trunk, which can alone supply the sap by which the whole must flourish, receives a deadly wound? Palpable effects of the Convention of Cintra, and self-contradicting consequences even in the matter especially aimed at, may be seen in the necessity which it entailed of leaving 8,000 British troops to protect Portuguese traitors from punishment by the laws of their country. A still more serious and fatal contradiction lies in this—that the English army was made an instrument of injustice, and was dishonoured, in order that it might be hurried forward to uphold a cause which could have no life but by justice and honour. The nation knows how that army languished in the heart of Spain: that it accomplished nothing except its retreat, is sure: what great service it might have performed, if it had moved from a different impulse, we have shewn.

It surely then behoves those who are in authority—to look to the state of their own minds. There is indeed an inherent impossibility that they should be equal to the arduous duties which have devolved upon them: but it is not unreasonable to hope that something higher might be aimed at; and that the People might see, upon great occasions,—in the practice of its Rulers—a more adequate reflection of its own wisdom and virtue. Our Rulers, I repeat, must begin with their own minds. This is a precept of immediate urgency; and, if attended to, might be productive of immediate good. I will follow it with further conclusions directly referring to future conduct.

I will not suppose that any ministry of this country can be so abject, so insensible, and unwise, as to abandon the Spaniards and Portuguese while there is a Patriot in arms; or, if the people should for a time be subjugated, to deny them assistance the moment they rise to require it again. I cannot think so unfavourably of my country as to suppose this possible. Let men in power, however, take care (and let the nation be equally careful) not to receive any reports from our army—of the disposition of the Spanish people—without mistrust. The British generals, who were in Portugal (the whole body of them,* according to the statement of Sir Hew Dalrymple), approved of the Convention of Cintra; and have thereby shewn that *their* communications are not to be relied upon in this case. And indeed there is not any information, which we can receive upon this subject, that is so little trust-worthy as that which comes from our army—or from any part of it. The opportunities of notice, afforded to soldiers in actual service, must necessarily be very limited; and a thousand things stand in the way of their power to make a right use of these. But a retreating army, in the country of an ally;—harassed and dissatisfied; willing to find a reason for its failures in any thing but itself, and actually not without much solid ground for complaint; retreating; sometimes, perhaps, fugitive; and, in its disorder, tempted (and even forced) to commit offences upon the people of the district through which it passes; while they, in their turn, are filled with fear and inconsiderate anger;—an army, in such a condition, must needs be incapable of seeing objects as they really are; and, at the same time, all things must change in its presence, and put on their most unfavourable appearances.

Deeming it then not to be doubted that the British government will continue its endeavours to support its allies; one or other of two maxims of policy follows obviously from the painful truths which we have been considering:—Either, first, that we should put forth to the utmost our strength as a military

* From this number, however, must be excepted the gallant and patriotic General Ferguson. For that officer has had the virtue publicly and in the most emphatic manner, upon two occasions, to reprobate the whole transaction.

power—strain it to the very last point, and prepare (no erect mind will start at the proposition) to pour into the Peninsula a force of two hundred thousand men or more,—and make ourselves for a time, upon Spanish ground, principals in the contest; or, secondly, that we should direct our attention to giving support rather in *Things* than in Men.

The former plan, though requiring a great effort and many sacrifices, is (I have no doubt) practicable: its difficulties would yield to a bold and energetic Ministry, in despite of the present constitution of Parliament. The Militia, if they had been called upon at the beginning of the rising in the Peninsula, would (I believe)—almost to a man—have offered their services: so would many of the Volunteers in their individual capacity. They would do so still. The advantages of this plan would be—that the power, which would attend it, must (if judiciously directed) insure unity of effort; taming down, by its dignity, the discords which usually prevail among allied armies; and subordinating to itself the affections of the Spanish and Portuguese by the palpable service which it was rendering to their Country. A further encouragement for adopting this plan he will find, who perceives that the military power of our Enemy is not in substance so formidable, by many—many degrees of terror, as outwardly it appears to be. The last campaign has not been wholly without advantage; since it has proved that the French troops are indebted, for their victories, to the imbecility of their opponents far more than to their own discipline or courage—or even to the skill and talents of their Generals. There is a superstition hanging over us which the efforts of our Army (not to speak of the Spaniards) have, I hope, removed.— But their mighty numbers!—In that is a delusion of another kind. In the former instance, year after year we imagined things to be what they were not: and in this, by a more fatal and more common delusion, the thought of what things really are—precludes the thought of what in a moment they may become: the mind, overlaid by the present, cannot lift itself to attain a glimpse of the future.

All—which is comparatively inherent, or can lay claim to any degree of permanence, in the tyranny which the French Nation maintains over Europe—rests upon two foundations:—First; Upon the despotic rule which has been established in France over a powerful People who have lately passed from a state of revolution, in which they supported a struggle begun for domestic liberty, and long continued for liberty and national independence:—and, secondly, upon the personal character of the Man by whom that rule is exercised.

As to the former; every one knows that Despotism, in a general sense, is but another word for weakness. Let one generation disappear; and a people over whom such rule has been extended, if it have not virtue to free itself, is condemned to embarrassment in the operations of its government, and to perpetual languor; with no better hope than that which may spring from the diseased activity of some particular Prince on whom the authority may happen to devolve. This, if it takes a regular hereditary course: but,—if the succession be interrupted, and the supreme power frequently usurped or given by election,—worse evils follow. Science and Art must dwindle, whether the power be hereditary or not: and the virtues of a Trajan or an Antonine are a hollow support for the feeling of contentment and happiness in the hearts of their subjects: such virtues are even a painful mockery;—something that is, and may vanish in a moment, and leave the monstrous crimes of a Caracalla or a Domitian in its place,—men, who are probably leaders of a long procession of their kind. The feebleness of despotic power we have had before our eyes in the late condition of Spain and Prussia; and in that of France before the Revolution; and in the present condition of Austria and Russia. But, in a *new-born* arbitrary and military Government (especially if, like that of France, it have been immediately preceded by a popular Constitution), not only this weakness is not found; but it possesses, for the purposes of external annoyance, a preternatural vigour. Many causes contribute to this: we need only mention that, fitness—real or supposed—being necessarily the chief (and almost sole) recommendation to offices of trust, it is clear that such offices will in general be ably filled; and their duties, comparatively, well executed: and that, from the conjunction of absolute civil and military authority in a single Person, there naturally follows promptness of decision; concentration of effort; rapidity of motion; and confidence that the movements made will be regularly supported. This is all which need now be said upon the subject of this first basis of French Tyranny.

For the second—namely, the personal character of the Chief; I shall at present content myself with noting (to prevent misconception) that this basis is not laid in any superiority of talents in him, but in his utter rejection of the restraints of morality—in wickedness which acknowledges no limit but the extent of its own power. Let any one reflect a moment; and he will feel that a new world of forces is opened to a Being who has made this desperate leap. It is a tremendous principle to be adopted, and steadily adhered to, by a man in the station which Buonaparte occupies; and he has taken the full benefit of it. What there is in this principle of weak, perilous, and self-destructive— I may find a grateful employment in endeavouring to shew upon some future occasion. But it is a duty which we owe to the present moment to proclaim—in vindication of the dignity of human nature, and for an admonition to men of prostrate spirit—that the dominion, which this Enemy of mankind holds, has neither been acquired nor is sustained by endowments of intellect which are rarely bestowed, or by uncommon accumulations of knowledge; but that it has risen from circumstances over which he had no influence; circumstances which, with the power they conferred, have stimulated passions whose natural food hath been and is ignorance; from the barbarian impotence and insolence of a mind—originally of ordinary constitution—lagging, in moral sentiment and knowledge, three hundred years behind the age in which it acts. In such manner did the power originate; and, by the forces which I have described, is it maintained. This should be declared: and it should be added—that the crimes of Buonaparte are more to be abhorred than those of other denaturalized creatures whose actions are painted in History; because the Author of those crimes is guilty with less temptation, and sins in the presence of a clearer light.

No doubt in the command of almost the whole military force of Europe (the subject which called upon me to make these distinctions) he has, *at this moment*, a third source of power which may be added to these two. He himself rates this last so high—either is, or affects to be, so persuaded of its pre-eminence—that he boldly announces to the world that it is madness, and even impiety, to resist him. And sorry may we be to remember that there are British Senators, who (if a judgement may be formed from the language which they speak) are inclined to accompany him far in this opinion. But the enormity of this power has in it nothing *inherent* or *permanent*. Two signal overthrows in pitched battles would, I believe, go far to destroy it. Germans, Dutch, Italians, Swiss, Poles, would desert the army of Buonaparte, and flock to the standard of his Adversaries, from the moment they could look towards it with that confidence which one or two conspicuous victories would inspire. A regiment of 900 Swiss joined the British army in Portugal; and, if the French had been compelled to surrender as Prisoners of War, we should have seen that all those troops, who were not native Frenchmen, would (if encouragement had been given) have joined the British: and the opportunity that was lost of demonstrating this fact—was not among the least of the mischiefs which attended the termination of the campaign.—In a word; the vastness of Buonaparte's military power is formidable— not because it is impossible to break it; but because it has not yet been penetrated. In this respect it may not inaptly be compared to a huge pine-forest (such as are found in the Northern parts of this Island), whose ability to resist the storms is in it's skirts: let but the blast once make an inroad; and it levels the forest, and sweeps it away at pleasure. A hundred thousand men, such as fought at Vimiera and Corunna, would accomplish three such victories as I have been anticipating. This Nation *might* command a military force which would drive the French out of the Peninsula: I do not say that we could sustain there a military force which would prevent their re-entering; but that we could transplant thither, by a great effort, one which would expel them:—*This* I maintain: and it is matter of thought in which infirm minds may find both reproach and instruction. The Spaniards could then take possession of their own fortresses; and have leisure to give themselves a blended civil and military organization, complete and animated by liberty; which, if once accomplished, they would be able to protect themselves. The oppressed Continental Powers also, seeing such unquestionable proof that Great Britain was sincere and earnest, would lift their heads again; and, by so doing, would lighten the burthen of war which might remain for the Spaniards.

In treating of this plan—I have presumed that a General might be placed at the head of this great military power who would not sign a Treaty like that of the Convention of Cintra, and say (look at the proceedings of the Board of Inquiry) that he was determined to this by "British interests;" or frame *any* Treaty in the country of an Ally (save one purely military for the honourable preservation, if necessary, of his own army or part of it) to which the sole, or even the main, inducement was—our interests contradistinguished from those of that Ally;—a General and a Ministry whose policy would be comprehensive enough to perceive that the true welfare of Britain is best promoted by the independence, freedom, and honour of other Nations; and that it is only by the diffusion and prevalence of these virtues that French Tyranny can be ultimately reduced; or the influence of France over the rest of Europe brought within its natural and reasonable limits.

If this attempt be "above the strain and temper" of the country, there remains only a plan laid down upon the other principle; namely, service (as far as is required) in *things* rather than in men; that is, men being secondary

3359 principle *M.Y.* i. 343: principles 1809.

to things. It is not, I fear, possible that the moral sentiments of the British Army or Government should accord with those of Spain in her present condition. Commanding power indeed (as hath been said), put forth in the repulse of the common enemy, would tend, more effectually than any thing save the prevalence of true wisdom, to prevent disagreement, and to obviate any temporary injury which the moral spirit of the Spaniards might receive from us: at all events—such power, should there ensue any injury, would bring a solid compensation. But from a middle course—an association sufficiently intimate and wide to scatter every where unkindly passions, and yet unable to attain the salutary point of decisive power—no good is to be expected. Great would be the evil, at this momentous period, if the hatred of the Spaniards should look two ways. Let it be as steadily fixed upon the French, as the Pilot's eye upon his mark. Military stores and arms should be furnished with unfailing liberality: let Troops also be supplied; but let these act separately,—taking strong positions upon the coast, if such can be found, to employ twice their numbers of the Enemy; and, above all, let there be Floating Armies—keeping the Enemy in constant uncertainty where he is to be attacked. The peninsular frame of Spain and Portugal lays that region open to the full shock of British warfare. Our Fleet and Army should act, wherever it is possible, as parts of one body—a right hand and a left; and the Enemy ought to be made to feel the force of both.

But—whatever plans be adopted—there can be no success, unless the execution be entrusted to Generals of competent judgement. That the British Army swarms with those who are incompetent—is too plain from successive proofs in the transactions at Buenos Ayres, at Cintra, and in the result of the Board of Inquiry.—Nor must we see a General appointed to command—and required, at the same time, to frame his operations according to the opinion of an inferior Officer: an injunction (for a recommendation, from such a quarter, amounts to an injunction) implying that a man had been appointed to a high station—of which the very persons, who had appointed him, deemed him unworthy; else they must have known that he would endeavour to profit by the experience of any of his inferior officers, from the suggestions of his own understanding: at the same time—by denying to the General-in-Chief the free use of his own judgement, and by the act of announcing this presumption of his incompetence to the man himself—such an indignity is put upon him, that his passions must of necessity be rouzed; so as to leave it scarcely possible that he could draw any benefit, which he might otherwise have drawn, from the local knowledge or talents of the individual to whom he was referred: and, lastly, this injunction virtually involves a subversion of all military subordination. In the better times of the House of Commons— a minister, who had presumed to write such a letter as that to which I allude, would have been impeached.

The Debates in Parliament, and measures of Government, every day furnish new proofs of the truths which I have been attempting to establish—of the utter want of general principles;—new and lamentable proofs! This moment (while I am drawing towards a conclusion) I learn, from the newspaper reports, that the House of Commons has refused to declare that the Convention of Cintra *disappointed the hopes and expectations of the Nation*.

The motion, according to the letter of it, was ill-framed; for the Convention might have been a very good one, and still have disappointed the hopes and expectations of the Nation—as those might have been unwise: at all events, the words ought to have stood—the *just* and *reasonable* hopes of the Nation. But the hacknied phrase of '*disappointed hopes and expectations*'—should not have been used at all: it is a centre round which much delusion has gathered. The Convention not only did not satisfy the Nation's hopes of good; but sunk it into a pitfall of unimagined and unimaginable evil. The hearts and understandings of the People tell them that the language of a proposed parliamentary resolution, upon this occasion, ought—not only to have been different in the letter—but also widely different in the spirit: and the reader of these pages will have deduced, that no terms of reprobation could in severity exceed the offences involved in—and connected with—that instrument. But, while the grand keep of the castle of iniquity was to be stormed, we have seen nothing but a puny assault upon heaps of the scattered rubbish of the fortress; nay, for the most part, on some accidental mole-hills at its base. I do not speak thus in disrespect to the Right Hon. Gentleman who headed this attack. His mind, left to itself, would (I doubt not) have prompted something worthier and higher: but he moves in the phalanx of Party;— a spiritual Body; in which (by strange inconsistency) the hampering, weakening, and destroying, of every individual mind of which it is composed—is the law which must constitute the strength of the whole. The question was—whether principles, affecting the very existence of Society, had not been violated; and an arm lifted, and let fall, which struck at the root of Honour; with the aggravation of the crime having been committed at this momentous period. But what relation is there between these principles and actions, and being in Place or out of it? If the People would constitutionally and resolutely assert their rights, their Representatives would be taught another lesson; and for their own profit. Their understandings would be enriched accordingly: for it is there—there where least suspected—that the want, from which this country suffers, chiefly lies. They err, who suppose that venality and corruption (though now spreading more and more) are the master-evils of this day: neither these nor immoderate craving for power are so much to be deprecated, as the non-existence of a widely-ranging intellect; of an intellect which, if not efficacious to infuse truth as a vital fluid into the heart, might at least make it a powerful tool in the hand. Outward profession,—which, for practical purposes, is an act of most desirable subservience,—would then wait upon those objects to which inward reverence, though not felt, was known to be due. Schemes of ample reach and true benefit would also promise best to ensure the rewards coveted by personal ambition: and men of baser passions, finding it their interest, would naturally combine to perform useful service under the direction of strong minds: while men of good intentions would have their own pure satisfaction; and would exert themselves with more upright—I mean, more hopeful— cheerfulness, and more successfully. It is not therefore inordinate desire of wealth or power which is so injurious—as the means which are and must be employed, in the present intellectual condition of the Legislature, to sustain and secure that power: these are at once an effect of barrenness, and a cause; acting, and mutually re-acting, incessantly. An enlightened Friend has, in conversation, observed to the Author of these pages—that formerly the principles of men were better than they who held them; but that now (a far worse evil!) men are better than their principles. I believe it:—of the deplorable quality and state of principles, the public proceedings in our Country furnish daily new proof. It is however some consolation, at this present crisis, to find—that, of the thoughts and feelings uttered during the two debates which led me to these painful declarations, such—as approach towards truth which has any dignity in it—come from the side of his Majesty's Ministers.—But note again those contradictions to which I have so often been obliged to advert. The Ministers advise his Majesty publicly to express sentiments of disapprobation upon the Convention of Cintra; and, when the question of the merits or demerits of this instrument comes before them in Parliament, the same persons— who, as advisers of the crown, lately condemned the treaty—now, in their character of representatives of the people, by the manner in which they received this motion, have pronounced an encomium upon it. For, though (as I have said) the motion was inaccurately and inadequately worded, it was not set aside upon this ground. And the Parliament has therefore persisted in withholding, from the insulted and injured People and from their Allies, the only reparation which perhaps it may be in its power to grant; has refused to signify its repentance and sorrow for what bath been done; without which, as a previous step, there can be no proof—no gratifying intimation even, to this Country or to its Allies, that the future efforts of the British Parliament are in a sincere spirit. The guilt of the transaction therefore being neither repented of, nor atoned for; the course of evil is, by necessity, persevered in.—But let us turn to a brighter region.

The events of the last year, gloriously destroying many frail fears, have placed—in the rank of serene and immortal truths—a proposition which, as an object of belief, hath in all ages been fondly cherished; namely—That a numerous Nation, determined to be free, may effect its purpose in despite of the mightiest power which a foreign Invader can bring against it. These events also have pointed out how, in the ways of Nature and under the guidance of Society, this happy end is to be attained: in other words, they have shewn that the cause of the People, in dangers and difficulties issuing from this quarter of oppression, is safe while it remains not only in the bosom but in the hands of the People; or (what amounts to the same thing) in those of a government which, being truly *from* the People, is faithfully *for* them. While the power remained with the provincial Juntas, that is, with the body natural of the community (for those authorities, newly-generated in such adversity, were truly living members of that body); every thing prospered in Spain. Hopes of the best kind were opened out and encouraged; liberal opinions countenanced; and wise measures arranged: and last, and (except as proceeding from these) least of all,—victories in the field, in the streets of the city, and upon the walls of the fortress.

I have heretofore styled it a blessing that the Spanish People became their own masters at once. It *was* a blessing; but not without much alloy: as the same disinterested generous passions, which preserved (and would for a season still have preserved) them from a bad exercise of their power, impelled them to

3477 intimation even, to *M.Y.* i. 343: intimation, even to 1809.

part with it too soon; before labours, hitherto neither tried nor thought-of, had created throughout the country the minor excellences indispensible for the performance of those labours; before powerful minds, not hitherto of general note, had found time to shew themselves; and before men, who were previously known, had undergone the proof of new situations. Much therefore was wanting to direct the general judgement in the choice of persons, when the second delegation took place; which was a removal (the first, we have seen, had not been so) of the power from the People. But, when a common centre became absolutely necessary, the power ought to have passed from the provincial Assemblies into the hands of the Cortes; and into none else. A pernicious Oligarchy crept into the place of this comprehensive—this constitutional—this saving and majestic Assembly. Far be it from me to speak of the Supreme Junta with ill-advised condemnation: every man must feel for the distressful trials to which that Body has been exposed. But eighty men or a hundred, with a king at their head veiled under a cloud of fiction (we might say, with reference to the difficulties of this moment, begotten upon a cloud of fiction), could not be an image of a Nation like that of Spain, or an adequate instrument of their power for their ends. The Assembly, from the smallness of its numbers, must have wanted breadth of wing to extend itself and brood over Spain with a quickening touch of warmth every where. If also, as hath been mentioned, there was a want of experience to determine the judgment in choice of persons; this same smallness of numbers must have unnecessarily increased the evil—by excluding many men of worth and talents which were so far known and allowed as that they would surely have been deputed to an Assembly upon a larger scale. Gratitude, habit, and numerous other causes must have given an undue preponderance to birth, station, rank, and fortune; and have fixed the election, more than was reasonable, upon those who were most conspicuous for these distinctions;—men whose very virtue would incline them superstitiously to respect established things, and to mistrust the People—towards whom not only a frank confidence but a forward generosity was the first of duties. I speak not of the vices to which such men would be liable, brought up under the discipline of a government administered like the old Monarchy of Spain: the matter is both ungracious and too obvious.

But I began with hope; and hope has inwardly accompanied me to the end. The whole course of the campaign, rightly interpreted, has justified my hope. In Madrid, in Ferrol, in Corunna, in every considerable place, and in every part of the country over which the French have re-extended their dominion,—we learn, from their own reports, that the body of the People have shewed against them, to the last, the most determined hostility. Hence it is clear that the lure, which the invading Usurper found himself constrained lately to hold out to the inferior orders of society in the shape of various immunities, has totally failed: and therefore he turns for support to another quarter, and now attempts to cajole the wealthy and the privileged. But this class has been taught, by late Decrees, what it has to expect from him; and how far he is to be confided-in for its especial interests. Many individuals, no doubt, he will seduce; but the bulk of the class, even if they could be insensible to more liberal feelings, cannot but be his enemies. This change, therefore, is not merely shifting ground; but retiring to a position which he himself has previously undermined. Here is confusion; and a power warring against itself.

So will it ever fare with foreign Tyrants when (in spite of domestic abuses) a People, which has lived long, feels that it has a Country to love; and where the heart of that People is sound. Between the native inhabitants of France and Spain there has existed from the earliest period, and still does exist, an universal and utter dissimilitude in laws, actions, deportment, gait, manners, customs: join with this the difference in the language, and the barrier of the Pyrenees; a separation and an opposition in great things, and an antipathy in small. Ignorant then must he be of history and of the reports of travellers and residents in the two countries, or strangely inattentive to the constitution of human nature, who (this being true) can admit the belief that the Spaniards, numerous and powerful as they are, will live under Frenchmen as their lords and masters. Let there be added to this inherent mutual repulsiveness—those recent indignities and horrible outrages; and we need not fear to say that such reconcilement is impossible; even without that further insuperable obstacle which we hope will exist, an establishment of a free Constitution in Spain.—The intoxicated setter-up of Kings may fill his diary with pompous stories of the acclamations with which his solemn puppets are received; he may stuff their mouths with impious asseverations; and hire knees to bend before them, and lips to answer with honied greetings of gratitude and love: these cannot remove the old heart, and put a new one into the bosom of the spectators. The whole is a pageant seen for a day among men in its passage to the "Limbo large and broad" whither, as to their proper home, fleet

> All the unaccomplish'd works of Nature's hand,

> Abortive, monstrous, or unkindly mix'd,
> *Dissolv'd on earth.*

Talk not of the perishable nature of enthusiasm; and rise above a craving for perpetual manifestations of things. He is to be pitied whose eye can only be pierced by the light of a meridian sun, whose frame can only be warmed by the heat of midsummer. Let us hear no more of the little dependence to be had in war upon voluntary service. The things, with which we are primarily and mainly concerned, are inward passions; and not outward arrangements. These latter may be given at any time; when the parts, to be put together, are in readiness. Hatred and love, and each in its intensity, and pride (passions which, existing in the heart of a Nation, are inseparable from hope)—these elements being in constant preparation—enthusiasm will break out from them, or coalesce with them, upon the summons of a moment. And these passions are scarcely less than inextinguishable. The truth of this is recorded in the manners and hearts of North and South Britons, of Englishmen and Welshmen, on either border of the Tweed and of the Esk, on both sides of the Severn and the Dee; an inscription legible, and in strong characters, which the tread of many and great blessings, continued through hundreds of years, has been unable to efface. The Sicilian Vespers are to this day a familiar game among the boys of the villages on the sides of Mount Etna, and through every corner of the Island; and "Exterminate the French!" is the action in their arms, and the word of triumph upon their tongues. He then is a sorry Statist, who desponds or despairs (nor is he less so who is too much elevated) from any considerations connected with the quality of enthusiasm. Nothing is so easy as to sustain it by partial and gradual changes of its object; and by placing it in the way of receiving new interpositions according to the need. The difficulty lies—not in kindling, feeding, or fanning the flame; but in continuing so to regulate the relations of things—that the fanning breeze and the feeding fuel shall come from no unworthy quarter, and shall neither of them be wanting in appropriate consecration. The Spaniards have as great helps towards ensuring this, as ever were vouchsafed to a People.

What then is to be desired? Nothing but that the Government and the higher orders of society should deal sincerely towards the middle class and the lower: I mean, that the general temper should be sincere.—It is not required that every one should be disinterested, or zealous, or of one mind with his fellows. Selfishness or slackness in individuals, and in certain bodies of men also (and at times perhaps in all), have their use: else why should they exist? Due circumspection and necessary activity, in those who are sound, could not otherwise maintain themselves. The deficiencies in one quarter are more than made up by consequent overflowings in another. "If my Neighbour fails," says the true Patriot, "more devolves upon me." Discord and even treason are not, in a country situated as Spain is, the pure evils which, upon superficial view, they appear to be. Never are a people so livelily admonished of the love they bear their country, and of the pride which they have in their common parent, as when they hear of some parricidal attempt of a false brother. For this cause chiefly, in times of national danger, are their fancies so busy in suspicion; which under such shape, though oftentimes producing dire and pitiable effects, is notwithstanding in its general character no other than that habit which has grown out of the instinct of self-preservation—elevated into wakeful and affectionate apprehension for the whole, and ennobling its private and baser ways by the generous use to which they are converted. Nor ever has a good and loyal man such a swell of mind, such a clear insight into the constitution of virtue, and such a sublime sense of its power, as at the first tidings of some atrocious act of perfidy; when, having taken the alarm for human nature, a second thought recovers him; and his faith returns—gladsome from what has been revealed within himself, and awful from participation of the secrets in the profaner grove of humanity which that momentary blast laid open to his view.

Of the ultimate independence of the Spanish Nation there is no reason to doubt: and for the immediate furtherance of the good cause, and a throwing-off of the yoke upon the first favourable opportunity by the different tracts of the country upon which it has been re-imposed, nothing is wanting but sincerity on the part of the government towards the provinces which are yet free. The first end to be secured by Spain is riddance of the enemy: the second, permanent independence: and the third, a free constitution of government; which will give their main (though far from sole) value to the other two; and without which little more than a formal independence, and perhaps scarcely that, can be secured. Humanity and honour, and justice, and all the sacred feelings connected with atonement, retribution, and satisfaction; shame that will not sleep, and the sting of unperformed duty; and all the powers of the mind, the memory that broods over the dead and turns to the living, the understanding, the imagination, and the reason;—demand and enjoin that the wanton oppressor should be driven, with confusion and dismay, from the country which he has so heinously abused.

This cannot be accomplished (scarcely can it be aimed at) without an accompanying and an inseparable resolution, in the souls of the Spaniards, to be and remain their own masters; that is, to preserve themselves in the rank of Men; and not become as the Brute that is driven to the pasture, and cares not who owns him. It is a common saying among those who profess to be lovers of civil liberty, and give themselves some credit for understanding it,—that, if a Nation be not free, it is mere dust in the balance whether the slavery be bred at home, or comes from abroad; be of their own suffering, or of a stranger's imposing. They see little of the under-ground part of the tree of liberty, and know less of the nature of man, who can think thus. Where indeed there is an indisputable and immeasurable superiority in one nation over another; to be conquered may, in course of time, be a benefit to the inferior nation: and, upon this principle, some of the conquests of the Greeks and Romans may be justified. But in what of really useful or honourable are the French superior to their Neighbours? Never far advanced, and, now barbarizing apace, they may carry—amongst the sober and dignified Nations which surround them—much to be avoided, but little to be imitated.

There is yet another case in which a People may be benefited by resignation or forfeiture of their rights as a separate independent State; I mean, where—of two contiguous or neighbouring countries, both included by nature under one conspicuously defined limit—the weaker is united with, or absorbed into, the more powerful; and one and the same Government is extended over both. This, with due patience and foresight, may (for the most part) be amicably effected, without the intervention of conquest; but—even should a violent course have been resorted to, and have proved successful—the result will be matter of congratulation rather than of regret, if the countries have been incorporated with an equitable participation of natural advantages and civil privileges. Who does not rejoice that former partitions have disappeared,—and that England, Scotland, and Wales, are under one legislative and executive authority; and that Ireland (would that she had been more justly dealt with!) follows the same destiny? The large and numerous Fiefs, which interfered injuriously with the grand demarcation assigned by nature to France, have long since been united

3671 (for the most part) 1809: always G.
3673 be G^{2}, 1809: furnish G.
3674–5 if the countries ... privileges G^{2}, 1809: if arrangements be made for incorporating the conquered Country according to the principles of justice that is for an equitable participation of natural advantages and civil privileges G.
3680 by nature G^{2}, 1809: *om.* G.

and consolidated. The several independent Sovereignties of Italy (a country, the boundary of which is still more expressly traced out by nature; and which has no less the further definition and cement of country which Language prepares) have yet this good to aim at: and it will be a happy day for Europe, when the natives of Italy and the natives of Germany (whose duty is, in like manner, indicated to them) shall each dissolve the pernicious barriers which divide them, and form themselves into a mighty People. But Spain, excepting a free union with Portugal, has no benefit of this kind to look for: she has long since attained it. The Pyrenees on the one side, and the Sea on every other; the vast extent and great resources of the territory; a population numerous enough to defend itself against the whole world, and capable of great increase; language; and long duration of independence;—point out and command that the two nations of the Peninsula should be united in friendship and strict alliance; and, as soon as it may be effected without injustice, form one independent and indissoluble sovereignty. The Peninsula cannot be protected but by itself: it is too large a tree to be framed by nature for a station among underwoods; it must have power to toss its branches in the wind, and lift a bold forehead to the sun.

Allowing that the "regni novitas" should either compel or tempt the Usurper to do away some ancient abuses, and to accord certain insignificant privileges to the People upon the purlieus of the forest of Freedom (for assuredly he will never suffer them to enter the body of it); allowing this, and much more; that the mass of the Population would be placed in a condition outwardly more thriving—would be *better off* (as the phrase in conversation is); it is still true that—in the act and consciousness of submission to an imposed lord and master, to a will not growing out of themselves, to the edicts of another People their triumphant enemy—there would be the loss of a sensation within for which nothing external, even though it should come close to the garden and the field—to the door and the fire-side, can make amends. The Artisan and the Merchant (men of classes perhaps least attached to their

3684 happy 1809: glorious G.
3686 the G^2, 1809: their G. which G^2, 1809: that G.
3687 mighty G^2, 1809: free and mighty G.
3688 Portugal G^2, 1809: Portugal an event most desirable G.
3688–9 she has ... attained it G^2, 1809: *om.* G.
3691 great 1809: mighty G.
3695 sovereignty. The Peninsula ... sun G^2, 1809: sovereignty of justice and without a pretext of expediency from unprincipled and sens[e]less ambition G.
3703 more G^2, 1809: more though most improbable G.
3706 not 1809: not residing in and G.

native soil) would not be insensible to this loss; and the Mariner, in his thoughtful mood, would sadden under it upon the wide ocean. The central or cardinal feeling of these thoughts may, at a future time, furnish fit matter for the genius of some patriotic Spaniard to express in his own noble language—as an inscription for the Sword of Francis the First; if that Sword, which was so ingloriously and perfidiously surrendered, should ever, by the energies of Liberty, be recovered, and deposited in its ancient habitation in the Escurial. The Patriot will recollect that,—if the memorial, then given up by the hand of the Government, had also been abandoned by the heart of the People, and that indignity patiently subscribed to,—his country would have been lost for ever.

There are multitudes by whom, I know, these sentiments will not be languidly received at this day; and sure I am—that, a hundred and fifty years ago, they would have been ardently welcomed by all. But, in many parts of Europe (and especially in our own country), men have been pressing forward, for some time, in a path which has betrayed by its fruitfulness; furnishing them constant employment for picking up things about their feet, when thoughts were perishing in their minds. While Mechanic Arts, Manufactures, Agriculture, Commerce, and all those products of knowledge which are confined to gross—definite—and tangible objects, have, with the aid of Experimental Philosophy, been every day putting on more brilliant colours; the splendour of the Imagination has been fading: Sensibility, which was formerly a generous

3713 a G^{2}, 1809: some G.

3714 express 1809: be expressed G.

3716–7 by … Liberty G^{2}, 1809: *om.* G.

3718 memorial G^{2}, 1809: monument G.

3721 There … not G^{3}, 1809: These sentiments will not I know [hope G^{2}] by tens of thousands G.

3726 when 1809: while G.

3727 *After* minds. *the following passage, eventually deleted entirely, appears in* G:

Lord Bacon two hundred years ago announced that knowledge was power and strenuously recommended the process of experiment and induction for attainment of knowledge. But the mind of this Philosopher was comprehensive and sublime and must have had intimate communion of the truth of which the experimentalists who deem themselves his disciples are for the most part ignorant viz. that knowledge of facts conferring power over the combinations of things in the material world has no determinate connection with power over the faculties of the mind. Nay so far is such encrease from being a necessary result that it is scarcely possible to [? strengthen] and unite the two species of power in such a manner that the more noble shall not lag behind in proportion to the rapid and eager advancement of the less noble. Let it not be supposed that I am blind to the power of intellect which has been [? put forth] in the improvement of experimental philosophy and the mechanic arts [? or under subjects] the various and great benefits which have proceeded from them or may proceed from these [? inquiries but] in justice [*tear*] the principles which I have undertaken to maintain I am [*tear*]mpelled to direct the Readers attention to these truths, that he may not overlook the rights and titles of superiority inherent in things. For the same cause I nursling of rude Nature, has been chased from its ancient range in the wide domain of patriotism and religion with the weapons of derision by a shadow calling itself Good Sense: calculations of presumptuous Expediency—groping its way among partial and temporary consequences—have been substituted for the dictates of paramount and infallible Conscience, the supreme embracer of consequences: lifeless and circumspect Decencies have banished the graceful negligence and unsuspicious dignity of Virtue.

The progress of these arts also, by furnishing such attractive stores of outward accommodation, has misled the higher orders of society in their more

must add that great and even mighty as is the relative worth of the products of natural science and its industrious associates yet absolute and unconditional worth they have none. They are not even gifted with the power of self-preservation. Innumerable inventions and abilities of this kind and of a very high order perished with the dissolution of morals and consequent wearing-away of intellect, in the declining empire of Rome. Unless as far as these acquisitions are subservient through civil liberty to moral greatness and purity, they are of no more value in the eye of Reason than the shells and pebbles which Caligula gathered up from the shores of Britain and exhibited to his Slaves in the majestic City as a recompense of an expedition and the spoils of a Conquest. ▶

Having said this I will not follow it with a charge which I have not, at present, time to substantiate against these pursuits as the cause indirectly of a course of obtuse and mechanical habits of thinking on moral investigations and as a source directly of degrading moral habits, it is enough to suggest to the Reader that while we have been making large encrease of gains on one side these gains have withdrawn our attention from great loss on the other. G.

Lord Bacon two centuries ago announced that knowledge was power and justified by the wrong practice which had till that time generally prevailed and by the wants which were then most pressing he strenuously recommended physical investigation to be carried on by induction and experiment for the attainment of knowledge. But knowledge of facts conferring power over the combinations of things in the material world has no necessary connection with encrease of power in the constitution and faculties of the mind, either in the mind of the individual or in the general mind of the age. Nay so far … in such manner that … the less noble. Injustice … the products of natural science and the mechanic arts its industrious associates … Innumerable discoveries inventions … these acquisitions are subservient to moral greatness … as the cause directly of obtuse feeling towards the nobler moral impressions and of a course of (see the end of last sheet) mechanical thinking on moral investigations and as a source directly of degrading moral habits, thus countenancing and aggravating that evil which [? excess] [of which *del.*] (as I have heretofore proved) [? inseparably] adheres to the minds of ordinary practical statesmen it is enough to suggest that while we have been making large gains on one side … on the other. G².

3727–8 Agriculture, Commerce 1809: agriculture and commerce G.

3730 the splendour … has 1809: religion and the splendour … have G.

3732–3 range … derision 1809: range with the weapons of sneer and derision G.

3734 calculations of G², 1809: *om.* G.

3739 also G2, 1809: also (this I venture to assert because no train of reasoning is required to establish the truth) G.

disinterested exertions for the service of the lower. Animal comforts have been rejoiced over, as if they were the end of being. A neater and more fertile garden; a greener field; implements and utensils more apt; a dwelling more commodious and better furnished;—let these be attained, say the actively benevolent, and we are sure not only of being in the right road, but of having successfully terminated our journey. Now a country may advance, for some time, in this course with apparent profit: these accommodations, by zealous encouragement, may be attained: and still the Peasant or Artisan, their master, be a slave in mind; a slave rendered even more abject by the very tenure under which these possessions are held: and—if they veil from us this fact, or reconcile us to it—they are worse than worthless. The springs of emotion may be relaxed or destroyed within him; he may have little thought of the past, and less interest in the future.—The great end and difficulty of life for men of all classes, and especially difficult for those who live by manual labour, is a union of peace with innocent and laudable animation. Not by bread alone is the life of Man sustained; not by raiment alone is he warmed;—but by the genial and vernal inmate of the breast, which at once pushes forth and cherishes; by self-support and self-sufficing endeavours; by anticipations, apprehensions, and active remembrances; by elasticity under insult, and firm resistance to injury; by joy, and by love; by pride which his imagination gathers in from afar; by patience, because life wants not promises; by admiration; by gratitude which—debasing him not when his fellow-being is its object—habitually expands itself, for his elevation, in complacency towards his Creator.

3743 field 1809: Croft G.
3744 benevolent G2, 1809: charitable G.
3746–8 a country … encouragement 1809: all these G.
3748–50 a slave … held: 1809: an abject Slave G.
3750–1 or … it G^2, 1809: *om.* G.
3753 future. G^3, 1809: future. Having no craving he may appear to be contented and deem himself so, but the fullness of his mind is not like the fullness of the pool in the mountains or of the Lake in the [? Vale] ample measure of living and circulating waters, receiving and discharging—its contents are like the basons [basons (*pots of the Lyn*) G^2] which the Wanderer by the side of the brooks finds scooped out in the hard rock by the floods which have passed away; such only may be his mind and the stores which it contains—fed by no springs within itself agitated by by [sic] no breezes, exhaled by no sunshine—tranquil, but sullen [joyless G^2] in its tranquillity. G.
3753–5 The great … animation] *In G, written in Wordsworth's hand on the address panel, crossing the address, and with so much alteration as to be almost illegible.*
3757 inmate of 1809: inmate in G.
3758 anticipations] *del. from* G. remembrances; G^2, 1809: remembrances; by hopes which if not [? manifold] are continuous and which when embodied in action [? fail] not for want of [? alacrity] G.

Now, to the existence of these blessings, national independence is indispensible; and many of them it will itself produce and maintain. For it is some consolation to those who look back upon the history of the world to know—that, even without civil liberty, society may possess—diffused through its inner recesses in the minds even of its humblest members—something of dignified enjoyment. But, without national independence, this is impossible. The difference, between inbred oppression and that which is from without, is *essential*; inasmuch as the former does not exclude, from the minds of a people, the feeling of being self-governed; does not imply (as the latter does, when patiently submitted to) an abandonment of the first duty imposed by the faculty of reason. In reality: where this feeling has no place, a people are not a society, but a herd; man being indeed distinguished among them from the brute; but only to his disgrace. I am aware that there are too many who think that, to the bulk of the community, this independence is of no value; that it is a refinement with which they feel they have no concern; inasmuch as, under the best frame of Government, there is an inevitable dependence of the poor upon the rich—of the many upon the few—so unrelenting and imperious as to reduce this other, by comparison, into a force which has small influence, and is entitled to no regard. Superadd civil liberty to national independence; and this position is overthrown at once: for there is no more certain mark of a sound frame of polity than this; that, in all individual instances (and it is upon these generalized that this position is down), the dependence is in reality far more strict on the side of the wealthy; and the labouring man leans less upon others than any man in the community.—But the case before us is of a country not internally free, yet supposed capable of repelling an external enemy who attempts its subjugation. If a country have put on chains of its own forging; in the name of virtue, let it be conscious that to itself it is accountable: let it not have cause to look beyond its own limits for reproof: and,—in the name of humanity,—if it be self-depressed, let it have its pride and some hope within itself. The poorest Peasant, in an unsubdued land, feels this pride. I do not appeal to the example of Britain or of Switzerland, for the one is free, and the other lately was free (and, I trust, will ere long be so again): but talk with the Swede; and you will see the joy he finds in these sensations. With him animal courage (the substitute for many and the friend of all the manly virtues) has space to move in; and is at once elevated by his im-

3766 those ... look G[2], 1809: him ... looks G.
3767 possess G[2], 1809: have G.
3768 even ... members G[2], 1809: of men G.
3769–76 The difference ... disgrace. 1809: *om.* G.
3778 they feel 1809: *om.* G.
3781 has ... and G[2], 1809: *om.* G.

agination, and softened by his affections: it is invigorated also; for the whole courage of his Country is in his breast.

In fact: the Peasant, and he who lives by the fair reward of his manual labour, has ordinarily a larger proportion of his gratifications dependent upon these thoughts—than, for the most part, men in other classes have. For he is in his person attached, by stronger roots, to the soil of which he is the growth: his intellectual notices are generally confined within narrower bounds: in him no partial or antipatriotic interests counteract the force of those nobler sympathies and antipathies which he has in right of his Country; and lastly the belt or girdle of his mind has never been stretched to utter relaxation by false philosophy, under a conceit of making it sit more easily and gracefully. These sensations are a social inheritance to him; more important, as he is precluded from luxurious—and those which are usually called refined—enjoyments.

Love and admiration must push themselves out towards some quarter: otherwise the moral man is killed. Collaterally they advance with great vigour to a certain extent—and they are checked: in that direction, limits hard to pass are perpetually encountered: but upwards and downwards, to ancestry and to posterity, they meet with gladsome help and no obstacles; the tract is interminable—Perdition to the Tyrant who would wantonly cut off an independent Nation from its inheritance in past ages; turning the tombs and burial-places of the Forefathers into dreaded objects of sorrow, or of shame and reproach, for the Children! Look upon Scotland and Wales: though, by the union of these with England under the same Government (which was effected without conquest in one instance), ferocious and desolating wars, and more injurious intrigues, and sapping and disgraceful corruptions, have been prevented; and tranquillity, security, and prosperity, and a thousand interchanges of amity, not otherwise attainable, have followed;—yet the flashing eye, and the agitated voice, and all the tender recollections, with which the names of Prince Llewellin and William Wallace are to this day pronounced by the fire-side and on the public road, attest that these substantial blessings have not been purchased without the relinquishment of something most salutary to the moral nature of Man: else the remembrances would not cleave so faithfully to their abiding-place in the human heart. But, if these affections be of general interest, they are of especial interest to Spain; whose history, written and traditional, is pre-eminently stored with the sustaining food of such affections: and in no country are they more justly and generally prized, or more feelingly cherished.

In the conduct of this argument I am not speaking *to* the humbler ranks of society: it is unnecessary: *they* trust in nature, and are safe. The People of Madrid, and Corunna, and Ferrol, resisted to the last; from an impulse which, in their hearts, was its own justification. The failure was with those who stood higher in the scale. In fact; the universal rising of the Peninsula, under the pressure and in the face of the most tremendous military power which ever existed, is evidence which cannot be too much insisted upon; and is decisive upon this subject, as involving a question of virtue and moral sentiment. All ranks were penetrated with one feeling: instantaneous and universal was the acknowledgement. If there have been since individual fallings-off; those have been caused by that kind of after-thoughts which are the bastard offspring of selfishness. The matter was brought home to Spain; and no Spaniard has offended herein with a still conscience.—It is to the worldlings of our own country, and to those who think without carrying their thoughts far enough, that I address myself. Let them know, there is no true wisdom without imagination; no genuine sense ;—that the man, who in this age feels no regret for the ruined honour of other Nations, must be poor in sympathy for the honour of his own Country; and that, if he be wanting here towards that which circumscribes the whole, he neither has—nor can have— a social regard for the lesser communities which Country includes. Contract the circle, and bring him to his family; such a man cannot protect *that* with dignified love. Reduce his thoughts to his own person; he may defend himself,—what *he* deems his honour; but it is the *action* of a brave man from the impulse of the brute, or the motive of a coward.

But it is time to recollect that this vindication of human feeling began from an *hypothesis*,—that the *outward* state of the mass of the Spanish people would be improved by the French usurpation. To this I now give an unqualified denial. Let me also observe to those men, for whose infirmity this hypothesis was tolerated,—that the true point of comparison does not lie between what the Spaniards have been under a government of their own, and what they may become under French domination; but between what the Spaniards may do (and, in all likelihood, will do) for themselves, and what Frenchmen would do for them. But,—waiving this,—the sweeping away of the most splendid monuments of art, and rifling of the public treasuries in the conquered countries, are an apt prologue to the tragedy which is to ensue. Strange that there are

3854 love *M.Y.* i. 343: loves 1809.

men who can be so besotted as to see, in the decrees of the Usurper concerning feudal tenures and a worn-out inquisition, any other evidence than that of insidiousness and of a constrained acknowledgement of the strength which he felt he had to overcome. What avail the lessons of history, if men can be duped thus? Boons and promises of this kind rank, in trustworthiness, many degrees lower than amnesties after expelled kings have recovered their thrones. The fate of subjugated Spain may be expressed in these words, pillage—depression—and helotism—for the supposed aggrandizement of the imaginary freeman its master. There would indeed be attempts at encouragement, that there might be a supply of something to pillage: studied depression there would be, that there might arise no power of resistance: and lastly helotism;—but of what kind? that a vain and impious Nation might have slaves, worthier than itself, for work which its own hands would reject with scorn.

What good can the present arbitrary power confer upon France itself? Let that point be first settled by those who are inclined to look farther. The earlier proceedings of the French Revolution no doubt infused health into the country; something of which survives to this day: but let not the now-existing Tyranny have the credit of it. France neither owes, nor can owe, to this any rational obligation. She has seen decrees without end for the increase of commerce and manufactures; pompous stories without number of harbours, canals, warehouses, and bridges: but there is no worse sign in the management of affairs than when that, which ought to follow as an effect, goes before under a vain notion that it will be a cause.—Let us attend to the springs of action, and we shall not be deceived. The works of peace cannot flourish in a country governed by an intoxicated Despot; the motions of whose distorted benevolence must be still more pernicious than those of his cruelty. "*I have bestowed; I have created; I have regenerated; I have been pleased to organize;*"—this is the language perpetually upon his lips, when his ill-fated activities turn that way. Now commerce, manufactures, agriculture, and all the peaceful arts, are of the nature of virtues or intellectual powers: they cannot be given; they cannot be stuck in here and there; they must spring up; they must grow of themselves: they may be encouraged; they thrive better with encouragement, and delight in it; but the obligation must have bounds nicely defined; for they are delicate, proud, and independent. But a Tyrant has no joy in any thing which is endued with such excellence: he sickens at the sight of it: he turns away from it, as an insult to his own attributes. We have seen the present ruler of France publicly addressed as a Providence upon earth; styled, among innumerable other blasphemies, the supreme Ruler of things; and heard him say, in his answers, that he approved of the language of those who thus saluted him. (*See* Appendix E.)—Oh folly to think that plans of reason can prosper under such countenance! If this be the doom of France, what a monster would be the double-headed tyranny of Spain!

It is immutably ordained that power, taken and exercised in contempt of right, never can bring forth good. Wicked actions indeed have oftentimes happy issues: the benevolent economy of nature counter-working and diverting evil; and educing finally benefits from injuries, and turning curses to blessings. But I am speaking of good in a direct course. All good in this order—all moral good—begins and ends in reverence of right. The whole Spanish People are to be treated not as a mighty multitude with feeling, will, and judgment; not as rational creatures;—but as objects without reason; in the language of human law, insuperably laid down not as Persons but as Things. Can good come from this beginning; which, in matter of civil government, is the fountain-head and the main feeder of all the pure evil upon earth? Look at the past history of our sister Island for the quality of foreign oppression: turn where you will, it is miserable at best; but, in the case of Spain!—it might be said, engraven upon the rocks of her own Pyrenees,

Per me si va nella città dolente;
Per me si va nell' eterno dolore;
Per me si va tra la perduta gente.

So much I have thought it necessary to speak upon this subject; with a desire to enlarge the views of the short-sighted, to chear the desponding, and stimulate the remiss. I have been treating of duties which the People of Spain feel to be solemn and imperious; and have referred to springs of action (in the sensations of love and hatred, of hope and fear),—for promoting the fulfilment of these duties,—which cannot fail. The People of Spain, thus animated, will move now; and will be prepared to move, upon a favourable summons, for ages. And it is consolatory to think that,—even if many of the leading persons of that country, in their resistance to France, should not look beyond the two first objects (viz. riddance of the enemy, and security of national independence);—it is, I say, consolatory to think that the conduct, which can alone secure either of these ends, leads directly to a free internal Government. We have therefore both the passions and the reason of these men on our side in two stages of the common journey: and, when this is the case, surely we are justified in expecting some further companionship and support from their reason—acting independent of their partial interests, or in opposition to them. It is obvious that, to the narrow policy of this class (men loyal to the Nation and to the King, yet jealous of the People), the most dangerous failures, which have hitherto taken place, are to be attributed: for, though from acts of open treason Spain may suffer and has suffered much, these (as I have proved) can never affect the vitals of the cause. But the march of Liberty has begun; and they, who will not lead, may be borne along.—At all events, the road is plain. Let members for the Cortes be assembled from those Provinces which are not in the possession of the Invader: or at least (if circumstances render this impossible at present) let it be announced that such is the intention, to be realized the first moment when it shall become possible. In the mean while speak boldly to the People: and let the People write and speak boldly. Let the expectation be familiar to them of open and manly institutions of law and liberty according to knowledge. Let them be universally trained to military exercises, and accustomed to military discipline: let them be drawn together in civic and religious assemblies; and general communication of those assemblies with each other be established through the country: so that there may be one zeal and one life in every part of it.

With great profit might the Chiefs of the Spanish Nation look back upon the earlier part of the French Revolution. Much, in the outward manner, might there be found worthy of qualified imitation: and, where there is a difference in the inner spirit (and there is a mighty difference!), the advantage is wholly on the side of the Spaniards.— Why should the People of Spain be dreaded by their leaders? I do not mean the profligate and flagitious leaders; but those who are well-intentioned, yet timid. That there are numbers of this class who have excellent intentions, and are willing to make large personal sacrifices, is clear; for they have put every thing to risk—all their privileges, their honours, and possessions—by their resistance to the Invader. Why then should they have fears from a quarter—whence their safety must come, if it come at all?—Spain has nothing to dread from Jacobinism. Manufactures and Commerce have there in far less degree than elsewhere—by unnaturally clustering the people together—enfeebled their bodies, inflamed their passions by intemperance, vitiated from childhood their moral affections, and destroyed their imaginations. Madrid is no enormous city, like Paris; overgrown, and disproportionate; sickening and bowing down, by its corrupt humours, the frame of the body politic. Nor has the pestilential philosophism of France made any progress in Spain. No flight of infidel harpies has alighted upon their ground. A Spanish understanding is a hold too strong to give way to the meagre tactics of the "Systême de la Nature;" or to the pellets of logic which Condillac has cast in the foundry of national vanity, and tosses about at hap-hazard— self-persuaded that he is proceeding according to art. The Spaniards are a people with imagination: and the paradoxical reveries of Rousseau, and the flippancies of Voltaire, are plants which will not naturalise in the country of Calderon and Cervantes. Though bigotry among the Spaniards leaves much to be lamented; I have proved that the religious habits of the nation must, in a contest of this kind, be of inestimable service.

Yet further: contrasting the present condition of Spain with that of France at the commencement of her revolution, we must not overlook one characteristic; the Spaniards have no division among themselves by and through themselves; no numerous Priesthood—no Nobility—no large body of powerful Burghers—from passion, interest, and conscience—opposing the end which is known and felt to be the duty and only honest and true interest of all. Hostility, wherever it is found, must proceed from the seductions of the Invader: and these depend solely upon his power: let that be shattered; and they vanish.

And this once again leads us directly to that immense military force which the Spaniards have to combat; and which, many think, more than counterbalances every internal advantage. It is indeed formidable: as revolutionary appetites and energies must needs be; when, among a people numerous as the people of France, they have ceased to spend themselves in conflicting factions within the country for objects perpetually changing shape; and are carried out of it under the strong controul of an absolute despotism, as opportunity invites, for a definite object—plunder and conquest. It is, I allow, a frightful spectacle—to see the prime of a vast nation propelled out of their territory with the rapid sweep of a horde of Tartars; moving from the impulse of like savage instincts; and furnished, at the same time, with those implements of physical destruction which have been produced by science and civilization. Such are the motions of the French armies; unchecked by any thought which philosophy and the spirit of society, progressively humanizing, have called forth—to determine or regulate the application of the murderous and desolating apparatus with which by philosophy and science they have been provided. With a like perversion of things, and the same mischievous reconcilement of forces in their nature adverse, these revolutionary impulses and these appetites of barbarous (nay, what is far worse, of barbarized) men are embodied in a new frame of polity; which possesses the consistency of an ancient Government, without its embarrassments and weaknesses. And at the head of all is the mind of one man who acts avowedly upon the principle that every thing, which can be done safely by the supreme power of a state, may be done (See *Appendix F.*); and who has, at his command, the greatest part of the continent of Europe—to fulfil what yet remains unaccomplished of his nefarious purposes.

Now it must be obvious to a reflecting mind that every thing which is desperately immoral, being in its constitution monstrous, is of itself perishable: decay it cannot escape; and, further, it is liable to sudden dissolution: time would evince this in the instance before us; though not, perhaps, until infinite and irreparable harm had been done. But, even at present, each of the sources of this preternatural strength (as far as it is formidable to Europe) has its corresponding seat of weakness; which, were it fairly touched, would manifest itself immediately.—The power is indeed a Colossus: but, if the trunk be of molten-brass, the members are of clay; and would fall to pieces upon a shock which need not be violent. Great Britain, if her energies were properly called forth and directed, might (as we have already maintained) give this shock. "Magna parvis obscurantur" was the appropriate motto (the device a Sun Eclipsed) when Lord Peterborough, with a handful of men opposed to fortified cities and large armies, brought a great part of Spain to acknowledge a sovereign of the House of Austria. We have *now* a vast military force; and,—even without a Peterborough or a Marlborough,—at this precious opportunity (when, as is daily more probable, a large portion of the French force must march northwards to combat Austria) we might easily, by expelling the French from the Peninsula, secure an immediate footing there for liberty; and the Pyrenees would then be shut against them for ever. The disciplined troops of Great Britain might overthrow the enemy in the field; while the Patriots of Spain, under wise management, would be able to consume him slowly but surely.

For present annoyance his power is, no doubt, mighty: but liberty—in which it originated, and of which it is a depravation—is far mightier; and the good in human nature is stronger than the evil. The events of our age indeed have brought this truth into doubt with some persons: and scrupulous observers have been astonished and have repined at the sight of enthusiasm, courage, perseverance, and fidelity, put forth seemingly to their height,—and all engaged in the furtherance of wrong. But the minds of men are not always devoted to this bad service as strenuously as they appear to be. I have personal knowledge that, when the attack was made which ended in the subjugation of Switzerland, the injustice of the undertaking was grievously oppressive to many officers of the French army; and damped their exertions. Besides, were it otherwise, there is no just cause for despondency in the perverted alliance of these qualities with oppression. The intrinsic superiority of virtue and liberty, even for politic ends, is not affected by it. If the tide of success were, by any effort, fairly turned ;—not only a general desertion, as we have the best reason to believe, would follow among the troops of the enslaved nations; but a moral change would also take place in the minds of the native French soldiery. Occasion would be given for the discontented to break out; and, above all, for the triumph of human nature, it would *then* be seen whether men fighting in a bad cause,—men without magnanimity, honour, or justice,—could recover; and stand up against champions who by these virtues were carried forward in good fortune, as by these virtues in adversity they had been sustained. As long as guilty actions thrive, guilt is strong: it has a giddiness and transport of its own; a hardihood not without superstition, as if Providence were a party to its success. But there is no independent spring at the heart of the machine which can be relied upon for a support of these motions in a change of circumstances. Disaster opens the eyes of conscience; and, in the minds of men who have been employed in bad actions, defeat and a feeling of punishment are inseparable.

On the other hand; the power of an unblemished heart and a brave spirit is shewn, in the events of war, not only among unpractised citizens and peasants; but among troops in the most perfect discipline. Large bodies of the British army have been several times broken—that is, technically vanquished—in Egypt, and elsewhere. Yet they, who were conquered as formal soldiers, stood their ground and became conquerors as men. This paramount efficacy of moral causes is not willingly admitted by persons high in the profession of arms; because it seems to diminish their value in society—by taking from the importance of their art: but the truth is indisputable: and those Generals are as blind to their own interests as to the interests of their country, who, by submitting to inglorious treaties or by other misconduct, hazard the breaking down of those

4103 nature, it *M.Y.* i. 545: nature. It 1809.

personal virtues in the men under their command—to which they themselves, as leaders, are mainly indebted for the fame which they acquire.

Combine, with this moral superiority inherent in the cause of Freedom, the endless resources open to a nation which shews constancy in defensive war; resources which, after a lapse of time, leave the strongest invading army comparatively helpless. Before six cities, resisting as Saragossa hath resisted during her two sieges, the whole of the military power of the adversary would melt away. Without any advantages of natural situation; without fortifications; without even a ditch to protect them; with nothing better than a mud wall; with not more than two hundred regular troops; with a slender stock of arms and ammunition; with a leader inexperienced in war;—the Citizens of Saragossa began the contest. Enough of what was needful—was produced and created; and—by courage, fortitude, and skill, rapidly matured—they baffled for sixty days, and finally repulsed, a large French army with all its equipments. In the first siege the natural and moral victory were both on their side; nor less so virtually (though the termination was different) in the second. For, after another resistance of nearly three months, they have given the enemy cause feelingly to say, with Pyrrhus of old,—"A little more of such conquest, and I am destroyed."

If evidence were wanting of the efficacy of the principles which throughout this Treatise have been maintained,—it has been furnished in overflowing measure. A private individual, I had written; and knew not in what manner tens of thousands were enacting, day after day, the truths which, in the solitude of a peaceful vale, I was meditating. Most gloriously have the Citizens of Saragossa proved that the true army of Spain, in a contest of this nature, is the whole people. The same city has also exemplified a melancholy—yea a dismal truth; yet consolatory, and full of joy; that,—when a people are called suddenly to fight for their liberty, and are sorely pressed upon, —their best field of battle is the floors upon which their children have played; the chambers where the family of each man has slept (his own or his neighbours'); upon or under the roofs by which they have been sheltered; in the gardens of their recreation; in the street, or in the market-place; before the Altars of their Temples; and among their congregated dwellings—blazing, or up-rooted.

The Government of Spain must never forget Saragossa for a moment. Nothing is wanting, to produce the same effects every where, but a leading mind such as that city was blessed with. In the latter contest this has been proved;

for Saragossa contained, at that time, bodies of men from almost all parts of Spain. The narrative of those two sieges should be the manual of every Spaniard: he may add to it the ancient stories of Numantia and Saguntum: let him sleep upon the book as pillow; and, if he be a devout adherent to the religion of his country, let him wear it in his bosom for his crucifix to rest upon.

Beginning from these invincible feelings, and the principles of justice which are involved in them; let nothing be neglected, which policy and prudence dictate, for rendering subservient to the same end those qualities in human nature which are indifferent or even morally bad; and for making the selfish propensities contribute to the support of wise arrangements, civil and military.—Perhaps there never appeared in the field more steady soldiers—troops which it would have been more difficult to conquer with such knowledge of the art of war as then existed—than those commanded by Fairfax and Cromwell: let us see from what root these armies grew. "Cromwell," says Sir Philip Warwick, "made use of the zeal and credulity of these persons" (that is—such of the people as had, in the author's language, the fanatic humour); "teaching them (as they too readily taught themselves) that they engaged for God, when he led them against his vicegerent the King. And, where this opinion met with a natural courage, it made them bolder—and too often crueller; and, where natural courage wanted, zeal supplied its place. And at first they chose rather to die than flee; and custom removed fear of danger: and afterwards—finding the sweet of good pay, and of opulent plunder, and of preferment suitable to activity and merit—the lucrative part made gain seem to them a natural member of godliness. And I cannot here omit" (continues the author) "a character of this army which General Fairfax gave unto myself; when, complimenting him with the regularity and temperance of his army, he told me, The best common soldiers he had—came out of our army and from the garrisons he had taken in. So (says he) I found you had made them good soldiers; and I have made them good men. But, upon this whole matter, it may appear" (concludes the author) "that the spirit of discipline of warr may beget that spirit of discipline which even Solomon describes as the spirit of wisdom and obedience." Apply this process to the growth and maturity of an armed force in Spain. In making a comparison of the two cases; to the sense of the insults and injuries which, as Spaniards and as human Beings, they have received and have to dread,—and to the sanctity which an honourable resistance has already conferred upon their misfortunes,—add the devotion of that people to their religion as Catholics;—and it will not be doubted that the superiority of the radical feeling is, on their side, immeasurable. There is (I cannot refrain from observing) in the Catholic religion, and in the character of its Priesthood especially, a source of animation and fortitude in desperate struggles—which may be relied upon as one of the best hopes of the cause. The narrative of the first siege of Zaragoza, lately published in this country, and which I earnestly recommend to the reader's perusal, informs us that,—"In every part of the town where the danger was most imminent, and the French the most numerous,—was Padre St. Iago Sass, curate of a parish in Zaragoza. As General Palafox made his rounds through the city, he often beheld Sass alternately playing the part of a Priest and a Soldier; sometimes administering the sacrament to the dying; and, at others, fighting in the most determined manner against the enemies of his country.—He was found so serviceable in inspiring the people with religious sentiments, and in leading them on to danger, that the General has placed him in a situation where both his piety and courage may continue to be as useful as before; and he is now both Captain in the army, and Chaplain to the commander-in-chief."

The reader will have been reminded, by the passage above cited from Sir Philip Warwick's memoirs, of the details given, in the earlier part of this tract, concerning the course which (as it appeared to me) might with advantage be pursued in Spain: I must request him to combine those details with such others as have since been given: the whole would have been further illustrated, if I could sooner have returned to the subject; but it was first necessary to examine the grounds of hope in the grand and disinterested passions, and in the laws of universal morality. My attention has therefore been chiefly directed to these laws and passions; in order to elevate, in some degree, the conceptions of my readers; and with a wish to rectify and fix, in this fundamental point, their judgements. The truth of the general reasoning will, I have no doubt, be acknowledged by men of uncorrupted natures and practised understandings; and the conclusion, which I have repeatedly drawn, will be acceded to; namely, that no resistance can be prosperous which does not look, for its chief support, to these principles and feelings. If, however, there should be men who still fear (as I have been speaking of things under combinations which are transitory) that the action of these powers cannot be sustained; to such I answer that,—if there be a necessity that it should be sustained at the point to which it first ascended, or should recover that height if there have been a fall,—nature will

4163 where *Errata*: were 1809.

provide for that necessity. The cause is in Tyranny: and that will again call forth the effect out of its holy retirements. Oppression, its own blind and predestined enemy, has poured this of blessedness upon Spain,—that the enormity of the outrages, of which she has been the victim, has created an object of love and of hatred—of apprehensions and of wishes—adequate (if that be possible) to the utmost demands of the human spirit. The heart that serves in this cause, if it languish, must languish from its own constitutional weakness; and not through want of nourishment from without. But it is a belief propagated in books, and which passes currently among talking men as part of their familiar wisdom, that the hearts of the many *are* constitutionally weak; that they *do* languish; and are slow to answer to the requisitions of things. I entreat those, who are in this delusion, to look behind them and about them for the evidence of experience. Now this, rightly understood, not only gives no support to any such belief; but proves that the truth is in direct opposition to it. The history of all ages; tumults after tumults; wars, foreign or civil, with short or with no breathing-spaces, from generation to generation; wars—why and wherefore? yet with courage, with perseverance, with self-sacrifice, with enthusiasm—with cruelty driving forward the cruel man from its own terrible nakedness, and attracting the more benign by the accompaniment of some shadow which seems to sanctify it; the senseless weaving and interweaving of factions—vanishing and reviving and piercing each other like the Northern Lights; public commotions, and those in the bosom of the individual; the long calenture of fancy to which the Lover is subject; the blast, like the blast of the desart, which sweeps perennially through a frightful solitude of its own making in the mind of the Gamester; the slowly quickening but ever quickening descent of appetite down which the Miser is propelled; the agony and cleaving oppression of grief; the ghost-like hauntings of shame; the incubus of revenge; the life-distemper of ambition;—these inward existences, and the visible and familiar occurrences of daily life in every town and village; the patient curiosity and contagious acclamations of the multitude in the streets of the city and within the walls of the theatre; a procession, or a rural dance; a hunting, or a horse-race; a flood, or a fire; rejoicing and ringing of bells for an unexpected gift of good fortune, or the coming of a foolish heir to his estate;—these demonstrate incontestibly that the passions of men (I mean, the soul of sensibility in the heart of man)—in all quarrels, in all contests, in all quests, in all delights, in all employments which are either

4213 of fancy *M.Y.* i. 343: *om.* 1809.

sought by men or thrust upon them—do immeasurably transcend their objects. The true sorrow of humanity consists in this;—not that the mind of man fails; but that the course and demands of action and of life so rarely correspond with the dignity and intensity of human desires: and hence that, which is slow to languish, is too easily turned aside and abused. But—with the remembrance of what has been done, in the face of the interminable evils which are threatened—a Spaniard can never have cause to complain of this, while a follower of the Tyrant remains in arms upon the Peninsula.

Here then they, with whom I *hope*, take their stand. There is a spiritual community binding together the living and the dead; the good, the brave, and the wise, of all ages. We would not be rejected from this community; and therefore do we hope. We look forward with erect mind, thinking and feeling: it is an obligation of duty: take away the sense of it, and the moral being would die within us.—Among the most illustrious of that fraternity, whose encouragement we participate, is an Englishman who sacrificed his life in devotion to a cause bearing a stronger likeness to this than any recorded in history. It is the elder Sidney—a deliverer and defender, whose name I have before uttered with reverence; who, treating of the war in the Netherlands against Philip the Second, thus writes: "If her Majesty," says he, "were the fountain; I wold fear, considering what I daily find, that we shold wax dry. But she is but a means whom God useth. And I know not whether I am deceaved; but I am fully persuaded, that, if she shold withdraw herself, other springs wold rise to help this action. For, methinks, I see the great work indeed in hand against the abusers of the world; wherein it is no greater fault to have confidence in man's power, than it is too hastily to despair of God's work."

The pen, which I am guiding, has stopped in my hand; and I have scarcely power to proceed.—I will lay down one principle; and then shall contentedly withdraw from the sanctuary.

When wickedness acknowledges no limit but the extent of her power, and advances with aggravated impatience like a devouring fire; the only worthy or adequate opposition is—that of virtue submitting to no circumscription of her endeavours save that of her rights, and aspiring from the impulse of her own ethereal zeal. The Christian exhortation for the individual is here the precept for nations—"Be ye therefore perfect; even as your Father, which is in Heaven, is perfect."

4249 abusers *M.Y.* i. 343: abuses 1809.

Upon a future occasion (if what has been now said meets with attention) I shall point out the steps by which the practice of life may be lifted up towards these high precepts. I shall have to speak of the child as well as the man; for with the child, or the youth, may we begin with more hope: but I am not in despair even for the man; and chiefly from the inordinate evils of our time. There are (as I shall attempt to shew) tender and subtile ties by which these principles, that love to soar in the pure region, are connected with the ground-nest in which they were fostered and from which they take their flight.

The outermost and all-embracing circle of benevolence has inward concentric circles which, like those of the spider's web, are bound together by links, and rest upon each other; making one frame, and capable of one tremor; circles narrower and narrower, closer and closer, as they lie more near to the centre of self from which they proceeded, and which sustains the whole. The order of life does not require that the sublime and disinterested feelings should have to trust long to their own unassisted power. Nor would the attempt consist either with their dignity or their humility. They condescend, and they adopt: they know the time of their repose; and the qualities which are worthy of being admitted into their service—of being their inmates, their companions, or their substitutes. I shall strive to shew that these principles and movements of wisdom—so far from towering above the support of prudence, or rejecting the rules of experience, for the better conduct of those multifarious actions which are alike necessary to the attainment of ends good or bad—do instinctively prompt the sole prudence which cannot fail. The higher mode of being does not exclude, but necessarily includes, the lower; the intellectual does not exclude, but necessarily includes, the sentient; the sentient, the animal; and the animal, the vital—to its lowest degrees. Wisdom is the hidden root which thrusts forth the stalk of prudence; and these uniting feed and uphold "the bright consummate flower"—National Happiness—the end, the conspicuous crown, and ornament of the whole.

I have announced the feelings of those who hope: yet one word more to those who despond. And first; *he* stands upon a hideous precipice (and it will be the same with all who may succeed to him and his iron sceptre)—he who has outlawed himself from society by proclaiming, with word and act, that he acknowledges no mastery but power. This truth must be evident to all who

4294 word and act *M.Y.* i. 545: act and deed 1809.

breathe—from the dawn of childhood, till the last gleam of twilight is lost in the darkness of dotage. But take the tyrant as he is, in the plenitude of his supposed strength. The vast country of Germany, in spite of the rusty but too strong fetters of corrupt princedoms and degenerate nobility,— Germany—with its citizens, its peasants, and its philosophers—will not lie quiet under the weight of injuries which has been heaped upon it. There is a sleep, but no death, among the mountains of Switzerland. Florence, and Venice, and Genoa, and Rome,—have their own poignant recollections, and a majestic train of glory in past ages. The stir of emancipation may again be felt at the mouths as well as at the sources of the Rhine. Poland perhaps will not be insensible; Kosciusko and his compeers may not have bled in vain. Nor is Hungarian loyalty to be overlooked. And, for Spain itself, the territory is wide: let it be overrun: the torrent will weaken as the water spreads. And, should all resistance disappear, be not daunted: extremes meet: and how often do hope and despair almost touch each other—though unconscious of their neighbourhood, because their faces are turned different ways! yet, in a moment, the one shall vanish; and the other begin a career in the fulness of her joy.

But we may turn from these thoughts: for the present juncture is most auspicious. Upon liberty, and upon liberty alone, can there be permanent dependence; but a temporary relief will be given by the share which Austria is about to take in the war. Now is the time for a great and decisive effort; and, if Britain does not avail herself of it, her disgrace will be indelible, and the loss infinite. If there be ground of hope in the crimes and errors of the enemy, he has furnished enough of both: but imbecility in his opponents (above all, the imbecility of the British) has hitherto preserved him from the natural consequences of his ignorance, his meanness of mind, his transports of infirm fancy, and his guilt. Let us hasten to redeem ourselves. The field is open for a commanding British military force to clear the Peninsula of the enemy, while the better half of his power is occupied with Austria. For the South of Spain, where the first effort of regeneration was made, is yet free. Saragossa (which, by a truly efficient British army, might have been relieved) has indeed fallen; but leaves little to regret; for consummate have been her fortitude and valour. The citizens and soldiers of Saragossa are to be envied: for they have completed the circle of their duty; they have done all that could be wished—all that could be prayed for. And, though the cowardly malice of the enemy gives too much reason to fear that their leader Palafox (with the fate of Toussaint) will soon be among the dead, it is the high privilege of men who have performed what he has performed—that they cannot be missed; and, in moments of weakness only, can they be lamented: their actions represent them every where and for ever. Palafox has taken his place as parent and ancestor of innumerable heroes.

Oh! that the surviving chiefs of the Spanish people may prove worthy of their situation! With such materials,—their labour would be pleasant, and their success certain. But—though heads of a nation venerable for antiquity, and having good cause to preserve with reverence the institutions of their elder forefathers—they must not be indiscriminately afraid of new things. It is their duty to restore the good which has fallen into disuse; and also to create, and to adopt. Young scions of polity must be engrafted on the time-worn trunk: a new fortress must be reared upon the ancient and living rock of justice. Then would it be seen, while the superstructure stands inwardly immoveable, in how short a space of time the ivy and wild plant would climb up from the base, and clasp the naked walls; the storms, which could not shake, would weather-stain; and the edifice, in the day of its youth, would appear to be one with the rock upon which it was planted, and to grow out of it.

But let us look to ourselves. Our offences are unexpiated: and, wanting light, we want strength. With reference to this guilt and to this deficiency, and to my own humble efforts towards removing both, I shall conclude with the words of a man of disciplined spirit, who withdrew from the too busy world—not out of indifference to its welfare, or to forget its concerns—but retired for wider compass of eye-sight, that he might comprehend and see in just proportions and relations; knowing above all that he, who hath not first made himself master of the horizon of his own mind, must look beyond it only to be deceived. It is Petrarch who thus writes: "Hæc dicerem, et quicquid in rem praesentem et indignatio dolorque dictarent; nisi obtorpuisse animos, actumque de rebus nostris, crederem. Nempe, qui aliis iter rectum ostendere solebamus, nunc (quod exitio proximum est) coeci coecis ducibus per abrupta rapimur; alienoque circumvolvimur exemplo; quid velimus, nescii. Nam (ut coeptum exequar) totum hoc malum, seu nostrum proprium seu potius omnium gentium commune, IGNORATIO FINIS facit. Nesciunt inconsulti homines quid agant: ideo quicquid agunt, mox ut coeperint, vergit in nauseam. Hinc ille discursus sine termino; hinc, medio calle, discordie; et, ante exitum, DAMNATA PRINCIPIA; et expleti nihil."

4366 expleti *M.Y.* i. 343: explete 1809.

As an act of respect to the English reader—I shall add, to the same purpose, the words of our own Milton; who, contemplating our ancestors in his day, thus speaks of them and their errors:— "Valiant, indeed, and prosperous to win a field; but, to know the end and reason of winning, injudicious and unwise. Hence did their victories prove as fruitless, as their losses dangerous; and left them still languishing under the same grievances that men suffer conquered. Which was indeed unlikely to go otherwise; unless men more than vulgar bred up in the knowledge of ancient and illustrious deeds, invincible against many and vain titles, impartial to friendships and relations, had conducted their affairs."

THE END

[Wordsworth's] APPENDICES

A (see text page 279).

WHEN this passage was written, there had appeared only unauthorized accounts of the Board of Inquiry's proceedings. Neither from these however, nor from the official report of the Board (which has been since published), is any satisfactory explanation to be gained on this question—or indeed on any other question of importance. All, which is to be collected from them, is this: the Portuguese General, it appears, offered to unite his whole force with the British on the single condition that they should be provisioned from the British stores; and, accordingly, rests his excuse for not co-operating on the refusal of Sir Arthur Wellesley to comply with this condition. Sir A. W. denies the validity of his excuse; and, more than once, calls it a *pretence*; declaring that, in his belief, Gen. Freire's real motive for not joining was—a mistrust in the competence of the British to appear in the field against the French. This however is mere surmise; and therefore cannot have much weight with those who sincerely sought for satisfaction on this point: moreover, it is a surmise of the individual whose justification rests on making it appear that the difficulty did not arise with himself; and it is right to add, that the only *fact* produced goes to discredit this surmise; viz, that Gen. Freire did, without any delay, furnish the whole number of troops which Sir Arthur engaged to feed. However the Board exhibited so little anxiety to be satisfied on this point, that no positive information was gained.

A reference being here first made to the official report of the Board of Inquiry; I shall make use of the opportunity which it offers to lay before the reader an outline of that Board's proceedings; from which it will appear how far the opinion—pronounced, by the national voice, upon the transactions in Portugal—ought, in sound logic, to be modified by any part of those proceedings.

We find in the warrant under which the Board of Inquiry was to act, and which defined its powers, that an inquiry was to be made into the conditions of the "armistice and convention; and into all the causes and circumstances, whether arising from the operations of the British army, or otherwise, which led to them."

Whether answers to the charges of the people of England were made possible by the provisions of this warrant—and, secondly, whether even these provisions have been satisfied by the Board of Inquiry—will best appear by involving those charges in four questions, according to the following scale, which supposes a series of concessions impossible to those who think the nation justified in the language held on the transactions in Portugal.

1. Considering the perfidy with which the French army had entered Portugal; the enormities committed by it during its occupation of that country; the vast military power of which that army was a part, and the use made of that power by its master; the then existing spirit of the Spanish, Portuguese, and British nations; in a word, considering the especial nature of the service, and the individual character of this war;—was it lawful for the British army, under any conceivable circumstances, so long as it had the liberty of re-embarking, to make *any conceivable* convention? i.e. Was the negative evil of a total failure in every object for which it had been sent to Portugal of worse tendency than the positive evil of acknowledging in the French army a fair title to the privileges of an honourable enemy by consenting to a mode of treaty which (in its very name, implying a reciprocation of concession and respect) must be under any limitations as much more indulgent than an ordinary capitulation, as that again must (in its severest form) be more indulgent than the only favour which the French marauders could presume upon obtaining—viz. permission to surrender at discretion?

To this question the reader need not be told that these pages give a naked unqualified denial; and that to establish the reasonableness of that denial is one of their main purposes: but, for the benefit of the men accused, let it be supposed granted; and then the second question will be

2. Was it lawful for the English army, in the case of its being reduced to the supposed dilemma of either re-embarking or making *some* convention, to make that *specifical convention* which it did make at Cintra?

This is of necessity and *à fortiori* denied; and it has been proved that neither to this, nor any other army, could it be lawful to make such a convention—not merely under the actual but under any conceivable circumstances; let however this too, on behalf of the parties accused, be granted; and then the third question will be

3. Was the English Army reduced to that dilemma?

4. Finally, this also being conceded (which not even the Gener-

als have dared to say), it remains to ask by whose and by what misconduct did an army—confessedly the arbiter of its own movements and plans at the opening of the campaign—forfeit that free agency—either to the extent of the extremity supposed, or of any approximation to that extremity?

Now of these four possible questions in the minds of all those who condemn the convention of Cintra, it is obvious that the King's warrant supposes only the three latter to exist (since, though it allows inquiry to be made into the individual convention, it no where questions the tolerability of a convention *in genere*); and it is no less obvious that the Board, acting under that warrant, has noticed only the last—i.e. by what series of military movements the army was brought into a state of difficulty which justified a convention (the Board taking for granted throughout—1st, That such a state could exist; 2ndly, That it actually did exist; and 3rdly, That—if it existed, and accordingly justified *some imaginable* convention—it must therefore of necessity justify *this* convention).

Having thus shewn that it is on the last question only that the nation could, in deference to the Board of Inquiry, surrender or qualify any opinion which it had previously given—let us ask what answer is gained, from the proceedings of that Board, to the charge involved even in this last question (premising however—first—that this charge was never explicitly made by the public, or at least was enunciated only in the form of a conjecture—and 2ndly that the answer to it is collected chiefly from the depositions of the parties accused)? Now the whole sum of their answer amounts to no more than this—that, in the opinion of some part of the English staff, an opportunity was lost on the 21st of exchanging the comparatively slow process of reducing the French army by siege for the brilliant and summary one of a *coup-de-main.*

This opportunity, be it observed, was offered only by Gen. Junot's presumption in quitting his defensive positions, and coming out to meet the English army in the field; so that it was an advantage so much over and above what might fairly have been calculated upon: at any rate, if *this* might have been looked for, still the accident of battle, by which a large part of the French army was left in a situation to be cut off, (to the loss of which advantage Sir A. Wellesley ascribes the necessity of a convention) could surely never have been anticipated; and therefore the British army was, even after that loss, in as prosperous a state as it had from the first any right to expect. Hence it is to be inferred, that Sir A. W. must have entered on this campaign with a predetermination to grant a convention in any case, excepting in one single case which he knew to be in the gift of only very extraordinary good fortune. With respect to him, therefore, the charges—pronounced by the national voice—are not only confirmed, but greatly aggravated. Further, with respect to the General who superseded him, all those—who think that such an opportunity of terminating the campaign was really offered, and, through his refusal to take advantage of it, lost—are compelled to suspect in him a want of military skill, or a wilful sacrifice of his duty to the influence of personal rivalry, accordingly as they shall interpret his motives.

The whole which we gain therefore from the Board of Inquiry is—that what we barely suspected is ripened into certainty—and that on all, which we assuredly knew and declared without needing that any tribunal should lend us its sanction, no effort has been made at denial, or disguise, or palliation.

Thus much for the proceedings of the Board of Inquiry, upon which their decision was to be grounded. As to the decision itself, it declares that no further military proceedings are necessary; "because" (say the members of the board), "however some of us may differ in our sentiments respecting the fitness of the convention in the relative situation of the two armies, it is our unanimous declaration that unquestionable zeal and firmness appear throughout to have been exhibited by Generals Sir H. Dalrymple, Sir H. Burrard, and Sir A. Wellesley." In consequence of this decision, the Commander-in-Chief addressed a letter to the Board—reminding them that, though the words of his Majesty's warrant expressly enjoin that the *conditions* of the Armistice and Convention should be strictly examined and reported upon, they have altogether neglected to give any opinion upon those conditions. They were therefore called upon then to declare their opinion, whether an armistice was adviseable; and (if so) whether the terms of *that* armistice were such as ought to be agreed upon;—and to declare, in like manner, whether a convention was adviseable; and (if so) whether the terms of *that* convention were such as ought to have been agreed upon.

To two of these questions—viz. those which relate to the particular armistice and convention made by the British Generals—the members of the Board (still persevering in their blindness to the other two which express doubt as to the lawfulness of *any* armistice or convention) severally return answers which convey an approbation of the armistice and convention by four members, a disapprobation of the convention by the remaining three, and further a disapprobation of the armistice by one of those three.

Now it may be observed—first—that, even if the investigation had not been a public one, it might have reasonably been concluded, from the circumstance of the Board having omitted to report any opinion concerning the terms of the armistice and the convention, that those terms had not occupied enough of its attention to justify the Board in giving any opinion upon them—whether of approbation or disapprobation; and, secondly,—this conclusion, which might have been made *à priori*, is confirmed by the actual fact that no examination or inquiry of this kind appears throughout the report of its proceedings: and therefore any opinion subsequently given, in consequence of the requisition of the Commander-in-Chief, can lay claim to no more authority upon these points—than the opinion of the same men, if they had never sat in a public court upon this question. In this condition are all the members, whether they approve or disapprove of the convention. And with respect to the three who disapprove of the convention,—over and above the general impropriety of having, under these circumstances, pronounced a verdict at all in the character of members of that Board—they are subject to an especial charge of inconsistency in having given such an opinion, in their second report, as renders nugatory that which they first pronounced. For the reason—assigned, in their first report, for deeming no further military proceedings necessary—is because it appears that unquestionable *zeal and firmness* were exhibited throughout by the several General Officers; and the reason—assigned by those three who condemn the convention—is that the Generals did not insist upon the terms to which they were entitled; that is (in direct opposition to their former opinions), the Generals shewed a want of firmness and zeal. If then the Generals were acquitted, in the first case, solely upon the ground of having displayed firmness and zeal; a confessed want of firmness and zeal, in the second case, implies conversely a ground of censure—rendering (in the opinions of these three members) further military proceedings absolutely necessary. They,—who are most aware of the unconstitutional frame of this Court or Board, and of the perplexing situation in which its members must have found themselves placed,—will have the least difficulty in excusing this inconsistency: it is however to be regretted; particularly in the instance of the Earl of Moira;—who, disapproving both of the Convention and Armistice, has assigned for that disapprobation unanswerable reasons drawn—not from hidden sources, unapproachable except by judicial investigation—but from facts known to all the world.—The reader will excuse this long note; to which however I must add one word:—Is it not strange that, in the general decision of the Board, zeal and firmness—nakedly considered, and without question of their union with judgment and such other qualities as can alone give them any value—should be assumed as sufficient grounds on which to rest the acquittal of men lying under a charge of military delinquency?

B (see text page 283).

It is not necessary to add, that one of these fears was removed by the actual landing of ten thousand men, under Sir J. Moore, pending the negociation: and yet no change in the terms took place in consequence. This was an important circumstance; and, of itself, determined two of the members of the Board of Inquiry to disapprove of the convention: such an accession entitling Sir H. Dalrymple (and, of course, making it his duty) to insist on more favourable terms. But the argument is complete without it.

C (see text page 286)*)*.

I was unwilling to interrupt the reader upon a slight occasion; but I cannot refrain from adding here a word or two by way of comment.—I have said at page [282], speaking of Junot's army, that the British were to encounter the same men, &c. Sir Arthur Wellesley, before the Board of Inquiry, disallowed this supposition; affirming that Junot's army had not then reached Spain, nor could be there for some time. Grant this: was it not stipulated that a messenger should be sent off, immediately after the conclusion of the treaty, to Buonaparte—apprising him of its terms, and when he might expect his troops; and would not this enable him to hurry forward forces to the Spanish frontiers, and to bring them into action—knowing that these troops of Junot's would be ready to support him? What did it matter whether the British were again to measure swords with these identical men; whether these men were even to appear again upon Spanish ground? It was enough, that, if these did not, others would—who could not have been brought to that service, but that these had been released and were doing elsewhere some other service for their master; enough that every thing was provided by the British to land them as near the Spanish frontier (and as speedily) as they could desire.

D (see text page 316).

This attempt, the reader will recollect, is not new to our country;—it was accomplished, at one æra of our history, in that memorable act of an English Parliament, which made it unlawful for any man to ask his neighbour to join him in a petition for redress of grievances; and which thus denied the people "the benefit of tears and prayers to their own infamous deputies!" For the deplorable state of England and Scotland at that time—see the annals of Charles the Second, and his successor.—We must not forget however that to this state of things, as the cause of those measures which the nation afterwards resorted to, we are originally indebted for the blessing of the Bill of Rights.

E (see text page 364).

I allude here more especially to an address presented to Buonaparte (October 27th, 1808) by the deputies of the new departments of the kingdom of Italy; from which address, as given in the English journals, the following passages are extracted:—

"In the necessity, in which you are to overthrow—to destroy—to disperse your enemies as the wind dissipates the dust, you are not an exterminating angel; but you are the being that extends his thoughts— that measures the face of the earth—to re-establish universal happiness upon better and surer bases."

* * * * * *

"We are the interpreters of a million of souls at the extremity of your kingdom of Italy."—"Deign, *Sovereign Master of all Things*, to hear (as we doubt not you will)" &c.

The answer begins thus:—

"I *applaud* the sentiments you express in the name of my people of Musora, Metauro, and Tronto."

F (see text page 367).

This principle, involved in so many of his actions, Buonaparte has of late explicitly avowed: the instances are numerous: it will be sufficient, in this place, to allege one—furnished by his answer to the address cited in the last note:—

"I am particularly attached to your Archbishop of Urbino: that prelate, animated with the true faith, repelled with indignation the advice—and braved the menaces—of those who wished to confound the affairs of Heaven, which never change, with the affairs of this world, which are modified according to circumstances of *force* and policy."

SUSPENSION OF ARMS

Agreed upon between Lieutenant-General Sir Arthur Wellesley, K.B. *on the one part, and the General-of-Division* Kellermann *on the other part; each having powers from the respective Generals of the French and English Armies.*

Head-Quarters of the English Army, August 22, 1808.

Article I. There shall be, from this date, a Suspension of Arms between the armies of his Britannic Majesty, and his Imperial and Royal Majesty, Napoleon I. for the purpose of negociating a Convention for the evacuation of Portugal by the French army.

Art. II. The Generals-in-Chief of the two armies, and the Commander-in-Chief of the British fleet at the entrance of the Tagus, will appoint a day to assemble, on such part of the coast as shall be judged convenient, to negociate and conclude the said Convention.

Art. III. The river of Sirandre shall form the line of demarkation to be established between the two armies; Torres Vedras shall not be occupied by either.

Art. IV. The General-in-Chief of the English army undertakes to include the Portuguese armies in this suspension of arms; and for them the line of demarkation shall be established from Leyria to Thomar.

Art. V. It is agreed provisionally that the French army shall not, in any case, be considered as prisoners of war; that all the individuals who compose it shall be transported to France with their arms and baggage, and the whole of their private property, from which nothing shall be exempted.

Art. VI. No individual, whether Portuguese, or of a nation allied to France, or French, shall be called to account for his political conduct; their respective property shall be protected; and they shall be at liberty to withdraw from Portugal, within a limited time, with their property.

ART. VII. The neutrality of the port of Lisbon shall be recognised for the Russian fleet: that is to say, that, when the English army or fleet shall be in possession of the city and port, the said Russian fleet shall not be disturbed during its stay; nor stopped when it wishes to sail; nor pursued, when it shall sail, until after the time fixed by the maritime law.

ART. VIII. All the artillery of French calibre, and also the horses of the cavalry, shall be transported to France.

ART. IX. This suspension of arms shall not be broken without forty- eight hours' previous notice.

Done and agreed upon between the above-named Generals, the day and year above-mentioned.

(Signed) ARTHUR WELLESLEY.
KELLERMANN, General-of-Division.

Additional Article.

The garrisons of the places occupied by the French army shall be included in the present Convention, if they have not capitulated before the 25th instant.

(Signed) ARTHUR WELLE5LEY.
KELLERMANN, General-of-Division.
(A true Copy.)
A. J. DALRYMPLE, Captain, Military Secretary.

DEFINITIVE CONVENTION FOR THE EVACUATION OF PORTUGAL BY THE FRENCH ARMY

The Generals commanding in chief the British and French armies in Portugal, having determined to negociate and conclude a treaty for the evacuation of Portugal by the French troops, on the basis of the agreement entered into on the 22d instant for a suspension of hostilities, have appointed the under-mentioned officers to negociate the same in their names; viz.—on the part of the General-in-Chief of the British army, Lieutenant-Colonel MURRAY, Quarter-

Master General; and, on the part of the General-in-Chief of the French army, Monsieur Kellermann, General-of-Division; to whom they have given authority to negociate and conclude a convention to that effect, subject to their ratification respectively, and to that of the Admiral commanding the British fleet at the entrance of the Tagus.

Those two officers, after exchanging their full powers, have agreed upon the articles which follow:

Article I. All the places and forts in the kingdom of Portugal, occupied by the French troops, shall be delivered up to the British army in the state in which they are at the period of the signature of the present Convention.

Art. II. The French troops shall evacuate Portugal with their arms and baggage; they shall not be considered as prisoners of war; and, on their arrival in France, they shall be at liberty to serve.

Art. III. The English Government shall furnish the means of conveyance for the French army; which shall be disembarked in any of the ports of France between Rochefort and L'Orient, inclusively.

Art. IV. The French army shall carry with it all its artillery, of French calibre, with the horses belonging to it, and the tumbrils supplied with sixty rounds per gun. All other artillery, arms, and ammunition, as also the military and naval arsenals, shall be given up to the British army and navy in the state in which they may be at the period of the ratification of the Convention.

Art. V. The French army shall carry with it all its equipments, and all that is comprehended under the name of property of the army; that is to say, its military chest, and carriages attached to the Field Commissariat and Field Hospitals; or shall be allowed to dispose of such part of the same, on its account, as the Commander-in-Chief may judge it unnecessary to embark. In like manner, all individuals of the army shall be at liberty to dispose of their private property of every description; with full security hereafter for the purchasers.

Art. VI. The cavalry are to embark their horses; as also the Generals and other officers of all ranks. It is, however, fully understood, that the means of conveyance for horses, at the disposal of the British Commanders, are very limited; some additional conveyance may be procured in the port of Lisbon; the number of horses to be embarked by the troops shall not exceed six hundred; and the number embarked by the Staff shall not exceed two hundred. At all events every facility will be given to the French army to dispose of the horses, belonging to it, which cannot be embarked.

ART. VII. In order to facilitate the embarkation, it shall take place in three divisions; the last of which will be principally composed of the garrisons of the places, of the cavalry, the artillery, the sick, and the equipment of the army. The first division shall embark within seven days of the date of the ratification; or sooner, if possible.

ART. VIII. The garrison of Elvas and its forts, and of Peniche and Palmela, will be embarked at Lisbon; that of Almaida at Oporto, or the nearest harbour. They will be accompanied on their march by British Commissaries, charged with providing for their subsistence and accommodation.

ART. IX. All the sick and wounded, who cannot be embarked with the troops, are entrusted to the British army. They are to be taken care of, whilst they remain in this country, at the expence of the British Government; under the condition of the same being reimbursed by France when the final evacuation is effected. The English government will provide for their return to France; which shall take place by detachments of about one hundred and fifty (or two hundred) men at a time. A sufficient number of French medical officers shall be left behind to attend them.

ART. X. As soon as the vessels employed to carry the army to France shall have disembarked it in the harbours specified, or in any other of the ports of France to which stress of weather may force them, every facility shall be given them to return to England without delay; and security against capture until their arrival in a friendly port.

ART. XI. The French army shall be concentrated in Lisbon, and within a distance of about two leagues from it. The English army will approach within three leagues of the capital; and will be so placed as to leave about one league between the two armies.

ART. XII. The forts of St. Julien, the Bugio, and Cascais, shall be occupied by the British troops on the ratification of the Convention. Lisbon and its citadel, together with the forts and batteries, as far as the Lazaretto or Tarfuria on one side, and fort St. Joseph on the other, inclusively, shall be given up on the embarkation of the second division; as shall also the harbour; and all armed vessels in it of every description, with their rigging, sails, stores, and ammunition. The fortresses of Elvas, Almaida, Peniche, and Palmela, shall be given up as soon as the British troops can arrive to occupy them. In the mean time, the General-in-Chief of the British army will give notice of the present Convention to the garrisons of those places, as also to the troops before them, in order to put a stop to all further hostilities.

Art. XIII. Commissioners shall be named, on both sides, to regulate and accelerate the execution of the arrangements agreed upon.

Art. XIV. Should there arise doubts as to the meaning of any article, it will be explained favourably to the French army.

Art. XV. From the date of the ratification of the present Convention, all arrears of contributions, requisitions, or claims whatever, of the French Government, against the subjects of Portugal, or any other individuals residing in this country, founded on the occupation of Portugal by the French troops in the month of December 1807, which may not have been paid up, are cancelled; and all sequestrations laid upon their property, moveable or immoveable, are removed; and the free disposal of the same is restored to the proper owners.

Art. XVI. All subjects of France, or of powers in friendship or alliance with France, domiciliated in Portugal, or accidentally in this country, shall be protected: their property of every kind, moveable and immoveable, shall be respected: and they shall be at liberty either to accompany the French army, or to remain in Portugal. In either case their property is guaranteed to them; with the liberty of retaining or of disposing of it, and passing the produce of the sale thereof into France, or any other country where they may fix their residence; the space of one year being allowed them for that purpose.

It is fully understood, that the shipping is excepted from this arrangement; only, however, in so far as regards leaving the port; and that none of the stipulations above-mentioned can be made the pretext of any commercial speculation.

Art. XVII. No native of Portugal shall be rendered accountable for his political conduct during the period of the occupation of this country by the French army; and all those who have continued in the exercise of their employments, or who have accepted situations under the French Government, are placed under the protection of the British Commanders: they shall sustain no injury in their persons or property; it not having been at their option to be obedient, or not, to the French Government: they are also at liberty to avail themselves of the stipulations of the 16th Article.

Art. XVIII. The Spanish troops detained on board ship in the Port of Lisbon shall be given up to the Commander-in-Chief of the British army; who engages to obtain of the Spaniards to restore such French subjects, either military or civil, as may have been detained in Spain, without being taken in battle, or in consequence of military operations, but on occasion of the occurrences of the 29th of last May, and the days immediately following.

Art. XIX. There shall be an immediate exchange established for all ranks of prisoners made in Portugal since the commencement of the present hostilities.

Art. XX. Hostages of the rank of field-officers shall be mutually furnished on the part of the British army and navy, and on that of the French army, for the reciprocal guarantee of the present Convention. The officer of the British army shall be restored on the completion of the articles which concern the army; and the officer of the navy on the disembarkation of the French troops in their own country. The like is to take place on the part of the French army.

Art. XXI. It shall be allowed to the General-in-Chief of the French army to send an officer to France with intelligence of the present Convention. A vessel will be furnished by the British Admiral to convey him to Bourdeaux or Rochefort.

Art. XXII. The British Admiral will be invited to accommodate His Excellency the Commander-in-Chief, and the other principal officers of the French army, on board ships of war.

Done and concluded at Lisbon this 30th day of August, 1808.

(Signed) George Murray,
Quarter-Master-General.
Kellermann,
Le Général de Division.

We, the Duke of Abrantes, General-in-Chief of the French army, have ratified and do ratify the present Definitive Convention in all its articles, to be executed according to its form and tenor.

(Signed) The Duke of Abrantes.

Head-Quarters—Lisbon, 30th August, 1808.

Additional Articles to the Convention of the 30th of August, 1808.

Art. I. The individuals in the civil employment of the army made prisoners, either by the British troops, or by the Portuguese, in any part of Portugal, will be restored, as is customary, without exchange.

Art. II. The French army shall be subsisted from its own magazines up to the day of embarkation; the garrisons up to the day of the evacuation of the fortresses.

The remainder of the magazines shall be delivered over, in the usual form, to the British Government; which charges itself with the subsistence of the men and horses of the army from the above-mentioned periods till they arrive in France; under the condition of their being reimbursed by the French Government for the excess of the expense beyond the estimates, to be made by both parties, of the value of the magazines delivered up to the British army.

The provisions on board the ships of war, in possession of the French army, will be taken in account by the British Government in like manner with the magazines in the fortresses.

ART. III. The General commanding the British troops will take the necessary measures for re-establishing the free circulation of the means of subsistence between the country and the capital.

Done and concluded at Lisbon this 30th day of August, 1808.

(Signed) GEORGE MURRAY,
Quarter-Master-General.
KELLERMANN,
Le Général de Division.

We, Duke of Abrantes, General-in-Chief of the French army, have ratified and do ratify the additional articles of the Convention, to be executed according to their form and tenor.

The Duke of ABRANTES.

(A true Copy.)
A. J. DALRYMPLE, Captain, Military Secretary.

Articles of a Convention entered into between Vice-Admiral SENIAVIN, *Knight of the Order of St. Alexander and other Russian Orders, and Admiral Sir* CHARLES COTTON, *Bart. for the Surrender of the Russian Fleet, now anchored in the River Tagus.*

ART. I. The ships of war of the Emperor of Russia, now in the Tagus (as specified in the annexed list), shall be delivered up to Admiral Sir Charles Cotton, immediately, with all their stores as they now are; to be sent to England, and there held as a deposit by His Britannic Majesty, to be restored to His Imperial Majesty within six months after the conclusion of a peace between His Britannic Majesty and His Imperial Majesty the Emperor of all the Russias.

ART. II. Vice-Admiral Seniavin, with the officers, sailors, and marines, under his command, to return to Russia, without any condition or stipulation respecting their future services; to be conveyed thither in men of war, or proper vessels, at the expence of His Britannic Majesty.

Done and concluded on board the ship Twerday, in the Tagus, and on board His Britannic Majesty's ship Hibernia, off the mouth of that river, the 3d day of September 1808.

(Signed) DE SENIAVIN.
(Signed) CHARLES COTTON.
(Counter-signed) By command of the Admiral,
L. SASS, Assesseur de Collège.
(Counter-signed) By command of the Admiral,
JAMES KENNEDY, Secretary.

[De Quincey's] POSTSCRIPT

ON SIR JOHN MOORE'S LETTERS.

Whilst the latter sheets of this work were passing through the press, there was laid before Parliament a series of correspondence between the English Government and its servants in Spain; amongst which were the letters of Sir John Moore. That these letters, even with minds the least vigilant to detect contradictions and to make a commentary from the past actions of the Spaniards, should have had power to alienate them from the Spanish cause—could never have been looked for; except indeed by those who saw, in the party spirit on this question, a promise that more than ordinary pains would be taken to misrepresent their contents and to abuse the public judgment. But however it was at any rate to have been expected—both from the place which Sir J. Moore held in the nation's esteem previously to his Spanish campaign, and also especially from that which (by his death in battle) he had so lately taken in its affections—that they would weigh a good deal in depressing the general sympathy with Spain: and therefore the Author of this work was desirous that all which these letters themselves, or other sources of information, furnished to mitigate and contradict Sir J. M.'s opinions—should be laid before the public: but—being himself at a great distance from London, and not having within his reach all the documents necessary for this purpose—he has honoured the friend, who corrects the press errors, by making over that task to him; and the reader is therefore apprised, that the Author is not responsible for any thing which follows.

* * * * * *

Those, who have not examined these letters for themselves, will have collected enough of their general import, from conversation and the public prints, to know that they pronounce an opinion unfavourable to the Spaniards. They will perhaps have yet to learn that this opinion is not supported by any body of *facts* (for of facts only three are given; and those, as we shall see, misrepresented); but solely by the weight of Sir John Moore's personal authority. This being the case, it becomes the more important to assign the value of that authority, by making such deductions from the present public estimate of it, as are either fairly to be presumed from his profession and office, or directly inferred from the letters under consideration.

As reasons for questioning *à priori* the impartiality of these letters,—it might be suggested (in reference to what they would be likely *omit*)—first—that they are the letters of a *soldier*; that is, of a man trained (by the prejudices of his profession) to despise, or at least to rate secondary, those resources which for Spain must be looked to as supreme and, secondly, that they are the letters of a *general*; that is, of a soldier removed by his rank from the possibility of any extensive intercourse with the lower classes; concerning whom the question chiefly was. But it is more important to remark (in reference to what they would be likely to *mis-state*)—thirdly—that they are the letters of a *commander-in-chief*; standing—from the very day when he took the field—in a dilemma which compelled him to risk the safety of his army by advancing, or its honour by retreating; and having to make out an apology, for either issue, to the very persons who had imposed this dilemma upon him.—The reader is requested to attend to this. Sir John Moore found himself in Leon with a force "which, if united," (to quote his own words) "would not exceed 26,000 men." Such a force, after the defeat of the advanced armies,—he was sure—could effect nothing; the best result he could anticipate was an inglorious retreat. That he should be in this situation at the very opening of the campaign, he saw, would declare to all Europe that somewhere there must be blame: but where? with himself he knew that there was none: the English Government (with whom he must have seen that least a part of the blame lay—for sending him so late, and with a force so lamentably incommensurate to the demands of the service) it was not for him—holding the situation that he did—openly to accuse (though, by implication, he often does accuse them); and therefore it became his business to look to the Spaniards; and, in their conduct, to search for palliations of that inefficiency on his part—which else the persons, to whom he was writing, would understand as charged upon themselves. Writing with such a purpose—and under a double fettering of his faculties; first from anxious forebodings of calamity or dishonour; and secondly from the pain he must have felt at not being free to censure those with whom he could not but be aware that the embarrassments of his situation had, at least in part, originated—we might expect that it would not be difficult for him to find, in the early events of the campaign, all which he sought; and to deceive himself into a belief, that, in stating these events without any commentary or even hints as to the relative circumstances under which they took place (which only could give to the naked facts their value and due meaning), he was making no misrepresentations,— and doing the Spaniards no injustice.

These suggestions are made with the greater earnestness, as it is probable that the honourable death of Sir John Moore will have given so much more weight to his opinion on any subject—as, if these suggestions be warranted, it is entitled on this subject to less weight—than the opinion of any other individual equally intelligent, and not liable (from high office and perplexity of situation) to the same influences of disgust or prejudice.

That these letters *were* written under some such influences, is plain throughout: we find, in them, reports of the four first events in the campaign; and, in justice to the Spaniards, it must be said that all are virtually mis-statements. Take two instances:

1. The main strength and efforts of the French were, at the opening of the campaign, directed against the army of Gen. Blake. The issue is thus given by Sir J. M.:—"Gen. Blake's army in Biscay has been defeated—dispersed; and its officers and men are flying in every direction." Could it be supposed that the army, whose matchless exertions and endurances are all merged in this over-charged (and almost insulting) statement of their result, was, 'mere peasantry' (Sir J. M.'s own words) and opposed to greatly superior numbers of

veteran troops? Confront with this account the description given by an eye-witness (Major-Gen. Leith) of their constancy and the trials of their constancy; remembering that, for ten successive days, they were engaged (under the pressure of similar hardships, with the addition of one not mentioned here, viz.—a want of cloathing) in continued actions with the French:—"Here I shall take occasion to state another instance of the patience (and, I will add, the chearfulness) of the Spanish soldiers under the greatest privations—After the action of Soronosa on the 31st ult., it was deemed expedient by Gen. Blake, for the purpose of forming a junction with the second division and the army of Asturias, that the army should make long, rapid, and continued marches through a country at any time incapable of feeding so numerous an army, and at present almost totally drained of provisions. From the 30th of October to the present day (Nov. 6), with the exception of a small and partial issue of bread at Bilboa on the morning of the 1st of November, this army has been totally destitute of bread, wine, or spirits; and has literally lived on the scanty supply of beef and sheep which those mountains afford. Yet never was there a symptom of complaint or murmur; the soldiers' minds appearing to be entirely occupied with the idea of being led against the enemy at Bilboa."—"It is impossible for me to do justice to the gallantry and energy of the divisions engaged this day. The army are loud in expressing their desires to be led against the enemy at Bilboa; the universal exclamation is—The bayonet! the bayonet! lead us back to Soronosa."

2. On the 10th of November the Estramaduran advanced-guard, of about 12,000 men, was defeated at Burgos by a division of the French army *selected* for the service—and having a vast superiority in cavalry and artillery. This event, with the same neglect of circumstances as in the former instance, Sir J. M. thus reports:—"The French, after beating the army of Estramadura, are advanced at Burgos." Now surely to any unprejudiced mind the bare fact of 2,000 men (chiefly raw levies) having gone forward to meet and to find out the main French army—under all the oppression which, to the ignorant of the upper and lower classes throughout Europe, there is in the name of Bonaparte—must appear, under any issue, a title to the highest admiration, such as would have made this slight and incidental mention of it impossible.

The two next events—viz. the forcing of the pass at Somosierra by the Polish horse, and the partial defeat of Castanos—are, as might be shewn even from the French bulletins, no less misrepresented. With respect to the first,—

Sir J. Moore, overlooking the whole drama of that noble defence, gives only the catastrophe; and his account of the second will appear, from any report, to be an exaggeration.

It may be objected that—since Sir J. M. no where alleges these events as proving any thing against the Spaniards, but simply as accounting for his own plans (in which view, howsoever effected, whether with or without due resistance, they were entitled to the same value)—it is unfair to say that, by giving them uncircumstantially, he has misrepresented them. But it must be answered, that, in letters containing elsewhere (though not immediately in connexion with these statements) opinions unfavourable to the Spaniards, to omit any thing making *for* them—*is* to misrepresent in effect. And, further, it shall now be shewn that even those three charges—which Sir J. M. *does* allege in proof of his opinions—are as glaringly misstated.

The first of these charges is the most important: I give it to the reader in the words of Sir John Moore:—"The French cavalry from Burgos, in small detachments, are over-running the province of Leon; raising contributions; to which the inhabitants submit without the least resistance." Now here it cannot be meant that no efforts at resistance were made by individuals or small parties; because this would not only contradict the universal laws of human nature,—but would also be at utter variance with Sir J. M.'s repeated complaints that he could gain no information of what was passing in his neighbourhood. It is meant therefore that there was no regular or organised resistance; no resistance such as might be made the subject of an official report. Now we all know that the Spaniards have every where suffered deplorably from a want of cavalry; and, in the absence of that, hear from a military man (Major-Gen. Brodrick) *why* there was no resistance: "—At that time I was not aware how remarkably the plains of Leon and Castille differ from any other I have seen; nor how strongly the circumstances, which constitute that difference, enforce the opinion I ventured to express." (He means the necessity of cavalry reinforcements from England.) "My road from Astorga lay through a vast open space, extending from 5 to 20 or more miles on every side; without a single accident of ground which could enable a body of infantry to check a pursuing enemy, or to cover its own retreat. In such ground, any corps of infantry might be insulted, to the very gates of the town it occupied, by cavalry far inferior in numbers; *contributions raised under their eyes*, and the whole neighbourhood exhausted of its resources, *without the possibility of their opposing any resistance to such incursions.*"

The second charge is made on the retreat to Corunna: "the Gallicians, though armed," Sir J. M. says, "made no attempt to stop the passage of the French through the mountains." That they were armed—is a proof that they had an *intention* to do so (as one of our journals observed): but what encouragement had they in that intention from the sight of a regular force—more than 30,000 strong—abandoning, without a struggle, passes where (as an English general asserts) "a body of a thousand men might stop an army of twenty times the number?"

The third charge relates to the same province: it is a complaint that 'the people run away; the villages are deserted;' and again, in his last letter,—"They abandoned their dwellings at our approach; drove away their carts, oxen, and every thing which could be of the smallest aid to the army." To this charge, in so far as it may be thought to criminate the Spaniards, a full answer is furnished by their accuser himself in the following memorable sentence in another part of the very same letter:—"I am sorry to say that the army, whose conduct I had such reason to extol in its march through Portugal and on its arrival in Spain, has totally changed its character since it began to retreat." What do we collect from this passage? Assuredly that the army ill-treated the Gallicians; for there is no other way in which an army, as a body, can offend—excepting by an indisposition to fight; and that interpretation (besides that we are all sure that no English army could *so* offend) Sir J. Moore expressly guards against in the next sentence.

The English army then treated its ally as an enemy: and,—though there are alleviations of its conduct in its great sufferings,—yet it must be remembered that these sufferings were due—not to the Gallicians— but to circumstances over which they had no controul—to the precipitancy of the retreat, the inclemency of the weather, and the poverty of the country; and that (knowing this) they must have had a double sense of injustice in any outrages of an English army, from contrasting them with the professed objects of that army in entering Spain—It is to be observed that the answer to the second charge would singly have been some answer to this; and, reciprocally, that the answer to this is a full answer to the second.

Having thus shewn that, in Sir J. Moore's very inaccurate statements of facts, we have some further reasons for a previous distrust of any opinion which is supported by those statements,—it is now time to make the reader acquainted with the real terms and extent of that opinion. For it is far less to be feared that, from his just respect for him who gave it, he should allow it an undue weight in his judgment—than that, reposing on the faithfulness of the abstracts and reports of these letters, he should really be still ignorant of its exact tenor.

The whole amount then of what Sir John Moore has alleged against the Spaniards, in any place but one, is comprised in this sentence:—"The enthusiasm, of which we have heard so much, no where appears: whatever good-will there is (and I believe amongst the lower orders there is a great deal) is taken no advantage of." It is true that, in that one place (viz. in his last letter written at Corunna), he charges the Spaniards with "apathy and indifference:" but, as this cannot be reconciled with his concession of *a great deal of good-will*, we are bound to take that as his real and deliberate opinion which he gave under circumstances that allowed him most coolness and freedom of judgment.—The Spaniards then were wanting in enthusiasm. Now what is meant by enthusiasm? Does it mean want of ardour and zeal in battle? This Sir J. Moore no where asserts; and, even without a direct acknowledgement of their good conduct in the field (of which he had indeed no better means of judging than we in England), there is involved in his statement of the relative numbers of the French and Spaniards—combined with our knowledge of the time during which they maintained their struggle—a sufficient testimony to that; even if the events of the first campaign had not made it superfluous. Does it mean then a want of good-will to the cause? So from this, we have seen that Sir J. M. admits that there was, in that class where it was most wanted, 'a great deal' of good-will. And, in the present condition of Spain, let it be recollected what it is that this implies. We see, in the intercepted letter to Marshal Soult (transmitted by Sir J. M.), that the French keep accurate registers of the behaviour of the different towns; and this was, no doubt, well known throughout Spain. Therefore to shew any signs of good-will—much more to give a kind welcome to the English (as had been done at Badajoz and Salamanca)—was, they knew, a pledge of certain punishment on any visit from the French. So that goodwill, manifested in these circumstances, was nothing less than a testimony of devotion to the cause.

Here then, the reader will say, I find granted—in the courage and the good-will of the Spaniards—all the elements of an enthusiastic resistance; and cannot therefore imagine what more could be sought for except the throwing out and making palpable of their enthusiasm to the careless eye in some signal outward manifestations. In this accordingly we learn what interpretation we are to give to Sir J. M.'s charge:—there were no tumults on his entrance into Spain; no insurrections; they did not, as he says, "rally round" the English army. But, to determine how far this disappointment of his expectations tells against the Spaniards, we must first know how far those expectations were reasonable. Let the reader consider, then,

First; what army was this round which the Spaniards were to rally? If it was known by the victory of Vimiera, it was known also to many by the Convention of Cintra: for, though the government had never ventured to communicate that affair officially to the nation, dark and perplexing whispers were however circulated about it throughout Spain. Moreover, it must surely demand some superstition in behalf of regular troops—to see, in an army of 26,000 men, a dignity adequate to the office here claimed for it of awakening a new vigour and enthusiasm in such nation as Spain; not to mention that an English army, however numerous, had no right to consider itself as other than a tributary force—as itself tending to a centre—and attracted rather than attracting.

Secondly; it appears that Sir J. M. has overlooked one most important circumstance;—viz. that the harvest, in these provinces, had been already reaped; the English army could be viewed only as gleaners. Thus, as we have already seen, Estramadura had furnished an army which had marched before his arrival; from Salamanca also—the very place in which he makes his complaint—there had gone out a battalion to Biscay which Gen. Blake had held up, for its romantic gallantry, to the admiration of his whole army.

Yet, thirdly, it is not meant by any means to assert that Spain has put forth an energy adequate to the service—or in any tolerable proportion to her own strength. Far from it! But upon whom does the blame rest? Not surely upon the people—who, as long as they continued to have confidence in their rulers, could not be expected (after the early fervours of their revolution had subsided) much to overstep the measure of exertion prescribed to them—but solely upon the government. Up to the time when Sir J. M. died, the Supreme Junta had adopted no one grand and comprehensive measure for calling out the strength of the nation;—scarcely any of such ordinary vigour as, in some countries, would have been adopted to meet local disturbances among the people. From their jealousy of popular feeling,—they had never taken any steps, by books or civic assemblies, to make the general enthusiasm in the cause available by bringing it within the general consciousness; and thus to create the nation into an organic whole. Sir J. M. was fully aware of this:—"The Spanish Government," he says, "do not seem ever to have contemplated the possibility of a second attack:" and accordingly, whenever he is at leisure to make distinctions, he does the people the justice to say—that the failure was with those who should have "taken advantage" of their good will. With the people therefore will for ever remain the glory of having resisted heroically with means utterly inadequate; and with the government the whole burthen of the disgrace that the means were thus inadequate.

But, further,—even though it should still be thought that, in the three provinces which Sir J. Moore saw, there may have been some failures with the people,—it is to be remembered that these were the very three which had never been the theatre of French outrages; which therefore had neither such a vivid sense of the evils which they had to fear, nor so strong an animation in the recollection of past triumphs: we might accordingly have predicted that, if any provinces should prove slack in their exertions, it would be these three. So that, after all, (a candid inquirer into this matter will say) admitting Sir J. M.'s description to be faithful with respect to what he saw, I can never allow that the conduct of these three provinces shall be held forth as an exponent of the general temper and condition of Spain. For that therefore I must look to other authorities.

Such an inquirer we might then refer to the testimonies of Gen. Leith and of Capt. Pasley for Biscay and Asturias; of Mr. Vaughan (as cited by Lord Castlereagh) for the whole East and South; of Lord Cochrane (himself a most gallant man, and giving *his* testimony under a trying comparison of the Spaniards with English Sailors) for Catalonia in particular; of Lord W. Bentinck for the central provinces; and, for all Spain, we might appeal even to the Spanish military reports—which, by the discrimination of their praises (sometimes giving severe rebukes to particular regiments, &c.) authenticate themselves.

But, finally, we are entitled—after the *actions* of the Spaniards—to dispense with such appeals. Spain might justly deem it a high injury and affront, to suppose that (after her deeds performed under the condition of her means) she could require any other testimony to justify her before all posterity. What those deeds have been, it cannot surely now be necessary to inform the reader:

and therefore the remainder of this note shall be employed in placing before him the present posture of Spain—under two aspects which may possibly have escaped his notice.

First, Let him look to that part of Spain which is now in the possession of the enemy;—let him bear in mind that the present campaign opened at the latter end of last October; that the French were then masters of the country up to the Ebro; that the contest has since lain between a veteran army (rated, on the lowest estimate, at 113,000 men—with a prodigious superiority in cavalry, artillery, &c.) opposed (as to all *regular* opposition) by unpractised Spaniards, split into three distinct armies, having no communication with each other, making a total of not more than 80,000 men;—and then let him inquire what progress, in this time and with these advantages, the French have been able to make (comparing it, at the same time, with that heretofore made in Prussia, and elsewhere): the answer shall be given from the *Times* newspaper of April 8th—"It appears that, at the date of our last accounts from France as well as Spain, about one half of the Peninsula was still unsubdued by the French arms. The provinces, which retain their independence, form a sort of irregular or broken crescent; of which one horn consists in parts of Catalonia and Valencia, and the other horn includes Asturias (perhaps we may soon add Gallicia). The broader surface contains the four kingdoms of Andalusia (Seville, Grenada, Cordova, and Murcia), and considerable parts of Estramadura, and La Mancha; besides Portugal."—The writer might have added that even the provinces, occupied by the French, cannot yet be counted substantially as conquests: since they have a military representation in the south; large proportions of the defeated armies having retreated thither.

Secondly, Let him look to that part of Spain which yet remains unsubdued.—It was thought no slight proof of heroism in the people of Madrid, that they prepared for their defence—not as the foremost champions of Spain (in which character they might have gained an adventitious support from the splendour of their post; and, at any rate, would have been free from the depression of preceding disasters)—but under a full knowledge of recent and successive overthrows; their advanced armies had been defeated; and their last stay, at Somosierra, had been driven in upon them. But the Provinces in the South have many more causes for dejection: they have heard, since these disasters, that this heroic city of Madrid has fallen; that their forts in Catalonia have been wrested from them; that an English army just moved upon the horizon of Spain—to draw upon itself the gaze and expectations of the people, and then to vanish like an apparition; and, finally, they have heard of the desolation of Saragossa. Under all this accumulation of calamity, what has been their conduct? In Valencia redoubled preparations of defence; in Seville a decree for such energetic retaliation on the enemy,—as places its authors, in the event of his success, beyond the hopes of mercy; in Cadiz—on a suspicion that a compromise was concerted with their enemy—tumults and clamours of the people for instant vengeance; every where, in their uttermost distress, the same stern and unfaultering attitude of defiance as at the glorious birth of their resistance.

In this statement, then, of the past efforts of Spain—and of her present preparations for further efforts—will be found a full answer to all the charges alleged, by Sir John Moore in his letters, against the people of Spain, even if we did not find sufficient ground for rejecting them in an examination of these letters themselves.

* * * * * *

The author of the above note—having, in justice to the Spaniards, spoken with great plainness and freedom—feels it necessary to add a few words, that it may not thence be concluded that he is insensible to Sir J. Moore's claims upon his respect. Perhaps—if Sir J. M. could himself have given us his commentary upon these letters, and have restricted the extension of such passages as (from want of vigilance in making distinctions or laxity of language) are at variance with concessions made elsewhere—they would have been found not more to differ from the reports of other intelligent and less prejudiced observers, than we might have expected from the circumstances under which they were written. Sir J. M. has himself told us (in a letter published since the above note was written) that he thinks the Spaniards "a fine people;" and that acknowledgement, from a soldier, cannot be supposed to exclude courage; nor, from a Briton, some zeal for national independence. We are therefore to conclude that, when Sir J. M. pronounces opinions on "the Spaniards" not to be reconciled with this and other passages, he speaks—not of the Spanish people—but of the Spanish government. And, even for what may still remain charged uncandidly upon the people, the writer does not forget that there are infinite apologies to be found in Sir J. Moore's situation: the earliest of these letters were written under great anxiety and disturbance of mind from the anticipation of calamity;—and the latter (which are the most severe) under the actual pressure of calamity; and calamity of that sort which would be the most painful to the feelings of a gallant soldier, and most likely to vitiate his judgment with respect to those who had in part (however innocently) occasioned it. There may be pleaded also for him—that want of leisure which would make it difficult to compare the different accounts he received, and to draw the right inferences from them. But then these apologies for his want of fidelity—are also reasons before-hand for suspecting it: and there are now (May 18th) to be added to these reasons, and their confirmations in the letters themselves, fresh proofs in the present state of Gallicia, as manifested by the late re-capture of Vigo, and the movements of the Marquis de la Romana; all which, from Sir J. Moore's account of the temper in that province, we might have confidently pronounced impossible. We must therefore remember that what in him were simply mis-statements—are now, when repeated with our better information, calumnies; and calumnies so much the less to be excused in us, as we have already (in our conduct towards Spain) given her other and no light matter of complaint against ourselves.

END OF THE APPENDIX.

EDITORIAL APPENDICES

APPENDIX I

Address on The Convention of Cintra

In the Wordsworth Library, Grasmere, is preserved a single manuscript sheet, in the hand of either Mary Wordsworth or Sara Hutchinson, which gives, in a much amended draft, the fragment printed here. It is clear from parallels of wording and substance that the document is connected with *Cintra*: cf. *Cintra*, 1085: 'the transaction, considered as a military transaction', and *Address*, 1: 'To what extent, as a military measure, it may be arraigned …'; *Cintra*, 1098: 'looking at this issue merely as an affair between two armies', and *Address*, 5–6: 'Considered, then, as an affair between two armies'; and especially Wordsworth's claim (*Cintra*, 1488 ff.) that, as a private citizen, he is entitled to speak upon public and military matters, and the similar claim in *Address*, 11–42. Since the last words of the fragment define it as part of an 'address', we conjecture that it is part of a draft of an address which Wordsworth proposed to deliver (either orally or in print: note 'reader', 3) at the public meeting projected by himself and his Lake District friends in protest against the Convention (see *Cintra*, Introd.). We have provided a title accordingly.

The draft, even in the edited form presented here, is in the tortuous manner of *Cintra* itself, and is sometimes, especially in the paragraph 11–28, not absolutely coherent or even grammatical (see 32–3: 'the health … are the condition'). The manuscript is inadequately punctuated, and almost all the commas in our text, and some other pointing, are editorial.

[Address on The Convention of Cintra]

To what extent, as a military measure, it may be arraigned; and under what conditions this charge of incompetence may be justly preferred against those who condemn this as a military measure (and the reader will recollect that it is as such only that I have lately been speaking of it); I will now, in justification of the sentence which I passed upon it above, proceed to determine.—Considered, then, as an affair between two armies, the measure resolves itself into three elementary parts—

1st. Matters which, to be justly appreciated, require professional skill and a thorough knowledge of all local circumstances and exigences of the time;—whoever decides upon these matters without such qualifications is obnoxious to the charge: but on these I have given no opinion.

2ndly. A class of measures, and those general ones, on which certain men may claim a right to give judgement from the joint consideration, first, that the facts are of high interest—secondly, that the evidence of the facts is, in its kind, unquestionable (coming only either from the mouths of the men arraigned—or universally acknowledged to be unimpeachable authority)—in its kind unquestionable, and in its degree complete;—thirdly, that the law, these conditions being presumed, includes in it's constitution the warrant for its own application—inasmuch as it is nothing more than an abstract from every parallel case found in history—the [?train] of conduct held in such cases—and [*tear*]ons pronounced by all men who, in recording such [? cases, have] taken neither the narrow view of a purely military scrutiny, nor the wide and comprehensive one of moral man appealing to elementary and universal principles

MS. *begins*: Arraigning it for the present *del.*
1–3 and under … measure *ins.*
4 such *del. and restored*; in this light *ins. and del.*
4 have … of it *subs. for* [1] am now viewing it [2] am now looking at it
4–7 I will now … parts—*subs. for the following, which is undeleted except as indicated*: [will appear from the *del.*] [my own *del.*] [for the *subs. for* in] justification of the sentence which I have passed upon it above I am now called upon to [shew *del.*] state: and this I shall do by shewing that
6 resolves *subs. for* divides
7 elementary *subs. for* dif[ferent]
9 on these I have not presumed to give an opinion *del. after* time;—
16 or *del. after* authority)
21 all men *subs. for* men

of his nature, but have spoken in the character of politicians and calculators of gross general expediency:—Such character, and the consequent right to pronounce sentence upon this second class of measures, I may surely claim, if I have any right to speak to the public at all upon public affairs; and, accordingly, I have spoken without reserve.

3rdly. and lastly: a class of military measures of paramount importance, sinking the rest, in comparison with them, into insignificance— measures which, though formally military, are in their [ ] moral; which cannot be thought of in separation from moral feelings and powers;—where the health of the moral feelings and powers are the condition of the military strength:—These are measures which every man may be entitled to decide upon who has little or no acquaintance with past ages, and only a general knowledge, with a deep feeling of the struggle as a contest of justice with the most atrocious oppression.—On the rights of this class of judges I most earnestly insist; to them I chiefly appeal; theirs is the authority of most weight; by the principles of courage—independence—honor—and dignity inherent in them is the question mainly to be tried; and to encourage these principles, and to sustain them by calling them to their proper exercise—is one of the primary objects of this present address.

27 affairs *subs. for* measures
33 military *subs. for* moral —this is a division of the subject *del. after* measures

APPENDIX II

CONTENTS OF THE CORNELL MANUSCRIPT OF DE QUINCEY'S 'POSTSCRIPT ON SIR JOHN MOORE'S LETTERS' (HEALEY ITEM 2804)

pp. 1–16: a fairly clean version of *Ap. Cintra*, 566–end. This is the longest continuous draft in the MS.; most (but not all) of the emendations are in the direction of the text of 1809; the order of paragraphs is identical with that of 1809; there is one large–scale variant at 678–87.

pp. 17–18: a version of 850–end.

p. 19: versions of 672–4, 678–77.

p. 20: details of proof–corrections to the text of 1809, pp. 193–200

pp. 21–4: a version of 519–75.

pp. 25–7: a version of 734–72–840, omitting 745–51.

pp. 28–31: a version of 566–647.

p. 32: summaries of arguments developed elsewhere: on internal inconsistencies in Moore's letters (cf. 700–04, 853–6); on parts of Spain not under French control (cf. 773–84); on the guilt of governments; on testimony other than Moore's; on the 'energy and patriotism of Spain' (cf. 823–43).

p. 33: a version of 832–43; and a short passage similar in drift to 801–10.

pp. 34–6: versions of 529–75 and 609–19.

p. 37: extracts from Moore's letters, with dates of letters and of their publication.

p. 38: a discussion of Moore's veracity, hinting at the matter of 529–41; and a draft combining the matter of 745–51 and 610–5.

pp. 39–40: a version of 793–830. At the top of p. 40, upside-down, a version of 519–20; at the bottom, upside-down, a version of497–8.

p. 41: two passages which are evidently drafts of De Quincey's note on Saragossa; see *Cintra*, 2705 ff., and n. The upper third of the page, written upside-down, reads after emendation as follows:

> & if carefully examined it is not Saragossa—a walled city—that he has possessed himself of—but Saragossa a lazarhouse and a tomb!
>
> it is thought necessary therefore to account to the reader for retaining the here referred to

> the passage relating to that city by stating that the great distance of the author from London made it impossible for his friend (to whom the correcting of the proof–sheets has been entrusted) to wait for the slight alterations occasionally demanded in the allusions to passing occurrences without very long and inconvenient

The lower two–thirds of the page reads after emendation as follows:

> for the proof of which assertion the reader who may [?inconsiderately] have adopted any opinion pronounced upon the Army or the Heroic Governor of Saragossa in the calumnious statement of their enemy, is referred with entire confidence to the facts detailed (though no doubt with the greatest possible injustice to the Spaniards) in the same document.
>
> Whilst this sheet was under revisal, the 33rd bulletin of the French Army in Spain was received in London—announcing, in sum, that three divisions of that Army had at length possessed themselves of the ruins of Saragossa.—It is thought proper therefore to inform the reader that, from the author's great distance from London, it was not possible to apply to him for an alteration without considerable inconvenience, and this the reviser deemed the less necessary as being well assured that his friend would make no further alteration than [?] declare, in a more full and solemn tribute of honor to Saragossa, that of all the high anticipations [?] of her she had most faithfully acquitted herself; having then only ceased to be the champion of the Spanish cause when she became its glorious martyr: since even upon the testimony of her [?base] and calumnious enemy

p. 41 verso: In a large hand:

Convention of Cintra
all in confusion
Is this Wordsworths
hand or my Fathers

p. 42: a version of 572–75; a space for examples; a version of 688–95.

pp. 43–5: a version of 696–800.

p.46: versions of 605–15 and 616–8.

p. 47: a version of 576–84. p. 47 ends: 'For Sir D. Baird, it is still more difficult to find an excuse, who, in'; and p. 46 begins: 'this instance, had—in the letter of Capt. Pasley of the Engineers—a fuller testimony to the merits of this army than was Sir J. M.

'2. The defeat of the Estramaduran advanced–guard' etc.

It is clear that the order of pp. 46 and 47, recto and verso of one sheet, should be reversed.

pp. 48–9: a version of 529–65.

pp. 50–1: a version of 700–51–804, omitting 734–44.

pp. 52–3: a version of 656–97.

p. 54: versions of 685–7, 667–70.

pp. 55^r, 55^v: extracts from *The Courier*, 12 November 1808, for Appendices E and F.

pp. 56–7: *Cintra*, 4288–94, transcribed by De Quincey. See Introd.

p. 58: version of, or notes for, 529–65.

p. 59: versions of, or notes for, 730–2, 745–7, 754–65. Upside-down, near the bottom, a version of 861–4. Last line of page: 'that approach to equality which makes [?superiority pleasant]'.

p. 60: versions of 626–9, 572–5; and this passage, apparently referring to Moore's comments on the defeat of Blake (576 ff.):

> The true reason for all these misrepresentations must be sought in these two circumstances:
>
> 1st that the English army, in it's upper ranks, was in many sympathies and communities of thinking more nearly allied to it's enemy than it's ally: thus we find Sir J. M. more than once quoting with approbation intercepted French letters—2nd—It was a gallant [?army]

p. 61: a version of 872–end.

p. 62: a version of 850–72; at the foot, upside–down, a version of 566–71. The order of pp. 61 and 62, recto and verso of the same sheet, should perhaps be reversed, though the verbal connection is not quite exact.

pp. 63–5: a version of 785–846. p. 63, beginning 'of Gen. Leith and Capt. Pasley', may be intended to follow p. 27, which ends (in its third line) 'refer to the testimonies'.

pp. 66^r, 66^v: a version of 529–65. These pages are numbered (by De Quincey) 3 and 4, and seem to be intended to precede the version of 566 ff. beginning on p. 1, the first ten pages of which are numbered 5–14 by De Quincey.

p. 67: versions of 808–10, 823–37.

pp. 68–71: extracts from and summaries of official correspondence on the campaign.

pp. 72–4: versions of 495–517, 525–33, 529–30.

COMMENTARY: *CINTRA*

Title–page. Qui didicit … ducis.] Horace, *Ars Poetica*, 312–15. On the earlier form of the title–page, see Introd.

Motto. See textual n., and cf. *M.Y.* i. 328. The passage is from *An Advertisement touching the Controversies of the Church of England*, in Bacon, *Works* (London, 1740), iv. 460. This edition, 'To which is prefixed, A New Life of the Author, By Mr. Mallet', gives the text as Wordsworth wished it to be printed. From Jordan, pp. 192–5 (31 May 1809), it appears that De Quincey prepared the passage for the press; he explains that 'M[r] Wordsworth said that the reason why he did not send me the extract was that he did not exactly know where to look for it.' This letter also indicates Mallet's edition as a source of Wordsworth's version; De Quincey, in a long discussion of the readings 'hate' and 'zeal', is concerned lest Mallet's 'hate' should be less authentic than 'zeal', which he transcribed from other, supposedly more authoritative, texts. Wordsworth was seeking a copy of 'Lord Bacon's Works' in July 1808 (*M.Y.* i. 257).

Advertisement

6–7. two portions … Courier] *Cintra*, 1–187, appeared in *The Courier* for Tuesday, 27 Dec. 1808, p. 2, cols. 2–4, under the heading: 'Concerning the Convention of Cintra, in Reference to the Principles by which the Independence and Freedom of Nations must be Preserved or Recovered.' It was signed 'G.'. *Cintra*, 188–503, appeared in *The Courier* for Friday, 13 Jan. 1809, p. 1, col. 4,–p. 2, col. 4, under the heading, 'Concerning the Convention of Cintra, in Relation to the Principles by which alone the Independence and Freedom of Nations can be Maintained or Recovered. Section II. Continued from Tuesday's Courier, 27th ult.' It is again signed 'G.', and concludes with '(To be continued)'.

9–11. otherwise … work] This seems to refer to the promise at *Cintra*, 228 ff, to cite from Spanish documents, which is repeated at 497–503 and not fulfilled until 504 ff. It is not, however, clear what this has to do with the 'previous publication', except that the reprinting of the Spanish documents would have been an uneconomical way to fill the columns of the newspaper from which Wordsworth had already taken the citations.

13. pressure of public business] Wordsworth probably refers to the examination of Mrs. Clarke before a Committee of the House of Commons. Mary Anne Clarke (1776–1852), *née* Thompson, mistress of Frederick, Duke of York, from about 1803, was under examination from 1 February until 20 March 1809, on the ground that she had received money for using her influence with the Duke in connection with promotions in the Army. The charges were brought before the House by Colonel Gwylym Lloyd Wardle on 27 January; those against the Duke were not proved, but he resigned his appointment as Commander–in–Chief. Reports of the examination occupy most of the space in *The Courier* from 2 February, except on rare occasions such as 22 February, when the debate on the Convention of Cintra is fully reported. On the 'loss of several sheets' (11), see Introd.

23–29. I must ... corrected.] An insertion made on ? 26 March 1809 (*M.Y.* i. 300). Wordsworth's letter reads 'a change' instead of 'changes' (28).

29. On the additions, see Introd.; for examples of corrections see notes on *Cintra*, 2298–9, 3795, 4061, etc.

Concerning the Convention of Cintra

67–8. This just and necessary war] Cf. Freeholders, 431, 498–500. A commonplace of the time; see, for instance, the royal 'Proclamation, for General Fast', in *London Gazette*, No. 16214 (31 Dec. 1808—3 Jan. 1809), p. 1: 'We, taking into Our most serious Consideration the just and necessary War in which We are engaged ... do ... hereby command, that a Publick Day of Fasting and Humiliation be observed ... on Wednesday the Eighth Day of February next ensuing.' In the nineties Coleridge had toyed with the phrase in his political writings: see *Collected Works*, i, ed. L. Patton and P. Mann (London and Princeton, 1971), pp. 51, 54, 69, 287.

69–70. before the Treaty ... Switzerland] Between 1798 and 1802.

72 ff. and this justice etc.] Wordsworth draws on his own reactions to the war with France: see *Prel.* X. 228 ff.; and with 'and that enemy ambition' (75–9), cf. *Prel.* X. 792 if. The tone of *Cintra*, in passages such as 'Their conduct was herein consistent [against] the spirit of selfish tyranny and lawless ambition' (84–9), is more confident than that of *Prel.* X. 798–805. See also *L.Y.*, pp. 56–7 (Dec. 1821):

> If I were addressing those who have dealt so liberally with the words Renegado Apostate, etc., I should retort the charge upon them, and say, *you* have been deluded by *Places* and *Persons*, while I have stuck to *Principles*—I abandoned France, and her Rulers, when *they* abandoned the struggle for Liberty, gave themselves up to Tyranny, and endeavoured to enslave the world. I disapproved of the war against France at its commencement ... but after Bonaparte had violated the Independence of Switzerland, my heart turned against him, and

against the Nation that could submit to be the Instrument of such an outrage.

Cf. also the drift of Coleridge's 'France: An Ode'.

95. evil communications] I Cor. 15 : 33: 'Evil communications corrupt good manners.'

127. the moment of the rising] In Madrid, 2 May 1808; subsequently Asturias (24 May) and Galicia (30 May). Asturian envoys were in London seeking British assistance by 7 June.

131. We have inspected, or had reports on, nine copies of 1809 in an effort to establish the correct reading here. In all copies the last letter of the group which we print as 'of a' is printed without a space between it and 'of', and is followed by a space for about three letters. In the copies in the British Museum (Ashley 4628), Yale University Library, and New York Public Library, the letter is certainly 'a'; it is almost certainly 'a' in the copies in the British Museum (C. 114. d. 2), Wordsworth Library (Grasmere), and Turnbull Library (Wellington, New Zealand); in the copies at St. John's College, Cambridge, and Cornell, all that survives is a form like a Greek iota which, from the angle of the spur at the foot, is probably the remains of an 'a'. In the Bodleian copy, Godw. Pamph. 1980 (15), the letter can be read as a 't' at first glance, because of a smear emerging to the right of the minim; but the smear is too low to be the cross of a 't', the spur is that of an 'a' not a 't', and we think that the bow of an 'a' can be seen impressed into the paper but not inked. Wells (pp. 68–9) reports copies reading 'oft' as well as copies reading 'ofa', but his descriptions of those reading 'oft' are so qualified that we suspect that the true reading is 'ofa' in each instance. If a clear case of 'oft' should be found, we should assume an attempt to emend 'of a' (as in *Courier*) to 'of the', which is the reading of most reprints of *Cintra* (Wells, p. 68), though no copy of 1809 known to us or reported by Wells gives authority for this reading. It would indeed be remarkable if such an attempt should be made to emend a text already satisfactory in sense, with a damaged type (Wells, p. 68) replacing another damaged type, and without the necessary 'he'; it seems much more likely that in all copies the uncertain letter is 'a' in various states. Our text accordingly reads 'of a', and our assumption is that 1809 rightly repeats, or attempts to repeat, the reading of *Courier*, the only errors lying in the spacing of the types and in the use of a defective type for 'a'.

132–3. 'this corruptible ... immortality'] 1 Cor. 15: 53.

147–51. Britain and Spain were technically at war in 1808. A peace treaty was signed on 14 January 1809 (*Courier*, 28 Mar. 1809).

159–61. See Introd., sect. I.

174–5. their Sovereign] Charles IV (abdicated 19 March 1808); or more likely his son, Ferdinand VII, who is constantly referred to in Spanish documents of the kind cited below (504 ff.) as the lawful sovereign of Spain.

186. victory of Vimiera] 21 August 1808. Modern authorities give the place-name as 'Vimiero'; we have preserved Wordsworth's spelling throughout.

207–8. opposition ... Marathon] The defence of Thermopylae by the Spartans under Leonidas against the Persians took place in 480 B.C.; see Herodotus, *Hist.* vii. 175–228, especially 210–28. Cf. 429 below. In 490 B.C. the Athenians and Plataeans defeated a Persian rearguard near Marathon, and thereby secured the defence of Athens (Herodotus, vi. 102–17).

241. present disaster] At the date of writing, presumably 3 January 1809 (see Introd., sect. II), the most obvious 'disaster' was the ill–fortune of Sir John Moore's army in Spain.

273 ff. paper entitled "Precautions"] Printed in *Courier*, 4 July 1808, under the heading: 'Precautions which it will be proper to observe throughout the different Provinces of Spain, in the necessity to which they have been driven by the French, of resisting the unjust and violent possession which their Armies are endeavouring to take of the Kingdom'. The original reads 'or even the hope' (279). Clause 2 reads: 'A war of partisans is the system which suits us; the embarrassing and wasting the enemy's armies by want of provisions, destroying bridges, throwing up entrenchments in proper situations, and other similar means. The situation of Spain, its many mountains, and the passes which they present, its rivers and torrents, and even the collocation of its provinces, invite us to carry on this species of warfare successfully.'

334. Thirdly, ... See note to line 356 below

338. battle of Rio Seco] 13–14 July 1808; the French under Bessières defeated the army of Galicia under Blake and Cuesta, mainly because of the latter's incompetence. This battle, which cleared French communications from Bayonne into Spain, was the only notable French success in the early stages of the war.

338–41. returned ... troops.] *Courier*, 9 Aug. 1808, quotes a letter from Blake to Bessières dated 28 July 1808:

> Signior Marshal—I have received your Excellency's letter with due respect, and renew to you my acknowledgments for your having set at liberty the 400 or 500 prisoners taken in the battle of Rio Seco, whom your Excellency calls peasants of Gallicia. They are, however, real soldiers. They are recruits incorporated in the regiments of the line, though they did not wear uniforms. I explain this circumstance, not to exempt myself from acknowledging the generous conduct of your Excellency towards these men, but lest any equivocal idea should, at another time, bring on them a treatment they would not deserve.

340. Blake] Joachim Blake, of Irish descent, general of the Galician forces.

356–478. not merely ... the latter.] Coleridge to Thomas Poole, 3 Feb. 1809 (*C.L.* iii. 174), claims that in the instalments of *Cintra* which appeared in *The Courier* for 13 January 1809, 'The two last Columns of the second, excepting the concluding Paragraph, were written all but a few sentences by me.' The passage concerned is that indicated above. Coleridge summarizes its content in a letter to Stuart of 8–9 January 1809 (*C.L.* iii. 164). [According to *EOT* 3: 98–103 the passage which Coleridge claims to have re-composed from Wordsworth's notes may begin at line 334—RG.]

400. moral qualities ... nature] Cf. *E.E.* II. 55 ff., and n.

404. bodies of the Angels] *Paradise Lost*, VI. 328–3. [c.f. Sonnets to National Independence and Liberty, XXX]

428. Abdiel] *Paradise Lost*, V. 800 ff.; VI. ill ff.

429. Leonidas] Commander of the Spartans against Xerxes at Thermopylae, 480 B.C. (Herodotus, *Hist.* vii. 204). Cf. 231–2 above.

461. late Austrian or Prussian resistance to France] Resistance crushed by Napoleon's campaigns of 1805–6, in his victories at Ulm, Austerlitz, Jena, and Auerstädt.

482–3. all knowledge ... repose] Cf. *Reply to Mathetes*, 427–9.

487 "the sea-mark ... sail"] *Othello*, v. ii. 267.

504. the first to rise] Apart from the riots in Madrid on 2 May 1808; see 127, n.

506–24. "Loyal Asturians ... to arms!"] *The Times*, 29 June 1808, almost verbatim, under heading 'Proclamation of the Council General of the Principality of Asturias'.

524–42. Supreme Junta ... against him."] *Courier*, 8 July 1808, almost verbatim.

544. manifesto of the Court] *Courier*, 11 Aug. 1808: 'Manifesto of the Prince Regent of Portugal against France, Or Justificatory Exposition of the conduct of the Court of Portugal with respect to France, from the commencement of the Revolution to the time of the Invasion of Portugal, and of the motives that compelled it to declare War against the Emperor of the French, in consequence of that Invasion, and the subsequent Declaration of War, made after the Report of the Minister of Foreign Affairs.' The document lists, inter alia, the following French demands: '1st, To shut up the ports of Portugal against England; 2d, to detain all Englishmen who resided in Portugal; and 3d, to confiscate all English property; or, in case of refusal, to expose itself to an immediate war with France and Spain.' It proceeds: 'General Junot, without any previous declaration, without the consent of the Prince Regent of Portugal, entered the kingdom with the vanguard of his army, assuring the people in the country that he was marching through it, to succour his Royal Highness against an invasion of the English, and that he entered Portugal as the General of a friendly and allied power.' On the behaviour of the Portuguese court under French pressure, see Introd.

546–77. Address of the Supreme Junta ... to action."] *Courier*, 8 July 1808, under heading 'Address to the People of Portugal'. The latter portion of the document is quoted in part below, *Cintra*, 824–35.

579–92. proclamation ... shot."] All but the first sentence quoted appears in *Courier*, 15 Aug. 1808, in a fuller version than Wordsworth gives here. *The Times* of the same date supplies the missing sentence as: 'You yourselves have asked him for a king, who, aided by this all–powerful and great Monarch, might be able to recover your unhappy country, and place it in the rank to which it belongs.' Neither journal gives Wordsworth's version exactly.

592–624. bulletins ... in chief."] *Courier*, 10 Oct. 1808, under heading: 'The following Bulletins, relative to the commencement of the resistance to the French in Portugal, were since published by the authority of General Junot'. 'We entered ... burned.' (595–8) is from No. II, dated 2 July 1808; 'The spirit ... Portugal.' (598–601) is from No. III, dated 7 July 1808; the remaining passages, quoted with omissions and adaptations, are from No. IV, dated 18 July 1808. Beia was sacked by Maransin on 26 June, Guerda (Guarda) and Alpedrinha by Loison in early July. These events took place as outlying French detachments fought their way back Lisbon for concentration there when Junot found himself isolated Portugal by the Spanish revolt.

609. 13000 dead] So *Courier*, 10 Oct. 1808; *The Times* of same date reads '3000 dead'.

625–31. Address ... course."] *Courier*, 1 Oct. 1808, reporting 'a general and extraordinary Junta of the Province of Biscay [at Bilbao] and under the Presidency ... of his Excellency Don Joseph Domingo De Massaredo, Captain–General of the Navy, Minister for Maritime Affairs, &c,':

> Biscayans! his Majesty has ordered me to assemble you, 1st, To know from yourselves what share you have had in the insurrection excited in the city of Bilboa; whether you approved of, or abhorred it.—2d. To assure you in case you disapprove of it, that his Majesty has consigned to oblivion, the mistakes and errors of the insurgents, and that he will punish only the heads and beginners of the insurrection, with regard to whom the law must take its course, for the purpose of preventing them in future from disturbing your repose and prosperity.

644–66. address ... enemies, &c."] *The Times*, 28 June 1808, in different translation. 'Resolved to get together something like a representative body which might vote away the liberty of Spain, Napoleon nominated, in the Madrid Gazette of May 24,

150 persons who were to go to Bayonne and there ask him to grant them a king … no less than ninety–one of the nominees were base enough to obey the orders given them, to go to Bayonne and there crave as a boon that the weak and incompetent Joseph Bonaparte might be set to govern their unhappy country' (Oman, i. 63–4).

668–77. address … exist?"] *The Times*, 30 June 1808, in this translation, with minor variants. This passage is the basis of the opening lines of *Nat. Ind. and Lib.* II. xxvii (*P.W.* iii. 137).

719–22. Council … correction."] *The Times*, 30 Aug. 1808, under heading: 'Proclamation of the Council of Castile, to the People of Madrid, on the Departure of the French', dated 5 August 1808: 'Let us, therefore [i.e. because of Spanish victories outside Madrid], cast off our lethargy, and purify our manners, which were arrived almost at the pitch of complete corruption. Let us acknowledge the calamities which the kingdom and this great capital have endured, as a punishment necessary for our correction.'

722–9. General Morla … loaded."] Morla was in command in Cadiz in 1808, and, according to Napier (i. 172–3), who accuses him of double dealing, declined British assistance there. The passage is quoted from an address dated 15 June 1808, in *Courier*, 16 July 1808.

731–41. "The defence … formed them."] *Courier*, 15 Sept. 1808, almost verbatim.

745–54. The names … progenitors."] *Courier*, 1 July 1808, under heading: 'Address from the Council of Leon to the Spanish nation.'

761–71. "Life or Death … enjoy."] We have not found the source of this quotation.

774–82. The next … disgrace."] From Clause 9 of *Precautions*, verbatim from *Courier*, 4 July 1808; see n. on 273 ff.

789–99. "All Europe … preserved."] *Courier*, 12 July 1808, with minor variants.

803–24. Address … just cause."] *The Times*, 30 June 1808, in this translation.

824–35. address … like men."] *Courier*, 8 July 1808, continuing almost immediately after the passage quoted in 546–7. With omissions and slight adaptation. Cf. 2846–50.

836–47. "Precautions … laws, &c. &c."] From Clause 11 of the document; *Courier*, 4 July 1808, almost verbatim. The italics are Wordsworth's.

848–57. proclamation … herself."] *The Times*, 4 Aug. 1808, almost verbatim.

864–5. the voice … God] Cf. *E.S.* 855—62: 'The voice that issues from this Spirit is that Vox Populi which the Deity inspires', whereas there is nothing infallible in 'the clamour of that small though loud portion of the community ... which, under the name of the Public, passes itself, upon the unthinking, as the People.'.

882–3. the knowledge ... forefathers] Similarly, *Prel.* (1850), VI. 448–50: 'Past and future [are] the wings / On whose support harmoniously conjoined / Moves the great spirit of human knowledge'. Cited in *E.S.* 851–3.

886–9. The stream ... strengthen it] Cf. *Llandaff*, 273–5.

897. those heights of magnanimity] Cf. 75 ff.

924–33. dispatches ... cannon, &c. &c."] Reprinted from the *Gazette* of 2 September in *Courier*, 3 Sept. 1808. The 'second letter' is dated 'Vimiera, Aug. 21, 1808'. Wordsworth quotes verbatim. The first letter (17 Aug. 1808) describes the action against Laborde at Roliça. The 'official communication' (933) does not seem to be reprinted; but cf. Courier, 5 Sept. 1808: 'After this action [Vimiera], on the next day, Gen. KELLERMAN arrived at Sir ARTHUR WELLESLEY's headquarters, to treat for terms of submission.'

925–6. two several engagements] Roliça and Vimiera (17 and 21 Aug. 1808).

943. losses ... sustained in Spain] Primarily in the defeat of Dupont at Baylen in mid–July; see n. on 1452.

950. Maida] Some 210 miles south of Naples; scene of an engagement between British and French troops on 4 July 1806, in which the British force under General Sir John Stuart was successful.

957–63. proclamation ... England."] *The Times*, 3 Sept. 1808:

> His Britannic Majesty our most gracious King and Master has, in compliance with the wishes and ardent supplication for succour from all parts of Portugal, sent to your aid a British army directed to co-operate with his fleet already on your coast. The English soldiers who land upon your shore do so with equal sentiments of friendship, faith, and honour. The glorious struggle in which you are engaged is for all that is dear to man; the protection of your wives and children; the restoration of your lawful Princes; the independence, nay, the very existence of your kingdom; and the preservation of your holy religion. Objects like these can only be attained by distinguished examples of fortitude and constancy. The noble struggle against the tyranny and usurpation of France will be jointly maintained by Portugal, Spain, and England; and, in contributing to the success of a cause so just and glorious, the views of his Britannic Majesty are the same as those by which you are yourselves animated.

985–90. Sir Arthur ... disappointed.] *Courier*, 18 Nov. 1808, citing a dispatch of Wellesley dated 16 Aug. 1808, read before the Board of Inquiry:

> It had been the wish of [the Portuguese] Government that the British stores should be employed for the maintenance of the Portuguese troops; and the dispatch stated the refusal of compliance on the part of Sir Arthur Wellesley, who intimated to the Portuguese General that the British forces would not be under

> the necessity of obtaining bread from them, but would require that nation to supply the British with beef, wine, and forage. It also contained an account of … some extraordinary messages sent respecting the supplies, in which General Friere expressed his anxiety on that subject. Sir Arthur Wellesley received a proposition from General Friere, respecting a new plan of operations, which went to separate the Portuguese from the British troops; and the pretext for this proceeding was the probable want of supplies, notwithstanding Sir Arthur Wellesley had expressly stated to him the contrary. Sir Arthur Wellesley attributed this wish of General Friere to his apprehension that the British were not sufficiently strong for the enemy. … If Sir Arthur had been furnished with the supplies, he would have acceded to the request, but he found that the British Commissariat had not sufficient stores to enable him to do so. Besides, he did not believe that the motives stated by General Friere were what led to his determination.

Wellesley's and Freire's motives are analysed by Napier, i. 197–8. Oman calls Freire 'a pretentious and incapable person . . . a self-willed and shifty man' (i. 212, 233). He was murdered by his own troops at Braga in March 1809, during the second French invasion of Portugal (Oman, ii. 233).

997–1044. Now there is … event.] Cf. editorial comment in *Courier*, 22 Sept. 1808:

> There is [in the Convention] a studied abstinence from any thing that can in the least degree wound even the *feelings* of the enemy, as if we were *fearful* he would not accept the conditions. … Could we imagine the French General to have sat down for the purpose of inventing terms of an agreement which should not only wipe off every stain which his character had sustained from a previous defeat, but which would transfer that stain from his own to his adversary's character, he could not have done it more effectively than by the present convention. Nothing that can gratify the pride and vanity of Junot and his Master is omitted.—The former is the *Duke of Abrantes*, and the latter *is his Imperial and Royal Majesty Napoleon the First!!*—Oh! this hateful Convention.

Again, *Courier*, 27 Sept. 1808, editorial comment:

> In the very outset of the negociation we acknowledge Junot as Duke of Abrantes—This was a most singular imprudence. … At the very time we were reconquering the Country for its legitimate Sovereign, from the Usurper of his authority, we recognise as legal an act of that Usurper against the legitimate Sovereign—we recognise Junot as the rightful possessor of a Portuguese title and territory, bestowed upon him, not by the Prince Regent of Portugal, from whom alone such a gift could have justly proceeded, but from Bonaparte, who had no right to grant it.

Cf. also Southey to Humphrey Senhouse, 15 Oct. 1808 (*Life and Correspondence*, iii. 175): 'the high treason against all moral feeling, in recognising Junot by his usurped title'.

1048–50. The night before … news.] *Courier*, 16 Sept. 1808: 'The Park and Tower Guns were fired between eight and nine o'clock.—Undoubtedly it is a matter of great and deep rejoicing, that the main object of the expedition has been accomplished. …

But here joy and congratulation cease; for it must be confessed that the terms were not such as the public had expected.'

1052. such a burst ... indignation] Meetings of public bodies demanding inquiry into the Convention are reported in *The Times*, 13 Oct. 1808 (City of London); 20 Oct. (Reading, Winchester); 21 Oct. (City of Westminster); 29 Oct. (Essex); 4 Nov. (Hampshire); 12 Nov. (Middlesex); 17 Nov. (Rochester); and others. It was from Lord Lonsdale's pressure against such a meeting in Westmorland that *Cintra* arose; see Introd.

1085–6. the Russian fleet] See the Convention between Seniavin and Cotton, Appendix, 472–94.

1085–90. the Russian fleet ... Sweden] Cf. *Courier*, 16 Sept. 1808: 'As to the Russian Fleet, nine sail of the line, and of the Russian line, more or less, are of little importance to such a Navy as ours.—But holding in deposit is not a term to be found in our Naval Dictionary. ... And the Seamen! they are to be sent back to Russia without conditions; of course they may serve immediately against us and our Allies, as the French may'; *The Times*, 16 Sept. 1808: 'Are then the Russian Officers and seamen to be indeed sent home by us—or, in other words, to be conveyed to attack the King of SWEDEN, our most faithful Ally?' Oman (i. 224) calls 'our most faithful Ally' 'the hairbrained King of Sweden'. Cf. *Nat. Ind. and Lib.* I. vii, and Wordsworth's and de Selincourt's notes (*P.W.* iii. 112, 453–4); II. xx and xxi (*P.W.* iii. 133–4).

1090. a French army] See Convention, arts. II–X, pages 387–8, above.

1090–3. a French army ... it] Cf. *Courier*, 16 Sept. 1808: 'But still, whatever inconveniences we might have been subject to [after Vimiera], the enemy were subject to the same, if not to greater, and their force was inferior:—the country all round them was hostile.' Junot's communications had been cut by the Spanish uprising in general and by the defeat of Dupont at Baylen in particular.

1094–6. to be transported ... immediately!] Cf. *Courier*, 16 Sept. 1808: 'But here we find the French obtaining the favourable terms of being allowed to evacuate Portugal, retaining their baggage, that is, their plunder ... the moment they reach France they may set out upon their march to resume hostilities against this very Portugal which they have but just evacuated'; *The Times*, 20 Oct. 1808: 'For see, now, the result of the memorable Armistice and Convention of Cintra: the first body of the French troops were embarked on board the British transports about the 8th of last month, six weeks ago. These men, therefore, may be in Spain; and notwithstanding the arts which have been used to conceal the terms of the Portuguese Convention, the Spaniards may have already learned them from the bayonets of those troops which we have sent to aid in their destruction.'

1098. as an affair between two armies] Cf. *Address*, 6 (p. 405, above).

1118–20. The motive … famine] *Courier*, 17 Sept. 1808, quoting a letter from Dalrymple to Castlereagh of 3 September 1808:

> my own opinion in favour of the expediency of expelling the French army from Portugal by means of the Convention … was principally founded on the great importance of time, which the season of the year rendered peculiarly valuable…. When the suspension of arms was agreed upon, the army under the command of Sir John Moore had not arrived, and doubts were even entertained whether so large a body of men could be landed on an open and dangerous beach; and that being effected, whether the supply of so large an army with provisions from the ships could be provided for, under all the disadvantages to which the shipping were exposed.

Cf. *Courier*, 16 Sept. 1808: 'A respectable Morning Paper hints, that a fleet of transports off the coast of Portugal was in a dangerous state; that the difficulty of landing provisions from the victuallers was very great, and highly precarious, from the state of the surf; besides which considerable dread was entertained in respect of the approaching equinox.'

1122. The nation … discretion] Cf. *Courier*, 16 Sept. 1808: the British public 'expected from the decisive victory of the 21st, gained by a British force which had afterwards been strengthened by 15,000 men, that Junot would have been compelled to an unconditional surrender'.

1124–9. It has … termination.] *Courier*, 15 Dec. 1808, reporting Colonel Torrens under examination by Sir Arthur Wellesley:

> Immediately after we had defeated the right column of the French army, which had made its attack on our left, Sir Arthur Wellesley rode to Sir Harry Burrard, and said, "Sir Harry, now is your time to advance, the enemy are completely beaten, and we shall be in Lisbon in three days. We have a large body of troops which have not been in action: let us move them from the right on the road to Torres Verdas [*sic*], and I'll follow the enemy with the left." Sir H. Burrard replied that he thought a great deal had been done, very much to the credit of the troops; but that he did not think it advisable to move off the ground in pursuit of the enemy. [Ibid., reporting Wellesley:] On the 21st the enemy being completely defeated at all points, he had repeatedly proposed to Sir H. Burrard to advance in pursuance of his original plan of operations. His reasons for thinking that to advance would be beneficial, were before the Court … [but this opportunity having been lost on 21 August, he did not consider the Convention an unreasonable solution, since the French had recovered by 22 August].

1125–9. Sir Arthur … termination] *Courier*, 22 Nov. 1808: 'Q[uestion]. Did you consider the army under your command adequate to the dispersion of Junot's force, when you advised Sir Harry Burrard to march to cut off the enemy's retreat?—

A[nswer, by Wellesley]. I did consider the force which marched under my command to be sufficient to drive the French from Lisbon, and from the forts upon the Tagus.'

1136. his letter] Presumably that of 3 September 1808, cited in n. on 1118–20.

1136. A want of cavalry] *Courier*, 13 Dec. 1808, reporting Burrard: 'The want of cavalry, and the insufficiency of the artillery horses to drag the artillery, appeared to him to be insuperable objections to advancing. ... The difficulties which arose from the want of cavalry were rendered evident by that action [Vimiera] ...'; *Courier*, 22 Nov. 1808, reporting Dalrymple: 'the great loss which we sustained in our very small body of cavalry'; *Courier*, 3 Jan. 1809 (report of Board of Inquiry): 'a superior cavalry retarding our advance ... the want of a sufficient body of cavalry was the cause of [the enemy's] suffering but little loss in the plain. ... He succeeded in effecting his retreat in good order, owing principally to [Wellesley's] want of cavalry.'

1138–9. certain failures ... horses] *Courier*, 22 Nov. 1808, reporting Dalrymple's narrative to the Board of Inquiry: 'It was ... hard to move with rapidity when, as it was stated by Sir A. Wellesley, the artillery horses were by no means in proper condition—when a great proportion of them were horses furnished by the Irish Commissariat from the cast horses of the cavalry, many of them blind and lame.'

1142. difficulties] *Courier*, 18 Nov. 1808, reporting Wellesley's dispatch to Castlereagh of 1 August 1808: 'he had commenced his disembarkation in that river on the day of writing that letter, but ... the landing was attended with some difficulty, and it would have been quite impossible, had it not been for the zeal of the people of the country, and the activity of the Officers of the navy and army'; *Courier*, 21 Nov. 1808, reporting Wellesley's narrative to the Board of Inquiry: 'The landing [at Mondego Bay] was ... attended with considerable difficulties, on account of the surf.' Naval witnesses were called by the Board to testify to the difficulties (*Courier*, 22 and 23 Nov. 1808).

1146–7. heavy ordnance ... needed.] *Courier*, 26 Nov. 1808: 'Major General SPENCER answered [to Wellesley], that the *Alfred* was ordered for the express purpose of supplying whatever heavy ordnance the Commander in Chief might require'; *Courier*, 15 Dec. 1808: 'how did you propose to get heavy cannon?—[Wellesley.] From the ships. It had been so settled before I left England, and a store-ship lay off for that purpose.'

1158. the proclamation] See 957–63, and n.

1176–8. in Sir Hew ... enemies] Wordsworth thought that this passage might be libellous (*M.Y.* i. 341).

1185. talents, genius] See *E.S.* 1, textual n., and n. In 1812, H.C.R notes, W 'observed of himself that he has comparatively but little talent [compared with Coleridge]; genius is his characteristic quality'. H.C.R. corroborates and expands on this judgement.

1195. "bold, bad men"] Spenser, *Faerie Queene*, i. i. 37, and Shakespeare, *Henry VIII*, II. ii. 44. Cf. *Prel.* VII. 322, where the quotation is directly from Spenser; but the reference to Wolsey in Shakespeare is nearer Wordsworth's meaning in the present passage.

1218–9. Phocion, Epaminondas, and Philopœmen] All subjects of Lives by Plutarch (Epaminondas in *Pelopidas*). There do not seem to be any obvious verbal borrowings from Plutarch. Phocion is said to have refused a present of 100 talents from Alexander and bribes from Harpalus (*Phocion*, XVIII, XXI). Note also *Pelopidas*, IV. 3: 'And the true reason for the superiority of the Thebans was their virtue, which led them not to aim in their actions at glory or wealth, which are naturally attended by bitter envying and strife; on the contrary, they were both filled from the beginning with a divine desire to see their country become most powerful and glorious in their day and by their efforts, and to this end they treated one another's successes as their own' (trans. Perrin, in Loeb edn., London, 1917, v. 349). On Philopœmen see the Life, III: 'it was the energy, sagacity, and indifference to money in Epaminondas which he strenuously imitated' (ed. cit., x. 261); and Life, IV, on his intense interest in military matters. 'Wordsworth was seeking a translation of Plutarch's *Lives* in July 1808 (*M.Y.* i. 257).

1219–20. Sidney ... *dealing*] Fulke Greville, *The Life of the Renowned Sr. Philip Sidney* (London, 1652), in *Works*, ed. Grosart (privately printed, 1870), iv. 38: 'Besides which honour of unequal nature and education, his very waies in the world, did generally adde reputation to his prince and Country, by restoring amongst us the ancient majestie of noble and true dealing.' Wordsworth was seeking Greville's *Life* in February 1809 (*M.Y.* i. 289), though he had quoted from it in 1806 (*P.W.* iii. 122, 456–7).

1223. Lord Peterborough] Charles Mordaunt, third Earl of Peterborough (1658–1735), commanded British forces in Spain in 1705–6, with notable incompetence, according to modern authorities. Wordsworth's favourable opinion probably derives from the *Memoirs of an English Officer ... By Capt. George Carleton* (London, 1727), edited by Walter Scott in 1809, and read by Wordsworth early in that year (*M.Y.* i. 303). An edition of 1743 is recorded in Rydal Mount Catalogue, lot 96. Coleridge refers to the book favourably in 1809 (*C.L.* iii. 200, cf. iii. 241). See n. on 4582–5.

1252, fn. Cf. *M.Y.* i. 289 (Feb. 1809): 'Buonaparte may rather be said *to inflict upon* than *to propose* terms to his adversaries.'

1257. it has been urged] Perhaps from *Courier*, 25 Nov. 1808 (examination of General Ferguson):

> He was then asked—Suppose the Armistice had been rejected upon the 22d, and the French attacked in their positions, whether it was not his opinion, that from the known character of the French General, and the mode in which French armies were accustomed to conduct themselves, the city of Lisbon would not have been in great danger of destruction?—General Ferguson replied, that he had no reason to suppose that a French army and a French commander would have acted at all differently from what any other army or any other Commander would have done in similar circumstances.

1267. further effusion of human blood] *Courier*, 15 Dec. 1808, reporting Dalrymple's answer to questions on Junot's motives for accepting the Convention: Junot 'doubtless thought he saw some advantages in it to the French interest which I could not discern, exclusively of the great motive that must influence upon all such occasions—to spare the useless effusion of blood'.

1286–7. ignoble ease and darling sloth] *Paradise Lost*, II. 227: 'Counsel'd ignoble ease, and peaceful sloath'.

1308. submit or yield] *Paradise Lost*, I. 108: 'And courage never to submit or yield'.

1321–2. purified and exalted] Cf. *P.L.B.* 130–1, and [115]: 'affections strengthened and purified'; 'taste exalted' (by the perception of general truth in poetry). So *E.S.* 715–16.

1353–62. manifesto ... contributions] See n. on 544. *Courier*, 11 Aug. 1808:

> General Junot, without any previous declaration, without the consent of the Prince Regent of Portugal, entered the kingdom with the vanguard of his army, assuring the people of the country that he was marching through it, to succour his Royal Highness against an invasion of the English, and that he entered Portugal as the General of a friendly and allied power. [Whereupon the Prince Regent, though he could have resisted, removed to Brazil, so that his resistance should not be made an excuse for reprisals on his people. Since then he has heard of] pillage and plunder practised in [Portugal] ... the raising of an exorbitant contribution demanded from a country which opposed no kind of resistance to the entry of the French troops.

1388–90. but I will ... power?] Cf. the drift of the passage from *Courier*, 4 Jan. 1809, cited in n. on 2860–7.

1409–15. The nation ... submission] Cf. *Courier*, 16 Sept. 1808, cited in n. on 1122.

1417–20. our Generals ... Spain] *Courier*, 22 Nov. 1808, reporting Dalrymple:

> If, however, he had understood that the objects of the expedition were merely limited to Portugal, and that there was no other motive for it, except the reduction of that particular force which occupied that country; he would allow, in such

> a case, that the Convention would be improper, for if the British army had no ulterior object, or nothing else to do, there could be no question but that by the delay of many months, they would be able completely to reduce the French force under Junot; but he always conceived that a co-operation with the Spanish army was not only the ultimate, but by many degrees the principal object for which the expedition was originally intended; and as to the expulsion of the French from Portugal, he only considered that as a preliminary step to a co-operation of the British army in the defence of Spain.

Courier, 23 Nov. 1808, reporting Wellesley: 'The object of the British Government ... had been to lose as little time as possible in Portugal, and to proceed to co–operate with the Spanish armies. By this Convention, there were liberated for the same purpose 4000 Spaniards, who were on board of the Russian fleet.'

1452. Baylen] On 13 July 1808, and following days, the Spaniards under Castanos defeated the French under Dupont at Baylen, and a convention was agreed by 22 July. Wordsworth's observation on 'justice' refers to the fact that Dupont's force became prisoners of war, whereas Junot's did not. According to Napier, i. 125, 'The French troops, instead of being sent to France [according to the terms of the Convention], were maltreated, and numbers of them murdered in cold blood ... all who survived the march to Cadiz ... were cast into some hulks, where the greatest number perished in lingering torments: a few hundreds ... contrived to escape.' Cf. Oman, i. 200ff.

1454–6. And was ... Junot?] Cf. *Courier*, 17 Sept. 1808: 'in reading the first of these Articles [of the Convention], our readers we fear will be immediately disposed to compare it with the very different result of the operations of the Spanish army against DUPONT—DUPONT'S was a larger army than JUNOT'S, and the army of CASTANOS was an army composed almost of raw levies; yet these levies forced DUPONT to an unconditional surrender, and to disgorge all the plunder they had acquired.'

1461–4. noble letter ... executioners] Two letters, dated Cadiz, 10 and 14 August 1808, are printed in *Courier*, 12 Sept. 1808. The drift of the first is that transport out of Spain, required by the terms of Dupont's surrender to Castanos, cannot be provided; that Castanos had no means of guaranteeing to Dupont safe passage through the British blockade, that Castanos must have known this, and that Dupont must have known it also. The substance of Wordsworth's summary is in this letter, but he draws verbally on Morla's recapitulation in the second: 'Your Excellency will lay aside such false expectations and congratulate yourself that the Spanish people, as I have already said, have so noble a character, that they will abstain from exercising the vile office of executioners.' A glance at the complete text in the sources quoted, or in Oman, i. 624–5, will show that Oman's characterization of the letter as 'most shameless and cynical' is more apt than Wordsworth's 'noble'. Morla was subsequently concerned in the surrender of Madrid to Napoleon in early December.

1467–71. A Portugueze … necessary.] *Courier*, 21 Nov. 1808, reporting documents read to the Board of Inquiry:

> a letter from a Portuguese General, whose name we could not collect, who was also a Member of the Regency appointed by the PRINCE REGENT. He protested against the Armistice, and said, that from the 19th of June, when he had taken the command in the Algarves, he had been able to drive the French completely out in that province, to free the province of Alentejo, and to establish his head-quarters on the South of the Tagus. He therefore could not be convinced that such an Armistice was absolutely necessary.

1473–6. Another letter … by them.] Courier, 21 Nov. 1808:

> The next letter that was read was a sort of protest against the Convention, addressed by a Judge of a district in Portugal (the name of which we did not hear) to Sir Hew Dalrymple. This letter, although coming from an individual, was allowed to be his act as a Magistrate speaking the sentiments of the people of his district. It inveighed against the Convention, as leaving the crimes of the French in Portugal unpunished; as giving no indemnification for all the murders, robberies, and atrocities which had been committed by them.

Wordsworth, not unnaturally, omits the passage immediately following in The *Courier*: 'Next followed a letter from the same Judge to Sir Hew Dalrymple, dated only ten days after. In this second letter, the Judge expressed his satisfaction and unqualified admiration of the British, and made an invocation to the genius of Pope and Milton.'

1478–80. Wordsworth hints at the King's rebuff to the City of London; see n. on 2231–8.

1483–4. each has written … ***man.***] Cf. *The Times*, 21 Sept. 1808: 'We do not say that the proofs of [Wellesley's] guilt are conclusive; but they are such, that the grand inquest of his country has found "a true bill against him." His own hand-writing stares him in the face.'

1488–1522. I am entitled … one of them.] Cf. *Address*, 12 ff.

1545. Radice … tendit] Vergil, *Georgics*, ii. 292. Lines 126–33 of this poem are cited in *M. Y.* i. 302 (? 26 Mar. 1809), as part of the draft of a note which Wordsworth eventually cancelled.

1549–53. I will … abolished.] Cf. the passage from *Courier*, 22 Sept. 1808, cited in n. on 997–1044.

> Junot found a salve for his injured pride by remembering that he had slipped a mention of Napoleon as 'Emperor of the French,' into the text of the suspension of hostilities: in this he thought that he had won a great success, for the British Government had hitherto refused to recognize any such title, and had constantly irritated its adversaries by alluding to the master of the Continent as 'General Bonaparte,' or the 'actual head of the French executive' [Oman, i. 272, where it

is pointed out that the objectionable phrase did not recur in the Convention].

1561–6. We enter … agreement.] Cf. *Courier*, 24 Sept. 1808: 'Why were not the Portuguese our Allies consulted? It is true that the battle of Vimiera was gained by British valour: but surely it would have been but delicate and proper to have made the Portuguese a party to the Negociations'; Southey to Humphrey Senhouse, 15 Oct. 1808 (*Life and Correspondence*, iii. 175): '[Dalrymple] presuming to grant stipulations for the Portuguese which no government ever pretended to have power to make for an independent ally …'.

1580. power is the measure of right] Cf. 4019–21, and Appendix F; *M.Y.* i. 299–300 (26 Mar. 1809): 'the blasphemous address to Buonaparte made by some Italian deputies … and his answer [containing] the avowal which he has so repeatedly made to the Spaniards, that power is, in his estimation, the measure of right'.

1645–50. one of those … nation."] *Courier*, 26 Sept. 1808, under heading: 'Protest Made by Bernardin Freire de Andrade, General of the Portuguese Troops.' Wordsworth quotes with minor omissions and adaptations.

1671–3. It was … intended.] *Courier*, 22 Nov. 1808: 'As to the hoisting of the English colours, instead of the Portuguese, on the entrance of the British into Lisbon, [Dalrymple] declared it was entirely without his knowledge; and when he heard of it, he ordered the Portuguese to be hoisted.'

1777–85. Sir Hew … to them."] *Courier*, 21 Nov. 1808:

> Sir Hew Dalrymple, in his answer to General Beresford, declared that he was determined that no Article of the Convention should be violated by the French; that their conduct on this occasion had been most shameful, and had evinced a want of probity and honour which was most disgraceful to them. It seemed to be their intention to go away, leaving all their debts unpaid, and carrying off a considerable part of their plunder, by calling it public money, and saying it belonged to their military chest. As to any plunder that could be identified, it must be restored. He regretted, however, much, that part of their plunder, which was in money, it would be difficult, if not impossible, to identify.

1796–1803. "How … senseless?"] See n. on 1461–4. This passage is adapted from Morla's letter of 14 August 1808:

> It is with extreme surprise that I received your Excellency's letter of yesterday, in which you make a demand of the equipages, money, horses and various commodities belonging to you and the General who accompanied you, which the populace of Santa Maria plundered and destroyed … [He regrets the action of the mob, indeed he had made suggestions previously for the safety of Dupont and his baggage.] But it never was my intention, still less of the Supreme Junta, that your Excellency and your army should carry out of Spain the fruit of your rapacity, cruelty, and impiety. How could your Excellency conceive this possible? How could you imagine us to be so stupid and senseless? Can a capitulation, which speaks only of your equipage, give you a property in the treasures which your

> army has accumulated by means of assassinations, cruelty, and sacrilege of the most horrid kind, at Cordova, and other cities? [etc., etc.]

The Times, 12 Sept. 1808, reprints a dispatch from Madrid dated 23 August 1808:

> On the 14th inst. General Dupont arrived with the Staff of his army at the port of Santa Maria, in order to embark in the armed vessels, in which they were to remain till means could be found to transport them to France. The people beheld with indignation the robbers of their riches, the sacrilegious plunderers of the temples, and the profaners of every law, human and divine; but they repressed their just indignation through respect for the Government. But while the baggage was actually embarking, it happened that there fell out of a bag a chalice and a paten; the sight of these sacred utensils about to be thus sacrilegiously transported, roused their sentiments of zeal for our holy religion, the instantaneous effects of which it was impossible to repress. [The French were attacked and the loot recovered.] Nevertheless, the insolent Dupont had the audacity to make a formal demand of his Excellency the Governor of Cadiz, that he and his army should be indemnified for the loss they had sustained. This occasioned the letter of General Morla.

1826. How must … glory] *Paradise Lost*, I. 571–3: 'And now his heart / Distends with pride, and hardning in his strength / Glories.'

1830–49. But, as to … the old.] Cf. Coleridge to T. G. Street, 7 Dec. 1808 (*C.L.* iii. 137): 'Buonaparte were a fool, if he sent Junot's army immediately into Spain—they are doing him more service in France, where every Soldier with his Plunder is acting the part of a Recruiting Serjeant.'

1849–51. "What an effect … tournois!"] See n. on 1461–4. Wordsworth quotes Morla's letter of 10 August 1808 verbatim.

1882. I have animadverted] See 1325 ff. Cf. *The Times*, 18 Oct. 1808, commenting on a proclamation to the inhabitants of Lisbon signed by Lieutenant-General John Hope: 'Our Commanders have, in fact, assumed the civil government of Lisbon.… We believe, that most of the people of England thought, that the duty of the British army in Portugal was to beat and drive away the French … instead of which, having liberated JUNOT'S army at Lisbon, we have, it appears, most kindly condescended to take their places.'

1902–4. See n. on 2231–8.

1907. the persons] Cf. 1482–4, 2226 ff.

1928. their motion … suspended] For the phrasing cf. 'Tintern Abbey', 44–5 (*P. W.* ii. 260).

1932–9. "I protest … men."] *Courier*, 26 Sept. 1808, with minor variants.

1987. the Spaniards] Spanish troops under General Caraffa, who had entered Portugal as part of Junot's invading force, stationed at Lisbon and discreetly disarmed by Junot on 9 June 1808, after the first Portuguese rising in Oporto, which had been viewed favourably by Spain. Wordsworth conveniently ignores the reason for the presence of these troops in Lisbon.

1996. occurrences of the 29th of last May] Like Wordsworth, we are unable to identify these events. Oman, i. 627, says that 'the persons intended were primarily General Quesnel, his staff, and escort, who had been seized in Portugal and then taken into Spain. The clause also covered some French officers and commissaries who had been seized at Badajoz and elsewhere while making their way to Lisbon, at the moment when the insurrection broke out.' But Oman, i. 208, appears to indicate that the capture of Quesnel took place on 6 June; unless, therefore, the capture of the 'officers and commissaries' took place on 29 May, the clause remains dark.

2005. a few weeks before] During the first rising in Madrid, 2 May 1808. With Wordsworth's comment (2003–7), cf. *The Times*, 27 Sept. 1808: 'We may ... easily judge what kind of wretches these are whose liberation JUNOT has thus bargained for, by the surrender of honourable Spanish troops. They are spies, assassins, and corrupters, employed by BUONAPARTE, and seized to answer for their crimes.'

2030–2. and the people ... effected.] *Courier*, 18 Nov. 1808; cited above, n. on 1142.

2053. if not ... despair."] Probably suggested by *Paradise Lost*, I. 187–91: 'Consult ... / What reinforcement we may gain from Hope, / If not what resolution from despare.'

2067. we announced] In the proclamation of Cotton and Wellesley; see 957–63, n.

2172. sentence ... countrymen] See textual n. The alteration, which resulted in the cancel N1, was made because Wordsworth feared that the uncancelled text was libellous; see *M. Y.* i. 327–34, 336–7. 'The change, sent by M Wordsworth [*M. Y.* i. 329], was adopted—only leaving out the word already which, M St[uart] observed, had occurred just before' (Jordan, p. 153; 9 May 1809).

2231–8. City of London ... investigation."] On Tuesday, 4 October 1808, at Guildhall, Mr. Waithman moved:

> That an Humble and Dutiful Address and Petition be presented to his Majesty, expressing our grief and astonishment at the extraordinary and disgraceful Convention lately entered into by the Commanders of his Majesty's Forces in Portugal and the Commander of the French Army in Lisbon, praying his Majesty to institute such an Enquiry into this dishonourable and unprecedented transaction, as will lead to the discovery and punishment of those by whose misconduct and incapacity the Cause of the Country and its Allies have been so shamefully sacrificed. ... The question was ... put and carried unanimously, not a single hand having been held up against it [*Courier*, 5 Oct. 1808].

The Address and Petition were presented to the King on 12 October (*Courier*, 13 Oct.

1808); the operative paragraph reads:

> We therefore humbly pray your Majesty, in justice to the outraged feelings of a brave, injured, and indignant people, whose blood and treasure have been thus expended, as well as to retrieve the wounded honour of the country, and to remove from its character so foul a stain in the eyes of Europe, that your Majesty will be graciously pleased immediately to institute such an inquiry into this dishonourable and unprecedented transaction, as will lead to the discovery and punishment of those by whose misconduct and incapacity the cause of the Country and its Allies have been so shamefully sacrificed. [The King's reply reads:] I am fully sensible of your loyalty and attachment to my Person and Government. I give credit to the motives which have dictated your Petition and Address, but I must remind you that it is inconsistent with the principles of British Justice to pronounce judgment without previous investigation. I should have hoped that recent occurrences would have convinced you, that I am at all times ready to institute inquiries on occasions in which the character of the Country, or the honour of my Arms is concerned, and that the interposition of the City of London could not be necessary for inducing me to direct due inquiry to be made into a transaction, which has disappointed the hopes and expectations of the Nation [*Courier*, 13 Oct. 1808].

2239–65. Upon … land.] A deleted draft of this passage (see Introd. and textual notes) appears in Wordsworth's hand at the head of his letter to Daniel Stuart of 'Sunday Evening' (5 Feb. 1809; p.m. 9 Feb. 1809; *M.Y.* i. 288; B.M. Add. MS. 34046, fol. 207). In the letter Wordsworth says that he has had to 'recompose' the passage, presumably to include the reference to 'menaces … recently thrown out in the lower House of Parliament' concerning the freedom of the press (2245–7). The 'menaces' arose from the initial debate (27 Jan. 1809) on the case of the Duke of York and Mrs. Clarke, when Mr. Secretary Canning, speaking in favour of an Inquiry by a Committee of the House, rather than a private one, attacked the national press for its 'calumnies … against his Royal Highness'; they were

> only a part of a system of abuse, which for foulness and aspersion had never before disgraced the press of this country, so that it might create a doubt amongst those who love the freedom of the press, whether liberty was not on such terms too dearly purchased. But, by the proceedings of that day, the doubt would be renewed [? removed], as it would appear that the evil was only transient, whilst the good was permanent. Every man must be sensible of the cowardliness, the baseness, and the wretchedness of the calumnies which had been vented in the publications of the day during the last six months against the Duke of York … those in the highest station … should not be attacked with such slanderous malevolence [*Courier*, 28 Jan. 1809].

The Courier of the same date comments in its editorial:

> But we warn the public to prepare for some measures, which seem to be desired if not in contemplation, to fetter the Press of this Country, *the only free Press in the World*—Our warning is founded upon some expressions that fell in the course of last night's debate—It is supposed that the free discussion of the

> Cintra Convention has given mortal offence—The Press will be fettered, upon the old pretence of its being licentious—but let the public recollect, that there are laws in existence sufficiently powerful to punish any offence of which the Press may be guilty.

The Times, 30 Jan. 1809, carries similar editorial comment.

2241. I have ... animadverted] See 1902 ff.

2254 ff. If the persons, etc.] Cf. *The Times*, 20 Oct. 1808:

> But, we are subverting the maxims of the English law: we "are condemning unheard." Strange assertion! Have we the power to condemn? And is there no difference between condemnation and accusation? We condemn no one, but we accuse all, connected in any way either with the Armistice ... or the Convention. It belongs, therefore, to persons accused, against whom there is presumptive evidence of guilt, such as the signature of their names [cf. *Cintra*, 1483–4, 1907] or the sanction of their approbation, to prove their innocence.

2300. unjust [tribunals]] Cf. *Prel.* X. 378; *Samson Agonistes*, 695.

2305. "head and front"] *Othello*, I. iii. 80: 'The very head and front of my offending'. Cf. *Subl. and Beaut.* 159.

2309. crude consistence] *Paradise Lost*, II. 941; the quotation following is from *Paradise Lost*, X. 293 ff.:

> The aggregated Soyle
> Death with his Mace petrific, cold and dry,
> As with a Trident smote, and fix't as firm
> As *Delos* floating once; the rest his look
> Bound with *Gorgonian* rigor not to move.

2330–5. under the cover ... framed it.] A passage rewritten by De Quincey because Wordsworth thought it possibly libellous: 'speaking of the King's reproof to the City of London, I said they had been condemned under a sophism insidiously or ignorantly applied. Pray was that altered? If not surely it ought to be—some way in this manner, "as might be said if the words were not entitled to deference by having been put into his Majesty's mouth insidiously or ignorantly, etc."' (*M.Y.* i. 340–1). De Quincey writes on 13 May 1809 (Jordan, p. 163): 'The "insidiously or ignorantly employed" &c. passage—I had altered myself according to Mr. Wordsworth's direction; clumsily enough, I fear; but not so as by any torture, I think, to be racked into a libel.'

2343–5. And now ... conduct.] Cf. *E.E.* III. 11–24.

2350. One of their body] The incident is referred to in Castlereagh's speech of 19 January 1809 in the House of Commons (*Courier*, 21 Jan. 1809):

> But the Hon. Gentleman thought an extreme contrast existed between the disapprobation expressed by his Majesty in his Speech of some parts of the Convention of Cintra, and the part which Government took in ushering in to the Public, by the usual mark of approbation and joy (the firing of guns) the intelligence which they had received of the evacuation of Portugal by the French. Was it

> unnatural that Government, feeling that the great object of the expedition had been thus attained, should afford to the Public their testimony that such a great good had been accomplished?

2354–7. Was not the *positive* ... disapprobation?] *The Times*, 14 Oct. 1808, makes a similar point by juxtaposing the clause from the King's reply to the City ('I must remind you that it is inconsistent with the principles of British justice, to pronounce judgment without previous investigation') with the presentation of Wellesley to the King on his return from Portugal: 'is "a gracious reception at Court" ... no prejudication of a man against whom there are apparent, we do not mean to say conclusive, proofs of guilt?'

2361–5. a document ... nations."] Printed in *Courier*, 21 Jan. 1809, under head–note: 'The following are the terms in which his MAJESTY has expressed his disapprobation to Sir H. DALRYMPLE, of certain parts of the Convention of Cintra':

> The King has taken into his consideration the Report of the Board of Inquiry, together with the documents and opinions thereunto annexed. While his Majesty adopts the unanimous opinion of the Board, that no farther Military proceeding is necessary to be had upon the transactions referred to in their investigation, his Majesty does not intend thereby to convey an expression of his Majesty's satisfaction at the Terms and Conditions of the Armistice and Convention. When those instruments were first laid before his Majesty, the King, reserving for investigation those parts of the Definitive Convention in which his Majesty's immediate interests were concerned, caused it to be signified to Sir Hew Dalrymple, by his Majesty's Secretary of State, that his Majesty, nevertheless, felt himself compelled at once to express his disapprobation of those articles, in which stipulations were made, directly affecting the interests and feelings of the Spanish and Portuguese nations. At the close of the Enquiry, the King, abstaining from any observations upon other parts of the Convention, repeats his disapprobation of those articles; his Majesty deeming it necessary that his sentiments should be clearly understood, as to the impropriety and danger of the unauthorised admission, into Military Conventions, of articles of such a description, which, especially when incautiously framed, may lead to the most injurious consequences. His Majesty cannot forbear further to observe, that Lieutenant–General Sir Hew Dalrymple's delaying to transmit for his information the Armistice concluded on 22d Aug. until the 4th September, when he, at the same time, transmitted the ratified Convention, was calculated to produce great public inconvenience, and that such inconvenience did in fact result therefrom.

The King's disapproval was similarly referred to in the Speech from the Throne opening the Parliamentary session (*Courier*, 19 Jan. 1809).

2401–2. to which ... light;") Cf. *Prel.* XI. 383–5: 'All these were spectacles and sounds to which / I often would repair and thence would drink, / As at a fountain.' The quotation is from *Paradise Lost*, VII. 364–5: 'Hither as to thir Fountain other Starrs / Repairing, in thir gold'n Urns draw Light.'

2405. Sidneys] Philip (1554–86) and Algernon (1622–82).

2413. weighed … wanting] Dan. 5:27: 'Thou art weighed in the balances, and art found wanting.' Cf. *Prel.* III. 65–6.

2426. animating] De Quincey on 1 April 1809 (Jordan, p. 136) suggested that this should be 'animated'. Wordsworth means that the 'efforts of the Peninsula' animated Englishmen: cf. 124–6: 'we were instantaneously animated' by 'the rising of the people of the Pyrenean peninsula'.

2432–3. "DICTATED … RETREAT."] *Courier*, 15 Nov. 1808, reporting an 'Exposition of the Situation of the French Empire', delivered by M. Crelet, Minister of the Interior, on 3 November 1808: 'What presage does the heroic army of Portugal afford, which, contending against double its numbers, was able to erect trophies of victory upon the very ground where it fought with so much disadvantage, and to dictate the conditions of a glorious retreat.' *The Times*, 16 Nov. 1808, comments that this passage 'contains a melancholy truth'.

2450–1. For, when … Demon] Cf. *The Friend*, No. 7 (28 Sept. 1809), p. 111: 'Sir Philip Sidney … was so deeply convinced that the Principles diffused through the majority of a Nation are the true Oracles from which Statesmen are to learn wisdom, and that "when the People speak loudly it is from their being strongly possessed either by the Godhead or the Dæmon," that in the Revolution of the Netherlands he considered the universal adoption of one set of Principles, as a proof of the divine Presence.' Coleridge goes on to cite the passage from Sidney's letter to Walsingham used by Wordsworth in 4245–51 below, and to recommend *Cintra* to his readers. The passage cited above reappears in essentials in *On the Constitution of Church and State* (3rd edn., London, 1839), pp. 43–4. It is not quite clear whether Coleridge is adapting *Cintra*, or Wordsworth adapting Coleridge, or whether both have a common source in Sidney, which we have not found.

2451. discover] Wells (p. 75) reports that in a copy owned by him and corrected in De Quincey's hand, this word has been altered to 'distinguish'. As we have found no Wordsworthian authority for this emendation, and as the text is intelligible, we have preferred to let the reading of 1809 stand.

2473. illustrated] 'illuminated, made famous'. Cf. *Reply to Mathetes*, 45.

2514–8. for the mind … before it] Cf. *Prel.* VIII. 756: 'all objects, being / Themselves capacious, also found in me / Capaciousness and amplitude of mind; / Such is the strength and glory of our Youth'; *Prel.* p. 576: 'He feels that, be his mind however great / In aspiration, the universe in which / He lives is equal to his mind, that each / Is worthy of the other'; *P. 1815*, 352—7; Owen, *Wordsworth as Critic*, ch. VIII.

2551. two masters … served] Matt. 6:24: 'No man can serve two masters.' Cf. *E.S.* 90–1.

2552. take place of] 'take precedence of' (*O.E.D.*, s.v. *place*, sb., sense 27 c); so *R.M.* 444–5; *Subl. and Beaut.* 163. Knight (*Prose Works*, i. 209), evidently not understanding the idiom, prints 'take the place of'.

2583–90. Boy of Saragossa … Virgin] Cf. *Courier*, 7 Jan. 1809:

> Letters from Valencia state the following trait of the most heroic valour, on the part of a boy, fourteen years of age, which deserves to be recorded in the military annals of his country:—
>
> During the last inlistment in Saragossa, the said boy was rejected as unfit for service, but animated by the most fervent patriotism, and anxious to share in the glory of the gallant defenders of their country, he continued to mix with the troops who attacked the French, and behaved with so much intrepidity and valour, that he took a stand of colours, which, in the sight of the army, he carried to the church of Pilar, placed them on the high altar, and rejoined the troops, who were still closely engaged with the enemy.—*Corunna Diary, December 30.*

2638–9. "shake … horror"] From the Address of the Junta of Seville to the people of Madrid, 809 above.

2639. Cf. Matt. 4:4: 'Man shall not live by bread alone, but by every word that proceedeth out of the mouth of God'; Deut. 8:3; 3755 below.

2641. abominations …. sanctuary] Ezek. 5:11: 'thou hast defiled my sanctuary … with all thine abominations.'

2652–6. wherever … love.] For the image cf. *E.E.* I. 67–77.

2664. I have shewn] See 2566–618.

2674–93. citizen of Seville … glorious!"] We have not found the source of this passage.

2705 ff. This passage, as the footnote to 2706 states, was written in February 1809, before the fall of Saragossa (20 Feb.) was reported in Britain. On 10 March De Quincey first read reports of the fall, which he received at first with incredulity, but which were soon confirmed (Jordan, pp. 112, 117; 14 and 21 Mar. 1809). He consequently thought it incumbent upon him to alter or annotate this passage:

> On the passage relating to Saragossa I have, in consequence [*here a lacuna of about nine lines*] I thought of substituting—Saragossa!—She also, the wasted and twice [ ] city, has borne witness—in her glorious martyrdom—to the efficacy of these passions. [ ] had pledged herself to the same self-devotion. The Multitudes of men, who were [ ]ed in the fields of Baylen—!—or something to that purpose. But this, on consideration, seemed improper on 2 accounts; 1st. that it was to do a grievous injustice to Saragossa; and 2ndly. that, as [the] pamphlet could not be supposed to have been written since that news was received, it looked too much like an artifice to make [ ] thing. Therefore, on the whole, I have thought it right to do as follows:—[ ] footnote, as from

> a friend of the author's employed to correct the press errors [that, whilst that sheet was passing through the press, the 33[d] bulletin had been received—containing an account of the enemy's having possessed himself of the ruins of Saragossa;—that, in a pamphlet adverting perpetually to passing occurrences, it seemed necessary to notice this,—that it's date might be [ ];—but that, from the distance of the author it was impossible to [ ] [wi]thout occasioning a very serious delay:—that, finally, this was the less necessary as the friend of the author was well assured that he would wish to make no other change than to declare, in a more full and solemn tribute to Saragossa, that all which had been prophesied of her she had faithfully ratified: and that, for the truth of this assertion, the reader—if unwarily he had adopted the *conclusions* of the French,—was referred with the greatest confidence the statements made even by that base enemy upon which those conclusions professed to be grounded [*here another lacuna of about nine lines*] [Jordan, p. 117; Mar. 1809].

On 25 March (Jordan, p. 119), De Quincey says that, as he has received no instruction on the subject, he proposes to print the note; but on ?26 March (*M.Y.* i. 298), Wordsworth brushes aside De Quincey's efforts in this matter, and orders him 'to *cancel* the page with the footnote'. This instruction, and Wordsworth's seeming misunderstanding of the drift of the note, brought De Quincey to the verge of a quarrel with him, and on 1 April (Jordan, p. 132) he complains 'of the very great injustice which [Wordsworth] had done me in what relates to Saragossa'. The rupture was healed in subsequent correspondence. Fragmentary drafts of De Quincey's proposed note are preserved in the Cornell MS. of De Quincey's Postscript on Moore's letters; see our Appendix II.

2706, fn. This replaces De Quincey's suggested footnote; see previous note and *M.Y.* i. 309.

2723–5. Magnus … alto.] Vergil, *Ecl.* iv. 5–7: [in T F Royd's Everyman's library translation: 'A mighty roll of generations new / Is now arising. Justice now returns / And Saturn's realm, and from high heaven descends / A worthier race of men'].

2792–8. "compelled … Spain."] Cf. 731–41, and n.

2785. eye … off] Acts 9:18: 'there fell from his eyes as it had been scales.'.

2802–3. progressive … species] Cf. Prospectus to *The Recluse* (*P. Exc.* 122–3): 'the progressive powers … / Of the whole species'.

2804. "amplitude … deeds"] *Paradise Regained*, II. 139: 'And amplitude of mind to greatest Deeds'.

2818. "noble rage"] Gray, *Elegy Written in a Country Church-Yard*, 51.

2828. "For ye are in a dream;"] We have not found the source of this quotation.

2830–1. "in the eclipse … dark."] *Lycidas*, 101: 'Built in th'eclipse, and rigg'd with curses dark.'

2841–5. a general … terms] The general was Wellesley; see *M.Y.* 289 (? 5 Feb.

1809), referring to an article in *The Courier*: 'What you say upon Wellesley, as to the french being *entitled* to such terms …'. Wellesley was received at Court on his return from the Peninsula, and received votes of thanks in the Lords (23 Jan. 1809; Earl of Liverpool's motion) and Commons (25 Jan. 1809; Castlereagh's motion). Attempts to have Burrard's name included in these votes (motions of Lord Moira and Mr. Whitbread) were discussed and eventually withdrawn.

2845, 2855. the French army … terms … "Because … broken."] *Courier*, 21 Nov. 1808: Wellesley agreed with Dalrymple 'in the propriety of signing a Convention for the evacuation of Portugal, because … by the customs of war, the French army, being then unbroken, had a fair claim to treat for the evacuation of Portugal'. See also n. on 3348.

2846–50. "Ye have … nation."] From the Address of the Junta of Seville the Portuguese of 30 May 1808; see 546–77, 824–35. More or less verbatim from *Courier*, 8 July 1808.

2852–3. "Our enemies … destroyed."] *Courier*, 12 July 1808, under heading 'Proclamation of the Supreme Junta of Seville': 'The positions they [the French] have taken are exactly those in which they can be conquered and defeated in the easiest manner.' The passage quoted above, 789–99, follows almost immediately.

2860–7. The French army … light] The Board of Inquiry pointed out that the generals had cited the example of procedure in Egypt in 1801, when a similar convention was granted to the French. On this parallel *Courier*, 4 Jan. 1809 (see n. on 3173–5), comments:

> we wish they had rather referred to the practise of Bonaparte, who as the most successful Captain of the times, is consequently the highest authority. Has it been policy to send back to their country with their arms, equipments, and even plunder, the armies whom he has "signally defeated." Has not on the contrary, the signal defeat of an army and its annihilation been with him one and the same thing, except when on some occasions he has gained greater advantages by a Treaty, such as at Marengo, thereby extirpating the army wholly. After he had signally defeated the Prussians at Jena, he would make no convention to spare any of them.—The Prussian General Blucher, with his brave army, was pursued even to annihilation. At Ulm, the Austrians had one of their finest armies, nearly equal in numbers to the French, strongly posted in chosen situations, commanded by chosen Generals, equipped in the best manner. This army had not been signally defeated; it was unbroken. And yet Bonaparte would not send it back by Convention into Austria with arms, ammunition, and baggage, as an unbroken and even a triumphant army. No, he insisted on making the whole prisoners of war, and he wholly annihilated the army. … What a pity our Generals could not feel the wisdom of pursuing the same policy at Cintra, having so rare and glorious an opportunity before them! Had Bonaparte been in their situation, he would have talked as much as they about his love of tranquillity and sparing of the effusion of

> innocent blood; but he would have fought his enemies day and night, hotly and vigorously attacking them until they were all either slain or surrendered prisoners at discretion. Had our own Commanders acted in this way, we should not now have had to contemplate Junot's army at Vittoria, preparing under very different circumstances to revenge upon the British their disgrace at Vimiera.

2865–6. at Ulm … Prussia] The fortress of Ulm under Mack von Leiberich surrendered to Napoleon in October 1805. Napoleon's Prussian campaign took place in October 1806. Lübeck was the scene of Blucher's surrender, 7 November 1806. Switzerland was occupied in 1798. Cf. *Nat. Ind. and Lib.* I. xxvii (*P.W.* iii. 122).

2899. "heroic wisdom;"] Milton, Digression to *History of Britain*, in *Works*, x (New York, 1932), 324, and xviii (New York, 1938), 254: 'But to do this and to know these exquisit proportions, the heroic wisdom which is requir'd surmounted far the principles of narrow politicians.' Cf. nn. on 3358, 4369–76. Wordsworth was seeking Milton's Prose Works in July 1808 (*M.Y.* i. 257).

2930. is to increase] Altered by De Quincey from 'or to increase'; see Jordan, pp. 97, 137.

2998–9. the tendency … intellect] Some alteration, 'omitting what is said about "shutting out from common sympathies and genuine knowledge"', was made by Wordsworth on ? 26 March 1809 (*M.Y.* i. 300).

3048. "I see … they are:"] Coleridge, 'Dejection: An Ode', 38.

3068. "inspired by nature and by fortune taught;"] Adapted or misquoted from Dryden, *Absolom and Achitophel*, 883: 'Endew'd by nature and by learning taught'. The following passage, 3071–73, may have been suggested by Dryden's description of Achitophel, *Abs. Ach.* 153–63, 198–9, though there are no obvious verbal parallels except Wordsworth's 'Great talents' and Dryden's 'Great Wits' (*Abs. Ach.* 163). Cf. also the character of Oswald as presented in *The Borderers*; note especially *P. Bord.*: 'to such a mind those enterprizes which are the most extraordinary will in time appear the most inviting … he frequently breaks out into what has the appearance of greatness.'

3083. those already] Altered by De Quincey from 'those which I have already' (Jordan, p. 97; 5 Mar. 1809).

3087–100. The Empire … leads.] Cf. *R.M.* 249–54, 429–46.

3173–5. the necessity … country.] *Courier*, 4 Jan. 1809, reprints extracts from the Report of the Board of Inquiry with interspersed comments. Among these is the following:

> [Report:] It appears, that pains were taken to misrepresent and raise a clamour in Portugal against this Convention; but when it was generally known, and its effects felt, the people of Lisbon, and of the country, seem to have expressed

> their gratitude and thanks for the benefits attending it. [Comment:] Gratitude and thanks, by being so discontented as to render it necessary that we should leave 10,000 men in Portugal to keep them quiet!

3176. the English army] Altered by De Quincey from 'this army', 'for the sake of euphony; but, on reading the whole paragraph over, it seems to me to improve the emphasis of the passage, from a feeling of the opposition between what is *English*—and *dishonor*' (Jordan, p. 110; 14 Mar. 1809).

3198, fn. See *M.Y.* i. 300–1 (26 Mar. 1809): 'I have done injustice to Gen. Ferguson, by not mentioning in the body of the work his marked disapprobation of the Convention of Cintra.' Wordsworth proposed to mention Ferguson in a projected note on 'the French Bulletin on Saragossa' (*M.Y.* i. 301–2), but later abandoned the note (*M.Y.* i. 305); whereupon De Quincey took the opportunity of introducing this note into the body of the work rather than into the Appendix (Jordan, p. 158; 5 Apr. 1809), adapting Wordsworth's suggested phrasing (*M.Y.* i. 302). In the debate on the Convention in the Commons, Ferguson 'was aware that many General Officers of great eminence had approved of this Convention. He was not of rank to be consulted upon it; but if he had been so consulted, he had no hesitation in saying, that it should have met his decided negative' (*Courier*, 22 Feb. 1809).

3199. Sir Hew Dalrymple ... Cintra] Wellesley stated to Castlereagh that he was in disagreement on details, but approved the general plan for a French evacuation of Portugal. Dalrymple repeated before the Board that the negotiations had begun two hours before his arrival (*Courier*, 21 Nov. 1808, and elsewhere). Again (*Courier*, 23 Nov. 1808), Wellesley stated: 'That the Negociation should not originally extend beyond the suspension of hostilities. ... That instead of private property, the words arms and baggage should be substituted. ... That nothing should be introduced about the Russian Fleet.—On the two first of these the Commander differed from him.' Castlereagh, in the debate on the Convention, asserted that 'it was rather presumptuous to oppose the opinion of the whole Staff in Portugal with respect to the propriety of granting to the French the liberty of retiring from that country' (*Courier*, 22 Feb. 1809).

3214 ff. Wordsworth's 'two maxims of policy' were mentioned as 'two extreme opinions' by Castlereagh in the debate on the campaign in Spain in the Commons on 24 February 1809: one was that Spain 'was sufficiently powerful as to men; and that our co–operation need go no further than supplies of arms, money, clothing, ammunition, and whatever other necessaries might be wanting'; the other, 'that there was no medium between a great effort, and the whole effort, and ... that not a soldier should be kept at home ... [this] would be in itself impracticable' (cf. *Cintra*, 3223–

4). The Government rejected both these policies. In the same debate Mr. Windham recommended a force of 100,000 men (cf. *Cintra*, 3331), based on Gibraltar; such a force (though he 'disliked the practice') could be recruited 'from the militia' (cf. *Cintra*, 3225–6). 'The effect of such an army, ably conducted [cf. *Cintra*, 3345 ff.], was not to be spoken lightly of ... when we talked of Buonaparte's numbers, we must recollect where these numbers were to act [cf. *Cintra*, 3241]. A force raised to the greatest possible amount to which the mind and means of the country,—then elevated above itself and exalted to something of a preternatural greatness ... could have carried it, should have been placed in Spain' (cf. *Cintra*, 3271–20). Since no single newspaper report we have seen gives all the above details, we cite the report in Cobbett's *Parliamentary Debates*, xii (1809), cols. 1078–9, 1111–12. That Wordsworth studied this debate as well as that of 21 February on the Convention (see n. on 3405–8) is clear from his reference to 'the two debates' (3462).

3229. power, which] Altered by De Quincey from 'power, that' (Jordan, p. 110; 14 Mar. 1809).

3254. every one ... weakness] Cf. *Prel.* X. 160–8: 'the commonplaces of the Schools, / A theme for boys ... that tyrannic Power is weak'.

3263–7. Trajan ... Antonine ... Caracalla ... Domitian] Emperors of Rome in A.D. 98–117, 138–61, 211–17, and 81–96 respectively.

3285–6. his utter rejection ... morality] Cf. 1823–8; Coleridge to Sir George Beaumont, 14 Dec. 1808 (*C.L.* iii. 147): 'reflect only on the enormous power, which for a small time a mere Individual can acquire by the total emancipation of the will from all the Laws of general Morality. What then must be the power, when one pre–eminently wicked Man wields the whole strength and cunning of a wicked Nation?'; *C.N.B.* ii. 3230 (1807–10): 'What then is the secret of the French Power? of the vicious French? Consistency, unanimity in vice & energy'; passage from *The Friend*, No. 6 (21 Sept. 1809), 84–5, cited in n. to *E.E.* III. 14–15. The association of Napoleon with the Miltonic Satan is common in Coleridge's writings of this and later dates.

3313–5. And sorry ... opinion] Cf. *Freeholders*, 482–5: 'the Opposition were taking counsel from their fears, and recommending despair they continued to magnify without scruple the strength of the Enemy, and to expose, misrepresent, and therefore increase the weaknesses of their country.'

3320–1. A regiment of 900 Swiss] Oman, i. 238, reports that members of the 4th Swiss battalion in Junot's force deserted to the British before and during the battle of Roliça (17 Aug. 1808), and after the Convention of Cintra. They numbered 985, according to a French return of 15 July (Oman, i. 235, 243). We have not found

Wordsworth's source for this information.

3348. "British interests;"] *Courier*, 15 Dec. 1808, reporting Wellesley under interrogation by Lord Moira, who hinted that Junot would not have signed the Convention had he not considered this a better course than continuing to fight, which (as the British generals admitted under examination) he could have done after 22 August 1808:

> When I considered the expediency of allowing the French to evacuate Portugal by sea, I took into my contemplation British interests and British objects only, with the objects of our allies as connected with those of Great Britain. I considered that the French army, from the relative situation of the two armies in Portugal, and from its having the military possession of the country, had a fair military right to withdraw by sea with their arms and baggage; and I do not think it necessary for me to account for the motives which induced General Junot to prefer the evacuation by sea to another line of operations.

3358. "above the strain and temper"] Milton, Digression to *History of Britain*, in *Works*, x (New York, 1932), 324: 'what wonder then if they sunke as those unfortunate Britans before them, entangl'd and oppress'd with things too hard and generous above thir straine and temper.' Cf. 2899, and n.

3384. those who are incompetent] Cf. the comments on the Army in *M.Y.* i. 296 (?26 Mar. 1809). Daniel Stuart, seeking possible libels in *Cintra*, thought this passage libellous, but deferred to the judgement of De Quincey and of Baldwin, the printer of the pamphlet. For details, see Jordan, pp. 164–6 (16 May 1809). Wordsworth was displeased by De Quincey's opposition to Stuart in this matter (*M.Y.* i. 342–4); De Quincey defended himself at length in late May (Jordan, pp. 196–8).

3385. transactions at Buenos Ayres] An expedition sent against Buenos Ayres under General Beresford in 1806 had surrendered to the local inhabitants. A second force under Lt.–Gen. John Whitelocke attacked Buenos Ayres in June July 1807, but withdrew, by agreement with the Spanish commander, after sustaining considerable losses in prisoners. Whitelocke was court–martialled (Jan.–Mar. 1808) and cashiered.

3394–5. announcing ... himself] Altered by De Quincey from 'making this avowal of incompetence ... himself', 'since, as it stood, the *incompetence* seemed to be the minister's—not Sir H[ew] D[alrymple]'s incompetence', and for other reasons (Jordan, pp. 110–11; 14 Mar. 1809).

3400. such a letter] Sir Hew Dalrymple reported to the Board of Inquiry that

> He afterwards, upon the 2d of August, received another dispatch from Lord Castlereagh ... pointing out to him the general outlines of the measures to be pursued, after the French force should have been subdued or expelled from Portugal. ... He saw no reason for assuming the responsibility of measures which ap-

> peared to have been confided peculiarly to Sir Arthur Wellesley. Sir A. had been recommended by Lord Castlereagh to his most particular confidence; and great confidence was expressed in the dispatch to have been given by Government to his well-known talents, and a sort of wish that every attention which the rules of the service would allow should be paid to his advice and opinion. He, for his part, felt perfectly disposed to pay every attention to the opinion of a man of Sir Arthur Wellesley's talents, who had also distinguished himself by an important victory [*Courier*, 22 Nov. 1808].

This matter raised adverse comment in the debate on the Convention in the Commons: from Lord Henry Petty, moving the motion referred to below (3405–8), from General Tarleton, and from Wellesley himself, who said that he 'should have felt uncomfortable' had he been aware of such instructions from Castlereagh (*The Times*, 22 Feb. 1809).

3405–8. This moment ... Nation.] The motion was moved in the House of Commons on 21 February 1809 by Lord Henry Petty: 'That the Convention of Cintra, and also that entered into by Adm. Cotton, had disappointed the hopes and expectations of the country—and this resolution the Noble Lord announced his intention to follow up with another, "that these events were to be attributed to the misconduct of his Majesty's Ministers."' It was lost, after debate, by 203 votes to 153 (*Courier*, 22 Feb. 1809).

3456. An enlightened Friend] Presumably Coleridge, who makes this observation in his *Lay Sermon* of 1817 (2nd edn., London, 1839, p. 310): 'A long and attentive observation had convinced me that formerly men were worse than their principles, but that at present the principles are worse than the men.' The germ of this appears to be in *C.N.B.* ii. 2627: 'Pasley remarked last night (2nd Aug. 1805) ... that *men* themselves in the present Age were not so much degraded, as their *sentiments* ... almost all men nowadays act and feel more nobly than they think.'

3473–4. in withholding] Altered by De Quincey from 'to withhold', the altered version 'seeming to me the English idiom' (Jordan, p. 110; 14 Mar. 1809).

3510. the second delegation] The transfer of power from local Juntas to the Supreme Junta at Aranjuez in the summer of 1808; see Oman, i. 342–66.

3519. begotten ... fiction] Cf. *E.S.* 552–4 [WW's joke about Ossian as a 'Phantom begotten by the snug embrace of an impudent Highlander upon a cloud of tradition'].

3522–3. breadth of wing ... every where.] Perhaps suggested by *Paradise Lost*, 1. 19–22: 'Thou ... with mighty wings outspread / Dove–like satst brooding on the vast Abyss / And mad'st it pregnant.'

3537 ff. But I began, etc.] See Introd.

3539. In Madrid ... Corunna] Madrid was reoccupied by the French under

Napoleon in early December 1808. Corunna surrendered to Soult on 19 January 1809, after the embarkation of Sir John Moore's army, and Ferrol on 26 January. As Soult marched south in February into Portugal, Galicia rose in revolt, at the instance of local ecclesiastics and of the Marquis de la Romana, who was gradually assembling a force about Monterey at this time.

3568. The intoxicated setter–up of Kings] Cf. 'an intoxicated Despot', 3893 below, and *Burns*, 478–9 ['the downfall of an intoxicated despot'].

3573–7. "Limbo ... earth.] *Paradise Lost*, III. 495, 455–7. Cf. *Burns*, 457–8.

3594. Sicilian Vespers] On 31 March 1282 the people of Palermo rose against their French rulers (under Charles I of Anjou), and a general revolt spread through Sicily, with considerable slaughter of the French population. We have not found the source of Wordsworth's information; but it may well have been Coleridge, whose obscure entry in *C.N.B.* ii. 2675, as illuminated by Miss Coburn's note, indicates that he knew details of the event.

3699. "regni novitas"] *Aeneid*, i. 563–4: 'Res dura et regni novitas me talia cogunt / Moliri, et late fines custode tueri' [where Dido is using the 'newness of the kingdom' to excuse the reception experienced by the Trojans].

3715. Sword of Francis the First] *Courier*, 12 May 1808, from the Madrid Gazette of 5 April:

> His Imperial Highness, the Grand Duke of Berg, having intimated to his Excellency Don Pedro Cevallos, First Secretary of State, that his Imperial Majesty the Emperor of the French and King of Italy, would be pleased in the possession of the Sword that Francis I. King of France, surrendered in the famous battle of Pavia, in the reign of the Emperor Charles V. in Spain, which was kept in due estimation in the Royal Armory, since the year 1525, desiring that it might thus be represented to our Lord the King. His Majesty being informed of this, and desirous of availing himself of every opportunity to testify to his intimate Ally the Emperor of the French, his high regard for his august person, and the admiration his unheard of deeds inspire him with, immediately ordered the aforementioned sword to be remitted to his Imperial and Royal Majesty.

'Perfidious' (cf. 3717) occurs twice in a Spanish document on this subject printed in *The Times*, 10 Sept. 1808. Wordsworth queries 'deposited Escurial' (3718) in *M.Y.* i. 300 (? 26 Mar. 1809).

3727, textual n. Lord Bacon ... power] From *Meditationes Sacrae: De Haeresibus*, in *Works* (London, 1740; see n. on *Cintra*, motto), ii. 402: certain heretics 'statuunt ... latiores terminos scientiae Dei quam potestatis, vel potius ejus partis potestatis Dei (nam & ipsa scientia potestas est) qua scit, quam ejus qua movet & agit, ut praesciat quaedam otiose, quae non praedestinet & praeordinet'. The rest of the general Baconian doctrine in Wordsworth's sentence does not appear in the *De Haeresibus*.

3727 (on 2nd page of textual note), shells and pebbles ... a Conquest] The episode occurred in A.D. 40 during Caligula's visit to Gaul. See Suetonius, *Caligula*, XLVI; Dio Cassius, *Roman History*, LIX, which mentions, as Suetonius does not, that Caligula behaved 'as if he were going to conduct a campaign in Britain', and that the shells were taken to Rome 'for the purpose of exhibiting the booty to the people there as well' (trans. Cary, Loeb edn., London, 1924, vii. 339). Wordsworth's version seems to derive from inaccurate recollection, or reporting, of this account; no authority known to us places the episode in Britain. He refers to it in a letter of 1791 (*E.Y.* p. 56).

3753, textual n. pots of the Lyn] *pots* = 'the deep circular holes which the action of a river forms amongst the rocks of the Duddon', cited as Lakeland usage in *E.D.D.*, s.v. *pot*, sb.[2] Wordsworth could have observed the Devon river Lyn during his walk with Cottle and Coleridge in May 1798 (Moorman, i. 373).

3755. Not by bread ... sustained] Matt. 4:4; cf. 2639 above.

3769–76. The difference ... disgrace] Added on 28 March 1809 (*M.Y.* i. 304, reading 'mind' for 'minds').

3795. Swede] 'or Norwegian', following, was deleted, according to *M.Y.* i. 300.

3804. his intellectual ... bounds] Cf. *P.L.B.* 80: 'the sameness and narrow circle of their intercourse'.

3805–6. of those nobler ... Country] Supplied by De Quincey to cover an omission in the manuscript, in which the sentence ended with 'force' (Jordan, p. 135; 1 Apr. 1809; cf. *M.Y.* i. 315).

3811–2. Love ... killed] Cf. *Exc.* IV. 763: 'We live by Admiration, Hope, and Love'; and *Prel.* p. 571, lines 3–5.

3825–60. Prince Llewellin, *ob.* 1240, Prince of North Wales, active against English pressure on North Wales under King John, 1211–15, and subsequently in Wales generally, until the last years of his life, 1237–40. William Wallace (? 1272–1305) engaged in similar operations on behalf of Scotland against Edward I, from 1297 until his capture and execution in 1305. Cf. *Prel.* I. 213–19.

3866. the sweeping away] Napoleon 'extorted from [Joseph Bonaparte] fifty of the choicest pictures of the royal gallery at Madrid; but in compensation Joseph was invited to annex all that he might choose from the private collections of the exiled Spanish nobility and the monasteries of the capital' (Oman, ii. 16). We have not found Wordsworth's source. *Courier*, 30 Aug. 1808, prints a dispatch from Madrid, dated 3 August, on the departure of the French: Joseph 'goes laden with the rich booty of the Royal Palaces, the cash of the Treasury, and Chest of Consolidation'.

3869. feudal tenures ... inquisition] *Courier*, 7 Jan. 1809, reports a decree of

Napoleon dated Madrid, 4 December 1808, abolishing 'the feudal rights ... in Spain' and 'All personal dues, all exclusive rights of fishery, or other rights of the same nature, on the coasts, rivers, and banks of rivers, all bannalities of mills'. Another decree of the same date abolishes 'The Tribunal of the Inquisition ... as contrary to the Civil Sovereignty and Authority'. Cf. Oman, i. 475–6. In March 1809 Wordsworth's landlord, Mr. Crump, praised such activities of Napoleon (*M.Y.* i. 306).

3893–4. an intoxicated Despot] Cf. 3568 and n.

3919. not as Persons but as Things] A distinction common in Coleridge's political writings; see John Colmer, *Coleridge: Critic of Society* (Oxford, 1969), pp. 100, 141.

3926. Per me ... gente.] Dante, *Inferno*, III. 1–3 [In H. F. Cary's translation: 'Through me you pass into the city of woe: / Through me you pass into eternal pain: / Through me among the people lost for aye.' RG].

3982. Systême ... Condillac] Paul Heinrich Dietrich, Baron D'Holbach (1723–89), contributor to the *Encyclopédie*, published *Le Système de la Nature*, an attack on Christianity, and religion in general, in 1770. The item 'Systime [*sic*] de la Nature' appears as item 126 in manuscript 'Inventory of Books, Prints, and Pictures, of the late Wm Wordsworth, Esq. of Rydal Mount taken by me [John Hudson], this 7th day of May 1850', preserved in the Wordsworth Library, Grasmere. Étienne Bonnot de Condillac (1715–80), follower of Locke and friend of Rousseau; Wordsworth perhaps refers especially to his *Logique* (1780).

4030. The power ... clay] Dan. 2:32–3: 'The image's ... belly and his thighs of brass, ... his feet part of iron and part of clay.'

4033. "Magna ... Austria.] See n. on 1223. The Carleton *Memoirs*, pp. 160–1, read: 'Accordingly, next Morning, the first of May, 1706, while the Sun was under a total Eclypse, in a suitable Hurry and Confusion, they [King Philip's forces] broke up ... [In commemoration of the subsequent relief of Barcelona,] The next Orders were for recasting all the damag'd brass Cannon which the Enemy had left; upon every one of which was, by order, a Sun eclyps'd, with this Motto under it: *Magna parvis obscurantur.*'

4053. I have personal knowledge] How and when Wordsworth acquired such knowledge we have not discovered.

4061 ff. a moral change ... This paramount efficacy ... who, by submitting] Altered on 28 March 1809 (*M. Y.* i. 304).

4076–7. Large bodies ... elsewhere.] See Jordan, pp. 134–6 (1 Apr. 1809): 'It is said, in speaking of the English Troops, that they were *broken* at *Corunna*—in

Egypt—and *elsewhere*.' De Quincey challenges the statement with respect to Corunna, and remarks that 'many [will read the pamphlet] who were present in that battle and who therefore, if it be a misstatement, will instantly detect it.' On the affair in Egypt, his recollection is that 'the Scotch Regiment—which was penetrated by the French Cavalry—was scarcely broken; and if it was—and that should be thought equivalent to being *vanquished*, still it restored itself as *technically* as it was defeated—viz. by *rallying* into groupes—and taking advantage of the French who found themselves unable to act from the *ruins* among which the Scotch Reg. had been posted.' He thinks that the reference to Corunna at least ought to be deleted. Wordsworth agrees, after argument (*M.Y.* i. 319, 320).

4090. Saragossa] The first siege of Saragossa, by Lefebvre–Desnouettes and Verdier, lasted from June to August 1808; it ended with the withdrawal of the French. The second siege began on 20 December 1808 under Moncey and Mortier; it continued under Mortier, Junot, and eventually Lannes, until the fall of the city on 20 February 1809.

4092 ff. The details mentioned here may have been gathered from R. Vaughan's *Narrative of the Siege of Zaragoza* (see 4161 and n.):

> [p. 2:] The walls of Zaragoza appear to have been constructed merely to facilitate the means of levying taxes upon every article brought into the town for sale; the gates ... are of the most simple construction, and the *alignment* between them, is in some places preserved by the mud-wall of a garden, in others by ... the remains of an old Moorish wall, which has a slight parapet, but without any platform even for musquetry. ... [p. 4:] At the time when Don J. Palafox assumed the command in Aragon, he had very little acquaintance with military affairs; for though he had been in the Spanish guards all his life, he had never seen actual service. ... [p. 5:] Palafox mustered the regular troops quartered at Zaragoza, and found that they amounted to two hundred and twenty men. ... [p. 9:] Zaragoza['s] fortifications consisted merely of mud-walls; it was destitute of heavy artillery, and without troops that could undertake sorties against the enemy's works. ... [p. 19:] [Palafox] caused corn-mills worked by horses, to be established in various parts of the city, and ordered the monks to be employed under skilful directors in manufacturing gunpowder. All the sulphur which the place afforded was put into immediate requisition, the earth of the streets was carefully washed in order to furnish saltpetre; and charcoal was made of the stalks of hemp [cf. *Cintra*, 4097] ... [pp. 26–7:] For eleven successive days the most sanguinary conflict was continued from street, to street, from house, to house, and from room to room, (the enraged populace always gaining by degrees upon the disciplined troops of the French,) until the space occupied by the enemy was gradually reduced to about one-eighth part of the city [cf. *Cintra*, 4113–8].

4095. a leader inexperienced in war] Joseph Palafox is criticized by Oman for his 'refusal to make sorties on a large scale during the first half of the [second] siege, while he was still in possession of great masses of superfluous fighting–men ...if [he] had saved up all the volunteers whom he lost by tens and twenties in small and fruitless attacks on the trenches, he could have built up with them a column–head that would have pierced through the French line at any point that he chose' (Oman, ii. 141).

4102. Pyrrhus ... destroyed."] After the battle of Asculum, 279 B.C.; Plutarch, *Pyrrhus*, XXI.

4112–5. their best field ... up–rooted.] In the first siege the Spaniards had successfully exploited a technique of house–to–house fighting; in the second, they continued these tactics, but they were successfully, though laboriously, countered by the French, who advanced by mining buildings, occupying them when the mines had cleared them, and using them as bases for further mining. See Oman, ii. 123 ff.

4121–2. bodies ... Spain.] This is confirmed by the analysis in Oman, ii. 622–4; but we have not found the source of Wordsworth's information. Vaughan's *Narrative* (1st edn., p. 13; see n. on 4726) says of the first siege that 'In the last few days of the month of June, four hundred soldiers of the regiment of Estramadura, small parties from other corps, and a few artillerymen, contrived to reinforce Zaragoza. To the artillerymen were added, two hundred of the militia of Logrono. ...'

4123. Numantia and Saguntum] Numantia, near Soria in Old Castile, was much besieged by the Romans in the wars of 154–133 B.C., until reduced by famine in the siege under Scipio Aemilianus, 134–133 B.C. (Appian, *Iber.* 84–98). Saguntum, mod. Sagunto, near Valencia, in alliance with Rome just before the second Punic War, was attacked and taken by Hannibal in 219 B.C. after a siege of eight months (Livy, XXI. vi–xv). Cf. Southey to Grosvenor C. Bedford, 9 Nov. 1808 (*Life and Correspondence*, iii. 182): 'there will be many and dreadful defeats of the patriots [in Spain], and such scenes as have never been witnessed in Europe since the destruction of Saguntum and Numantia may perhaps be renewed there.'

4134–51. "Cromwell ... obedience."] *Memoires of the Reigne of King Charles I* (London, 1701), pp. 252—3: 'Now from [Cromwell's] personall temper wee will reflect on the temper of his whole army; for they had all either naturally the phanatick humour, or soon imbibed it ... he himselfe ... made use of the zeal and credulity of those persons', etc., with omissions and minor variants.

4161. The narrative] Charles Richard Vaughan, *Narrative of the Siege of Zaragoza* (three editions, all dated London, 1809). Vaughan's Preface is dated 25 January 1809. The passage cited is on pp.27–8 of the second and third editions; it does not appear in the first. After 'of his country.—' (4168), Wordsworth omits: 'from his energy of character and uncommon bravery, the commander in chief reposed the utmost confidence in him during the siege: wherever any thing difficult or hazardous was to be done, Sass was selected for its execution; and the introduction of a supply of powder, so essentially necessary to the defence of the town, was effected in the most complete manner, by this clergyman, at the head of forty of the bravest men in Zaragoza.'

4201–6. the hearts ... civil] Emended on ? 6 March 1809, not exactly as printed here (*M.Y.* i. 294—5).

4224–30. the passions ... human desires] Cf. *Exc.* IV. 136–9: ''tis a thing impossible to frame / Conceptions equal to the soul's desires; / And the most difficult of tasks to keep / Heights which the soul is competent to gain.'

4245–51. "If ... work."] Sidney to Sir Francis Walsingham, 24 Mar. 1586, in *Works*, ed. Feuillerat, iii (Cambridge, 1923), 166; verbally as Wordsworth gives it, except 'faithfully' for Wordsworth's 'fully'.

4255–9. When wickedness ... zeal] Cf. *Exc.* IV. 307–19, especially 313–16: 'Virtue / Will, to her efforts, tolerate no bounds / That are not lofty as her rights; aspiring / By impulse of her own ethereal zeal.'

4260–1 Be ye . . . perfect] Matt. 5:48.

4263. I shall point out] This obscure promise is perhaps most easily explained as reflecting a projected continuation of *Cintra*; see Introd. De Quincey on 5 April 1809 (Jordan, p. 139) questions it, and observes that 'no direction is given [by Wordsworth] for erasing it.' Wordsworth may have retained it through oversight, or because he thought the promise would be honoured in *The Prelude*, or in *The Recluse* generally, or because he was already meditating matter which shortly appeared in *R.M.*, where he deals with childhood, with his rejection of 'despair even for the man' (or at least the young man), and with 'the inordinate evils of our time'.

4268–70. Cf. the imagery of 'To a Skylark' (*P.W.* ii. 266).

4272–4. circles ... self] Emended on ? 6 March 1809 (*M.Y.* i. 295).

4288–9. "the bright consummate flower"] *Paradise Lost*, V. 479–82: 'So from the root / Springs lighter the green stalk, from thence the leaves / More aerie, last the bright consummate floure / Spirits odorous breathes.'

4306. Kosciusko] Tadeusz Andrzej Bonawentura Kosciusko (1746–1817), Polish soldier and statesman, fought for the Americans in the War of Independence, and commanded Polish forces against Russia and Prussia in 1794, until his defeat at Maciejowice, 10 October 1794. After his release from Russia in 1796 he continued to work in the political field for the independence of Poland. [For his disillusionment with Napoleon's predatory instincts as regards Poland, see Helen Maria Williams in *A Narrative of the Events which have taken place in France; with an account of the* *present state of society and public opinion* (2nd ed. London: John Murray, 1816), 149–52.]

4316. Austria] See *M.Y.* i. 302 for a potential alteration. Austrian troops advanced against the French on 9 April 1809.

4332. Palafox] Jose de Palafox y Melzi (1780–1847), Captain General of Aragon and commander of Saragossa during its two sieges. He was captured at the end of the second, and imprisoned at Vincennes until December 1813. Cf. *Nat. Ind. and Lib.* II. xiii, xvi, xxii, xxiii (*P.W.* iii. 131 ff.).

4332. Toussaint] Pierre-Dominique Toussaint L'Ouverture, a leader against local French authority in Haiti in 1791; governor and commander-in-chief under French authority against Spanish and British intervention in the mid-nineties; self-appointed governor-general in 1801; captured in April 1802 by Napoleon's forces, and died in prison in the Château de Joux, 7 April 1803. Cf. *Nat. Ind. and Lib.* I. viii (*P.W.* iii. 112).

4358–67. "Hæc ... nihil."] Petrarch, *De Vita Solitaria*, I, in *Prose*, ed. G. Martellotti *et al.* (Milan and Naples, 1955), p. 394, with an omission after 'nauseam' (4958). Coleridge's *Prospectus to The Friend*, dated 2 February 1809, concludes with a quotation from this work, ed. cit., p. 328. [Petrarch's quotation communicates the utmost political despair. Translated by Ted Kenney (formerly Kennedy Professor of Latin in the University of Cambridge) the passage runs:

> This is what I should be saying, with whatever else grief and indignation at the present state of affairs might dictate, were it not that I believe that our minds have become numbed and that it is all up with us. I mean that we who once used to show others the right way, now (and this is close on utter ruin) are being blindly carried away headlong by blind leaders and are enmeshed by foreign example, not knowing what we want. For, to finish what I have begun, this evil, whether it is peculiar to us or common to all nations, is wholly caused by ignorance of our goal. When ill-advised, men do not know what to do, so that whatever they do, as soon as it is begun, turns to disgust. Hence comes that running this way and that; hence, in mid-way, dissension; and before any result is reached, principles have gone to the devil and nothing has been fully achieved.]

4370–77. "Valiant ... affairs."] Milton, Digression to *History of Britain*, in Works, x (New York, 1932), 325. Cf. n. on 2899.

COMMENTARY: APPENDIX

4. report of the Board] On 21 March 1809 (Jordan, p. 116), De Quincey says that 'the *Appendix* A which I got about that time [14 March] from the [*tear*] it was quite necessary shou[ld be] remodeled since the appearance of an official Report of the Board of Inquiry's proceedings.' The Board's summary of the evidence it had heard, and its conclusions, had been published in *Courier*, 3 Jan. 1809; but De Quincey is here referring to a *Copy of the Proceedings upon the Inquiry relative to the Armistice and Convention, &c. made and concluded in Portugal, in August 1808, between the Commanders of the British and French Armies;—held at the Royal Hospital at Chelsea, on Monday the 14th of November; and continued by Adjournments until the 27th of December 1808. Ordered by the House of Commons, to be printed, 81st January 1809*. This publication contains a full verbatim report of the Inquiry, and full texts of relevant documents; the 'Report' itself, i.e. the matter printed in newspapers of 3 January, begins on p. 111. How far De Quincey's remodelling proceeded cannot now be determined; it may have been confined to 'verify[ing] some quotations' and the like (Jordan, p. 116), though Wordsworth's 'thanks for … trouble about the note on the Board of Inquiry' and 'The note on the Board of Inquiry is a clencher for that business' (*M.Y.* i. 300, 348) might suggest more thorough recasting. In the absence of firm evidence, we have assumed that De Quincey's revisions were minimal, and in the following notes we have quoted newspaper reports as Wordsworth's probable source; but we have added references to the *Copy*, and occasionally drawn on its texts of written documents.

7–19. the Portuguese General … feed] This matter is summarized by the Board: 'It appears, that hitherto the Portuguese had moved on [Wellesley's] left, extending towards the Tagus, but they now [16 August 1808] raised such difficulties about subsistence and proceeding on the manner Sir A. Wellesley thought most advisable, that he dispensed with their co–operation, on condition they would send him 1600 men, to be at his disposal, and to whom he was to furnish bread' (*Courier*, 3 Jan. 1809; *Copy*, pp. 113–14). Wellesley's narrative to the Board (*Copy*, p. 27) states:

> Colonel Trant … informed me of the General's [Freire's] intention to halt at Leyria, unless I should consent to supply the Portuguese troops with provisions from the British commissariat on the march to Lisbon … I pointed out the impossibility of my complying with the demand for provisions … I then proposed to him,

> that ... he should send to join me 1,000 regular infantry, all his light troops and his cavalry, which troops I engaged to feed [cf. *Ap. Cintra*, 20] as the utmost I could undertake to perform in that way. These troops, in numbers 1,000 regular infantry, 400 light troops, and 250 cavalry, joined me at Alcobaça.

Wellesley to Castlereagh, 16 Aug. 1808 (*Copy*, p. 155) gives the above information, and proceeds: 'General Freire has been apprized of this state of the resources; and yet he perseveres in his plan; and I acknowledge that I can attribute it only to his apprehensions, which, however, he has never hinted to me, that we are not sufficiently strong for the enemy. I don't believe the motive stated [by Freire] is that which has caused the determination to which I have adverted.'

28–32. the warrant ... to them."] *Courier*, 15 Nov. 1808; *Copy*, p. 10. The operative part reads:

> We think it necessary that an enquiry should be made . . . into the conditions of the said Armistice and Convention, and into all the causes and circumstances (whether arising from the previous operations of the British army or otherwise), which led to them, and into the conduct, behaviour, and proceedings of the said Lieutenant-General Sir Hew Dalrymple, and of any other officer or officers who may have held the command of our troops in Portugal; and of any other person or persons, as far as the same were connected with the said Armistice and Convention, in order that the said General Officers [of the Board] may report to Us, touching the matters aforesaid for our better information.

97–100. Now the whole ... coup-de-main.] This matter is summarized by the Board (*Courier*, 8 Jan. 1809; *Copy*, pp. 119—20):

> It is further urged by the Generals, as much more than probable, that if the enemy had been required to lay down their arms, and surrender prisoners of war, they would not have complied; but if driven to extremity, that they would have retired upon Lisbon, reinforced by six thousand Russians, who must have been thus compelled to share their fate; and in the temporary attack of this city, much calamity and destruction must have ensued.
>
> Also, that masters of the Russian fleet, and of the boats and shipping in the Tagus, the passage of the river was ensured to them: that they could have defended, for a considerable time its East Bank, and prevented the occupation of the Tagus by our fleet: that with the strong fortresses of Alentejo in their possession, they could have protracted a destructive war, to the great detriment of Portugal and the Spanish cause, by finding employment for the greater part of the British Army, for the remainder of the year, and whose difficulties and losses in such operation [*sic*] must have been very considerable.

106–7. Sir A. Wellesley ascribes] See n. on *Cintra*, 1268–73.

126.–30. "because ... Wellesley."] *Courier*, 3 Jan. 1809; *Copy*, p. 121; reading 'howsoever' and spelling Christian names in full.

131. the Commander-in-Chief] Frederick, Duke of York. The letter reads in part (*Courier*, 3 Jan. 1809; *Copy*, pp. 121–2):

> upon a due consideration of the whole matter, it certainly appears that your opinion upon the conditions of the Armistice and Convention, which the words of his Majesty's warrant expressly enjoin should be strictly examined, enquired into, and reported upon, has been altogether omitted. [The Board is asked] to subjoin to the opinion … already given … whether, under all the circumstances which appear in evidence before you, on the relative situation of the two armies, on the 22d of August, 1808, it is your opinion that an Armistice was advisable, and if so, whether the terms of that Armistice were such as ought to have been agreed upon [; and similarly with regard to the Convention].

The Armistice was then approved by all members of the Board except the Earl of Moira; the Convention was approved by Nugent, Heathfield, Craig, and Dundas, disapproved by Nicholls, Pembroke, and Moira. Those who disapproved gave reasons, Nicholls and Pembroke briefly, Moira at length. The burden of their disapproval is that the British case was greatly strengthened by the arrival of reinforcements, so that harder terms might well have been extracted from the French. See 193–6.

190–31. the actual landing] *Courier*, 3 Jan. 1809; *Copy*, p. 116: 'It appears that Sir J. Moore did arrive at Mondego on the 20th [August]—that he began to disembark—that on the 22d he received an order from Sir H. Burrard, to re-embark such as he had landed, and proceed to Maciera—that he arrived on the 24th at Maciera Bay, and that he disembarked his corps on the days from the 25th to the 29th.'

193. two of the members] In fact all three who disapproved (Nicholls, Pembroke, Moira) mentioned the reinforcement by Moore's corps (*Courier*, Jan. 1809; *Copy*, pp. 122–8).

194–6. such … terms.] 'I think, considering the great increase of our force from the first suspension of hostility to the definitive signing of the Convention, added to the defeat the enemy had suffered, Sir Hew Dalrymple was fully entitled to have insisted upon more favourable terms' (Nicholls disapproving of the Convention; see previous n.).

203–5. Sir Arthur Wellesley … time] *Courier*, 23 Nov. 1808, reporting Wellesley's comments on Dalrymple's narrative:

> The object of the British Government … he conceived, had been to lose as little time as possible in Portugal, and to proceed to co-operate with the Spanish armies. By this Convention, there were liberated for the same purpose 4000 Spaniards, who were on board of the Russian fleet. Besides these, 16,000 British troops had been rendered disposable for the same purpose; and, of the French liberated, who, it was alledged, would so speedily find their way into Spain, not a single man had arrived there, or could expect to be brought to the frontiers of Spain for some time to come.

In the debate in the Commons on the Convention Lord Henry Petty alleged that 'the only French Officer who had been taken at the battle of Corunna was found, to the grief, shame, and disgust of our brave army, to be one who was also taken prisoner at the battle of Vimiera' (*The Times*, 22 Feb. 1809).

221. that memorable act] Wordsworth evidently refers to 'An Act against Tumults and Disorders, upon Pretence of preparing or presenting public Petitions, or other Addresses, to his Majesty or the Parliament' (1661; 13 Charles II, st. 1, c. 5):

> ... no Person or Persons whatsoever shall, from and after the First of *August*, one thousand six hundred sixty and one, solicite, labour, or procure the getting of Hands, or other Consent, of any Persons above the Number of Twenty or more, to any Petition, Complaint, Remonstrance, Declaration, or other Addresses to the King, or both or either Houses of Parliament, for Alteration of Matters established by Law in Church or State, unless the Matter thereof have been first consented unto and ordered by Three or more Justices of that County, or by the major Part of the Grand Jury of the County, etc. [*Statutes at Large*, London, 1786, iii. 189].

For the Bill of Rights (1689), which lays it down that 'it is the Right of the Subjects to petition the King', see *Statutes at Large*, iii. 416–19. Cf. *M.Y.* i. 299. We have not traced the quotation '"the benefit ... deputies!" 'On 6 April De Quincey reported (Jordan, p. 138): 'The note upon Charles II[nd's] parliaments, I have not placed at the foot of the page, but in the Appendix:—it seemed to me quite *digressional* enough to warrant (or even require) this.'

230–51. an address ... policy] Verbatim from *Courier*, 12 Nov. 1808, under heading: 'Paris, Oct. 29. The Deputies of the new Departments of the Kingdom of Italy, the Musora, the Tronto and the Metauro, presented the day before yesterday to the Emperor and King, pronounced the following Speech.' The note, or at least the quotation, is evidently due to De Quincey, who was asked to supply the quotation by Wordsworth (*M.Y.* i. 299–300). De Quincey's transcript of the quotation is in the Cornell MS. (see n. on 495 ff., below), p. 55. The passage quoted in Appendix F (249–51) is also from *Courier*, 12 Nov. 1808, almost verbatim.

252–494. The text of these documents was taken from official prints (perhaps the *Copy of the Proceedings* mentioned above, n. to 4) supplied to the printer by De Quincey (Jordan, p. 157; 10 May 1809); though on 28 March (Jordan, p. 121) he mentioned transcribing 'the Armistice & Convention from authorised copies'. The version given here differs slightly from that printed in *Courier*, 17 Dec. 1808.

495 ff. The Postscript on Moore's letters, as the text makes clear (550–7), is the work of De Quincey. In the Cornell Wordsworth Collection is preserved a manuscript of De Quincey (item 2804 in the Catalogue of G. H. Healey) which shows various parts of the work in various stages of development and which contains other matter connected with its compilation. To attempt a complete critical apparatus would, we are convinced, be pointless in an edition of Wordsworth's prose; we have therefore confined ourselves to the summary of the contents of the manuscript which is given in our Appendix II.

499. the letters of Sir John Moore] Moore's letters to Castlereagh, and other relevant documents, were laid on the table of the House of Commons in late March 1809. *The Courier* began to print them on 24 March, and Wordsworth saw them there (*M.Y.* i. 307). Since, however, De Quincey refers to *The Times* (*Ap. Cintra*, 868), since *The Times* gives a fuller presentation of the letters than *The Courier*, and since De Quincey on 12 May 1809 praises *The Times* at the expense of *The Courier* (Jordan, p. 160), we have usually preferred to give references to *The Times* as De Quincey's probable source. Most of the documents are conveniently collected in Cobbett's *Parliamentary Debates*, xiii (1809), ccxc ff. De Quincey's criticisms in this Postscript are often based on the views of Wordsworth expressed in his letter of 29 March 1809 (*M.Y.* i. 307 if.); parallels are noted below. De Quincey admits that he wrote 'making a point to prepare the course of what I was saying to receive nearly all of M[r]. Wordsworth's thoughts … and sometimes his words' (Jordan, p. 167).

537–41. the letters … upon him] Cf. *M.Y.* i. 307: 'First to remind the reader of the situation in which Sir J. Moore stood, and of the purpose for which these Letters were written—namely, under a conviction that his army could accomplish nothing; and to save himself and it from reproach in that quarter by which he had been sent—the Ministry.'

543. "which … 26,000 men"] Moore's letter of 5 December 1808 (*The Times*, 25 Mar. 1809): 'which when united does not exceed 26,000 men'. Transcribed by De Quincey in Cornell MS., p.37. Moore means the junction of his own force with Sir David Baird's corps, which had landed at Corunna on 13 October 1808 but which did not join Moore until 20 December.

548–53. the English Government … Spaniards] Cf. *M.Y.* i. 307: 'Now it was clear that the best way to succeed in this, was not to charge those who had sent him with blame, but to fling the whole upon the Spaniards.'

578–9. "Gen. Blake's … direction."] Moore's letter of 24 November 1808; *The Times*, 25 Mar. 1809; transcribed in Cornell MS., p.37; criticized by Wordsworth, *M.Y.* i. 307. Blake was defeated by Lefebvre at Zornosa on 31 October 1808, and by Victor at Espinosa on 11 November, after some Spanish success on 10 November. There followed a disastrous retreat through the mountains until the remnant of Blake's army reached Leon, where he gave up his command to La Romana.

581. 'mere peasantry'] Moore's letter of 24 November 1808; *The Times*, 25 Mar.

1809; Cornell MS., p. 37.

584. Major-Gen. Leith] 'Military Agent ... in the Asturias' (*The Times*, 25 Mar. 1809, whence the following extract, 587–604, is taken); Cornell MS., p. 71. This was among the third body of papers laid on the table of the House of Commons; *The Times* prints only an extract (of which De Quincey gives most), 'as it gives an interesting account of the sufferings of General BLAKE and his army, and the resolution with which they were sustained'.

605–7. The Estramaduran force, under the Conde de Belvedere, numbered just under 11,000, according to Oman, i. 421. They were opposed by Soult with some 22,000 men, including 4,500 cavalry; the total French force available in the advance on Burgos was nearly 70,000. De Quincey's information is from Lord William Bentinck to Castlereagh, 14 Nov. 1808 (*The Times*, 24 Mar. 1808; Cornell MS., p. 68).

609–10. "The French ... at Burgos."] Moore's letter of 24 November 1808; *The Times*, 25 Mar. 1809; Cornell MS., p. 37. Criticized by Wordsworth, *M.Y.* i. 307. With what follows (610–15), cf. *M.Y.* i. 307: Moore 'seems to be surprized that these raw levies could not stand their ground, upon all occasions, against the practised troops of Buonaparte'.

616–21. The two next ... exaggeration] Moore's letters of 29 November and 5 December 1808 (*The Times*, 25 Mar. 1809; Cornell MS., p. 37): 'I received yesterday evening a letter ... announcing the total defeat of the army of Castanos and Palafox ... I had the honour to address your Lordship on the 29th November, and to inform you with the determination I had come to in consequence of the defeat of the army of General Castanos. ... The French attacked and carried the pass of Soma Sierra on the 29th.' Cf. *M.Y.* i. 307: 'the fate [fact MS.] of Castanos is totally misrepresented—inasmuch as his centre only was defeated, his two wings being untouched.' On the Polish cavalry at Somosierra, where a squadron was wiped out by Spanish artillery, in one of Napoleon's more theatrical military gestures, and where French infantry carried the day, see Oman, i. 456 ff. Castanos was defeated by Lannes at Tudela on 23 November 1808. According to Oman, 1. 443, and Napier, i. 403, the Spanish right wing was defeated, and the left wing appears to have been 'untouched' mainly because it failed to fight. Oman, i. 442, says that 'Palafox was not on the field'; Napier, i. 403, that he fled to Saragossa 'with the right wing and the centre'.

633–5. "The French cavalry ... resistance."] Moore's letter of 24 November 1808; *The Times*, 25 Mar. 1809. With De Quincey's comment, cf. *M.Y.* i. 308: 'This fact I cannot believe upon the evidence of any General,—because my knowledge of human nature teaches me beforehand that it is impossible. That the resistance might fall far below what a superficial thinker would expect I can easily believe—things of this sort, where regular arrangements have not been made to preclude such inactivity … depend upon accident.'

644–55. "—At that time … ***incursions.***"] Broderick's letter to Castlereagh dated Reynosa, 10 September 1808 (*The Times*, 25 Mar. 1809), almost verbatim.

656–8. "the Gallicians … mountains."] Moore's letter of 13 January 1809 (*The Times*, 10 Apr. 1809): 'The people of the Galicias, though armed', etc.

662–3. "a body … number?"] *The Times*, 23 Mar. 1809; printed as a translation of 'part of the following enclosure, &c. which we know not how has found its way into these Documents'. After the translation, *The Times* inserts the following comment: 'We cannot help again expressing our surprize at the introduction of such a document as this in an official correspondence. If it is meant to attack General Moore, why not do it openly? if not, to what purpose is it to tell Lord William Bentinck, in French, that a small force can defend Gallicia against a large one?' The original is an enclosure in Castlereagh to Lord William Bentinck, 30 Sept. 1808 (also printed in *The Times*, 23 Mar. 1809); it is a memorandum, in French, from the Marquis de la Romana (see 879 below, and n.), designed for the general assistance of British forces in Spain. The French text (Cobbett, *Parliamentary Debates*, xiii, ccciv) reads: '… la grande route qui mène de Castille en Galice, et qui est tellement rétrécie par les montagnes de droite et de gauche qu'un Corps de mille hommes pourrait arrêter une armée de vingt mille.' Why De Quincey attributes this to 'an English general', and why, in his transcript from *The Times's* translation (Cornell MS., p. 68), he marks off the phrase 'an army of twenty times the number' as a quotation, we have not discovered.

665. 'the people … deserted;'] Moore's letter of 31 December 1808; *The Times*, 25 Mar. 1809; Cornell MS., p. 71.

665–7. "They abandoned … army."] Moore's letter of 13 January 1809; *The Times*, 10 Apr. 1809; and so "I am sorry … retreat" (670–72).

697–700. "The enthusiasm … advantage of."] Moore's letter of 24 November 1808; *The Times*, 25 Mar. 1809; Cornell MS., p. 37.

701. "apathy and indifference:"] Moore's letter of 13 January 1809 (*The Times*, 10 Apr. 1809): 'I was sensible … that the apathy and indifference of the Spaniards would never have been believed.'

716. letter to Marshal Soult] A letter from Berthier to Soult, dated Chamartin, 10 December 1808, sent with Moore to Castlereagh, 16 Dec. 1808; *The Times*, 25 Mar. 1809. The passage referred to seems to be: 'Valladolid is a fine city, and has conducted itself well', which is hardly an 'accurate register of the behaviour of the different towns'.

720. Badajoz and Salamanca] Moore concentrated his own forces at Salamanca in November–December 1808; Badajoz was the base of Hope's corps. In Moore to Castlereagh, 8 Dec. 1808 (*Courier*, 24 Mar. 1809; not in *The Times*), Moore says that in Salamanca 'no one stirs, and yet they are well inclined.' We have not found any source for a similar view of Badajoz, nor anything to contradict it.

730. "rally round"] Probably from Moore's letter of 5 December 1808 (*The Times*, 25 Mar. 1809): 'it was my intention ... to march upon Madrid, from whence, getting behind the Tagus, we should have given the Spaniards an opportunity of rallying round us, and have shared their fortunes'; cf. also his letter of 24 November 1808 (ibid.): 'if the Spaniards, roused by their misfortunes, assemble round us, and become once more enthusiastic and determined, there may still be hopes of expelling the French.' Neither passage is transcribed in the Cornell MS.

765–7. "The Spanish Government ... attack:"] Moore's letter of 24 November 1808; *The Times*, 25 Mar. 1809; Cornell MS., p. 37.

785. Leith] See n. on 584 above.

786. Pasley] De Quincey extracted the 'testimony' from Broderick to Castlereagh, 22 Nov. 1808 (*The Times*, 25 Mar. 1809); his note (Cornell MS., p. 69) says that the letter 'states the substance of Captn. Pasley's of the Royal Engineers detail of Blake's actions in Biscay'. Broderick gives 'details [of actions in Biscay] contained in a letter I received yesterday from Capt. Pasley of the Royal Engineers. [There follows a factual report of the battle of 31 October 1808 between Blake and Lefebvre.] The Asturians, who principally composed the beaten wing, being raw troops, and one of their Generals killed, and the other wounded, and several of their officers having gone off, Captain Pasley remarks, that their conduct on that day ought not to excite surprize. They had fought very well on the former days.' For Pasley see *M.Y.* i. 370, n. 2.

786. Mr. Vaughan] Castlereagh to Moore, 16 Dec. 1808 (*The Times*, 23 Mar. 1809): 'Mr. Vaughan, who has travelled over the greater part of Spain, describes the southern and eastern provinces as full of ardour and enthusiasm.' Cornell MS., p. 68. Charles Vaughan, author of the *Narrative of the Siege of Zaragoza* (see n. on *Cintra*, 4161); for a brief account of his exploits in Spain see Oman, i. iv—vi.

787. Cochrane] In the frigates *Impérieuse* and *Cambrian* he bombarded Duhesme's force aimed at Barcelona in July and August 1808. In early November a French force under St. Cyr marched to relieve Duhesme, and on 7 November besieged Rosas, which held out until 5 December. The Spanish garrison was materially assisted by the guns of Cochrane's ships and by British sailors and marines therefrom. Cochrane's observations can be found in his dispatch to Collingwood, 5 Dec. 1808, printed in the *London Gazette*, No. 16235 (7–11 Mar. 1809), p. 307:

> The Garrison [of Rosas, on 23 November 1808,] consisted of about Eighty Spaniards, and were on the Point of surrendering; accordingly I threw myself into it, with Fifty Seamen and Thirty Marines of the Imperieuse ... The Spanish Garrison being changed, gave good Assistance; and Lieutenant Bourman, of the Regiment of Ultonia, who succeeded to the Command of the Spanish Soldiers in the Castle on Captain Fitzgerald's being wounded in the Hand, deserves every Thing his Country can do for an active and gallant Officer. Innocenti Maranger, Cadet of the same Regiment, particularly distinguished himself by his Zeal and Vigilance. As to the Officers, Seamen, and Marines of this Ship, the Fatigues they underwent, and the gallant Manner in which they behaved, deserve every Praise.

We have not found this dispatch reprinted in the newspapers that we have consulted; at the relevant date they are still almost wholly occupied with the affairs of the Duke of York. From Jordan, p. 177, it appears that De Quincey sometimes read the *Gazette* itself.

789. Bentinck] Letter to Castlereagh, 14 Nov. 1808 (*The Times*, 24 Mar. 1809; Cornell MS., p. 68): 'This army [of Castanos and Palafox] is also in want of clothing, of money, and of provisions. Its spirit, however, is represented to be excellent; and Colonel Graham, in whose opinion I have great reliance, speaks very confidently of the event of a battle … Notwithstanding I think ill of the present moment, and that the Spaniards have not the means at present to repel the danger that threatens, still I have confidence in the unconquerable spirit of the nation.' Earlier, Bentinck says: 'I must not disguise from your Lordship that I think very unfavourably of the affairs of Spain.' Bentinck was the British military representative in Madrid in late 1808.

811–19. "It appears ... Portugal."] Almost verbatim from *The Times*, 8 Apr. 1809.

824–30. Madrid was attacked by Napoleon on 2 December 1808, and capitulated on 4 December. The authorities appear to have envisaged a house-to-house defence as in Saragossa, but the city was unsuited to such tactics.

832–3. forts in Catalonia] Rosas fell on 5 December 1808 (see above, n. on 787). St. Cyr moved about the Barcelona district until March 1809, but we have not discovered what other 'forts' he took.

837–43. Preparations for the defence of Valencia as of 9 December 1808 are reported in *The Times*, 11 Jan. 1809, but De Quincey seems to refer to a later report which we have not discovered. He writes on 1 April 1809 (Jordan, pp. 136–7): 'Last night I read, with great pleasure, the Decree for giving no quarter to the French Troops (under particular limitations)'; *Courier*, 31 Mar. 1809, reports this decree of 7 February 1809 under the heading: 'Decree of the Supreme Junta against the

French'; after listing various atrocities, it decrees: 'That no quarter shall be given to any French soldier, Officer, or General, who may be made prisoner in any town or district, in which acts contrary to the laws of war have been committed by the enemy, but that such persons shall be immediately put to the sword, as an example to their companions, and a satisfaction to outraged humanity.' *The Times*, 23 Mar. 1809, reports 'serious tumults' in Cadiz,

> from a suspicion on the part of the people, too well justified by fatal experience in other quarters, that their magistrates were unfaithful to the cause of their country. The immediate occasion is understood to be the following:—Some of the French prisoners, who, under that description, had been so long confined at Cadiz, made the suspicious offer of their services to garrison the town, and to make this proposal palatable, declared themselves to be Poles, and not Frenchmen. The Marquis de Villel, Governour of the place, was disposed to accept of this offer, against which the inhabitants mutinied.

A longer report in *Courier*, 25 Mar. 1809, citing a dispatch from Cadiz of 22 February.

860. "a fine people:"] Moore's letter of 28 November to J. H. Frere; *The Times*, 15 Apr. 1809.

879. Vigo] Its capture in early February 1809 is reported in a French bulletin of 17 February (*The Times*, 6 Mar. 1809). The recapture, on 27 March, by local forces with the assistance of the British navy, is reported in *The Times*, 14 Apr. 1809. A dispatch from Captain George M'Kinley ends: 'It also becomes most gratifying that I am enabled to inform you of the spirit and determination of the Spaniards to expel from their country the invaders of all that is dear to a brave and loyal people ... The ardour of the peasantry is beyond all description.'

879. Marquis de la Romana] Pedro Caro y Sureda, commanded Spanish troops in French service in Denmark, rescued thence with his troops by the British navy in August 1808. He returned to Spain and took over Blake's command in November 1808, after Blake's failures at Zornosa and Espinosa. Sir John Moore made more or less abortive attempts to co-operate with him during his Spanish campaign. He had been building up forces about Monterey since January 1809; at the time of which De Quincey is writing, he was pursuing Fabian tactics further east, and captured Villa-franca from a small French garrison on 17 March.

Also from Humanities-Ebooks

All in PDF Ebook Format

Jared Curtis, ed. ***The Fenwick Notes of William Wordsworth*** *

Jared Curtis, ed., ***The Poems of William Wordsworth: Collected Reading Texts from the Cornell Wordsworth,*** **3 volumes** **

Richard Gravil, ed., ***Master Narratives: Tellers and Telling in the English Novel***

Richard Gravil and Molly Lefebure, eds, ***The Coleridge Connection: Essays for Thomas McFarland***

W. J. B. Owen and J. W. Smyser, eds, ***Wordsworth's Political Writings*****

W. J. B. Owen, ***Understanding The Prelude***

Richard Gravil and W. J. B. Owen, eds, ***William Wordsworth: Concerning the Convention of Cintra*** *

Pamela Perkins, ed. ***Francis Jeffrey: Highland and Continental Tours*** *

Under Consideration

It is proposed to publish further volumes of Wordsworth's prose from the Owen and Smyser edition. Feedback is invited on whether this should be by way of a new edition of volumes two and three (but with textual notes converted to endnotes and commentary converted to footnotes), or as a volume of *Wordsworth's Critical Prose* and a volume of his *Topographical and Ethical Prose* in the format adopted for *Wordsworth's Political Writings*. Either way, line numbers would be omitted.

* also in paperback from Lulu ** in paperback from Troubador.co.uk

http://www.humanities-ebooks.co.uk

www.ingramcontent.com/pod-product-compliance
Lightning Source LLC
Chambersburg PA
CBHW081324090726
47907CB00010B/2363

* 9 7 8 1 8 4 7 6 0 0 7 7 6 *